KV-029-652

MAN'S BOOK

MADE AND PRINTED IN
GREAT BRITAIN BY ODHAMS (WATFORD) LTD.
WATFORD, HERTS.

S.960.R.N.

ODDS AGAINST
Dick Francis

★

A RING OF ROSES
John Blackburn

★

THE CONCRETE KIMONO
John Paddy Carstairs

ODHAMS BOOKS LIMITED
LONG ACRE, LONDON

CONTENTS

ODDS AGAINST

Dick Francis

"Odds Against" is published by Michael Joseph Ltd.

The Author

As a former champion jockey nobody knows better than Dick Francis the perils and excitement of the steeplechasing world. In 1956 he narrowly missed winning the Grand National on the Queen Mother's Devon Loch. Despite his retirement from racing he is still very much in the racing game, both as a racing correspondent and as a judge at horse shows. His stories *Nerve* and *For Kicks* were included in two of the earlier volumes of Man's Book.

CHAPTER ONE

I WAS never particularly keen on my job before the day I got shot and nearly lost it, along with my life. But the ·38 slug of lead which made a pepper-shaker out of my intestines left me with fire in my belly in more ways than one. Otherwise I should never have met Zanna Martin, and would still be held fast in the spider-threads of departed joys, of no use to anyone, least of all myself.

It was the first step to liberation, that bullet, though I wouldn't have said so at the time. I stopped it because I was careless. Careless because bored.

I woke up gradually in hospital, in a private room for which I got a whacking great bill a few days later. Even before I opened my eyes I began to regret I had not left the world completely. Someone had lit a bonfire under my navel.

A fierce conversation was being conducted in unhushed voices over my head. With woolly wits, the anaesthetic still drifting inside my skull like puff-ball clouds in a summer sky, I tried unenthusiastically to make sense of what was being said.

'Can't you give him something to wake him more quickly?'

'No.'

'We can't do much until we have his story, you must see that. It's nearly seven hours since you finished operating. Surely . . .'

'And he was all of four hours on the table before that. Do you want to finish off what the shooting started?'

'Doctor . . .'

'I am sorry, but you'll have to wait.'

There's my pal, I thought. They'll have to wait. Who wants to hurry back into the dreary world? Why not go to sleep for a month and take things up again after they've put the bonfire out? I opened my eyes reluctantly.

It was night. A globe of electric light shone in the centre of the ceiling. That figured. It had been morning when Jones-boy found me still seeping gently on to the office linoleum and went to telephone, and it appeared that about twelve hours had passed since they stuck the first blessed needle into my arm. Would a twenty-four hour start, I wondered, be enough for a panic-stricken ineffectual little crook to get himself undetectably out of the country?

There were two policemen on my left, one in uniform, one not. They were both sweating, because the room was hot. The doctor stood on the right, fiddling with a tube which ran from a bottle into my elbow. Various other tubes sprouted disgustingly from my abdomen, partly covered by a light sheet. Drip and drainage, I thought sardonically. How absolutely charming.

Radnor was watching me from the foot of the bed, taking no part in the argument still in progress between medicine and the law. I wouldn't have thought I rated the boss himself attendant at the bedside, but then I suppose it wasn't every day that one of his employees got himself into such a spectacular mess.

He said, 'He's conscious again, and his eyes aren't so hazy. We might get some sense out of him this time.' He looked at his watch.

The doctor bent over me, felt my pulse, and nodded. 'Five minutes, then. Not a second more.'

The plain clothes policeman beat Radnor to it by a fraction of a second. 'Can you tell us who shot you?'

I still found it surprisingly difficult to speak, but not as impossible as it had been when they asked me the same question that morning. Then, I had been too far gone. Now, I was apparently on the way back. Even so, the policeman had plenty of time to repeat his question, and to wait some more, before I managed an answer.

'Andrews.'

It meant nothing to the policeman, but Radnor looked astonished and also disappointed.

'Thomas Andrews?' he asked.

'Yes.'

Radnor explained to the police. 'I told you that Halley here and another of my operatives set some sort of a trap intending to clear up an intimidation case we are investigating. I understand they were hoping for a big fish, but it seems now they caught a tiddler. Andrews is small stuff, a weak sort of youth used for running errands. I would never have thought he would carry a gun, much less that he would use it.'

Me neither. He had dragged the revolver clumsily out of his jacket pocket, pointed it shakily in my direction, and used both hands to pull the trigger. If I hadn't seen that it was only Andrews who had come to nibble at the bait I wouldn't have ambled unwarily out of the darkness of the washroom to tax him with breaking into the Cromwell Road premises of Hunt Radnor Associates at one o'clock in the morning. It simply hadn't occurred to me that he would attack me in any way.

By the time I realized that he really meant to use the gun and was not waving it about for effect, it was far too late. I had barely begun to turn to flip the light switch when the bullet hit, in and out diagonally through my body. The force of it spun me on to my knees and then forward on to the floor.

As I went down he ran for the door, stiff-legged, crying out, with circles of white showing wild round his eyes. He was almost as horrified as I was at what he had done.

'At what time did the shooting take place?' asked the policeman formally.

After another pause I said, 'One o'clock, about.'

The doctor drew in a breath. He didn't need to say it; I knew I was lucky to be alive. In a progressively feeble state I'd lain on the floor through a chilly September night looking disgustedly at a telephone on which I couldn't summon help. The office telephones all worked through a switchboard. This might have been on the moon as far as I was concerned, instead of along the passage, down the curving stairs and through the door to the reception desk, with the girl who worked the switches fast asleep in bed.

The policeman wrote in his notebook. 'Now sir, I can get a description of Thomas Andrews from someone else so as not to trouble you too much now, but I'd be glad if you can tell me what he was wearing.'

'Black jeans, very tight. Olive green jersey. Loose black jacket.' I paused. 'Black fur collar, black and white checked lining. All shabby . . . dirty.' I tried again. 'He had gun in jacket pocket right side . . . took it with him . . . no gloves . . . can't have a record.'

'Shoes?'

'Didn't see. Silent, though."

'Anything else?'

I thought. 'He had some badges . . . place names, skull and crossbones, things like that . . . sewn on his jacket, left sleeve.'

'I see. Right. We'll get on with it then.' He snapped shut his notebook, smiled briefly, turned, and walked to the door, followed by his uniformed ally, and by Radnor, presumably for Andrews' description.

The doctor took my pulse again, and slowly checked all the tubes. His face showed satisfaction.

He said cheerfully, 'You must have the constitution of a horse.'

'No,' said Radnor, coming in again and hearing him. 'Horses are really quite delicate creatures. Halley has the constitution of a jockey. A steeplechase jockey. He used to be one. He's got a body like a shock absorber . . . had to have to deal with all the fractures and injuries he got racing.'

'Is that what happened to his hand? A fall in a steeplechase?'

Radnor's glance flicked to my face and away again, uncomfortably. They never mentioned my hand to me in the office if they could help it. None of them, that is, except my fellow trapsetter Chico Barnes, who didn't care what he said to anyone.

'Yes,' Radnor said tersely. 'That's right.' He changed the subject. 'Well, Sid, come and see me when you are better. Take your time.' He nodded uncertainly to me, and he and the doctor, with a joint backward glance, ushered each other out of the door.

So Radnor was in no hurry to have me back. I would have smiled if I'd had the energy. When he first offered me a job I guessed that somewhere in the background my father-in-law was pulling strings; but I had been in a why-not mood at the time. Nothing mattered very much.

'Why not?' I said to Radnor, and he put me on his payroll as an investigator, Racing Section, ignoring my complete lack of experience and explaining to the rest of the staff that I was there in an advisory capacity, owing to my intimate knowledge of the game. They had taken it very well, on the whole. Perhaps they realized, as I did, that my employment was an act of pity. Perhaps they thought I should be too proud to accept that sort of pity. I wasn't. I didn't care one way or the other.

Radnor's agency ran Missing Persons, Guard, and Divorce departments, and also a section called Bona Fides, which was nearly as big as the others put together. Most of the work was routine painstaking enquiry stuff, sometimes leading to civil or divorce action, but oftener merely to a discreet report sent to the client. Criminal cases, though accepted, were rare. The Andrews business was the first for the three months.

The Racing Section was Radnor's special baby. It hadn't existed, I'd been told, when he bought the agency with an Army gratuity after the war and developed it from a dingy three-roomed affair into something like a national institution. Radnor printed 'Speed, Results, and Secrecy' across the top of his stationery; promised them, and delivered them. A life-long addiction to racing, allied to six youthful rides in point-to-points, had led him not so much to ply for hire from the Jockey Club and the National Hunt Committee as to indicate that his agency was at their disposal. The Jockey Club and the National Hunt Committee tentatively wet their feet, found the water beneficial, and plunged right in. The Racing Section blossomed. Eventually private business outstripped the official, especially when Radnor began supplying pre-race guards for fancied horses.

By the time I joined the firm 'Bona Fides: Racing', had proved so successful that it had spread from its own big office into the room next door. For a reasonable fee a trainer could check on the character and background of a prospective owner, a bookmaker on a client, a client on a bookmaker, anybody on anybody. The phrase 'O.K.'d by Radnor' had passed into racing slang. Genuine, it meant. Trustworthy. I had even heard it applied to a horse.

They had never given me a Bona Fides assignment. This work was done by a bunch of inconspicuous middle-aged retired policemen who took minimum time to get maximum results. I'd never been sent to sit all night outside the box of a hot favourite, though I would have done it willingly. I had never been put on a racecourse security patrol. If the Stewards asked for operators to keep tabs on undesirables at race meetings, I didn't go. If anyone had to watch for pickpockets in Tattersalls, it wasn't me. Radnor's two unvarying excuses for giving me nothing to do were first that I was too well known to the whole racing world to be inconspicuous, and second, that even if I didn't seem to care, he was not going to be the one to give an ex-champion jockey tasks which meant a great loss of face.

As a result I spent most of my time kicking around the office reading other people's reports. When anyone asked me for the informed advice I was supposedly there to give, I gave it; if anyone asked what I would do in a certain set of circumstances, I told them. I got to know all the operators and gossiped with them when they came into the office. I always had the time.

If I took a day off and went to the races, nobody complained. I sometimes wondered whether they even noticed.

At intervals I remarked to Radnor that he didn't have to keep me, as I so obviously did nothing to earn my salary. He replied each time that he was satisfied with the arrangement, if I was. I had the impression that he was waiting for something, but if it wasn't for me to leave, I didn't know what. On the day I walked into Andrews' bullet I had been with the agency in this fashion for exactly two years.

A nurse came in to check the tubes and take my blood pressure. She was starched and efficient. She smiled but didn't speak. I waited for her to say that my wife was outside asking about me anxiously. She didn't say it. My wife hadn't come. Wouldn't come. If I couldn't hold her when I was properly alive, why should my near-death bring her running? Jenny. My wife. Still my wife in spite of three years' separation. Regret, I think, held both of us back from the final step of divorce: we had been through passion, delight, dissension, anger and explosion. Only regret was left, and it wouldn't be strong enough to bring her to the hospital. She'd seen me in too many hospitals before. There was no more drama, no more impact, in my form recumbent, even with tubes. She wouldn't come. Wouldn't telephone. Wouldn't write. It was stupid of me to want her to.

Time passed slowly and I didn't enjoy it, but eventually all the tubes except the one in my arm were removed and I began to heal. The police didn't find Andrews, Jenny didn't come, Radnor's typists sent me a get-well card, and the hospital sent the bill.

Chico slouched in one evening, his hands in his pockets and the usual derisive grin on his face. He looked me over without haste and the grin, if anything, widened.

'Rather you than me, mate,' he said.

'Go to bloody hell.'

He laughed. And well he might. I had been doing his job for him because he had a date with a girl, and Andrews' bullet should have been his bellyache, not mine.

'Andrews,' he said musingly. 'Who'd have thought it? Sodding little weasel. All the same, if you'd done what I said and stayed in the washroom, and taken his photo quiet like on the old infra-red, we'd have picked him up later nice and easy and you'd have been lolling on your arse around the office as usual instead of sweating away in here.'

'You needn't rub it in,' I said. 'What would you have done?'

He grinned. 'The same as you, I expect. I'd have reckoned it would only take the old one-two for that little worm to come across with who sent him.'

'And now we don't know.'

'No.' He sighed. 'And the old man ain't too sweet about the whole thing. He did know I was using the office as a trap, but he didn't think it would work, and now this has happened he doesn't like it. He's leaning over backwards, hushing the whole thing up. They might have sent a bomb, not a sneak thief, he said. And of course Andrews bust a window getting in, which I've probably got to pay for. Trust the little sod not to know how to pick a lock.'

'I'll pay for the window,' I said.

'Yeah,' he grinned. 'I reckoned you would I if I told you.'

He wandered round the room, looking at things. There wasn't much to see.

"What's in that bottle dripping into your arm?'

'Food of some sort, as far as I can gather. They never give me anything to eat.'

'Afraid you might bust out again, I expect.'

'I guess so,' I agreed.

He wandered on. 'Haven't you got a telly then? Cheer you up a bit wouldn't it, to see some other silly buggers getting shot?' He looked at the chart on the bottom of the bed. 'Your temperature was 102 this morning, did they tell you? Do you reckon you're going to kick it?'

'No.'

'Near thing, from what I've heard. Jones-boy said there was enough of your life's blood dirtying up the office floor to make a tidy few black puddings.'

I didn't appreciate Jones-boy's sense of humour.

Chico said, 'Are you coming back?'

'Perhaps.'

He began tying knots in the cord of the window blind. I watched him, a thin figure imbued with so much energy that it was difficult for him to keep still. He had spent two fruitless nights watching in the washroom before I took his place, and I knew that if he hadn't been dedicated to his job he couldn't have borne such inactivity. He was the youngest of Radnor's team. About twenty-four, he believed, though as he had been abandoned as a child on the steps of a police station in a push-chair, no one knew for certain.

If the police hadn't been so kind to him, Chico sometimes said, he would have taken advantage of his later opportunities and turned deliquent. He never grew tall enough to be a copper. Radnor's was the best he could do. And he did very well by Radnor. He put two and two together quickly and no one on the staff had faster physical reactions. Judo and wrestling were his hobbies, and along with the regular throws and holds he had been taught some strikingly dirty tricks. His smallness bore no relation whatever to his effectiveness in his job.

'How are you getting on with the case?' I asked.

'What case? Oh . . . that. Well since you got shot the heat's off, it seems. Brinton's had no threatening calls or letters since the other night. Whoever was leaning on him must have got the wind up. Anyway, he's feeling a bit safer all of a sudden and he's carping a lot to the old man about fees. Another day or two, I give it, and there won't be no one holding his hand at night. Anyway, I've been pulled off it. I'm flying from Newmarket to Ireland tomorrow, sharing a stall with a hundred thousand pounds' worth of stallion.'

Escort duty was another little job I never did. Chico liked it, and went often. As he had once thrown a fifteen stone would-be nobbler over a seven foot wall, he was always much in demand.

'You ought to come back,' he said suddenly.

'Why?' I was surprised.

'I don't know . . .' he grinned. 'Silly, really, when you do sweet eff-all, but everybody seems to have got used to you being around. You're missed, kiddo, you'd be surprised.'

'You're joking, of course.'

'Yeah . . .' He undid the knots in the window cord, shrugged, and thrust his hands into his trouser pockets. 'God, this place gives you the willies. It reeks of warm disinfectant. Creepy. How much longer are you going to lie here rotting?'

'Days,' I said mildly. 'Have a good trip.'

'See you.' He nodded, drifting in relief to the door. 'Do you want anything? I mean, books or anything?'

'Nothing, thanks.'

'Nothing . . . that's just your form, Sid, mate. You don't want nothing.' He grinned and went.

I wanted nothing. My form. My trouble. I'd had what I wanted most in the world and lost it irrevocably. I'd found nothing else to want. I stared at the ceiling, waiting for time to pass. All I wanted was to get back on to my feet and stop feeling as though I had eaten a hundredweight of green apples.

Three weeks after the shooting I had a visit from my father-in-law. He came in the late afternoon, bringing with him a small parcel which he put without comment on the table beside the bed.

'Well, Sid, how are you?' He settled himself into an easy chair, crossed his legs and lit a cigar.

'Cured, more or less. I'll be out of here soon.'

'Good. Good. And your plans are . . . ?'

'I haven't any.'

'You can't go back to the agency without some . . . er . . . convalescence,' he remarked.

'I suppose not.'

'You might prefer somewhere in the sun,' he said, studying the cigar. 'But I would like it if you could spend some time with me at Aynsford.'

I didn't answer immediately.

'Will . . . ?' I began and stopped, wavering.

'No,' he said. 'She won't be there. She's gone out to Athens to stay with Jill and Tony. I saw her off yesterday. She sent you her regards.'

'Thanks,' I said dryly. As usual I did not know whether to be glad or sorry that I was not going to meet my wife. Nor was I sure that this trip to see her sister Jill was not as diplomatic as Tony's job in the Corps.

'You'll come, then? Mrs Cross will look after you splendidly.'

'Yes, Charles, thank you. I'd like to come for a little while.'

He gripped the cigar in his teeth, squinted through the smoke, and took out his diary.

'Let's see, suppose you leave here in, say, another week . . . No point in hurrying out before you're fit to go . . . that brings us to the twenty-sixth . . . hm . . . now, suppose you come down a week on Sunday, I'll be at home all that day. Will that suit you?'

'Yes, fine, if the doctors agree.'

'Right, then.' He wrote in the diary, put it away and took the cigar carefully out of his mouth, smiling at me with the usual inscrutable blankness in his eyes. He sat easily in his dark city suit, Rear-Admiral Charles Roland, R.N., retired, a man carrying his sixty-six years lightly. War photographs showed him tall, straight, bony almost, with a high forehead and thick dark hair. Time had greyed the hair, which in receding left his forehead higher than ever, and had added weight where it did no harm. His manner was ordinarily extremely charming and occasionally patronizingly offensive. I had been on the receiving end of both.

He relaxed in the arm-chair, talking unhurriedly about steeple-chasing.

'What do you think of that new race at Sandown? I don't know about you, but I think it's framed rather awkwardly. They're bound to get a tiny field with those conditions, and if Devil's Dyke doesn't run after all the whole thing will be a non-crowd puller *par excellence*.'

His interest in the game only dated back a few years, but recently to his pleasure he had been invited by one or two courses to act as a Steward. Listening to his easy familiarity with racing problems and racing jargon, I was in a quiet inward way amused. It was impossible to forget his reaction long ago to Jenny's engagement to a jockey, his unfriendly rejection of me as a future son-in-law, his absence from our wedding, the months afterwards of frigid disapproval, the way he had seldom spoken to or even looked at me.

I believed at the time that it was sheer snobbery, but it wasn't as simple as that. Certainly he didn't think me good enough, but not only, or even mainly, on a class distinction level; and probably we would never have understood each other, or come eventually to like each other, had it not been for a wet afternoon and a game of chess.

Jenny and I went to Aynsford for one of our rare, painful Sunday visits. We ate our roast beef in near silence, Jenny's father staring rudely out of the window and drumming his fingers on the table. I made up my mind that we wouldn't go again. I'd had enough. Jenny could visit him alone.

After lunch she said she wanted to sort out some of her books now that we had a new book-case, and disappeared upstairs. Charles Roland and I looked at each other in dislike, the afternoon stretching drearily ahead and the downpour outside barring retreat into the garden and park beyond.

'Do you play chess?' he asked in a bored, expecting-the-answer-no voice.

'I know the moves,' I said.

He shrugged (it was more like a squirm), but clearly thinking that it would be less trouble than making conversation, he brought a chess set out and gestured to me to sit opposite him. He was normally a good player, but that afternoon he was bored and irritated and inattentive, and I beat him quite early in the game. He couldn't believe it. He sat staring at the board, fingering the bishop with which I'd got him in a classic discovered check.

'Where did you learn?' he said eventually, still looking down.

'Out of a book.'

'Have you played a great deal?'

'No, not much. Here and there.' But I'd played with some good players.

'Hm.' He paused. 'Will you play again?'

'Yes, if you like.'

We played. It was a long game and ended in a draw, with practically every piece off the board. A fortnight later he rang up and asked us, next time we came, to stay overnight. It was the first twig of the olive branch. We went more often and more willingly to Aynsford after that. Charles and I played chess occasionally and won a roughly equal number of games, and he began rather tentatively to go to the races. Ironically from then on our mutual respect grew strong enough to survive even the crash of Jenny's and my marriage, and Charles's interest in racing expanded and deepened with every passing year.

'I went to Ascot yesterday,' he was saying, tapping ash off his cigar. 'It wasn't a bad crowd, considering the weather. I had a drink with that handicapper fellow, John Pagan. Nice chap. He was very pleased with himself because he got six abreast over the last in the handicap hurdle. There was an objection after the three mile chase—flagrant bit of crossing on the run-in. Carter swore blind he was leaning and couldn't help it, but you can never believe a word he says. Anyway, the Stewards took it away from him. The only thing they could do. Wally Gibbons rode a brilliant finish in the handicap hurdle and then made an almighty hash of the novice chase.'

'He's heavy-handed with novices,' I agreed.

'Wonderful course, that.'

'The tops.' A wave of weakness flowed outwards from my

stomach. My legs trembled under the bedclothes. It was always happening. Infuriating.

'Good job it belongs to the Queen and is safe from the land-grabbers.' He smiled.

'Yes, I suppose so . . .'

'You're tired,' he said abruptly. 'I've stayed too long.'

'No,' I protested. 'Really, I'm fine.'

He put out the cigar, however, and stood up. 'I know you too well, Sid. Your idea of fine is not the same as anyone else's. If you're not well enough to come to Aynsford a week on Sunday you'll let me know. Otherwise I'll see you then.'

'Yes, O.K.'

He went away, leaving me to reflect that I did still tire infernally easily. Must be old age, I grinned to myself, old age at thirty-one. Old tired battered Sid Halley, poor old chap. I grimaced at the ceiling.

A nurse came in for the evening jobs.

'You've got a parcel,' she said brightly, as if speaking to a retarded child. 'Aren't you going to open it?'

I had forgotten about Charles's parcel.

'Would you like me to open it for you? I mean, you can't find things like opening parcels very easy with a hand like yours.'

She was only being kind. 'Yes,' I said. 'Thank you.'

She snipped through the wrappings with scissors from her pocket and looked dubiously at the slim dark book she found inside.

'I suppose it is meant for you? I mean somehow it doesn't seem like things people usually give patients.'

She put the book into my right hand and I read the title embossed in gold on the cover. *Outline of Company Law.*

'My father-in-law left it on purpose. He meant it for me.'

'Oh well, I suppose it's difficult to think of things for people who can't eat grapes and such.' She bustled around, efficient and slightly bullying, and finally left me alone again.

Outline of Company Law. I riffled through the pages. It was certainly a book about company law. Solidly legal. Not light entertainment for an invalid. I put the book on the table.

Charles Roland was a man of subtle mind, and subtlety gave him much pleasure. It hadn't been my parentage that he had objected to so much as what he took to be Jenny's rejection of his mental standards in choosing a jockey for a husband. He'd never met a jockey before, disliked the idea of racing, and took it for granted that everyone engaged in it was either a rogue or a moron. He'd wanted both his daughters to marry clever men, clever more than handsome or well-born or rich, so that he could enjoy their company. Jill had obliged him with Tony, Jenny disappointed him with me: that was how he saw it, until he found that at least I could play chess with him now and then.

Knowing his subtle habits, I took it for granted that he had not idly brought such a book and hadn't chosen it or left it by mistake. He meant me to read it for a purpose. Intended it to be useful to me—or to him—later on. Did he think he could manoeuvre me into business, now that I hadn't distinguished myself at the agency? A nudge, that book was. A nudge in some specific direction.

I thought back over what he had said, looking for a clue. He'd been insistent that I should go to Aynsford. He'd sent Jenny to Athens. He'd talked about racing, about the new race at Sandown, about Ascot, John Pagan, Carter, Wally Gibbons . . . nothing there that I could see had the remotest connection with company law.

I sighed, shutting my eyes. I didn't feel too well. I didn't have to read the book, or go wherever Charles pointed. And yet . . . why not? There was nothing I urgently wanted to do instead. I decided to do my stodgy homework. Tomorrow.

Perhaps.

CHAPTER TWO

FOUR days after my arrival at Aynsford I came downstairs from an afternoon's rest to find Charles delving into a large packing case in the centre of the hall. Strewn round on the half-acre of parquet was a vast amount of wood shavings, white and curly, and arranged carefully on a low table beside him were the first trophies out of the lucky dip, appearing to me to be dull chunks of rock.

I picked one of them up. One side had been ground into a smooth face and across the bottom of this was stuck a neat label. 'Porphyry' it said, and beneath, 'Carver Mineralogy Foundation.'

'I didn't know you had an obsessive interest in quartz.'

He gave me one of his blank stares, which I knew didn't mean that he hadn't heard or understood what I'd said, but that he didn't intend to explain.

'I'm going fishing,' he said, plunging his arms back into the box.

So the quartz was bait. I put down the porphyry and picked up another piece. It was small, the size of a squared-off egg, and beautiful, as clear and translucent as glass. The label said simply 'Rock Crystal'.

'If you want something useful to do,' said Charles, 'you can write out what sort they all are on the plain labels you will find on my desk, and then soak the Foundation's label off and put the new ones on. Keep the old ones, though. We'll have to replace them when all this stuff goes back.'

'All right,' I agreed.

The next chunk I picked up was heavy with gold. 'Are these valuable?' I asked.

'Some are. There's a booklet somewhere. But I told the Foundation they'd be safe enough. I said I'd have a private detective in the house all the time guarding them.'

I laughed and began writing the new labels, working from the inventory. The lumps of quartz overflowed from the table on to the floor before the box was empty.

'There's another box outside,' Charles observed.

'Oh no!'

'I collect quartz,' said Charles with dignity, 'and don't you forget it. I've collected it for years. Years. Haven't I?'

'Years,' I agreed. 'You're an authority. Who wouldn't be an authority on rocks, after a life at sea.'

'I've got exactly one day to learn them in,' said Charles smiling. 'They've come later than I asked. I'll have to be word perfect by tomorrow night.'

He fetched the second lot, which was much smaller and was fastened with important looking seals. Inside were uncut gem quartz crystals, mounted on small individual black plinths. Their collective value was staggering. The Carver Foundation must have taken the private detective bit seriously. They'd have held tight to their rocks if they'd seen my state of health.

We worked for some time changing the labels while Charles muttered their names like incantations under his breath. 'Chrysoprase, Aventurine, Agate, Onyx, Chalcedony, Tiger-eye, Carnelian, Citrine, Rose, Plasma, Basanite, Bloodstone, Chert. Why the hell did I start this?'

'Well, why?'

I got the blank stare again. He wasn't telling. 'You can test me on them,' he said.

We carried them piece by piece into the dining-room, where I found the glass-doored book shelves on each side of the fire had been cleared of their yards of leather-bound classics.

'They can go up there later,' said Charles, covering the huge dining-room table with a thick felt. 'Put them on the table for now.'

When they were all arranged he walked slowly round learning them. There were about fifty altogether. I tested him after a while, at his request, and he muddled up and forgot about half of them. They were difficult, because so many looked alike.

He sighed. 'It's time we had a noggin and you went back to bed.' He led the way into the little sitting-room he occasionally referred to as the wardroom, and poured a couple of stiffish brandies. He raised his glass to me and appreciatively took a mouthful. There was a suppressed excitement in his expression, a glint in the unfathomable eyes. I sipped the brandy, wondering with more interest what he was up to.

'I have a few people coming for the week-end,' he said casually, squinting at his glass. 'A Mr and Mrs Rex van Dysart, a Mr and Mrs Howard Kraye, and my cousin Viola, who will act as hostess.'

'Old friends?' I murmured, having only ever heard of Viola.

'Not very,' he said smoothly. 'They'll be here in time for dinner tomorrow night. You'll meet them then.'

'But I'll make it an odd number . . . I'll go up before they come and stay out of your way for most of the week-end.'

'No,' he said sharply. Much too vehemently. I was surprised. Then it came to me suddenly that all he had been doing with his rocks and his offer of a place for my convalescence was to engineer a meeting between me and the weekend guests. He offered me rest. He offered Mr Van Dysart, or perhaps Mr Kraye, rocks. Both of us had swallowed the hook. I decided to give the line a tug, to see just how determined was the fisherman.

'I'd be better upstairs. You know I can't eat normal meals.' My diet at that time consisted of brandy, beef juice, and some vacuum-packed pots of stuff which had been developed for feeding astronauts. Apparently none of these things affected the worst shot-up bits of my digestive tract.

'People loosen up over the dinner table . . . they talk more, and you get to know them better.' He was carefully unpersuasive.

'They'll talk to you just as well if I'm not there—better in fact. And I couldn't stand watching you all tuck into steaks.'

He said musingly, 'You can stand anything, Sid. But I think you'd be interested. Not bored, I promise you. More brandy?'

I shook my head, and relented. 'All right, I'll be there at dinner, if you want it.'

He relaxed only a fraction. A controlled and subtle man. I smiled at him, and he guessed that I'd been playing him along.

'You're a bastard,' he said.

From him, it was a compliment.

The transistor beside my bed was busy with the morning news as I slowly ate my breakfast pot of astronaut paste.

'The race meeting scheduled for today and tomorrow at Seabury,' the announcer said, 'has had to be abandoned. A tanker carrying liquid chemical crashed and overturned at dusk yesterday afternoon on a road crossing the racecourse. There was considerable damage to the turf, and after an examination this morning the Stewards regretfully decided that it was not fit to be raced on. It is hoped to replace the affected turf in time for the next meeting in a fortnight's time, but an announcement will be made about this at a later date. And here is the weather forecast . . .'

Poor Seabury, I thought, always in the wars. It was only a year since their stable block had been burned down on the eve of a meeting. They had had to cancel then too, because temporary stables could not be erected overnight, and the National Hunt Committee in consultation with Radnor had decided that indiscriminate stabling in the surrounding district was too much of a security risk.

It was a nice track to ride on, a long circuit with no sharp bends, but there had been trouble with the surface in the Spring; a drain of some sort had collapsed during a hurdle race. The forefeet of one unfortunate horse had gone right through into it to a depth of about eighteen inches and he had broken a leg. In the resulting pile-up two more horses had been ruinously injured and one jockey badly concussed. Maps of the course didn't even warn that the drain existed, and I'd heard trainers wondering whether there were any more antique waterways ready to collapse with as little notice. The executive, on their side, naturally swore there weren't.

For some time I lay day-dreaming, racing round Seabury again in my mind, and wishing uselessly, hopelessly, achingly, that I could do it again in fact.

Mrs Cross tapped on the door and came in. She was a quiet,

unobtrusive mouse of a woman with soft brown hair and a slight outward cast in her grey-green eyes. Although she seemed to have no spirit whatever and seldom spoke, she ran the place like oiled machinery, helped by a largely invisible squad of 'dailies'. She had the great virtue to me of being fairly new in the job and impartial on the subject of Jenny and me. I wouldn't have trusted her predecessor, who had been fanatically fond of Jenny, not to have added cascara to my beef juice.

'The Admiral would like to know if you are feeling well today, Mr Halley,' said Mrs Cross primly, picking up my breakfast tray.

'Yes, I am, thank you.' More or less.

'He said, then, when you're ready would you join him in the dining-room?'

'The rocks?'

She gave me a small smile. 'He was up before me this morning, and had his breakfast on a tray in there. Shall I tell him you'll come down?'

'Please.'

When she had gone, and while I was slowly dressing, the telephone bell rang. Not long afterwards, Charles himself came upstairs.

'That was the police,' he said abruptly, with a frown. 'Apparently they've found a body and they want you to go and identify it.'

'Whose body, for heaven's sake?'

'They didn't say. They said they would send a car for you immediately, though. I gathered they really rang here to locate you.'

'I haven't any relatives. It must be a mistake.'

He shrugged. 'We'll know soon, anyway. Come down now and test me on the quartz. I think I've got it taped at last.'

We went down to the dining-room, where I found he was right. He went round the whole lot without a mistake. I changed the order in which they stood, but it didn't throw him. He smiled, very pleased with himself.

'Word perfect,' he said. 'Let's put them up on the shelves now. At least, we'll put all the least valuable ones up there, and the gem stones in the bookcase in the drawing-room—that one with the curtains inside the glass doors.'

'They ought to be in a safe.' I had said it yesterday evening as well.

'They were quite all right on the dining-room table last night, in spite of your fears.'

'As the consultant private detective in the case I still advise a safe.'

He laughed. 'You know bloody well I haven't got a safe. But as consultant private detective you can guard the things properly tonight. You can put them under your pillow. How's that?'

'O.K.' I nodded.

'You're not serious?'

'Well no . . . they'd be too hard under the pillow.'

'Damn it . . .'

'But upstairs, either with you or me, yes. Some of those stones really are valuable. You must have had to pay a big insurance premium on them.'

'Er . . . no,' admitted Charles. 'I guaranteed to replace anything which was damaged or lost.'

I goggled. 'I know you're rich, but . . . you're an absolute nut. Get them insured at once. Have you any idea what each specimen is worth?'

'No, as a matter of fact . . . no. I didn't ask.'

'Well, if you've got a collector coming to stay, he'll expect you to remember how much you paid for each.'

'I thought of that,' he interrupted. 'I inherited them all from a distant cousin. That covers a lot of ignorance, not only costs and values but about crystalography and distribution and rarity, and everything specialized. I found I couldn't possibly learn enough in one day. Just to be able to show some familiarity with the collection should be enough.'

'That's fair enough. But you ring the Carver Foundation at once and find out what the stones are worth just the same, and then get straight on to your broker. The trouble with you, Charles, is that you are too honest. Other people aren't. This is the bad rough world you're in now, not the Navy.'

'Very well,' he said amicably. 'I'll do as you say. Hand me that inventory.'

He went to telephone and I began putting the chunks of quartz on the empty bookshelves, but before I had done much the front door bell rang. Mrs Cross went to answer it and presently came to tell me that a policeman was asking for me.

I put my useless deformed left hand into my pocket, as I always did with strangers, and went into the hall. A tall heavy young man in uniform stood there, giving the impression of trying not to be overawed by his rather grand surroundings. I remembered how it felt.

'Is it about this body?' I asked.

'Yes, sir, I believe you are expecting us.'

'Whose body is it?'

'I don't know, sir. I was just asked to take you.'

'Well . . . where to?'

'Epping Forest, sir.'

'But that's miles away,' I protested.

'Yes, sir,' he agreed, with a touch of gloom.

'Are you sure it's me that's wanted?'

'Oh, positive, sir.'

'Well, all right. Sit down a minute while I get my coat and say where I'm going.'

The policeman drove on his gears, which I found tiring. It took two hours to go from Aynsford, west of Oxford, to Epping Forest, and it was much too long. Finally, however, we were met at a cross-roads by another policeman on a motor cycle, and followed him down a twisting secondary road. The forest stretched away all round, bare-branched and mournful in the grey damp day.

Round the bend we came on a row of two cars and a van, parked. The motor cyclist stopped and dismounted, and the policeman and I got out.

'ETA 12.15,' said the motor cyclist looking at his watch. 'You're late. The brass has been waiting here twenty minutes.'

'Traffic like caterpillars on the A40,' said my driver defensively.

'You should have used your bell,' the motor cyclist grinned. 'Come on. It's over this way.'

He led us down a barely perceptible track into the wood. We walked on dead brown leaves, rustling. After about half a mile we came to a group of men standing round a screen made of hessian. They were stamping their feet to keep warm and talking in quiet voices.

'Mr Halley?' One of them shook hands, a pleasant capable looking man in middle age who introduced himself as Chief-Inspector Cornish. 'We're sorry to bring you here all this way, but we want you to see the er . . . remains . . . before we move them. I'd better warn you, it's a perfectly horrible sight.' He gave a very human shudder.

'Who is it?' I asked.

'We're hoping you can tell us that, for sure. We think . . . but we'd like you to tell us without us putting it into your head. All right? Now?'

I nodded. He showed me round the screen.

It was Andrews. What was left of him. He had been dead a long time, and the Epping Forest scavengers seemed to have found him tasty. I could see why the police had wanted me to see him *in situ*. He was going to fall to pieces as soon as they moved him.

'Well?'

'Thomas Andrews,' I said.

They relaxed. 'Are you sure? Positive?'

'Yes.'

'It's not just the clothes?'

'No. The shape of the hair-line. Protruding ears. Exceptionally rounded helix, vestigial lobes. Very short eyebrows, thick near the nose. Spatulate thumbs, white marks across nails. Hair growing on backs of phalanges.'

'Good,' said Cornish. 'That's conclusive, I'd say. We made a preliminary identification fairly early because of the clothes—they were detailed on the wanted-for-questioning list, of course. But our first enquiries were negative. He seems to have no family, and no one could remember that he had any distinguishing marks—no tattoos, no scars, no operations, and as far as we could find out he hadn't been to a dentist all his life.'

'It was intelligent of you to check all that before you gave him to the pathologist,' I remarked.

'It was the pathologist's idea, actually.' He smiled.

'Who found him?' I asked.

'Some boys. It's usually boys who find bodies.'

'When?'

'Three days ago. But obviously he's been here weeks, probably from very soon after he took a pot at you.'

'Yes. Is the gun still in his pocket?'

Cornish shook his head. 'No sign of it.'

'You don't know yet how he died?' I asked.

'No not yet. But now you've identified him we can get on with it.'

We went out from behind the screen and some of the other men went in with a stretcher. I didn't envy them.

Cornish turned to walk back to the road with me, the driver

following at a short distance. We went fairly slowly, talking about Andrews, but it seemed more like eight miles than eight hundred yards. I wasn't quite ready for jolly country rambles.

As we reached the cars he asked me to lunch with him. I shook my head, explained about the diet, and suggested a drink instead.

'Fine,' he said. 'We could both do with one after that.' He jerked his head in the direction of Andrews. 'There's a good pub down the road this way. Your driver can follow us.'

He climbed into his car and we drove after him.

In the bar, equipped with a large brandy and water for me and a whisky and sandwiches for him, we sat at a black oak table, on chintzy chairs, surrounded by horse brasses, hunting horns, warming pans and pewter pots.

'It's funny, meeting you like this,' said Cornish, in between bites. 'I've watched you so often racing. You've won a tidy bit for me in your time. I hardly missed a meeting on the old Dunstable course, before they sold it for building. I don't get so much racing now, it's so far to a course. Nowhere now to slip along to for a couple of hours in an afternoon.' He grinned cheerfully and went on, 'You gave us some rare treats at Dunstable. Remember the day you rode that ding-dong finish on Brushwood?'

'I remember,' I said.

'You literally picked that horse up and carried him home.' He took another bite. 'I never heard such cheering. There's no mistake about it, you were something. Pity you had to give it up.'

'Yes . . .'

'Still, I suppose that's a risk you run, steeplechasing. There is always one crash too many.'

'That's right.'

'Where was it you finally bought it?'

'At Stratford on Avon, two years ago last May.'

He shook his head sympathetically, 'Rotten bad luck.'

I smiled. 'I'd had a pretty good run, though, before that.'

'I'll say you did.' He smacked his palm on the table. 'I took the Missus down to Kempton on Boxing Day, three or four years ago . . .' He went on talking with enjoyment about races he had watched, revealing himself as a true enthusiast, one of the people without whose interest all racing would collapse. Finally, regretfully, he finished his whisky and looked at his watch. 'I'll have to get back. I've enjoyed meeting you. It's odd how things turn out, isn't it? I don't suppose you ever thought when you were riding that you would be good at this sort of work.'

'What do you mean, good?' I asked, surprised.

'Hm? Oh, Andrews, of course. That description of his clothes you gave after he had shot you. And identifying him today. Most professional. Very efficient.' He grinned.

'Getting shot wasn't very efficient,' I pointed out.

He shrugged. 'That could happen to anyone, believe me . . . I shouldn't worry about that.'

I smiled, as the driver jerked me back to Aynsford, at the thought that anyone could believe me good at detective work. There was a simple explanation of my being able to describe and identify—I had read so many of the Missing Persons and Divorce files. The band of ex-policemen who compiled them knew what to base identification on, the unchanging things like ears and hands, not hair colour or the wearing of spectacles or a moustache. One of them had told me without pride that wigs, beards, face-padding, and the wearing of or omission of cosmetics made no impression on him, because they were not what he looked at. 'Ears and fingers,' he said, 'they can't disguise those. They never think of trying. Stick to ears and fingers, and you don't go far wrong.'

Ears and fingers were just about all there was left of Andrews to identify. The unappetising gristly bits.

The driver decanted me at Charles's back door and I walked along the passage to the hall. When I had one foot on the bottom tread of the staircase Charles himself appeared at the drawing-room door.

'Oh, hullo, I thought it might be you. Come in here and look at these.'

Reluctantly leaving the support of the banisters I followed him into the drawing-room.

'There,' he said, pointing. He had fixed up a strip of light inside his bookcase and it shone down on to the quartz gems, bringing them to sparkling life. The open doors with their red silk curtains made a softly glowing frame. It was an eye-catching and effective arrangement, and I told him so.

'Good. The light goes on automatically when the doors are open . . . nifty, don't you think?' He laughed. 'And you can set your mind at rest. They are now insured.'

'That's good.'

He shut the doors of the bookcase and the light inside went

out. The red curtains discreetly hid their treasure. Turning to me more seriously, he said, 'Whose body?'

'Andrews.'

'The man who shot you? How extraordinary. Suicide?'

'No. I don't think so. The gun wasn't there, anyway.'

He made a quick gesture towards the chair. 'My dear Sid, sit down, sit down. You look like d . . . er . . . a bit worn out. You shouldn't have gone all that way. Put your feet up, I'll get you a drink.' He fussed over me like a mother hen, fetching me first water, then brandy, and finally a cup of warm beef juice from Mrs Cross, and sat opposite me watching while I despatched it.

'Do you like that stuff?' he asked.

'Yes, luckily.'

'We used to have it when we were children. A ritual once a week. My father used to drain it out of the Sunday joint, propping the dish on the carving fork. We all loved it, but I haven't had any for years.'

'Try some?' I offered him the cup.

He took it and tasted it. 'Yes, it's good. Takes me back sixty years . . .' He smiled companionably, relaxing in his chair, and I told him about Andrews and the long-dead state he was in.

'It sounds,' he said slowly, 'as if he might have been murdered.'

'I wouldn't be surprised. He was young and healthy. He wouldn't just lie down and die of exposure in Essex.'

Charles laughed.

'What time are your guests expected?' I asked, glancing at the clock. It was just after five.

'About six.'

'I think I'll go up and lie on my bed for a while, then.'

'You are all right, Sid, aren't you? I mean, really all right?'

'Oh yes. Just tired.'

'Will you come down to dinner?' There was the faintest undercurrent of disappointment in his casual voice. I thought of all his hard work with the rocks and the amount of manoeuvring he had done. Besides, I was getting definitely curious myself about his intentions.

'Yes,' I nodded, getting up. 'Lay me a teaspoon.'

I made it upstairs and lay on my bed, sweating. And cursing. Although the bullet had missed everything vital in tearing holes through my gut, it had singed and upset a couple of nerves, and they had warned me in the hospital that it would be some time before I felt well. It didn't please me that so far they were right.

I heard the visitors arrive, heard their loud cheerful voices as they were shown up to their rooms, the doors shutting, the bath waters running, the various bumps and murmurs from the adjoining rooms; and eventually the diminishing chatter as they finished changing and went downstairs past my door. I heaved myself off the bed, took off the loose-waisted slacks and jersey shirt I felt most comfortable in, and put on a white cotton shirt and dark grey suit.

My face looked back at me, pale, gaunt and dark-eyed, as I brushed my hair. A bit of death's head at the feast. I grinned nastily at my reflection. It was only a slight improvement.

CHAPTER THREE

By the time I got to the foot of the stairs, Charles and his guests were coming across the hall from the drawing-room to the dining-room. The men all wore dinner jackets and the women, long dresses. Charles deliberately hadn't warned me, I reflected. He knew my convalescent kit didn't include a black tie.

He didn't stop and introduce me to his guests, but nodded slightly and went straight on into the dining-room, talking with charm to the rounded, fluffy little woman who walked beside him. Behind came Viola and a tall dark girl of striking good looks. Viola, Charles's elderly widowed cousin, gave me a passing half-smile, embarrassed and worried. I wondered what was the matter: normally she greeted me with affection, and it was only a short time since she had written warm wishes for my recovery. The girl beside her barely glanced in my direction, and the two men bringing up the rear didn't look at me at all.

Shrugging, I followed them into the dining-room. There was no mistaking the place laid for me: it consisted, in actual fact, of a spoon, a mat, a glass, and a fork, and it was situated in the centre of one of the sides. Opposite me was an empty gap. Charles seated his guests, himself in his usual place at the end of the table, with fluffy Mrs van Dysart on his right, and the striking Mrs Kraye on his left. I sat between Mrs Kraye and Rex van Dysart. It was only gradually that I sorted everyone out. Charles made no introductions whatever.

The groups at each end of the table fell into animated chat and paid me as much attention as a speed limit. I began to think I would go back to bed.

The manservant whom Charles engaged on these occasions served small individual tureens of turtle soup. My tureen, I found, contained more beef juice. Bread was passed, spoons clinked, salt and pepper were shaken and the meal began. Still no one spoke to me, though the visitors were growing slightly curious. Mrs van Dysart flicked her sharp china blue eyes from Charles to me and back again, inviting an introduction. None came. He went on talking to the two women with almost overpowering charm, apparently oblivious.

Rex van Dysart on my left offered me bread with lifted eyebrows and a faint non-committal smile. He was a large man with a flat white face, heavy black rimmed spectacles and a domineering manner. When I refused the bread he put the basket down on the table, gave me the briefest of nods, and turned back to Viola.

Even before he brought quartz into his conversation I guessed it was for Howard Kraye that the show was being put on; and I disliked him on sight with a hackle-raising antipathy that disconcerted me. If Charles was planning that I should ever work for, or with, or near Mr Kraye, I thought, he could think again.

He was a substantial man of about forty-eight to fifty, with shoulders, waist and hips all knocking forty-four. The dinner jacket sat on him with the ease of a second skin, and when he shot his cuffs occasionally he did so without affectation, showing off noticeably well manicured hands.

He had tidy grey-brown hair, straight eyebrows, narrow nose, small firm mouth, rounded freshly shaven chin, and very high unwrinkled lower eyelids, which gave him a secret, shuttered look. A neat enclosed face like a mask, with perhaps something rotten underneath. You could almost smell it across the dinner table. I guessed, rather fancifully, that he knew too much about too many vices. But on top he was smooth. Much too smooth. In my book, a nasty type of phony. I listened to him talking to Viola.

'. . . So when Doria and I got to New York I looked up those fellows in that fancy crystal palace on First Avenue and got them moving. You have to give the clothes-horse diplomats a lead, you know, they've absolutely no initiative of their own. Look, I told them, unilateral action is not only inadvisable, its impracticable. But they are so steeped in their own brand of pragmatism that informed opinion has as much chance of osmosing as mercury through rhyolite . . .'

Viola was nodding wisely while not understanding a word. The pretentious rigmarole floated comfortably over her sensible head and left her unmoved. But its flashiness seemed to me to be part of a gigantic confidence trick: one was meant to be enormously impressed. I couldn't believe that Charles had fallen under his spell. It was impossible. Not my subtle, clever, cool-headed father-in-law. Mr van Dysart, however, hung on every word.

By the end of the soup his wife at the other end of the table could contain her curiosity no longer. She put down her spoon, and with her eyes on me said to Charles in a low but clearly audible voice, 'Who is that?'

All the heads turned towards him, as if they had been waiting for the question. Charles lifted his chin and spoke distinctly, so that they should all hear the answer.

'That,' he said, 'is my son-in-law.' His tone was light, amused, and infinitely contemptuous; and it jabbed raw on a nerve I had thought long dead. I looked at him sharply, and his eyes met mine, blank and expressionless.

My gaze slid up over and past his head to the wall behind him. There for some years, and certainly that morning, had hung an oil painting of me on a horse going over a fence at Cheltenham. In its place there was now an old-fashioned seascape, brown with Victorian varnish.

Charles was watching me. I looked back at him briefly and said nothing. I suppose he knew I wouldn't. My only defence against his insults long ago had been silence, and he was counting on my instant reaction being the same again.

Mrs van Dysart leaned forward a little, and with waking malice murmured, 'Do go on, Admiral.'

Without hesitation Charles obeyed her, in the same flaying voice. 'He was fathered, as far as he knows, by a window cleaner on a nineteen-year-old unmarried girl from the Liverpool slums. She later worked, I believe, as a packer in a biscuit factory.'

'Admiral, no!' exclaimed Mrs van Dysart breathlessly.

'Indeed yes,' nodded Charles. 'As you might guess, I did my best to stop my daughter making such an unsuitable match. He is small, as you see, and he has a crippled hand. Working class and undersized . . . but my daughter was determined. You know what girls are.' He sighed.

'Perhaps she was sorry for him,' suggested Mrs van Dysart.

'Maybe,' said Charles. He hadn't finished, and wasn't to be deflected. 'If she had met him as a student of some sort, one might have understood it . . . but he isn't even educated. He finished school at fifteen to be apprenticed to a trade. He has been unemployed now for some time. My daughter, I may say, has left him.'

I sat like stone, looking down at the congealed puddle at the bottom of my soup dish, trying to loosen the clamped muscles in my jaw, and to think straight. Not four hours ago he'd shown concern for me and had drunk from my cup. As far as I could ever be certain of anything, his affection for me was genuine and unchanged. So he must have a good reason for what he was doing to me now. At least I hoped so.

I glanced at Viola. She hadn't protested. She was looking unhappily down at her place. I remembered her embarrassment out in the hall, and I guessed that Charles had warned her what to expect. He might have warned me too, I thought grimly.

Not unexpectedly, they were all looking at me. The dark and beautiful Doria Kraye raised her lovely eyebrows and in a flat, slightly nasal voice, remarked, 'You don't take offence, then.' It was half-way to a sneer. Clearly she thought I ought to take offence, if I had any guts.

'He is not offended,' said Charles easily. 'Why should the truth offend?'

'Is it true then,' asked Doria down her flawless nose, 'that you are illegitimate, and all the rest?'

I took a deep breath and eased my muscles.

'Yes.'

There was an uncomfortable short silence. Doria said, 'Oh,' blankly, and began to crumble her bread.

On cue, and no doubt summoned by Charles's foot on the bell, the manservant came in to remove the plates, and conversation trickled back to the party like cigarette smoke after a cancer scare.

I sat thinking of the details Charles had left out: the fact that my twenty-year-old father, working overtime for extra cash, had fallen from a high ladder and been killed three days before his wedding day, and that I had been born eight months later. The fact that my young mother, finding that she was dying from some obscure kidney ailment, had taken me from grammar school at fifteen, and because I was small for my age had apprenticed me to a racehorse trainer in Newmarket, so that I should have a home and someone to turn to when she had gone. They had been good enough people, both of them, and Charles knew that I thought so.

The next course was some sort of fish smothered in mushroom coloured sauce. My astronaut's delight, coming at the same time, didn't look noticeably different, as it was not in its pot, but out on a plate. Dear Mrs Cross, I thought fervently, I could kiss you. I could eat it this way with a fork, single-handed. The pots needed to be held; in my case inelegantly hugged between forearm and chest; and at that moment I would have starved rather than take my left hand out of my pocket.

Fluffy Mrs van Dysart was having a ball. Clearly she relished the idea of me sitting there practically isolated, dressed in the wrong clothes, and an object of open derision to her host. With her fair frizzy hair, her baby-blue eyes and her rose pink silk dress embroidered with silver, she looked as sweet as sugar icing. What she said showed that she thoroughly understood the pleasures of keeping a whipping boy.

'Poor relations are such a problem, aren't they?' she said to Charles sympathetically, and intentionally loud enough for me to hear. 'You can't neglect them in our position, in case the Sunday papers get hold of them and pay them to make a smear. And it's especially difficult if one has to keep them in one's own house . . . one can't, I suppose, put them to eat in the kitchen, but there are so many occasions when one could do without them. Perhaps a tray upstairs is the best thing.'

'Ah, yes,' nodded Charles smoothly, 'but they won't always agree to that.'

I half choked on a mouthful, remembering the pressure he had exerted to get me downstairs. And immediately I felt not only reassured but deeply interested. This, then, was what he had been so industriously planning, the destruction of me as a man in the eyes of his guests. He would no doubt explain why in his own good time. Meanwhile I felt slightly less inclined to go back to bed.

I glanced at Kraye, and found his greenish-amber eyes steady on my face. It wasn't as overt as in Mrs van Dysart's case, but it was there: pleasure. My toes curled inside my shoes. Interested or not, it went hard to sit tight before that loathsome, taunting half-smile. I looked down, away blotting him out.

He gave a sound half-way between a cough and a laugh, turned his head, and began talking down the table to Charles about the collection of quartz.

'So sensible of you, my dear chap, to keep them all behind glass, though most tantalizing to me from here. Is that a geode, on the middle shelf? The reflection, you know . . . I can't quite see.'

'Er . . .' said Charles, not knowing any more than I did what a geode was. 'I'm looking forward to showing them to you. After dinner, perhaps? Or tomorrow?'

'Oh, tonight, I'd hate to postpone such a treat. Did you say that you had any felspar in your collection?'

'No,' said Charles uncertainly.

'No, well, I can see it is a small specialized collection. Perhaps you are wise in sticking to silicon dioxide.'

Charles glibly launched into the cousinly-bequest alibi for ignorance, which Kraye accepted with courtesy and disappointment.

'A fascinating subject, though, my dear Roland. It repays study. The earth beneath our feet, the fundamental sediment from the Triassic and Jurassic epochs, is our priceless inheritance, the source of all our life and power . . . There is nothing which interests me so much as land.'

Doria on my right gave the tiniest of snorts, which her husband didn't hear. He was busy constructing another long, polysyllabic and largely unintelligible chat on the nature of the universe.

I sat unoccupied through the steaks, the meringue pudding, the cheese and the fruit. Conversations went on on either side of me and occasionally past me, but a deaf mute could have taken as much part as I did. Mrs van Dysart commented on the difficulties of feeding poor relations with delicate stomachs and choosey appetites. Charles neglected to tell her that I had been shot and wasn't poor, but agreed that a weak digestion in dependants was a moral fault. Mrs van Dysart loved it. Doria occasionally looked at me as if I were an interesting specimen of low life. Rex van Dysart again offered me the bread; and that was that. Finally Viola shepherded Doria and Mrs Van Dysart out to have coffee in the drawing-room and Charles offered his guests port and brandy. He passed me the brandy bottle with an air of irritation and compressed lips in disapproval when I took some. It wasn't lost on his guests.

After a while he rose, opened the glass bookcase doors, and showed the quartz to Kraye. Piece by piece the two discussed their way along the rows, with van Dysart standing beside them exhibiting polite interest and hiding his yawns of boredom. I stayed sitting down. I also helped myself to some more brandy.

Charles kept his end up very well and went through the whole lot without a mistake. He then transferred to the drawing-room, where his gem cabinet proved a great success. I tagged along, sat in an unobtrusive chair and listened to them all talking, but I came to no conclusions except that if I didn't soon go upstairs I wouldn't get there under my own steam. It was eleven o'clock and I had had a long day. Charles didn't look round when I left the room.

Half an hour later, when his guests had come murmuring up to their rooms, he came quietly through my door and over to the bed. I was still lying on top in my shirt and trousers, trying to summon some energy to finish undressing.

He stood looking down at me, smiling.

'Well?' he said.

'It is you,' I said, 'who is the dyed-in-the-wool, twenty-four carat, unmitigated bastard.'

He laughed. 'I thought you were going to spoil the whole thing when you saw your picture had gone.' He began taking off my shoes and socks. 'You looked as bleak as the Bering Strait in December. Pyjamas?'

'Under the pillow.'

He helped me undress in his quick neat naval fashion.

'Why did you do it?' I said.

He waited until I was lying between the sheets, then he perched on the edge of the bed.

'Did you mind?'

'Hell, Charles . . . of course. At first anyway.'

'I'm afraid it came out beastlier than I expected, but I'll tell you why I did it. Do you remember that first game of chess we had? When you beat me out of sight? You know why you won so easily?'

'You weren't paying enough attention.'

'Exactly. I wasn't paying enough attention, because I didn't think you were an opponent worth bothering about. A bad tactical error.' He grinned. 'An admiral should know better. If you underrate a strong opponent you are at a disadvantage. If you grossly underrate him, if you are convinced he is of absolutely no account, you prepare no defence and are certain to be defeated.'

He paused for a moment, and went on. 'It is therefore good strategy to delude the enemy into believing you are too weak to be considered. And that is what I was doing tonight on your behalf.'

He looked at me gravely. After some seconds I said, 'At what game, exactly, do you expect me to play Howard Kraye?'

He sighed contentedly, and smiled. 'Do you remember what he said interested him most?'

I thought back. 'Land.'

Charles nodded. 'Land. That's right. He collects it. Chunks of it, yards of it, acres of it . . .' He hesitated.

'Well?'

'You can play him,' he said slowly, 'for Seabury Racecourse.'

The enormity of it took my breath away.

'What?' I said incredulously. 'Don't be silly. I'm only . . .'

'Shut up,' he interrupted. 'I don't want to hear what you think you are only. You're intelligent, aren't you? You work for a detective agency? You wouldn't want Seabury to close down? Why shouldn't you do something about it?'

'But I imagine he's after some sort of take-over bid, from what you say. You want some powerful city chap or other to oppose him, not . . . me.'

'He is very much on his guard against powerful chaps in the city, but wide open to you.'

I stopped arguing because the implications were pushing into the background my inadequacy for such a task.

'Are you sure he is after Seabury?' I asked.

'Someone is,' said Charles. 'There has been a lot of buying and selling of the shares lately, and the price per share is up although they haven't paid a dividend this year. The Clerk of the Course told me about it. He said that the directors are very worried. On paper, there is no great concentration of shares in any one name, but there wasn't at Dunstable either. There, when it came to a vote on selling out to a land developer, they found that about twenty various nominees were in fact all agents for Kraye. He carried enough of the other shareholders with him, and the racecourse was lost to housing.'

'It was all legal, though?'

'A wangle; but legal, yes. And it looks like happening again.'

'But what's to stop him, if it's legal?'

'You might try.'

I stared at him in silence. He stood up and straightened the bedcover neatly. 'It would be a pity if Seabury went the way of Dunstable.' He went towards the door.

'Where does van Dysart fit in?' I asked.

'Oh,' he said, turning, 'nowhere. I met them only a week or two ago. They're on a visit from South Africa, and I was sure they wouldn't know you. And it was Mrs van Dysart I wanted. She has a tongue like a rattlesnake. I knew she would help me tear you to pieces.' He grinned. 'She'll give you a terrible week-end, I'm glad to say.'

'Thanks very much,' I said sarcastically.

'I was a bit worried that Kraye would know you by sight,' he said thoughtfully. 'But he obviously doesn't, so that's all right. And I didn't mention your name tonight, as you probably noticed. I am being careful not to.' He smiled. 'And he doesn't know my daughter married Sid Halley . . . I've given him several opportunities of mentioning it, because of course none of this would have been possible if he'd known, but he hasn't responded at all. As far as Kraye is concerned,' he finished with satisfaction, 'you are a pathetic cypher.'

I said, 'Why didn't you tell me all this before? When you so carefully left me that book on company law for instance? Or at least this evening when I came back from seeing Andrews, so that I could have been prepared, at dinner?'

He opened the door and smiled across the room, his eyes blank again.

'Sleep well,' he said. 'Good night, Sid.'

Charles took the two men out shooting the following morning, and Viola drove their wives into Oxford to do some shopping and visit an exhibition of Venetian glass. I took the opportunity of having a good look round the Krayes' bedroom.

It wasn't until I'd been there for more than ten minutes that it struck me that two years earlier I wouldn't have dreamed of doing such a thing. Now I had done it as a matter of course, without thinking twice. I grinned sardonically. Evidently even in just sitting around in a detective agency one caught an attitude of mind. I realized, moreover, that I had instinctively gone about my search methodically and with a careful touch. In an odd way it was extremely disconcerting.

I wasn't of course looking for anything special: just digging a little into the Krayes' characters. I wouldn't even concede in my own mind that I was interested in the challenge Charles had so elaborately thrown down. But all the same I searched, and thoroughly.

Howard Kraye slept in crimson pyjamas with his initials embroidered in white on the pocket. His dressing-gown was of crimson brocade with a black quilted collar and black tassels on the belt. His washing things, neatly arranged in a large fitted toilet case in the adjoining bathroom, were numerous and ornate. He used pine scented after-shave lotion, cologne friction rub, lemon hand cream, and an oily hair dressing, all from gold-topped cut-glass bottles. There were also medicated soap tablets, special formula toothpaste, talcum powder in a gilt container, deodorant, and a supersonic looking electric razor. He wore false teeth and had a spare set. He had brought a half full tin of laxatives, some fruit salts, a bottle of mouth wash, some antiseptic foot powder, penicillin throat lozenges, a spot sealing stick, digestive tablets and an eye bath. The body beautiful, in and out.

All his clothes, down to his vests and pants, had been made to measure, and he had brought enough to cover every possibility of a country week-end. I went through the pockets of his dinner-jacket and the three suits hanging beside it, but he was a tidy man and they were all empty, except for a nail file in each breast pocket. His six various pairs of shoes were hand-made and nearly new. I looked into each shoe separately, but except for trees they were all empty.

In a drawer I found neatly arranged his stock of ties, handkerchiefs, and socks: all expensive. A heavy chased silver box contained cuff links, studs, and tie pins; mostly of gold. He had avoided jewels, but one attractive pair of cuff links was made from pieces of what I now knew enough to identify as tiger-eye. The backs of his hairbrushes were beautiful slabs of the gem stone, smoky quartz. A few brown and grey hairs were lodged in between the bristles.

There remained only his luggage, four lavish suitcases standing in a neat row beside the wardrobe. I opened each one. They were all empty except for the smallest, which contained a brown calf attaché case. I looked at it carefully before I touched it, but as Kraye didn't seem to have left any tell-tales like hairs or pieces of cotton attached, I lifted it out and put it on one of the beds. It was locked, but I had learnt how to deal with such drawbacks. A lugubrious ex-police sergeant on Radnor's payroll gave me progressively harder lessons in lock-picking every time he came into the office between jobs, moaning all the while about the damage the London soot did to his chrysanthemums. My one-handedness he had seen only as a challenge, and had invented a couple of new techniques and instruments entirely for my benefit. Recently he had presented me with a collection of fine delicate keys which he had once removed from a burglar, and had bullied me until I carried them with me everywhere. They were in my room. I went and fetched them and without much trouble opened the case.

It was as meticulously tidy as everything else, and I was particularly careful not to alter the position or order of any of the papers. There were several letters from a stockbroker, a bunch of share transfer certificates, various oddments, and a series of typed sheets, headed with the previous day's date, which were apparently an up to the minute analysis of his investments. He seemed to be a rich man and to do a good deal of buying and selling. He had money in oils, mines, property and industrial stocks. There was also a sheet headed simply S.R., on which every transaction was a purchase. Against each entry was a name and the address of a bank. Some names occurred three or four times, some only once.

Underneath the papers lay a large thick brown envelope inside which were two packets of new ten pound notes. I didn't count, but there couldn't have been fewer than a hundred of them. The envelope was at the bottom of the case, except for a writing board with slightly used white blotting paper held by crocodile and gold corners. I pulled up the board and found underneath it two more sheets of paper, both covered with dates, initials, and sums of money.

I let the whole lot fall back into place, made sure that everything looked exactly as I had found it, relocked the case, and put it back into its covering suitcase.

The divine Doria, I found, was far from being as tidy as her husband. All her things were in a glorious jumble, which made leaving them undisturbed a difficult job, but also meant that she would be less likely than her husband to notice if anything were slightly out of place.

Her clothes, though they looked and felt expensive, were bought ready-made and casually treated. Her washing things consisted of a plastic zipped case, a flannel, a tooth brush, bath essence, and a puffing bottle of talc. Almost stark beside Howard's collection. No medicine. She appeared to wear nothing in bed, but a pretty white quilted dressing-gown hung half off a hanger behind the bathroom door.

She had not completely unpacked. Suitcases propped on chairs and stools still held stirred-up underclothes and various ultra feminine equipment which I hadn't seen since Jenny left.

The top of the dressing-table, though the daily seemed to have done her best to dust it, was an expensive chaos. Pots of cosmetics, bottles of scent and hair spray stood on one side, a box of tissues, a scarf, and the cluttered tray out of the top of a dressing-case filled the other. The dressing-case itself, of crocodile with gold clips, stood on the floor. I picked it up and put it on the bed. It was locked. I unlocked it, and looked inside.

Doria was quite a girl. She possessed two sets of false eyelashes, spare finger nails, and a hair piece on a tortoiseshell headband. Her big jewel case, the one tidy thing in her whole luggage, contained on the top layer the sapphire and diamond earrings she had worn the previous evening, along with a diamond sunburst brooch and a sapphire ring; and on the lower layer a second necklace, bracelet, earrings, brooch and ring all of gold, platinum, and citrine. The yellow jewels were uncommon, barbaric in design, and had no doubt been made especially for her.

Under the jewel case were four paper-back novels so pornographic in content as to raise doubts about Kraye's ability as a lover. Jenny had held that a truly satisfied woman didn't need to read dirty sex. Doria clearly did.

Alongside the books was a thick leather covered diary to which the beautiful Mrs Kraye had confided the oddest thoughts. Her life seemed to be as untidy as her clothes, a mixture of ordinary social behaviour, dream fantasy and a perverted marriage relationship. If the diary were to be believed, she and Howard obtained deeper pleasure, both of them, from him beating her, than from the normal act of love. Well, I reflected, at least they were well matched. Some of the divorces which Hunt Radnor Associates dealt with arose because one partner alone was pain fixated, the other being revolted.

At the bottom of the case were two other objects of interest. First, coiled in a brown velvet bag, the sort of leather strap used by schoolmasters, at whose purpose, in view of the diary, it was easy to guess; and second, in a chocolate box, a gun.

CHAPTER FOUR

TELEPHONING for the local taxi to come and fetch me, I went to Oxford and bought a camera. Although the shop was starting a busy Saturday afternoon, the boy who served me tackled the problem of a one-handed photographer with enthusiasm and as if he had all the time in the world. Between us we sorted out a miniature German sixteen millimetre camera, three inches long by one and a half wide, which I could hold, set, snap and wind with one hand with the greatest ease.

He gave me a thorough lesson in how to work it, added an inch to its length in the shape of a screwed-on photo electric light meter, loaded it with film, and slid it into a black case so small that it made no bulge in my trouser pocket. He also offered to change the film later if I couldn't manage it. We parted on the best of terms.

When I got back everyone was sitting round a cosy fire in the drawing-room, eating crumpets. Very tantalising. I loved crumpets.

No one took much notice when I went in and sat down on the fringe of the circle except Mrs van Dysart, who began sharpening her claws. She got in a couple of quick digs about spongers marrying girls for their money, and Charles didn't say that I hadn't. Viola looked at me searchingly, worry opening her mouth. I winked, and she shut it again in relief.

I gathered that the morning's bag had been the usual mixture (two brace of pheasant, five wild duck and a hare), because Charles preferred a rough shoot over his own land to organised affairs with beaters. The women had collected a poor opinion of Oxford shop assistants and a booklet on the manufacture of fifteenth-century Italian glass. All very normal for a country week-end. It was my snooping which seemed unreal. That, and the false position Charles had steered me into.

Kraye's gaze, and finally his hands, strayed back to the gem bookshelves. Again the door was opened, Charles' trick lighting working effectively, and one by one the gems were brought out, passed round and closely admired. Mrs van Dysart seemed much attached to a spectacular piece of rose quartz, playing with it to make light strike sparks from it, and smoothing her fingers over the glossy surface.

'Rex, you must collect some of this for me!" she ordered, her will showing like iron inside the fluff: and masterful looking Rex nodded his meek agreement.

Kraye was saying, 'You know, Roland, these are really remarkably fine specimens. Among the best I've ever seen. Your cousin must have been extremely fortunate and influential to acquire so many fine crystals.'

'Oh, indeed he was,' agreed Charles equably.

'I should be interested if you ever think of realizing on them . . . a first option, perhaps?'

'You can have a first option by all means,' smiled Charles. 'But I shan't be selling them, I assure you.'

'Oh well, so you say now. But I don't give up easily . . . I shall try you later. But don't forget, my first option?'

'Certainly,' said Charles. 'My word on it.'

Kraye smiled at the stone he held in his hands, a magnificent raw amethyst like a cluster of petrified violets.

'Don't let this fall into the fire,' he said. 'It would turn yellow.' He then treated everyone to a lecture on amethysts which would have been interesting had he made any attempt at simplicity: but blinding by words was with him either a habit or a policy. I wasn't certain which.

'. . . Manganese, of course occurring in geodes or agate nodules in South America or Russia, but with such a worldwide distribution it was only to be expected that elementary societies should ascribe to it supra rational inherencies and attributes . . .'

I suddenly found him looking straight at me, and I knew my expression had not been one of impressed admiration. More like quizzical sarcasm. He didn't like it. There was a quick flash in his eyes.

'It is symptomatic of the slum mentality,' he remarked, 'to scoff at what it can't comprehend.'

'Sid,' said Charles sharply, unconsciously giving away half my name, 'I'm sure you must have something else to do. We can let you go until dinner.'

I stood up. The natural anger rose quickly, but only as far as my teeth. I swallowed. 'Very well,' I muttered.

'Before you go, Sid,' said Mrs van Dysart from the depths of a sofa, '. . . Sid, what a deliciously plebeian name, so suitable . . . Put these down on the table for me.'

She held out both hands, one stone in each and another

balanced between them. I couldn't manage them all, and dropped them.

'Oh dear,' said Mrs van Dysart, acidly sweet, as I knelt and picked them up, putting them one by one on the table, 'I forgot you were disabled, so silly of me.' She hadn't forgotten. 'Are you sure you can't get treatment for whatever is wrong with you? You ought to try some exercises, they'd do you the world of good. All you need is a little perseverance. You owe it to the Admiral, don't you think, to *try*?'

I didn't answer, and Charles at least had the grace to keep quiet.

'I know of a very good man over here,' went on Mrs van Dysart. 'He used to work for the army at home . . . excellent at getting malingerers back into service. Now he's the sort of man who'd do you good. What do you think, Admiral, shall I fix up for your son-in-law to see him?'

'Er . . .' said Charles, 'I don't think it would work.'

'Nonsense.' She was brisk and full of smiles. 'You can't let him lounge about doing nothing for the rest of his life. A good bracing course of treatment, that's what he needs. Now,' she said turning to me, 'so that I know exactly what I'm talking about when I make an appointment, let's see this precious crippled hand of yours.'

There was a tiny pause. I could feel their probing eyes, their unfriendly curiosity.

'No,' I said calmly. 'Excuse me, but no.'

As I walked across the room and out of the door her voice floated after me. 'There you are, Admiral, he doesn't *want* to get better. They're all the same . . .'

I lay on my bed for a couple of hours re-reading the book on company law, especially, now, the section on take-overs. It was no easier than it had been in the hospital, and now that I knew why I was reading it, it seemed more involved, not less. If the directors of Seabury were worried, they would surely have called in their own investigator. Someone who knew his way round the stock markets like I knew my way round the track. An expert. I wasn't at all the right sort of person to stop Kraye, even if indeed anyone could stop him. And yet . . . I stared at the ceiling, taking my lower lip between my teeth . . . and yet I did have a wild idea . . .

Viola came in, knocking as she opened the door.

'Sid, dear, are you all right? Can I do anything for you?' She shut the door, gentle, generous, and worried.

I sat up and swung my legs over the side of the bed. 'No thanks, I'm fine.'

She perched on the arm of an easy chair, looked at me with her kind, slightly mournful brown eyes, and said a little breathlessly, 'Sid, why are you letting Charles say such terrible things about you? It isn't only when you are there in the room, they've been, oh, almost sniggering about you behind your back. Charles and that frightful Mrs van Dysart . . . What has happened between you and him? When you nearly died he couldn't have been more worried if you'd been his own son . . . but now he is so cruel, and terribly unfair.'

'Dear Viola, don't worry. It's only some game that Charles is playing, and I go along with him.'

'Yes,' she said, nodding. 'He warned me. He said that you were both going to lay a smoke screen and that I was on no account to say a single word in your defence the whole weekend. But it wasn't true, was it? When I saw your face, when Charles said that about your poor mother, I knew you didn't know what he was going to do.'

'Was it so obvious?' I said ruefully. 'Well, I promise you I haven't quarrelled with him. Will you just be a dear and do exactly as he asked? Don't say a single word to any of them about . . . um . . . the more successful bits of my life history, or about my job at the agency, or about the shooting. You didn't today, did you, on the trip to Oxford?' I finished with some anxiety.

She shook her head. 'I thought I'd talk to you first.'

'Good,' I grinned.

'Oh dear,' she cried, partly in relief, partly in puzzlement. 'Well in that case, Charles asked me to pop in and make sure you would come down to dinner.'

'Oh he did, did he? Afraid I'll throw a boot at him, I should think, after sending me out of the room like that. Well, you just pop back to Charles and say that I'll come down to dinner on condition that he organizes some chemmy afterwards, and includes me out.'

Dinner was a bit of a trial: with their smoked salmon and pheasant the guests enjoyed another round of Sid-baiting. Both the Krayes, egged on by Charles and the fluffy harpy beside him, had developed a pricking skill at this novel weekend parlour game, and I heartily wished Charles had never thought of it. However, he kept his side of the bargain by digging out the chemmy shoe, and after the coffee, the brandy, and another inspection of the dining-room quartz, he settled his guests firmly round the table in the drawing-room.

Upstairs, once the shoe was clicking regularly and the players were well involved, I went and collected Kraye's attaché case and took it along to my room.

Because I was never going to get another chance and did not want to miss something I might regret later, I photographed every single paper in the case. All the stockbroker's letters and all the investment reports. All the share certificates, and also the two separate sheets under the writing board.

Although I had an ultra-bright light bulb and the exposure meter to help me to get the right setting, I took several pictures at different light values of the papers I considered the most important, in order to be sure of getting the sharpest possible result. The little camera handled beautifully, and I found I could change the films in their tiny cassettes without much difficulty. By the time I had finished I had used three whole films of twenty exposures on each. It took me a long time, as I had to put the camera down between each shot to move the next paper into my pool of light, and also had to be very careful not to alter the order in which the papers had lain in the case.

The envelope of ten pound notes kept me hoping like crazy that Howard Kraye would not lose heavily and come upstairs for replacements. It seemed to me at the time a ridiculous thing to do, but I took the two flat blocks of tenners out of the envelope, and photographed them as well. Putting them back I flipped through them: the notes were new, consecutive, fifty to a packet. One thousand pounds to a penny.

When everything was back in the case I sat looking at the contents for a minute, checking their position against my visual memory of how they looked when I first saw them. At last satisfied, I shut the case, locked it, rubbed it over to remove any finger marks I might have left, and put it back where I had found it.

After that I went downstairs to the dining-room for the brandy I had refused at dinner. I needed it. Carrying the glass, I listened briefly outside the drawing-room door to the murmurs and clicks from within and went upstairs again, to bed.

Lying in the dark I reviewed the situation. Howard Kraye, drawn by the bait of a quartz collection, had accepted an invitation to a quiet week-end in the country with a retired admiral.

With him he had brought a selection of private papers. As he had no possible reason to imagine that anyone in such innocent surroundings would spy on him, the papers might be very private indeed. So private that he felt safest when they were with him? Too private to leave at home? It would be nice to think so.

At that point, imperceptibly, I fell asleep.

The nerves in my abdomen wouldn't give up. After about five hours of fighting them unsuccessfully I decided that staying in bed all morning thinking about it was doing no good, and got up and dressed.

Drawn partly against my will, I walked along the passage to Jenny's room, and went in. It was the small sunny room she had had as a child. She had gone back to it when she left me and it was all hers alone. I had never slept there. The single bed, the relics of childhood, girlish muslin frills on curtains and dressing-table, everything shut me out. The photographs round the room were of her father, her dead mother, her sister, brother-in-law, dogs and horses, but not of me. As far as she could, she had blotted out her marriage.

I walked slowly round touching her things, remembering how much I had loved her. Knowing, too, that there was no going back, and that if she walked through the door at that instant we would not fall into each other's arms in tearful reconciliation.

Removing a one-eyed teddy bear I sat down for a while on her pink armchair. It's difficult to say just where a marriage goes wrong, because the accepted reason often isn't the real one. The rows Jenny and I had had were all ostensibly caused by the same thing: my ambition. Grown finally too heavy for flat racing, I had switched entirely to steeplechasing the season before we married, and I wanted to be champion jumping jockey. To this end I was prepared to eat little, drink less, go to bed early, and not make love if I were racing the next day. It was unfortunate that she liked late-night parties and dancing more than anything else. At first she gave them up willingly, then less willingly, and finally in fury. After that, she started going on her own.

In the end she told me to choose between her and racing. But by then I was indeed champion jockey, and had been for some time, and I couldn't give it up. So Jenny left. It was just life's little irony that six months later I lost the racing as well. Gradually since then I had come to realize that a marriage didn't break up just because one half liked parties and the other didn't. I thought now that Jenny's insistence on a gay time was the result of my having failed her in some basic, deeply necessary way. Which did nothing whatsoever for my self-respect or my self-confidence.

I sighed, stood up, replaced the teddy bear, and went downstairs to the drawing-room. Eleven o'clock on a windy autumn morning.

Doria was alone in the big comfortable room, sitting on the window seat and reading the Sunday papers, which lay around her on the floor in a haphazard mess.

'Hello,' she said, looking up. 'What hole did you crawl out of?'

I walked over to the fire and didn't answer.

'Poor little man, are his feelings hurt then?'

'I do have feelings, the same as anyone else.'

'So you actually can talk?' she said mockingly. 'I'd begun to wonder.'

'Yes, I can talk.'

'Well, now, tell me all your troubles, little man.'

'Life is just a bowl of cherries.'

She uncurled herself from the window seat and came across to the fire, looking remarkably out of place in skin-tight leopard printed pants and a black silk shirt.

She was the same height as Jenny, the same height as me, just touching five foot six. As my smallness had always been an asset for racing, I never looked on it as a handicap for life in general, either physical or social. Neither had I ever really understood why so many people thought that height for its own sake was important. But it would have been naïve not to take note of the widespread extraordinary assumption that the mind and heart could be measured by tallness. The little man with the big emotion was a stock comic figure. It was utterly irrational. What difference did three or four inches of leg bone make to a man's essential nature? Perhaps I had been fortunate in coming to terms early with the effect of poor nutrition in a difficult childhood; but it did not stop me understanding why other short men struck back in defensive aggression. There were the pinpricks, for instance, of girls like Doria calling one 'little' and intending it as an insult.

'You've dug yourself into a cushy berth here, haven't you?' she said, taking a cigarette from the silver box on the mantelpiece.

'I suppose so.'

'If I were the Admiral I'd kick you out.'

'Thank you,' I said, neglecting to offer her a light. With a mean look she found a box of matches and struck one for herself.

'Are you ill, or something?'

'No. Why?'

'You eat those faddy health foods, and you look such a sickly little creature . . . I just wondered.' She blew the smoke down her nose. 'The Admiral's daughter must have been pretty desperate for a wedding ring.'

'Give her her due,' I said mildly. 'At least she didn't pick a rich father-figure twice her age.'

I thought for a moment she meant to go into the corny routine of smacking my face, but as it happened she was holding the cigarette in the hand she needed.

'You little shit,' she said instead. A charming girl, altogether.

'I get along.'

'Not with me, you don't.' Her face was tight. I had struck very deep, it seemed.

'Where is everyone else?' I asked, gesturing around the empty room.

'Out with the Admiral somewhere. And you can take yourself off again too. You're not wanted in here.'

'I'm not going. I live here, remember?'

'You went quick enough last night,' she sneered. 'When the Admiral says jump, you jump. But fast, little man. And that I like to see.'

'The Admiral,' I pointed out, 'is the hand that feeds. I don't bite it.'

'Boot-licking little creep.'

I grinned at her nastily and sat down in an arm-chair. I still didn't feel too good. Pea green and clammy, to be exact. Nothing to be done though, but wait for it to clear off.

Doria tapped ash off her cigarette and looked at me down her nose, thinking up her next attack. Before she could launch it, however, the door opened and her husband came in.

'Doria,' he said happily, not immediately seeing me in the arm-chair, 'where have you hidden my cigarette case? I shall punish you for it.'

She made a quick movement towards me with her hand and Howard saw me and stopped dead.

'What are you doing here?' he said brusquely, the fun-and-games dying abruptly out of his face and voice.

'Passing the time.'

'Clear out then. I want to talk to my wife.'

I shook my head and stayed put.

'Short of picking him up and throwing him out bodily,' said Doria, 'you won't get rid of him. I've tried.'

Kraye shrugged. 'Roland puts up with him. I suppose we can too.' He picked up one of the newspapers and sat down in an arm-chair facing me. Doria wandered back to the window-seat, pouting. Kraye straightened up the paper and began to read the front page. Across the back page, the racing page, facing me across the fireplace, the black, bold headlines jumped out.

'ANOTHER HALLEY?'

Underneath, side by side, were two photographs; one of me, and the other of a boy who had won a big race the day before.

It was by then essential that Kraye should not discover how Charles had misrepresented me; it had gone much too far to be explained away as a joke. The photograph was clearly printed for once. I knew it well. It was an old one which the papers had used several times before, chiefly because it was a good likeness. Even if none of the guests read the racing column, as Doria obviously hadn't, it might catch their eye in passing, through being in such a conspicuous place.

Kraye finished reading the front page and began to turn the paper over.

'Mr Kraye,' I said. 'Do you have a very big quartz collection yourself?'

He lowered the paper a little and gave me an unenthusiastic glance.

'Yes, I have,' he said briefly.

'Then could you please tell me what would be a good thing to give the Admiral to add to his collection? And where would I get it, and how much would it cost?'

The paper folded over, hiding my picture. He cleared his throat and with strained politeness started to tell me about some obscure form of crystal which the Admiral didn't have. Press the right button, I thought . . . Doria spoilt it. She walked jerkily over to Kraye and said crossly, 'Howard, for God's sake. The little creep is buttering you up. I bet he wants something. You're a sucker for anyone who will talk about rocks.'

'People don't make fools of me,' said Kraye flatly, his eyes narrowing in irritation.

'No. I only want to please the Admiral,' I explained.

'He's a sly little beast,' said Doria. 'I don't like him.'

Kraye shrugged, looked down at the newspaper and began to unfold it again.

'It's mutual,' I said casually. 'You Daddy's doll.'

Kraye stood up slowly and the paper slid to the floor, front page up.

'What did you say?'

'I said I didn't think much of your wife.'

He was outraged, as well he might be. He took a single step across the rug, and there was suddenly something more in the room than three guests sparring round a Sunday morning fire.

Even though I was as far as he knew an insignificant fly to swat, a clear quality of menace flowed out of him like a radio signal. The calm social mask had disappeared, along with the wordy, phony, surface personality. The vague suspicion I had gained from reading his papers, together with antipathy I had felt for him all along, clarified into belated recognition: this was not just a smooth speculator operating near the legal border-line, but a full-blown, powerful, dangerous big-time crook.

Trust me, I thought, to prod an anthill and find a hornets' nest. Twist the tail of a grass snake and find a boa constrictor. What on earth would he be like, I wondered, if one did more to cross him than disparage his choice of wife.

'He's sweating,' said Doria, pleased. 'He's afraid of you.'

'Get up,' he said.

As I was sure that if I stood up he would simply knock me down again, I stayed where I was.

'I'll apologize,' I said.

'Oh no,' said Doria, 'that's much too easy.'

'Something subtle,' suggested Kraye, staring down.

'I know!' Doria was delighted with her idea. 'Let's get that hand out of his pocket.'

They both saw from my face that I would hate that more than anything. They both smiled. I thought of bolting, but it meant leaving the paper behind.

'That will do very nicely,' said Kraye. He leant down, twined one hand into the front of my jersey shirt and the other into my hair, and pulled me to my feet. The top of my hand reached about to his chin. I wasn't in much physical shape for resisting, but I took a half-hearted swipe at him as I came up. Doria caught my swinging arm and twisted it up behind my back, using both of hers and an uncomfortable amount of pressure. She was a strong healthy girl with no inhibitions about hurting people.

'That'll teach you to be rude to me,' she said with satisfaction.

I thought of kicking her shins, but it would only have brought more retaliation. I also wished Charles would come back at once from wherever he was.

He didn't.

Kraye transferred his grip from my hair to my left forearm and began to pull. That arm was no longer much good, but I did my best. I tucked my elbow tight against my side, and my hand stayed in my pocket.

'Hold him harder,' he said to Doria. 'He's stronger than he looks.' She levered my arm up another inch and I started to roll round to get out of it. But Kraye still had his grasp on the front of my jersey, with his forearm leaning across under my throat, and between the two of them I was properly stuck. All the same, I found I couldn't just stand still and let them do what I so much didn't want them to.

'He squirms, doesn't he?' said Doria cheerfully.

I squirmed and struggled a good deal more; until they began getting savage with frustration, and I was panting. It was my wretched stomach which finished it. I began to feel too ill to go on. With a terrific jerk Kraye dragged my hand out.

'Now,' he said triumphantly.

He gripped my elbow fiercely and pulled the jersey sleeve up from my wrist. Doria let go of my right arm and came to look at their prize. I was shaking with rage, pain, humiliation . . . heaven knows what.

'Oh,' said Doria blankly. 'Oh.'

She was no longer smiling, and nor was her husband. They looked steadily at the wasted, flabby, twisted hand, and at the scars on my forearm, wrist and palm, not only the terrible jagged marks of the original injury but the several tidier ones of the operations I had had since. It was a mess, a right and proper mess.

'So that's why the Admiral lets him stay, the nasty little beast,' said Doria, screwing up her face in distaste.

'It doesn't excuse his behaviour,' said Kraye. 'I'll make sure he keeps that tongue of his still, in future.'

He stiffened his free hand and chopped the edge of it across the worst part, the inside of my wrist. I jerked in his grasp.

'Ah . . .' I said. 'Don't.'

'He'll tell tales to the Admiral,' said Doria warningly, 'if you hurt him too much. It's a pity, but I should think that's about enough.'

'I don't agree, but . . .'

There was a scrunch on the gravel outside, and Charles' car swept past the window, coming back.

Kraye let go of my elbow with a shake. I went weakly down on my knees on the rug, and it wasn't all pretence.

'If you tell the Admiral about this, I'll deny it,' said Kraye, 'and we know who he'll believe.'

I did know who he'd believe, but I didn't say so. The newspaper which had caused the whole rumpus lay close beside me on the rug. The car doors slammed distantly. The Krayes turned away from me towards the window, listening. I picked up the paper, got to my feet, and set off for the door. They didn't try to stop me in any way. They didn't mention the newspaper either. I opened the door, went through, shut it, and steered a slightly crooked course across the hall to the wardroom. Upstairs was too far. I shut the wardroom door behind me, hid the newspaper, slid into Charles' favourite arm-chair, and waited for my various miseries, mental and physical, to subside.

Some time later Charles came in to fetch some fresh cartons of cigarettes.

'Hullo,' he said over his shoulder, opening the cupboard. 'I thought you were still in bed. Mrs Cross said you weren't very well this morning. It isn't at all warm in here. Why don't you come into the drawing-room?'

'The Krayes . . .' I stopped.

'They won't bite you.' He turned round, cigarettes in hand. He looked at my face. 'What's so funny?' and then more sharply, looking closer. 'What's the matter?'

'Oh, nothing. Have you seen today's *Sunday Hemisphere*?'

'No, not yet. Do you want it? I thought it was in the drawing-room with the other papers.'

'No, it's in the top drawer of your desk. Take a look.'

Puzzled, he opened the drawer, took out the paper, and unfolded it. He went to the racing section unerringly.

'My God!' he said, aghast. 'Today of all days.' His eyes skimmed down the page and he smiled. 'You've read this, of course?'

I shook my head. 'I just took it to hide it.'

He handed me the paper. 'Read it then. It'll be good for your ego. They don't let you die! "Young Finch",' he quoted, ' "showed much of the judgment and miraculous precision of the great Sid". How about that? And that's just the start.'

'Yeah, how about it?' I grinned. 'Count me out for lunch, if you don't mind, Charles. You don't need me there any more.'

'All right, if you don't feel like it. They'll be gone by six at the latest, you'll be glad to hear.' He smiled and went back to his guests.

I read the newspaper before putting it away again. As Charles had said, it was good for the ego. I thought the columnist, whom I'd known for years, had somewhat exaggerated my erstwhile powers. A case of the myth growing bigger than the reality. But still, it was nice. Particularly in view of the galling, ignominious end to the rough-house in which the great Sid had so recently landed himself.

On the following morning Charles and I changed back the labels on the chunks of quartz and packed them up ready to return to the Carver Foundation. When we had finished we had one label left over.

'Are you sure we haven't put one stone in the box without changing the label?' said Charles.

'Positive.'

'I suppose we'd better check. I'm afraid that's what we've done.'

We took all the chunks out of the big box again. The gem collection, which Charles under protest had taken to bed with him each night, was complete; but we looked through them again too to make sure the missing rock had not got among them by mistake. It was nowhere to be found.

'St Luke's Stone,' I read from the label. 'I remember where that was, up on the top shelf on the right hand side.'

'Yes,' agreed Charles, 'a dull looking lump about the size of a fist. I do hope we haven't lost it.'

'We have lost it,' I remarked. 'Kraye's pinched it.'

'Oh no,' Charles exclaimed. 'You can't be right.'

'Go and ring up the Foundation, and ask them what the stone is worth.'

He shook his head doubtfully, but went to the telephone, and came back frowning.

'They say it hasn't any intrinsic value, but it's an extremely rare form of meteorite. It never turns up in mines or quarrying of course. You have to wait for it to fall from the heavens, and then find it. Very tricky.'

'A quartz which friend Kraye didn't have.'

'But he surely must know I'd suspect him?' Charles protested.

'You'd never have missed it, if it had really been part of your cousin's passed-on collection. There wasn't any gap on the shelf just now. He'd moved the others along. He couldn't know you would check carefully almost as soon as he had gone.'

Charles sighed. 'There isn't a chance of getting it back.'

'No,' I agreed.

'Well, it's a good thing you insisted on the insurance,' he said. 'Carver's valued that boring-looking lump more than all the rest put together. Only one other meteorite like it has ever been found: the St Mark's Stone.' He smiled suddenly. 'We seem to have mislaid the equivalent of the penny black.'

CHAPTER FIVE

Two days later I went back through the porticoed columned doorway of Hunt Radnor Associates, a lot more alive than when I last came out.

I got a big hullo from the girl on the switchboard, went up the curving staircase very nearly whistling, and was greeted by a barrage of ribald remarks from the Racing Section. What most surprised me was the feeling I had of coming home: I had never thought of myself as really belonging to the agency before, even though down at Aynsford I had realized that I very much didn't want to leave it. A bit late, that discovery. The skids were probably under me already.

Chico grinned widely. 'So you made it.'

'Well . . . Yes.'

'I mean, back here to the grindstone.'

'Yeah.'

'But,' he cast a rolling eye at the clock, 'late as usual.'

'Go stuff yourself,' I said.

Chico threw out an arm to the smiling department. 'Our Sid is back, his normal charming bloody self. Work in the agency can now begin.'

'I see I still haven't got a desk,' I observed, looking round. No desk. No roots. No real job. As ever.

'Sit on Dolly's, she's kept it dusted for you.'

Dolly looked at Chico, smiling, the mother-hunger showing too vividly in her great blue eyes. She might be the second-best head of department the agency possessed, with a cross-referencing filing-index mind like a computer, she might be a powerful, large, self-assured woman of forty-odd with a couple of marriages behind her and an ever hopeful old bachelor at her heels, but she still counted her life a wasteland because her body couldn't produce children. Dolly was a terrific worker, overflowing with intensely female vitality, excellent drinking company, and very, very sad.

Chico didn't want to be mothered. He was prickly about mothers. All of them in general, not just those who abandoned their tots in push-chairs at police stations near Barnes Bridge. He jollied Dolly along and deftly avoided her tentative maternal invitations.

I hitched a hip on to a long accustomed spot on the edge of Dolly's desk, and swung my leg.

'Well, Dolly my love, how's the sleuthing trade?' I said.

'What we need,' she said with mock tartness, 'is a bit more work from you and a lot less lip.'

'Give me a job, then.'

'Ah, now.' She pondered. 'You could . . .' she began, then stopped. 'Well, no . . . perhaps not. And it had better be Chico who goes to Lambourn; some trainer there wants a doubtful lad checked on . . .'

'So there's nothing for me?'

'Er . . . well . . .' said Dolly. 'No.' She had said no a hundred times before. She had never once said yes.

I made a face at her, picked up her telephone, pressed the right button, and got through to Radnor's secretary.

'Joanie? This is Sid Halley. Yes . . . back from Beyond, that's it. Is the old man busy? I'd like a word with him.'

'Big deal,' said Chico.

Joanie's prim voice said, 'He's got a client with him just now. When she's gone I'll ask him, and ring you back.'

'O.K.' I put down the receiver.

Dolly raised her eyebrows. As head of the department she was my immediate boss, and in asking direct for a session with Radnor I was blowing agency protocol a raspberry. But I was certain that her constant refusal to give me anything useful to do was a direct order from Radnor. If I wanted the drain unblocked I would have to go and pull out the plug. Or go on my knees to stay at all.

'Dolly, love, I'm tired of kicking my heels. Even against your well-worn desk, though the view from here is ravishing.' She was wearing, as she often did, a cross-over cream silk shirt: it crossed over at a point which on a young girl would have caused a riot. On Dolly it still looked pretty potent, owing to the generosity of nature and the disposal of her arrangements.

'Are you chucking it in?' said Chico, coming to the point.

'It depends on the old man,' I said. 'He may be chucking me out.'

There was a brief, thoughtful silence in the department. They all knew very well how little I did. How little I had been content to do. Dolly looked blank, which wasn't helpful.

Jones-boy clattered in with a tray of impeccable unchipped tea mugs. He was sixteen; noisy, rude, anarchistic, callous, and probably the most efficient office boy in London. His hair grew robustly nearly down to his shoulders, wavy and fanatically clean, dipping slightly in an expensive styling at the back. From behind he looked like a girl, which never disconcerted him. From in front his bony, acned face proclaimed him unprepossessingly male. He spent half his pay packet and his Sundays in Carnaby Street and the other half on week nights chasing girls. According to him, he caught them. No girls had so far appeared in the office to corroborate his story.

Under the pink shirt beat a stony heart; inside the sprouting head hung a big 'So What?' Yet it was because this amusing, ambitious, unsocial creature invariably arrived well before his due hour to get his office arrangements ready for the day that he had found me before I died. There was a moral there, somewhere.

He gave me a look. 'The corpse has returned, I see.'

'Thanks to you,' I said idly, but he knew I meant it. He didn't care, though.

He said, 'Your blood and stuff ran through a crack in the linoleum and soaked the wood underneath. The old man was wondering if it would start dry rot or something.'

'Jones-boy,' protested Dolly, looking sick. 'Get the hell out of here, and shut up.'

The telephone rang on her desk. She picked it up and listened, said, 'All right,' and disconnected.

'The old man wants to see you. Right away.'

'Thanks.' I stood up.

'The flipping boot?' asked Jones-boy interestedly.

'Keep your snotty nose out,' said Chico.

'And balls to you . . .'

I went out smiling, hearing Dolly start to deal once again with the running dog fight Chico and Jones-boy never tired of. Downstairs, across the hall, into Joanie's little office and through into Radnor's.

He was standing by the window, watching the traffic doing its nut in the Cromwell Road. This room, where the clients poured out their troubles, was restfully painted a quiet grey, carpeted and curtained in crimson and furnished with comfortable armchairs, handy little tables with ashtrays, pictures on the walls, ornaments, and vases of flowers. Apart from Radnor's small desk in the corner, it looked like an ordinary sitting-room, and indeed everyone believed that he had bought the room intact with the lease, so much was it what one would expect to find in a graceful, six-storeyed, late Victorian town house. Radnor had a theory that people exaggerated and distorted facts less in such peaceful surroundings than in the formality of a more orthodox office.

'Come in, Sid,' he said. He didn't move from the window, so I joined him there. He shook hands.

'Are you sure you're fit enough to be here? You haven't been as long as I expected. Even knowing you . . .' he smiled slightly, with watching eyes.

I said I was all right. He remarked on the weather, the rush-hour and the political situation, and finally worked round to the point we both knew was at issue.

'So, Sid, I suppose you'll be looking around a bit now?'

Laid on the line, I thought.

'If I wanted to stay here . . .'

'If? Hm, I don't know.' He shook his head very slightly.

'Not on the same terms, I agree.'

'I'm sorry it hasn't worked out.' He sounded genuinely regretful, but he wasn't making it easy.

I said with careful calm. 'You've paid me for nothing for two years. Well, give me a chance now to earn what I've had. I don't really want to leave.'

He lifted his head slightly like a pointer to a scent, but he said nothing. I ploughed on.

'I'll work for you for nothing, to make up for it. But only if it's real, decent work. No more sitting around. It would drive me mad.'

He gave me a hard stare and let out a long breath like a sigh. 'Good God. At last,' he said. 'And it took a bullet to do it.'

'What do you mean?'

'Sid, have you ever seen a zombie wake up?'

'No,' I said ruefully, understanding him. 'It hasn't been as bad as that?'

He shrugged one shoulder. 'I saw you racing, don't forget. You notice when a fire goes out. We've had the pleasant, flippant ashes drifting round this office, that's all.' He smiled deprecatingly at his flight of fancy: he enjoyed making pictures of words. It wasted a lot of office time, on the whole.

'Consider me alight again, then,' I grinned. 'And I've brought a puzzle back with me. I want very much to sort it out.'

'A long story?'

'Fairly, yes.'

'We'd better sit down, then.'

He waved me to an arm-chair, sank into one himself, and prepared to listen with the stillness and concentration which sent him time and time again to the core of a problem.

I told him about Kraye's dealing in racecourses. Both what I knew and what I guessed. When at length I finished he said calmly, 'Where did you get hold of this?'

'My father-in-law, Charles Roland, tossed it at me while I was staying with him last week-end. He had Kraye as a house guest.' The subtle old fox, I thought, throwing me in at the deep end: making me wake up and swim.

'And Roland got it from where?'

'The Clerk of the Course at Seabury told him that the directors were worried about too much share movement, that it was Kraye who got control of Dunstable, and they were afraid he was at it again.'

'But the rest, what you've just told me, is your own supposition?'

'Yes.'

'Based on your appraisal of Kraye over one week-end?'

'Partly on what he showed me of his character, yes. Partly on what I read of his papers . . .' With some hesitation I told him about my snooping and the photography. '. . . The rest, I suppose, a hunch.'

'Hmm. It needs checking . . . Have you brought the films with you?'

I nodded, took them out of my pocket, and put them on the little table beside me.

'I'll get them developed.' He drummed his fingers lightly on the arm of the chair, thinking. Then, as if having made a decision, said more briskly, 'Well, the first thing we need is a client.'

'A client?' I echoed absent-mindedly.

'Of course. What else? We are not the police. We work strictly for profit. Ratepayers don't pay the overheads and salaries in this agency. The clients do.'

'Oh . . . yes, of course.'

'The most likely client in this case is either Seabury Racecourse executive, or perhaps the National Hunt Committee. I think I should sound out the Senior Steward first, in either case. No harm in starting at the top.'

'He might prefer to try the police,' I said, 'free.'

'My dear Sid, the one thing people want when they employ private investigators is privacy. They pay for privacy. When the police investigate something, everyone knows about it. When we do, they don't. That's why we sometimes get criminal cases when it would undoubtedly be cheaper to go to the police.'

'I see. So you'll try the Senior Steward . . .'

'No,' he interrupted. 'You will.'

'I?'

'Naturally. It's your case.'

'But it's your agency . . . he is used to negotiating with you.'

'You know him too,' he pointed out.

'I used to ride for him, and that puts me on a bad footing for this sort of thing. I'm a jockey to him, an ex-jockey. He won't take me seriously.'

Radnor shrugged a shoulder. 'If you want to take on Kraye, you need a client. Go and get one.'

I knew very well that he never sent even senior operatives, let alone inexperienced ones, to arrange or angle for an assignment, so that for several moments I couldn't really believe that he intended me to go. But he said nothing else, and eventually I stood up and went towards the door.

'Sandown Races are on today,' I said tentatively. 'He's sure to be there.'

'A good opportunity.' He looked straight ahead, not at me.

'I'll try it, then.'

'Right.'

He wasn't letting me off. But then he hadn't kicked me out either. I went through the door and shut it behind me, and while I was still hesitating in disbelief I heard him inside the room give a sudden guffaw, a short, sharp, loud, triumphant snort of laughter.

I walked back to my flat, collected the car, and drove down to Sandown. It was a pleasant day, dry, sunny, and warm for November, just right for drawing a good crowd for steeple-chasing.

I turned in through the racecourse gates, spirits lifting, parked the car (a Mercedes S.L.230 with automatic gears, power assisted steering, and a strip on the back saying NO HAND SIGNALS), and walked round to join the crowd outside the weighing room door. I could no longer go through it. It had been one of the hardest things to get used to, the fact that all the changing rooms and weighing rooms which had been my second homes for fourteen years were completely barred to me from the day I rode my last race. You didn't lose just a job when you handed in your jockey's licence, you lost a way of life.

There were a lot of people to talk to at Sandown, and as I hadn't been racing for six weeks I had a good deal of gossip to catch up on. No one seemed to know about the shooting, which was fine by me, and I didn't tell them. I immersed myself very happily in the racecourse atmosphere and for an hour Kraye retreated slightly into the background.

Not that I didn't keep an eye on my purpose, but until the third race the Senior Steward, Viscount Hagbourne, was never out of a conversation long enough for me to catch him.

Although I had ridden for him for years and had found him undemanding and fair, he was in most respects still a stranger. An aloof, distant man, he seemed to find it difficult to make ordinary human contacts, and unfortunately he had not proved a great success as Senior Steward. He gave the impression, not of power in himself, but of looking over his shoulder at power behind: I'd have said he was afraid of incurring the disapproval of the little knot of rigidly determined men who in fact ruled racing themselves, regardless of who might be in office at the time. Lord Hagbourne postponed making decisions until it was almost too late to make them, and there was still a danger after that that he would change his mind. But all the same he was the front man until his year of office ended, and with him I had to deal.

At length I fielded him neatly as he turned away from the Clerk of the Course and forestalled a trainer who was advancing upon him with a grievance. Lord Hagbourne, with one of his rare moments of humour, deliberately turned his back on the grievance and consequently greeted me with more warmth than usual.

'Sid, nice to see you. Where have you been lately?'

'Holidays,' I explained succinctly. 'Look, sir, can I have a talk with you after the races? There's something I want to discuss urgently.'

'No time like the present,' he said, one eye on the grievance. 'Fire away.'

'No, sir. It needs time and all your attention.'

'Hm?' The grievance was turning away. 'Not today, Sid, I have to get home. What is it? Tell me now.'

'I want to talk to you about the take-over bid for Seabury Racecourse.'

He looked at me, startled. 'You want . . .?'

'That's right. It can't be said out here where you will be needed at any moment by someone else. If you could just manage twenty minutes at the end of the afternoon . . . ?'

'Er . . . what is your connection with Seabury?'

'None in particular, sir. I don't know if you remember, but I've been connected' (a precise way of putting it) 'with Hunt Radnor Associates for the last two years. Various . . . er . . . facts about Seabury have come our way and Mr Radnor thought you might be interested. I am here as his representative.'

'Oh, I see. Very well, Sid, come to the Stewards' tea room after the last. If I'm not there, wait for me. Right?'

'Yes. Thank you.'

I walked down the slope and then up the iron staircase to the jockeys' box in the stand, smiling at myself. Representative. A nice big important word. It covered anything from an ambassador down. Commercial travellers had rechristened themselves with its rolling syllables years ago . . . they had done it because of the jokes, of course. It didn't sound the same, somehow, starting off with 'Did you hear the one about the representative who stopped at a lonely farmhouse . . . ?' Rodent officers, garbage disposal and sanitary staff: pretty new names for rat-catchers, dustmen and road sweepers. So why not for me?

'Only idiots laugh at nothing,' said a voice in my ear. 'What the hell are you looking so pleased about all of a sudden? And where the blazes have you been this last month?'

'Don't tell me you've missed me?' I grinned, not needing to look round. We went together through the door of the high-up jockeys' box, two of a kind, and stood looking out over the splendid racecourse.

'Best view in Europe.' He sighed. Mark Witney, thirty-eight years old, racehorse trainer. He had a face battered like a boxer's from too many racing falls and in the two years since he hung up his boots and stopped wasting he had put on all of three stone. A fat, ugly man. We had a host of memories in common, a host of hard ridden races. I liked him a lot.

'How's things?' I said.

'Oh, fair, fair. They'll be a damn sight better if that animal of mine wins the fifth.'

'He must have a good chance.'

'He's a damn certainty, boy. A certainty. If he doesn't fall over his god-damned legs. Clumsiest sod this side of Hades.' He lifted his race glasses and looked at the number board. 'I see poor old Charlie can't do the weight again on that thing of Bob's . . . That boy of Plumtree's is getting a lot of riding now. What do you think of him?'

'He takes too many risks,' I said. 'He'll break his neck.'

'Look who's talking . . . No, seriously, I'm considering taking him on. What do you think?' He lowered his glasses. 'I need someone available regularly from now on and all the ones I'd choose are already tied up.'

'Well, you could do better, you could do worse, I suppose. He's a bit flashy for me, but he can ride, obviously. Will he do as he's told?'

He made a face. 'You've hit the bull's eye. That's the snag. He always knows best.'

'Pity.'

'Can you think of anyone else?'

'Um . . . what about that boy Cotton? He's too young really. But he's got the makings . . .' We drifted on in amiable chat, discussing his problem, while the box filled up around us and the horses went down to the start.

It was a three mile chase, and one of my ex-mounts was favourite. I watched the man who had my old job ride a very pretty race, and with half my mind thought about housing estates.

Sandown itself had survived, some years ago, a bid to cover its green tempting acres with little boxes. Sandown had powerful friends. But Hurst Park, Manchester and Birmingham racecourses had all gone under the rolling tide of bricks and mortar, lost to the double-barrelled persuasive arguments that shareholders liked capital gains and people needed houses. To defend itself from such a fate Cheltenham Racecourse had transformed itself from a private, dividend-paying company into a non-profit-making Holdings Trust, and other racecourses had followed their lead.

But not Seabury. And Seabury was deep in a nasty situation. Not Dunstable, and Dunstable Racecourse was now a tidy dormitory for the Vauxhall workers of Luton.

Most British racecourses were, or had been, private companies, in which it was virtually impossible for an outsider to acquire shares against the will of the members. But four, Dunstable, Seabury, Sandown and Chepstow, were public companies, and their shares could be bought on the open market, through the Stock Exchange.

Sandown had been played for in a straightforward and perfectly honourable way, and plans to turn it into suburban housing had been turned down by the local and county councils. Sandown flourished, made a good profit, paid a ten per cent dividend, and was probably now impregnable. Chepstow was surrounded by so much other open land that it was in little danger from developers. But little Dunstable had been an oasis inside a growing industrial area.

Seabury was on the flat part of the south coast, flanked on every side by miles of warm little bungalows representing the dreams and savings of people in retirement. At twelve bungalows to the acre—elderly people liked tiny gardens—there must be room on the spacious racecourse for over three thousand more. Add six or seven hundred pounds to the building price of each bungalow for the plot it stood on, and you scooped something in the region of two million . . .

The favourite won and was duly cheered. I clattered down the iron staircase with Mark, and we went and had a drink together.

'Are you sending anything to Seabury next week?' I asked. Seabury was one of his nearest meetings.

'Perhaps. I don't know. It depends if they hold it at all, of course. But I've got mine entered at Lingfield as well, and I think

I'll send them there instead. It's a much more prosperous looking place, and the owners like it better. Good lunch and all that. Seabury's so dingy these days. I had a hard job getting old Carmichael to agree to me running his horse there at the last meeting—and look what happened. The meeting was off and we'd missed the other engagement at Worcester too. It wasn't my fault, but I'd persuaded him that he stood more chance at Seabury, and he blamed me because in the end the horse stayed at home eating his head off for nothing. He says there's a jinx on Seabury, and I've a couple more owners who don't like me entering their horses there. I've told them that it's a super track from the horses' point of view, but it doesn't make much difference, they don't know it like we do.'

We finished our drinks and walked back towards the weighing room. His horse scrambled home in the fifth by a whisker and I saw him afterwards in the unsaddling enclosure beaming like a Hallowe'en turnip.

After the last race I went to the Stewards' tea room. There were several Stewards with their wives and friends having tea, but no Lord Hagbourne. The Stewards pulled out a chair, gave me a welcome, and talked as ever, about the racing. Most of them had ridden as amateurs in their day, one against me in the not too distant past, and I knew them all well.

'Sid, what do you think of the new type hurdles?'

'Oh, much better. Far easier for a young horse to see.'

'Do you know of a good young chaser I could buy?'

'Didn't you think Hayward rode a splendid race?'

'I watched the third down at the Pond, and believe me that chestnut took off outside the wings . . .'

'. . . do you think we ought to have had him in, George?'

'. . . heard that Green bust his ribs again yesterday . . .'

'Don't like that breed, never did, not genuine . . .'

'Miffy can't seem to go wrong, he'd win with a carthorse . . .'

'Can you come and give a talk to our local pony club, Sid? I'll write you the details . . . what date would suit you?'

Gradually they finished their tea, said good-bye, and left for home. I waited. Eventually he came, hurrying, apologizing, explaining what had kept him.

'Now,' he said, biting into a sandwich. 'What's it all about, eh?'

'Seabury.'

'Ah yes, Seabury. Very worrying. Very worrying indeed.'

'A Mr Howard Kraye has acquired a large number of shares . . .'

'Now hold on a minute, Sid. That's only a guess, because of Dunstable. We've been trying to trace the buyer of Seabury shares through the Stock Exchange, and we can find no definite lead to Kraye.'

'Hunt Radnor Associates do have that lead.'

He stared. 'Proof?'

'Yes.'

'What sort?'

'Photographs of share transfer certificates.' And heaven help me, I thought, if I've messed them up.

'Oh,' he said sombrely. 'While we weren't sure, there was some hope we were wrong. Where did you get these photographs?'

'I'm not at liberty to say, sir. But Hunt Radnor Associates would be prepared to make an attempt to forestall the takeover of Seabury.'

'For a fat fee, I suppose,' he said dubiously.

'I'm afraid so, sir, yes.'

'I don't connect you with this sort of thing, Sid.' He moved restlessly and looked at his watch.

'If you would forget about me being a jockey, and think of me as having come from Mr Radnor, it would make things a lot easier. How much is Seabury worth to National Hunt racing?'

He looked at me in surprise, but he answered the question, though not in the way I meant.

'Er . . . well you know it's an excellent course, good for horses and so on.'

'It didn't show a profit this year, though.'

'There was a great deal of bad luck.'

'Yes. Too much to be true, don't you think?'

'What do you mean?'

'Has it ever occurred to the National Hunt Committee that bad luck can be . . . well . . . arranged?'

'You aren't seriously suggesting that Kraye . . . I mean that anyone would damage Seabury on purpose? In order to make it show a loss?'

'I am suggesting that it is a possibility. Yes.'

'Good God.' He sat down rather abruptly.

'Malicious damage,' I said. 'Sabotage, if you like. There's a great deal of industrial precedent. Hunt Radnor Associates investigated a case of it only last year in a small provincial brewery where the fermentation process kept going wrong. A prosecution resulted, and the brewery was able to remain in business.'

He shook his head. 'It is quite ridiculous to think that Kraye would be implicated in anything like that. He belongs to one of my clubs. He's a wealthy, respected man.'

'I know, I've met him,' I said.

'Well then, you must be aware of what sort of person he is.'

'Yes.' Only too well.

'You can't seriously suggest . . .' he began.

'There would be no harm in finding out,' I interrupted. 'You'll have studied the figures. Seabury's quite a prize.'

'How do you see the figures, then?' It seemed he genuinely wanted to know, so I told him.

'Seabury Racecourse has an issued share capital of eighty thousand pounds in fully paid-up one pound shares. The land was bought when that part of the coast was more or less uninhabited, so that this sum bears absolutely no relation to the present value of the place. Any company in that position is just asking for a take-over.

'A buyer would in theory need fifty-one per cent of the shares to be certain of gaining control, but in practice, as was found at Dunstable, forty would be plenty. It could probably be swung on a good deal less, but from the point of view of the buyer, the more he got his hands on before declaring his intentions, the bigger would be his profit.

'The main difficulty in taking over a racecourse company—it's only natural safeguard, in fact—is that the shares seldom come on the market. I understand that it isn't always by any means possible to buy even a few on the Stock Exchange, as people who own them tend to be fond of them, and as long as the shares pay any dividend, however small, they won't sell. But it's obvious that not everyone can afford to have bits of capital lying around unproductively, and once the racecourse starts showing a loss, the temptation grows to transfer to something else.

'Today's price of Seabury shares is thirty shillings, which is about four shillings higher than it was two years ago. If Kraye can manage to get hold of a forty per cent holding at an average price of thirty shillings, it will cost him only about forty-eight thousand pounds.

'With a holding that size, aided by other shareholders tempted by a very large capital gain, he can out-vote any opposition, and sell the whole company to a land developer. Planning permission would almost certainly be granted, as the land is not beautiful, and is surrounded already by houses. I estimate that a developer would pay roughly a million for it, as he could double that by selling off all those acres in tiny plots. There's the capital gains tax, of course, but Seabury shareholders stand to make eight hundred per cent on their original investment, if the scheme goes through. Four hundred thousand gross for Mr Kraye, perhaps. Did you ever find out how much he cleared at Dunstable?'

He didn't answer.

I went on, 'Seabury used to be a busy, lively, successful place, and now it isn't. It's a suspicious coincidence that as soon as a big buyer comes along the place goes downhill fast. They paid a dividend of only sixpence per share last year, a gross yield of under one and three-quarters per cent at today's price, and this year they showed a loss of three thousand, seven hundred and fourteen pounds. Unless something is done soon, there won't be a next year.'

He didn't reply at once. He stared at the floor for a long time with the half-eaten sandwich immobile in his hand.

Finally he said, 'Who did the arithmetic? Radnor?'

'No . . . I did. It's very simple. I went to Company House in the City yesterday and looked up the Seabury balance sheets for the last few years, and I rang for a quotation of today's share price from a stockbroker this morning. You can easily check it.'

'Oh, I don't doubt you. I remember now, there was a rumour that you made a fortune on the Stock Exchange by the time you were twenty.'

'People exaggerate so,' I smiled. 'My old governor, where I was apprenticed, started me off investing, and I was a bit lucky.'

'Hm.'

There was another pause while he hesitated over his decision. I didn't interrupt him, but I was much relieved when finally he said, 'You have Radnor's authority for seeing me, and he knows what you have told me?'

'Yes.'

'Very well.' He got up stiffly and put down the unfinished sandwich. 'You can tell Radnor that I agree to an investigation being made, and I think I can vouch for my colleagues agreeing. You'll want to start at once, I suppose.'

I nodded.

'The usual terms?'

'I don't know,' I said. 'Perhaps you would get on to Mr Radnor about that.'

As I didn't know what the usual terms were, I didn't want to discuss them.

'Yes, all right. And Sid . . . it's understood that there is to be no leak about this? We can't afford to have Kraye slapping a libel or slander action on us.'

'The agency is always discreet,' I said, with an outward and an inward smile. Radnor was right. People paid for privacy. And why not?

CHAPTER SIX

THE Racing Section was quiet when I went in next morning, mostly because Chico was out on an escort job. All the other heads were bent studiously over their desks, including Dolly's.

She looked up and said with a sigh, 'You're late again.' It was ten to ten. 'The old man wants to see you.'

I made a face at her and retraced my way down the staircase. Joanie looked pointedly at her watch.

'He's been asking for you for half an hour.'

I knocked and went in. Radnor was sitting behind his desk, reading some papers, pencil in hand. He looked at me and frowned.

'Why are you so late?'

'I had a pain in me tum,' I said flippantly.

'Don't be funny,' he said sharply, and then, more reasonably, 'Oh . . . I suppose you're not being funny.'

'No. But I'm sorry about being late.' I wasn't a bit sorry, however, that it had been noticed: before, no one would have said a thing if I hadn't turned up all day.

'How did you get on with Lord Hagbourne?' Radnor asked. 'Was he interested?'

'Yes. He agreed to an investigation. I said he should discuss terms with you.'

'I see.' He flicked a switch on the small box on his desk. 'Joanie, see if you can get hold of Lord Hagbourne. Try the London flat number first.'

'Yes, sir,' her voice came tinnily out of the speaker.

'Here,' said Radnor, picking up a shallow brown cardboard box. 'Look at these.'

The box contained a thick wad of large glossy photographs. I looked at them one by one and heaved a sigh of relief. They had all come out sharp and clear, except some of the ones I had duplicated at varying exposures.

The telephone on Radnor's desk rang once, quietly. He lifted the receiver.

'Oh, good morning, Lord Hagbourne. Radnor here. Yes, that's right . . .' He gestured to me to sit down, and I stayed there listening while he negotiated terms in a smooth, civilized, deceptively casual voice.

'And of course in a case like this, Lord Hagbourne, there's one other thing: we make a small surcharge if our operatives have to take out of the ordinary risks . . . Yes, as in the Canlas case, exactly. Right then, you shall have a preliminary report from us in a few days. Yes . . . goodbye.'

He put down the receiver, bit his thumb-nail thoughtfully for a few seconds, and said finally, 'Right, then, Sid. Get on with it.'

'But . . .' I began.

'But nothing,' he said. 'It's your case. Get on with it.'

I stood up, holding the packet of photographs. 'Can I . . . can I use Bona Fides and so on?'

He waved his hand permissively. 'Sid, use every resource in the agency you need. Keep an eye on expenses though, we don't want to price ourselves out of business. And if you want leg work done, arrange it through Dolly or the other department heads. Right?'

'Won't they think it odd? I mean . . . I don't amount to much around here.'

'And whose fault is that? If they won't do what you ask, refer them to me.' He looked at me expressionlessly.

'All right.' I walked to the door. 'Er . . . who . . .' I said, turning the knob, 'gets the danger money? The operative or the agency?'

'You said you would work for nothing,' he observed dryly.

I laughed. 'Just so. Do I get expenses?'

'That car of yours drinks petrol.'

'It does twenty,' I protested.

'The agency rate is based on thirty. You can have that. And other expenses, yes. Put in a chit to accounts.'

'Thanks.'

He smiled suddenly, the rare sweet smile so incongruous to his military bearing, and launched into another elaborate metaphor.

'The tapes are up,' he said. 'What you do with the race depends on your skill and timing, just as it always used to. I've backed you with the agency's reputation for getting results, and I can't afford to lose my stake. Remember that.'

'Yes,' I said soberly. 'I will.'

I thought, as I took my stupidly aching stomach up two storeys to Bona Fides, that it was time Radnor had a lift installed: and was glad I wasn't bound for Missing Persons away in the rarefied air of the fifth floor. There was a lot more character, I supposed, in the splendidly proportioned, solidly built town house that Radnor had chosen on a corner site in the Cromwell Road, but a flat half-acre of modern office block would have been easier on his staff. And about ten times as expensive, no doubt.

The basement, to start at the bottom, was—except for the kitchen—given over entirely to files and records. On the ground floor, besides Radnor himself and Joanie, there were two interview-cum-waiting rooms, and also the Divorce Section. On the first floor, the Racing Section, Accounts, another interview room and the general secretarial department. Up one was Bona Fides, and above that, on the two smaller top floors, Guard and Missing Persons. Missing Persons alone had room to spare. Bona Fides, splitting at the seams, was encroaching on Guard. Guard was sticking in its toes.

Jones-boy, who acted as general messenger, must have had legs like iron from pounding up and down the stairs, though thanks to a tiny service lift used long ago to take nursery food to top floor children, he could have his tea trays up from landing to landing instead of carrying them.

In Bona Fides there was the usual chatter of six people talking on the telephone all at once. The department head, receiver glued to one ear and finger stuck in the other, was a large bald-headed man with half-moon spectacles sitting half way down a prominent nose. As always, he was in his shirt sleeves, teamed with a frayed pullover and baggy grey flannels. No tie. He seemed to have an inexhaustible supply of old clothes but never any new ones, and Jones-boy had a theory that his wife dressed him from jumble sales.

I waited until he had finished a long conversation with a managing director about the character of the proposed production manager of a glass factory. The invaluable thing about Jack Copeland was his quick and comprehensive grasp of what dozens of jobs entailed. He was speaking to the glass manufacturer as if he had grown up in the industry: and in five minutes, I knew, he might be advising just as knowledgeably on the suitability of a town clerk. His summing up of a man went far beyond the basic list of honesty, conscientiousness, normality and prudence, which was all that many employers wanted. He liked to discover his subject's reaction under stress, to find out what he disliked doing, and what he often forgot. The resulting footnotes to his reports were usually the most valuable part of them, and the faith large numbers of industrial firms had in him bore witness to his accuracy.

He wielded enormous power but did not seem conscious of it, which made him much liked. After Radnor, he was the most important person in the agency.

'Jack,' I said, as he put down the receiver. 'Can you check a man for me, please?'

'What's wrong with the Racing Section, pal?' he said, jerking his thumb towards the floor.

'He isn't a racing person.'

'Oh? Who is it?'

'A Howard Kraye. I don't know if he has a profession. He speculates on the stock market. He is a rabid collector of quartz.' I added Kraye's London address.

He scribbled it all down fast.

'O.K., Sid. I'll put one of the boys on to it and let you have a prelim. Is it urgent?'

'Fairly.'

'Right.' He tore the sheet off the pad. 'George? You still doing that knitting wool client's report? When you've finished, here's your next one.'

'George,' I said. 'Be careful.'

They both looked at me, suddenly still.

'An unexploded bomb,' I observed. 'Don't set him off.'

George said cheerfully, 'Makes a nice change from knitting wool. Don't worry, Sid. I'll walk on eggs.'

Jack Copeland peered at me closely through the half specs. 'You've cleared it with the old man, I suppose?'

'Yes.' I nodded. 'It's a query fraud. He said to check with him if you wanted to.'

He smiled briefly. 'No need, I guess. Is that all then?'

'For the moment, yes, thanks.'

'Just for the record, is this your own show, or Dolly's, or whose?'

'I suppose . . . mine.'

'Uh-huh,' he said, accenting the second syllable. 'The wind of change, if I read it right?'

I laughed. 'You never know.'

Down in the Racing Section I found Dolly supervising the reshuffling of the furniture. I asked what was going on, and she gave me a flashing smile.

'It seems you're in, not out. The old man just rang to say you needed somewhere to work, and I've sent Jones-boy upstairs to pinch a table from Missing Persons. That'll do for now, won't it? There isn't a spare desk in the place.'

A series of bangs from outside heralded the return of Jones-boy, complete with a spindly plywood affair in a sickly lemon colour. 'How that lot ever find a missing person I'll never know. I bet they don't even find their missing junk.'

He disappeared and came back shortly with a chair.

'The things I do for you!' he said, setting it down in front of me. 'A dim little bird in the typing pool is now squatting on a stool. I chatted her up a bit.'

'What this place needs is some more equipment,' I murmured.

'Don't be funny,' said Dolly. 'Every time the old man buys one desk he takes on two assistants. When I first came here fifteen years ago we had a whole room each, believe it or not . . .'

The rearranged office settled down again, with my table wedged into a corner next to Dolly's desk. I sat behind it and spread out the photographs to sort them. The people who developed and printed all the agency's work had come up with their usual excellent job, and it amazed me that they had been able to enlarge the tiny negatives up to nine by seven inch prints, and get a clearly readable result.

I picked out all the fuzzy ones, the duplicates at the wrong exposures, tore them up, and put the pieces in Dolly's waste paper basket. That left me with fifty-one pictures of the contents of Kraye's attaché case. Innocent enough to the casual eye, but they turned out to be dynamite.

The two largest piles, when I had sorted them out, were

Seabury share transfer certificates, and letters from Kraye's stockbroker. The paper headed S.R. revealed itself to be a summary in simple form of the share certificates, so I added it to that pile. I was left with the photographs of the bank notes, of share dealings which had nothing to do with Seabury, and the two sheets of figures I had found under the writing board at the bottom of the case.

I read through all the letters from the stockbroker, a man called Ellis Bolt, who belonged to a firm known as Charing, Street and King. Bolt and Kraye were on friendly terms; the letters referred sometimes to social occasions on which they had met; but for the most part the typewritten sheets dealt with the availability and prospects of various shares (including Seabury), purchases made or proposed, and references to tax, stamp duty, and commission.

Two letters had been written in Bolt's own hand. The first, dated ten days ago, said briefly:

Dear H.
Shall wait with interest for the news on Friday.
E

The second, which Kraye must have received on the morning he went to Aynsford, read:

Dear H.
I have put the final draft in the hands of the printers, and the leaflets should be out by the end of next week, or the Tuesday following at the latest. Two or three days before the next meeting, anyway. That should do it, I think. There would be a lot of unrest should there be another hitch, but surely you will see to that.
E

'Dolly,' I said. 'May I borrow your phone?'

'Help yourself.'

I rang upstairs to Bona Fides. 'Jack? Can I have a run-down on another man as well? Ellis Bolt, stockbroker, works for a firm called Charing, Street and King.' I gave him the address. 'He's a friend of Kraye's. Same care needed, I'm afraid.'

'Right. I'll let you know.'

I sat staring down at the two harmless looking letters.

'Shall wait with interest for the news on Friday'. It could mean any news, anything at all. It also could mean the News; and on the radio on Friday I had heard that Seabury Races were off because a lorry carrying chemicals had overturned and burned the turf.

The second letter was just as tricky. It could easily refer to a shareholders' meeting at which a hitch should be avoided at all costs. Or it could refer to a race meeting—at Seabury—where another hitch could affect the sale of shares yet again.

It was like looking at a conjuring trick: from one side you saw a normal object, but from the other, a sham.

If it were a sham, Mr Ellis Bolt was in a criminal career up to his eyebrows. If it was just my suspicious mind jumping to hasty conclusions I was doing an old-established respectable stockbroker a shocking injustice.

I picked up Dolly's telephone again and got an outside line.

'Charing, Street and King, good morning,' said a quiet female voice.

'Oh, good morning. I would like to make an appointment to see Mr Bolt and discuss some investments. Would that be possible?'

'Certainly, yes. This is Mr Bolt's secretary speaking. Could I have your name?'

'Halley. John Halley.'

'You would be a new client, Mr Halley?'

'That's right.'

'I see. Well, now, Mr Bolt will be in the office tomorrow afternoon, and I could fit you in at three thirty. Would that suit you?'

'Thank you. That's fine. I'll be there.'

I put down the receiver and looked tentatively at Dolly.

'Would it be all right with you if I go out for the rest of the day?'

She smiled. 'Sid, dear, you're very sweet, but you don't have to ask my permission. The old man made it very clear that you're on your own now. You're not accountable to me or anyone else in the agency, except the old man himself. I'll grant you I've never known him give anyone quite such a free hand before, but there you are, my love, you can do what you like. I'm your boss no longer.'

'You don't mind?' I asked.

'No,' she said thoughtfully. 'Come to think of it, I don't. I've a notion that what the old man has always wanted of you in this agency is a partner.'

'Dolly!' I was astounded. 'Don't be ridiculous.'

'He's not getting any younger,' she pointed out.

I laughed. 'So he picked on a broken-down jockey to help him out.'

'He picks on someone with enough capital to buy a partnership, someone who's been to the top of one profession and has the time in years to get to the top of another.'

'You're raving, Dolly dear. He nearly chucked me out yesterday morning.'

'But you're still here, aren't you? More here than ever before. And Joanie said he was in a fantastically good mood all day yesterday, after you'd been in to see him.'

I shook my head, laughing. 'You're too romantic. Jockeys don't turn into investigators any more than they turn into . . .'

'Well, what?' she prompted.

'Into auctioneers, then . . . or accountants.'

She shook her head. 'You've already turned into an investigator, whether you know it or not. I've been watching you these two years, remember? You look as if you're doing nothing, but you've soaked up everything the bloodhounds have taught you like a hungry sponge. I'd say, Sid love, if you don't watch out, you'll be part of the fixtures and fittings for the rest of your life.'

But I didn't believe her, and I paid no attention to what she had said.

I grinned. 'I'm going down to take a look at Seabury Racecourse this afternoon. Like to come?'

'Are you kidding?' she sighed. Her in-tray was six inches deep. 'I could have just done with a ride in that rocket car of yours, and a breath of sea air.'

I stacked the photographs together and returned them to the box, along with the negatives. There was a drawer in the table, and I pulled it open to put the photographs away. It wasn't empty. Inside lay a packet of sandwiches, some cigarettes, and a flat half bottle of whisky.

I began to laugh. 'Someone,' I said, 'will shortly come rampaging down from Missing Persons looking for his Missing Lunch.'

Seabury Racecourse lay about half a mile inland, just off a trunk road to the sea. Looking backwards from the top of the stands one could see the wide silver sweep of the English Channel. Between and on both sides the crowded rows of little houses seemed to be rushing towards the coast like Gadarene swine. In each little unit a retired schoolmaster or civil servant or clergyman—or their widows—thought about the roots they had pulled up from wherever it had been too cold or too dingy for their old age, and sniffed the warm south salt-laden air.

They had made it. Done what they'd always wanted. Retired to a bungalow by the sea.

I drove straight in through the open racecourse gates and stopped outside the weighing room. Climbing out, I stretched and walked over to knock on the door of the racecourse manager's office.

There was no reply. I tried the handle. It was locked. So was the weighing room door, and everything else.

Hands in pockets, I strolled round the end of the stands to look at the course. Seabury was officially classified in Group Three: that is to say, lower than Doncaster and higher than Windsor when it came to receiving aid from the Betting Levy Board.

It had less than Grade Three stands: wooden steps with corrugated tin roofs for the most part, and draughts from all parts of the compass. But the track itself was a joy to ride on, and it had always seemed a pity to me that the rest of the amenities didn't match it.

There was no one about near the stands. Down at one end of the course, however, I could see some men and a tractor, and I set off towards them, walking down inside the rails, on the grass. The going was just about perfect for November racing, soft but springy underfoot, exactly right for tempting trainers to send their horses to the course in droves. In ordinary circumstances, that was. But as things stood at present, more trainers than Mark Witney were sending their horses elsewhere. A course which didn't attract runners didn't attract crowds to watch them. Seabury's gate receipts had been falling off for some time, but its expenses had risen; and therein lay its loss.

Thinking about the sad tale I had read in the balance sheets, I reached the men working on the course. They were digging up a great section of it and loading it on to a trailer behind the tractor. There was a pervasive unpleasant smell in the air.

An irregular patch about thirty yards deep, stretching nearly the whole width of the course, had been burned brown and killed. Less than half of the affected turf had already been removed, showing the greyish chalky mud underneath, and there was still an enormous amount to be shifted. I didn't think there were enough men working on it for there to be a hope of its being re-turfed and ready to race on in only eight days' time.

'Good afternoon,' I said to the men in general. 'What a horrible mess.'

One of them thrust his spade into the earth and came over, rubbing his hands on the sides of his trousers.

'Anything you want?' he said, with fair politeness.

'The racecourse manager. Captain Oxon.'

His manner shifted perceptibly towards the civil. 'He's not here today, sir. Hey! . . . aren't you Sid Halley?'

'That's right.'

He grinned, doing another quick change, this time towards brotherhood. 'I'm the foreman. Ted Wilkins.' I shook his outstretched hand. 'Captain Oxon's gone up to London. He said he wouldn't be back until tomorrow.'

'Never mind,' I said. 'I was just down in this part of the world and I thought I'd drop in and have a look at the poor old course.'

He turned with me to look at the devastation. 'Shame, isn't it?'

'What happened, exactly?'

'The tanker overturned on the road over there.' He pointed, and we began to walk towards the spot, edging round the dug-up area. The road, a narrow secondary one, ran across near the end of the racecourse, with a wide semi-circle of track on the far side of it. During the races the hard road surface was covered thickly with tan or peat, or with thick green matting, which the horses galloped over without any trouble. Although not ideal, it was an arrangement to be found on many courses throughout the country, most famously with the Melling Road at Aintree, and reaching a maximum with five road crossings at Ludlow.

'Just here,' said Ted Wilkins, pointing. 'Worst place it could possibly have happened, right in the middle of the track. The stuff just poured out of the tanker. It turned right over, see, and the hatch thing was torn open in the crash.'

'How did it happen?' I asked. 'The crash, I mean?'

'No one knows, really.'

'But the driver? He wasn't killed, was he?'

'No, he wasn't even hurt much. Just shook up a bit. But he couldn't remember what happened. Some people in a car came driving along after dark and nearly ran into the tanker. They found the driver sitting at the side of the road, holding his head and moaning. Concussion, it was, they say. They reckon he hit his head somehow when his lorry went over. Staggers me how he got out of it so lightly, the cab was fair crushed, and there was glass everywhere.'

'Do tankers often drive across here? Lucky it's never happened before, if they do.'

'They used not to,' he said, scratching his head. 'But they've been over here quite regularly now for a year or two. The traffic on the London road's getting chronic, see?'

'Oh . . . did it come from a local firm, then?'

'Down the coast a bit. Intersouth Chemicals, that's the firm it belonged to.'

'How soon do you think we'll be racing here again?' I asked, turning back to look at the track. 'Will you make it by next week?'

He frowned. 'Strictly between you and me, I don't think there's a bleeding hope. What we needed, as I said to the Captain, was a couple of bulldozers, not six men with spades.'

'I would have thought so too.'

He sighed. 'He just told me we couldn't afford them and to shut up and get on with it. And that's what we've done. We'll just about have cut out all the dead turf by next Wednesday, at this rate of going on.'

'That doesn't leave any time for new turf to settle,' I remarked.

'It'll be a miracle if it's laid, let alone settled,' he agreed gloomily.

I bent down and ran my hand over a patch of brown grass. It was decomposing and felt slimy. I made a face, and the foreman laughed.

'Horrible, isn't it? It stinks, too.'

I put my fingers to my nose and wished I hadn't. 'Was it slippery like this right from the beginning?'

'Yes, that's right. Hopeless.'

'Well, I won't take up any more of your time,' I said, smiling.

'I'll tell Captain Oxon you came. Pity you missed him.'

'Don't bother him. He must have a lot to worry about just now.'

'One bloody crisis after another,' he nodded. 'So long, then.' He went back to his spade and his heart-breaking task, and I retraced the quarter mile up the straight to the deserted stands.

I hesitated for a while outside the weighing room, wondering whether to pick the lock and go in, and knowing it was mainly nostalgia that urged me to do it, not any conviction that it would be a useful piece of investigation. There would always be the temptation, I supposed, to use dubious professional skills for one's own pleasure. Like doctors sniffing ether. I contented myself with looking through the windows.

The deserted weighing room looked the same as ever: a large bare expanse of wooden board floor, with a table and some upright chairs in one corner, and the weighing machine itself on the left. Racecourse weighing machines were not all of one universal design. There weren't any left of the old type where the jockeys stood on a platform while weights were added to the balancing arm. That whole process was much too slow. Now there were either seats slung from above, in which one felt much like a bag of sugar, or chairs bolted to a base plate on springs: in both these cases the weight was quickly indicated by a pointer which swung round a gigantic clock face. In essence, modern kitchen scales vastly magnified.

The scales at Seabury were the chair-on-base-plate type, which I'd always found simplest to use. I recalled a few of the before-and-after occasions when I had sat on that particular spot. Some good, some bad, as always with racing.

Shrugging, I turned away. I wouldn't, I thought, ever be sitting there again. And no one walked over my grave.

Climbing into the car, I drove to the nearest town, looked up the whereabouts of Intersouth Chemicals, and an hour later was speaking to the personnel manager. I explained that on behalf of the National Hunt Committee I had just called in passing to find out if the driver of the tanker had fully recovered, or had remembered anything else about the accident.

The manager, fat and fiftyish, was affable but unhelpful. 'Smith's left,' he said briefly. 'We gave him a few days off to get over the accident, and then he came back yesterday and said his wife didn't fancy him driving chemicals any more, and he was packing it in.' His voice held a grievance.

'Had he been with you long?' I asked sympathetically.

'About a year.'

'A good driver, I suppose?'

'Yes, about average for the job. They have to be good drivers, or we don't use them, you see. Smith was all right, but nothing special.'

'And you still don't really know what happened?'

'No,' he sighed. 'It takes a lot to tip one of our tankers over. There was nothing to learn from the road. It was covered with oil and petrol and chemical. If there had ever been any marks, skid marks I mean, they weren't there after the breakdown cranes had lifted the tanker up again, and the road was cleared.'

'Do your tankers use that road often?'

'They have done recently, but not any more after this. As a matter of fact, I seem to remember it was Smith himself who found that way round. Going over the racecourse missed out some bottle-neck at a junction, I believe. I know some of the drivers thought it a good idea.'

'They go through Seabury regularly, then?'

'Sure, often. Straight line to Southampton and round to the oil refinery at Fawley.'

'Oh? What exactly was Smith's tanker carrying?'

'Sulphuric acid. It's used in refining petrol, among other things.'

Sulphuric acid. Dense; oily; corrosive to the point of charring. Nothing more instantly lethal could have poured out over Seabury's turf. They could have raced had it been a milder chemical, put sand or tan on the dying grass and raced over the top. But no one would risk a horse on ground soaked with vitriol.

I said, 'Could you give me Smith's address? I'll call round and see if his memory has come back.'

'Sure.' He searched in a file and found it for me. 'Tell him he can his his job back if he's interested. Another of the men gave notice this morning.'

I said I would, thanked him, and went to Smith's address, which proved to be two rooms upstairs in a suburban house. But Smith and his wife no longer lived in them. Packed up and gone yesterday, I was told by a young woman in curlers. No, she didn't know where they went. No, they didn't leave a forwarding address, and if I was her I wouldn't worry about his health as he'd been laughing and drinking and playing records to all hours the day after the crash, his concussion having cured itself pretty quick. Reaction, he'd said when she complained of the noise, against not being killed.

It was dark by then, and I drove slowly back into London against the stream of headlights pouring out. Back to my flat in a modern block, a short walk from the office, down the ramp into the basement garage, and up in the lift to the fifth floor, home.

There were two rooms facing south, bedroom and sitting-room, and two behind them, bathroom and kitchen, with windows into an inner well. A pleasant sunny place, furnished in blond wood and cool colours, centrally heated, cleaning included in the rent. A regular order of groceries arrived week by week directly into the kitchen through a hatch, and rubbish disappeared down a chute. Instant living. No fuss, no mess, no strings. And damnably lonely, after Jenny.

Not that she had ever been in the place, she hadn't. The house in the Berkshire village where we had mostly lived had been too much of a battleground, and when she walked out I sold it, with relief. I'd moved into the new flat shortly after going to the agency, because it was close. It was also expensive: but I had no fares to pay.

I mixed myself a brandy with ice and water, sat down in an arm-chair, put my feet up, and thought about Seabury. Seabury, Captain Oxon, Ted Wilkins, Intersouth Chemicals, and a driver called Smith.

After that I thought about Kraye. Nothing pleasant about him, nothing at all. A smooth, phony crust of sophistication hiding ruthless greed; a seething passion for crystals, ditto for land, an obsession with the cleanliness of his body to compensate for the murk in his mind; unconventional sexual pleasures; and the abnormal quality of being able to look carefully at a crippled hand and *then hit it*.

No, I didn't care for Howard Kraye one little bit.

CHAPTER SEVEN

'Chico,' I said. 'How would you overturn a lorry on a predetermined spot?'

'Huh? That's easy. All you'd need would be some heavy lifting gear. A big hydraulic jack. A crane. Anything like that.'

'How long would it take?'

'You mean, supposing the lorry and the crane were both in position?'

'Yes.'

'Only a minute or two. What sort of lorry?'

'A tanker.'

'A petrol job?'

'A bit smaller than the petrol tankers. More the size of milk ones.'

'Easy as kiss your hand. They've got a low centre of gravity, mind. It'd need a good strong lift. But dead easy, all the same.'

I turned to Dolly. 'Is Chico busy today, or could you spare him?'

Dolly leaned forward, chewing the end of a pencil and looking at her day's chart. The cross-over blouse did its stuff.

'I could send someone else to Kempton . . .' She caught the direction of my eyes and laughed, and retreated a whole half inch. 'Yes, you can have him.' She gave him a fond glance.

'Chico,' I said. 'Go down to Seabury and see if you can find any trace of heavy lifting gear having been seen near the racecourse last Friday . . . those little bungalows are full of people with nothing to do but watch the world go by . . . you might check whether anything was hired locally, but I suppose that's a bit much to hope for. The road would have to have been closed for a few minutes before the tanker went over, I should think. See if you can find anyone who noticed anything like that . . . detour signs, for instance. And after that, go to the council offices and see what you can dig up among their old maps on the matter of drains.' I told him the rough position of the subsiding trench which had made a slaughterhouse of the hurdle race, so that he should know what to look for on the maps. 'And be discreet.'

'Teach your grandmother to suck eggs,' he grinned.

'Our quarry is rough.'

'And you don't want him to hear us creep up behind him?'

'Quite right.'

'Little Chico,' he said truthfully, 'can take care of himself.'

After he had gone I telephoned Lord Hagbourne and described to him in no uncertain terms the state of Seabury's turf.

'What they need is some proper earth moving equipment, fast, and apparently there's nothing in the kitty to pay for it. Couldn't the Levy Board . . . ?'

'The Levy Board is no fairy godmother,' he interrupted. 'But I'll see what can be done. Less than half cleared, you say? Hmm. However, I understand that Captain Oxon assured Weatherbys that the course would be ready for the next meeting. Has he changed his mind?'

'I didn't see him, sir. He was away for the day.'

'Oh.' Lord Hagbourne's voice grew a shade cooler. 'Then he didn't ask you to enlist my help?'

'No.'

'I don't see that I can interfere then. As racecourse manager it is his responsibility to decide what can be done and what can't, and I think it must be left like that. Mm, yes. And of course he will consult the Clerk of the Course if he needs advice.'

'The Clerk of the Course is Mr Fotherton, who lives in Bristol. He is Clerk of the Course there, too, and he's busy with the meetings there tomorrow and Monday.'

'Er, yes, so he is.'

'You could ring Captain Oxon up in an informal way and just ask how the work is getting on,' I suggested.

'I don't know . . .'

'Well, sir, you can take my word for it that if things dawdle on at the same rate down there, there won't be any racing at Seabury next week-end. I don't think Captain Oxon can realize just how slowly those men are digging.'

'He must do,' he protested. 'He assured Weatherbys . . .'

'Another last minute cancellation will kill Seabury off,' I said with some force.

There was a moment's pause. Then he said reluctantly, 'Yes, I suppose it might. All right then. I'll ask Captain Oxon and Mr Fotherton if they are both satisfied with the way things are going.'

And I couldn't pin him down to any more direct action than that, which was certainly not going to be enough. Protocol would be the death of Seabury, I thought.

Monopolozing Dolly's telephone, I next rang up the Epping police and spoke to Chief-Inspector Cornish.

'Any more news about Andrews?' I asked.

'I suppose you have a reasonable personal interest.' His chuckle came down the wire. 'We found he did have a sister after all. We called her at the inquest yesterday for identification purposes as she is a relative, but if you ask me she didn't really know. She took one look at the bits in the mortuary and was sick on the floor.'

'Poor girl, you couldn't blame her.'

'No. She didn't look long enough though to identify anyone. But we had your identification for sure, so we hadn't the heart to make her go in again.'

'How did he die? Did you find out?'

'Indeed we did. He was shot in the back. The bullet ricocheted off a rib and lodged in the sternum. We got the experts to compare it with the one they dug out of the wall of your office. Your bullet was a bit squashed by the hard plaster, but there's no doubt that they are the same. He was killed with the gun he used on you.'

'And was it there, underneath him?'

'Not a sign of it. They brought in "murder by persons unknown". And between you and me, that's how it's likely to stay. We haven't a lead to speak of.'

'What lead do you have?' I asked.

His voice had a smile in it. 'Only something his sister told us. She has a bedsitter in Islington, and he spent the evening there before breaking into your place. He showed her the gun. She says he was proud of having it; apparently he was a bit simple. All he told her was that a big chap had lent it to him to go out and fetch something, and he was to shoot anyone who got in his way. She didn't believe him. She said he was always making things up, always had, all his life. So she didn't ask him anything about the big chap, or about where he was going, or anything at all.'

'A bit casual,' I said. 'With a loaded gun under her nose.'

'According to the neighbours she was more interested in a stream of men friends than in anything her brother did.'

'Sweet people, neighbours.'

'You bet. Anyway we checked with anyone we could find who had seen Andrews the week he shot you, and he hadn't said a word to any of them about a gun or a "big chap", or an errand in Cromwell Road.'

'He didn't go back to his sister afterwards?'

'No, she'd told him she had a guest coming.'

'At one in the morning? The neighbours must be right. You tried the racecourses, of course? Andrews was quite well known there, as a sort of spivvy odd-job messenger boy.'

'Yes, we mainly tried the racecourses. No results. Everyone seemed surprised that such a harmless person should have been murdered.'

'Harmless!'

He laughed. 'If you hadn't thought him harmless, you'd have kept out of his way.'

'You're so right,' I said with feeling. 'But now I see a villain in every respectable citizen. It's very disturbing.'

'Most of them are villains, in one way or another,' he said cheerfully. 'Keeps us busy. By the way, what do you think of Sparkle's chances this year in the Hennessy . . . ?'

When eventually I put the telephone down Dolly grabbed it with a sarcastic 'Do you mind?' and asked the switchboard girl to get her three numbers in a row, 'without interruptions from Halley'. I grinned, got the packet of photographs out of the plywood table drawer, and looked through them again. They didn't tell me any more than before. Ellis Bolt's letters to Kraye. Now you see it, now you don't. A villain in every respectable citizen. Play it secretly, I thought, close to the chest, in case the eyes looking over your shoulder give you away. I wondered why I was so oppressed by a vague feeling of apprehension, and decided in irritation that a bullet in the stomach had made me nervous.

When Dolly finished her calls I took the receiver out of her hand and got through to my bank manager.

'Mr Hopper? This is Sid Halley . . . yes, fine thanks, and you? Good. Now, would you tell me just how much I have in both my accounts, deposit and current?'

'They're quite healthy, actually,' he said in his gravelly bass voice. 'You've had several dividends in lately. Hang on a minute, and I'll send for the exact figures.' He spoke to someone in the background and then came back. 'It's time you re-invested some of it.'

'I do have some investments in mind,' I agreed. 'That's what I want to discuss with you. I'm planning to buy some shares this time from another stockbroker, not through the bank. Er . . . please don't think that I'm dissatisfied; how could I be, when you've done so well for me. It's something to do with my work at the agency.'

'Say no more. What exactly do you want?'

'Well, to give you as a reference,' I said. 'He's sure to want one, but I would be very grateful if you would make it as impersonal and as strictly financial as possible. Don't mention either my past occupation or my present one. That's very important.'

'I won't, then. Anything else?'

'Nothing . . . oh, yes. I've introduced myself to him as John Halley. Would you refer to me like that if he gets in touch with you?'

'Right. I'll look forward to hearing from you one day what it's all about. Why don't you come in and see me? I've some very good cigars.' The deep voice was amused. 'Ah, here are the figures . . .' He told me the total, which for once was bigger than I expected. That happy state of affairs wouldn't last very long, I reflected, if I had to live for two years without any salary from Radnor. And no one's fault but my own.

Giving Dolly back her telephone with an ironic bow, I went upstairs to Bona Fides. Jack Copeland's mud coloured jersey had a dark blue darn on the chest and a fraying stretch of ribbing on the hip. He was picking at a loose thread and making it worse.

'Anything on Kraye yet?' I asked. 'Or is it too early?'

'George has got something on the prelim, I think,' he answered. 'Anybody got any scissors?' A large area of jersey disintegrated into ladders. 'Blast.'

Laughing, I went over to George's desk. The prelim was a sheet of handwritten notes in George's concertina'd style. 'Leg mat, 2 yrs. 2 prev, 1 div, 1 sui dec.' it began, followed by a list of names and dates.

'Oh, yeah?' I said.

'Yeah.' He grinned. 'Kraye was legally married to Doria Dawn, née Eastman, two years ago. Before that he had two other wives. One killed herself; the other divorced him for cruelty.' He pointed to the names and dates.

'So clear,' I agreed. 'When you know how.'

'If you weren't so impatient you'd have a legible typed report. But as you're here . . .' He went on down the page, pointing. 'Geologists think him a bit eccentric . . . quartz has no intrinsic value, most of it's much too common, except for the gem stones, but Kraye goes round trying to buy chunks of it if they take his fancy. They know him quite well along the road at the Geology Museum. But not a breath of any dirty work. Clubs . . . he belongs to these three, not over-liked, but most members think he's a brilliant fellow, talks very well. He gambles at Crockfords, ends up about all square over the months. He travels, always first-class, usually by boat, not air. No job or profession, can't trace him on any professional or university lists. Thought to live on investments, playing the stock market, etc. Not much liked, but considered by most a clever, cultured man, by one or two a hypocritical gasbag.'

'No talk of him being crooked in any way?'

'Not a word. You want him dug deeper?'

'If you can do it without him finding out.'

George nodded. 'Do you want him tailed?'

'No, I don't think so. Not at present.' A twenty-four-hour tail was heavy on man-power and expensive to the client, quite apart

from the risk of the quarry noticing and being warned of the hunt.
'Anything on his early life?' I asked.

George shook his head. 'Nothing. Nobody who knows him now has known him longer than about ten years. He either wasn't born in Britain, or his name at birth wasn't Kraye. No known relatives.'

'You've done marvels, George. All this in one day.'

'Contacts, chum, contacts. A lot of phoning, a bit of pubbing, a touch of gossip with the local tradesmen . . . nothing to it.'

Jack, moodily poking his fingers through the cobweb remains of his jersey, looked at me over the half-moon specs and said that there wasn't a prelim on Bolt yet because ex-sergeant Carter, who was working on it, hadn't phoned in.

'If he does,' I said, 'let me know? I've an appointment with Bolt at three thirty. It would be handy to know the set-up before I go.'

'O.K.'

After that I went down and looked out of the windows of the Racing Section for half an hour, idly watching life go by in the Cromwell Road and wondering just what sort of mess I was making of the Kraye investigation. A novice chaser in the Grand National, I thought wryly; that was me. Though, come to think of it, I had once ridden a novice in the National, and got round, too. Slightly cheered, I took Dolly out to a drink and a sandwich in the snack bar at the Air Terminal, where we sat and envied the people starting off on their travels. So much expectation in the faces, as if they could fly away and leave their troubles on the ground. An illusion, I thought sourly. Your troubles flew with you; a drag in the mind . . . a deformity in the pocket.

I laughed and joked with Dolly, as usual. What else can you do?

The firm of Charing, Street and King occupied two rooms in a large block of offices belonging to a bigger firm, and consisted entirely of Bolt, his clerk and a secretary.

I was shown the door of the secretary's office, and went into a dull, tidy, fog-coloured box of a room with cold fluorescent lighting and a close-up view of the fire-escape through the grimy window. A woman sat at a desk by the right hand wall, facing the window, with her back towards me. A yard behind her chair was a door with ELLIS BOLT painted on a frosted glass panel. It occurred to me that she was most awkwardly placed in the room, but that perhaps she liked sitting in a potential draught and having to turn round every time someone came in.

She didn't turn round, however. She merely moved her head round a fraction towards me and said 'Yes?'

'I have an appointment with Mr Bolt,' I said. 'At three thirty.'

'Oh, yes, you must be Mr Halley. Do sit down. I'll see if Mr Bolt is free now.'

She pointed to an easy chair a step ahead of me, and flipped a switch on her desk. While I listened to her telling Mr Bolt I was there, in the quiet voice I had heard on the telephone, I had time to see she was in her late thirties, slender, upright in her chair, with a smooth wing of straight, dark hair falling down beside her cheek. If anything, it was too young a hair style for her. There were no rings on her fingers, and no nail varnish either. Her clothes were dark and uninteresting. It seemed as though she were making a deliberate attempt to be unattractive, yet her profile, when she half turned and told me Mr Bolt would see me, was pleasant enough. I had a glimpse of one brown eye quickly cast down, the beginning of a smile on pale lips, and she presented me again squarely with the back of her head.

Puzzled, I opened Ellis Bolt's door and walked in. The inner office wasn't much more inspiring than the outer; it was larger and there was a new green square of carpet on the linoleum, but the greyish walls pervaded, along with the tidy dullness. Through the two windows was a more distant view of the fire-escape of the building across the alley. If a drab conventional setting equalled respectability, Bolt was an honest stockbroker; and Carter, who had phoned in just before I left, had found nothing to suggest otherwise.

Bolt was on his feet behind his desk, hand outstretched. I shook it, he gestured me to a chair with arms, and offered me a cigarette.

'No, thank you, I don't smoke.'

'Lucky man,' he said benignly, tapping ash off one he was half through, and settling his pin-striped bulk back into his chair.

His face was rounded at every point, large round nose, round cheeks, round heavy chin: no planes, no impression of bone structure underneath. He had exceptionally heavy eyebrows, a full mobile mouth, and a smug self-satisfied expression.

'Now, Mr Halley, I believe in coming straight to the point. What can I do for you?'

He had a mellifluous voice, and he spoke as if he enjoyed the sound of it.

I said, 'An aunt has given me some money now rather than leave it to me in her will, and I want to invest it.'

'I see. And what made you come to me? Did someone recommend . . . ?' He tailed off, watching me with eyes that told me he was no fool.

'I'm afraid . . .' I hesitated, smiling apologetically to take the offence out of the words, 'that I literally picked you with a pin. I don't know any stockbrokers. I didn't know how to get to know one, so I picked up a classified directory and stuck a pin into the list of names, and it was yours.'

'Ah,' he said paternally, observing the bad fit of Chico's second best suit, which I had borrowed for the occasion, and listening to me reverting to the accent of my childhood.

'Can you help me?' I asked.

'I expect so, I expect so. How much is this er, gift?' His voice was minutely patronizing, his manner infinitesimally bored. His time, he suspected, was being wasted.

'Fifteen hundred pounds.'

He brightened a very little. 'Oh, yes, definitely, we can do something with that. Now, do you want growth mainly or a high rate of yield?'

I looked vague. He told me quite fairly the difference between the two, and offered no advice.

'Growth, then,' I said, tentatively. 'Turn it into a fortune in time for my old age.'

He smiled without much mirth, and drew a sheet of paper towards him.

'Could I have your full name?'

'John Halley . . . John Sidney Halley,' I said truthfully. He wrote it down.

'Address?' I gave it.

'And your bank?' I told him that too.

'And I'll need a reference, I'm afraid.'

'Would the bank manager do?' I asked. 'I've had an account there for two years . . . he knows me quite well.'

'Excellent.' He screwed up his pen. 'Now, do you have any idea what companies you'd like shares in, or will you leave it to me?'

'Oh, I'll leave it to you. If you don't mind, that is. I don't know anything about it, you see, not really. Only it seems silly to leave all that money around doing nothing.'

'Quite, quite.' He was bored with me. I thought with amusement that Charles would appreciate my continuing his strategy of the weak front. 'Tell me, Mr Halley, what do you do for a living?'

'Oh . . . um . . . I work in a shop,' I said. 'In the men's wear. Very interesting, it is.'

'I'm sure it is.' There was a yawn stuck in his throat.

'I'm hoping to be made an assistant buyer next year,' I said eagerly.

'Splendid. Well done.' He'd had enough. He got cumbrously to his feet and ushered me to the door. 'All right, Mr Halley, I'll invest your money safely for you in good long term growth stock, and send you the papers to sign in due course. You'll hear from me in a week or ten days. All right?'

'Yes, Mr Bolt, thank you very much indeed,' I said respectfully. He shut the door gently behind me.

There were now two people in the outer office. The woman with her back still turned, and a spare, middle-aged man with a primly folded mouth, and tough stringy tendons pushing his collar away from his neck. He was quite at home, and with an incurious, unhurried glance at me he went past into Bolt's office. The clerk, I presumed.

The woman was typing addresses on envelopes. The twenty or so that she had done lay in a slithery stack on her left: on her right an open file provided a list of names. I looked over her shoulder casually, and then with quickened interest. She was working down the first page of a list of Seabury shareholders.

'Do you want something, Mr Halley?' she asked politely, pulling one envelope from the typewriter and inserting another with a minimum of flourish.

'Well, er, yes,' I said diffidently. I walked round to the side of her desk and found that one couldn't go on round to the front of it: a large old fashioned table with bulbous legs filled all the space between the desk and the end of the room. I looked at this arrangement with some sort of understanding and with compassion.

'I wondered,' I said, 'if you could be very kind and tell me something about investing money, and so on. I didn't like to ask

Mr Bolt too much, he's a busy man. And I'd like to know a bit about it.'

'I'm sorry, Mr Halley.' Her head was turned away from me, bent over the Seabury investors. 'I've a job to do, as you see. Why don't you read the financial columns in the papers, or get a book on the subject?'

I had a book all right. *Outline of Company Law.* One thing I had learned from it was that only stockbrokers—apart from the company involved—could send circulars to shareholders. It was illegal if private citizens did it. Illegal for Kraye to send letters to Seabury shareholders offering to buy them out: legal for Bolt.

'Books aren't as good as people at explaining things,' I said. 'If you are busy now, could I come back when you've finished work and take you out for a meal? I'd be so grateful if you would, if you possibly could.'

A sort of shudder shook her. 'I'm sorry, Mr Halley, but I'm afraid I can't.'

'If you will look at me, so that I can see all of your face,' I said, 'I will ask you again.'

Her head went up with a jerk at that, but finally she turned round and looked at me.

I smiled. 'That's better. Now, how about coming out with me this evening?'

'You guessed?'

I nodded. 'The way you've got your furniture organized . . . Will you come?'

'You still want to?'

'Well, of course. What time do you finish?'

'About six, tonight.'

'I'll come back. I'll meet you at the door, down in the street.'

'All right,' she said. 'If you really mean it, thank you. I'm not doing anything else tonight . . .'

Years of hopeless loneliness showed raw in the simple words. Not doing anything else, tonight or most nights. Yet her face wasn't horrific; not anything as bad as I had been prepared for. She had lost an eye, and wore a false one. There had been some extensive burns and undoubtedly some severe fracture of the facial bones, but plastic surgery had repaired the damage to a great extent, and it had all been a long time ago. The scars were old. It was the inner wound which hadn't healed.

Well . . . I knew a bit about that myself, on a smaller scale.

CHAPTER EIGHT

SHE came out of the door at ten past six wearing a neat well cut dark overcoat and with a plain silk scarf covering her hair, tied under her chin. It hid only a small part of the disaster to her face, and seeing her like that, defenceless, away from the shelter she had made in her office, I had an uncomfortably vivid vision of the purgatory she suffered day in and day out on the journeys to work.

She hadn't expected me to be there. She didn't look round for me when she came out, but turned directly up the road towards the tube station. I walked after her and touched her arm, Even in low heels she was taller than I.

'Mr Halley!' she said. 'I didn't think . . .'

'How about a drink first?' I said. 'The pubs are open.'

'Oh no . . .'

'Oh yes. Why not?' I took her arm and steered her firmly across the road into the nearest bar. Dark oak, gentle lighting, brass pump handles, and the lingering smell of lunchtime cigars: a warm beckoning stop for city gents on their way home. There were already half a dozen of them, prosperous and dark-suited, adding fizz to their spirits.

'Not here,' she protested.

'Here.' I held a chair for her to sit on at a small table in a corner, and asked her what she would like to drink.

'Sherry, then . . . dry . . .'

I took the two glasses over one at a time, sherry for her, brandy for me. She was sitting on the edge of the chair, uncomfortably, and it was not the one I had put her in. She had moved round so that she had her back to everyone except me.

'Good luck, Miss . . . ?' I said, lifting my glass.

'Martin. Zanna Martin.'

'Good luck, Miss Martin.' I smiled.

Tentatively she smiled back. It made her face much worse: half the muscles on the disfigured right side didn't work and could do nothing about lifting the corner of her mouth or crinkling the skin round the socket of her eye. Had life been even ordinarily kind she would have been a pleasant looking, assured woman in her late thirties with a loving husband and a growing family:

years of heartbreak had left her a shy, lonely spinster who dressed and moved as though she would like to be invisible. Yet, looking at the sad travesty of her face, one could neither blame the young men who hadn't married her nor condemn her own efforts at effacement.

'Have you worked for Mr Bolt long?' I asked peaceably, settling back lazily into my chair and watching her gradually relax into her own.

'Only a few months . . .' She talked for some time about her job in answer to my interested questions, but unless she was supremely artful, she was not aware of anything shady going on in Charing, Street and King. I mentioned the envelopes she had been addressing, and asked what was going into them.

'I don't know yet,' she said. 'The leaflets haven't come from the printers.'

'But I expect you typed the leaflet anyway,' I said idly.

'No, actually I think Mr Bolt did that one himself. He's quite helpful in that way, you know. If I'm busy he'll often do letters himself.'

Will he, I thought. Will he, indeed. Miss Martin, as far as I was concerned, was in the clear. I bought her another drink and extracted her opinion about Bolt as a stockbroker. Sound, she said, but not busy. She had worked for other stockbrokers, it appeared, and knew enough to judge.

'There aren't many stockbrokers working on their own any more,' she explained, 'and . . . well . . . I don't like working in a big office, you see . . . and it's getting more difficult to find a job which suits me. So many stockbrokers have joined up into partnerships of three or more; it reduces overheads terrifically, of course, and it means that they can spend more time in the House . . .'

'Where are Mr Charing, Mr Street, and Mr King?' I asked.

Charing and Street were dead, she understood, and King had retired some years ago. The firm now consisted simply and solely of Ellis Bolt. She didn't really like Mr Bolt's offices being contained inside of those of another firm. It wasn't private enough, but it was the usual arrangement nowadays. It reduced overheads so much . . .

When the city gents had mostly departed to the bosoms of their families, Zanna Martin and I left the pub and walked through the empty city streets towards the Tower. We found a quiet little restaurant where she agreed to have dinner. As before, she made a straight line for a corner table and sat with her back to the room.

'I'm paying my share,' she announced firmly when she had seen the prices on the menu. 'I had no idea this place was so expensive, or I wouldn't have let you choose it . . . Mr Bolt mentioned that you worked in a shop.'

'There's Aunty's legacy,' I pointed out. 'The dinner's on Aunty.'

She laughed. It was a happy sound if you didn't look at her, but I found I was already able to talk to her without continually, consciously thinking about her face. One got used to it after a very short while. Some time, I thought, I would tell her so.

I was still on a restricted diet, which made social eating difficult enough without one-handedness thrown in, but did very well on clear soup and Dover sole, expertly removed from the bone by a waiter. Miss Martin, shedding inhibitions visibly, ordered lobster cocktail, fillet steak, and peaches in kirsch. We drank wine, coffee and brandy, and took our time.

'Oh!' she said ecstatically at one point. 'It is so long since I had anything like this. My father used to take me out now and then, but since he died . . . well, I can't go to places like this myself . . . I sometimes eat in a café round the corner from my rooms, they know me there . . . it's very good food really, chops, eggs and chips . . . you know . . . things like that.' I could picture her there, sitting alone, with her ravaged head turned to the wall. Lonely unhappy Zanna Martin. I wished I could do something—anything —to help her.

Eventually, when she was stirring her coffee, she said simply, 'It was a rocket, this.' She touched her face. 'A firework. The bottle it was standing in tipped over just as it went off, and it came straight at me. It hit me on the cheek bone and exploded . . . It wasn't anybody's fault . . . I was sixteen.'

'They made a good job of it,' I said.

She shook her head, smiling the crooked tragic smile. 'A good job from what it was, I suppose, but . . . they said if the rocket had struck an inch higher it would have gone through my eye into my brain and killed me. I often wish it had.'

She meant it. Her voice was calm. She was stating a fact.

'Yes,' I said.

'It's strange, but I've almost forgotten about it this evening, and that doesn't often happen when I'm with anyone.'

'I'm honoured.'

She drank her coffee, put down her cup, and looked at me thoughtfully.

She said, 'Why do you keep your hand in your pocket all the time?'

I owed it to her, after all. I put my hand palm upward on the table, wishing I didn't have to.

She said 'Oh!' in surprise, and then, looking back at my face, 'So you do know. That's why I feel so . . . so easy with you. You do understand.'

I shook my head. 'Only a little. I have a pocket; you haven't. I can hide.' I rolled my hand over (the back of it was less off-putting), and finally retreated it on to my lap.

'But you can't do the simplest things,' she exclaimed. Her voice was full of pity. 'You can't tie your shoe-laces, for instance. You can't even eat steak in a restaurant without asking someone else to cut it up for you . . .'

'Shut up,' I said abruptly. 'Shut up, Miss Martin. Don't you dare to do to me what you can't bear yourself.'

'Pity . . .' she said, biting her lip and staring at me unhappily. 'Yes, it's so easy to give . . .'

'And embarrassing to receive.' I grinned at her. 'And my shoes don't have shoe-laces. They're out of date, for a start.'

'You can know as well as I do what it feels like, and yet do it to someone else . . .' She was very upset.

'Stop being miserable. It was kindness. Sympathy.'

'Do you think,' she said hesitantly, 'that pity and sympathy are the same thing?'

'Very often, yes. But sympathy is discreet and pity is tactless. Oh . . . I'm so sorry.' I laughed. 'Well . . . it was sympathetic of you to feel sorry I can't cut up my own food, and tactless to say so. The perfect example.'

'It wouldn't be so hard to forgive people for just being tactless,' she said thoughtfully.

'No,' I agreed, surprised. 'I suppose it wouldn't.'

'It might not hurt so much . . . just tactlessness?'

'It mightn't . . .'

'And curiosity . . . that might be easier, too, if I just thought of it as bad manners, don't you think? I mean tactlessness and bad manners wouldn't be so hard to stand. In fact *I* could be sorry for *them*, for not knowing better how to behave. Oh why, why didn't I think of that years ago, when it seems so simple now. So sensible.'

'Miss Martin,' I said with gratitude. 'Have some more brandy . . . you're a liberator.'

'How do you mean?'

'Pity is bad manners and can be taken in one's stride, as you said.'

'You said it,' she protested.

'Indeed I didn't, not like that.'

'All right,' she said with gaiety. 'We'll drink to a new era. A bold front to the world. I will put my desk back to where it was before I joined the office, facing the door. I'll let every caller see me. I'll . . .' Her brave voice nearly cracked. 'I'll just think poorly of their manners if they pity me too openly. That's settled.'

We had some more brandy. I wondered inwardly whether she would have the same resolve in the morning, and doubted it. There had been so many years of hiding. She too, it seemed, was thinking along the same lines.

'I don't know that I can do it alone. But if you will promise me something, then I can.'

'Very well,' I said incautiously. 'What?'

'Don't put your hand in your pocket tomorrow. Let everyone see it.'

I couldn't. Tomorrow I would be going to the races. I looked at her, appalled, and really understood only then what she had to bear, and what it would cost her to move her desk. She saw the refusal in my face, and some sort of light died in her own. The gaiety collapsed, the defeated, defenceless look came back, the liberation was over.

'Miss Martin . . .' I swallowed.

'It doesn't matter,' she said tiredly. 'It doesn't matter. And anyway, it's Saturday tomorrow. I only go in for a short while to see to the mail and anything urgent from today's transactions. There wouldn't be any point in changing the desk.'

'And on Monday?'

'Perhaps.' It meant no.

'If you'll change it tomorrow and do it all next week, I'll do what you ask,' I said, quaking at the thought of it.

'You can't,' she said sadly. 'I can see that you can't.'

'If you can, I must.'

'But I shouldn't have asked you . . . you work in a shop.'

'Oh.' That I had forgotten. 'It won't matter.'

An echo of her former excitement crept back.

'Do you really mean it?'

I nodded. I had wanted to do something—anything—to help her. Anything. My God.

'Promise?' she said doubtfully.

'Yes. And you?'

'All right,' she said, with returning resolution. 'But I can only do it if I know you are in the same boat . . . I couldn't let you down then, you see.'

I paid the bill, and although she said there was no need, I took her home. We went on the Underground to Finchley. She made straight for the least conspicuous seat and sat presenting the good side of her face to the carriage. Then, laughing at herself, she apologized for doing it.

'Never mind,' I said, 'the new era doesn't start until tomorrow,' and hid my hand like a proper coward.

Her room was close to the station (a deliberately short walk, I guessed) in a large prosperous looking suburban house. At the gate she stopped.

'Will . . . er . . . I mean, would you like to come in? It's not very late . . . but perhaps you are tired.'

She wasn't eager, but when I accepted she seemed pleased.

'This way, then.'

We went through a bare tidy garden to a black painted front door adorned with horrible stained glass panels. Miss Martin fumbled endlessly in her bag for her key and I reflected idly that I could have picked that particular lock as quickly as she opened it legally. Inside there was a warm hall smelling healthily of air freshener, and at the end of a passage off it, a door with a card saying 'Martin'.

Zanna Martin's room was a surprise. Comfortable, large, close carpeted, newly decorated, and alive with colour. She switched on a standard lamp and a rosy table lamp, and drew burnt orange curtains over the black expanse of french windows. With satisfaction she showed me the recently built tiny bathroom leading out of her room, and the suitcase-sized kitchen beside it, both of which additions she had paid for herself. The people who owned the house were very understanding, she said. Very kind. She had lived there for eleven years. It was home.

Zanna Martin had no mirrors in her home. Not one.

She bustled in her little kitchen, making more coffee: for something to do, I thought. I sat relaxed on her long comfortable modern sofa and watched how, from long habit, she leant forward most of the time so that the heavy shoulder length dark hair swung down to hide her face. She brought the tray and set it down, and sat on the sofa carefully on my right. One couldn't blame her.

'Do you ever cry?' she said suddenly.

'No.'

'Not . . . from frustration?'

'No.' I smiled. 'Swear.'

She sighed. 'I used to cry often. I don't any more, though. Getting older, of course. I'm nearly forty. I've got resigned now to not getting married . . . I knew I was resigned to it when I had the bathroom and kitchen built. Up to then, you see, I'd always pretended to myself that one day . . . one day, perhaps . . . but I don't expect it any more, not any more.'

'Men are fools,' I said inadequately.

'I hope you don't mind me talking like this? It's so seldom that I have anyone in here, and practically never anyone I can really talk to . . .'

I stayed for an hour, listening to her memories, her experiences, her whole shadowed life. What, I chided myself, had ever happened to me that was one tenth as bad. I had had far more ups than downs.

At length she said, 'How did it happen with you? Your hand . . .'

'Oh, an accident. A sharp bit of metal.' A razor sharp racing horse-shoe attached to the foot of a horse galloping at thirty miles an hour, to be exact. A hard kicking slash as I rolled on the ground from an easy fall. One of those things.

Horses race in thin light shoes called plates, not the heavy ones they normally wear: blacksmiths change them before and after, every time a horse runs. Some trainers save a few shillings by using the same racing plates over and over again, so that the leading edge gradually wears down to the thickness of a knife. But jagged knives, not smooth. They can cut you open like a hatchet.

I'd really known at once when I saw my stripped wrist with the blood spurting out in a jet and the broken bones showing white, that I was finished as a jockey. But I wouldn't give up hope, and insisted on the surgeons sewing it all up, even though they wanted to take my hand off there and then. It would never be any good, they said; and they were right. Too many of the tendons and nerves were severed. I persuaded them to try twice later on to rejoin and graft some of them and both times it had been a useless agony. They had refused to consider it again.

Zanna Martin hesitated on the brink of asking for details, and fortunately didn't. Instead she said, 'Are you married? Do you know, I've talked so much about myself, that I don't know a thing about you.'

'My wife's in Athens, visiting her sister.'

'How lovely,' she sighed. 'I wish . . .'

'You'll go one day,' I said firmly. 'Save up, and go in a year or two. On a bus tour or something. With people anyway. Not alone.'

'I looked at my watch, and stood up. 'I've enjoyed this evening a great deal. Thank you so much for coming out with me.'

She stood and formally shook hands, not suggesting another meeting. So much humility, I thought: so little expectation. Poor, poor Miss Martin.

'Tomorrow morning . . .' she said tentatively, at the door.

'Tomorrow,' I nodded. 'Move that desk. And I . . . I promise I won't forget.'

I went home cursing that fate had sent me someone like Zanna Martin. I had expected Charing, Street and King's secretary to be young, perhaps pretty, a girl I could take to a café and the pictures and flirt with, with no great involvement on either side. Instead it looked as if I should have to pay more than I'd meant to for my inside information on Ellis Bolt.

CHAPTER NINE

'Now look,' said Lord Hagbourne, amidst the bustle of Kempton races, 'I've had a word with Captain Oxon and he's satisfied with the way things are going. I really can't interfere any more. Surely you understand that?'

'No, sir, I don't. I don't think Captain Oxon's feelings are more important than Seabury Racecourse. The course should be put right quickly, even if it means overruling him.'

'Captain Oxon,' he said with a touch of sarcasm, 'knows more about his job than you do. I give more weight to his assurance than to your quick look at the track.'

'Then couldn't you go and see for yourself? While there is still time.'

He didn't like being pushed. His expression said so, plainly. There was no more I could say, either, without risking him ringing up Radnor to cancel the whole investigation.

'I may . . . er . . . I may find time on Monday,' he said at last, grudgingly. 'I'll see. Have you found anything concrete to support your idea that Seabury's troubles were caused maliciously?'

'Not yet, sir.'

'A bit far-fetched, if you ask me,' he said crossly. 'I said so to begin with, if you remember. If you don't turn something up pretty soon . . . it's all expense, you know.'

He was intercepted by a passing Steward who took him off to another problem, leaving me grimly to reflect that so far there was a horrid lack of evidence of any sort. What there was, was negative.

George had still found no chink in Kraye's respectability, ex-sergeant Carter had given Bolt clearance, and Chico had come back from Seabury with no results all along the line.

We'd met in the office that morning, before I went to Kempton.

'Nothing,' said Chico. 'I wagged me tongue off, knocking at every front door along that road. Not a soggy flicker. The bit which crosses the racecourse wasn't closed by diversion notices, that's for sure. There isn't much traffic along there, of course. I counted it. Only forty to the hour, average. Still, that's too much for at least some of the neighbours not to notice if there'd been anything out of the ordinary.'

'Did anyone see the tanker, before it overturned?'

'They're always seeing tankers, nowadays. Several complaints about it, I got. No one noticed that one, especially.'

'It can't be coincidence . . . just at that spot at that time, where it would do most harm. And the driver packing up and moving a day or two afterwards, with no forwarding address.'

'Well . . .' Chico scratched his ear reflectively. 'I got no dice with the hiring of lifting gear either. There isn't much to be had, and what there was was accounted for. None of the little bungalows saw anything in that line, except the breakdown cranes coming to lift the tanker up again.'

'How about the drains?'

'No drains,' he said. 'A blank back to Doomsday.'

'Good.'

'Come again?'

'If you'd found them on a map, the hurdle race accident would have been a genuine accident. This way, they reek of tiger traps.'

'A spot of spade work after dark? Dodgy stuff.'

I frowned. 'Yes. And it had to be done long enough before the race meeting for the ground to settle, so that the line of the trench didn't show . . .'

'And strong enough for a tractor to roll over it.'

'Tractor?'

'There was one on the course yesterday, pulling a trailer of dug up turf.'

'Oh yes, of course. Yes, strong enough to hold a tractor . . . but wheels wouldn't pierce the ground like a horse's legs. The weight is more spread.'

'True enough.'

'How fast was the turf-digging going?' I asked.

'Fast? You're joking.'

It was depressing. So was Lord Hagbourne's shilly-shallying. So, acutely, was the whole day, because I kept my promise to Zanna Martin. Pity, curiosity, surprise, embarrassment and revulsion, I encountered the lot. I tried hard to look on some of the things that were said as tactlessness or bad manners, but it didn't really work. Telling myself it was idiotic to be so sensitive didn't help either. If Miss Martin hadn't kept her side of the bargain, I thought miserably, I would throttle her.

Half way through the afternoon I had a drink in the big upstairs bar with Mark Witney.

'So that's what you've been hiding all this time in pockets and gloves,' he said.

'Yes.'

'Bit of a mess,' he commented.

'I'm afraid so.'

'Does it hurt still?'

'No, only if I knock it. And it aches sometimes.'

'Mm,' he said sympathetically. 'My ankle still aches too. Joints are always like that; they mend, but they never forgive you.' He grinned. 'The other half? There's time; I haven't a runner until the fifth.'

We had another drink, talking about horses, and I reflected that it would be easy if they were all like him.

'Mark,' I said as we walked back to the weighing room, 'do you remember whether Dunstable ran into any sort of trouble before it packed up?'

'That's going back a bit.' He pondered. 'Well, it certainly wasn't doing so well during the last year or two, was it? The attendances had fallen off, and they weren't spending any money on paint.'

'But no specific disasters?'

'The Clerk of the Course took an overdose, if you call that a disaster. Yes, I remember now, the collapse of the place's prosperity was put down to the Clerk's mental illness. Brinton, I think his name was. He'd been quietly going loco and making hopeless decisions all over the place.'

'I'd forgotten,' I said glumly. Mark went into the weighing room and I leant against the rails outside. A suicidal Clerk of the Course could hardly have been the work of Kraye, I thought. It might have given him the idea of accelerating the demise of Seabury, though. He'd had plenty of time over Dunstable, but owing to a recent political threat of nationalization of building land, he might well be in a hurry to clinch Seabury. I sighed, disregarded as best I could a stare of fascinated horror from the teenage daughter of a man I used to ride for, and drifted over to look at the horses in the parade ring.

At the end of the too-long afternoon I drove back to my flat, mixed a bigger drink than usual, and spent the evening thinking without any world-shattering results. Late the next morning, when I was similarly engaged, the door bell rang, and I found Charles outside.

'Come in,' I said with surprise: he rarely visited the flat, and was seldom in London at week-ends. 'Like some lunch? The restaurant downstairs is quite good.'

'Perhaps. In a minute.' He took off his overcoat and gloves and accepted some whisky. There was something unsettled in his manner, a ruffling of the smooth urbane exterior, a suggestion of a troubled frown in the high domed forehead.

'O.K.,' I said. 'What's the matter?'

'Er . . . I've just driven up from Aynsford. No traffic at all, for once. Such a lovely morning, I thought the drive would be . . . oh damn it,' he finished explosively, putting down his glass with a bang. 'To get it over quickly . . . Jenny telephoned from Athens last night. She's met some man there. She asked me to tell you she wants a divorce.'

'Oh,' I said. How like her, I thought, to get Charles to wield the axe. Practical Jenny, eager for a new fire, hacking away the dead wood. And if some of the wood was still alive, too bad.

'I must say,' said Charles, relaxing, 'you make a thorough job of it.'

'Of what?'

'Of not caring what happens to you.'

'I do care.'

'No one would suspect it,' he sighed. 'When I tell you your wife wants to divorce you, you just say, "Oh." When that happened,' he nodded to my arm, 'the first thing you said to me afterwards when I arrived full of sorrow and sympathy was, if I remember correctly, and I do, "Cheer up, Charles. I had a good run for my money."'

'Well, so I did.' Always, from my earliest childhood, I had instinctively shied away from too much sympathy. I didn't want it. I distrusted it. It made you soft inside, and an illegitimate child couldn't afford to be soft. One might weep at school, and one's spirit would never recover from so dire a disgrace. So the poverty and the sniggers, and later the lost wife and the smashed career had to be passed off with a shrug, and what one really felt about it had to be locked up tightly inside, out of view. Silly, really, but there it was.

We lunched companionably together downstairs, discussing in civilized tones the mechanics of divorce. Jenny, it appeared, did not want me to use the justified grounds of desertion: I, she said, should 'arrange things' instead. I must know how to do it, working for the agency. Charles was apologetic: Jenny's prospective husband was in the Diplomatic Service like Tony, and would prefer her not to be the guilty party.

Had I, Charles enquired delicately, already been . . . er . . . unfaithful to Jenny? No, I replied, watching him light his cigar, I was afraid I hadn't. For much of the time, owing to one thing and another, I hadn't felt well enough. That, he agreed with amusement, was a reasonable excuse.

I indicated that I would fix things as Jenny wanted, because it didn't affect my future like it did hers. She would be grateful, Charles said. I thought she would very likely take it for granted, knowing her.

When there was little else to say on that subject, we switched to Kraye. I asked Charles if he had seen him again during the week.

'Yes, I was going to tell you. I had lunch with him in the Club on Thursday. Quite accidentally. We both just happened to be there alone.'

'That's where you met him first, in your club?'

'That's right. Of course he thanked me for the week-end, and so on. Talked about the quartz. Very interesting collection, he said. But not a murmur about the St Luke's Stone. I would have liked to have asked him straight out, just to see his reaction.' He tapped off the ash, smiling. 'I did mention you, though, in passing, and he switched on all the charm and said you had been extremely insulting to him and his wife, but that of course you hadn't spoiled his enjoyment. Very nasty, I thought it. He was causing bad trouble for you. Or at least, he intended to.'

'Yes,' I said cheerfully. 'But I did insult him, and I also spied on him. Anything he says of me is fully merited.' I told Charles how I had taken the photographs, and all that I had discovered or guessed during the past week. His cigar went out. He looked stunned.

'Well, you wanted me to, didn't you?' I said. 'You started it. What did you expect?'

'It's only that I had almost forgotten . . . this is what you used to be like, always. Determined. Ruthless, even.' He smiled. 'My game for convalescence has turned out better than I expected.'

'God help your other patients,' I said, 'if Kraye is standard medicine.'

We walked along the road towards where Charles had left his car. He was going straight home again.

I said, 'I hope that in spite of the divorce I shall see something of you? I should be sorry not to. As your ex-son-in-law, I can hardly come to Aynsford any more.'

He looked startled. 'I'll be annoyed if you don't, Sid. Jenny will be living all round the world, like Jill. Come to Aynsford whenever you want.'

'Thank you,' I said. I meant it, and it sounded like it.

He stood beside his car, looking down at me from his straight six feet.

'Jenny,' he said casually, 'is a fool.'

I shook my head. Jenny was no fool. Jenny knew what she needed, and it wasn't me.

When I went into the office (on time) the following morning, the girl on the switchboard caught me and said Radnor wanted me straight away.

'Good morning,' he said. 'I've just had Lord Hagbourne on the telephone telling me it's time we got results and that he can't go to Seabury today because his car is being serviced. Before you explode, Sid . . . I told him that you would take him down there now, at once, in your own car. So get a move on.'

I grinned. 'I bet he didn't like that.'

'He couldn't think of an excuse fast enough. Get round and collect him before he comes up with one.'

'Right.'

I made a quick detour up to the Racing Section where Dolly was adjusting her lipstick. No cross-over blouse today. A disappointment.

I told her where I was going, and asked if I could use Chico.

'Help yourself,' she said resignedly. 'If you can get a word in edgeways. He's along in Accounts arguing with Jones-boy.'

Chico, however, listened attentively and repeated what I had asked him. 'I'm to find out exactly what mistakes the Clerk of the Course at Dunstable made, and make sure that they and nothing else were the cause of the course losing money.'

'That's right. And dig out the file on Andrews and the case you were working on when I got shot.'

'But that's all dead,' he protested, 'the file's down in records in the basement.'

'Send Jones-boy down for it,' I suggested, grinning. 'It's probably only a coincidence, but there is something I want to check. I'll do it tomorrow morning. O.K.?'

'If you say so, chum.'

Back at my flat, I filled up with Extra and made all speed round to Beauchamp Place. Lord Hagbourne, with a civil but cool good morning, lowered himself into the passenger seat, and we set off for Seabury. It took him about a quarter of an hour to get over having been manoeuvred into something he didn't want to do, but at the end of that time he sighed and moved in his seat, and offered me a cigarette.

'No, thank you, sir. I don't smoke.'

'You don't mind if I do?' He took one out.

'Of course not.'

'This is a nice car,' he remarked, looking round.

'It's nearly three years old now. I bought it the last season I was riding. It's the best I've ever had, I think.'

'I must say,' he said inoffensively, 'that you manage extremely well. I wouldn't have thought that you could drive a car like this with only one effective hand.'

'Its power makes it easier, actually. I took it across Europe last Spring . . . good roads, there.'

We talked on about cars and holidays, then about theatres and books, and he seemed for once quite human. The subject of Seabury we carefully by-passed. I wanted to get him down there in a good mood; the arguments, if any, could take place on the way back; and it seemed as if he was of the same mind.

The state of Seabury's track reduced him to silent gloom. We walked down to the burnt piece with Captain Oxon, who was bearing himself stiffly and being pointedly polite. I thought he was a fool: he should have fallen on the Senior Steward and begged for instant help.

Captain Oxon, whom I had not met before, though he said he knew me by sight, was a slender pleasant looking man of about fifty, with a long pointed chin and a slight tendency to watery eyes. The present offended obstinacy of his expression looked more like childishness than real strength. A colonel manqué, I thought uncharitably, and no wonder.

'I know it's not really my business,' I said, 'but surely a bulldozer would shift what's left of the burnt bit in a couple of hours? There isn't time to settle new turf, but you could cover the whole area with some tons of tan and race over it quite easily, like that. You must be getting tan anyway, to cover the road surface. Surely you could just increase the order?'

Oxon looked at me with irritation. 'We can't afford it.'

'You can't afford another cancellation at the last minute,' I corrected.

'We are insured against cancellations.'

'I doubt whether an insurance company would stand this one,' I said. 'They'd say you could have raced if you'd tried hard enough.'

'It's Monday now,' remarked Lord Hagbourne thoughtfully. 'Racing's due on Friday. Suppose we call in a bulldozer tomorrow; the tan can be unloaded and spread on Wednesday and Thursday. Yes, that seems sound enough.'

'But the cost . . .' began Oxon.

'I think the money must be found,' said Lord Hagbourne. 'Tell Mr Fotherton when he comes over that I have authorized the expenditure. The bills will be met, in one way or another.

But I do think there is no case for not making an effort.'

It was on the tip of my tongue to point out that if Oxon had arranged for the bulldozer on the first day he could have saved the price of casual labour for six hand-diggers for a week, but as the battle was already won, I nobly refrained. I continued to think, however, that Oxon was a fool. Usually the odd custom of giving the managerships of racecourses to ex-army and navy officers worked out well, but conspicuously not in this case.

The three of us walked back up to the stands, Lord Hagbourne pausing and pursing his lips at their dingy appearance. I reflected that it was a pity that Seabury had a Clerk of the Course whose heart and home were far away on the thriving course at Bristol. If I'd been arranging things, I'd have seen to it a year ago, when the profits turned to loss, that Seabury had a new Clerk entirely devoted to its own interests, someone moreover whose livelihood depended on it staying open. The bungle, delay, muddle, too much politeness and failure to take action showed by Seabury executive had been of inestimable value to the quietly burrowing Kraye.

Mr Fotherton might have been worried, as he said, but he had done little except mention it in passing to Charles in his capacity as Steward at some other meeting. Charles, looking for something to divert my mind from my stomach, and perhaps genuinely anxious about Seabury, had tossed the facts to me. In his own peculiar way, naturally.

The casualness of the whole situation was horrifying. I basely wondered whether Fotherton himself had a large holding in Seabury shares and therefore a vested interest in its demise. Planning a much closer scrutiny of the list of shareholders, I followed Lord Hagbourne and Captain Oxon round the end of the stands, and we walked the three hundred yards or so through the racecourse gates and down the road to where Captain Oxon's flat was situated above the canteen in the stable block.

On Lord Hagbourne's suggestion he rang up a firm of local contractors while we were still there, and arranged for the urgent earth-moving to be done the following morning. His manner was still ruffled, and it didn't improve things when I declined the well-filled ham and chutney sandwiches he offered, though I would have adored to have eaten them, had he but known. I had been out of hospital for a fortnight, but I had another fortnight to go before things like new bread, ham, mustard and chutney were due back on the agenda. Very boring.

After the sandwiches Lord Hagbourne decided on a tour of inspection, so we all three went first round the stable block, into the lads' hostel, through the canteen to the kitchen, and into all the stable administrative offices. Everywhere the story was the same. Except for the rows of wooden boxes which had been thrown up cheaply after the old ones burned down, there was no recent maintenance and no new paint.

Then we retraced our steps up the road, through the main gate, and across to the long line of stands with the weighing room, dining-rooms, bars and cloakrooms built into the back. At one end were the secretary's office, the press room and the Stewards' room: at the other, the first-aid room and a store. A wide tunnel like a passage ran centrally through the whole length of the building, giving secondary access on one side to many of the rooms, and on the other to the steps of the stands themselves. We painstakingly covered the lot, even down to the boiler room and the oil bunkers, so I had my nostalgic look inside the weighing room and changing room after all.

The whole huge block was dankly cold, very draughty, and smelt of dust. Nothing looked new, not even the dirt. For inducing depression it was hard to beat, but the dreary buildings along in the cheaper rings did a good job of trying.

Captain Oxon said the general dilapidation was mostly due to the sea air, the racecourse being barely half a mile from the shore, and no doubt in essence he was right. The sea air had had a free hand for far too long.

Eventually we returned to where my car was parked inside the gate, and looked back to the row of stands: forlorn, deserted, decaying on a chilly early November afternoon, with a salt-laden drizzle just beginning to blur the outlines.

'What's to be done?' said Lord Hagbourne glumly, as we drove through the rows of bungalows on our way home.

'I don't know.' I shook my head.

'The place is dead.'

I couldn't argue. Seabury had suddenly seemed to me to be past saving. The Friday and Saturday fixtures could be held now, but as things stood the gate money would hardly cover expenses. No company could go on making a loss indefinitely. Seabury could plug the gap at present by drawing on their reserve funds, but as I'd seen from their balance sheets at Company House, the reserves only amounted to a few thousands. Matters were bound to get worse. Insolvency waited round a close corner. It might be more realistic to admit that Seabury had no future and to sell the land at the highest price offered as soon as possible. People were, after all, crying out for flat land at the seaside. And there was no real reason why the shareholders shouldn't be rewarded for their long loyalty and recent poor dividends and receive eight pounds for each one they had invested. Many would gain if Seabury came under the hammer, and no one would lose. Seabury was past saving: best to think only of the people who would benefit.

My thoughts stopped with a jerk. This, I realized, must be the attitude of the Clerk, Mr Fotherton, and of the Manager, Oxon, and of all the executive. This explained why they had made surprisingly little attempt to save the place. They had accepted defeat easily and seen it not only to be harmless, but to many, usefully profitable. As it had been with other courses, big courses like Hurst Park and Birmingham, so it should be with Seabury.

What did it matter that yet another joined the century's ghost ranks of Cardiff, Derby, Bournemouth, Newport? What did it matter if busy people like Inspector Cornish of Dunstable couldn't go racing much because their local course had vanished? What did it matter if Seabury's holiday makers went to the Bingo halls instead?

Chasing owners, I thought, should rise up in a body and demand that Seabury should be preserved, because no racecourse was better for their horses. But of course they wouldn't. You could tell owners how good it was, but unless they were horsemen themselves, it didn't register. They only saw the rotten amenities of the stands, not the splendidly sited well-built fences that positively invited their horses to jump. They didn't know how their horses relished the short springy turf underfoot, or found the arc and cambers of the bends perfect for maintaining an even speed. Corners at many other racecourses threw horses wide and broke up their stride, but not those at Seabury. The original course builder had been brilliant, and regular visits from the Inspector of Courses had kept his work fairly intact. Fast, true run, unhazardous racing, that's what Seabury gave.

Or had done, before Kraye.

Kraye and the executive's inertia between them . . . I stamped on the accelerator in a surge of anger and the car swooped up the side of the South Downs like a bird. I didn't often drive fast any more: I did still miss having two hands on the wheel. At the top, out of consideration for my passenger's nerves, I let the speedometer ribbon slide back to fifty.

He said, 'I feel like that about it too.'

I glanced at him in surprise.

'The whole situation is infuriating,' he nodded. 'Such a good course basically, and nothing to be done.'

'It could be saved,' I said.

'How?'

'A new attitude of mind . . .' I tailed off.

'Go on,' he said. But I couldn't find the words to tell him politely that he ought to chuck out all the people in power at Seabury; too many of them were probably his ex-school chums or personal friends.

'Suppose,' he said after a few minutes, 'that you had a free hand, what would you do?'

'One would never get a free hand. That's half the trouble. Someone makes a good suggestion, and someone else squashes it. They end up, often as not, by doing nothing.'

'No, Sid, I mean you personally. What would you do?'

'I?' I grinned. 'What I'd do would have the National Hunt Commission Committee swooning like Victorian maidens.'

'I'd like to know.'

'Seriously?'

He nodded. As if he could ever be anything else but serious.

I sighed. 'Very well then. I'd pinch every good crowd-pulling idea that any other course has thought of, and put them all into operation on the same day.'

'What, for instance?'

'I'd take the whole of the reserve fund and offer it as a prize for a big race. I'd make sure the race was framed to attract the really top chasers. Then I'd go round to their trainers personally and explain the situation, and beg for their support. I'd go to some of the people who sponsor Gold Cup races and cajole them into giving five hundred pound prizes for all the other races on that day. I'd make the whole thing into a campaign. I'd get Save Seabury discussed on television, and in the sports columns of newspapers. I'd get people interested and involved. I'd make helping Seabury the smart thing to do. I'd get someone like the Beatles to come and present the trophies. I'd advertise free car-parking and free race cards, and on the day I'd have the whole place bright with flags and bunting and tubs of flowers to hide the lack of paint. I'd make sure everyone on the staff understood that a friendly welcome must be given to the customers. And I'd insist that the catering firm used its imagination. I'd fix the meeting for the beginning of April, and pray for a sunny Spring day. That,' I said, running down, 'would do for a start.'

'And afterwards?' He was non-committal.

'A loan, I suppose. Either from a bank or from private individuals. But the executive would have to show first that Seabury could be a success again, like it used to be. No one falls over himself to lend to a dying business. The revival has to come before the money, if you see what I mean.'

'I do see,' he agreed slowly, 'but . . .'

'Yes. But. It always comes to But. But no one at Seabury is going to bother.'

We were silent for a long way.

Finally I said, 'This meeting on Friday and Saturday . . . it would be a pity to risk another last-minute disaster. Hunt Radnor Associates could arrange for some sort of guard on the course. Security patrols, that kind of thing.'

'Too expensive,' he said promptly. 'And you've not yet proved that it is really needed. Seabury's troubles still look like plain bad luck to me.'

'Well . . . a security patrol might prevent any more of it.'

'I don't know. I'll have to see.' He changed the subject then, and talked firmly about other races on other courses all the way back to London.

CHAPTER TEN

DOLLY lent me her telephone with resignation on Tuesday morning, and I buzzed the switchboard for an internal call to Missing Persons.

'Sammy?' I said. 'Sid Halley, down in Racing. Are you busy?'

'The last teenager has just been retrieved from Gretna. Fire away. Who's lost?'

'A man called Smith.'

Some mild blasphemy sped three storeys down the wire.

I laughed. 'I think his name really is Smith. He's a driver by trade. He's been driving a tanker for Intersouth Chemicals for the last year. He left his job and his digs last Wednesday; no forwarding address.' I told him about the crash, the suspect concussion and the revelry by night.

'You don't think he was planted on purpose on the job a year ago? His name likely wouldn't be Smith in that case . . . make it harder.'

'I don't know. But I think it's more likely he was a bona fide Intersouth driver who was offered a cash payment for exceptional services rendered.'

'O.K., I'll try that first. He might give Intersouth as a reference, in which case they'll know if he applies for another job somewhere, or I might trace him through his union. The wife might have worked, too. I'll let you know.'

'Thanks.'

'Don't forget, when the old man buys you a gold-plated executive desk I want my table back.'

'You'll want for ever,' I said smiling. It had been Sammy's lunch.

On the table in question lay the slim file on the Andrews case that Jones-boy had unearthed from the basement. I looked round the room.

'Where's Chico?' I asked.

Dolly answered. 'Helping a bookmaker to move house.'

'He's doing *what*?' I goggled.

'That's right. Long-standing date. The bookmaker is taking his safe with him and wants Chico to sit on it in the furniture van. It had to be Chico, he said. No one else would do. The paying customer is always right, so Chico's gone.'

'Damn.'

She reached into a drawer. 'He left you a tape,' she said.

'Undamn, then.'

She grinned and handed it to me, and I took it over to the recorder, fed it through on to the spare reel, and listened to it in the routine office way, through the earphones.

'After wearing my plates down to the ankles,' said Chico's cheerful voice, 'I found out that the worst things your Clerk of the Course did at Dunstable were to frame a lot of races that did the opposite of attract any decent runners, and be stinking rude to all and sundry. He was quite well liked up to the year before he killed himself. Then everyone says he gradually got more and more crazy. He was so rude to people who worked at the course that half of them wouldn't put up with it and left. And the local tradesmen practically spat when I mentioned his name. I'll fill you in when I see you, but there wasn't anything like Seabury—no accidents or damage or anything like that.'

Sighing, I wiped the tape clean and gave it back to Dolly. Then I opened the file on my table and studied its contents.

A Mr Mervyn Brinton of Reading, Berks., had applied to the agency for personal protection, having had reason to believe that he was in danger of being attacked. He had been unwilling to say why he might be attacked, and refused to have the agency make enquiries. All he wanted was a bodyguard. There was a strong possibility, said the report, that Brinton had tried a little amateurish blackmail, which had backfired. He had at length revealed that he possessed a certain letter, and was afraid of being attacked and having it stolen. After much persuasion by Chico Barnes, who pointed out that Brinton could hardly be guarded for the rest of his life, Brinton had agreed to inform a certain party that the letter in question was lodged in a particular desk drawer in the Racing Section of Hunt Radnor Associates. In fact it was not; and had not at any time been seen by anyone working for the agency. However, Thomas Andrews came, or was sent, to remove the letter, was interrupted by J. S. Halley (whom he wounded by shooting), and subsequently made his escape. Two days later Brinton telephoned to say he no longer required a bodyguard, and as far as the agency was concerned the case was then closed.

The foregoing information had been made available to the police in their investigation into the shooting of Halley.

I shut the file. A drab little story, I thought, of a pathetic little man playing out of his league.

Brinton.

The Clerk of the Course at Dunstable had also been called Brinton.

I sat gazing at the short file. Brinton wasn't an uncommon name. There was probably no connection at all. Brinton of Dunstable had died a good two years before Brinton of Reading had asked for protection. The only visible connection was that at different ends of the scale both the Dunstable Brinton and Thomas Andrews had earned their living on the racecourse. It wasn't much. Probably nothing. But it niggled.

I went home, collected the car, and drove to Reading.

A nervous grey-haired elderly man opened the front door on a safety chain, and peered through the gap.

'Yes?'

'Mr Brinton?'

'What is it?'

'I'm from Hunt Radnor Associates. I'd be most grateful for a word with you.'

He hesitated, chewing an upper lip adorned with an untidy pepper and salt moustache. Anxious brown eyes looked me up and down and went past me to the white car parked by the kerb.

'I sent a cheque,' he said finally.

'It was quite in order,' I assured him.

'I don't want any trouble . . . it wasn't my fault that that man was shot.' He didn't sound convinced.

'Oh, no one blames you for that,' I said. 'He's perfectly all right now. Back at work, in fact.'

His relief showed, even through the crack. 'Very well,' he said, and pushed the door shut to take off the chain.

I followed him into the front room of his tall terrace house. The air smelt stale and felt still, as if it had been hanging in the same spot for days. The furniture was of the hard-stuffed and brown shellacked substantial type that in my plywood childhood I had thought the peak of living, unobtainable; and there were cases of tropical butterflies on the walls, and carved ornaments from somewhere like Java or Borneo on several small tables. A life abroad, retirement at home, I thought. From colour and heat to suburban respectability in Reading.

'My wife has gone out shopping,' he said, still nervously. 'She'll be back soon.' He looked hopefully out of the lace curtained window, but Mrs Brinton didn't oblige him by coming to his support.

I said, 'I just wanted to ask you, Mr Brinton, if you were by any chance related to a Mr William Brinton, one-time Clerk of Dunstable racecourse.'

He gave me a long agonized stare, and to my consternation sat down on his sofa and began to cry, his shaking hands covering his eyes and the tears splashing down on to his tweed-clad knees.

'Please . . . Mr Brinton . . . I'm so sorry,' I said awkwardly.

He snuffled and coughed, and dragged a handkerchief out to wipe his eyes. Gradually the paroxysm passed, and he said indistinctly, 'How did you find out? I told you I didn't want anyone asking questions . . .'

'It was quite accidental. Nobody asked any questions, I promise you. Would you like to tell me about it? Then I don't think any questions will need to be asked at all, from anyone else.'

'The police . . .' he said doubtfully, on a sob. 'They came before. I refused to say anything, and they went away.'

'Whatever you tell me will be in confidence.'

'I've been such a fool . . . I'd like to tell someone, really.'

I pictured the strung up, guilt-ridden weeks he'd endured, and the crying fit became not only understandable but inevitable.

'It was the letter, you see,' he said sniffing softly. 'The letter William began to write to me, though he never sent it . . . I found it in a whole trunk of stuff that was left when he . . . killed himself. I was in Sarawak then, you know, and they sent me a cable. It was a shock . . . one's only brother doing such a . . . a terrible thing. He was younger than me. Seven years. We weren't very close, except when we were children. I wish . . . but it's too late now. Anyway, when I came home I fetched all his stuff round from where it had been stored and put it up in the attic here, all his racing books and things. I didn't know what to do with them, you see. I wasn't interested in them, but it seemed . . . I don't know . . . I couldn't just burn them. It was months before I bothered to sort them out, and then I found the letter . . .' His voice faltered and he looked at me appealingly, wanting to be forgiven.

'Kitty and I had found my pension didn't go anywhere near as far as we'd expected. Everything is so terribly expensive. The rates . . . we decided we'd have to sell the house again though we'd only just bought it, and Kitty's family are all close. And then . . . I thought . . . perhaps I could sell the letter instead.'

'And you got threats instead of money,' I said.

'Yes. It was the letter itself which gave me the idea . . .' He chewed his moustache.

'And now you no longer have it,' I said matter of factly, as if I knew for certain and wasn't guessing. 'When you were first threatened you thought you could still sell the letter if Hunt Radnor kept you safe, and then you got more frightened and gave up the letter, and then cancelled the protection because the threats had stopped.'

He nodded unhappily. 'I gave them the letter because that man was shot . . . I didn't realize anything like that would happen. I was horrified. It was terrible. I hadn't thought it could be so dangerous, just selling a letter . . . I wish I'd never found it. I wish William had never written it.'

So did I, as it happened.

'What did the letter say?' I asked.

He hesitated, his fear showing. 'It might cause more trouble. They might come back.'

'They won't know you've told me,' I pointed out. 'How could they?'

'I suppose not.' He looked at me, making up his mind. There's one thing about being small: no one is ever afraid of you. If I'd been big and commanding I don't think he'd have risked it. As it was, his face softened and relaxed and he threw off the last threads of reticence.

'I know it by heart,' he said. 'I'll write it down for you, if you like. It's easier than saying it.'

I sat and waited while he fetched a ball point pen and a pad of large writing paper and got on with his task. The sight of the letter materializing again in front of his eyes affected him visibly, but whether to fear or remorse or sorrow, I couldn't tell. He covered one side of the page, then tore it off the pad and shakily handed it over.

I read what he had written. I read it twice. Because of these short desperate sentences, I reflected unemotionally, I had come within spitting distance of St Peter.

'That's fine,' I said. 'Thank you very much.'

'I wish I'd never found it,' he said again. 'Poor William.'

'Did you go to see this man?' I asked, indicating the letter as I put it away in my wallet.

'No, I wrote to him . . . he wasn't hard to find.'

'And how much did you ask for?'

Shame-faced, he muttered, 'Five thousand pounds.'

Five thousand pounds had been wrong, I thought. If he'd asked fifty thousand, he might have had a chance. But five thousand didn't put him among the big-power boys, it just revealed his mediocrity. No wonder he had been stamped on, fast.

'What happened next?' I asked.

'A big man came for the letter, about four o'clock one afternoon. It was awful. I asked him for the money and he just laughed in my face and pushed me into a chair. No money, he said, but if

I didn't hand over the letter at once he'd . . . he'd teach me a thing or two. That's what he said, teach me a thing or two. I explained that I had put the letter in my box at the bank and that the bank was closed and that I couldn't get it until the next morning. He said that he would come to the bank with me the next day, and then he went away . . .'

'And you rang up the agency almost at once? Yes. What made you choose Hunt Radnor?'

He looked surprised. 'It was the only one I knew about. Are there any others? I mean, most people have heard of Hunt Radnor, I should think.'

'I see. So Hunt Radnor sent you a bodyguard, but the big man wouldn't give up.'

'He kept telephoning . . . then your man suggested setting a trap in his office, and in the end I agreed. Oh, I shouldn't have let him, I was such a fool. I knew all the time, you see, who was threatening me, but I couldn't tell your agency because I would have had to admit I'd tried to get money . . . illegally.'

'Yes. Well, there's only one more thing. What was he like, the man who came and threatened you?'

Brinton didn't like even the memory of him. 'He was very strong. Hard. When he pushed me it was like a wall. I'm not . . . I mean, I've never been good with my fists, or anything like that. If he'd started hitting me I couldn't have stopped him . . .'

'I'm not blaming you for not standing up to him,' I pointed out. 'I just want to know what he looked like.'

'Very big,' he said vaguely. 'Huge.'

'I know it's several weeks ago now, but can't you possibly remember more than that? How about his hair? Anything odd about his face? How old? What class?'

He smiled for the first time, the sad wrinkles folding for a moment into some semblance of faded charm. If he'd never taken his first useless step into crime, I thought, he might still have been a nice gentle innocuous man, fading without rancour towards old age, troubled only by how to make a little pension go a long way. No tearing, destructive guilt.

'It's certainly easier when you ask questions like that. He was beginning to go bald, I remember now. And he had big blotchy freckles on the backs of his hands. It's difficult to know about his age. Not a youth, though; more than thirty, I think. What else did you ask? Oh yes, class. Working class, then.'

'English?'

'Oh yes, not foreign. Sort of cockney, I suppose.'

I stood up, thanked him, and began to take my leave. He said, begging me still for reassurance, 'There won't be any more trouble?'

'Not from me or the agency.'

'And the man who was shot?'

'Not from him either.'

'I tried to tell myself it wasn't my fault . . . but I haven't been able to sleep. How could I have been such a fool? I shouldn't have let that young man set any trap . . . I shouldn't have called in your agency . . . and it cost another chunk of our savings . . . I ought never to have tried to get money for that letter . . .'

'That's true, Mr Brinton, you shouldn't. But what's done is done, and I don't suppose you'll start anything like that again.'

'No, no,' he said with pain. 'I wouldn't. Ever. These last few weeks have been . . .' His voice died. Then he said more strongly, 'We'll have to sell the house now. Kitty likes it here, of course. But what I've always wanted myself is a little bungalow by the sea.'

When I reached the office I took out the disastrous letter and read it again, before adding it to the file. Being neither the original nor a photocopy, but only a reproduction from memory, it wasn't of the slightest use as evidence. In the older Brinton's small tidy script, a weird contrast to the heart-broken contents, it ran:

Dear Mervy, dear big brother,

I wish you could help me, as you did when I was little. I have spent fifteen years building up Dunstable racecourse, and a man called Howard Kraye is making me destroy it. I have to frame races which nobody likes. Very few horses come now, and the gate receipts are falling fast. This week I must see that the race-card goes to the printers too late, and the Press room telephones will all be out of order. There will be a terrible muddle. People must think I am mad. I can't escape him. He is paying me as well, but I must do as he says. I can't help my nature, you know that. He has found out about a boy I was living with, and I could be prosecuted. He wants the racecourse to sell for housing. Nothing can stop him getting it. My racecourse, I love it.

I know I shan't send this letter. Mervy, I wish you were here. I haven't anyone else. Oh dear God, I can't go on much longer, I really can't.

At five to six that afternoon I opened the door of Zanna Martin's office. Her desk was facing me and so was she. She raised her head, recognized me, and looked back at me in a mixture of pride and embarrassment.

'I did it,' she said. 'If you didn't, I'll kill you.'

She had combed her hair even further forward, so that it hung close round her face, but all the same one could see the disfigurement at first glance. I had forgotten, in the days since Friday, just how bad it was.

'I felt the same about you,' I said grinning.

'You really did keep your promise?'

'Yes, I did. All day Saturday and Sunday, most of yesterday and most of today, and very nasty it is, too.'

She sighed with relief. 'I'm glad you've come. I nearly gave it up this morning. I thought you wouldn't do it, and you'd never come back to see if I had, and that I was being a proper idiot.'

'Well, I'm here,' I said. 'Is Mr Bolt in?'

She shook her head. 'He's gone home. I'm just packing up.

'Finished the envelopes?' I said.

'Envelopes? Oh, those I was doing when you were here before? Yes, they're all done.'

'And filled and sent?'

'No, the leaflets haven't come back from the printers yet, much to Mr Bolt's disgust. I expect I'll be doing them tomorrow.'

She stood up, tall and thin, put on her coat and tied the scarf over her hair.

'Are you going anywhere this evening?' I asked.

'Home,' she said decisively.

'Come out to dinner,' I suggested.

'Aunty's legacy won't last long, the way you spend. I think Mr Bolt has already invested your money. You'd better save every penny until after settlement day.'

'Coffee, then, and the flicks?'

'Look,' she said hesitantly, 'I sometimes buy a hot chicken on my way home. There's a fish and chip shop next to the station that sells them. Would you . . . would you like to come and help me eat it? In return, I mean, for Friday night.'

'I'd enjoy that,' I said, and was rewarded by a pleased half-incredulous laugh.

'Really?'

'Really.'

As before, we went to Finchley by Underground, but this time she sat boldly where her whole face showed. To try to match her fortitude, I rested my elbow on the seat arm between us. She looked at my hand and then at my face, gratefully, almost as if we were sharing an adventure.

As we emerged from the tube station she said, 'You know, it makes a great deal of difference if one is accompanied by a man, even . . .' she stopped abruptly.

'Even,' I finished, smiling, 'if he is smaller than you and also damaged.'

'Oh dear . . . and much younger, as well.' Her real eye looked at me with rueful amusement. The glass one stared stonily ahead. I was getting used to it again.

'Let me buy the chicken,' I said, as we stopped outside the shop. The smell of hot chips mingled with diesel fumes from a passing lorry. Civilization, I thought. Delightful.

'Certainly not.' Miss Martin was firm and bought the chicken herself. She came out with it wrapped in newspaper. 'I got a few chips and a packet of peas,' she said.

'And I,' I said firmly, as we came to an off-licence, 'am getting some brandy.' What chips and peas would do to my digestion I dared not think.

We walked round to the house with the parcels and went through into her room. She moved with a light step.

'In that cupboard over there,' she said, pointing, as she peeled off her coat and scarf, 'there are some glasses and a bottle of sherry. Will you pour me some? I expect you prefer brandy, but have some sherry if you'd like. I'll just take these things into the kitchen and put them to keep hot.'

While I unscrewed the bottle and poured the drinks I heard her lighting her gas stove and unwrapping the parcels. There was dead quiet as I walked across the room with her sherry, and when I reached the door I saw why. She held the chicken in its piece of greaseproof paper absently in one hand: the bag of chips lay open on the table with the box of peas beside it: and she was reading the newspaper they had all been wrapped in.

She looked up at me in bewilderment.

'You,' she said. 'It's you. This is you.'

I looked down where her finger pointed. The fish and chip shop had wrapped up her chicken in the *Sunday Hemisphere*.

'Here's your sherry,' I said, holding it out to her.

She put down the chicken and took the glass without appearing to notice it.

'Another Halley,' she said. 'It caught my eye. Of course I read it. And it's your picture, and it even refers to your hand. You are Sid Halley.'

'That's right.' There was no chance of denying it.

'Good heavens. I've known about you for years. Read about you. I saw you on television, often. My father loved watching the racing, we always had it on when he was alive . . .' She broke off and then said with increased puzzlement, 'Why on earth did you say your name was John and that you worked in a shop? Why did you come to see Mr Bolt? I don't understand.'

'Drink your sherry, put the chicken in the oven before it freezes and I'll tell you.' There was nothing else to do: I didn't want to risk her brightly passing on the interesting titbit of news to her employer.

Without demur she put the dinner to heat, came to sit on the sofa, opposite to where I apprehensively waited in an arm-chair, and raised her eyebrows in expectation.

'I don't work in a shop,' I admitted. 'I am employed by a firm called Hunt Radnor Associates.'

Like Brinton, she had heard of the agency. She stiffened her whole body and began to frown. As casually as I could, I told her about Kraye and the Seabury shares; but she was no fool and she went straight to the heart of things.

'You suspect Mr Bolt, too. That's why you went to see him.'

'Yes, I'm afraid so.'

'And me? You took me out simply and solely to find out about him?' Her voice was bitter.

I didn't answer at once. She waited, and somehow her calmness was more piercing than tears or temper could have been. She asked so little of life.

At last I said, 'I went to Bolt's office as much to take out his secretary as to see Bolt himself, yes.'

The peas boiled over, hissing loudly. She stood up slowly. 'At least that's honest.'

She went into the tiny kitchen and turned out the gas under the saucepan.

I said, 'I came to your office this afternoon because I wanted to look at those leaflets Bolt is sending to Seabury shareholders. You told me at once that they hadn't come from the printers. I didn't need to accept your invitation to supper after that. But I'm here.'

She stood in the kitchen doorway, holding herself straight with an all too apparent effort.

'I suppose you lied about that too,' she said in a quiet rigidly controlled voice, pointing to my arm. 'Why? Why did you play such a cruel game with me? Surely you could have got your information without that. Why did you make me change my desk round? I suppose you were laughing yourself sick all day Saturday thinking about it.'

I stood up. Her hurt was dreadful.

I said, 'I went to Kempton races on Saturday.'

She didn't move.

'I kept my promise.'

She made a slight gesture of disbelief.

'I'm sorry,' I said helplessly.

'Yes. Good night Mr Halley. Good night.'

I went.

CHAPTER ELEVEN

RADNOR held a Seabury conference the next morning, Wednesday, consisting of himself, Dolly, Chico and me: the result, chiefly, of my having the previous afternoon finally wrung grudging permission from Lord Hagbourne to arrange a twenty-four hour guard at Seabury for the coming Thursday, Friday and Saturday.

The bulldozing had been accomplished without trouble, and a call to the course that morning had established that the tan was arriving in regular lorry loads and was being spread. Racing, bar any last minute accidents, was now certain. Even the weather was co-operating. The glass was rising; the forecast was dry, cold and sunny.

Dolly proposed a straight patrol system, and Radnor was inclined to agree. Chico and I had other ideas.

'If anyone intended to sabotage the track,' Dolly pointed out, 'they would be frightened off by a patrol. Same thing if they were planning something in the stands themselves.'

Radnor nodded. 'Safest way of making sure racing takes place. I suppose we'll need at least four men to do it properly.'

I said, 'I agree that we need a patrol tonight, tomorrow night and Friday night, just to play safe. But tomorrow, when the course will be more or less deserted . . . what we need is to pinch them at it, not to frighten them off. There's no evidence yet that could be used in a court of law. If we could catch them in mid-sabotage, so to speak, we'd be much better off.'

'That's right,' said Chico. 'Hide and pounce. Much better than scaring them away.'

'I seem to remember,' said Dolly with a grin, 'that the last time you two set a trap the mouse shot the cheese.'

'Oh God, Dolly, you slay me,' said Chico, laughing warmly and for once accepting her affection.

Even Radnor laughed. 'Seriously, though,' he said. 'I don't see how you can. A racecourse is too big. If you are hiding you can only see a small part of it. And surely if you show yourself your presence would act like any other patrol to stop anything plainly suspicious being done? I don't think it's possible.'

'Um,' I said. 'But there's one thing I can still do better than anyone else in this agency.'

'And what's that?' said Chico, ready to argue.

'Ride a horse.'

'Oh,' said Chico. 'I'll give you that, chum.'

'A horse,' said Radnor thoughtfully. 'Well, that's certainly an idea. Nobody's going to look suspiciously at a horse on a race-course, I suppose. Mobile, too. Where would you get one?'

'From Mark Witney. I could borrow his hack. Seabury's his local course. His stables aren't many miles away.'

'But can you still . . . ?' began Dolly, and broke off. 'Well, don't glare at me like that, all of you. I can't ride with two hands, let alone one.'

'A man called Gregory Philips had his arm amputated very high up,' I said, 'and went on racing in point-to-points for years.'

'Enough said,' said Dolly. 'How about Chico?'

'He can wear a pair of my jodhpurs. Protective colouring. And lean nonchalantly on the rails.'

'Stick insects,' said Chico cheerfully.

'That's what you want, Sid?' said Radnor.

I nodded. 'Look at it from the worst angle: we haven't anything on Kraye that will stand up. We might not find Smith, the tanker driver, and even if we do, he has everything to lose by talking and nothing to gain. When the racecourse stables burned down a year ago, we couldn't prove it wasn't an accident; an illicit cigarette end. Stable lads do smoke, regardless of bans.

'The so-called drain which collapsed—we don't know if it was dug a day, a week, or six weeks before it did its work. That letter William Brinton of Dunstable wrote to his brother, it's only a copy from memory that we've got, no good at all for evidence. All it proves, to our own satisfaction, is that Kraye is capable of anything. We can't show it to Lord Hagbourne, because I obtained it in confidence, and he still isn't a hundred per cent convinced that Kraye has done more than buy shares. As I see it, we've just got to give the enemy a chance to get on with their campaign.'

'You think they will, then?'

'It's awfully likely, isn't it? This year there isn't another Seabury meeting until February. A three months' gap. And if I read it right, Kraye is in a hurry now because of the political situation. He won't want to spend fifty thousand buying Seabury and then find building land has been nationalized overnight. If I were him, I'd want to clinch the deal and sell to a developer as quickly as possible. According to the photographs of the share transfers, he already holds twenty-three per cent of the shares. This is almost certainly enough to swing the sale of the company if it comes to a vote. But he's greedy. He'll want more. But he'll only want more if he can get it soon. Waiting for February is too risky. So yes, I do think that if we give him a chance he will organize some more damage this week.'

'It's a risk,' said Dolly. 'Suppose something dreadful happens and we neither prevent it nor catch anyone doing it?'

They kicked it round among the three of them for several minutes, the pros and cons of the straight patrols versus cat and mouse. Finally Radnor turned back to me and said 'Sid?'

'It's your agency,' I said seriously. 'It's your risk.'

'But it's your case. It's still your case. You must decide.'

I couldn't understand him. It was all very well for him to have given me a free hand so far, but this wasn't the sort of decision I would have ever expected him to pass on.

Still . . . 'Chico and I, then,' I said. 'We'll go along tonight and stay all day tomorrow. I don't think we'll let even Captain Oxon know we're there. Certainly not the foreman, Ted Wilkins, or any of the other men. We'll come in from the other side from the stands, and I'll borrow the horse for mobility. Dolly can arrange official patrol guards with Oxon for tomorrow night . . . suggest he gives them a warm room, Dolly. He ought to have the central heating on by then.'

'Friday and Saturday?' asked Radnor, non-committally.

'Full guards, I guess. As many as Lord Hagbourne will sub for. The racecourse crowds make cat and mouse impossible.'

'Right,' said Radnor, decisively. 'That's it, then.'

When Dolly, Chico, and I had got as far as the door he said, 'Sid, you wouldn't mind if I had another look at those photographs? Send Jones-boy down with them if you're not needing them.'

'Sure,' I agreed. 'I've pored over them till I know them by heart. I bet you'll spot something at once that I've missed.'

'It often works that way,' he said, nodding.

The three of us went back to the Racing Section, and via the switchboard I traced Jones-boy, who happened to be in Missing Persons. While he was on his way down I flipped through the packet of photographs yet again. The share transfers, the summary with the list of bank accounts, the letters from Bolt, the ten pound notes, and the two sheets of dates, initials and figures from the very bottom of the attaché case. It had been clear all along that these last were lists either of receipts or expenditure: but by now I was certain they were the latter. A certain W.L.B. had received regular sums of fifty pounds a month for twelve months, and the last date for W.L.B. was four days before William Leslie Brinton, Clerk of Dunstable Racecourse, had taken the quickest way out. Six hundred pounds and a threat; the price of a man's soul.

Most of the other initials meant nothing to me, except the last one, J.R.S., which looked as if they could be the tanker driver's. The first entry for J.R.S., for one hundred pounds, was dated the day before the tanker overturned at Seabury, the day before Kraye went to Aynsford for the week-end.

In the next line, the last of the whole list, a further sum of one hundred and fifty pounds was entered against J.R.S. The date of this was that of the following Tuesday, three days ahead when I took the photographs. Smith had packed up and vanished from his job and his digs on that Tuesday.

Constantly recurring amongst the other varying initials were two christian names, Leo and Fred. Each of these was on the regular pay-roll, it seemed. Either Leo or Fred, I guessed, had been the big man who had visited and frightened Mervyn Brinton. Either Leo or Fred was the 'Big Chap' who had sent Andrews with a gun to the Cromwell Road.

I had a score to settle with either Leo or Fred.

Jones-boy came in for the photographs. I tapped them together back into their box and gave them to him.

'Where, you snotty nosed little coot, is our coffee?' said Chico rudely. We had been downstairs when Jones-boy did his rounds.

'Coots are bald,' observed Dolly dryly, eyeing Jones-boy's luxuriant locks.

Jones-boy unprintably told Chico where he could find his coffee.

Chico advanced a step, saying, 'You remind me of the people sitting on the walls of Jerusalem.' He had been raised in a church orphanage, after all.

Jones-boy also knew the more basic bits of Isaiah. He said callously, 'You did it on the doorstep of the Barnes cop shop, I believe.'

Chico furiously lashed out a fist to Jones-boy's head. Jones-boy jumped back, laughed insultingly, and the box he was holding flew high out of his hand, opening as it went.

'Stop it you two, damn you,' shouted Dolly, as the big photographs floated down on to her desk and on to the floor.

'Babes in the Wood,' remarked Jones-boy, in great good humour from having got the best of the slanging match. He helped Dolly and me pick up the photographs, shuffled them back into the box in no sort of order, and departed grinning.

'Chico,' said Dolly severely, 'you ought to know better.'

'The bossy-mother routine bores me sick,' said Chico violently.

Dolly bit her lip and looked away. Chico stared at me defiantly, knowing very well he had started the row and was in the wrong.

'As one bastard to another,' I said mildly, 'pipe down.'

Not being able to think of a sufficiently withering reply fast enough Chico merely scowled and walked out of the room. The show was over. The office returned to normal. Typewriters clattered, someone used the tape recorder, someone else the telephone. Dolly sighed and began to draw up her list for Seabury. I sat and thought about Leo. Or Fred. Unproductively.

After a while I ambled upstairs to Bona Fides, where the usual amount of telephone shouting filled the air. George, deep in a mysterious conversation about moth-balls, saw me and shook his head. Jack Copeland, freshly attired in a patchily faded green sleeveless pullover, took time out between calls to say that they were sorry, but they'd made no progress with Kraye. He had, Jack said, very craftily covered his tracks about ten years back. They would keep digging, if I liked. I liked.

Up in Missing Persons Sammy said it was too soon for results on Smith.

When I judged that Mark Witney would be back in his house after exercising his second lot of horses, I rang him up and asked him to lend me his hack, a pensioned-off old steeplechaser of the first water.

'Sure,' he said. 'What for?'

I explained what for.

'You'd better have my horse box as well,' he commented. 'Suppose it pours with rain all night? Give you somewhere to keep dry, if you have the box.'

'But won't you be needing it? The forecast says clear and dry anyway.'

'I won't need it until Friday morning. I haven't any runners until Seabury. And only one there, I may say, in spite of it being so close. The owners just won't have it. I have to go all the way to Banbury on Saturday. Damn silly with another much better course on my door-step.'

'What are you running at Seabury?'

He told me, at great and uncomplimentary length, about a half blind, utterly stupid, one paced habitual non-jumper with which he proposed to win the novice chase. Knowing him, he probably would. We agreed that Chico and I should arrive at his place at about eight that evening, and I rang off.

After that I left the office, went across London by Underground to Company House in the City, and asked for the files of Seabury Racecourse. In a numbered chair at a long table, surrounded by earnest men and women clerks poring over similar files and making copious notes, I studied the latest list of investors. Apart from Kraye and his various aliases, which I now recognized on sight from long familiarity with the share transfer photographs, there were no large blocks in single ownership. No one else held more than three per cent of the total: and as three per cent meant that roughly two and a half thousand pounds was lying idle and not bringing in a penny in dividends, it was easy to see why no one wanted a larger holding.

Fotherton's name was not on the list. Although this was not conclusive, because a nominee name like 'Mayday Investments' could be anyone at all, I was more or less satisfied that Seabury's Clerk was not gambling on Seabury's death. All the big share movements during the past year had been to Kraye, and no one else.

A few of the small investors, holding two hundred or so shares each, were people I knew personally. I wrote down their names and addresses, intending to ask them to let me see Bolt's circular letter when it arrived. Slower than via Zanna Martin, but surer.

My mind shied away from Zanna Martin. I'd had a bad night thinking about her. Her and Jenny, both.

Back in the office I found it was the tail-end of the lunch hour, with nearly all the desks still empty. Chico alone was sitting behind his, biting his nails.

'If we're going to be up all night,' I suggested, 'we'd better take the afternoon off for sleep.'

'No need.'

'Every need. I'm not as young as you.'

'Poor old grandpa.' He grinned suddenly, apologizing for the morning. 'I can't help it. That Jones-boy gets on my wick.'

'Jones-boy can look after himself. It's Dolly . . .'

'It's not my bloody fault she can't have kids.'

'She wants kids like you want a mother.'

'But I don't . . .' he began indignantly.

'Your own,' I said flatly. 'Like you want your own mother to have kept you and loved you. Like mine did.'

'You had every advantage, of course.'

'That's right.'

He laughed. 'Funny thing is I like old Dolly, really. Except for the hen bit.'

'Who wouldn't?' I said amicably. 'You can sleep on my sofa.'

He sighed. 'You're going to be less easy than Dolly to work for, I can see that.'

'Eh?'

'Don't kid yourself, mate. Sir, I mean.' He was lightly ironic.

The other inmates of the office drifted back, including Dolly, with whom I fixed for Chico to have the afternoon free. She was cool to him and unforgiving, which I privately thought would do them both good.

She said, 'The first official patrol will start on the racecourse tomorrow at six p.m. Shall I tell them to find you and report?'

'No,' I said definitely. 'I don't know where I'll be.'

'It had better be the usual then,' she said. 'They can report to the old man at his home number when they are starting the job, and again at six a.m. when they go off and the next lot take over.'

'And they'll ring him in between if anything happens?' I said.

'Yes. As usual.'

'It's as bad as being a doctor,' I said smiling.

Dolly nodded, and half to herself she murmured, 'You'll find out.'

Chico and I walked round to my flat, pulled the curtains, and did our best to sleep. I didn't find it easy at two-thirty in the afternoon: it was the time for racing, not rest. It seemed to me that I had barely drifted off when the telephone rang: I looked at my watch on my way to answer it in the sitting-room and found it was only ten to five. I had asked for a call at six.

It was not the telephone exchange, however, but Dolly.

'A message has come for you by hand, marked very urgent. I thought you might want it before you go to Seabury.'

'Who brought it?'

'A taxi driver.'

'Shunt him round here, then.'

'He's gone, I'm afraid.'

'Who's the message from?'

'I've no idea. It's a plain brown envelope, the size we use for interim reports.'

'Oh. All right, I'll come back.'

Chico had drowsily propped himself up on one elbow on the sofa.

'Go to sleep again,' I said. 'I've got to go and see something in the office. Won't be long.'

When I reached the Racing Section again I found that whatever had come for me, something else had gone. The shaky lemon coloured table. I was deskless again.

'Sammy said he was sorry,' explained Dolly, 'but he has a new assistant and nowhere to park him.'

'I had things in the drawer,' I complained. Shades of Sammy's lunch, I thought.

'They're here,' Dolly said, pointing to a corner of her desk. 'There was only the Brinton file, a half bottle of brandy, and some pills. Also I found this on the floor.' She held out a flat crackly cellophane and paper packet.

'The negatives of those photographs are in here,' I said, taking it from her. 'They were in the box, though.'

'Until Jones-boy dropped it.'

'Oh yes.' I put the packet of negatives inside the Brinton file and pinched a large rubber band from Dolly to snap round the outside.

'How about that mysterious very urgent message?' I asked.

Dolly silently and considerately slit open the envelope in question, drew out the single sheet of paper it contained and handed it to me. I unfolded it and stared at it in disbelief.

It was a circular, headed Charing, Street and King, Stockbrokers, dated with the following day's date, and it ran:

Dear Sir or Madam,

We have various clients wishing to purchase small parcels of shares in the following lists of minor companies. If you are considering selling your interests in any of these, we would be grateful if you would get in touch with us. We would assure you of a good fair price, based on today's quotation.

There followed a list of about thirty companies, of which I had heard of only one. Tucked in about three-quarters of the way down was Seabury Racecourse.

I turned the page over. Zanna Martin had written on the back in a hurried hand.

This is only going to Seabury shareholders. Not to anyone owning shares in the other companies. The leaflets came from the printers this morning, and are to be posted tomorrow. I hope it is what you want. I'm sorry about last night.

Z.M.

'What is it?' asked Dolly.

'A free pardon,' I said light-heartedly, slipping the circular inside the Brinton file along with the negatives. 'Also confirmation that Ellis Bolt is not on the side of the angels.'

'You're a nut,' she said. 'And take these things off my desk. I haven't room for them.'

I put the pills and brandy in my pocket and picked up the Brinton file.

'Is that better?'

'Thank you, yes.'

'So long, then, my love. See you Friday.'

On the walk back to the flat I decided suddenly to go and see Zanna Martin. I went straight down to the garage for my car without going up and waking Chico again, and made my way eastwards to the City for the second time that day. The rush hour traffic was so bad that I was afraid I would miss her, but in fact she was ten minutes late leaving the office and I caught her up just before she reached the Underground station.

'Miss Martin,' I called. 'Would you like a lift home?'

She turned round in surprise.

'Mr Halley!'

'Hop in.'

She hopped. That is to say, she opened the door, picked up the Brinton file which was lying on the passenger seat, sat down, tidily folded her coat over her knees, and pulled the door shut again. The bad side of her face was towards me, and she was very conscious of it. The scarf and the hair were gently pulled forward.

I took a pound and a ten shilling note out of my pocket and gave them to her. She took them, smiling.

'The taxi-man told our switchboard girl you gave him that for bringing the leaflet. Thank you very much.' I swung out through the traffic and headed for Finchley.

She answered obliquely. 'That wretched chicken is still in the oven, stone cold. I just turned the gas out yesterday, after you'd gone.'

'I wish I could stay this evening instead,' I said, 'but I've got a job on for the agency.'

'Another time,' she said tranquilly. 'Another time, perhaps. I understand that you couldn't tell me at first who you worked for, because you didn't know whether I was an . . . er, an accomplice of Mr Bolt's, and afterwards you didn't tell me for fear of what actually happened, that I would be upset. So that's that.'

'You are generous.'

'Realistic, even if a bit late.'

We went a little way in silence. Then I asked. 'What would happen to the shares Kraye owns if it were proved he was sabotaging the company? If he were convicted, I mean. Would his shares be confiscated, or would he still own them when he came out of jail?'

'I've never heard of anyone's shares being confiscated,' she said, sounding interested. 'But surely that's a long way in the future?'

'I wish I knew. It makes a good deal of difference to what I should do now.'

'How do you mean?'

'Well . . . an easy way to stop Kraye buying too many more shares would be to tell the racing press and the financial press that a take-over is being attempted. The price would rocket. But Kraye already holds twenty-three per cent, and if the law couldn't take it away from him, he would either stick to that and vote for a sell out, or if he got cold feet he could unload his shares at the higher price and still make a fat profit. Either way, he'd be sitting pretty financially, in jail or out. And either way Seabury would be built on.'

'I suppose this sort of thing's happened before?'

'Take-overs, yes, several. But only one other case of sabotage. At Dunstable. Kraye again.'

'Haven't any courses survived a take-over bid?'

'Only Sandown, publicly. I don't know of any others, but they may have managed it in secrecy.'

'How did Sandown do it?'

'The local council did it for them. Stated loudly that planning permission would not be given for building. Of course the bid collapsed then.'

'It looks as though the only hope for Seabury, in that case, is that the council there will act in the same way. I'd try a strong lobby, if I were you.'

'You're quite a girl, Miss Martin,' I said smiling. 'That's a very good idea. I'll go and dip a toe into the climate of opinion at the Town Hall.'

She nodded approvingly. 'No good lobbying against the grain. Much better to find out which way people are likely to move before you start pushing!'

Finchley came into sight. I said, 'You do realize, Miss Martin, that if I am successful at my job, you will lose yours?'

She laughed. 'Poor Mr Bolt. He's not at all bad to work for. But don't worry about my job. It's easy for an experienced stock-broker's secretary to get a good one, I assure you.'

I stopped at her gate, looking at my watch. 'I'm afraid I can't come in. I'm already going to be a bit late.'

She opened the door without ado and climbed out. 'Thank you for coming at all.' She smiled, shut the door crisply, and waved me away.

I drove back to my flat as fast as I could, fuming slightly at the traffic. It wasn't until I switched off the engine down in the garage and leaned over to pick it up that I discovered the Brinton file wasn't there. And then remembered Miss Martin holding it on her lap during the journey, and me hustling her out of the car. Zanna Martin still had Brinton's file. I hadn't time to go back for it, and I couldn't ring her up because I didn't know the name of the owner of the house she lived in. But surely, I reassured myself, surely the file would be safe enough where it was until Friday.

CHAPTER TWELVE

Chico and I sat huddled together for warmth in some gorse bushes and watched the sun rise over Seabury Racecourse. It had been a cold clear night with a tingle of nought degrees centigrade about it, and we were both shivering.

Behind us, among the bushes and out of sight, Revelation, one-time winner of the Cheltenham Gold Cup, was breakfasting on meagre patches of grass. We could hear the scrunch when he bit down close to the roots, and the faint chink of the bridle as he ate. For some time Chico and I had been resisting the temptation to relieve him of his nice warm rug.

'They might try something now,' said Chico hopefully. 'First light, before anyone's up.'

Nothing had moved in the night, we were certain of that. Every hour I had ridden Revelation at a careful walk round the whole of the track itself, and Chico had made a plimsoll-shod inspection of the stands, at one with the shadows. There had been no one about. Not a sound but the stirring breeze, not a glimmer of light but from the stars and a waning moon.

Our present spot, chosen as the sky lightened and some concealment became necessary, lay at the farthest spot from the stands, at the bottom of the semi-circle of track cut off by the road which ran across the course. Scattered bushes and scrub filled the space between the track and boundary fence, enough to shield us from all but closely prying eyes. Behind the boundary fence were the little back gardens of the first row of bungalows. The sun rose bright and yellow away to our left and the birds sang around us. It was half past seven.

'It's going to be a lovely day,' said Chico.

At ten past nine there was some activity up by the stands and the tractor rolled on to the course pulling a trailer. I unshipped my race glasses, balanced them on my bent up knees, and took a look. The trailer was loaded with what I guessed were hurdles, and was accompanied by three men on foot.

I handed the glasses to Chico without comment, and yawned.

'Lawful occasions,' he remarked, bored.

We watched the tractor and trailer lumber slowly round the far end of the course, pause to unload, and return for a refill. On its second trip it came close enough for us to confirm that it was in fact the spare hurdles that were being dumped into position, four or five at each flight, ready to be used if any were splintered in the races. We watched for a while in silence. Then I said slowly, 'Chico, I've been blind.'

'Huh?'

'The tractor,' I said. 'The tractor. Under our noses all the time.'

'So?'

'So the sulphuric acid tanker was pulled over by a tractor. No complicated lifting gear necessary. Just a couple of ropes or chains slung over the top of the tanker and fastened round the axles. Then you unscrew the hatches and stand well clear. Someone drives the tractor at full power up the course, over goes the tanker and out pours the juice. And Bob's your uncle!'

'Every racecourse has a tractor,' said Chico thoughtfully.

'That's right.'

'So no one would look twice at a tractor on a racecourse. Quite. No one would remark on any tracks it left. No one would mention seeing one on the road. So if you're right, and I'd say you certainly are, it wouldn't necessarily have been that tractor, the racecourse tractor, which was used.'

'I'll bet it was, though.' I told Chico about the photographed initials and payments. 'Tomorrow I'll check the initials of all the workmen here from Ted Wilkins downwards against that list. Any one of them might have been paid just to leave the tractor on the course, lying handy. The tanker went over on the evening before the meeting, like today. The tractor would have been in use then too. Warm and full of fuel. Nothing easier. And afterwards, straight on up the racecourse, and out of sight.'

'It was dusk,' agreed Chico. 'As long as no one came along the road in the minutes it took to unhitch the ropes or chains afterwards, they were clear. No traffic diversions, no detours, nothing.'

We sat watching the tractor lumbering about, gloomily realizing we couldn't prove a word of it.

'We'll have to move,' I said presently. 'There's a hurdle just along there, about fifty yards away, where those wings are. They'll be down here over the road soon.'

We adjourned with Revelation back to the horse box half a mile away down the road to the west and took the opportunity to eat our own breakfast. When we had finished Chico went back first, strolling along confidently in my jodhpurs, boots and polo-necked jersey, the complete horseman from head to foot. He had never actually sat on a horse in his life.

After a while I followed on Revelation. The men had brought the hurdles down into the semi-circular piece of track and had laid them in place. They were now moving farther away up the course, unloading the next lot. Unremarked, I rode back to the bushes and dismounted. Of Chico there was no sign for another half-hour, and then he came whistling across from the road with his hands in his pockets.

When he reached me he said, 'I had another look round the stands. Rotten security, here. No one asked me what I was doing. There are some women cleaning here and there, and some are working in the stable block, getting the lads' hostel ready, things like that. I said good morning to them, and they said good morning back.' He was disgusted.

'Not much scope for saboteurs,' I said morosely. 'Cleaners in the stands and workmen on the course.'

'Dusk tonight,' nodded Chico. 'That's the most likely time now.'

The morning ticked slowly away. The sun rose to its low November zenith and shone straight into our eyes. I passed the time by taking a photograph of Revelation and another of Chico. He was fascinated by the tiny camera and said he couldn't wait to get one like it. Eventually I put it back into my breeches pocket, and shading my eyes against the sun took my hundredth look up the course.

Nothing. No men, no tractor. I looked at my watch. One o'clock. Lunch hour. More time passed.

Chico picked up the race-glasses and swept the course.

'Be careful,' I said idly. 'Don't look at the sun with those. You'll hurt your eyes.'

'Do me a favour.'

I yawned, feeling the sleepless night catch up.

'There's a man on the course,' he said. 'One. Just walking.'

He handed me the glasses and I took a look. He was right. One man was walking alone across the racecourse; not round the track but straight across the rough grass in the middle. He was too far away for his features to be distinguishable and in any case he was wearing a fawn duffle coat with the hood up. I shrugged and lowered the glasses. He looked harmless enough.

With nothing better to do we watched him reach the far side, duck under the rails, and move along until he was standing behind one of the fences with only his head and shoulders in our sight.

Chico remarked that he should have attended to nature in the gents before he left the stands. I yawned again, smiling at the same time. The man went on standing behind the fence.

'What on earth is he doing?' said Chico, after about five minutes.

'He isn't doing anything,' I said, watching through the glasses. 'He's just standing there looking this way.'

'Do you think he's spotted us?'

'No, he couldn't. He hasn't any binocs, and we are in the bushes.'

Another five minutes passed in inactivity.

'He must be doing *something,*' said Chico, exasperated.

'Well, he isn't,' I said.

Chico took a turn with the glasses. 'You can't see a damn thing against the sun,' he complained. 'We should have camped up the other end.'

'In the car park?' I suggested mildly. 'The road to the stables and the main gates runs along the other end. There isn't a scrap of cover.'

'He's got a flag,' said Chico suddenly. 'Two flags. One in each hand. White on the left, orange on the right. He seems to be waving them alternately. He's just some silly nit of a racecourse attendant practising calling up the ambulance and the vet.' He was disappointed.

I watched the flags waving, first white, then orange, then white, then orange, with a gap of a second or two between each wave. It certainly wasn't any form of recognizable signalling: nothing like semaphore. They were, as Chico had said, quite simply the flags used after a fall in a race: white to summon the ambulance for the jockey, orange to get attention for a horse. He didn't keep it up very long. After about eight waves altogether he stopped, and in a moment or two began to walk back across the course to the stands.

'Now what,' said Chico, 'do you think all that was in aid of?'

He swept the glasses all round the whole racecourse yet again. 'There isn't a soul about except him and us.'

'He's probably been standing by a fence for months waiting for a chance to wave his flags, and no one has been injured anywhere near him. In the end, the temptation proved too much.'

I stood up and stretched, went through the bushes to Revelation, undid the head collar with which he was tethered to the bushes, unbuckled the surcingle and pulled off his rug.

'What are you doing?' said Chico.

'The same as the man with the flags. Succumbing to an intolerable temptation. Give me a leg up.' He did what I asked, but hung on to the reins.

'You're mad. You said in the night that they might let you do it after this meeting, but they'd never agree to it before. Suppose you smash the fences?'

'Then I'll be in almighty trouble,' I agreed. 'But here I am on a super jumper looking at a heavenly course on a perfect day, with everyone away at lunch.' I grinned. 'Leave go.'

Chico took his hand away. 'It's not like you,' he said doubtfully.

'Don't take it to heart,' I said flippantly, and touched Revelation into a walk.

At this innocuous pace the horse and I went out on to the track and proceeded in the direction of the stands. Anti-clockwise, the way the races were run. Still at a walk we reached the road and went across its uncovered tarmac surface. On the far side of the road lay the enormous dark brown patch of tan, spread thick and firm where the burnt turf had been bulldozed away. Horses would have no difficulty in racing over it.

Once on the other side, on the turf again, Revelation broke into a trot. He knew where he was. Even with no crowds and no noise the fact of being on a familiar racecourse was exciting him. His ears were pricked, his step springy. At fourteen he had been already a year in retirement, but he moved beneath me like a four-year-old. He too, I guessed fancifully, was feeling the satanic tug of pleasure about to be illicitly snatched.

Chico was right, of course. I had no business at all to be riding on the course so soon before a meeting. It was indefensible. I ought to know better. I did know better. I eased Revelation gently into a canter.

There were three flights of hurdles and three fences more or less side by side up the straight, and the water jump beyond that. As I wasn't sure that Revelation would jump the fences in cold blood on his own (many horses won't), I set him at the hurdles.

Once he had seen these and guessed my intention I doubt if I could have stopped him, even if I'd wanted to. He fairly ate up the first flight and stretched out eagerly for the second. After that I gave him a choice, and of the two obstacles lying ahead, he opted for the fence. It didn't seem to bother him that he was on his own. They were excellent fences and he was a Gold Cup winner, born and bred for the job and being given an unexpected, much missed treat. He flew the fence with all his former dash and skill.

As for me, my feelings were indescribable. I'd sat on a horse a few times since I'd given up racing, but never found an opportunity of doing more than riding out quietly at morning exercise with Mark's string. And here I was, back in my old place, doing again what I'd ached for in two and a half years. I grinned with irrepressible joy and got Revelation to lengthen his stride for the water jump.

He took it with feet to spare. Perfect. There were no irate shouts from the stands on my right, and we swept away on round the top bend of the course, fast and free. Another fence at the end of the bend—Revelation floated it—and five more stretching away down the far side. It was at the third of these, the open ditch, that the man had been standing and waving the flags.

It's an undoubted fact that emotions pass from rider to horse, and Revelation was behaving with the same reckless exhilaration which gripped me: so after two spectacular leaps over the next two fences we both sped onwards with arms open to fate. There ahead was the guard rail, the four foot wide open ditch and the four foot six fence rising on the far side of it. Revelation, knowing all about it, automatically put himself right to jump.

It came, the blinding flash in the eyes, as we soared into the air. White, dazzling, brain shattering light, splintering the day into a million fragments and blotting out the world in a blaze as searing as the sun.

I felt Revelation falling beneath me and rolled instinctively, my eyes open and quite unable to see. Then there was the rough crash on the turf and the return of vision from light to blackness and up through grey to normal sight.

I was on my feet before Revelation, and I still had hold of the reins. He struggled up, bewildered and staggering, but apparently unhurt. I pulled him forward into an unwilling trot to make sure of his legs, and was relieved to find them whole and sound. It only remained to remount as quickly as possible, and this was infuriatingly difficult. With two hands I could have jumped up easily: as it was I scrambled untidily back into the saddle at the third attempt, having lost the reins altogether and bashed my stomach on the pommel of the saddle into the bargain. Revelation behaved very well, all things considered. He trotted only fifty yards or so in the wrong direction before I collected myself and the reins into a working position and turned him round. This time we by-passed the fence and all subsequent ones: I cantered him first down the side of the track, slowed to a trot to cross the road, and steered then not on round the bottom semi-circle but off to the right, heading for where the boundary fence met the main London road.

Out of the corner of my eye I saw Chico running in my direction across the rough grass. I waved him towards me with a sweep of the arm and reined in and waited for him where our paths converged.

'I thought you said you could bloody well ride,' he said, scarcely out of breath from the run.

'Yeah,' I said. 'I thought so once.'

He looked at me sharply. 'You fell off. I was watching. You fell off like a baby.'

'If you were watching . . . the horse fell, if you don't mind. There's a distinction. Very important to jockeys.'

'Nuts,' he said. 'You fell off.'

'Come on,' I said, walking Revelation towards the boundary fence. 'There's something to find,' I told Chico what. 'In one of those bungalows, I should think. At a window or on the roof, or in a garden.'

'Sods,' said Chico forcefully. 'The dirty sods.'

I agreed with him.

It wasn't very difficult, because it had to be within a stretch of only a hundred yards or so. We went methodically along the boundary fence towards the London road, stopping to look carefully into every separate little garden, and at every separate little house. A fair number of inquisitive faces looked back.

Chico saw it first, propped into a high leafless branch of a tree growing well back in the second to last garden. Traffic whizzed along the London road only ten yards ahead, and Revelation showed signs of wanting to retreat.

'Look,' said Chico, pointing upwards.

I looked, fighting a mild battle against the horse. It was five feet high, three feet wide, and polished to a spotless brilliance. A mirror.

'Sods,' said Chico again.

I nodded, dismounted, led Revelation back to where the traffic no longer fretted him, and tied the reins to the fence. Then Chico and I walked along to the London road and round into the road of bungalows. Napoleon Close, it said. Napoleon wasn't *that* close, I reflected, amused.

We rang the door of the second bungalow. A man and a woman both came to the door to open it, elderly, gentle, inoffensive and enquiring.

I came straight to the point, courteously. 'Do you know you have a mirror in your tree?'

'Don't be silly,' said the woman, smiling as at an idiot. She had flat wavy grey hair and was wearing a sloppy black cardigan over a brown wool dress. No colour sense, I thought.

'You'd better take a look,' I suggested.

'It's not a mirror, you know,' said the husband, puzzled. 'It's a placard. One of those advertisement things.'

'That's right,' said his wife contrapuntally. 'A placard.'

'We agreed to lend our tree . . .'

'For a small sum, really . . . only our pension . . .'

'A man put up the framework . . .'

'He said he would be back soon with the poster . . .'

'A religious one, I believe. A good cause . . .'

'We wouldn't have done it otherwise . . .'

Chico interrupted. 'I wouldn't have thought it was a good place for a poster. Your tree stands farther back than the others. It isn't conspicuous.'

'I did think . . .' began the man doubtfully, shuffling in his checked woolly bedroom slippers.

'But if he was willing to pay rent for your particular tree, you didn't want to put him off,' I finished. 'An extra quid or two isn't something you want to pass on next door.'

They wouldn't have put it so bluntly, but they didn't demur.

'Come and look,' I said.

They followed me round along the narrow path beside their bungalow wall and into their own back garden. The tree stood half way to the racecourse boundary fence, the sun slanting down through the leafless branches. We could see the wooden back of the mirror, and the ropes which fastened it to the tree trunk. The man and his wife walked round to the front, and their puzzlement increased.

'He said it was for a poster,' repeated the man.

'Well,' I said as matter of factly as I could, 'I expect it is for a poster, as he said. But at the moment, you see, it is a mirror. And it's pointing straight out over the racecourse; and you know how mirrors reflect the sunlight? We just thought it might not be too safe, you know, if anyone got dazzled, so we wondered if you would mind us moving it?'

'Why, goodness,' agreed the woman, looking with more awareness at our riding clothes, 'no one could see the racing with light shining in their eyes.'

'Quite. So would you mind if we turned the mirror round a bit?'

'I can't see that it would hurt, Dad,' she said doubtfully.

He made a nondescript assenting movement with his hand, and Chico asked how the mirror had been put up in the tree in the first place. The man had brought a ladder with him, they said, and no, they hadn't one themselves. Chico shrugged, placed me beside the tree, put one foot on my thigh, one on my shoulder, and was up in the bare branches like a squirrel. The elderly couple's mouths sagged open.

'How long ago?' I asked. 'When did the man put up the mirror?'

'This morning,' said the woman, getting over the shock. 'He came back just now, too, with another rope or something. That's when he said he'd be back with the poster.'

So the mirror had been hauled up into the tree while Chico and I had been obliviously sitting in the bushes, and adjusted later when the sun was at the right angle in the sky. At two o'clock. The time, the next day, of the third race, the handicap steeplechase. Some handicap, I thought, a smash of light in the eyes.

White flag: a little bit to the left. Orange flag: a little bit to the right. No flag: dead on target.

Come back tomorrow afternoon and clap a religious poster over the glass as soon as the damage was done, so that even the quickest search wouldn't reveal a mirror. Just another jinx on Seabury racecourse. Dead horses, crushed and trampled jockeys. A jinx. Send my horses somewhere else, Mr Witney, something always goes wrong at Seabury.

I was way out in one respect. The religious poster was not due to be put in place the following day.

CHAPTER THIRTEEN

'I THINK,' I said gently to the elderly couple, 'that it might be better if you went indoors. We will explain to the man who is coming what we are doing to his mirror.'

Dad glanced up the path towards the road, put his arm protectively round his wife's woolly shoulders, and said gratefully, 'Er . . . yes . . . yes.'

They shuffled rapidly through the back door into the bungalow just as a large man carrying an aluminium folding ladder and a large rolled up paper came barging through their front gate. There had been the squeak of his large plain dark blue van stopping, the hollow crunch of the handbrake being forcibly applied, the slam of the door and the scrape of the ladder being unloaded. Chico in the tree crouched quite still, watching.

I was standing with my back to the sun, but it fell full on the big man's face when he came into the garden. It wasn't the sort of face one would naturally associate with religious posters. He was a cross between a heavyweight wrestler and Mount Vesuvius. Craggy, brutally strong, and not far off erupting.

He came straight towards me across the grass, dropped the ladder beside him, and said enquiringly, 'What goes on?'

'The mirror,' I said. 'Comes down.'

His eyes narrowed in sudden awareness and his body stiffened.

'There's a poster going over it,' he began quite reasonably, lifting the paper roll. Then with a rush the lava burst out, the paper flew wide, and the muscles bunched into action.

It wasn't much of a fight. He started out to hit my face, changed his mind, and ploughed both fists in below the belt. It was quite a long way down for him. Doubling over in pain on to the lawn, I picked up the ladder, and gave him a swinging swipe behind the knees.

The ground shook with the impact. He fell on his side, his coat swinging open. I lunged forward, snatching at the pistol showing in the holster beside his ribs. It came loose, but he brushed me aside with an arm like a telegraph pole. I fell, sprawling. He rolled over into a crouch, picked up the gun from the grass and sneered down into my face. Then he stood up like a released spring and on the way with force and deliberation booted his toe-cap into my navel. He also clicked back the catch on his gun.

Up in the tree Chico yelled. The big man turned and took three steps towards him, seeing him for the first time. With a choice of targets, he favoured the one still in a state to resist. The hand with the pistol pointed at Chico.

'Leo,' I shouted. Nothing happened. I tried again.

'Fred!'

The big man turned his head a fraction back to me and Chico jumped down on to him from ten feet up.

The gun went off with a double crash and again the day flew apart in shining splintering fragments. I sat on the ground with my knees bent up, groaning quietly, cursing fluently, and getting on with my business.

Drawn by the noise, the inhabitants of the bungalows down the line came out into their back gardens and looked in astonishment over the fences. The elderly couple stood palely at their window, their mouths again open. The big man had too big an audience now for murder.

Chico was overmatched for size and nearly equalled in skill. He and the big man threw each other round a bit while I crept doubled up along the path into the front garden as far as the gate, but the battle was a foregone conclusion, bar the retreat.

He came alone, crashing up the path, saw me hanging on to the gate and half raised the gun. But there were people in the road now, and more people peering out of opposite windows. In scorching fury he whipped at my head with the barrel, and I avoided it by leaving go of the gate and collapsing on the ground again. Behind the gate, with the bars nice and comfortingly between me and his boot.

He crunched across the pavement, slammed into the van, cut his cogs to ribbons and disappeared out on to the London road in a cloud of dust.

Chico came down the garden path staggering, with blood sloshing out of a cut eyebrow. He looked anxious and shaken.

'I thought you said you could bloody well fight,' I mocked him.

He came to a halt beside me on his knees. 'Blast you.' He put his fingers to his forehead and winced at the result.

I grinned at him.

'You were running away,' he said.

'Naturally.'

'What have you got there?' He took the little camera out of my hand. 'Don't tell me,' he said, his face splitting into an unholy smile. 'Don't tell me.'

'It's what we came for, after all.'

'How many?'

'Four of him. Two of the van.'

'Sid, you slay me, you really do.'

'Well,' I said, 'I feel sick.' I rolled over and retched what was left of my breakfast on to the roots of the privet hedge. There wasn't any blood. I felt a lot better.

'I'll go and get the horse-box,' said Chico, 'and pick you up.'

'You'll do nothing of the sort,' I said, wiping my mouth on a handkerchief. 'We're going back into the garden. I want that bullet.'

'It's half way to Seabury,' he protested, borrowing my handkerchief to mop the blood off his eyebrow.

'What will you bet?' I said. I used the gate again to get up, and after a moment or two was fairly straight. We presented a couple of reassuring grins to the audience, and retraced our way down the path into the back garden.

The mirror lay in sparkling pointed fragments all over the lawn.

'Pop up the tree and see if the bullet is there, in the wood. It smashed the mirror. It might be stuck up there. If not, we'll have to comb the grass.'

Chico went up the aluminium ladder that time.

'Of all the luck,' he called. 'It's here.' I watched him take a penknife out of his pocket and carefully cut away at a section just off-centre of the back board of the ex-mirror. He came down and held the little misshapen lump out to me on the palm of his hand. I put it carefully away in the small waist pocket of my breeches.

The elderly couple had emerged like tortoises from their bungalow. They were scared and puzzled, understandably. Chico offered to cut down the remains of the mirror, and did, but we left them to clear up the resulting firewood.

As an afterthought, however, Chico went across the garden and retrieved the poster from a soggy winter rosebed. He unrolled it and showed it to us, laughing.

'Blessed are the meek: for they shall inherit the earth.'

'One of them,' said Chico, 'has a sense of humour.'

Much against his wishes, we returned to our observation post in the scrubby gorse.

'Haven't you had enough?' he said crossly.

'The patrols don't get here till six,' I reminded him. 'And you yourself said that dusk would be the likely time for them to try something.'

'But they've already done it.'

'There's nothing to stop them from rigging up more than one booby trap,' I pointed out. 'Especially as that mirror thing wouldn't have been one hundred per cent reliable, even if we hadn't spotted it. It depended on the sun. Good weather forecast, I know, but weather forecasts are as reliable as a perished hot-water bottle. A passing cloud would have wrecked it. I would think they have something else in mind.'

'Cheerful,' he said resignedly. He led Revelation away along the road to stow him in the horse box, and was gone a long time.

When he came back he sat down beside me and said, 'I went all round the stables. No one stopped me or asked what I was doing. Don't they have *any* security here? The cleaners have all gone home, but there's a woman cooking in the canteen. She said I was too early, to come back at half past six. There wasn't anyone about in the stands block except an old geyser with snuffles mucking about with the boiler.'

The sun was lower in the sky and the November afternoon grew colder. We shivered a little and huddled inside our jerseys.

Chico said, 'You guessed about the mirror before you set off round the course.'

'It was a possibility, that's all.'

'You could have ridden along the boundary fence, looking into the gardens like we did afterwards, instead of haring off over all those jumps.'

I grinned faintly. 'Yes. As I told you, I was giving in to temptation.'

'Screwy. You must have known you'd fall.'

'Of course I didn't. The mirror mightn't have worked very effectively. Anyway, it's better to test a theory in a practical way. And I just wanted to ride round there. I had a good excuse if I were hauled up for it. So I went. And it was grand. So shut up.'

He laughed. 'All right.' Restlessly he stood up again and said he would make another tour. While he was gone I watched the racecourse with and without the binoculars, but not a thing moved on it.

He came back quietly and dropped down beside me.

'As before,' he said.

'Nothing here, either.'

He looked at me sideways. 'Do you feel as bad as you look?'

'I shouldn't be surprised,' I said. 'Do you?'

He tenderly touched the area round his cut eyebrow. 'Worse. Much worse. Soggy bad luck, him slugging away at your belly like that.'

'He did it on purpose,' I said idly; 'and it was very informative.'

'Huh?'

'It showed he knew who I was. He wouldn't have needed to have attacked us like that if we'd just been people come over from the racecourse to see if we could shift the mirror. But when he spoke to me he recognized me, and he knew I wouldn't be put off by any poster eyewash. And his sort don't mildly back down and retreat without paying you off for getting in their way. He just hit where he knew it would have most effect. I actually saw him think it.'

'But how did he know?'

'It was he who sent Andrews to the office,' I said. 'He was the man Mervyn Brinton described; big, going a bit bald, freckles on the backs of his hands, cockney accent. He was strong-arming Brinton, and he sent Andrews to get the letter that was supposed to be in the office. Well . . . Andrews knew me, and I knew him. He must have gone back and told our big friend Fred that he had shot me in the stomach. My death wasn't reported in the papers, so Fred knew I was still alive and would put the finger on Andrews at once. Andrews wasn't exactly a good risk to Fred, just a silly spiv with no sense, so Fred, I guess, marched him straight off to Epping Forest and left him for the birds. Who did a fair job, I'll give them that.'

'Do you think,' said Chico slowly, 'that the gun Fred had today . . . is that why you wanted the bullet?'

I nodded. 'That's right. I tried for the gun too, but no dice. If I'm going on with this sort of work, pal, you'll have to teach me a spot of judo.'

He looked down doubtfully. 'With that hand?'

'Invent a new sport,' I said. 'One-armed combat.'

'I'll take you to the club,' he said smiling. 'There's an old Jap there who'll find a way if anyone can.'

'Good.'

Up at the far end of the racecourse a horse box turned in off the main road and trundled along towards the stables. The first of the next day's runners had apparently arrived.

Chico went to have a look.

I sat on in fading daylight, watching nothing happen, hugging myself against the cold and the re-awakened grinding ache in my gut, and thinking evil thoughts about Fred. Not Leo. Fred.

There were four of them, I thought. Kraye, Bolt, Fred and Leo.

I had met Kraye: he knew me only as Sid, a despised hanger-on in the home of a retired admiral he had met at his club and had spent a week-end with.

I had met Bolt: he knew me as John Halley, a shop assistant wanting to invest a gift from an aunt.

I had met Fred: he knew my whole name, and that I worked for the agency, and that I had turned up at Seabury.

I did not know if I had met Leo. But Leo might know *me*. If he had anything to do with racing, he definitely did.

It would be all right, I thought, as long as they did not connect all the Halleys and Sids too soon. But there was my wretched hand, which Kraye had pulled out of my pocket, which Fred could have seen in the garden, and which Leo, whoever he was, might have noticed almost anywhere in the last six days, thanks to my promise to Zanna Martin. Zanna Martin, who worked for Bolt. A proper merry-go-round, I thought wryly.

Chico materialized out of the dusk. 'It was Ping Pong, running in the first tomorrow. All above board,' he said. 'And nothing doing anywhere, stands or course. We might as well go.'

It was well after five. I agreed, and got up stiffly.

'That Fred,' said Chico, casually giving me a hand, 'I've been thinking. I've seen him before, I'm certain. At race meetings. He's not a regular. Doesn't work for a bookie, or anything like that. But he's about. Cheap rings, mostly.'

'Let's hope he doesn't burrow,' I said.

'I don't see why he should,' he said seriously. 'He can't possibly think you'd connect him with Andrews or with Kraye. All you caught him doing was fixing a poster in a tree. If I were him, I'd be sleeping easy.'

'I called him Fred,' I said.

'Oh,' said Chico glumly. 'So you did.'

We reached the road and started along it towards the horse box.

'Fred must be the one who does all the jobs,' said Chico. 'Digs the false drains, sets fire to stables, and drives tractors to pull over tankers. He's big enough for anything.'

'He didn't wave the flags. He was up the tree at the time.'

'Um. Yes. Who did?'

'Not Bolt,' I said. 'It wasn't fat enough for Bolt, even in a duffle coat. Possibly Kraye. More likely Leo, whoever he is.'

'One of the workmen, or the foreman. Yes. Well, that makes two of them for overturning tankers and so on.'

'It would be easier for two,' I agreed.

Chico drove the horse box back to Mark's, and then, to his obvious delight, my Merc back to London.

CHAPTER FOURTEEN

CHIEF-INSPECTOR CORNISH was pleased but trying to hide it.

'I suppose you can chalk it up to your agency,' he said, as if it were debatable.

'He walked slap into us, to be fair.'

'And slap out again,' he said dryly.

I grimaced. 'You haven't met him.'

'You want to leave that sort to us,' he said automatically. 'Where were you, then?'

'That's a point,' he admitted, smiling.

He picked up the matchbox again and looked at the bullet. 'Little beauty. Good clear markings. Pity he has a revolver, though, and not an automatic. It would have been nice to have had cartridge cases as well.'

'You're greedy,' I said.

He looked at the aluminium ladder standing against his wall, and at the poster on his desk, and at the rush-job photographs. Two clear prints of the van showing its number plates and four of Fred in action against Chico. Not exactly posed portraits, those, but four different, characteristic and recognizable angles taken in full sunlight.

'With all this lot to go on, we'll trace him before he draws breath.'

'Fine,' I said. And the sooner Fred was immobilized the better, I thought. Before he did any more damage to Seabury. 'You'll need a tiger net to catch him. He's a very tough baby and he knows judo. And unless he has the sense to throw it away, he'll still have that gun.'

'I'll remember,' he said. 'And thanks.' We shook hands amicably as I left.

It was results day at Radnor's, too. As soon as I got back Dolly said Jack Copeland wanted me up in Bona Fides. I made the journey.

Jack gleamed at me over the half moons, pleased with his department. 'George's got him. Kraye. He'll tell you.'

I went over to George's desk. George was fairly smirking, but after he'd talked for two minutes, I allowed he'd earned it.

'On the off chance,' he said, 'I borrowed a bit of smooth quartz Kraye recently handled in the Geology Museum and got Sammy to do the prints on it. Two or three different sets of fingers came out, so we photographed the lot. None of them were on the British files, but I've given them the run around with the odd pal in Interpol and so on, just in case. And brother, have we hit pay dirt or have we.'

'We have?' I prompted, grinning.

'And how. Your friend Kraye is in the ex-con library of the state of New York.'

'What for?'

'Assault.'

'Of a girl?' I asked.

George raised his eyebrows. 'A girl's father. Kraye had beaten the girl, apparently with her permission. She didn't complain. But her father saw the bruises and raised the roof. He said he'd get Kraye on a rape charge, though it seems the girl had been perfectly willing on that count too. But it looked bad for Kraye, so he picked up a chair and smashed it over the father's head and scarpered. They caught him boarding a plane for South America and hauled him back. The father's brain was damaged. There are long medical details, but what it all boils down to is that he couldn't co-ordinate properly afterwards. Kraye got off on the rape charge, but served four years for attacking the father.

'Three years after that he turned up in England with some money and a new name, and soon acquired a wife. The one who divorced him for cruelty. Nice chap.'

'Yes indeed,' I said. 'What was his real name?'

'Wilbur Potter,' said George sardonically. 'And you'll never guess. He was a geologist by profession. He worked for a construction firm, surveying. Always moving about. Character assessment: slick, a pusher, a good talker. Cut a few corners, always had more money than his salary, threw his weight about, but nothing indictable. The assault on the father was his first brush with the law. He was thirty-four at that time.'

'Messy,' I said. 'The whole thing.'

'Very,' George agreed.

'But sex violence and fraudulent take-overs aren't much related,' I complained.

'You might as well say it is impossible to have boils and cancer at the same time. Something drastically wrong with the constitution, and two separate symptoms.'

'I'll take your word for it,' I said.

Sammy up in Missing Persons had done more than photograph Kraye's fingerprints, he had almost found Smith.

'Intersouth rang us this morning,' he purred. 'Smith gave them as a reference. He's applied for a driving job in Birmingham.'

'Good,' I said.

'We should have his address by this afternoon.'

Downstairs in Racing I reached for Dolly's telephone and got through to Charing, Street and King.

'Mr Bolt's secretary speaking,' said the quiet voice.

'Is Mr Bolt in?' I asked.

'I'm afraid not . . . er, who is that speaking, please?'

'Did you find you had a file of mine?'

'Oh . . .' she laughed. 'Yes, I picked it up in your car. I'm so sorry.'

'Do you have it with you?'

'No,' she said. 'I didn't bring it here. I thought it might be better not to risk Mr Bolt seeing it, as it's got Hunt Radnor Associates printed on the outside along with a red sticker saying "Ex Records, care of Sid Halley".'

'Yes, it would have been a disaster,' I agreed with feeling.

'I left it at home. Do you want it in a hurry?'

'No, not really. As long as it's safe, that's the main thing. How would it be if I came over to fetch it the day after tomorrow—Sunday morning? We could go for a drive, perhaps, and have some lunch?'

There was a tiny pause. Then she said strongly, 'Yes, please. Yes.'

'Have the leaflets gone out?' I asked.

'They went yesterday.'

'See you on Sunday, Miss Martin.'

I put down Dolly's telephone to find her looking at me quizzically. I was again squatting on the corner of her desk, the girl from the typing pool having in my absence reclaimed her chair.

'The mouse got away again, I understand,' she said.

'Some mouse.'

Chico came into the office. The cut on his eyebrow looked red and sore, and all the side of his face showed greyish bruising.

'Two of you,' said Dolly disgustedly, 'and he knocked you about like kids.'

Chico took this a lot better than if she had fussed maternally over his injury.

'It took more than two Lilliputians to peg down Gulliver,' he said with good humour. (They had a large library in the children's orphanage.)

'But only one David to slay Goliath.'

Chico made a face at her, and I laughed.

'And how are our collywobbles today?' he asked me ironically.

'Better than your looks.'

'You know why Sid's best friends don't know him?' said Chico.

'Why?' said Dolly, seriously.

'He suffers from Halley-tosis.'

'Oh God,' said Dolly. 'Take him away someone. Take him away. I can't stand it.'

On the ground floor I sat in a padded maroon arm-chair in Radnor's drawing-room office and listened to him saying there were no out-of-the-ordinary reports from the patrols at Seabury.

'Fison has just been on the telephone. Everything is normal for a race day, he says. The public will start arriving very shortly. He and Thom walked all round the course just now with Captain Oxon for a thorough check. There's nothing wrong with it, that they can see.'

There might be something wrong with it that they couldn't see. I was uneasy.

'I might stay down there tonight, if I can find a room,' I said.

'If you do, give me a ring again at home, during the evening.'

'Sure.' I had disturbed his dinner, the day before, to tell him about Fred and the mirror.

'Could I have those photographs back, if you've finished with them?' I asked. 'I want to check that list of initials against the racecourse workmen at Seabury.'

'I'm sorry, Sid, I haven't got them.'

'Are they back upstairs . . . ?'

'No, no, they aren't here at all. Lord Hagbourne has them.'

'But why?' I sat up straight, disturbed.

'He came here yesterday afternoon. I'd say on balance he is almost down on our side of the fence. I didn't get the usual caution about expenses, which is a good sign. Anyway, what he wanted was to see the proofs you told him we held which show it is Kraye who is buying the shares. Photographs of share transfer certificates. He knew about them. He said you'd told him.'

'Yes, I did.'

'He wanted to see them. That was reasonable, and I didn't want to risk tipping him back into indecision, so I showed them to him. He asked me very courteously if he could take them to show them to the Seabury executive. They held a meeting this morning, I believe. He thought they might be roused to some effective action if they could see for themselves how big Kraye's holding is.'

'What about the other photographs? The others that were in the box.'

'He took them all. They were all jumbled up, and he was in a hurry. He said he'd sort them out himself later.'

'He took them to Seabury?' I said uneasily.

'That's right. For the executive meeting this morning.' He looked at his watch. 'The meeting must be on at this moment, I should think. If you want them you can ask him for them as soon as you get there. He should have finished with them by then.'

'I wish you hadn't let him take them,' I said.

'It can't do any harm. Even if he lost them we'd still have the negatives. You could get another print done tomorrow, of your list.'

The negatives, did he but know it, were inaccessibly tucked into a mislaid file in Finchley. I didn't confess. Instead I said, unconvinced, 'All right. I suppose it won't matter. I'll get on down there, then.'

I packed an overnight bag in the flat. The sun was pouring in through the windows, making the blues and greens and blond wood furniture look warm and friendly. After two years the place was at last beginning to feel like home. A home without Jenny. Happiness without Jenny. Both were possible, it seemed. I certainly felt more myself than at any time since she left.

The sun was still shining, too, at Seabury. But not on a very large crowd. The poor quality of the racing was so obvious as to be pathetic: and it was in order that such a rotten gaggle of weedy quadrupeds could stumble and scratch their way round to the winning post, I reflected philosophically, that I had tried to pit my inadequate wits against Lord Hagbourne, Captain Oxon, the Seabury executive, Kraye, Bolt, Fred, Leo, old Uncle Tom Cobley and all.

There were no mishaps all day. The horses raced nonchalantly over the tan patch at their speedy crawl, and no light flashed in their eyes as they knocked hell out of the fences on the far side. Round One to Chico and me.

As the fine weather put every one in a good mood a shred of Seabury's former vitality temporarily returned to the place: enough, anyway, for people to notice the dinginess of the stands and remark that it was time something was done about it. If they felt like that, I thought, a revival shouldn't be impossible.

The Senior Steward listened attentively while I passed on Zanna Martin's suggestion that Seabury council should be canvassed, and surprisingly said that he would see it was promptly done.

In spite of these small headways, however, my spine wouldn't stop tingling. Lord Hagbourne didn't have the photographs.

'They are only mislaid, Sid,' he said soothingly. 'Don't make such a fuss. They'll turn up.'

He had put them down on the table round which the meeting had been held, he said. After the official business was over, he had chatted, standing up. When he turned back to pick up the box, it was no longer there. The whole table had been cleared. The ashtrays were being emptied. The table was required for lunch. A white cloth was being spread over it.

What, I asked, had been the verdict of the meeting, anyway? Er, um, it appeared the whole subject had been shelved for a week or two: no urgency was felt. Shares changed hands slowly, very slowly. But they had agreed that Hunt Radnor could carry on for a bit.

I hesitated to go barging into the executive's private room just to look for a packet of photographs, so I asked the caterers instead. They hadn't seen it, they said, rushing round me. I tracked down the man and woman who had cleared the table after the meeting and laid it for lunch.

Any amount of doodling on bits of paper, said the waitress, but no box of photographs, and excuse me love, they're waiting for these sandwiches. She agreed to look for it, looked, and came back shaking her head. It wasn't there, as far as she could see. It was quite big, I said despairingly.

I asked Mr Fotherton, Clerk of the Course; I asked Captain Oxon, I asked the secretary, and anyone else I could think of who had been at the meeting. None of them knew where the photographs were. All of them, busy with their racing jobs, said much the same as Lord Hagbourne.

'Don't worry, Sid, they're bound to turn up.'

But they didn't.

I stayed on the racecourse until after the security patrols changed over at six o'clock. The incomers were the same men who had been on watch the night before, four experienced and sensible ex-policemen, all middle-aged. They entrenched themselves comfortably in the Press room, which had windows facing back and front, effective central heating, and four telephones; better headquarters than usual on their night jobs, they said.

Between the last race (three-thirty) and six o'clock, apart from hunting without success for the photographs and driving Lord Hagbourne round to Napoleon Close for a horrified first-hand look at the smashed-up mirror, I persuaded Captain Oxon to accompany me on a thorough nook and cranny check-up of all the racecourse buildings.

He came willingly enough, his stiffness of earlier in the week having been thawed, I supposed, by the comparative success of the day; but we found nothing and no one that shouldn't have been there.

I drove into Seabury and booked into the Seafront Hotel, where I had often stayed in the past. It was only half full. Formerly, on racing nights, it had been crammed. Over a brandy in the bar the manager lamented with me the state of trade.

'Race meetings used to give us a boost every three weeks nearly all the winter. Now hardly anyone comes, and I hear they didn't even ask for the January fixture this year. I tell you, I'd like to see that place blooming again, we need it.'

'Ah,' I said. 'Then write to the Town Council and say so.'

'That wouldn't help,' he said gloomily.

'You never know. It might. Do write.'

'All right, Sid. Just to please you then. For old time's sake. Let's have another brandy on the house.'

I had an early dinner with him and his wife and afterwards went for a walk along the seashore. The night was dry and cold and the onshore breeze smelt of seaweed. The banked pebbles scrunched into trickling hollows under my shoes and the winter sand was as hard-packed as rock. Thinking about Kraye and his machinations, I had strolled quite a long way eastwards, away from the racecourse, before I remembered I had said I would ring Radnor at his home during the evening.

There was nothing much to tell him. I didn't hurry, and it was nearly ten o'clock when I got back to Seabury. The modernizations didn't yet run to telephones in all the bedrooms at the hotel, so I used the kiosk outside on the promenade, because I came to it first.

It wasn't Radnor who answered, but Chico, and I knew at once from his voice that things had gone terribly wrong.

'Sid . . .' he said. 'Sid . . . look, pal, I don't know how to tell you. You'll have to have it straight. We've been trying to reach you all the evening.'

'What . . . ?' I swallowed.

'Someone bombed your flat.'

'*Bombed*,' I said stupidly.

'A plastic bomb. It blew the street wall right out. All the flats round yours were badly damaged, but yours . . . well, there's nothing there. Just a big hole with disgusting black sort of cobwebs. That's how they knew it was a plastic bomb. The sort the French terrorists used . . . Sid, are you there?'

'Yes.'

'I'm sorry, pal. I'm sorry. But that's not all. They've done it to the office, too.' His voice was anguished. 'It went off in the Racing Section. But the whole place is cracked open. It's . . . it's bloody ghastly.'

'Chico.'

'I know. I know. The old man's round there now, just staring at it. He made me stay here because you said you'd ring, and in case the racecourse patrols want anything. No one was badly hurt, that's the only good thing. Half a dozen people were bruised and cut, at your flats. And the office was empty, of course.'

'What time . . . ?'

'The bomb in the office went off about an hour and a half ago, and the one in your flat was just after seven. The old man and I were round there with the police when they got the radio message about the office. The police seem to think that whoever did it was looking for something. The people who live underneath you heard someone moving about upstairs for about two hours shortly before the bomb went off, but they just thought it was you making more noise than usual. And it seems everything in your flat was moved into one pile in the sitting-room and the bomb put in the middle. The police said it meant that they hadn't found what they were looking for and were destroying everything in case they had missed it.'

'Everything . . .' I said.

'Not a thing was left. God, Sid, I wish I didn't have to . . . but there it is. Nothing that was there exists any more.'

The letters from Jenny when she loved me. The only photograph of my mother and father. The trophies I won racing. The lot. I leant numbly against the wall.

'Sid, are you still there?'

'Yes.'

'It was the same thing at the office. People across the road saw lights on and someone moving about inside, and just thought we were working late. The old man said we must assume they still haven't found what they were looking for. He wants to know what it is.'

'I don't know,' I said.

'You must.'

'No. I don't.'

'You can think on the way back.'

'I'm not coming back. Not tonight. It can't do any good. I think I'll go out to the racecourse again, just to make sure nothing happens there too.'

'All right. I'll tell him when he calls. He said he'd be over in Cromwell Road all night, very likely.'

We rang off and I went out of the kiosk into the cold night air. I thought that Radnor was right. It was important to know what it was that the bomb merchants had been looking for. I leaned against the outside of the box, thinking about it. Deliberately not thinking about the flat, the place that had begun to be home, and all that was lost. That had happened before, in one way or another. The night my mother died, for instance. And I'd ridden my first winner the next day.

To look for something, you had to know it existed. If you used bombs, destroying it was more important than finding it. What did I have, which I hadn't had long (or they would have searched before) which Kraye wanted obliterated.

There was the bullet which Fred had accidentally fired into the mirror. They wouldn't find that, because it was somewhere in a police ballistics laboratory. And if they had thought I had it, they would have looked for it the night before.

There was the leaflet Bolt had sent out, but there were hundreds of those, and he wouldn't want the one I had, even if he knew I had it. There was the letter Mervyn Brinton had re-written for me, but if it were that it meant . . .

I went back into the telephone box, obtained Mervyn Brinton's number from directory enquiries, and rang him up.

To my relief, he answered.

'You are all right, Mr Brinton?'

'Yes, yes. What's the matter?'

'You haven't had a call from the big man? You haven't told anyone about my visit to you, or that you know your brother's letter by heart?'

He sounded scared. 'No. Nothing's happened. I wouldn't tell anyone. I never would.'

'Fine,' I reassured him. 'That's just fine. I was only checking.'

So it was not Brinton's letter.

The photographs, I thought. They had been in the office all the time until Radnor gave them to Lord Hagbourne yesterday afternoon. No one outside the agency, except Lord Hagbourne and Charles, had known they existed. Not until this morning, when Lord Hagbourne took them to Seabury executive meeting, and lost them.

Suppose they weren't lost, but stolen. By someone who knew Kraye, and thought he ought to have them. From the dates on all those documents Kraye would know exactly when the photographs had been taken. And where.

My scalp contracted. I must assume, I thought, that they had now connected all the Halleys and Sids.

Suddenly fearful, I rang up Aynsford. Charles himself answered, calm and sensible.

'Charles, please will you do as I ask, at once, and no questions? Grab Mrs Cross, go out and get in the car and drive well away from the house, and ring me back at Seabury 79411. Got that? Seabury 79411.'

'Yes.' He said, and put down the telephone. Thank God, I thought, for a naval training. There might not be much time. The office bomb had exploded an hour and a half ago; London to Aynsford took the same.

Ten minutes later the bell began to ring. I picked up the receiver.

'They say you're in a call box,' Charles said.

'That's right. Are you?'

'No, the pub down in the village. Now, what's it all about?'

I told him about the bombs, which horrified him, and about the missing photographs.

'I can't think what else it can be that they are looking for.'

'But you said that they've got them.'

'The negatives,' I said.

'Oh. Yes. And they weren't in your flat or the office?'

'No. Quite by chance, they weren't.'

'And you think if they're still looking, that they'll come to Aynsford?'

'If they are desperate enough, they might. They might think

you would know where I keep things . . . And even have a go at making you tell them. I asked you to come out quick because I didn't want to risk it. If they are going to Aynsford, they could be there at any minute now. It's horribly likely they'll think of you. They'll know I took the photos in your house.'

'From the dates. Yes. Right. I'll get on to the local police and ask for a guard on the house at once.'

'Charles, one of them . . . well, if he's the one with the bombs, you'll need a squad.' I described Fred and his van, together with its number.

'Right.' He was still calm. 'Why would the photographs be so important to them? Enough to use bombs, I mean?'

'I wish I knew.'

'Take care.'

'Yes,' I said.

I did take care. Instead of going back into the hotel, I rang up.

The manager said, 'Sid, where on earth are you, people have been trying to reach you all the evening . . . the police too.'

'Yes, Joe, I know. It's all right. I've talked to the people in London. Now, has anyone actually called at the hotel, wanting me?'

'There's someone up in your room, yes. Your father-in-law, Admiral Roland.'

'Oh really? Does he look like an Admiral?'

'I suppose so,' he sounded puzzled.

'A gentleman?'

'Yes, of course.' Not Fred, then.

'Well, he isn't my father-in-law. I've just been talking to him in his house in Oxfordshire. You collect a couple of helpers and chuck my visitor out.'

I put down the receiver sighing. A man up in my room meant everything I'd brought to Seabury would very likely be ripped to bits. That left me with just the clothes I stood in, and the car . . .

I fairly sprinted round to where I'd left the car. It was locked, silent and safe. No damage. I patted it thankfully, climbed in, and drove out to the racecourse.

CHAPTER FIFTEEN

ALL was quiet as I drove through the gates and switched off the engine. There were lights on—one shining through the windows of the Press room, one outside the weighing room door, one high up somewhere on the stands. The shadows in between were densely black. It was a clear night with no moon.

I walked across to the Press room, to see if the security patrols had anything to report.

They hadn't.

All four of them were fast asleep.

Furious, I shook the nearest. His head lolled like a pendulum, but he didn't wake up. He was sitting slumped into his chair. One of them had his arms on the table and his head on his arms. One of them sat on the floor, his head on the seat of the chair and his arms hanging down. The fourth lay flat, face downwards, near the opposite wall.

The stupid fools, I thought violently. Ex-policemen letting themselves be put to sleep like infants. It shouldn't have been possible. One of their first rules in guard work was to take their own food and drink with them and not accept sweets from strangers.

I stepped round their heavily breathing hulks and picked up one of the Press telephones to ring Chico for reinforcements. The line was dead. I tried the three other instruments. No contact with the exchange on any of them.

I would have to go back and ring up from Seabury, I thought. I went out of the Press room but in the light pouring out before I shut the door I saw a dim figure walking towards me from the direction of the gate.

'Who's that?' he called imperiously, and I recognized his voice. Captain Oxon.

'It's only me, Sid Halley.' I shouted back. 'Come and look at this.'

He came on into the light, and I stood aside for him to go into the Press room.

'Good heavens. What on earth's the matter with them?'

'Sleeping pills. And the telephones don't work. You haven't seen anyone about who ought not to be?'

'No. I haven't heard anything except your car. I came down to see who had come.'

'How many lads are there staying overnight in the hostel? Could we use some of those to patrol the place while I ring the agency to get some more men?'

'I should think they'd love it,' he said, consideringly. 'There are about five of them. They shouldn't be in bed yet. We'll go over and ask them, and you can use the telephone from my flat to ring your agency.'

'Thanks,' I said. 'That's fine.'

I looked round the room at the sleeping men. 'I think perhaps I ought to see if any of them tried to write a message. I won't be a minute.'

He waited patiently while I looked under the head and folded arms of the man at the table and under the man on the floor, and all round the one with his head on the chair seat, but none of them had even reached for a pencil. Shrugging, I looked at the remains of their supper, lying on the table. Half eaten sandwiches on grease-proof paper, dregs of coffee in cups and thermos flasks, a couple of apple cores, some cheese sections and empty wrappings, and an unpeeled banana.

'Found anything?' asked Oxon.

I shook my head in disgust. 'Not a thing. They'll have terrible headaches when they wake up, and serve them right.'

'I can understand you being annoyed . . .' he began. But I was no longer really listening. Over the back of the chair occupied by the first man I had shaken was hanging a brown leather binoculars case: and on its lid were stamped three black initials: L.E.O. Leo. *Leo.*

'Something the matter?' asked Oxon.

'No.' I smiled at him and touched the strap of the binoculars. 'Are these yours?'

'Yes. The men asked if I could lend them some. For the dawn, they said.'

'It was very kind of you.'

'Oh. Nothing.' He shrugged, moving out into the night. 'You'd better make the phone call first. We'll tackle the boys afterwards.'

I had absolutely no intention of walking into his flat.

'Right,' I said.

We went out of the door, and I closed it behind us.

A familiar voice, loaded with satisfaction, spoke from barely a yard away. 'So you've got him, Oxon. Good.'

'He was coming . . .' began Oxon in anxious anger, knowing that 'got him' was an exaggeration.

'No,' I said, and turned and ran for the car.

When I was barely ten yards from it someone turned the lights on. The headlights of my own car. I stopped dead.

Behind me one of the men shouted and I heard their feet running. I wasn't directly in the beam, but silhouetted against it. I swerved off to the right, towards the gate. Three steps in that direction, and the headlights of a car turning in through it caught me straight in the eyes.

There were more shouts, much closer, from Oxon and Kraye. I turned, half dazzled, and saw them closing in. Behind me now the incoming car rolled forward. And the engine of my Mercedes purred separately into life.

I ran for the dark. The two cars, moving, caught me again in their beams. Kraye and Oxon ran where they pointed.

I was driven across and back towards the stands like a coursed hare, the two cars behind inexorably finding me with their lights and the two men running with reaching, clutching hands. Like a nightmare game of 'He', I thought wildly, with more than a child's forfeit if I were caught.

Across the parade ring, across the flat tarmac stretch beyond it, under the rails of the unsaddling enclosure and along the weighing room wall. Sometimes only a foot from hooking fingers. Once barely a yard from a speeding bumper. But I made it. Safe, panting, in the precious dark, on the inside of the door into the trainers' luncheon room and through there without stopping into the kitchen. And weaving on from there out into the members' lunch room, round acres of tables with upturned chairs, through the far door into the wide passage which cut like a tunnel along the length of the huge building, across it, and up a steep stone staircase emerging half way up the open steps of the stands, and sideways along them as far as I could go. The pursuit was left behind.

I sank down, sitting with one leg bent to run, in the black shadow where the low wooden wall dividing the Members from Tattersalls cut straight down the steps separating the stands into two halves. On top of the wall wire netting stretched up too high to climb: high enough to keep out the poorer customers from gate-crashing the expensive ring.

At the bottom of the steps lay a large expanse of Members' lawn stretching to another metal mesh fence, chest high, and beyond that lay the whole open expanse of racecourse. Half a mile across it to the London road to Seabury, with yet another barrier, the boundary fence, to negotiate.

It was too far. I knew I couldn't do it. Perhaps once, with two hands for vaulting, with a stomach which didn't already feel as if it were tearing into more holes inside. But not now. Although I always mended fast, it was only two weeks since I had found the short walk to Andrews' body very nearly too much; and Fred's well-aimed attentions on the previous day had not been therapeutic.

Looking at it straight: if I ran, it had to be successful. My kingdom for a horse, I thought. Any reasonable cowboy would have had Revelation hitched to the rails, ready for a flying leap into the saddle and a thundering exit. I had a hundred and fifty mile an hour little white Mercedes: and someone else was sitting in it.

To run and be caught running would achieve nothing and be utterly pointless.

Which left just one alternative.

The security patrol hadn't been drugged for nothing. Kraye wasn't at Seabury for his health. Some more damage had been planned for this night. Might already have been done. There was just a chance, if I stayed to look, that I could find out what it was. Before they found *me*. Naturally.

If I ever have any children, they won't get me playing hide and seek.

Half an hour later the grim game was still in progress. My own car was now parked on the racecourse side of the stands, on the tarmac in Tattersalls where the bookies had called the odds that afternoon. It was facing the stands with the headlights full on. Every inch of the steps was lit by them, and since the car had arrived there I had not been able to use that side of the building at all.

The other car was similarly parked inside the racecourse gates, its headlights shining on the fronts of the weighing room, bars, dining-rooms, cloakrooms and offices.

Presuming that each car still had a watching occupant, that left only Kraye and Oxon, as far as I could guess, to run me to ground: but I became gradually sure that there were three, not two, after me in the stands. Perhaps one of the cars was empty. But which? And it would be unlikely to have its ignition key in place.

Bit by bit I covered the whole enormous block. I didn't know what I was looking for, that was the trouble. It could have been anything from a plastic bomb downwards, but if past form was anything to go by, it was something which could appear accidental. Bad luck. A jinx. Open, recognizable sabotage would be ruinous to the scheme.

Without a surveyor I couldn't be certain that part of the steps would not collapse the following day under the weight of the crowd, but I could find no trace of any structural damage at all, and there hadn't been much time: only five or six hours since the day's meeting ended.

There were no large quantities of food in the kitchen: the caterers appeared to have removed what had been left over ready to bring fresh the next day. A large double-doored refrigerator was securely locked. I discounted the possibility that Kraye could have thought of large scale food poisoning.

All the fire extinguishers seemed to be in their places, and there were no smouldering cigarette ends near tins of paraffin. Nothing capable of spontaneous combustion. I supposed another fire, so soon after the stables, might have been too suspicious.

I went cautiously, carefully, every nerve-racking step of the way, peering round corners, easing through doors, fearing that at any moment one of them would pounce on me from behind.

They knew I was still there, because everywhere they went they turned on lights, and everywhere I went I turned them off. Opening a door from a lighted room on to a dark passage made one far too easy to spot; I turned off the lights before I opened any door. There had been three lights in the passage itself, but I had broken them early on with a broom from the kitchen.

Once when I was in the passage, creeping from the men's lavatories to the Tattersalls bar, Kraye himself appeared at the far end, the Members' end, and began walking my way. He came in through the faint glow from the car's headlights, and he hadn't seen me. One stride took me across the passage, one jump and a wriggle into the only cover available, the heap of equipment the bookmakers had left there out of the weather, overnight.

These were only their metal stands, their folded umbrellas, the boxes and stools they stood on: a thin, spiky, precarious heap. I crouched down beside them, praying I wouldn't dislodge anything.

Kraye's footsteps scraped hollowly as he trod toward my ineffective hiding place. He stopped twice, opening doors and looking into the store-rooms which were in places built back under the steps of the stands. They were mostly empty or nearly so, and offered nothing to me. They were too small, and all dead ends: if I were found in one of them, I couldn't get out.

The door of the bar I had been making for suddenly opened, spilling bright light into the passage between me and Kraye.

Oxon's voice said anxiously, 'He can't have got away.'

'Of course not, you fool,' said Kraye furiously. 'But if you'd had the sense to bring your keys over with you we'd have had him long ago.' Their voices echoed up and down the passage.

'It was your idea to leave so much unlocked. I could go back and fetch them.'

'He'd have too much chance of giving us the slip. But we're not getting anywhere with all this dodging about. We'll start methodically from this end and move down.'

'We did that to start with,' complained Oxon. 'And we missed him. Let me go back for the keys. Then as you said before we can lock all the doors behind us and stop him doubling back.'

'No,' said Kraye decisively. 'There aren't enough of us. You stay here. We'll go back to the weighing room and start all together.'

They began to walk away. The bar door was still open, lighting up the passage, which I didn't like. If anyone came in from the other end, he would see me for sure.

I shifted my position to crawl away along the wall for better concealment, and one of the bookmakers' metal tripods slid down and clattered off the side of the pile with an echoing noise like a dozen demented machine guns.

There were shouts from the two men down the passage.

'There he is.'

'Get him.'

I stood up and ran.

The nearest opening in the wall was a staircase up to a suite of rooms above the changing room and Members' dining-room. I hesitated a fraction of a second and then passed it. Up those steps were the executive's rooms and offices. I didn't know my way round up there, but Oxon did. He had a big enough advantage already in his knowledge of the building without my giving him a bonus.

I ran on, past the gent's cloaks, and finally in through the last possible door, that of a long bare dirty room smelling of beer. It was a sort of extra, subsidiary bar, and all it now contained was a bare counter backed by empty shelves. I nearly fell over a bucket full of crinkled metal bottle tops which someone had carelessly left in my way, and then wasted precious seconds to dart back to put the bucket just inside the door I'd come in by.

Kraye and Oxon were running. I snapped off the lights, and with no time to get clear through the far door out into the paddock, where anyway I would be lit by car headlights, I scrambled down behind the bar counter.

The door jerked open. There was a clatter of the bucket and a yell, and the sound of someone falling. Then the light snapped on again, showing me just how tiny my hiding place really was, and two bottle tops rolled across the floor into my sight.

'For God's sake,' yelled Kraye in anger. 'You clumsy, stupid fool. Get up. Get up.' He charged down the room to the far door, the board floor bouncing slightly under his weight. From the clanking, cursing, and clattering of bottle tops I imagined that Oxon was extricating himself from the bucket and following. If it hadn't been so dangerous it would have been funny.

Kraye yanked the outside door open, stepped outside and yelled across to the stationary car to ask where I had gone. I felt rather than saw Oxon run down the room to join him. I crawled round the end of the counter, sprinted for the door I had come in by, flipped off the light again, slammed the door, and ran back up the passage. There was a roar from Kraye as he fumbled back into the darkened room, and long before they had emerged into the passage again, kicking bottle tops in all directions, I was safe in the opening of a little off-shoot lobby to the kitchen.

The kitchens were safest to me because there were so many good hiding places and so many exits, but it wasn't much good staying there as I had searched them already.

I was fast running out of places to look. The boiler room had given me an anxious two minutes as its only secondary exit was into a dead end store-room containing, as far as I could see, nothing but vast oil tanks with pipes and gauges. They were hard against the walls: nowhere to hide. The boiler itself roared, keeping the central heating going all through the night.

The weighing room was even worse, because it was big and entirely without cover. It contained nothing it shouldn't have: tables, chairs, notices pinned on the walls, and the weighing machine itself. Beyond, in the changing room, there were rows of pegs with saddles on, the warm, banked-up coke stove in the corner, and a big wicker basket full of helmets, boots, weight cloths and other equipment left by the valets overnight. A dirty cup and saucer. A copy of *Playboy*. Several raincoats. Racing colours on pegs. A row of washed breeches hanging up to dry. It was the most occupied looking part of the stands, the place I felt most at home in and where I wanted to go to ground, like an ostrich in familiar sand. But on the far side of the changing room lay only the wash room, another dead end.

Opening out of the weighing room on the opposite side to the changing room was the Stewards' room, where in the past like all jockeys I'd been involved in cases of objections-to-the-winner. It was a bare room: large table, chairs round it, sporting pictures, small threadbare carpet. A few of the Stewards' personal possessions lay scattered about, but there was no concealment.

A few doors here and there were locked, in spite of Oxon having left the keys in his flat. As usual I had the bunch of lock-pickers in my pocket and with shortened breath I spent several sticky minutes letting myself into one well secured room off the Members' bar. It proved to be the liquor store: crates of spirits, champagne, wine and beer. Beer from floor to ceiling, and a porter's trolley to transport it. It was a temptation to lock myself in there, and wait for the caterers to rescue me in the morning. This was one door that Oxon would not expect to find me on the far side of.

In the liquor store I might be safe. On the other hand, if I were safe the racecourse might not be. Reluctantly I left again; but I didn't waste time locking up. With the pursuit out of sight, I risked a look upstairs. It was warm and quiet, and all the lights were on. I left them on, figuring that if the watchers in the cars saw them go out they would know too accurately where I was.

Nothing seemed to be wrong. On one side of a central lobby there was the big room where the executive held their meetings and ate their lunch. On the other side there was a sort of drawing-room furnished with light armchairs, with two cloakrooms leading off it at the back. At the front, through double glass doors, it led out into a box high up on the stands. The private box for directors and distinguished guests, with a superb view over the whole course.

I didn't go out there. Sabotaging the Royal Box wouldn't stop a race meeting to which royalty weren't going anyway. And besides, whoever was in my car would see me opening the door.

Retreating, I went back, right through the dining-board room and out into the servery on the far side. There I found a storeroom with plates, glass and cutlery, and in the storeroom also a second exit. A small service lift down to the kitchens. It worked with ropes, like the one in the office in the Cromwell Road . . . like the office lift *had* worked, before the bomb.

Kraye and Oxon were down in the kitchen. Their angry voices floated up the shaft, mingled with a softer murmuring voice which seemed to be arguing with them. Since for once I knew where they all were, I returned with some boldness to the ground again. But I was worried. There seemed to be nothing at all going wrong in the main building. If they were organizing yet more damage somewhere out on the course itself, I didn't see how I could stop it.

While I was still dithering rather aimlessly along the passage the kitchen door opened, the light flooded out, and I could hear Kraye still talking. I dived yet again for the nearest door and put it between myself and them.

I was, I discovered, in the ladies' room, where I hadn't been before: and there was no second way out. Only a double row of cubicles, all with the doors open, a range of washbasins, mirrors on the walls with a wide shelf beneath them, a few chairs, and a counter like that in the bar. Behind the counter there was a rail with coat hangers.

There were heavy steps in the passage outside. I slid instantly behind and under the counter and pressed myself into a corner The door opened.

'He won't be in here,' said Kraye. 'The light's still on.'

'I looked in here not five minutes ago, anyway,' agreed Oxon.

The door closed behind them and their footsteps went away. I began to breathe again and my thudding heart slowed down. But for a couple of seconds only. Across the room, someone coughed.

I froze. I couldn't believe it. The room had been empty when I came in, I was certain. And neither Kraye nor Oxon had stayed . . . I stretched my ears, tense, horrified.

Another cough. A soft, single cough.

Try as I could, I could hear nothing else. No breathing. No rustle of clothing, no movement. It didn't make sense. If someone in the room knew I was behind the counter, why didn't they do something about it? If they didn't know, why were they so unnaturally quiet?

In the end, taking a conscious grip on my nerves, I slowly stood up.

The room was empty.

Almost immediately there was another cough. Now that my ears were no longer obstructed by the counter, I got a clearer idea of its direction. I swung towards it. There was no one there.

I walked across the room and stared down at the wash basin. Water was trickling from one of the taps. Even while I looked at it the tap coughed. Almost laughing with relief I stretched out my hand and turned it off.

The metal was very hot. Surprised, I turned the water on again. It came spluttering out of the tap, full of air bubbles and very hot indeed. Steaming. How stupid, I thought, turning it off again, to have the water so hot at this time of night . . .

Christ, I thought. The boiler.

CHAPTER SIXTEEN

KRAYE and Oxon's so-called methodical end to end search which had just failed to find me in the ladies', was proceeding from the Members' end of the stands towards Tattersalls. The boiler, like myself, was in the part they had already put behind them. I switched out the ladies' room lights, carefully eased into the passage, and via the kitchen, the Members' dining-room, the gentlemen's cloaks and another short strip of passage returned to the boiler room.

Although there was no door through, I knew that on the far side of the inside wall lay to the left the weighing room and to the right the changing room, with the dividing wall between. From both those rooms, when it was quiet, as it was that night, one could quite clearly hear the boiler's muffled roar.

The light that I had switched off was on again in the boiler room. I looked round. It all looked as normal as it had before except . . . except that away to the right there was a very small pool of water on the floor.

Boilers. We had had a lesson on them at school. Sixteen or seventeen years ago, I thought hopelessly. But I remembered very well the way the master had begun the lesson.

'The first thing to learn about boilers,' he said, 'is that they explode.'

He was an excellent teacher: the whole class of forty boys listened from then on with avid interest. But since then the only acquaintance I'd had with boilers was down in the basement of the flats, where I sometimes drank a cup of orange tea with the caretaker. A tough ex-naval stoker, he was, and a confirmed student of racing form. Mostly we'd talked about horses, but sometimes about his job. There were strict regulations for boilers, he'd said, and regular official inspections every three months, and he was glad of it, working alongside them every day.

The first thing to learn about boilers is that they explode.

It's no good saying I wasn't frightened, because I was. If the boiler burst it wasn't simply going to make large new entrances into the weighing room and changing room, it was going to fill every cranny near it with scalding tornadoes of steam. Not a death I looked on with much favour.

I stood with my back against the door and tried desperately to remember that long ago lesson, and to work out what was going wrong.

It was a big steam boiler. An enormous cylinder nine feet high and five feet in diameter. Thick steel, with dark red anti-rust paint peeling off. Fired at the bottom not by coke, which it had been built for, but by the more modern roaring jet of burning oil. If I opened the fire door I would feel the blast of its tremendous heat.

The body of the cylinder would be filled almost to the top with water. The flame boiled the water. The resulting steam went out of the top under its own fierce pressure in a pipe which—I followed it with my eye—led into a large yellow-painted round-ended cylinder slung horizontally near the ceiling. This tank looked rather like a zeppelin. It was, if I remembered right, a calorifier. Inside it, the steam pipe ran in a spiral, like an immobile spring. The tank itself was supplied direct from the mains with the water which was to be heated, the water going to the central heating radiators, and to the hot taps in the kitchen, the cloakrooms and the jockeys' washrooms. The scorching heat from the spiral steam pipe instantly passed into the mains water flowing over it, so that the cold water entering the calorifier was made very hot in the short time before it left at the other end.

The steam, however, losing its heat in the process, gradually condensed back into water. A pipe led down the wall from the calorifier into a much smaller tank, an ordinary square one, standing on the floor. From the bottom of this yet another pipe tracked right back across the room and up near the boiler itself to a bulbous metal contraption just higher than my head. An electric pump. It finished the circuit by pumping the condensed water up from the tank on the floor and returning it to the boiler, steamed and condensed all over again. Round and round, continuously.

So far, so good. But if you interfered with the circuit so that the water didn't get back into the boiler, and at the same time kept the heat full on at the bottom, all the water inside the cylinder gradually turned to steam. Steam, which was strong enough to drive a liner, or pull a twelve coach train, but could in this case only get out at all through a narrow, closely spiralled pipe.

This type of boiler, built not for driving an engine but only for heating water, wasn't constructed to withstand enormous pressures. It was a toss-up, I thought, whether when all the water had gone the fast expanding air and steam found a weak spot to break out of before the flames burnt through the bottom. In either case, the boiler would blow up.

On the outside of the boiler there was a water gauge, a foot-long vertical glass tube held in brackets. The level of water in the tube indicated the level of water in the boiler. Near the top of the gauge a black line showed what the water level ought to be. Two thirds of the way down a broad red line obviously acted as a warning. The water in the gauge was higher than the red line by half an inch.

To put it mildly, I was relieved. The boiler wasn't bulging. The explosion lay in the future: which gave me more time to work out how to prevent it. As long as it would take Oxon and Kraye to decide on a repeat search, perhaps.

I could simply have turned out the flame, but Kraye and Oxon would notice that the noise had stopped, and merely light it again. Nothing would have been gained. On the other hand, I was sure that the flame was higher than it should have been at night, because the water in the ladies' tap was nearly boiling.

Gingerly I turned the adjusting wheel on the oil line. Half a turn. A full turn. The roaring seemed just as loud. Another turn: and that time there was a definite change. Half a turn more. It was perceptibly quieter. Slowly I inched the wheel around more, until quite suddenly the roar turned to a murmur. Too far. Hastily I reversed. At the point where the murmur was again a roar, I left it.

I looked consideringly at the square tank of condensed water on the floor. It was this, overflowing, which was making the pool of water; and it was overflowing because the contents were not being pumped back into the boiler. If they've broken the pump, I thought despairingly, I'm done. I didn't know the first thing about electric pumps.

Another sentence from that far away school lesson floated usefully through my mind. *For safety's sake, every boiler must have two sources of water.*

I chewed my lower lip, watching the water trickle down the side of the tank on to the floor. Even in the few minutes I had been there the pool had spread. One source of water was obviously knocked out. Where and what was the other?

There were dozens of pipes in the boiler room; not only oil pipes and water pipes, but all the electric cables were installed inside tubes as well. There were about six separate pipes with stop cocks on them. It seemed to me that all the water for the entire building came in through the boiler room.

Two pipes, apparently rising mains, led from the floor up the wall and into the calorifier. Both had stop-cocks, which I tested. Both were safely open. There was no rising main leading direct into the boiler.

By sheer luck I was half way round the huge cylinder looking for an inlet pipe when I saw the lever type door handle move down. I leapt for the only vestige of cover, the space between the boiler and the wall. It was scorching hot there: pretty well unbearable.

Kraye had to raise his voice to make himself heard over the roaring flame.

'You're sure it's still safe?'

'Yes, I told you, it won't blow up for three hours yet. At least three hours.'

'The water's runing out already,' Kraye objected.

'There's a lot in there.' Oxon's voice came nearer. I could feel my heart thumping and hear the pulse in my ears. 'The level's not down to the caution mark on the gauge yet,' he said. 'It won't blow for a long time after it goes below that.'

'We've got to find Halley,' Kraye said. 'Got to.' If Oxon moved another step he would see me. 'I'll work from this end; you start again from the other. Look in every cupboard. The little rat has gone to ground somewhere.'

Oxon didn't answer audibly. I had a sudden glimpse of his

sleeve as he turned, and I shrank back into my hiding place.

Because of the noise of the boiler I couldn't hear them go away through the door, but eventually I had to risk that they had. The heat where I stood was too appalling. Moving out into the ordinarily hot air in the middle of the room was like diving into a cold bath. And Oxon and Kraye had gone.

I slipped off my jacket and wiped the sweat off my face with my shirt sleeve. Back to the problem: water supply.

The pump *looked* all right. There were no loose wires, and it had an undisturbed, slightly greasy, slightly dirty appearance. With luck, I thought, they hadn't damaged the pump, they'd blocked the pipe where it left the tank. I took off my tie and shirt as well, and put them with my jacket on the grimy floor.

The lid of the tank came off easily enough, and the water, when I tested it, proved to be no more than uncomfortably hot. I drank some in my cupped palm. The running and the heat had made me very thirsty, and although I would have preferred it iced, no water could have been purer; or more tasteless, though I was not inclined to be fussy on that point.

I stretched my arm down into the water, kneeling beside the tank. As it was only about two feet deep I could touch the bottom quite easily, and almost at once my searching fingers found and gripped a loose object. I pulled it out.

It was a fine mesh filter, which should no doubt have been in place over the opening of the outlet pipe.

Convinced now that the pipe was blocked from this end, I reached down again into the water. I found the edge of the outlet, and felt carefully into it. I could reach no obstruction. Bending over further, so that my shoulder was half in the water, I put two fingers as far as they would go into the outlet. I could feel nothing solid, but there did seem to be a piece of string. It was difficult to get it between two fingers firmly enough to pull as hard as was necessary, but gradually with a series of little jerks I managed to move the plug backwards into the tank.

It came away finally so suddenly that I nearly over-balanced. There was a burp from the outlet pipe of the tank and on the other side of the room a sharp click from the pump.

I lifted my hand out of the water to see what had blocked the pipe, and stared in amazement. It was a large mouse. I had been pulling its tail.

Accidental sabotage, I thought. The same old pattern. However unlikely it was that a mouse should dive into a tank, find the filter conveniently out of place, and get stuck just inside the outlet pipe, one would have a hard job proving that it was impossible.

I carefully put the sodden little body out of sight in the small gap between the tank and wall. With relief I noticed that the water level was already going down slightly, which meant that the pump was working properly and the boiler would soon be more or less back to normal.

I splashed some more water out of the tank to make a larger pool should Kraye or Oxon glance in again, and replaced the lid. Putting on my shirt and jacket I followed with my eyes the various pipes in and out of the boiler. The lagged steam exit pipe to the calorifier. The vast chimney flue for the hot gases from the burning oil. The inlet pipe from the pump. The water gauge. The oil pipe. There had to be another water inlet somewhere, partly for safety, partly to keep the steam circuit topped up.

I found it in the end running alongside and behind the inlet pipe from the pump. It was a gravity feed from a stepped series of three small unobtrusive tanks fixed high on the wall. Filters, I reckoned, so that the mains water didn't carry its mineral salts into the boiler and fur it up. The filter tanks were fed by a pipe which branched off one of the rising mains and had its own stop cock.

Reaching up, I tried to turn it clockwise. It didn't move. The mains water was cut off. With satisfaction, I turned it on again.

Finally, with the boiler once more working exactly as it should, I took a look at the water gauge. The level had already risen to nearly half way between the red and black marks. Hoping fervently Oxon wouldn't come back for another check on it, I went over to the door and switched off the light.

There was no one in the passage. I slipped through the door, and in the last three inches before shutting it behind me stretched my hand back and put the light on again. I didn't want Kraye knowing I'd been in there.

Keeping close to the wall, I walked softly down the passage towards the Tattersalls end. If I could get clear of the stands there were other buildings out that way to give cover. The barns, cloakrooms and tote buildings in the silver ring. Beyond these lay the finishing straight, the way down to the tan patch and the bisecting road. Along that, bungalows, people, and telephones.

That was when my luck ran out.

CHAPTER SEVENTEEN

I WAS barely two steps past the door of the Tattersalls bar when it opened and the lights blazed out on to my tiptoeing figure. In the two seconds it took Oxon to realize what he was seeing I was six running paces down towards the way out. His shouts echoed in the passage mingled with others farther back, and I still thought that if Kraye too were behind me I might have a chance. But when I was within ten steps of the end another figure appeared there, hurrying, called by the noise.

I skidded nearly to a stop, sliding on one of the scattered bottle tops, and crashed through the only possible door, into the same empty bar as before. I raced across the board floor, kicking bottle tops in all directions, but I never got to the far door. It opened before I reached it: and that was the end.

Doria Kraye stood there, maliciously triumphant. She was dressed theatrically in white slender trousers and a shiny short white jacket. Her dark hair fell smoothly, her face was as flawlessly beautiful as ever: and she held rock steady in one elegant long-fingered hand the little .22 automatic I had last seen in a chocolate box at the bottom of her dressing-case.

'The end of the line, buddy boy,' she said. 'You stay just where you are.'

I hesitated on the brink of trying to rush her.

'Don't risk it,' she said. 'I'm a splendid shot. I wouldn't miss. Do you want a knee-cap smashed?'

There was little I wanted less. I turned round slowly. There were three men coming forward into the long room. Kraye, Oxon and Ellis Bolt. All three of them looked as if they had long got tired of the chase and were going to take it out on the quarry.

'Will you walk,' said Doria behind me, 'or be dragged?'

I shrugged. 'Walk.'

All the same, Kraye couldn't keep his hands off me. When, following Doria's instructions, I walked past him to go back out through the passage he caught hold of my jacket at the back of my neck and kicked my legs. I kicked back, which wasn't too sensible, as I presently ended up on the floor. There was nothing like little metal bottle tops for giving you a feeling of falling on little metal bottle tops, I thought, with apologies to Michael Flanders and Donald Swann.

'Get up,' said Kraye. Doria stood beside him, pointing at me with the gun.

I did as he said.

'Right,' said Doria. 'Now, walk down the passage and go into the weighing room. And Howard, for God's sake wait till we get there, or we'll lose him again. Walk, buddy boy. Walk straight down the middle of the passage. If you try anything, I'll shoot you in the leg.'

I saw no reason not to believe her. I walked down the centre of the passage with her too close behind for escape, and with the two men bringing up the rear.

'Stop a minute,' said Kraye, outside the boiler room.

I stopped. I didn't look round.

Kraye opened the door and looked inside. The light spilled out, adding to that already coming from the other open doors along the way.

'Well?' said Oxon.

'There's more water on the floor.' He sounded pleased, and shut the door without going in for a further look. Not all of my luck had departed, it seemed.

'Move,' he said. I obeyed.

The weighing room was as big and bare as ever. I stopped in the middle of it and turned round. The four of them stood in a row, looking at me, and I didn't at all like what I read in their faces.

'Go and sit there,' said Doria, pointing.

I went on across the floor and sat where she said, on the chair of the weighing machine. The pointer immediately swung round the clock face to show my weight. Nine stone seven. It was, I was remotely interested to see, exactly ten pounds less than when I had last raced. Bullets would solve any jockey's weight problem, I thought.

The four of them came closer. It was some relief to find that Fred wasn't among them, but only some. Kraye was emitting the same livid fury as he had twelve days ago at Aynsford. And then, I had merely insulted his wife.

'Hold his arms,' he said to Oxon. Oxon was one of those thin wiry men of seemingly limitless strength. He came round behind me, clamped his fingers round my elbows and pulled them back.

With concentration Kraye hit me several times in the face.

'Now,' he said, 'where are they?'

'What?' I said indistinctly.

'The negatives.'

'What negatives?'

He hit me again and hurt his own hand. Shaking it out and rubbing his knuckles, he said, 'You know what negatives. The films you took of my papers.'

'Oh, those.'

'Those.' He hit me again, but less hard.

'In the office,' I mumbled.

He tried a slap to save his knuckles. 'Office,' I said.

He tried with his left hand, but it was clumsy. After that he sucked his knuckles and kept his hands to himself.

Bolt spoke for the first time, in his consciously beautiful voice. 'Fred wouldn't have missed them, especially as there was no reason for them to be concealed. He's too thorough.'

If Fred wouldn't have missed them, the bombs had been pure spite. I licked the inside of a split lip and thought about what I would like to do to Fred.

'Where in the office?' said Kraye.

'Desk.'

'Hit him,' said Kraye. 'My hand hurts.'

Bolt had a go, but it wasn't his sort of thing.

'Try with this,' said Doria, offering Bolt the gun, but it was luckily so small he couldn't hold it effectively.

Oxon let go of my elbows, came round to the front, and looked at my face.

'If he's decided not to tell you, you won't get it out of him like that,' he said.

'I told you,' I said.

'Why not?' said Bolt.

'You're hurting yourselves more than him. And if you want my opinion, you won't get anything out of him at all.'

'Don't be silly,' said Doria scornfully. 'He's so small.'

Oxon laughed without mirth.

'If Fred said so, the negatives weren't at his office,' asserted Bolt again. 'Nor in his flat. And he didn't bring them with him. Or at least, they weren't in his luggage at the hotel.'

I looked at him sideways, out of an eye which was beginning to swell. And if I hadn't been so quick to have him flung out of my hotel room, I thought sourly, he wouldn't have driven through the racecourse gate at exactly the wrong moment. But I couldn't have foreseen it, and it was too late to help.

'They weren't in his car either,' said Doria. 'But this was.' She put her hand into her shining white pocket and brought out my baby camera. Kraye took it from her, opened the case, and saw what was inside. The veins in his neck and temples became congested with blood. In a paroxysm of fury he threw the little black toy across the room so that it hit the wall with a disintegrating crash.

'Sixteen millimetre,' he said savagely. 'Fred must have missed them.'

Bolt said obstinately, 'Fred would find a needle in a haystack. And those films wouldn't have been hidden.'

'He might have them in his pocket,' suggested Doria.

'Take your coat off,' Kraye said. 'Stand up.'

I stood up, and the base-plate of the weighing machine wobbled under my feet. Oxon pulled my coat down over the back of my shoulders, gave a tug to get the sleeves off, and passed the jacket to Kraye. His own hand he thrust into my trouser pockets. In the right one, under my tie, he found the bunch of lock pickers.

'Sit down,' he said. I did so, exploring with the back of my hand some of the damage to my face. It could have been worse, I thought resignedly, much worse. I would be lucky if that were all.

'What are those?' said Doria curiously, taking the jingling collection from Oxon.

Kraye snatched them from her and slung them after the camera. 'Skeleton keys,' he said furiously. 'What he used to unlock my cases.'

'I don't see how he could,' said Doria, 'with that . . . that . . . *claw.*' She looked down where it lay on my lap.

A nice line in taunts, I thought, but a week too late. Thanks to Zanna Martin, I was at last learning to live with the claw. I left it where it was.

'Doria,' said Bolt calmly, 'would you be kind enough to go over to the flat and wait for Fred to ring? He may already have found what we want at Aynsford.'

I turned my head and found him looking straight at me, assessingly. There was a detachment in the eyes, an unmoved quality in the rounded features; and I began to wonder whether his stolid coolness might not in the end prove even more difficult to deal with than Kraye's rage.

'Aynsford,' I repeated thickly. I looked at my watch. If Fred had really taken his bombs to Aynsford, he should by now be safely in the bag. One down, four to go. Five of them altogether, not four. I hadn't thought of Doria being an active equal colleague of the others. My mistake.

'I don't want to,' said Doria, staying put.

Bolt shrugged. 'It doesn't matter. I see that the negatives aren't at Aynsford, because the thought of Fred looking for them there doesn't worry Halley one little bit.'

The thought of what Fred might be doing at Aynsford or to Charles himself didn't worry any of them either. But more than that I didn't like the way Bolt was reasoning. In the circumstances, a clear-thinking opponent was something I could well have done without.

'We must have them,' said Kraye intensely. 'We must. Or be certain beyond doubt that they were destroyed.' To Oxon he said, 'Hold his arms again.'

'No,' I said, shrinking back.

'Ah, that's better. Well?'

'They were in the office.' My mouth felt stiff.

'Where?'

'In Mr Radnor's desk, I think.'

He stared at me, eyes narrowed, anger half under control, weighing up whether I were telling the truth or not. He certainly couldn't go to the office and make sure.

'Were,' said Bolt suddenly.

'What?' asked Kraye, impatiently.

'Were,' said Bolt. 'Halley said were. The negatives *were* in the office. Now that's very interesting indeed, don't you think?'

Oxon said, 'I don't see why.'

Bolt came close to me and peered into my face. I didn't meet his eyes, and anything he could read from my bruised features he was welcome to.

'I think he knows about the bombs,' he said finally.

'How?' said Doria.

'I should think he was told at the hotel. People in London must have been trying to contact him. Yes, I think we can take it for granted he knows about the bombs.'

'What difference does that make?' said Oxon.

Kraye knew. 'It means he thinks he is safe saying the negatives were in the office, because we can't prove they weren't.'

'They were,' I insisted, showing anxiety.

Bolt pursed his full moist lips. 'Just how clever is Halley?' he said.

'He was a jockey,' said Oxon flatly, as if that automatically meant an I.Q. of 70.

Bolt said, 'But they took him on at Hunt Radnor's.'

'I told you before,' said Oxon patiently, 'I asked various people about that. Radnor took him on as an adviser, but never gave him anything special to do, and if that doesn't show that he wasn't capable of much, I don't know what does. Everyone knows that his job is only a face saver. It sounds all right, but it means nothing really. Jobs are quite often given in that way to top jockeys when they retire. No one expects them to *do* much, it's just their name that's useful for a while. When their news value has gone, they get the sack.'

This all too true summing up of affairs depressed me almost as deeply as my immediate prospects.

'Howard?' said Bolt.

'I don't know,' said Kraye slowly. 'He doesn't strike me as being in the least clever. Very much the opposite. I agree he did take those photographs, but I think you are quite right in believing he doesn't know why we want them destroyed.'

That, too, was shatteringly correct. As far as I had been able to see, the photographs proved nothing conclusively except that Kraye had been buying Seabury shares under various names with Bolt's help. Kraye and Bolt could not be prosecuted for that. Moreover the whole of Seabury executive had seen the photographs at the meeting that morning, so their contents were no secret.

'Doria?' Bolt said.

'He's a slimy spying little creep, but if he was clever he wouldn't be sitting where he is.'

You couldn't argue with that, either. It had been fairly certain all along that Kraye was getting help from somebody working at Seabury, but even after knowing about Clerk of the Course Brinton's unwilling collaboration at Dunstable, I had gone on assuming that the helper at Seabury was one of the labourers. I hadn't given more than a second's flicker of thought to Oxon, because it didn't seem reasonable that it should be him. In destroying the racecourse he was working himself out of a job, and good jobs for forty year old ex-army captains weren't plentiful enough to be lost lightly. As he certainly wasn't mentally affected like Brinton, he wasn't being blackmailed into doing it against his will. I had thought him silly and self important, but not a rogue. As Doria said, had I been clever enough to suspect him, I wouldn't be sitting where I was.

Bolt went on discussing me as if I weren't there, and as if the decision they would come to would have ordinary everyday consequences.

He said, 'You may all be right, but I don't think so, because since Halley has been on the scene everything's gone wrong. It was he who persuaded Hagbourne to get the course put right, and he who found the mirror as soon as it was up. I took him without question for what he said he was when he came to see me—a shop assistant. You two took him for a wretched little hanger-on of no account. All that, together with the fact that he opened your locked cases and took good clear photographs on a miniature camera, adds up to just one thing to me. Professionalism. Even the way he sits there saying nothing is professional. Amateurs call you names and try to impress you with how much they know. All he has said is that the negatives were in the office. I consider we ought to forget every previous impression we have of him and think of him only as coming from Hunt Radnor.'

They thought about this for five seconds. Then Kraye said, 'We'll have to make sure about the negatives.'

Bolt nodded. If reason hadn't told me what Kraye meant, his wife's smile would have done. My skin crawled.

'How?' she said interestedly.

Kraye inspected his grazed knuckles. 'You won't beat it out of him,' said Oxon. 'Not like that. You haven't a hope.'

'Why not?' said Bolt.

Instead of replying, Oxon turned to me. 'How many races did you ride with broken bones?'

I didn't answer. I couldn't remember anyway.

'That's ridiculous,' said Doria scornfully. 'How could he?'

'A lot of them do,' said Oxon. 'And I'm sure he was no exception.'

'Nonsense,' said Kraye.

Oxon shook his head. 'Collar bones, ribs, forearms, they'll ride with cracks in any of those if they can keep the owners and trainers from finding out.'

Why couldn't he shut up, I thought savagely. He was making things much much worse; as if they weren't appalling enough already.

'You mean,' said Doria with sickening pleasure, 'that he can stand a great deal?'

'No,' I said. 'No.' It sounded like the plea it was. 'You can only ride with cracked bones if they don't hurt.'

'They must hurt,' said Bolt reasonably.

'No,' I said. 'Not always.' It was true, but they didn't believe it.

'The negatives were in the office,' I said despairingly. 'In the office.'

'He's scared,' said Doria delightedly. And that too was true.

It struck a chord with Kraye. He remembered Aynsford. 'We know where he's most easily hurt,' he said. 'That hand.'

'No,' I said in real horror.

They all smiled.

My whole body flushed with uncontrollable fear. Racing injuries were one thing: they were quick, one didn't expect them, and they were part of the job.

To sit and wait and know that a part of one's self which had already proved a burden was about to be hurt as much as ever was quite something else. Instinctively I put my arm up across my face to hide from them that I was afraid, but it must have been obvious.

Kraye laughed insultingly. 'So there's your brave clever Mr Halley for you. It won't take much to get the truth.'

'What a pity,' said Doria.

They left her standing in front of me holding the little pistol in an unswerving pink nailed hand while they went out and rummaged for what they needed. I judged the distance to the door, which was all of thirty feet, and wondered whether the chance of a bullet on the way wasn't preferable to what was going to happen if I stayed where I was.

Doria watched my indecision with amusement.

'Just try it, buddy boy. Just try it.'

I had read that to shoot accurately with an automatic pistol took a great deal of skill and practice. It was possible that all Doria had wanted was the power feeling of owning a gun and she couldn't aim it. On the other hand she was holding it high and with a nearly straight arm, close to where she could see along the sights. On balance, I thought her claim to be a splendid shot had too much probability to be risked.

It was a pity Doria had such a vicious soul inside her beautiful body. She looked gay and dashing in her white Courreges clothes, smiling a smile which seemed warm and friendly and was as safe as the yawn of a python. She was the perfect mate for Kraye, I thought. Fourth, fifth, sixth time lucky, he'd found a complete complement to himself. If Kraye could do it, perhaps one day I would too . . . but I didn't know if I would even see tomorrow.

I put the back of my hand up over my eyes. My whole face hurt, swollen and stiff, and I was developing a headache. I decided that if I ever got out of this I wouldn't try any more detecting. I had made a proper mess of it.

The men came back, Oxon from the Stewards' room lugging a wooden spoke-backed chair with arms, Kraye and Bolt from the changing room with the yard-long poker from the stove and the rope the wet breeches had been hung on to dry. There were still a couple of pegs clinging to it.

Oxon put the chair down a yard or two away and Doria waved the gun a fraction to indicate I should sit in it. I didn't move.

'God,' she said disappointedly, 'you really are a little worm, just like at Aynsford. Scared to a standstill.'

'He isn't a shop assistant,' said Bolt sharply. 'And don't forget it.'

I didn't look at him. But for him and his rejection of Charles' usefully feeble Halley image, I might have not been faced with quite the present situation.

Oxon punched me on the shoulder. 'Move,' he said.

I stood up wearily and stepped off the weighing machine. They stood close round me. Kraye thrust out a hand, twisted it into my shirt, and pushed me into the chair. He, Bolt and Oxon had a fine old time tying my arms and legs to the equivalent wooden ones with the washing line. Doria watched, fascinated.

I remembered her rather unusual pleasures.

'Like to change places?' I said tiredly.

It didn't make her angry. She smiled slowly, put her gun in a pocket, and leaned down and kissed me long and hard on the mouth. I loathed it. When at length she straightened up she had a smear of my blood on her lip. She wiped it off on to her hand,

and thoughtfully licked it. She looked misty-eyed and languorous, as if she had had a profound sexual experience. It made me want to vomit.

'Now,' said Kraye. 'Where are they?' He didn't seem to mind his wife kissing me. He understood her, of course.

I looked at the way they had tied the rope tightly round and round my left forearm, leaving the wrist bare, palm downwards. A hand, I thought. What good, anyway, was a hand that didn't work.

I looked at their faces, one by one. Doria, rapt. Oxon, faintly surprised. Kraye confident, flexing his muscles. And Bolt, calculating and suspicious. None of them within a mile of relenting.

'Where are they?' Kraye repeated, lifting his arm.

'In the office,' I said helplessly.

He hit my wrist with the poker. I'd hoped he might at least try to be subtle, but instead he used all his strength and with that one first blow smashed the whole shooting match to smithereens. The poker broke through the skin. The bones cracked audibly like sticks.

I didn't scream only because I couldn't get enough breath to do it. Before that moment I would have said I knew everything there was to know about pain, but it seems one can always learn. Behind my shut eyes the world turned yellow and grey, like sun shining through mist, and every inch of my skin began to sweat. There had never been anything like it. It was too much, too much. And I couldn't manage any more.

'Where are they?' said Kraye again.

'Don't,' I said. 'Don't do it.' I could hardly speak.

Doria sighed deeply.

I opened my eyes a slit, my head lolling weakly back, too heavy to hold up. Kraye was smiling, pleased with his efforts. Oxon looked sick.

'Well?' said Kraye.

I swallowed, hesitating still.

He put the tip of the poker on my shattered bleeding wrist and gave a violent jerk. Among other things it felt like a fizzing electric shock, up my arm into my head and down to my toes. Sweat started sticking my shirt to my chest and my trousers to my legs.

'Don't,' I said. 'Don't.' It was a croak; a capitulation; a prayer.

'Come on, then,' said Kraye, and jolted the poker again.

I told them. I told them where to go.

CHAPTER EIGHTEEN

THEY decided it should be Bolt who went to fetch the negatives.

'What is this place?' he said. He hadn't recognized the address.

'The home of . . . a . . . girl friend.'

He dispassionately watched the sweat run in trickles down my face. My mouth was dry. I was very thirsty.

'Say . . . I sent you,' I said, between jagged breaths. 'I . . . asked her . . . to keep them safe . . . They . . . are with . . . several other things . . . The package . . . you want . . . has a name on it . . . a make of film . . . Jigoro . . . Kano.'

'Jigoro Kano. Right,' Bolt said briskly.

'Give me . . .' I said, 'some morphine.'

Bolt laughed. 'After all the trouble you've caused us? Even if I had any, I wouldn't. You can sit there and sweat it out.'

I moaned. Bolt smiled in satisfaction and turned away.

'I'll ring you as soon as I have the negatives,' he said to Kraye. 'Then we can decide what to do with Halley. I'll give it some thought on the way up.' From his tone he might have been discussing the disposal of a block of worthless stocks.

'Good,' said Kraye. 'We'll wait for your call over in the flat.'

They began to walk towards the door. Oxon and Doria hung back, Doria because she couldn't tear her fascinated dilated eyes away from watching me, and Oxon for more practical reasons.

'Are you just going to leave him here?' he asked in surprise.

'Yes. Why not?' said Kraye. 'Come on, Doria darling. The best is over.'

Unwilling she followed him, and Oxon also.

'Some water,' I said. 'Please.'

'No,' said Kraye.

They filed past him out of the door. Just before he shut it he gave me a last look compounded of triumph, contempt and satisfied cruelty. Then he switched off all the lights and went away.

I heard the sound of a car starting up and driving off. Bolt was on his way. Outside the windows the night was black. Darkness folded round me like a fourth dimension. As the silence deepened I listened to the low hum of the boiler roaring safely on the far side of the wall. At least, I thought, I don't have to worry about that as well. Small, small consolation.

The back of the chair came only as high as my shoulders and gave no support to my head. I felt deathly tired. I couldn't bear to move: every muscle in my body seemed to have a private line direct to my left wrist, and merely flexing my right foot had me panting. I wanted to lie down flat. I wanted a long cold drink. I wanted to faint. I went on sitting in the chair, wide awake, with a head that ached and weighed a ton, and an arm which wasn't worth the trouble.

I thought about Bolt going to Zanna Martin's front door, and finding that his own secretary had been helping me. I wondered for the hundredth time what he would do about that: whether he would harm her. Poor Miss Martin, whom life had already hurt too much.

Not only her, I thought. In the same file was the letter Mervyn Brinton had written out for me. If Bolt should see that, Mervyn Brinton would be needing a bodyguard for life.

I thought about the people who had borne the beatings and brutalities of the Nazis and of the Japanese and had often died without betraying their secrets. I thought about the atrocities still going on throughout the world, and the ease with which man could break man. In Algeria, they said, unbelievable things had been done. Behind the Iron Curtain, brain washing wasn't all. In African jails, who knew?

Too young for World War Two, safe in a tolerant society, I had had no thought that I should ever come to such a test. To suffer or to talk. The dilemma which stretched back to antiquity. Thanks to Kraye, I now knew what it was like at first hand. Thanks to Kraye, I didn't understand how anyone could keep silent unto death.

I thought: I wanted to ride round Seabury racecourse again, and to go back into the weighing room, and to sit on the scales; and I've done all those things.

I thought: a fortnight ago I couldn't let go of the past. I was clinging to too many ruins, the ruins of my marriage and my racing career and my useless hand. They were gone for good now, all of them. There was nothing left to cling to. And every tangible memory of my life had blown away with a plastic bomb. I was rootless and homeless: and liberated.

What I refused to think about was what Kraye might still do during the next few hours.

Bolt had been gone for a good long time when at last Kraye came back. It had seemed half eternity to me, but even so I was in no hurry for it to end.

Kraye put the lights on. He and Doria stood just inside the doorway, staring across at me.

'You're sure there's time?' said Doria.

Kraye nodded, looking at his watch. 'If we're quick.'

'Don't you think we ought to wait until Ellis rings?' she said. 'He might have thought of something better.'

'He's late already,' said Kraye impatiently. They had clearly been arguing for some time. 'He should have rung by now. If we're going to do this, we can't wait any longer.'

'All right,' she shrugged. 'I'll go and take a look.'

'Be careful. Don't go in.'

'No,' she said. 'Don't fuss.'

They both came over to where I sat. Doria looked at me with interest, and liked what she saw.

'He looks ghastly, doesn't he? Serves him right.'

'Are you human?' I said.

A flicker of awareness crossed her lovely face, as if deep down she did indeed know that everything she had enjoyed that night was sinful and obscene, but she was too thoroughly addicted to turn back. 'Shall I help you?' she said to Kraye, not answering me.

'No. I can manage. He's not very heavy.'

She watched with a smile while her husband gripped the back of the chair I was sitting in and began to tug it across the floor towards the wall. The jerks were almost past bearing. I grew dizzy with the effort of not yelling my head off. There was no one close enough to hear me if I did. Not the few overnight stable lads fast asleep three hundred yards away. Only the Krayes, who would find it sweet.

Doria licked her lips, as if at a feast.

'Go on,' said Kraye. 'Hurry.'

'Oh, all right,' she agreed crossly, and went out through the door into the passage.

Kraye finished pulling me across the room, turned the chair round so that I was facing the wall with my knees nearly touching it and stood back, breathing deeply from the exertion.

On the other side of the wall the boiler gently roared. One could hear it more clearly at such close quarters. I knew I had no crashing explosion, no flying bricks, no killing steam to worry about. But the sands were running out fast, all the same.

Doria came back and said in a puzzled voice, 'I thought you said there would be water all down the passage.'

'That's right.'

'Well, there isn't. Not a drop. I looked into the boiler room and it's as dry as a bone.'

'It can't be. It's nearly three hours since it started overflowing. Oxon warned us it must be nearly ready to blow. You must be wrong.'

'I'm not,' she insisted. 'The whole thing looks perfectly normal to me.'

'It can't be.' Kraye's voice was sharp. He went off in a hurry to see for himself, and came back even faster.

'You're right. I'll go and get Oxon. I don't know how the confounded thing works.' He went straight on out of the main door, and I heard his footsteps running. There was no urgency except his own anger. I shivered.

Doria wasn't certain enough of the boiler's safety to spend any time near me, which was about the first really good thing which had happened the whole night. Nor did she find the back of my head worth speaking to: she liked to see her worms squirm. Perhaps she had even lost her appetite, now things had gone wrong. She waited uneasily near the door for Kraye to come back, fiddling with the catch.

Oxon came with him, and they were both running. They charged across the weighing room and out into the passage.

I hadn't much left anyway, I thought. A few tatters of pride, perhaps. Time to nail them to the mast.

The two men walked softly into the room and down to where I sat. Kraye grasped the chair and swung it violently round. The weighing room was quiet, undisturbed. There was only blackness through the window. So that was that.

I looked at Kraye's face, and wished on the whole that I hadn't. It was white and rigid with fury. His eyes were two black pits.

Oxon held the mouse in his hand. 'It must have been Halley,' he said, as if he'd said it before. 'There's no one else.'

Kraye put his right hand down on my left, and systematically began to take his revenge. After three long minutes I passed out.

I clung to the dark, trying to hug it round me like a blanket, and it obstinately got thinner and thinner, lighter and lighter, noisier and noisier, more and more painful, until I could no longer deny that I was back in the world.

My eyes unstuck themselves against my will.

The weighing room was full of people. People in dark uniforms. Policemen. Policemen coming through every door. Bright yellow lights at long last shining outside the window. Policemen carefully cutting the rope away from my leaden limbs.

Kraye and Doria and Oxon looked smaller, surrounded by the dark blue men. Doria in her brave white suit instinctively and unsuccessfully tried to flirt with her captors. Oxon, disconcerted to his roots, faced the facts of life for the first time.

Kraye's fury wasn't spent. His eyes stared in hatred across the room.

He shouted, struggling in strong restraining arms, 'Where did you send him? Where did you send Ellis Bolt?'

'Ah, Mr Potter,' I said into a sudden oasis of silence. 'Mr Wilbur Potter. Find out. But not from me.'

CHAPTER NINETEEN

Of course I ended up where I had begun, flat on my back in a hospital. But not for so long, that time. I had a pleasant sunny room with a distant view of the sea, some exceedingly pretty nurses, and a whole stream of visitors. Chico came first, as soon as they would let him, on the Sunday afternoon.

He grinned down at me.

'You look bloody awful.'

'Thanks very much.'

'Two black eyes, a scabby lip, a purple and yellow complexion and a three day beard. Glamorous.'

'It sounds it.'

'Do you want to look?' he asked, picking up a hand mirror from a chest of drawers.

I took the mirror and looked. He hadn't exaggerated. I would have faded into the background in a horror movie.

Sighing, I said, 'X certificate, definitely.'

He laughed, and put the mirror back. His own face still bore the marks of battle. The eyebrow was healing, but the bruise showed dark right down his cheek.

'This is a better room than you had in London,' he remarked, strolling over to the window. 'And it smells O.K. For a hospital, that is.'

'Pack in the small talk and tell me what happened,' I said.

'They told me not to tire you.'

'Don't be an ass.'

'Well, all right. You're a bloody rollicking nit in many ways, aren't you?'

'It depends how you look at it,' I agreed peaceably.

'Oh sure, sure.'

'Chico, give,' I pleaded. 'Come on.'

'Well, there I was harmlessly snoozing away in Radnor's armchair with the telephone on one side and some rather good chicken sandwiches on the other, dreaming about a willing blonde and having a ball, when the front door bell rang.' He grinned. 'I got up, stretched and went to answer it. I thought it might be you, come back after all and with nowhere to sleep. I knew it wouldn't be Radnor, unless he'd forgotten his key. And who else would be knocking on his door at two o'clock in the morning? But there was this fat geezer standing on the doorstep in his city pinstripes, saying you'd sent him. 'Come in, then,' I said, yawning my head off. He came in, and I showed him into Radnor's sort of study place, where I'd been sitting.

' "Sid sent you?" I asked him, "What for?"

'He said he understood your girl-friend lived here. God, mate, don't ever try snapping your mouth shut at the top of a yawn. I nearly dislocated my jaw. Could he see her, he said. Sorry it was so late, but it was extremely important.

' "She isn't here," I said. "She's gone away for a few days. Can I help you?"

' "Who are you?" he said, looking me up and down.

'I said I was her brother. He took a sharpish look at the sandwiches and the book I'd been reading, which had fallen on the floor, and he could see I'd been asleep, so he seemed to think everything was O.K., and he said, "Sid asked me to fetch something she is keeping for him. Do you think you could help me find it?"

' "Sure," I said. "What is it?"

'He hesitated a bit but he could see that it would look too weird if he refused to tell me, so he said "It's a packet of negatives. Sid said your sister had several things of his, but the packet I want has a name on it, a make of films. Jigoro Kano."

' "Oh?" I said innocently. "Sid sent you for a packet marked Jigoro Kano?"

' "That's right," he said, looking round the room. "Would it be in here?"

' "It certainly would," I said.'

Chico stopped, came over beside the bed, and sat on the edge of it, by my right toe.

'How come you know about Jigoro Kano?' he said seriously.

'He invented judo,' I said. 'I read it somewhere.'

Chico shook his head. 'He didn't really invent it. In 1882 he took all the best bits of hundreds of versions of ju-jitsu and put them into a formal sort of order, and called it judo.'

'I was sure you would know,' I said, grinning at him.

'You took a very sticky risk.'

'You had to know. After all, you're an expert. And there were all those years at your club. No risk. I knew you'd know. As long as I'd got the name right, that is. Anyway, what happened next?'

Chico smiled faintly.

'I tied him into a couple of knots. Arm locks and so on. He was absolutely flabbergasted. It was really rather funny. Then I put a bit of pressure on. You know. The odd thumb screwing down to a nerve. God, you should have heard him yell. I suppose he thought he'd wake the neighbours, but you know what London is. No one took a blind bit of notice. So then I asked him where you were, when you sent him. He didn't show very willing, I must say, so I gave him a bit more. Poetic justice, wasn't it, considering what they'd just been doing to you? I told him I could keep it up all night, I'd hardly begun. There was a whole bookful I hadn't touched on. It shook him, it shook him bad.'

Chico stood up restlessly and walked about the room.

'You know?' he said wryly. 'He must have had a lot to lose. He was a pretty tough cookie, I'll give him that. If I hadn't been sure that you'd sent him to me as a sort of SOS, I don't think I'd have had the nerve to hurt him enough to bust him.'

'I'm sorry,' I said.

He looked at me thoughtfully. 'We both learnt about it, didn't we? You on the receiving end, and me . . . I didn't like it. Doing it, I mean. I mean, the odd swipe or two and a few threats, that's usually enough, and it doesn't worry you a bit, you don't give it a second thought. But I've never hurt anyone like that before. Not seriously, on purpose, beyond bearing. He was crying, you see . . .'

Chico turned his back to me, looking out of the window.

There was a long pause. The moral problems of being on the receiving end were not so great, I thought. It was easier on the conscience altogether.

At last Chico said, 'He told me, of course. In the end.'

'Yes.'

'I didn't leave a mark on him, you know. Not a scratch . . . He said you were at Seabury racecourse. Well, I knew that was probably right, and that he wasn't trying the same sort of misdirection you had, because you'd told me yourself that you were going there. He said that you were in the weighing room and that the boiler would soon blow up. He said that he hoped it would kill you. He seemed half out of his mind with rage about you. How he should have known better than to believe you, he should have realized that you were as slippery as a snake, he'd been fooled once before . . . He said he'd taken it for granted you were telling the truth when you broke down and changed your story about the negatives being in the office, because you . . . because you were begging for mercy and morphine and God knows what.'

'Yes,' I said. 'I know all about that.'

Chico turned away from the window, his face lightening into a near grin, 'You don't say,' he said.

'He wouldn't have believed it if I'd given in sooner, or less thoroughly. Kraye would have done, but not him. It was very annoying.'

'Annoying,' said Chico. 'I like that word.' He paused, considering. 'At what moment exactly did you think of sending Bolt to me?'

'About half an hour before they caught me,' I admitted. 'Go on. What happened next?'

'There was a ball of string on Radnor's writing desk, so I tied old Fatso up with that in an uncomfortable position. Then there was the dicey problem of who to ring up to get the rescue squads on the way. I mean, the Seabury police might think I was some sort of nut, ringing up at that hour and telling such an odd sort of story. At the best, they might send a bobby or two out to have a look, and the Krayes would easily get away. And I reckoned you'd want them rounded up red-handed, so to speak. I couldn't get hold of Radnor on account of the office phones being plasticated. So, well, I rang Lord Hagbourne.'

'You didn't!'

'Well, yes. He was O.K., he really was. He listened to what I told him about you and the boiler and the Krayes and so on, and then he said, "Right", he'd see that half the Sussex police force turned up at Seabury racecourse as soon as possible.'

'Which they did.'

'Which they did,' agreed Chico. 'To find that my old pal Sid had dealt with the boiler himself, but was otherwise in a fairly ropy state.'

'Thanks,' I said. 'For everything.'

'Be my guest.'

'Will you do me another favour?'

'Yes, what?'

'I was supposed to take someone out to lunch today. She'll be wondering why I didn't turn up. I'd have got one of the nurses to ring her, but I still don't know her telephone number.'

'Are you talking about Miss Zanna Martin? The poor duck with the disaster area of a face?'

'Yes,' I said, surprised.

'Then don't worry. She wasn't expecting you. She knows you're here.'

'How?'

'She turned up at Bolt's office yesterday morning, to deal with the mail apparently, and found a policeman waiting on the doorstep with a search warrant. When he had gone she put two and two together smartly and trailed over to the Cromwell Road to find out what was going on. Radnor had gone down to Seabury with Lord Hagbourne, but I was there poking about in the ruins, and we sort of swapped info. She was a bit upset about you, mate, in a quiet sort of way. Anyhow, she won't be expecting you to take her out to lunch.'

'Did she say anything about having one of our files?'

'Yes. I told her to hang on to it for a day or two. There frankly isn't anywhere in the office to put it.'

'All the same, you go over to where she lives as soon as you get back, and collect it. It's the Brinton file. And take great care of it. The negatives Kraye wanted are inside it.'

Chico stared. 'You're not serious.'

'Why not?'

'But everyone . . . Radnor, Lord Hagbourne, even Kraye and Bolt, and the police . . . everyone has taken it for granted that what you said first was right, that they were in the office and were blown up.'

'It's lucky they weren't,' I said. 'Get some more prints made. We've still got to find out why they were so hellishly important. And don't tell Miss Martin they were what Kraye wanted.'

The door opened and one of the pretty nurses came in.

'I'm afraid you'll have to go now,' she said to Chico. She came close beside the bed and took my pulse. 'Haven't you any sense?' she exclaimed, looking at him angrily. 'A few quiet minutes was what we said. Don't talk too much, and don't let Mr Halley talk at all.'

'You try giving *him* orders,' said Chico cheerfully, 'and see where it gets you.'

'Zanna Martin's address,' I began.

'No,' said the nurse severely. 'No more talking.'

I told Chico the address.

'See what I mean?' he said to the nurse. She looked down at me and laughed. A nice girl behind the starch.

Chico went across the room and opened the door.

'So long, then, Sid. Oh, by the way, I brought this for you to read. I thought you might be interested.'

He pulled a glossy booklet folded lengthwise out of an inner pocket and threw it over on to the bed. It fell just out of my reach, and the nurse picked it up to give it me. Then suddenly she held on to it tight.

'Oh no,' she said. 'You can't give him that!'

'Why not?' said Chico. 'What do you think he is, a baby?'

He went out and shut the door. The nurse clung to the booklet, looking very troubled. I held out my hand for it.

'Come on.'

'I think I ought to ask the doctors . . .'

'In that case,' I said, 'I can guess what it is. Knowing Chico. So be a dear and hand it over. It's quite all right.'

She gave it to me hesitantly, waiting to see my reaction when I caught sight of the bold words on the cover.

'Artificial Limbs. The Modern Development.'

I laughed. 'He's a realist,' I said. 'You wouldn't expect him to bring fairy stories.'

CHAPTER TWENTY

When Radnor came the next day he looked tired, dispirited, and ten years older. The military jauntiness had gone from his bearing, there were deep lines around his eyes and mouth, and his voice was lifeless.

For some moments he stared in obvious distress at the white-wrapped arm which stopped abruptly four inches below the elbow.

'I'm sorry about the office,' I said.

'For God's sake . . .'

'Can it be rebuilt? How bad is it?'

'Sid . . .'

'Are the outside walls still solid, or is the whole place a write-off?'

'I'm too old,' he said, giving in, 'to start again.'

'It's only bricks and mortar that are damaged. You haven't got to start again. The agency is you, not the building. Everyone can work for you just as easily somewhere else.'

He sat down in an arm-chair, rested his head back, and closed his eyes.

'I'm tired,' he said.

'I don't suppose you've had much sleep since it happened.'

'I am seventy-one,' he said flatly.

I was utterly astounded. Until that day I would have put him in the late fifties.

'You can't be.'

'Time passes,' he said. 'Seventy-one.'

'If I hadn't suggested going after Kraye it wouldn't have happened,' I said with remorse. 'I'm so sorry . . . so sorry . . .'

He opened his eyes. 'It wasn't your fault. If it was anyone's it was my own. You wouldn't have let Hagbourne take those photographs to Seabury, if it had been left to you. I know you didn't like it, that I'd given them to him. Letting the photographs go to Seabury was the direct cause of the bombs, and it was my mistake, not yours.'

'You couldn't possibly tell,' I protested.

'I should have known better, after all these years. I think . . . perhaps I may not see so clearly . . . consequences, things like that.' His voice died to a low, miserable murmur. 'Because I gave the photographs to Hagbourne . . . you lost your hand.'

'No,' I said decisively. 'It's ridiculous to start blaming yourself for that. For heaven's sake snap out of it. No one in the agency can afford to have you in this frame of mind. What are Dolly and Jack Copeland and Sammy and Chico and all the others to do if you don't pick up the pieces?'

He didn't answer.

'My hand was useless, anyway,' I said. 'And if I'd been willing to give in to Kraye I needn't have lost it. It had nothing whatever to do with you.'

He stood up.

'You told Kraye a lot of lies,' he said.

'That's right.'

'But you wouldn't lie to me.'

'Naturally not.'

'I don't believe you.'

'Concentrate on it. It'll come in time.'

'You don't show much respect for your elders.'

'Not when they behave like bloody fools,' I agreed dryly.

He blew down his nostrils, smouldering inwardly. But all he said was, 'And you? Will you still work for me?'

'It depends on you. I might kill us all next time.'

'I'll take the risk.'

'All right then. Yes. But we haven't finished this time, yet. Did Chico get the negatives?'

'Yes. He had two sets of prints done this morning. One for him, and he gave me one to bring to you. He said you'd want them, but I didn't think . . .'

'But you did bring them?' I urged.

'Yes, they're outside in my car. Are you sure . . . ?'

'For heaven's sake,' I said in exasperation. 'I can hardly wait.'

By the following day I had acquired several more pillows, a bedside telephone, and a reputation for being a difficult patient.

The agency re-started work that morning, squeezing into Radnor's own small house. Dolly rang to say it was absolute hell, there was only one telephone instead of thirty, the blitz spirit was fortunately in operation, not to worry about a thing, there was a new word going round the office, it was Halley-lujah, and goodbye, someone else's turn now.

Chico rang a little later from a call box.

'Sammy found that driver, Smith,' he said. 'He went to see him in Birmingham yesterday. Now that Kraye's in jug Smith is willing to turn Queen's evidence. He agreed that he did take two hundred and fifty quid, just for getting out of his cab, unclipping the chains when the tanker had gone over, and sitting on the side of the road moaning and putting on an act. Nice easy money.'

'Good,' I said.

'But that's not all. The peach of it is he still has the money, most of it, in a tin box, saving it for a deposit on a house. That's what tempted him, apparently, needing money for a house. Anyway, Kraye paid him the second instalment in tenners, from one of the blocks you photographed in his case. Smith still has one of the actual tenners in the pictures. He agreed to part with that for evidence, but I can't see anyone making him give the rest back, can you?'

'Not exactly!'

'So we've got Kraye nicely tied up on malicious damage.'

'That's terrific,' I said. 'What are they holding him on now?'

'G.B.H. And the others for aiding and abetting.'

'Consecutive sentences, I trust.'

'You'll be lucky.'

I sighed. 'All the same, he still owns twenty-three per cent of Seabury's shares.'

'So he does,' agreed Chico gloomily.

'How bad exactly is the office?' I asked.

'They're surveying it still. The outside walls look all right, it's just a case of making sure. The inside was pretty well gutted.'

'We could have a better lay-out,' I said. 'And a lift.'

'So we could,' he said happily. 'And I'll tell you something else which might interest you.'

'What?'

'The house next door is up for sale.'

I was asleep when Charles came in the afternoon, and he watched me wake up, which was a pity. The first few seconds of consciousness were always the worst: I had the usual hellish time, and when I opened my eyes, there he was.

'Good God, Sid,' he said in alarm. 'Don't they give you anything?'

I nodded, getting a firmer grip on things.

'But with modern drugs, surely . . . I'm going to complain.'

'No.'

'But Sid . . .'

'They do what they can, I promise you. Don't look so upset. It'll get better in a few days. Just now it's a bore, that's all . . . Tell me about Fred.'

Fred had already been at the house when the police guard arrived at Aynsford. Four policemen had gone there, and it took all four to hold him, with Charles going back and helping as well.

'Did he do much damage?' I asked. 'Before the police got there?'

'He was very methodical, and very quick. He had been right through my desk, and all the wardroom. Every envelope, folder and notebook had been ripped apart, and the debris was all in a heap, ready to be destroyed. He'd started on the dining-room when the police arrived. He was very violent. And they found a box of plastic explosive lying on the hall table, and some more out in the van.' He paused. 'What made you think he would come?'

'They knew I took the photographs at Aynsford, but how would they know I got them developed in London? I was afraid they might think I'd had them done locally, and that they'd think you'd know where the negatives were, as it was you who inveigled Kraye down there in the first place.'

He smiled mischievously. 'Will you come to Aynsford for a few days when you get out of here?'

'I've heard that somewhere before,' I said. 'No thanks.'

'No more Krayes,' he promised. 'Just a rest.'

'I'd like to, but there won't be time. The agency is in a dicky state. And I've just been doing to my boss what you did to me at Aynsford.'

'What's that?'

'Kicking him out of depression into action.'

His smile twisted in amusement.

'Do you know how old he is?' I said.

'About seventy, why?'

I was surprised. 'I'd no idea he was that age, until he told me yesterday.'

Charles squinted at the tip of his cigar. He said, 'You always thought I asked him to give you a job, didn't you? And guaranteed your wages.'

I made a face at him, embarrassed.

'You may care to know it wasn't like that at all. I didn't know him personally, only by name. He sought me out one day in the club and asked me if I thought you'd be any good at working with him. I said yes, I thought you would. Given time.'

'I don't believe it.'

He smiled. 'I told him you played a fair game of chess. Also that you had become a jockey simply through circumstances, because you were small and your mother died, and that you could probably succeed at something else just as easily. He said that from what he'd seen of you racing you were the sort of chap he needed. He told me then how old he was. That's all. Nothing else. Just how old he was. But we both understood what he was saying.'

'I nearly threw it away,' I said. 'If it hadn't been for you . . .'

'Oh yes,' he said wryly. 'You have a lot to thank me for. A lot.'

Before he went I asked him to look at the photographs, but he studied them one by one and handed them back shaking his head.

Chief-Inspector Cornish rang up to tell me Fred was not only in the bag but sewn up.

'The bullets match all right. He drew the same gun on the men who arrested him, but one of them fortunately threw a vase at him and knocked it out of his hand before he could shoot.'

'He was a fool to keep that gun after he had shot Andrews.'

'Stupid. Crooks often are, or we'd never catch them. And he didn't mention his little murder to Kraye and the others, so they can't be pinched as accessories to that. Pity. But it's quite clear he kept it quiet. The Sussex force said that Kraye went berserk when he found out. Apparently he mostly regretted not having known about your stomach while he had you in his clutches.'

'Thank God he didn't!' I exclaimed with feeling.

Cornish's chuckle came down the wire. 'Fred was supposed to look for Brinton's letter at your agency himself, but he wanted to go to a football match up North or something, and sent Andrews instead. He said he didn't think there'd be a trap, or anything subtle like that. Just an errand, about on Andrews' level. He said he only lent him the gun for a lark, he didn't mean Andrews to use it, didn't think he'd be so silly. But then Andrews went back to him scared stiff and said he'd shot you, so Fred says he suggested a country ramble in Epping Forest and the gun went off by accident! I ask you, try that on a jury! Fred says he didn't tell Kraye because he was afraid of him.'

'What! Fred afraid?'

'Kraye seems to have made an adverse impression on him.'

'Yes, he's apt to do that,' I said.

I read Chico's booklet from cover to cover. One had to thank the thalidomide children, it appeared, for the speed-up of modern techniques. As soon as my arm had properly healed I could have a versatile gas-powered tool-hand with a swivelling wrist, activated by small pistons and controlled by valves, and operated by my shoulder muscles. The main snag to that, as far as I could gather, was that one always had to carry the small gas cylinders about, strapped on, like a permanent skin diver.

Much more promising, almost fantastic, was the latest invention of British and Russian scientists, the myo-electric arm. This worked entirely by harnessing the tiny electric currents generated in one's own remaining muscles, and the booklet cheerfully said it was easiest to fit on someone whose amputation was recent. The less one had lost of a limb, the better were one's chances of success. That put me straight in the guinea seats.

Finally, said the booklet with a justifiable flourish of trumpets, at St. Thomas's Hospital they had invented a miraculous new myo-electric hand which could do practically everything a real one could except grow nails.

I missed my real hand, there was no denying it. Even in its deformed state it had had its uses, and I suppose that any loss of so integral a part of oneself must prove a radical disturbance. My unconscious mind did its best to reject the facts: I dreamed each night that I was whole, riding races, tying knots, clapping . . . anything which required two hands. I awoke to the frustrating stump.

The doctors agreed to enquire from St Thomas's how soon I could go there.

On Wednesday morning I rang up my accountant and asked when he had a free day. Owing to an unexpected cancellation of plans, he said, he would be free on Friday. I explained where I was and roughly what had happened. He said that he would come to see me, he didn't mind the journey, a breath of sea air would do him good.

As I put the telephone down my door opened and Lord Hagbourne and Mr Fotherton came tentatively through it. I was sitting on the edge of the bed in a dark blue dressing-gown, my feet in slippers, my arm in a cradle inside a sling, chin freshly shaved, hair brushed, and the marks of Kraye's fists fading from my face. My visitors were clearly relieved at these encouraging signs of revival, and relaxed comfortably into the arm-chairs.

'You're getting on well, then, Sid?' said Lord Hagbourne.

'Yes, thank you.'

'Good, good.'

'How did the meeting go?' I asked. 'On Saturday?'

Both of them seemed faintly surprised at the question.

'Well, you did hold it, didn't you?' I said anxiously.

'Why yes,' said Fotherton. 'We did. There was a moderately good gate, thanks to the fine weather.' He was a thin, dry man with a long face moulded into drooping lines of melancholy, and on that morning he kept smoothing three fingers down his cheek as if he were nervous.

Lord Hagbourne said, 'It wasn't only your security men who were drugged. The stable lads all woke up feeling muzzy, and the old man who was supposed to look after the boiler was asleep on the floor in the canteen. Oxon had given them all a glass of beer. Naturally, your men trusted him.'

I sighed. One couldn't blame them too much. I might have drunk with him myself.

'We had the inspector in yesterday to go over the boiler thoroughly,' said Lord Hagbourne. 'It was nearly due for its regular check anyway. They said it was too old to stand much interference with its normal working, and that it was just as well it hadn't been put to the test. Also that they thought that it wouldn't have taken as long as three hours to blow up. Oxon was only guessing.'

'Charming,' I said.

'I sounded out Seabury Council,' said Lord Hagbourne. 'They're putting the racecourse down on their agenda for next month. Apparently a friend of yours, the manager of the Seafront Hotel, has started a petition in the town urging the council to take an interest in the racecourse on the grounds that it gives a seaside town prestige and free advertising is good for trade.'

'That's wonderful,' I said, very pleased.

Fotherton cleared his throat, looked hesitantly at Lord Hagbourne, and then at me.

'It has been discussed . . .' he began. 'It has been decided to ask you if you . . . er . . . would be interested in taking on . . . in becoming Clerk of the Course at Seabury.'

'Me?' I exclaimed, my mouth falling open in astonishment.

'It's getting too much for me, being Clerk of two courses,' he said, admitting it a year too late.

'You saved the place on the brink of the grave,' said Lord Hagbourne with rare decisiveness. 'We all know it's an unusual step to offer a Clerkship to a professional jockey so soon after he's retired, but Seabury executive are unanimous. They want you to finish the job.'

They were doing me an exceptional honour. I thanked them, and hesitated, and asked if I could think it over.

'Of course, think it over,' said Lord Hagbourne. 'But say yes.'

I asked them then to have a look at the box of photographs, which they did. They both scrutinized each print carefully, one by one, but they could suggest nothing at the end.

Zanna Martin came to see me the next afternoon, carrying some enormous, sweet-smelling bronze chrysanthemums. A transformed Zanna Martin, in a smart dark green tweed suit and shoes chosen for looks more than sturdy walking. Her hair had been re-styled so that it was shorter and curved in a bouncy curl on to her cheek. She had even tried a little lipstick and powder, and had tidied her eyebrows into a shapely line. The scars were just as visible, the facial muscles are wasted as ever, but Miss Martin had come to terms with them at last.

'How super you look,' I said truthfully.

She was embarrassed, but very pleased. 'I've got a new job. I had an interview yesterday, and they didn't even seem to notice my face. Or at least they didn't say anything. In a bigger office, this time. A good bit more than I've earned before, too.'

'How splendid,' I congratulated her sincerely.

'I feel new,' she said.

'I too.'

'I'm glad we met.' She smiled, saying it lightly. 'Did you get that file back all right? Your young Mr Barnes came to fetch it.'

'Yes, thank you.'

'Was it important?'

'Why?'

'He seemed very odd when I gave it to him. I thought he was going to tell me something about it. He kept starting to, and then he didn't.'

I would have words with Chico, I thought.

'It was only an ordinary file,' I said. 'Nothing to tell.'

On the off-chance, I got her to look at the photographs. Apart from commenting on the many examples of her own typing, and expressing surprise that anybody should have bothered to photograph such ordinary papers, she had nothing to say.

She rose to go, pulling on her gloves. She still automatically leaned forward slightly, so that the curl swung down over her cheek.

'Good-bye, Mr Halley. And thank you for changing everything for me. I'll never forget how much I owe you.'

'We didn't have that lunch,' I said.

'No.' She smiled, not needing me any more. 'Never mind. Some other time.' She shook hands. 'Good-bye.'

She went serenely out of the door.

'Good-bye, Miss Martin,' I said to the empty room. 'Good-bye, good-bye, good-bye.' I sighed sardonically at myself, and went to sleep.

Noel Wayne came loaded on Friday morning with a bulging brief-case of papers. He had been my accountant ever since I began earning big money at eighteen, and he probably knew more about me than anyone else on earth. Nearly sixty, bald except for a grey fringe over the ears, he was a small, round man with alert black eyes and a slow-moving mills-of-God mind. It was his advice more than my knowledge which had turned my earnings into a modest fortune via the stock markets, and I seldom did anything of any importance financially without consulting him first.

'What's up?' he said, coming straight to the point as soon as he had taken off his overcoat and scarf.

I walked over to the window and looked out. The weather had broken. It was drizzling, and a fine mist lay over the distant sea.

'I've been offered a job,' I said, 'Clerk of the Course at Seabury.'

'No!' he said, as astonished as I had been. 'Are you going to accept?'

'It's tempting,' I said. 'And safe.'

He chuckled behind me. 'Good. So you'll take it.'

'A week ago I definitely decided not to do any more detecting.'

'Ah.'

'So I want to know what you think about me buying a partnership in Radnor's agency.'

He choked.

'I didn't think you even liked the place.'

'That was a month ago. I've changed since then. And I won't be changing back. The agency is what I want.'

'But has Radnor *offered* a partnership?'

'No. I think he might have done eventually, but not since someone let a bomb off in the office. He's hardly likely to ask me to buy a half share of the ruins. And he blames himself for this.' I pointed to the sling.

'With reason?'

'No,' I said rather gloomily. 'I took a risk which didn't come off.'

'Which was?'

'Well, if you need it spelled out, that Kraye would only hit hard enough to hurt, not to damage beyond repair.'

'I see.' He said it calmly, but he looked horrified. 'And do you intend to take similar risks in future?'

'Only if necessary.'

'You always said the agency didn't do much crime work,' he protested.

'It will from now on, if I have anything to do with it. Crooks make too much misery in the world.' I thought of the poor Dunstable Brinton. 'And listen, the house next door is for sale. We could knock the two into one. Radnor's is bursting at the seams. The agency has expanded a lot even in the two years I've been there. There seems more and more demand for his sort of service. Then the head of Bona Fides, that's one of the departments, is a natural to expand as an employment consultant on the managerial level. He has a gift for it. And insurance—Radnor's always neglected that. We don't have an insurance investigation department. I'd like to start one. Suspect insurance claims; you know. There's a lot of work in that.'

'You're sure Radnor will agree, if you suggest a partnership?'

'He may kick me out. I'd risk it though. What do you think?'

'I think you've gone back to how you used to be,' he said thoughtfully. 'Which is good. Nothing but good. But . . . well, tell me what you really think about that.' He nodded at my chopped off arm. 'None of your flippant lies, either. The truth.'

I looked at him and didn't answer.

'It's only a week since it happened,' he said, 'and as you still look the colour of a grubby sheet I suppose it's hardly fair to ask. But I want to know.'

I swallowed. There were some truths which really couldn't be told. I said instead: 'It's gone. Gone, like a lot of other things I used to have. I'll live without it.'

'Live, or exist?'

'Oh live, definitely. Live.' I reached for the booklet Chico had brought, and flicked it at him. 'Look.'

He glanced at the cover and I saw the faint shock in his face. He didn't have Chico's astringent brutality. He looked up and saw me smiling.

'All right,' he said soberly. 'Yes. Invest your money in yourself.'

'In the agency,' I said.

'That's what I mean,' he said. 'In the agency. In yourself.'

He said he'd need to see the agency's books before a definite figure could be reached, but we spent an hour discussing the maximum he thought I should prudently offer Radnor, what return I could hope for in salary and dividends, and what I should best sell to raise the sum once it was agreed.

When we had finished I trotted out once more the infuriating photographs.

'Look them over, will you?' I said. 'I've shown them to everyone else without result. These photographs were the direct cause of the bombs in my flat and the office, and of me losing my hand, and I can't see why. It's driving me ruddy well mad.'

'The police . . .' he suggested.

'The police are only interested in the one photograph of a ten pound note. They looked at the others, said they could see nothing significant, and gave them back to Chico. But Kraye couldn't have been worried about that bank note, it was ten thousand to one we'd come across it again. No, it's something else. Something not obviously criminal, something Kraye was prepared to go to any lengths to obliterate immediately. Look at the time factor . . . Oxon only pinched the photographs just before lunch, down at Seabury. Kraye lived in London. Say Oxon rang him and told him to come and look: Oxon couldn't leave Seabury, it was a race day. Kraye ad to go to Seabury himself. Well, he went down and looked at the photographs and saw . . . what? What? My flat was being searched by five o'clock.'

Noel nodded in agreement. 'Kraye was desperate. Therefore there was something to be desperate about.' He took the photographs and studied them one by one.

Half an hour later he looked up and stared blankly out of the window at the wet grey skies. For several minutes he stayed completely still, as if in a state of suspended animation: it was his way of concentrated thinking. Finally he stirred and sighed. He moved his short neck as if it were stiff, and lifted the top photograph off the pile.

'This must be the one,' he said.

I nearly snatched it out of his hand.

'But it's only the summary of the share transfers,' I said in disappointment. It was the sheet headed S.R., Seabury Racecourse, which listed in summary form all Kraye's purchases of Seabury shares. The only noticeable factor in what had seemed to me merely a useful at-a-glance view of his total holding, was that it had been typed on a different typewriter, and not by Zanna Martin. This hardly seemed enough reason for Kraye's hysteria.

'Look at it carefully,' said Noel. 'The three left hand columns you can disregard, because I agree they are simply a tabulation of the share transfers, and I can't see any discrepancies.'

'There aren't,' I said. 'I checked that.'

'How about the last column, the small one on the right?'

'The banks?'

'The banks.'

'What about them?' I said.

'How many different ones are there?'

I looked down the long list, counting. 'Five. Barclays, Piccadilly. Westminster, Birmingham. British Linen Bank, Glasgow. Lloyds, Doncaster. National Provincial, Liverpool.'

'Five bank accounts, in five different towns. Perfectly respectable. A very sensible arrangement in many ways. He can move round the country and always have easy access to his money. I myself have accounts in three different banks: it avoids muddling my clients' affairs with my own.'

'I know all that. I didn't see any significance in his having several accounts. I still don't.'

'Hm,' said Noel. 'I think it's very likely that he has been evading income tax.'

'Is that all?' I said disgustedly.

Noel looked at me in amusement, pursing his lips. 'You don't understand in the least, I see.'

'Well, for heaven's sake, you wouldn't expect a man like Kraye to pay up every penny he was liable for like a good little citizen.'

'You wouldn't,' agreed Noel, grinning broadly.

'I'll agree he might be worried. After all, they sent Al Capone to jug in the end for tax evasion. But over here, what's the maximum sentence?'

'He'd only get a year, at the most,' he said, 'but . . .'

'And he would have been sure to get off with a fine. Which he won't do now, after attacking me. Even so, for that he'll only get three or four years, I should think, and less for the malicious damage. He'll be out and operating again far too soon. Bolt, I suppose, will be struck off, or whatever it is with stockbrokers.'

'Stop talking,' he said, 'and listen. While it's quite normal to have more than one bank account, an Inspector of Taxes, having agreed your tax liability, may ask you to sign a document stating that you have disclosed to him *all* your bank accounts. If you fail to mention one or two, it constitutes a fraud, and if you are discovered you can then be prosecuted. So, suppose Kraye has signed such a document, omitting one or two or even three of the five accounts? And then he finds a photograph in existence of his most private papers, listing all five accounts as undeniably his?'

'But no one would have noticed,' I protested.

'Quite. Probably not. But to him it must have seemed glaringly dangerous. Guilty people constantly fear their guilt will be visible to others. They're vibratingly sensitive to anything which can give them away. I see quite a lot of it in my job.'

'Even so . . . bombs are pretty drastic.'

'It would entirely depend on the sum involved,' he said primly.

'Huh?'

'The maximum fine for income tax evasion is twice the tax you didn't pay. If for example you amassed ten thousand pounds but declared only two, you could be fined a sum equal to twice the tax on eight thousand pounds. With surtax and so on, you might be left with almost nothing. A nasty set-back.'

'To put it mildly,' I said in awe.

'I wonder,' Noel said thoughtfuly, putting the tips of his fingers together, 'just how much undeclared loot Kraye has got stacked away in his five bank accounts?'

'It must be a lot,' I said, 'for bombs.'

'Quite so.'

There was a long silence. Finally I said, 'One isn't required either legally or morally to report people to the Inland Revenue.'

He shook his head.

'But we could make a note of those five banks, just in case?'

'If you like,' he agreed.

'Then I think I might let Kraye have the negatives and the new sets of prints,' I said. 'Without telling him I know why he wants them.'

Noel looked at me enquiringly, but didn't speak.

I grinned faintly. 'On condition that he makes a free, complete and outright gift to Seabury Racecourse Company of his twenty-three per cent holding.'

A RING OF ROSES

John Blackburn

"A Ring of Roses" is published by Jonathan Cape Ltd.

The Author

John Blackburn, an antiquarian bookseller, is the son of a north-country clergyman. He was educated at Haileybury and Durham University and served as a merchant seaman during the War. His first novel, *A Scent of New-Mown Hay*, was a Dollar Book Club and Literary Guild choice in the United States. He is married. His brother is Thomas Blackburn, the poet.

CHAPTER ONE

In the distance he heard the locomotive whistle and the train clanked slowly across what sounded like an iron bridge and ground to a halt. It was the sixth stop since they had left Berlin.

Billy Fenwick lay very stiffly in his upper berth of the sleeping compartment and he knew that it was the sixth stop because he'd counted every one of them. He also knew that the time was exactly twenty-five minutes to two and that they should be almost half way to the border by now. The wrist watch which he'd strapped to the rail of the bunk was a treasured possession, given to him on his ninth birthday, and every other minute he glanced at its luminous dial. Anything to pass the time, to stop him falling asleep, to keep him from staring at the window blind which, in the blue light cast by the little bulb over the door, looked like a sheet of shiny metal.

But he shouldn't be frightened because he was nine years old now. A great, big boy, as they kept telling him. Mummy had promised him that there were no monsters outside and it was just his imagination. Robin wasn't frightened and he was only five and a half. Billy leaned over the bunk and looked down at his brother, who was curled up fast asleep with his head buried in the pillow which had "Bundesbahn" embroidered across it in red silk. He looked so still that he might have been dead.

No, Robin wasn't frightened, but why should he be? Robin was too young to know why the blinds were pulled down so tightly. He couldn't picture the cold desert outside with its coils of rusting barbed wire and the tallow-faced people who stood and watched the trains. Robin didn't realize that at every stop there was danger, that at this very moment the people were coming toward them and, if the train didn't start again soon, one of them might raise his hand, open the window and begin to climb in. Billy stared across at the blind again. In the dim light he couldn't read the message which was written across it, but he knew what it said all right. "Allied personnel are ordered not to raise the blinds while the train is passing through East German territory." Daddy had told him that was because of something called a security agreement, but he knew better. It was because of the grey people who were waiting in the cold.

And two of them were there now. A dribble of sweat ran down his forehead as he listened. Yes, footsteps were coming across the tracks, somebody was speaking in a low guttural voice, somebody laughed, and there was a tapping noise just below the window. He pulled the blankets tightly up to his chin and tried not to scream, though he knew that at any moment the window would come down and he would see a hand slide in under the blind. The tapping stopped, there was another deep laugh and he could picture fingers fumbling for the window catch. Then the carriage creaked, the wheels started to turn, they were on their way again and he was safe.

Billy pushed down the blankets and grinned with relief. As long as the train was moving it was all right and there was nothing to be frightened of. Perhaps he'd been safe all the time really and it was just his imagination. After all Mummy and Daddy were in the next compartment and they wouldn't let anybody come in. Daddy was a major in the army. He'd reached 'field rank', as it was called, though that sounded silly, because he worked in an office and had nothing to do with any field. Daddy would stop anybody opening the window.

The train was going quite fast now, the carriage lurching and the wheels clicking sharply on the rails and reminding him of a Burl Ives song. 'Beneath this stone I'm forced to lie, the victim of a blue tail fly.' Billy nodded in time to the clicking wheels and he felt happy because he was going home. He'd liked Berlin at the beginning, but they'd been there far too long. One and a half years, almost a lifetime. Just a few more miles and he could forget about the grey people for ever.

But there might be another stop before the train crossed into West Germany. The seventh stop: the one that mattered, because there was something about seven. The seven days of the week, the seven deadly sins, the seven wonders of the world. He'd better make quite sure that the window was properly fastened just in case they stopped again before the border; the seventh stop.

Billy lowered himself over the side of the bunk, stepping very cautiously so as not to wake Robin, and ran his hand over the locking lever. Everything was all right, it was firmly in position and the blind was tightly drawn down. The train really was going fast too. The jerky tune had changed to a merry hum and the glasses were trembling in their holders above the wash-basin. Billy looked at the door. It would be fun to go out into the corridor for a moment, to show that he wasn't frightened, to prove that there was no danger as long as the train was moving. Besides, Hans might be outside and he liked talking to him. Hans was just a sleeping-car attendant now, but during the war he'd been a Luftwaffe pilot and had shot down over twenty Russian planes. Mummy had told him to take Hans's stories with a pinch of salt, but he enjoyed hearing them.

Putting on his watch, and again taking care not to wake Robin, Billy opened the door and stepped out of the compartment. With the lights winking on the glass panels, and the shiny metal floor, and the blue sign reading 'Toiletten' at the far end, the corridor made him think of a space-ship, a rocket speeding through emptiness. There was no sign of Hans, though; probably he'd gone to have a chat with the guard or one of the other attendants. That was a pity, but if he went to the lavatory and took his time, Hans might be back when he came out. Hans had been on the train when they went to Hanover in September and he'd never finished telling him the story about flying supplies through to Stalingrad. He'd like to hear the end of it.

Very slowly Billy walked down the corridor. Though the heating was on the floor felt icy cold under his bare feet and he gripped the hand-rail to steady himself against the lurch of the train. He stopped outside the lavatory and glanced at the blind covering the window of the outside door. It ran down from a roller and was held in position by a steel catch. Just one turn of that catch and the blind would shoot up and he would know what was really outside. Imagination, or the cold desert with its grey people who stood and waited for the trains to stop.

But no, he couldn't do it. The things behind the window were hideous, unspeakable, that was why the blinds were kept down. That was what the notice was for. Besides, he would be in trouble if anybody saw him. Hans might catch him or somebody might come out of one of the compartments. He looked cautiously at the door beside the lavatory. Number 18. That was occupied by Major Wood. Old 'Timber' Wood, as Daddy called him. He didn't like Major Wood, who had a fierce gingery moustache, always seemed to smell of whisky and pipe-smoke and kept twisting Billy's ear and saying, 'And how's the young hopeful, eh?' whenever they met. If the blind came up with a bang he could imagine old 'Timber' stomping out of the compartment in rank ill temper.

That was impossible, though. The train was making far too much noise for anyone to hear the blind go up, and in the buffet car he'd heard 'Timber' telling Daddy that he was assuring himself a good night's rest with a flask of Haig. 'A bedside bottle for the boy,' he'd called it. 'Timber' would be snoring soundly away and nothing would wake him till Hans knocked them up just before Hanover.

Yes, he had to know what was behind that window. Whatever the risk he had to look out. Very cautiously and with a mixture of dread and daring running through his head, Billy released the catch. The blind slid up quite soundlessly, but the glass was coated with rime and dirt on the outside and he could see nothing except a faint glimmer of light that might have been the moon.

He had to see out, though. He'd risked so much already and he must know the truth at last: whether it was just imagination, or if there really was a desert outside—an icy desert with here and there clumps of squat, prickly trees like the cactus plants Miss Murphy kept in the nature classroom, and always the people who stood and watched the trains. Almost as though somebody had taken hold of his hand he reached out for the locking lever and slid down the window. A blast of cold air beat on his face and made him close his eyes for a moment, but when he opened them he almost cried out with relief.

For there was no desert. There was just ordinary country, the same as he knew at home. The window only came half way down, but through it he could just make out the tops of pine trees and a ridge of hills stretching away in the moonlight. No, there was no desert, but the people might still be there. He had to know if they were just part of his imagination too and there was one way to find out. Quite a safe way, because the door opened against the direction of the train and wouldn't blow back. He turned the handle, pushed open the door, and leaned out into the nightmare.

CHAPTER TWO

'DARLING, you must try to relax. You must try to take it easy.' Tom Fenwick struggled to put a little confidence into his voice, though he felt none at all. 'They are bound to find Billy soon and he'll be all right. I can't tell you why, but somehow I just know that he will be all right.'

'You say that he'll be all right.' Mary Fenwick didn't look up at her husband. She just stood staring out of the window and her face was dead white under the make-up and had no expression at all. Tom's hand was on her shoulder, and through the costume he could feel her muscles tensed as though under shock treatment. 'Billy has been missing for four hours. We don't know what has become of him, but he probably fell from a moving train. And all you can do is to stand there and say that you know he's all right.'

'Mrs Fenwick, I'm sure that what the major says is correct.' Lieutenant Sutherland was not quite twenty years old and he felt horribly distressed and embarrassed. 'Please let me take you over to the hotel, Mrs Fenwick. Everything possible is being done to find your boy.' He glanced at his watch and then at Fenwick. 'Colonel Baxter has been waiting for over ten minutes, sir.'

'Yes, of course.' Tom followed his wife's set stare. In the thin winter sunlight the tall white buildings of Hanover looked safe and secure and cheerful: fairy-tale palaces mocking his terror. 'Mary,' he said. 'Please go to the hotel with Mr Sutherland. They'll let you know as soon as there's any news. Please do that for me, darling.' He watched her turn and move slowly away, her feet stumbling slightly on the carpet, and then he crossed to the door at the end of the reception room.

'Ah, there you are, Major.' Colonel Baxter of British Military Intelligence made the poor pretence of a smile as Tom came into the office. Under a brown leathery face which was tanned more by spirits than sun and wind, and the brusque manner of the military man who stood no nonsense from anyone, he concealed a very frightened soul. He was feeling frightened at the moment all right. He owed his position largely to the efforts of an ambitious and well-connected wife and he knew that one false move could hurl him into limbo. This business put him in one hell of a spot. If the boy had really fallen from the train he (Baxter) could expect a protest from the East German authorities at any moment, and only last month he had received a memo from London stating that the best possible relations must be maintained before the coming U.N. conference. If, on the other hand, his personal suspicions of what had happened were true, then . . . no, he wouldn't even consider that for the time being.

But this poor devil really was in a state. He studied Tom's face as he came towards him. 'Haunted' was the only word to describe his expression, and it made him think of a song from the First World War. 'I've seen them, hanging on the old barbed wire.'

'Do come in and sit down.' He motioned to the man who stood by the window. 'You know Herr von Zuler, I think.'

'Yes, we are old acquaintances, aren't we, Major?' Kurt von Zuler, liaison officer between the NATO forces and the Spionage-Abwehrdienst of West Germany dragged his steel foot across the floor and he looked what he was: hard and cold and efficient. He smelt slightly of scent, and the hand that took Tom's was bright with rings. 'And may I first say how sorry I am, Major. How very, very sorry about your son.'

'Thank you.' Tom sat down in front of the desk. The wall behind it was almost covered with photographs of Baxter: Baxter in uniform, Baxter in a bowler hat shaking hands with the Queen Mother, Baxter in tweeds with a shotgun under his arm, Baxter sitting in the front row of a cricket team. At any other time he might have found the man's vanity slightly amusing, but not now. Now he felt that he would never find anything amusing again. 'There's been no more news, I suppose?'

'No, nothing of any significance, I'm afraid, though we're getting our noses to what little scent there is. But do you mind if I recap a little for Herr von Zuler's benefit? His department have promised us the fullest possible co-operation.'

'Of course not.' Tom nodded but he didn't understand at all. Von Zuler worked for the counter-intelligence organization. What possible interest could he have in Billy's disappearance?

'Good. Now, let's see where we are.' Baxter studied the map which was spread out across his desk. 'The train left Charlottenburg station in West Berlin at ten forty-five last night. Shortly after it pulled out you and your family went along to the buffet car and stayed there for about half an hour. Correct?'

'Yes, it must have been about half an hour.' Tom tried to throw his mind back. 'Timber' Wood had been going to the rugger match at Hamburg and they'd had a couple of drinks to wish him luck. Mary and he had drunk gin and tonic and the boys Coca-Cola. 'I seem to remember looking at the clock over the bar and seeing it was about eleven twenty when we left to go back to our compartments.' Yes, that was right. They'd enjoyed those quick drinks very much and the kids had had a sleep during the afternoon and were bright and happy because they were going home. Billy had been tensed up about the journey, of course, but there was nothing new in that. It happened every time. Perhaps the poor little devil had had a kind of premonition that something was going to happen to him. Perhaps he'd known all the time. There'd been that odd, stiff-upper-lip look in his face when they kissed him good night, as though he wanted to say something but was holding it back in front of Robin. If only they'd made him tell them. If only Billy had slept with him and Mary with Robin. If only . . .

'And that's about all we really do know for sure, Herr von Zuler.' Baxter's voice cut into his thoughts. 'Major Fenwick and his family get back to their compartments at approximately eleven twenty. Allow about quarter of an hour to say good night and turn in. Correct, Major?' He watched Tom's nod and made a note on a sheet of paper beside the map.

'Yes, after about eleven thirty-five we know nothing. Nothing at all till the train was well across the border into West Germany. Correct again?'

'Quite correct.' Tom lowered his face from Baxter's stare. It had been well beyond the border when they'd heard the tapping. At first he had thought it was the attendant knocking them up, but he'd looked at his watch and seen it was only five fifteen and there was still an hour to go before Hanover. The train was lurching slightly and he'd felt it was just the door rattling till he saw Mary get out of her bunk to open it. As Robin came into the compartment another train had roared past them and he couldn't hear what he was saying. Then it was quiet again and his words had come rushing out. 'Billy's gone, Mummy. Billy's gone—gone—gone.'

'So your son must have left the train some time between about twelve thirty and five fifteen when your younger boy woke up and found him missing.' Baxter scribbled another note on his pad. 'I say twelve thirty because the buffet car closed at midnight and we should allow at least half an hour for the other passengers to settle down after that. Yes, somebody would have been bound to spot him if he'd come wandering out into the corridor before then. If our other theory is true, they wouldn't have risked trying anything till much later than that.'

'Your other theory, sir?' Tom looked up with a jerk. 'I don't understand. Who wouldn't have risked trying anything?'

'We'll come to that in a moment, Major Fenwick, but please help us to clear up a couple of points first. Will you allow me, Colonel?' Von Zuler leaned forward and pencilled two light crosses on the map.

'We've checked with the railway authorities, and during the times in question the train would have been between the western outskirts of Magdeburg in East Germany and Fallersleben, which is twelve kilometres on our side of the border. While passing through East Germany it made no less than seven signal stops. As you probably know, they often halt those trains deliberately to make things awkward for us, but in this case there might have been another reason.' He got up again, staring out at the Hanover skyline with the sunlight glinting on his ringed hand and his face set in a frown.

'Now, Major,' he said. 'Let's dispose of the obvious solution first. You said that Billy seemed anxious before he went to bed? Did he ever suffer from attacks of sleep-walking?'

'No, not to my knowledge.' Tom shook his head. 'When he was very young he used to have bad night terrors, but they seemed to pass by the time he was six.'

'I see. We can rule that out, then.' Von Zuler frowned at the tall buildings as though somehow they might tell him what he wanted to know. 'Yes, a nine-year-old boy,' he said and it almost sounded as though he were talking to himself. 'An imaginative, rather nervous, but perfectly normal nine-year-old boy who vanishes from a train that is passing through East German territory by reason of an agreement made with Russia just after the war. An agreement which is bitterly resented by the East German government, as you well know. It is quite definite that he did not leave the train on our side of the frontier. We've searched every metre of it.'

'But what about on the East German side? Have they searched between Magdeburg and the border yet?'

'They've promised to do so, but we haven't heard anything yet. They've got a fair distance to cover and I don't suppose they'll over-exert themselves on our behalf. Remember that they've been trying to have those trains stopped for years.'

'Excuse me one moment.' Baxter's pencil rapped sharply on the desk. 'Major Fenwick, this may seem a pointless question to you at the moment, but was your son friendly with the sleeping-car attendant, Hans Loser?'

'He knew him. Billy had often travelled on that train and

sometimes in Loser's carriage.' Tom stared blankly across the desk. His son was lost. He had vanished from a train without a trace. He was probably dead by now or lying horribly maimed beside some railway embankment. But, though Baxter and von Zuler seemed outwardly sympathetic, he had the feeling that to them his death might not be the worst possibility.

'Billy was a very sociable little boy,' he said. 'He chatted to Loser, that was all.'

'Thank you, Major. They were on friendly terms, in fact. Friendly enough for Billy to have come out of the compartment if Loser had knocked him up during the night and perhaps offered to show him something interesting?'

'I suppose so, but I don't see what you're driving at, sir. Loser could have had nothing to do with it. Why, he was genuinely upset when we found the boy was missing.'

'I am sure he seemed upset, Major Fenwick.' Von Zuler came back from the window, lighting a cigarette as he did so. 'Herr Loser is a glib liar, though not a very tenacious one, it appears.' He put on a pair of thick glasses and pulled out a notebook.

'After the police searched the train, Loser made a statement. He said that between three a.m. and three fifteen he had gone to the kitchen car to make himself a cup of coffee, but apart from that he had not left his seat in the corridor the whole night. He also stated that the blinds on all doors and windows were drawn down according to regulations.

'Well, that story wouldn't hold any water at all.' Von Zuler looked slightly embarrassed as he used the colloquial English phrase. 'If Billy had left the train by the compartment window, his brother is bound to have heard him. At some time during the journey he must have gone out into the corridor and, unless it was between three and a quarter-past, Loser was lying.'

'But why? What possible reason could he have had?' In the back of his mind Tom seemed to hear the roar of the train, to see the compartment door open, and Billy come blinking out into the corridor. He could also feel his own nails digging into his wrist.

'Loser says that he merely lied to protect his job. Our police know how to question witnesses and he was persuaded to change his statement after a time.' The German permitted himself a brief smile. 'He now says that as the end compartment of the next coach was unoccupied, he went and lay down in it from one a.m.

to five o'clock. When he came back he found one of the door blinds was up. He closed it, thinking he had failed to secure the catch earlier on, and thought no more about it till your son was found to be missing. He at first supposed that the whole story was some kind of practical joke on the part of the two boys and stuck to his version of having been in the corridor all the time apart from fifteen minutes. When it was clear that Billy really had disappeared he was too frightened to alter it.'

'So Billy did fall out through a door. He woke up in the night and walked along the corridor.' Tom could see it quite clearly now. Billy opening the door to look out, forcing it back against the wind and peering through the gap. Then he had slipped, or the train had braked suddenly and he had pitched head first into the night with the door slamming tight behind him. He could almost hear him screaming.

'He either fell, in which case the East German police will soon notify us that they have found him, or something else may have happened.' Baxter's voice was suddenly very gentle. 'Major Fenwick, by now you must have prepared yourself to hear that your son is dead. Naturally I hope that that is untrue, but if he is alive, there may be something which is almost as unpleasant. I want you to be prepared for that too. Excuse me, though.' He broke off and lifted the ringing telephone at his side.

'Oh, they are on the line at last, corporal. No, don't put the call through here. I'll take it next door. Be with you in a moment, gentlemen.' He got up and walked stiffly out of the room.

'And would you like me to finish what the colonel was about to tell you, Major Fenwick? As it happens it was I who put the idea into his mind.' Von Zuler's eyes were like blue pebbles behind the thick glasses and his cigarette was stuck to his lower lip and bobbed up and down as he spoke.

'I have a suspicious mind, I'm afraid, and when I heard that Loser had lied about his being in the corridor, I began to wonder if he had been lying for a rather more sinister reason than he stated. Our inquiries about him are very incomplete at the moment, but some of the things we have heard are interesting. It appears that Hans Loser has recently been in financial difficulties, and also that he has a mother and a sister living in East Berlin. You see what I'm implying, Major?'

'I think I do.' Tom nodded, but he didn't really see at all. 'You mean that Loser may have been working for some East German organization—that he has something to do with Billy's disappearance?'

'I think he may have done, but as I said, I have a suspicious mind and we can't be sure till we hear what the Vopo have had to say to Colonel Baxter. If my theory is correct, however, I think that what may have happened is this: Loser asked your son to come out of the compartment during one of those signal stops. He then opened the door of the corridor and handed him over to someone who was waiting outside. Kidnapped him, in fact, Herr Major.'

'Then Billy could still be alive.' Hope surged through Tom's head, but at the same instant he frowned at the absurdity of the idea. 'Kidnapped! But what possible reason could there be? Apart from my pay and a heavily mortgaged house in London we haven't a penny piece in the world.'

'No, you haven't much money, but you must not underestimate yourself, Major Fenwick.' Von Zuler grinned and dragged lightly on the cigarette. 'You have something which may be more valuable to them than money. I have looked through your army record and I understand that your memory for technical data is quite remarkable.'

'Yes, I have a good memory, but . . .'

'No, not just a good memory. A wonderful memory. Almost—how do you say—a photographic memory.' The German nodded approvingly; the headmaster complimenting a favoured pupil. 'And added to that, until last week you worked in the signals office in West Berlin which contains one of the new Haley-Moncelli decoding machines, on loan to your army from the British Foreign Office. We know that certain people in Russia would very much like to know the details of those machines and I am wondering—just wondering—if your remarkable memory could provide them with a circuit.'

'Yes I suppose I could.' Even as he spoke a diagram swam before Tom's eyes. 'I think I can remember the details of the circuit, but I still don't think they would have gone to such lengths. I mean what about the publicity this will cause? Whatever one hears, these people aren't monsters. And Billy was just a little boy—only nine—nobody would—' He heard his voice break into a stammer like a cracked gramophone record.

'Yes, only nine, Major. Nine years and three months almost to the day. Poor little boy, but a very important little boy if his father values his safety.' Von Zuler opened a cupboard beside the window and pulled out a bottle and two glasses. 'Ah, I thought Colonel Baxter probably kept something interesting here. We shouldn't really anticipate his hospitality, but in the circumstances . . .' He shrugged his shoulders and limped heavily across to the desk with the glasses in his hands.

'Well, cheers, Major. And let's drink to my theory being wrong —completely wrong. Let's pray that your Billy is just a naughty child who slipped out of a train when it was travelling very slowly and will soon be returned safe and sound to you.' He lifted his glass and knocked back the brandy in a single practised movement as the door opened.

'Sorry. Very sorry to have kept you waiting, gentlemen.' Baxter's normally tight, tanned face looked mottled and puffy and he spoke in jerks as though he had recently been running. He didn't appear to notice that they had helped themselves to his drinks, but flung himself down in his chair and stared at Tom.

'Well, Fenwick,' he said at last. 'I presume that von Zuler has told you his theory and I'm very, very sorry to say that it appears to be correct. The bastards! God, the bloody bastards!' A little tic was beating in his forehead and he raised his hand as though to control it.

'That was East German police headquarters on the telephone. They say that they have searched every foot of the line between Magdeburg and the frontier and there was no trace of your son. The man I talked to, a Colonel Behr, implied that the whole story was a lie; a Western trick to bring discredit on his government.' Baxter paused and blew his nose violently.

'Yes, Major, there are only two possible alternatives. I'm afraid Either your son has been kidnapped or he has completely vanished.'

CHAPTER THREE

'Yes, by all means give me a refill, waiter. Make it a double this time, please.' John Forest, chief correspondent of the Consolidated Press in Western Germany, beamed through the smoke of the cosy little bar. 'And you are sure I can't persuade you to have another, my boy? Quite sure?'

'No, I think I'd better not, thank you, sir.' Lieutenant

Sutherland drew back before his companion's smile. When he had come off duty a couple of hours ago he'd merely intended to have one drink, and by the most conservative reckoning he must have at least five beers and three glasses of schnapps inside him by now. Not that he hadn't needed them, of course, for it had been one hell of a day. He'd been called to the office hours before time, and the chief had been in a foul mood over this business of the Fenwick child. Naturally he, as the most junior commissioned member of the staff, had been delegated to look after the mother, and he still shuddered at the memory as he drained the remaining drop of lager in his glass. 'I've had a pretty tiring day, you see, and I don't want it to go to my head.'

'Yes, it must have been very difficult for you.' As though sensing his thoughts Forest nodded sympathetically. 'Poor woman. Poor, poor woman. I can quite imagine the state she must have been in; broke down in the car and was quite hysterical when you got her to the hotel. Sandhurst must have taught you a lot of useful things but not how to deal with situations of that kind, I imagine.'

'No, sir, I never thought I'd have to handle anything like that.' Sutherland shook his head. Forest really was a decent old boy, he thought. Friendly and sympathetic and understanding; very different from his chief. When he'd told the colonel how Mary Fenwick had screamed and sobbed in the hotel foyer till somebody found a doctor to give her a sedative, Baxter had merely nodded, told him to go and get on with his work and be sure to see he closed the door properly behind him. Yes, Forest was quite a different character, and Sutherland had been delighted and flattered when he'd come over and joined him in the Europa Bar. An important man, too; one of the chief Fleet Street correspondents in Germany. There was the typescript of a long, introspective novel in Sutherland's desk and a word from John Forest might go a good way to getting it published.

'You know, sir,' he said, 'I think that I will have just one more beer, if you don't mind.'

'But of course you will, my boy. And also another glass of schnapps to go with it. Lager beer should be drunk on its own only in very hot weather.' Forest crooked his finger at the waiter and beamed on Sutherland like a wicked uncle. And behind the smile he envied him. He envied Sutherland his youth, and his slim body, and his information. He himself was almost seventy years old, a hell of an age for a foreign correspondent, a hell of an age for any job, if it came to that, and he weighed eighteen stone—most of it sagging puffy flesh which shamed him bitterly each time he took a bath.

But, though he couldn't have Sutherland's body or his nineteen years, he'd have his information all right. He always got the information he wanted; partly because of his bland, friendly manner, and mainly just because he was there. That was the secret of success, the thing that really mattered, the reason the firm would never retire him till he asked them to: just being in the right place at the right moment. He remembered some of the times it had happened: in Berlin when he had seen the smoke from the Reichstag drifting across the city; off the North American coast when he had been on a ship called the *Morro Castle;* at Pearl Harbour when he had looked up from a breakfast table and heard the first wave of Japanese bombers come roaring in. Just being there when he was needed.

'But I understand that they haven't found the Fenwick child yet,' he said, studying Sutherland's face and noting with approval the slightly blurred expression that alcohol was giving it. He knew that the boy was under oath not to mention anything he heard in Baxter's office, and he made his voice sound slightly bored and indifferent. After all, there was no need to hurry: he still had three hours to make the morning editions. Just another drink, just a little more flattery and reassurance and the lieutenant would talk all right.

'No, they haven't found him yet, and between you and me, I don't think they will find him, sir.' Even as he spoke Sutherland knew that he was breaking regulations, but Forest's remark sounded completely innocent and the schnapps made a gentle murmur in his head.

'Really, how very interesting.' Forest knocked back the rest of his beer-chaser. One thing about his swollen body was that it seemed to give him an almost indestructible head for alcohol. Yes, he was on to something good all right. He'd sensed it that morning when his contact at Hanover had telephoned and told him that the military train from Berlin was an hour late. Not that that meant anything, of course. The East Germans were always halting those trains or sending them through on a roundabout route. But when it finally arrived at the station having been searched by the police because a child had disappeared, and the parents had been taken to Intelligence Headquarters, he'd hurried over from Bonn at once. Still not much to go on at that stage, but during the afternoon he learned that Kurt von Zuler had called on Baxter and that the father of the missing boy had worked at the Berlin signals office. Yes, he was on to something interesting, and it was a bit of luck finding Baxter's little office boy in the Europa Bar. He intended to make the most of it.

'But why should you say that they won't find him? Surely if he had fallen from the train in East Germany, the Vopo will recover the body at any moment.'

'They won't, but I can't tell you why I know.' Sutherland shook his head. 'It's all top secret at the moment, you see. All very, very hush hush.' He usually showed great respect for his elders and the omission of 'sir' proved his consumption of schnapps as much as his slurred speech.

'But naturally, my boy, very right and proper of you to keep your own counsel.' Forest nodded approvingly and beckoned to the waiter again. 'Give my friend a refill, please, Herr Ober.'

'Now, about that novel you've just finished, Mr. Sutherland. As it happens I'm rather pally with old Bill Seton of the Wayland Press. He's always on the look-out for young talent: why don't you send it to him?—mentioning my name, of course.

'Ah, there you are, Herr Ober. Yes, I will have just a spot more myself as well. Cheers, my boy. Here's to Seton liking—what was the title again? Yes, of course, "Best out of Five"; quite a catchy one.' He beamed across the table, a great jolly Friar Tuck without a sinister thought in his head.

'But what were you going to say about the Fenwick child? Why won't they find him and what do you think really happened?'

'But I told you. I can't say anything. Why, the colonel would have my guts for garters if I breathed a word.' Sutherland stared at his glass. It appeared to be almost empty again though he could only remember taking one sip since the waiter had topped it up.

'Don't be silly, my boy.' Forest's fin-like hand squeezed his arm reassuringly. 'The story is bound to be made public soon, and you needn't worry about Charlie Baxter. I went to school with his father and have known him for years. In any case, you have my word that he'll never know you've even spoken to me.'

'Well, if you're sure it's all right—that the colonel won't find out.' The murmur in Sutherland's head was a dull roar now and he felt slightly sick. 'If you promise.'

'Of course I promise, Mr Sutherland; anything you say to me is as safe as a confession. Now, just you tell me the full story about that missing child and I'll plan a nice letter to the Wayland Press.' Forest propped his huge head in his hand and nodded. 'That's it, my boy, start right at the beginning.'

It took Sutherland over half an hour to tell what he knew and Forest noted every slurred sentence. When at last he had finished he made an obvious excuse and moved heavily away to the lavatory. The light in the cubicle was over-bright and hurt his eyes, and even through the trousers his enormous weight made the seat feel like an instrument of torture. He pulled out a notebook and struggled to concentrate.

But was it remotely possible, he thought? Would even the M.V.D. have done anything like that? Could Sutherland's story be true, or had he got all his facts mixed up and alcohol given them pith?

And even if it were true, would they dare to print it at this stage? He stared at the notebook and shrugged his shoulders. That was the editor's responsibility, not his. His job was merely to tell the story and put it in the most lurid terms he could think of. Yes, a kidnapped child. A child whose father had been in charge of the signals office in West Berlin. That was the kind of angle they needed. A little, helpless child snatched from the train. He hunted for a catch-phrase to start the column. From the Bible perhaps. 'Better that a millstone . . .' No, far too long and flamboyant. Something short was what was wanted here. Something to make people sit up with a jerk as they opened the paper. Yes, that might do very nicely. He pulled out his pencil and began. 'A war on children . . .'

'Where are they holding him now? How much did they pay you? At which stop was the boy taken from the train? What is the name of the person who paid you, Loser?' The German intelligence sergeant had been shouting the questions for over three hours and he felt almost at the end of his tether. A child, he thought. God, a poor little child and this swine sold him. 'Come on, Loser. Just who paid you?'

'Nobody paid me anything. I had nothing to do with the boy's disappearance. You've got to believe me, Sergeant. For the love of God try to believe me.' Hans Loser swayed against the strap which held him to the chair and without it he would have crumpled to the floor. He wanted the light to stop hurting his eyes, he wanted a drink of water, he wanted a smoke, he wanted the questions to stop, but above all he wanted the bird-like thing in his chest to be still for just a moment. Yes, it was just like a bird. A trapped and terrified bird fluttering madly beside his heart, its wings beating against the cage of his ribs in its efforts to be free and now and again digging its beak into his flesh. He couldn't really blame the bird for wanting to be free, but if only it would stop for just a moment.

'I did lie at the beginning, Sergeant. I was frightened, you see, and I didn't tell them about going into the compartment. I didn't want to risk losing my job. Surely you can understand that. I have a sick wife and . . .'

'Yes, you have a sick wife. You need money, so you sell a child to pay your debts.' Sergeant Schmidt felt anger rising like a pressure gauge. If only I was on the other side, he thought. If only I worked for a force which had no sentimental conventions about human rights, there would be no difficulty in getting this swine to talk. One slow, accurate injection of—what was it—sodium pentothal would bring the truth out of him. Or better still—Schmidt had three children of his own and almost against his will his biceps flexed and knotted. 'Come on, Loser, tell me the truth. Who was it who first suggested the kidnapping to you?'

'There was nobody, nobody at all. How many times do I have to tell you that?' Loser's words were almost automatic as the sergeant stepped round from the desk and walked towards him, his huge body screening the light from his eyes. All he could really think about was lying down on a soft bed and waiting for the thing in his chest to find peace.

'How many times do I have to say that I know nothing? God, how many times?' With hardly any interest he watched the sergeant raise his arm and saw the hand swing down like a flail towards him.

'Stop it.' Von Zuler stood in the doorway and his face was crinkled with disgust. 'You were told to make this man talk, but not by those methods.'

'I'm sorry, sir.' Schmidt turned and looked at him. His voice was slightly slurred and his eyes looked glazed in the harsh lighting. 'I don't know what came over me, but I've been with him for over three hours, and before that Braun and Lang tried. I suppose I lost my temper, but you said we must get him to talk—that he was the one lead we'd got. Questions didn't seem any good, and when I thought about that poor kid . . .' He broke off and stared sheepishly at his hand.

'But perhaps you didn't ask your questions in the right way, Schmidt. In any case nobody ordered you to beat him up.' Von Zuler walked slowly towards the man in the chair. Loser's body was slumped far forward, hanging against the strap.

'Hullo, Hans,' he said and his voice was very gentle. 'My name is Kurt von Zuler and I have come to help you. As long as I remain in this room nobody will raise a finger against you, but you must help me in return. Now, just tell me who organized the kidnapping of the little English boy.' He stared down at Loser and then tilted his face into the light. For perhaps five seconds he studied it and then he turned and looked up at Schmidt.

'Well, Sergeant,' he said, 'you were quite right about one thing. This man was the one lead we had; the one person who might have told us what really happened on that train. It was essential that he should be made to tell us what he knew.' He drew back his hand, the rings sparkling in the light.

'But Loser won't tell us anything at all now, Sergeant. He won't say a word, and would you like to know why? Would you really like to know why?' His voice rose to a shout and his hand slashed out across the man's face. 'Loser won't talk, because you've just killed him.'

CHAPTER FOUR

Gregor Petrov, Chief of Department Nine of M.V.D., that section of the Soviet Intelligence Organization which dealt with Russia's satellite countries in Europe, was looking forward to his breakfast. For three years after the war he had been attached to the London embassy, and English food had become an essential part of his life. He beamed approvingly at the huge plate of bacon, eggs, mushrooms, two sausages and three—no, better still, four kidneys that his wife laid in front of him.

Yes, he'd been a clever chap when he married Shura, he thought. Not the most beautiful or intelligent of women perhaps, but a very good cook indeed. Though his position entitled him to a couple of servants she would never have allowed another person to prepare his breakfast. The bacon was just the crisp brown texture which he loved and the sausages were pink and bursting, as though inviting the knife. He patted his wife's backside with deep affection as she moved to her own place at the table, and tucked a napkin into his collar in anticipation of the feast.

The first day of November. He noted the date on the copy of *Pravda* neatly folded beside his coffee cup and glanced through the window. Another lovely morning and the Kremlin really looked beautiful at this time of year with the domes shimmering against the clear sky and the walls silvered by frost. Yes, he was very lucky. Just two more months to retirement; he was counting the hours to that day. Already a small villa in the Crimea had been reserved for him and soon he would spend his time lying on a beach or occasionally addressing some minor political meeting and presenting prizes to schoolchildren. The Minister had even hinted that there might be an official recognition of his services too. Not an Order of Lenin, of course. He could hardly expect anything of that sort, but some collective farm or small factory might be called after him. Shura would like that very much but the important things were still the long idle years of retirement with little to do except potter in the sun and contemplate secure old age and a long, devoted career.

Yes, the future really was bright. Petrov lifted his fork and prepared for pleasure. What should he start with first? A sliver of bacon? A piece of sausage? No, a kidney. His knife slid through the dark, leathery-looking crust to show pale blood inside. Shura knew how to cook them just as he wanted. He raised his fork to his mouth, savouring the faint, scented odour of urine and almost closed his eyes in anticipation. The kidney was within an inch of its destination when the door burst noisily open.

'My dear Tania, how many times must I tell you never to open my door without knocking?' Petrov scowled at his secretary and waved the speared kidney in admonition, but he didn't really feel annoyed. Tania Valina was too appealing to produce anger. At the moment her face was set in a frown of extreme self-importance and urgency, and she seemed slightly out of breath. Unlike Petrov, who regarded himself as a mere civil servant, she revelled in the cloak-and-dagger atmosphere of her job. Her face was thin and very young and with her well-developed body Petrov sometimes felt she was like two people sharing the same house: a pale Madonna upstairs and plump Mother Russia filling the ground floor and basement.

'And what is the idea of bursting in at this time of the morning?'

Still brandishing the kidney he consulted his watch. 'Why, it's barely eight fifteen and I'm not due at the office before nine. Like good Party members we should stick to the terms of our agreement.'

'Yes, of course, Mr Petrov, but I thought you should see this.' The girl held out a sheet of shiny grey paper. 'It's a photostat of the front page of the *London Morning Echo*. The Embassy just wired it through to us.'

'Oh very well, if I must, I must.' Petrov popped the kidney into his mouth and reached out. For a moment he glanced idly at the photostat and then his eyes bulged, his face went bright scarlet and he choked. He very nearly choked to death with the scarlet turning to dark purple and his breath gasping out like a steam engine under full pressure. When he finally managed to free himself of the kidney and swig back a cup of coffee, there were tears in his eyes and his forehead was damp with sweat.

'Gregor, I really must insist that you do not work during meals.' Shura frowned at him across the table. 'Your digestion is bad enough as it is. And, as for you Comrade Valina, you should be ashamed of yourself. You know perfectly well that my husband—'

'Please, please, my dear. Let me think for a moment.' Petrov put on his glasses and studied the paper. 'The bastards,' he said. 'Oh, the stupid, blundering bastards!' He pushed back his chair and stood up, looking sadly down at his plate as he did so. 'Excuse me, Shura. I'm afraid I won't have any time for breakfast this morning.' He turned and walked quickly out of the room with Tania behind him.

'Brr, it's freezing in here. Why can't they get the central heating fixed!' He bent down and switched on the electric fire of his study, seeing himself in the reflector and wincing slightly. Petrov's mother had once said that he had nice eyes and Shura told him he had an attractive smile, but he knew that his face looked as though it had been roughly modelled out of plasticine by a very untalented child.

'Now, get through to Berlin, at once, my dear. Yes, Vopo headquarters, and I want to speak to Colonel Behr. If he's not at the office have them put you through to his private number.' He sat down behind a desk which was almost covered by telephones and stared at the photostat again. The editor of the *Echo* had really gone to town on Forest's story. The headlines 'War on Children' were almost two inches deep and the sub-heading read 'British

Child Snatched From Train'. Beside the columns was an extremely savage cartoon of a Russian soldier carrying off a screaming baby.

'Yes, the fools, the stupid brainless fools.' The bronchitis from which he suffered badly gave his voice a harsh, sneering quality that he didn't intend, for if ever a man could be described as having a bark worse than his bite he was Gregor Petrov. 'What sort of publicity will this get us? What can the Minister say at the conference with this hanging over him? And all for an electronic decoder which will soon be obsolete anyway.' He shook his head in bewilderment as a telephone rang in front of him.

'Gregor Petrov speaking. Yes, of course I'll hold on.' He glanced through the window as he waited. A few minutes ago it had been a lovely morning, but now the sky looked grey and heavy with the promise of more snow.

'Ah, Minister. Yes, I have just seen the English paper and—' He broke off before the voice on the line. The Minister was almost screaming and his words were punctuated by dull thuds as though he were beating on his desk.

'No, Minister,' he said, when at last there was a break in the tirade. 'As I told you, I have seen a copy of the newspaper and, even if the story is true, no M.V.D. department had anything to do with the kidnapping.

'Yes, I quite realize that we cannot afford that kind of publicity before the U.N. conference, but I can only repeat that we had nothing to do with it.

'No, Minister, I'm not trying to deny that the policy of the German police is my responsibility, but I really can't be blamed for an act of pure insubordination. I have a line booked through to Berlin now and the matter will be given top priority. What's that you say?' As he listened the picture of a small white villa shone before Petrov's eyes and faded. Two months to go, but it could be two thousand years.

'Very well,' he said. 'At least I am grateful that you are so frank, Minister. Unless the child is returned in good health within the next twenty-four hours, I will take the full blame.' He put down the instrument and leaned back in his chair breathing deeply. He desperately wanted to close his eyes for a moment and try to imagine that the whole business was a bad dream, but already Tania was holding out another telephone. 'Berlin,' she said. 'Colonel Behr.'

'Thank you, my dear.' The instrument felt like a lead weight in his hand. 'That you, Gustav? Now, tell me quickly. That child which was taken from the British train: has he been injured in any way?

'What's that?' He grunted as though somebody had just punched him in the stomach. 'You're sure? Neither you nor your department had anything to do with it? You're quite sure about that, Gustav? Could some hot-heads have kidnapped him without central authority, do you suppose? You've checked on that too, have you? But what about the train attendant, Loser? They say that he was on your pay roll.' Petrov stared at the photostat as he listened.

Behr claimed that his department had never heard of Loser and that the railway line had been thoroughly searched and no trace of the child's body found. In his opinion the whole story was a propaganda stunt; a lie put out by the English. He started to give their possible reasons for this, but Petrov cut him short.

'Now listen to me, Gustav. In this case I do not believe that the English are lying and I am quite sure that the child is somewhere in East Germany; probably alive if the railway line was searched, as you say. I also think that he may have been kidnapped or, at any rate, that somebody is hiding him; a nine-year-old boy wandering about the countryside in pyjamas would hardly go unreported for long. But, wherever he is, I want that boy found, Gustav, and I'm holding you responsible for finding him. Yes, we've been friends for a long time, but if this Billy Fenwick doesn't turn up in the very near future I shall personally break you.' He replaced the telephone and looked across at Tania.

'That will set them to work,' he said, 'but I suppose we should go and look into things ourselves. Yes, book a couple of seats on the afternoon plane to Berlin.' He stood up and lit a cigarette, feeling slightly better for his threat to Behr, though he knew it was quite meaningless. If Billy Fenwick wasn't found quickly, it was he who would be broken.

'But just who is holding the boy, and where is he?' He muttered aloud to himself as he paced backwards and forwards across the room. The M.V.D. had nothing to do with it and neither had the East German police or intelligence organizations. He was also pretty certain that the English would not have made up the story for any propaganda purpose.

So what had happened and where was he? Petrov paused by the window. Heavy snow clouds were drifting in from the east and, though the room was warm, he had a premonition of bitter cold spreading across the world. 'Where,' he said, pulling his jacket a little more tightly around him, 'where, where, where?'

CHAPTER FIVE

THE important thing was not to look at the telephone or even to think about it. What she had to do was to try and keep calm, to imagine that Billy was staying with friends, as they'd told Robin, to pretend that everything was all right and smile as though nothing had happened.

Mary Fenwick watched Robin playing on the sitting-room carpet and she fought against the nightmare. He had emptied his toy chest and the contents were spread out in a jumble in front of him; toy soldiers, farmyard animals, a German doll with flaming red hair that he called 'Coppertop', a wooden train. Usually she only allowed him to take a few things out at a time, but now she had to let him do anything he liked. Anything to stop him asking questions, to stop him wondering when Billy was coming home, to stop him thinking about Billy.

It was such a nice room, too: the only room in the house that she'd managed to furnish properly so far. The house itself was a needless luxury, of course. The mortgage payments were far more than they could really afford and there was no reason for them to have a permanent home when they could be moved to the ends of the earth if the army said so. Still, they'd always wanted a place of their own and, when they heard that Tom would be based in London for at least two years, it had been heaven to have a home to come back to. Now she hated every inch of it.

And what almost made things worse was the way everybody had been so kind when they were told to leave Germany. Colonel Baxter had kept patting her arm and telling her to be 'a brave little lady,' and von Zuler had been clearly embarrassed as he broke the news.

'Mrs Fenwick,' he had said. 'I know that you will want to stay in Hanover to be as near as possible to the place where your son disappeared, but, believe me, it is better that you go back to England.' He had put a cigarette into his mouth as he spoke, not lighting it, but fiddling with the matches as though to avoid looking at her.

'If your son really has been kidnapped, and that seems probable now, the people responsible will contact your husband very soon. Because of certain international complications, it is not desirable that they do so in Germany, and I have been asked to put you on the next plane for London.'

Yes, everybody had been kind. The Lufthansa officials had treated them like royalty, and at London Airport there had been no customs formalities and a police car had driven them to Richmond. Now she was back in her own home, safe and secure, with thin winter sunlight glinting through the windows, a fire burning in the grate and her younger son playing happily in front of her.

'The train's crashed, Mummy.' Robin looked up. 'It was going too fast and came off the rails.' He had pushed it against a table leg and the locomotive and carriages lay in a piled heap.

'Yes, poor train.' Mary fought back the lump in her throat and tried to make her voice sound normal and cheerful. 'Put the train away for a rest, Robin, and play with the soldiers now.' Her eyes flickered towards the telephone and then moved quickly away as though the very sight of it might blind her. 'Let it ring,' she prayed. 'Oh, please God, let it ring soon.'

'The telephone will ring, Mrs Fenwick, and when it does, you will both have to be very brave indeed.' The man had been waiting at the house when they got there. An old, stout man with a heavy, aristocratic face, a grey moustache and a thick overcoat which he kept buttoned up though the room was warm.

'I am General Charles Kirk,' he had told them, 'and I represent the Foreign Office Intelligence Service. This isn't really our affair, of course, but as the decoder is F.O. property on loan to the army the Minister felt I should keep an eye on things.' As Mary watched Kirk's mild expression she had felt a sudden glow of hope. On the surface he looked ineffectual, almost foolish, but something told her that he was the man at the top, the man who would find Billy if it were humanly possible.

'Now, let's just run through the facts again, shall we? Looking at the brighter side first.' Kirk had lowered himself into a chair and Mary had noticed that his left hand was a mass of scar tissue and lacked three fingers.

'The East German authorities have told us that the railway line has been thoroughly searched and no trace of your son was found. That makes it pretty certain that he is alive, and highly likely that somebody is hiding him.

'But do you mind if I smoke, my dear?' He had bowed gratefully at Mary's nod and pulled out a very large cigar.

'Now, the only motive for kidnapping Billy would be to force your husband to hand over the details of that decoder. If the kidnappers are the M.V.D. or the East German Secret Police, I think you have every chance of recovering him in the near future. My opinion is that somebody was told to get the circuit at all costs and took his orders too literally. If that's so, we may not have much to worry about. With a U.N. meeting due to open next month, the Soviet government won't want any adverse publicity, and certain pressures are being brought to bear upon them already. The Americans, for instance, have promised to hold up their wheat shipments to Russia till Billy is returned to you, and very soon all U.K. ports will be closed to their ships. Yes, I imagine that by now Boris Birileff, their Foreign Minister, will have had a few quiet words with the M.V.D. chiefs and somebody will be wishing he had never been born.'

'But you said, if the kidnappers are the M.V.D. or the East German police, sir.' Tom leaned forward. 'Surely they must be. I mean, after all, who else could want to get hold of Billy?'

'Plenty of people, I'm afraid, Major.' Kirk broke off, lighting his cigar and staring up at the grey smoke drifting to the ceiling. 'International spy rings working for money rather than idealism exist behind the Iron Curtain as well as in the West, and it is quite possible that one of these has your son. That decoder is a very valuable piece of equipment, as you know, Major, and your remarkable memory makes you an obvious target for blackmail. And now I want to ask you a question. Think very carefully before you answer it.' His eyes were very thoughtful as he studied Tom's face and his torn hand drummed against the arm of the chair.

'If the persons who are holding Billy were to ring you up at this moment and ask for the details of the decoder, would you give them to them?'

'I'm afraid I don't have to think about the answer, sir.' There was a dark flush on Tom's face. 'In return for Billy's life I would tell them everything I knew.'

'Yes, I was hoping that you would say that, Major.' Kirk smiled approvingly. 'Any normal parent would do so of course, but very few would be so frank with me. As long as you are frank we have a chance, I think.' Once again he drew on his cigar and stared up at the smoke.

'So, you are not only prepared to betray your country, but would kill your child as well, eh?' He waved aside Tom's protest and nodded. 'Yes, you would kill him all right, my boy. Once these people got the circuit of the decoder they wouldn't take any chance of Billy talking. He would be dead and buried the moment they checked that your information was correct.'

'Then what can we do? For God's sake, General, is there nothing we can do?' Mary could feel tears running down her face but she hadn't got the strength to lift her hand and wipe them away.

'No, my dear, I'm afraid there is very little that we can do. There is, however, a great deal that the Russians can do; if they can be persuaded to help us.' Kirk pulled out a rolled newspaper from his pocket.

'As I said before, a great deal of pressure has already been put upon the Soviet government: the stopping of the American wheat supplies and the embargo on their ships entering our ports. There are also certain unofficial pressures which they won't like at all. Have you seen the midday edition yet?' He held out the newspaper showing headlines that read 'Paris Riots—Soviet Embassy Stoned'. The editor's comments on the Russian denial of the kidnapping were mild and reasonable, but slashed across the foot of the page in scarlet letters were the words 'Prove It'.

'No, Comrade Bírileff won't want to go before the United Nations with that kind of thing hanging over his head and, if we can keep the pressure up a little longer, I think that every Soviet agent and East German policeman will be looking for your son.' Again Kirk reached in his pocket and produced a long envelope.

'We have to give them time, though. Time to decide to help us, which will go very much against the grain, and time to get to work. You will have to supply that time, Major.'

He tore open the envelope and drew out a sheet of foolscap covered with figures and symbols.

'Now, unless my experience is worthless, I am sure that the people who are holding Billy will contact you before another day is past and demand the details of the decoder in return for his life. This is what you will give them.' He held out the paper. 'It is a slightly altered version of the first stage of the circuit, but without the other three stages nobody could know it is valueless.

Before handing over the other stages, you will demand proof that Billy is well; a letter in his handwriting and a photograph. That will get us a little of the time we need.'

'But that's all, General? That's all we can do?'

'Yes, I'm afraid that that's all that can be done at the moment.' Kirk smiled at Mary as he stood up. 'I can't promise anything, but I think it will work. As you know, your telephone has been disconnected for all except foreign calls, and you will just have to wait for it to ring.' He tightened his coat and moved to the door. 'Goodbye for the present and try not to worry. I am quite sure that it will ring very soon.'

'Mummy, Mummy, when is Billy coming home?' Robin's voice broke into Mary's thoughts and she looked up with a jerk. 'He's been away so long now, Mummy.'

'Yes, darling, it has been a long time, but he'll be coming back soon.' Again she struggled to hold back emotion, but this time it was no good. She just couldn't keep it up any longer.

'Oh darling, come here,' she said. 'Come to me, my little boy.' She pulled Robin to her, feeling his hair against her cheek and hearing nothing except her own sobs. For almost a minute she held him like that and then very gently pushed him away from her and stared across the room. Already Tom had got up from the sofa where he had been lying silent and motionless and was walking towards the little table by the window. On it, harsh and strident and threatening, like the opening bars of some very macabre modern symphony, the telephone had begun to ring.

At the top of a tall office building in Berlin, Major 'Timber' Wood paced the floor of his room like a huge caged animal. It was Sunday afternoon and, apart from a janitor in the basement, he was quite alone in the building and from time to time cursed angrily to himself to relieve his feelings, which were a mixture of compassion, self-pity and sheer murderous rage. At the moment rage was very much in the forefront.

'You bastards,' he said to the filing cabinets at the side of his desk. 'You bloody, unprintable bastards.' He turned and aimed a kick at the waste-paper basket and stumped back to his chair.

'A kid,' he thought bitterly. 'A poor, innocent, little kid.' They'd pay for it all right. If the government had one ounce of guts between them, the blasted Russians would be paying for it now. 'Timber' was too young to have taken part in the Korean War and had never heard a shot fired in anger in his life. A number of highly trained experts had attempted to show him the probable nature of any future world conflict, but their efforts had fallen on very stony ground. He still thought in terms of past glories; pennon-bearing tanks lumbering across the desert and massed infantry waiting to charge. 'Over the top, Sergeant. Give them a taste of the bayonet, lads.' 'Timber's' present command consisted of a pay corps corporal and three German clerks, but at the slightest nod from High Command he would have cheerfully hurled them at the Berlin wall.

Compassion. Yes, he felt a lot of that. Tom and Mary Fenwick were old friends and he'd been fond of Billy too. A funny little blighter, a bit shy and withdrawn at times, but with a most appealing smile. Strange—no, terrible to think that it was just the other day that he'd squeezed his ear and wished him good night on that damned train.

And where the hell was he now, and who had him? No, 'Timber' didn't even want to think about that, remembering lurid boyhood reading of blackmailers posting their victim's ears with the demands for ransom. Once again a picture of massed British infantry charging the Russian hordes flickered through his mind.

But self-pity was there too, for he had been on the train bound for the greatest honour of his life. The New Zealand rugby team had been touring Germany and he had been selected to play for a Combined Services fifteen against them. The moment the kidnapping story broke, all Berlin personnel had been ordered back to their posts and here he was behind his desk with the match played and lost without him.

Not that there was any reason for him to be at the office, of course. Sunday afternoons usually found him in the Marlborough Club, but he didn't fancy the place any more. It was full of reporters who kept asking him for his views on the kidnapping or how well he had known the Fenwicks. He'd almost taken a swipe at one of them last night.

No, work was the only thing that could help him take his mind off Billy, and he bent over the files on the desk. Colonel Mackenzie's account was overdrawn to the tune of a hundred and ninety-two pounds three and eightpence at the close of yesterday's business and Lieutenant Smith's three pounds and a penny. He'd have to be very tactful with the colonel, but one-pip lieutenants were quite a different matter. It would do Smith a power of good to be told exactly where he got off. He slipped a sheet of paper into the typewriter and then frowned as once again he heard the noise in the outer office.

Damn Herr Schlott! He'd promised to have the catch of that door fixed days ago and there it was, rattling as though in a full gale. Probably Schlott had forgotten it on purpose to annoy him. The man had been sullen, almost rude at times since he'd torn a strip off him for being late last month. He'd have something to say to Herr Schlott in the morning.

Rattle, rattle, rattle. No, he couldn't stand much more of that. 'Timber' pushed back his chair and stumped out to the reception office. With the lights off and the sky outside dark with snow clouds, the covered typewriters and filing cabinets looked slightly sinister and threatening objects in the gloom. The door was fastened, though. He had to give Schlott his due for that, but it was rattling all right—banging rather, as though somebody or something was beating against it. That was quite impossible, of course. Walther, the watchman, was the only other person in the building, and he'd have rung the bell if he wanted to speak to him.

Someone was there, though, or something. He could hear the sound of quick breathing through the woodwork and the rattle was more like a scratch at times, as though an animal were trying to get in.

'Timber' had few nerves in his big body, but he felt a slight twinge of trepidation as he slid back the catch and pulled open the door. It turned at once to pain and astonishment as a small figure who appeared to be dressed in rags hurled itself into his arms, treading hard on his toes as it did so.

'You,' was all he could say for a moment, staring down at the tear-stained face that was looking up at him through the dim light. 'My God, it really is you.'

'Yes, yes, it's me. And please, please take me home, Uncle "Timber",' said Billy Fenwick.

CHAPTER SIX

'DARLING, Billy's home, that's the only important thing. We've got our son back.' Tom Fenwick leaned forward and kissed his wife. 'He's safe and well and nothing else matters.'

'Yes, I suppose so. I suppose he is well, but why doesn't he tell us exactly what happened and where he's been?' Mary glanced over Tom's shoulder towards the door. Billy had been asleep for hours. He'd dropped off almost as soon as she tucked him into bed. She'd looked in at him at least six times and Tom was right: there was nothing to worry about, nothing to be frightened of any more, and she had to control herself and stop tiptoeing upstairs and peering in at him. All the same . . . 'We're his parents, darling,' she said. 'It's our right to know what happened to him.'

'And Kirk has told us that it's far better that we don't know—that Billy tells us nothing.' Tom leaned back on the sofa and lit a cigarette. The events of the day were still like a vague dream to him. The phone ringing, the operator announcing a call from Berlin, his hand reaching for the false circuit Kirk had given him and to his astonishment 'Timber' Wood's voice on the end of the line saying, 'Hold on, old boy. I've got somebody who wants to speak to you.' Then the room had seemed to tilt and there had been a great roaring in his head as he had heard Billy's voice. 'Daddy, Daddy, I'm with Uncle "Timber". Please come and take me home, Daddy.'

After that everything had happened very quickly and there had been more calls. From the duty officer at Tempelhof promising that transport for Billy would be laid on as soon as possible, from Colonel Baxter, finally from B.E.A. in London saying that the plane was on its way.

Kirk himself had taken them to the airport, uniformed police holding back the crowds who had gathered in the little suburban road and the newspaper cameramen who were trying to break through the cordon and get a shot at them. Though Kirk's car was provided with a motor-cycle escort it had been driven slowly and sedately along Western Avenue, and his cigar and an enormous heater had made the atmosphere barely supportable.

'Well, my dear,' he had said to Mary, 'that's it. All's well that ends well, eh? Your Billy is coming home, but there's no credit due to ourselves or the Russkis. There was no kidnapping either. He fell among friends, you see, and it's rather a touching little story.

'As far as we can make out—the boy's account is very incomplete and I'll explain why in a moment—this is what happened.' As he spoke Kirk had stared sadly out at the drab wilderness of the western suburbs: mean houses and small factories, and a thin layer of snow already turning to slush.

'It seems that Billy was unable to sleep on the train and at half past two—he is very definite about the time—he got out of bed and went into the corridor. There he opened a door.

'Yes, my dear, I know it was a very strange and disobedient thing to do, but he said that he had to see outside. He told our chaps in Berlin that he thought there were some kind of ghostly people standing beside the railway line and he had to prove he wasn't afraid of them. Quite a normal childish fantasy in the circumstances, I imagine.

'At any rate, he opened that door and leaned out. As he did so, the train braked violently and threw him forward on to the step. He managed to hang on there for some time—he has no idea how long, but finally his grip gave way and he dropped off.'

'And he wasn't injured, General? You are quite sure he wasn't injured?'

'No, apart from a slight concussion, he wasn't hurt at all and he is a very lucky boy indeed. The train must have been travelling slowly when he finally fell from it and he landed in a snow-drift, though he caught his head on something and was knocked out for a while. When he came round there was a woman bending over him.

'Billy was terrified at first, of course, but the woman was obviously friendly and, when he told her what had happened, she talked to him in English and took him to a house where he was given food and put to bed.' Kirk knocked an inch of ash from his cigar.

'And that's all that Billy can, or more probably will, tell us. From the time he reached that house, to when he found himself outside a West Berlin underground station near Major Wood's office, he says that he can remember nothing.'

'You say, "more probably will tell us," sir. Why should he lie or hide anything?' Tom glanced through the window. They were almost at the airport now, with signal gantries glowing against the evening sky.

'I've no idea, my boy, and our Berlin people won't venture an opinion as to whether he is lying or really has lost part of his memory.' Kirk pulled out a gleaming half-hunter watch. 'In a few minutes you can ask him yourselves, but I don't advise it. Children hate breaking promises, and I think your son made a very solemn promise indeed.' He replaced his watch and leaned back against the cushions.

'Both of you have lived in Berlin and you must realize what things are like in East Germany since they put up the wall. Before then, there was at least a sporting chance of getting out, if you were prepared to give up all your roots and possessions, of course. Now, there is no hope at all, except for the few; the very, very few, Mrs Fenwick.' Kirk had smiled at Mary, but through the smile Tom had seen how tired he was; too much worry, too much responsibility, too many decisions to be made.

'Yes, a very few people manage to get out nowadays, my dear. The handful who know and run the escape routes to the West: tunnels under the Spree River, basements extended into the Allied sectors, ways through the sewers and the disused railway tunnels where the barriers have been removed.'

'And you think that Billy was taken into West Berlin by one of those routes?'

'I can't be completely sure, Major, but in my own mind I'm almost certain that he was.' The lights glinted on Kirk's face as the car purred through the tunnel to the Central Airport. 'To me there seems no other possibility and this is what I imagine must have happened.

'As I said, Billy is a very lucky little boy. He fell into a snow-drift and he also fell among friends—powerful friends; people who run, or at least know about, one of those escape routes. When they discovered who Billy was, they helped him in every way and finally smuggled him into West Berlin. In return for their help, he promised to say nothing about them or what he had seen. Please don't make him break that promise, my dear. Believe me, the fewer people who know about those routes, the better it is.'

'I won't make him break it, General. All I'd like to do is to thank them for helping him.' Mary's words sounded almost automatic as though she were barely listening. Slowly and unhurriedly, as though speed were somehow too vulgar for its vast gleaming bulk, Kirk's car slid towards the main arrival building . . .

Midnight. The little clock on the mantelpiece started to strike and brought Tom back to the present. 'But, darling, you haven't been questioning Billy, have you?' he said. 'You haven't been pumping him—not after your promise to Kirk?'

'Yes, I've been pumping him, as you call it, Tom.' Mary frowned. 'After all, I am Billy's mother and I have a right to know what happened to him. And I'll tell you this, Tom: that child is terrified of something. I sensed it as soon as I saw him at the airport. Somebody has frightened him badly.'

'You think so? I must say it wasn't the impression I got. To me he almost seemed to be cocky.' Tom tried to recall exactly how it had been. The big gleaming hall with the reporters held back by a rope barrier and a group of officials hurrying to greet Kirk; the P.R.O. of the airline, a police inspector and somebody with the unlikely name of Sir Mason Toyne; a sense of waiting and expectancy, and then a door had opened and Billy had come into the hall.

And cocky really was the word to describe his manner. Billy had stood in the doorway for a moment, holding the hand of an air hostess, and then had run towards them. As he had run he had looked at the reporters, and the group beside Kirk and Tom had seen a fleeting look of pure pleasure and self-importance on his face, as though to say, 'Here I am, gentlemen, back from the dead. This is what you've been waiting for; the big moment.'

'Cocky!' Mary turned on him like a blight. 'Don't you realize that his manner was just an act, a pretence to try and show that he wasn't frightened? Tom, I'm his mother and I intend to find out exactly what happened to that child and why he is terrified out of his wits.'

'Yes, my dear, you've remarked several times that you're his mother. You are also a suspicious, over-imaginative woman and a demon where your children's welfare is concerned. There is nothing wrong with the boy; nothing at all.'

'Do you believe that, Tom? Do you really believe it? You may have been right about Billy's manner at the airport, but didn't you see his shoulders when he had a bath? They were covered with flea-bites.'

'And so what?' Tom suddenly felt as tired as Kirk had looked in the car. 'Isn't "flea-bite" a popular expression for something completely trivial and unimportant? I don't doubt for one moment that Billy has been in some pretty unsavoury places, but I still think that we owe nothing but deep gratitude to the people who helped him.'

'Do we? I wonder.' Mary got up and paced across the room. 'Darling, I may be crazy, but I'm sure something horrible happened to Billy. When I had put him to bed I asked him to tell me who were the people who had looked after him and he sort of cringed away as though I were about to hit him. I told him not to be silly and he looked up and said, "Mummy, please don't make me tell you. Please don't ask me. If I say anything, Hans will know and come for me. Iron Hans knows everything." '

'Hans?' Tom frowned. 'Did he mean Loser, the sleeping-car attendant? His name was Hans.'

'No, it wasn't Loser. I asked Billy that and he said, "Don't be silly, Mummy. Not that Hans. I mean Iron Hans. Little Iron Hans who can destroy the world." His voice sounded like a frightened old man's.'

'Got it!' Tom's frown changed to a grin. 'Iron Hans is a fairy-tale character, of course; from Grimm, I think, and Billy was reading it last term. You remember: the wild man covered with brown hair whom they find in a pool and shut up in an iron cage. Billy reads a lot and has far too much imagination, like his mother. He was just having a game with you, darling.'

'Perhaps you're right. I hope so, at any rate. And now let's go to bed. I've had about all I can take these last few days.' Mary gripped his arm as they walked upstairs, stepping very softly so as not to waken the children, but on the landing she paused and pushed open Billy's door. As she did so, Tom saw her body go rigid, and the next moment he was beside her with his hand reaching for the light switch.

Billy was sleeping heavily, with his head sunk deep in the pillow, and he appeared natural except for two things. His right hand was tearing and kneading at the sheet, and he was snoring. It wasn't like a child's snore. The noise he made didn't even sound human: it was a deep, grunting, coughing noise with a rasp and a whine in it which might have been made by some worn-out piece of machinery dragging an enormous burden up a steep hill.

'The thermometer, Tom. Get me the thermometer. It's in the dressing-table drawer; the top one on the right.' Mary's hand was on the child's forehead, but he didn't wake up. He just lay there quite naturally, apart from his clutching hand and the terrible guttural rasps of his snore.

'Have you got it?' She unbuttoned the pyjama jacket and slid the thermometer under Billy's arm, pressing it tight against the instrument while her other hand reached for his pulse. She didn't need a watch to tell her how fast it was, while all the time his snore rattled around the room, filling it.

'That should do it, darling.' She pulled out the thermometer, holding it to the light and shaking her head in disbelief as she did so. Her face looked much the same as when she had gone into the sleeping compartment and found Billy missing three days ago.

'Tom,' she said at last. 'Tom, this can't be true. Look for yourself.' She swayed against the bedpost as she handed the thermometer to him. 'As far as I can see, his temperature is over a hundred and seven.'

CHAPTER SEVEN

'THE flowers that bloom in the spring, tra-la . . .' Sir Marcus Levin, K.C.B., F.R.S., sang loudly and tunefully as he swung his Ferrari on to the dual carriageway and opened her up. 'Breathe promise of merry sunshine.'

Seventy miles an hour, eighty, ninety, a ton up, as the motorcycle maniacs called a hundred. Sir Marcus grinned fondly at the dashboard dials, revelling in speed and the sound of his rich baritone voice. 'As we merrily dance and we sing, tra-la . . .'

A hundred and ten now, and it felt as though he was barely moving. Very nice indeed, he gloated. Probably the nicest car that he, or anybody else for that matter, had ever owned. Almost seven thousand pounds' worth of car, but cheap at the price when one considered twelve cylinders, fuel injection and a custom-built body ordered to his own specification. He'd come a long, long way in his forty-five years.

'We welcome the hope that they bring, tra-la . . .' He negotiated a roundabout in an expert racing glide and charged up the next hill with his silencers blasting the early morning mist. 'Of a summer of roses and wine.'

Yes, a hell of a way he had come. All the way from his father's and grandfather's little shop in Lemberg, and most of it had been hell itself: a road to Calvary. He could remember the battle of the Warsaw ghetto, the Ruhr labour camps and Belsen. He could remember how he had slaved all day in a London factory and washed dishes every evening, trying to save a little money and praying that a British medical school would accept him on the strength of his single year at Warsaw University. After that had come the struggle for his degree and the fellowships at Cambridge and Edinburgh and New York, won in competition with men who had ten times his advantages of background, and would have left him standing if it hadn't been for his talent and ambition and Rachel. Yes, Rachel had always been beside him, urging him on.

Then, years later, he had knelt down in a big glittering room and felt a sword touch his shoulder. At that moment, he had seemed to see an old bearded face smiling at him and had had to fight to stop himself from saying aloud, 'Here I am, Father. Here I am, Jakob Levinski. Almost at the top, almost where you said I should go.' That had been the happiest time of his life, but it didn't last long. Three months later Rachel had died in a Vietnamese jungle, because the American plane which was supposed to have brought medical supplies had carried nothing except munitions and anti-Communist posters.

'Of a summer of roses and wine.' No, he didn't want to think about Rachel now. He'd loved her, he'd married her, and he'd dug her grave in rotting vegetation, because a little commonplace bug which penicillin could have wiped out in hours had burned her up. Rachel was only a memory and she wouldn't have wanted him to think about her. As she'd often said, only his career and his future mattered to her and, though he'd come a long way, he still had further to go. Sir Marcus Levin, Knight Commander of the Bath, Fellow of the Royal Society, and if he still wasn't recognized as one of the really top bacteriologists in the world, he very soon would be when his paper on the Enterin 165 Virus was read next month. Marcus Levin, who knew that he had been as emotionally and spiritually dead as old Marley's door-nail since the day that Rachel left him. He stopped singing as the car breasted the hill and whispered, 'To hell with the flowers that bloom in the spring.'

Still, it was going to be a nice day. Already the sun was climbing over the Surrey hills, the Thames valley was opening up in front of him, and wreaths of mist were drifting like smoke around the squat tower of Guildford Cathedral. He'd cursed when 'Jacko' Jackson had rung him up at six o'clock in the morning and asked him to come over to Richmond as a personal favour, but he felt quite pleased now. Not that he could ever have refused 'Jacko', of course. The man was his oldest friend, probably the best male friend he had ever had, though their relationship was eccentric to say the least. The bitter, ambitious Jew with a chip like a sack of cement on his shoulder, and the hearty, beer-swilling captain of the hospital rugger fifteen who had never suffered very much in his life and was called 'Jacko' not merely because his name was Jackson, but because his face resembled that of an amiable chimpanzee.

But 'Jacko' was wrong, of course. He had to be wrong, because his diagnosis was beyond the bounds of credibility. What he had seen in that child was merely a complicated case of pneumonia. 'Jacko' had jumped to conclusions and that was why he was a struggling G.P. earning about half the average national salary, and *he* was Sir Marcus Levin with fifty thousands pounds' worth of assets to his name and, like the car, worth every penny of them.

'Mark, old man, I've never asked you for many favours, but I'm begging for one now,' 'Jacko' had said. 'I don't want to call in the County Officer yet, nor even Redford Smith at the hospital, till I'm quite sure what it is. Please come over and give me your opinion, Mark. I hate to admit it, but I really am very worried indeed.

'What's that? Oh, yes, I've tried an injection of Genomycin; half a gramme just over an hour ago. There's been no change that I can see, though. Surely it should have started to lower his temperature by now?'

And 'Jacko' should have known better than that, of course. He couldn't even have been reading his *Lancet* lately. There had been an article on the antibiotic he'd used only a few weeks ago and it would take no effect for at least two hours from the time of administration. By now it should be working, though, and already the fever would be down and the breathing getting easier. When he got here the kid would probably be well over the crisis.

But it was getting pretty late. Marcus glanced at the dashboard clock. He'd promised 'Jacko' he'd be with him by seven and it was five past now. Damn Mrs Anderson! She'd seemed to think that her duties as housekeeper included those of a nannie in charge of a delicate and delinquent child. He'd crept downstairs in his socks, but she must have heard the telephone and was waiting by the dining-room door, tall and gaunt and imperious in a blue tartan dressing-gown.

'No, Sir Marcus,' she'd said, as always using the title with a flourish. 'It may be a matter of life or death, but you're not leaving the house till you've got something warm inside you. No, I'm very, very sorry, but I don't care if your new car has a dozen heaters in it. Now, just you go into the dining-room and wait for me, Sir Marcus.' He'd fretted for ten minutes while she prepared coffee and two boiled eggs and then stood grimly by the sideboard to see that he ate them.

But he was almost there at last. He swung the car into Richmond Park, narrowly missing a stag which was crossing the road, and he suddenly felt very glad that he had come. Apart from the pleasure of doing old 'Jacko' a good turn, apart from the lovely morning, there could be some useful publicity in the case. That Fenwick child had made the headlines once, and there was a good chance that he might do so again. Already he could picture them. 'Pneumonia Strikes Kidnapped Boy. Sir Marcus Levin Consulted.'

And here he was: Number 32 Park Approach with 'Jacko's' battered old Morris parked well out from the kerb. He drew up, picked up his case, and climbed purposefully out: a tall, imposing figure in his black coat, his Homburg hat and the thin sunlight glinting on his pearl tie-pin.

'Doctor . . . ?' Tom Fenwick opened the door almost as he touched the bell and tried to force his face into a smile. 'Dr Levin?'

'Yes, I'm Levin.' Marcus disliked professional soldiers on principle and normally would have put him in his place with 'Sir Marcus Levin', but he saw that this poor devil was on the point of collapse.

'My friend Dr Jackson asked me to come over and have a look at your boy; just to give a second opinion, you understand.' He bowed slightly and stepped into the little suburban hall, taking off his coat as he did so. He had cultivated a manner for every occasion and now radiated confidence. 'Doctor's here, so stop crying. Sir Marcus has arrived and there's no more need to worry. Everything will be all right because the expert has taken charge.'

'Now, Major Fenwick,' he said, studying Tom's face as he handed him his hat and coat. 'I understand that the patient is upstairs and I'll find my own way. And, while I'm making my examination, I want you to go and get a good, strong, alcoholic drink inside you; brandy, if you have it. Yes, that's an order, Major.' He turned as he heard 'Jacko's' voice at the top of the stairs and ran boyishly up to meet him.

'Mark, thank God you've come, old man.' 'Jacko's' face looked pinched and his handshake was clammy. 'I can't begin to say how grateful I am.'

'That's all right.' Once again strength and confidence gleamed in Marcus's eyes. 'Only sorry I couldn't get here earlier, but my dragon of a houskeeper insisted that I swallowed two large eggs before she let me out of the house. Now, let's have a look at your patient. He's in here, I suppose.' He started to move towards an open door on the landing.

'No, no, he's in the room at the end there. We put the mother in that one. She was hysterical, Mark, and I had to give her a sedative. It took the nurse and the husband to hold her down.'

'Take it easy, Jacko. Surely that was perfectly natural under the circumstances. The poor girl must have been under a hell of a strain lately. First the disappearance of her child and now this—this pneumonia, or whatever it is.' Marcus studied his friend with genuine concern. The old chap really was looking dreadful. He'd be needing a bit of medical attention himself if he didn't try to relax.

'Now, tell me about the kid. You gave him a shot of Genomycin two and a half hours back. The fever is a bit easier, I suppose?'

'No, Mark, it's no easier.' Jackson shook his head. 'Five minutes ago the temperature was still over a hundred and seven.

'Mark, I'm not an expert like you. I'm just a poor bloody G.P., but I'm prepared to swear that whatever is killing that boy is not pneumonia. Apart from the fever and the lung congestion, there are other things.'

'Well, let's have a look, shall we? And take it easy. Whatever happens, it can't be the end of the world.' Marcus frowned slightly. He didn't like the word *killing* at all. Now that he had arrived on the scene, 'Jacko' should feel that his worries were almost over. 'From what you told me of the case, everything points to pneumonia with complications. Exposure after he fell off that train, the time factors, the lung congestion and the vomiting. Still, even the best of us make mistakes and he certainly should be reacting to the antibiotic by now.' He pulled open the door and walked into the room, nodding to the nurse by the bed and sniffing the faint tang of antiseptic, corruption and oxygen.

'Thank you, nurse.' He leaned forward as she removed the little oxygen mask and studied Billy Fenwick's face. No, not at all a bad-looking kid apart from rather buck teeth which needed a brace. He was still snoring, but not very loudly, and there was a greyish tinge in the flushed cheeks. Marcus put his hand on the boy's forehead and sniffed his breath, like a terrier at a rat-hole.

'No,' he said. 'No, I think you may be right in saying that it isn't pneumonia. You've had a specimen of the sputum sent over for analysis? Good, that should tell us what we're up against at any rate. Let's have a look at these spots you mentioned. Probably a heat rash, I should think. He's almost burning up, isn't he?' He opened Billy's pyjama jacket and as he did so he stiffened. No, he thought, it's not possible. You're jumping to conclusions like 'Jacko', because it's your own subject. This child has never been out of Europe—it can't be possible. He pulled out a lens and studied the spots. They were rather beautiful: a ring of dark-red roses sprinkled on the pale skin.

'Tell me,' he said, 'was this rash there when you first examined him?' He looked at Jackson, but it was the nurse who answered.

'No, Sir Marcus.' She obviously enjoyed using the title and her voice had a comforting assurance similar to his own. 'It started to come up about two fifteen. His fever was very high then and I was sure it was just a sweat rash.'

'A sweat rash. Well, let's hope you're right, nurse. My God, I hope you are right.' The time factor was one thing in their favour at any rate. If what he suspected were true, the spots should have been the first symptom, not the second. Once again he stared down through the lens, praying that his suspicions were groundless, but as the tiny red blotches swam into perspective he knew that there was no mistake. The last time he had seen anything like them he had had to travel four hundred miles by jeep and helicopter and on horseback.

'Is there a telephone on this floor, nurse? In the next bedroom. Good, I don't want the father to hear what I have to say. Please go and get through to the County Health Officer. And hurry.' He shook his head at the question in her eyes and pulled down the bedclothes.

'And now, let's see, Jacko. Let's see if we really have a monster to deal with.' He ran his hand over the child's body, over the flat belly, past the tiny, undeveloped genitals and into the crotch, searching for the thing that he dreaded to find: the hall-mark which belonged to the greatest killer in history. It was there all right, just as he knew it would be, hard and throbbing under his fingers, and he could almost feel it growing. About as large as a walnut now, soon it would reach the size of a small orange and then burst. When it did so Billy Fenwick would probably be dead.

'Yes, Jacko, we've got our monster, I'm afraid.' Marcus stood up and went to the wash-basin, soaping his hands very carefully. 'No, there's not much point in replacing the oxygen mask. Give him a full adult shot of tetracyclin. I don't suppose it will do any good at this stage, but—' He shrugged his shoulders and walked out of the room. All jauntiness had left him and he looked much older than his forty-five years.

'Got him for me? Thanks.' He took the telephone from the nurse, lighting a cigarette as he did so. 'That you, Dr Lawrence? Yes, Marcus Levin here. What's that you say?' His voice was suddenly strident and foreign; the wailing of Israel against all Aryan stupidity.

'Yes, Doctor, I do realize the time, but I have not the slightest interest in the fact that you are just out of your bath. You will not ring me back, but listen very carefully to what I have to say.

'This is absolutely top priority and I am speaking from 32 Park Approach, Richmond, in connection with the Fenwick boy whom you must have heard about. I want the house isolated at once and you had better get on to the Foreign Office and the Ministry of Transport. We must round up all the boy's contacts of the last few days. As soon as I've put down this telephone, ring the Chief Constable.

'What's that, Dr Lawrence? Oh, yes, I think you can safely call it a national emergency.' He looked up at the nurse and nodded. 'You see, unless I'm wrong, we've got a case of bubonic plague on our hands.'

Plague—bubonic plague—*bacillus pestis*—the Black Virgin as they had called it—the Dark Lady of the Middle Ages returned to an English suburban street in the second half of the twentieth century to trouble the world. It was impossible, it had to be impossible. 'Jacko' Jackson shook his head in disbelief as he crossed the road towards the Bear Inn. The promise of a fine day had faded soon after nine o'clock, just about the time that Billy Fenwick died, and heavy clouds were drifting in with the promise of rain. Already a few drops were falling on the pavement.

Bubonic plague. He himself had known that it wasn't a case of pneumonia. But bubonic! Could old Mark really be certain at this stage? He revered Marcus Levin more than any other human being, but he didn't see how Mark could be so sure. Even with the rash, the bubo in the groin, and the lung congestion, nobody could be quite certain till full laboratory tests were made.

And where could the child have picked up the bug, if it came to that? Jackson ordered a pint of beer and carried it across to his usual seat by the saloon bar window. If he had been out East—

India or China, say—it would have been understandable, but there hadn't been a case of plague in Europe for years; unless you counted that chap from the research establishment near Salisbury not so long ago. Besides, if Mark was right about it being bubonic, it was acting very strangely. The rash and the swellings should have been the first symptoms and the lung congestion should have come later as a side effect. Jackson had not been a brilliant student, but at least he remembered that much.

Still, it wasn't his affair any more. His patient was dead, they'd removed the body, and the public health people had taken over. A decontamination squad had been at work when he left the house, the parents and the other boy had gone to the isolation hospital and the street outside had been almost blocked by police cars. Mark had driven off to the Central Laboratories soon after Billy died, and there was nothing for him to do except go home, attend to his practice and nurse his inoculation shot.

It had taken all right, that was one thing at least. He could feel his arm throbbing painfully as he lifted the tankard. He shouldn't really be drinking on top of it, of course, but a couple of pints wouldn't do any harm and he'd felt like stopping at the Bear before going home. The place was just beside the Laneham Park Rugby Ground and the members used it more as a club than a public house. The landlord was a former Welsh international and there were silver trophies along the top of the bar and the walls were covered with photographs of fifteens. He himself appeared in three of them. Apart from one enormously fat man chatting to the barman, the room was empty and Jackson was glad of that. Though the matter was no official concern of his any longer, he had to think about it.

Plague. The worst killer in history. Knocked out whole populations almost overnight: Marseilles, London, Bombay. Naples, where they had disinfected the sewers and blind rats had come pouring out into the streets. Right back in the Bible, too: the end of the Philistines and the Assyrian army dying before Jerusalem. Manson-Bahr said that was malignant malaria, not bubonic, but many authorities still disagreed with him.

Tetracyclin would stop it, if you got your patient in the early stages, of course, but they'd have to find every contact of the boy's and also the source of infection. Take a hell of a lot of doing. He glanced up as a board creaked a few yards away from him. The fat man had left the bar and was examining the photographs on the walls, nodding as he recognized a familiar face.

They'd have to be careful about security, too. The very word 'plague' carried the hint of panic and civil disorder. Already the newspapers would have heard that something was happening in Park Approach, and if the story broke before the original carrier was located, things could be pretty ugly. Yes, Lawrence had better have a good tale to fob them off with.

'Excuse me, sir, but am I addressing Dr Jackson?' The fat man had paused by his table and was beaming down at him. A whisky glass looked like a thimble in his great flabby hand.

'Yes, I'm Jackson.' 'Jacko' started to frown with annoyance at the interruption, but the man's expression was so friendly and pleasant that he had to smile back. 'I'm afraid I—'

'No, you don't know me, Doctor, but I know you all right—by reputation, of course. W. L. R. Jackson, the finest centre three-quarter Laneham Park ever had.

'But may I join you for a moment, Doctor? I would also count it an honour if I might buy you a drink.' He crooked a finger at the barman and lowered his vast bulk into a chair.

'Yes, this really is my lucky day, Doctor. Dr W. L. R. Jackson. The great W. L. R. Jackson.' He fumbled in his pocket and produced a visiting card. 'My name is Forest—John Forest—and I once saw you score three tries at Twickenham.'

CHAPTER EIGHT

'Come in, General Kirk, and welcome to my rather untidy castle.' Marcus Levin smiled and held out a beautifully manicured hand. 'We're all at sixes and sevens at the moment, I'm afraid, but at least pull up a chair and try to make yourself comfortable.'

'Thank you.' Kirk looked suspiciously around the office in the Central Laboratories and then relaxed. Though Levin seemed a flamboyant, over-dramatic fellow and his room was a maze of papers and scientific equipment, it was at least warm. He unwound his muffler and lowered himself into a chair by the desk.

'Now, Sir Marcus,' he said, 'before you try to put me in the picture, I should like to say that I shall quite understand any resentment you may feel about having an ignoramus on scientific matters hanging at your heels. No, it's true enough.' He waved aside Marcus's polite gesture of protest. 'My medical knowledge is confined to what is in *Dr Goodall's Family Physician* and I'll just have to try not to get in your way. The fact is that as the child appears to have picked up this—I don't know if "bug" is the right expression—in East Germany, it was decided that my department should co-operate with the health authorities.'

'I know that, General, and believe me, I appreciate your co-operation very much. We're going to need every bit of help we can get.' Marcus frowned at the papers on his desk. 'I gather that the Germans are rounding up all the boy's contacts and having them immunized.'

'All his contacts from the time he reached West Berlin. Before that we don't know whom he contacted, or rather who contacted him. The Minister has spoken personally to Moscow, however, and they've promised to do all they can to trace the boy's movements from the moment he fell from the train.' Kirk grinned slightly. 'Adversity makes strange bedfellows, as they say, and our friends behind the Iron Curtain don't want an epidemic of plague any more than we do.'

'But why haven't they got one, that's what I want to know?' Marcus's hand beat sharply on the desk. 'That child was bitten by an infected flea and he can't have been the only one. Somewhere, in East Germany probably, though it's not my job to say where, that bug, as you call it, is on the rampage, and unless we can find every carrier and, what is more important, the original source in the very near future, we're in real trouble.

'General Kirk, I wonder if you have any idea of the speed at which this thing travels? I've seen it myself in India and East Africa and it's quite frightening. The original carrier is usually *Xenopsylla cheopis,* of course, but, once established, droplet contact with an infected mammal . . .'

'Just a minute, Sir Marcus.' Kirk broke in shaking his head. 'I'm afraid you are going a bit fast for me. Could you just give me a general and very simple account of the working of this thing, *bacillus pestis*?'

'I'll try, but at this stage, we're not even sure that it is *bacillus pestis.*' Marcus slid a photograph across the desk. It showed a pink surface lightly dotted with what looked like small oval capsules stained purple.

'Now, General. That is a piece of animal tissue infected with the bacillus of true bubonic plague. The propagation and spread of the disease is carried out in a most beautiful manner.' He got up and paced in front of Kirk like a lecturer before a class. 'The bacillus lives in the body of the rat flea, *Xenopsylla cheopis,* which suffers no ill effects from its presence. The flea bites its host, however, the rat is infected, leaves its hole and dies. After a period of about three days, depending on climatic conditions, the flea, which relies on fresh blood for its existence, leaves the carcass of the rat and attaches itself to man and other animals. The incubation period in the human body is a further three days, after which the breath of an infected person can transmit the disease. The average mean duration of illness in fatal bubonic plague is five and a half days, making a total of eleven and a half for the full cycle.

'And now I'd like to show you something else.' Marcus slid another picture in front of Kirk. It looked almost the same as the first, though the capsules were stained a darker purple and they bulged slightly at one end like pears. 'As I said, eleven and a half days is the cycle of true bubonic plague. This little chap appears to take rather less than five.'

'And that's what killed Billy Fenwick? You mean it's not bubonic, as you thought?'

'Yes, that's what killed him, General, and though it's certainly some form of Eastern plague, it's like nothing I've seen or heard about before. Apart from the time sequence, it doesn't act like true bubonic. In normal cases the rash and the bubos, the swellings, should come first and the pulmonary congestion follow them as a side effect. That didn't happen with the Fenwick child. The damned thing is behaving in a way it has no right to do—no right at all.' Marcus scowled down at the photograph as though the creature's unorthodox behaviour were a personal affront.

'And what's it doing in Central Europe anyway? That's possibly the strangest thing of all. The fleas that carry bubonic are parasites of the black rat, which is almost non-existent except around a few dock areas. The most accepted theory is that it was wiped out by a larger brown variety: *ratus Norvegicus,* as it is wrongly called, which is usually free of them. That's why plague epidemics are so mercifully rare today. An attractive thought, isn't it, General? A war for the life of mankind being fought out in cellars, and sewers, and garbage heaps.'

'Yes, I suppose you could call it attractive.' Kirk was still staring at the photographs. 'But tell me, Doctor—sorry, Sir Marcus. These bulges in the second picture. What are they?'

'I just don't know, General Kirk, and please call me Doctor. I much prefer it.' Levin smiled, but his mind was far away, studying the bacillus through Kirk's eyes. 'I have a theory about them, but it's terribly far-fetched and I'd much rather discuss it when we have more facts to go on.

'Excuse me, though.' The telephone rang shrilly on his desk and he leaned forward to answer it. 'Oh, yes, please put him through at once.' He cupped his hand over the mouthpiece and looked at Kirk. 'It's the Semmelweiss Isolation Hospital in West Berlin. Major Wood, the man who found Billy Fenwick, was taken there this morning. It appears that they didn't manage to get him inoculated in time.

'Ah, good evening, Dr Heller,' he said in German. 'Yes, Marcus Levin here. He died, did he? I see, an hour ago. Yes, I was expecting that, but I didn't think it would be so soon.

'What's that? What's that you say, Doctor?' As Marcus listened, Kirk saw his hand tighten around the instrument.

'And you're sure about that? The tetracyclin had no effect whatsoever? It didn't even slow it down in any way?

'I see. Yes, of course we'll come up with something else in time. We're bound to. What I'm worried about is how much time have we got. Anyway, thank you for ringing, and I'll be in touch as soon as I have more news from our end. Goodbye, Doctor, and all the luck in the world.' He replaced the telephone and stared across the room for a moment. All his urbanity had left him and he suddenly looked what he was: a middle-aged Jew grown old before his time, who had almost been beaten to death in two concentration camps.

'General Kirk,' he said at last. 'I think I should put all my cards on the table. When I first examined that child, I thought that we had a slight variant of Eastern plague to deal with. I thought that the infection had probably taken place before the boy left the train, but the father assured me that there were no flea-marks on his body that night.

'All right. I was still more curious than bewildered. I had a species that developed faster than usual. *Bacillus pestis* often throws up strange variants. I could also accept the lung congestion coming before the rash and the bubo as some strange union of the bubonic and pneumonic forms of plague.

'But this!' He craned forward over the second photograph again, and there was the trace of a foreign accent in his voice which only happened when he was excited. 'These swellings you saw, and the fact that the bacilli are resistant to tetracyclin—the most effective antibiotic we have for the Pasteurella group—that makes me wonder if we are up against something unnatural: some kind of man-made mutant, in fact. Remember that the last person to die of Eastern plague in this country was a scientist working at the Porton Research Establishment.'

'You mean germ warfare, Doctor? If we are working on those lines, isn't it possible that the East Germans are doing so too?' Kirk shook his head and he sounded much more confident as he came to a familiar subject. 'Yes, it's possible, I suppose, but highly unlikely. I'm pretty well informed about what goes on in East Germany and I haven't heard of any such establishment.'

'Then either your information is incomplete or we've got a natural freak to deal with.' Levin broke off frowning as the door opened. 'What is it, Wilson? I told you we weren't to be disturbed for the next half-hour.'

'I know that, sir, but I think you had better look at the last slides we prepared.' Marcus's assistant could scarcely contain his excitement. 'Those bulges seem to be what you suspected. They are definitely opening . . . .'

'The devil they are!' Marcus was already moving to the door. 'Yes, you were quite right to interrupt me. You'd better come too, General. We may be going to see a piece of living history.

'Now, which is the earliest slide?' He glanced impatiently at the row of microscopes on the laboratory desk. 'The second from the right. Good.' He bent over the eye-piece, turning the fine adjustment till the picture slid into focus. As he did so, he could feel beads of sweat breaking out on his forehead.

For though it was thought to be impossible, though it was against the evidence of every recorded case, it was happening and he was watching it. He was looking at a miracle that might make his name live as long as medical text-books were read.

The things were dead, of course. The stain had killed them and, before they died, some of them had been dividing, reproducing themselves asexually. That was normal enough, but in the right-hand corner of the picture there were others which had not behaved normally at all. They had split open at the bulged ends to release a tiny, almost transparent speck which drifted beside them in the purple dye.

'We now come to sporulation in bacteria, gentlemen.' In the

back of his mind Marcus could hear an old, bored voice delivering a lecture he had probably given a hundred times before. 'The process of spore formation found in certain bacteria is a method of self-preservation. When placed in conditions where death would normally result, these organisms develop enormous powers of resistance and can remain dormant but alive almost indefinitely. If the spores are later returned to circumstances where the bacillus can grow, alterations take place in their structure, they germinate and normal reproduction is resumed.

'This process however is confined to certain species only and I am happy to say that *bacillus pestis,* for example, is not one of them. If it were, there is every probability that you and I would not be here today.'

But this culture was sporing. There was no doubt about it. Through the next microscope Marcus could see the whole surface of the slide covered with those tiny drifting dots. He tried to remember all he knew about plague—all he had learned in nineteen years of sweat and study and often incredible danger. None of it helped him at all.

The plague epidemics of classical times. At Alexandria where fifty thousand inhabitants had died almost overnight; at Carthage and Athens and Byzantium—all those outbreaks had been well documented, the symptoms laid out because, though no proper clinical methods existed, there were men of curious and scientific mind to record them. In China and India too there were records and, after the microscope was invented by van Loeuwenhoek, bacteriology had become a science.

Yes, almost all the major outbreaks had been recorded. All except one outbreak: the big one, the longest one, the one that had probably killed fifty million people and changed the economic structure of Europe. The symptoms had seemed to point to plague: tumours, dark patches which opened like mouths, vomiting from the lungs, but nobody could be certain what it was. There had been no accurate accounts because it had arrived in an age when reason was dead and men lived by superstition. Marcus lit a cigarette, dragging hard at it, and then turned to the third microscope. Wilson had added a different stain to the slide and the spores were much more visible—little reddish pinpoints floating around their parent bodies like moons.

No, they hadn't studied anything except dogma in the fourteenth century, and nobody could be completely sure what the epidemic had been. Its coming had been heralded by earthquakes, drought and dense fog. They had called it an act of God at first, and afterwards a sickness of the earth because the rats and mice came pouring out of their holes to die. They had said that cats, the creatures of the Devil, were responsible, and they'd killed them, allowing the rats to multiply. Then at last they thought that they had discovered the true cause: the well poisoners; and the pogroms had begun. Fifty thousand Jews killed in Burgundy alone, rabbis crucified head down like Peter, children hurled into the flames because their parents refused to allow them to be baptized.

But was it possible that the outbreak had not been true plague at all, but this—the thing he was looking at now? The means of self-preservation were there, and could it have lain dormant for centuries and then woken up for him to find? 'Sir Marcus Levin, the discoverer of—the isolator of—' As he considered the possibilities, the immunization shot in his arm seemed to burn and swell. It appeared to have taken all right, but was he really safe? Could any normal serum stop something which had managed to maintain itself for six hundred years?

'General Kirk,' he said. 'I think I may be on a completely wrong track . . . I hope I am, but I'd like you to look at this.' He drew back and motioned Kirk towards the microscope. 'If my very vague suspicions are correct, we have a real devil to deal with. Can you see them?' He watched Kirk fiddle with the adjustment and nod.

'Good. Now, look at the end of the rods. Can you see how they have split open and released spores? That was thought to be scientifically impossible, but you can see it happening, can't you?

'Well, I don't know what we're up against yet. I've only got a hunch at the moment, but if my hunch is right those things should have died six hundred years ago.' His hand came up and gripped Kirk's arm. 'I think that what you are looking at could be a return of the Black Death from the Middle Ages.'

It was really raining now. The clouds that had gathered over London in the morning had solidified into a huge, dark tent and there was not a breath of air. The rain dropped straight down out of the sky and bounced off the street and pavements like a forest of steel spikes standing upright.

'Your car should be round in a moment, sir. I sent a message to your chauffeur in the parking lot.' Marcus had said goodbye to Kirk in the laboratory and Wilson, his assistant, was escorting him out.

'Thank you, Dr Wilson.' Kirk's hat and muffler were at last adjusted to his satisfaction and he drew on a pair of thick gloves.

'Oh, I'm sorry. It's Mr Wilson, is it?' Kirk glanced keenly at him. Wilson was still young, barely in his middle twenties by the look of him, but his face was very intelligent. 'Just how long have you worked with Sir Marcus, Mr Wilson?'

'Seven years, General. He took me on as a lab. assistant after I left school.' There was a gleam of hero-worship in his eyes. 'I've been all over the world with Sir Marcus: India; Africa; Vietnam, where his wife died.'

'Yes, I've heard about that.' Kirk scowled out at the rain. It showed no sign of slackening and the gutters reminded him of brown mountain streams.

'Now, about this business of the bacillus producing spores. As I told Sir Marcus, I'm an ignoramus on medical matters and I understood very little of what he said. I did gather, however, that this sporulation, as you call it, has never been met with before in cases of plague.'

'No, General, it has never been met with before and that's what makes the whole business so incredible. It's like a creature suddenly changing its whole pattern. Almost as though you and I should start to grow another finger on our hands.' Wilson blushed scarlet as he remembered the torn talon on Kirk's left wrist. 'Oh, I'm sorry, sir. That was a stupid example.'

'It's quite all right.' Kirk smiled at him. 'I only wish I could grow another three on one of mine. But to get back to this plague mutation or whatever it is. A deadly disease—probably the most deadly disease there is—discovers a method of preserving itself almost indefinitely. A very nasty thought indeed. And what about the Black Death theory? Because there are so few records between the years 1342 and '88, Sir Marcus has put forward the possibility that this thing might be a return of the Black Death bacillus which, through its spores, has managed to maintain itself dormant but alive for more than six centuries. Do you agree with his view, Mr Wilson?'

'Do I agree?' Again Wilson reddened. 'Look, General Kirk, I'm just Sir Marcus's lab. assistant—his bottle-washer, if you like. It's not for me to question his judgment. After all he . . .'

'Yes, I know all that. Marcus Levin is an internationally known bacteriologist, but I'm still asking you, Mr Wilson.' A big pennon-bearing car had pulled up before the entrance, but Kirk ignored it. 'You have been trained in the subject, and I want your personal opinion. Has Sir Marcus any real scientific basis for saying that this may be a return of the Black Death bacillus?'

'I just can't answer that, General. This bug we've got is a freak. There's never been a case of sporulation in *bacillus pestis* before. Until we've had time to study it and also found the source—the first carrier—we can't be certain what it is. We don't know much about the Black Death either, if it comes to that. It was always thought to be a species of Eastern plague, but nobody can say for sure.'

'Thank you, Mr Wilson. That answers my question, I think.' Kirk nodded. 'There is not enough evidence at the moment to be certain about anything and Sir Marcus has jumped to conclusions.'

'Yes, I suppose you might say that, sir.' Wilson looked horribly embarrassed. 'The subject of the Black Death has always fascinated him; became a sort of personal challenge, if you like. He may have given it undue prominence in this case. All the same, he is a very fine scientist and I think we should trust his judgment.'

'You may be right, Mr Wilson, but thank you for what you've said.' Kirk held out his hand and smiled.

'And don't worry about it, my boy. You haven't been disloyal to your chief because you've told me nothing that I didn't suspect myself. Goodbye for the time being.' He turned and hurried down the steps to his waiting car.

'Thank you, Martin. Yes, it's back to the office again, I'm sorry to say.' He nodded to his chauffeur and leaned far back on the seat listening to the thunder of rain upon the roof.

Yes, he thought, Marcus Levin probably was jumping to conclusions. Even the most brilliant minds sometimes bypassed reason and gave way to unscientific hunches. And, if Levin were wrong, it meant that he could be wrong too. The thing might very well be a man-made mutant produced at some germ-warfare establishment which he hadn't heard about. He'd put every agent they had in East Germany to try and trace it, and he'd also have to talk to somebody in Moscow. He hated the very thought of that, but if there was going to be an epidemic there was no doubt that he'd get a hearing. After all, Russians and Germans could die of plague as easily as British children. The probability was that some fool of a scientist had let a culture get loose and was keeping quiet to protect his own skin. If so, the M.V.D. would soon get the truth out of him. The real drawback to the theory was the question why no cases had been reported in East Germany before now.

There was also the problem of the Fenwick child's contacts before he arrived at Major Wood's office. Colonel Baxter was convinced that he had been smuggled into West Berlin through one of the escape routes and the child's garbled version backed him up. It would be difficult to find the people who controlled the route, but it would have to be done. If Baxter didn't come up with a lead soon, he'd have to go to Germany himself.

And for the time being, the whole business had better be kept dark. Nothing had been released to the Press yet and it wouldn't be till they had more facts to go on. Kirk stared out at the evening crowds hurrying through the rain to buses and tube stations. The very word 'plague' had a ring of panic and they mustn't be told anything till the authorities were quite sure what they were up against. Panic! Apart from the riots and pogroms of the Middle Ages, there had been religious mania too: crazy theories that flagellation and sexual activity were its preventives; men and women copulating in the streets while others flogged themselves in graveyards.

No, there would be no public announcement till they knew exactly what they had to deal with. He pulled out a cigar and very carefully sliced off the end. He was just about to light it, when his eyes seemed to blur and he was sitting bolt upright shouting to his driver to stop.

At a newsvendor's stand at the end of Waterloo Bridge were two placards. They were already sodden with rain, but the word PESTILENCE was clearly visible on each of them.

That night, a man and a woman in Berlin, two men in London, a small child in Hanover and a soldier in Paris were starting to rot. They didn't know what was happening to them and neither did Iron Hans. He just sat in his cage and grinned.

CHAPTER NINE

'I AGREE, General Kirk. If this information is correct, and I stress the word "if", we must bury our differences for the time being.' The telephone was attached to a loudspeaker and microphone and Gregor Petrov paced up and down before the window as he spoke, staring out at the blizzard that was covering Berlin. As in London, the weather had promised to be fine at first, but at noon it had begun to rain and by early evening the rain had turned to sleet. Now thick snow swirled and eddied around the trees and the lamps of the Unter den Linden and was beginning to settle. Petrov liked watching the snow. It almost made him feel he was home in Moscow.

'Yes, General, a thorough investigation is being made at our end. You have my word for that. I would also like to say how much I—I—' he struggled for the correct English word—'how much I appreciate your speaking to me personally. I quite realize the embarrassment it must have caused you. Now, if you will just hold the line for a couple of minutes.' He switched off the microphone, but continued to stare out of the window. At least the snow is clean, he thought. Antiseptic drops of frozen moisture blanketing the earth and purifying it. That was rubbish, of course, but it made him feel slightly better to think about it. His own body was stale and damp with sweat, and the meal he'd eaten two hours ago was sour in his mouth.

Plague, he thought. Bubonic plague. In a bad epidemic thousands could die almost overnight, he'd heard; die horribly too: the bodies swelling, turning black and bursting like fruit that had been left to drop from the tree. Rats were supposed to be the carriers, weren't they? Scaly bodies wriggling through a hole in the wall, tearing open sacks of grain, fouling the contents, contaminating everything they touched. That stuff he'd eaten this evening: Königsberger Klops it was called; a typical Berliner dish. He'd enjoyed it very much, but were the ingredients all right? The meat, the flour that made the thick creamy coating, the sauce and the vegetables? Yes, a horrible death. Dark swellings in the flesh splitting open and starting to stink. Petrov struggled to push the thought out of his mind and turned back to the desk where Tania Valina was standing beside a tall man wearing the uniform of a Vopo colonel. He'd worked with Gustav Behr for years, he called him by his first name, but he didn't feel that he really knew him. Though Behr was always polite, always friendly, there was a coldness in his manner which repelled intimacy.

'Well, Gustav,' he said. 'You heard what this Kirk implied; is there any truth in it? Have your government, unknown to us been carrying out experiments in bacteriological warfare?'

'They have not.' The German's pale, rather scholarly face was almost devoid of expression. 'There have never been any such experiments in East Germany and no research establishment exists for the purpose.'

'Thank you.' Petrov nodded. 'So this—this thing, whatever it is, is not a man-made product from our side of the Iron Curtain, as they call it. On the other hand, if it is a natural outbreak, why have no more cases been reported by now? Either Kirk is lying or something very strange is going on.' He looked at Tania and grinned.

'And where do you think it comes from, my dear? From outer space, perhaps? Is it possible that the Martians are an extremely intelligent race of microbes who have just invaded us?' He shuffled back to the telephone, feeling slightly better for his little joke.

Less than three miles away from Behr's office, a woman named Ruth Eulenburg was trying to get to sleep. She wanted to sleep very badly because it was far the best cure for influenza and she was in for an attack all right. She'd felt it during the morning: aching joints, headache, and a throat that felt as though it had been scraped with a file. She'd done everything to stop it, taken huge doses of Vitamin C and aspirin and gone to bed, but the 'flu was winning hands down.

If only Wilhelm were with her it wouldn't be so bad. If only he hadn't gone away. From the bedroom walls the face of her husband seemed to stare across at her. If only Wilhelm would come home soon.

That was crazy, of course—the fever playing tricks with her mind and her eyes. Wilhelm couldn't ever come back. A bullet from a Vopo rifle had torn open his chest and he'd died in her arms. It might have been only yesterday when they'd come through. The old lorry lined with boiler plate and scrap iron lurching down the Muskauerstrasse towards the wall which had not been mortared then, and they'd gone slap through it. Seventeen of them lying in the back and Wilhelm crouched low down over the steering-wheel. For a moment the barbed wire had seemed to hold them, but somehow the lorry had torn over it, with the bullets thudding harmlessly against the iron plate, till they came to rest beside an American sentry box. She'd twisted her ankle as she jumped from the back and ran to the cab, wrenching open the door and shouting at the top of her voice, 'Darling, we made it—you made it—we're free—really free and in the West at last!' Then Wilhelm's body had fallen sideways and she'd seen the blood pouring from a rent in his coat.

Well, Wilhelm was dead. He'd died a hero and there was no point in thinking about him any more. She just had to concentrate on fighting off the 'flu because there was so much work to do. Another group would be coming through the new tunnel to the Ku'damm station next week and she had to make arrangements for meeting them. The Vopo would be bound to find it soon, but they should get a dozen parties through first. It had been a risk bringing that child out by it, but Gretel knew her business and was sure he wouldn't talk. She remembered how he had sobbed in her arms at the junction and she'd had to comfort him for half an hour before he promised to go and find the English major's office.

Yes, she had to be all right in the morning. If only she could sleep through, if only the aspirin would start to work, if only her head would stop throbbing, if only she could breathe. Ruth reached out and switched on her bedside radio. The little green dial glowed comfortingly and a Munich beer song thudded in time to her pulse. 'In der Nacht—schläft der Mensch—nicht gern alleine . . .' It died and an announcer's voice took over. 'Good morning, ladies and gentlemen. The time is now exactly one minute after midnight and before continuing our programme of light music, there is a news flash from London. The British Ministry of Health report that . . .'

'No, no, please God, no.' Ruth heard herself muttering aloud against the voice.

'All persons in any country who think they may have been in contact with this child are urged to get in touch with their doctor immediately.'

'No, no, no.' She was out of bed now, staring at her face under the dressing-table lamp and feeling sweat pour from her body and grow cold.

'I repeat that there is no cause for alarm as long as all contacts are inoculated.'

'No, no, it can't be true. It mustn't be true.' As the announcer broke off and a dance tune took over, Ruth staggered to the telephone. Somehow she seemed unable to control her hands and it took her a long time to dial the number she wanted.

'Professor Klee,' she said when at last somebody answered. 'Herr Professor, I know that I am not supposed to ring you, but I'm sick and I have to talk to you . . . No, no, please listen.'

Klee's voice sounded metallic and he appeared to be talking gibberish; something about a wrong number and replacing the telephone. He was obviously trying to protect himself, but she had to make him understand.

'Herr Professor, haven't you heard the news yet? About the little English boy that Clever Gretel sent us? We have to talk to her, Herr Professor. We have to know her real name, so we can find out exactly where the boy came from. Tell me her name, Professor Klee. Gretel—Clever Gretel . . .'

'This is the exchange. You have dialled a number which is unobtainable. Replace your instrument and re-dial please.' The West Berlin postal authorities were extremely proud of their recorded-instruction system, but Ruth Eulenburg still shook her head in disbelief. 'I know that you're there, Herr Professor, so listen to me. We must contact Gretel at once. We have to know what happened to that child. Gretel, Herr Professor. Clever, Clever Gretel . . .' Her knees buckled and she fell to the floor, dragging the telephone with her.

She was still repeating the name when they found her in the morning and she kept on repeating it in the ambulance. Just before she died she tried to say it again, but by that time she was too weak for anybody to hear her. 'Gretel—Gretel—Clever Gretel.'

CHAPTER TEN

'A RING, a ring of roses, a pocket full of posies . . .' Marcus Levin hummed as he watched the rats. He had sent his assistants off to an early breakfast, wanting to concentrate by himself, and he was quite alone in the laboratory.

'Atishoo, atishoo, we all fall down.' Almost every nursery rhyme recorded an historical event, and 'A Ring of Roses' was true to type. The animals in the first cage had been infected at six o'clock in the evening and they were dying already; one of them lying on its side and kicking feebly while its partner's efforts to escape were slackening at every minute. Marcus glanced at the clock and made a note on his pad. 'Though no accurate information is at present available in human subjects, the duration of the disease appears to be approximately three and a half days. In the case of rats . . .' The kicking had stopped now and the first animal was quite still. 'Twelve and a half hours.' Incredible but true.

A miasma, a contagion sent from the stars to infect the earth, the ancients had considered plague. A sickness of the soil which drove the creatures up into the daylight to die. That was happening in front of him, as he knew it would, though he hadn't expected the extreme violence that went with it. The six cages had been built to resemble underground sets, lined with clay and bricks and having a single exit blocked by three light wooden partitions. In every cage except the first the rats were still struggling to escape, tearing madly at the barriers and at each other in their efforts to get out. The big cross-bred albino in the fifth cage had killed its smaller neighbour and was busily gnawing at the second partition, though its strength seemed to be on the wane. Would human sufferers react with such violence, he wondered? 'Jacko' had kept the Fenwick child quiet with sedatives, but his hand, tearing and kneading at the bedclothes, appeared to imply that. He added another note on his pad. 'For the first seven hours after infection no apparent change in the animal was observed, but this was followed by a three-hour period of intense physical activity, aggression and the urge to escape. After this the organism slowly ran down into coma and death.' Marcus left the cages and bent over a microscope. A hanging droplet system had been used instead of dye and the things were alive and busily at work, dividing and reproducing themselves as was natural, but also preserving their race for posterity which they had no right to do. Even as he watched, more of those tiny dots burst from the parent bodies and circled around them: spores which in certain circumstances could lie dormant for centuries till moisture reached them, the creature awoke and became active again.

And had it happened like that? Was this a return from some past outbreak that had managed to maintain itself over the years, or was his original idea of a man-made mutation right, for all Kirk's assurance that no research establishment existed in East Germany? Marcus was strongly drawn towards the first possibility, though he had no real scientific grounds for this, but merely a hunch, an intuitive feeling. What he had to do was to study the thing and find the most efficient way of controlling and destroying it. The normal inoculation serum for bubonic seemed to be working all right, that was one point in their favour at any rate. The boy's parents and younger brother had been caught in time, though two more cases had been reported in Germany: the air hostess of the Lufthansa plane, and Major Wood's housekeeper. They'd have a job tracing all their contacts before it turned up again.

But even with effective inoculation, could they hold it back? The worst thing about orthodox plague was the speed at which it travelled, eleven and a half days from the beginning of the cycle to death of the patient, and this thing took less than five.

And they had found no antibiotic to touch it yet. He peered into the next microscope. Penicillin had been added to the culture but the creature was still thriving. They'd have to find the original source soon, or whole populations could be wiped out almost overnight.

The publicity wouldn't help either. Since those headlines 'Pestilence' had blazoned the news to London, the radio and television networks had issued sober and reassuring statements, but he doubted if they would be enough. Unless it could be announced that the outbreak was under control, public confidence would be at breaking point before long.

But where could that damned child have picked up the bug? Who was the original carrier? Marcus crossed to a shelf at the back of the room. Half his reference library on plague had been sent over to the laboratories and it was piled high with books. Sticker's *Die Geschichte der Pest,* Creighton's *A History of Epidemics in Britain,* Bulard's *De la Peste Orientale.* He grinned sadly at the titles. Sticker and Creighton and Bulard had been trained observers, men of science who had patiently recorded every detail. What would they think of his blind intuition? All the same, none of them had seen anything like the little monster which was working away behind him. He opened a map of Central Germany and frowned down at it. Somewhere along that twisting roundabout line between Magdeburg and the border Billy Fenwick had fallen from the train. Somewhere in the area he must have met the carrier.

Magdeburg, Oberfeld, Raltona, Rudisheim, Helmstedt. Marcus's finger ran along the route and then stopped. Rudisheim? Just what did he remember about the name? Where had he heard it before? From the map it appeared to be a small unimportant town or just a village, but somehow it rang a loud bell in his memory. He pulled out a heavy leather-bound volume from the pile of books. Vogel's *The Great Pandemic of the Middle Ages,* translated into English by Nevison and Butt. Translated pretty inaccurately too. He'd always intended to buy an original edition, but somehow he had never got down to it. At least the index gave him what he wanted, though, and he flicked open a page. Yes, here it was.

> The outbreak of plague at Rudisheim near Magdeburg is of interest, not only because it appears to have been one of the earliest appearances of the scourge in Germany, but because of the spate of superstitious beliefs and legends which surrounded the district for generations.
>
> The first victim was said to be the abbot of a Benedictine monastery, one Rudolph von Ginter, a man greatly hated in the district on account of his cruel and profligate life. His death met with general rejoicing, being considered a punishment from heaven, and bonfires were lit in the streets to celebrate it. Within weeks, however, the rest of the religious community and most of the local population followed him to the grave.

Marcus lit a cigarette as he turned over the leaf. The next page was illustrated with a medieval woodcut, blurred and indistinct, but it seemed to show a forest clearing at night with a thin moon above the tree tops. In the foreground was the figure of a naked man bent almost double beneath a wizened, ape-like being which crouched upon his shoulders.

> For more than three hundred years, the monastery ruins and grounds were regarded as an accursed place in which it was unsafe to venture, and a mass of legends surrounded them. These included the Black Virgin or Plague Maiden who rode upon the shoulders of a dead man, scattering dark red roses in her way, and a monstrous creature with the shape of a rat and the size of a wolf that stalked the area by night and on which it was death to look.

Marcus shook his head in disgust. 'Don't walk through the

ruins, don't go near the park, For something pretty nasty may be waiting in the dark.' What the hell was he doing, poring over such rubbish? His place was at the microscope, not browsing through accounts of dead folklore. All the same, it must have been somewhere near Rudisheim that Billy Fenwick had vanished from the train. He read on.

> These stories and fears persisted until the middle of the eighteenth century, when coal was discovered in the neighbourhood and Rudisheim grew into a small but fairly important industrial centre. In 1825 the Lutheran authorities bought part of the monastery grounds and built a church upon the site. While digging the foundations a bronze casting of a man's head was discovered and some scholars claim that it may have been taken from the death mask of the former abbot, Rudolph von Ginter. This relic was kept in the church as an historical curiosity till the end of the last war, when it disappeared.

A sickness of the soil, a miasma, a visitation from the stars against one evil man which destroyed a neighbourhood. Marcus put down the book and paced across the room. Was it possible that that was how it had happened? Could it have existed so long? Tiny spores lying dormant in dry soil or rubble till one day something disturbed them and a drop of moisture brought back normal reproduction?

And, after all, what were legends and superstitions? Childish nonsense, or warnings that had once been based on reality? Symbolic stories to protect simple people? Was there still a Plague Maiden at Rudisheim? Could the sickness have lived on and something pretty nasty really be waiting in the dark? Marcus turned to the cages again. The big piebald rat was almost through the last barrier, but it looked very weak and there was a dribble of blood on its muzzle. He swung round as the door burst open.

'Hello, sir. Sorry to dash in like that, but I think you should see these at once.' Wilson laid a pile of morning papers on the table. 'It's making quite a stir.'

'Yes, quite a stir.' Marcus glanced at the first of them. Following last night's story, half the population of England appeared to think they might have been infected and hospitals had been deluged with demands for inoculation. In West Berlin, a laboratory had been broken into and a huge quantity of drugs stolen.

'Yes, I thought this might happen after those damned headlines,' he said. 'As always, you underestimate things, Peter.'

'Sorry, Sir Marcus, but you always used to say it was a good fault.' Wilson handed him a scribbled note. 'This came through to the switchboard just now. Another case in Berlin. The symptoms were about the same as the others.'

'Thanks.' Marcus held it under the light. 'Ruth Eulenburg—aged thirty-six—widow, living alone—no known connection with the Fenwick child established, but symptoms similar if not identical with those of Major Wood—found by police after telephone operator reported a woman sobbing and raving on the line—in ambulance kept repeating the name of somebody called Clever Gretel—died, seven a.m. Central European time.'

'And she kept saying that, did she? Clever Gretel.' Marcus laid down the paper and looked at Wilson. 'Name mean anything to you, Peter?'

'Well, not really mean anything, sir. She was obviously just raving. I think Gretel is a fairy-story character. Maybe Hans Andersen.'

'No, it's Grimm, not Andersen. Gretel was the woman who kept planning against imaginary misfortunes. As you say, it probably was just delirious raving, but the Fenwick boy raved too. He kept talking about somebody named Iron Hans who is another character from Grimm. Don't you think there could be a connection?' He put his hand on Wilson's arm and stared hard at him.

'And tell me something else, Peter. We've been together a long time and I want the truth. This theory of mine, about a return of the Black Death bacillus: do you think there is anything in it, or am I going right round the bend?'

'No, sir, of course you're not. All the same, I do feel that it's too early to say what it is yet. I think you may be playing a hunch—jumping to conclusions without any—'

'Without any real evidence or proper observation.' Marcus picked up the newspaper again. 'You're quite right, of course, but what else can I do? We've no time for a full investigation. Once this thing gets going it could start the worst epidemic since the fourteenth century. I've just got to play my hunch and hope that it's right.' He glanced over his shoulder at the cages. The big rat had crawled into the top compartment where an ultra-violet bulb simulated daylight, but it hadn't much longer to live. The blood from its jaw was a dark stream and it was staggering around in circles.

'Go and telephone General Kirk,' he said. 'The number is on my desk next door. Tell him I want a visa for East Germany straight away.' He stood watching the rat as Wilson hurried out of the room. It fell on its side kicking feebly, and he picked up his pad again.

'But who are they?' he thought, as he noted the time of the animal's death. 'Who are they, and what is the connection? Iron Hans and Clever Gretel?'

Six hundred miles from the Central Laboratories another rat was dying. It wasn't a sleek, glossy specimen like Marcus Levin's, but an old, bloated grandfather of the sewers with warts around the ears and the scars of a hundred underground battles on its skin. It crawled slowly up from a manmade hole, twisted round three times like a kitten chasing its own tail and then fell on its side. In her little warm room a few yards away Clever Gretel was smiling.

CHAPTER ELEVEN

'THIS is Captain Hanks again, ladies and gentlemen, and once more I do apologize for having to ask you to keep your seat belts fastened a little longer.' The pilot's voice on the loudspeakers was breezy and self-assured. 'There's still a bit of bad weather in front of us, but nothing to be alarmed about. We're not going through it, but just taking a look-see, as one might say.' He chuckled but, as though in answer, the plane bucked violently and Kirk swayed across the seat, his shoulder colliding with Marcus Levin's.

'Sorry about that, ladies and gentlemen. My fault really. I should have kept above it, but I was hoping to get you to Tempelhof on time.'

'Why can't the fellow keep quiet and concentrate on flying his blasted aeroplane?' Kirk scowled and mopped his forehead. His face was an unhealthy, mottled green. 'On time indeed! We're fifteen minutes late already, and my appointment is for noon sharp.

'No, no, none of your pills, Doctor. I'm just going to bear it, though I can't say I feel like grinning.' He brushed aside Marcus's offer and turned to von Zuler, who had joined them at Hanover.

'And before I keep that appointment, Herr von Zuler, I must have more facts. This man Petrov has offered to see us personally, which proves, to my satisfaction at least, that the Russians are prepared to co-operate with us if we are able to give them certain assurances.' He tucked away his handkerchief and stared gloomily out of the port-hole at the swirling mist.

'But what assurance can I give them? What can I say to Petrov? We think that the Fenwick boy fell from the train somewhere between Magdeburg and the border. We think that he picked up the bug somewhere in East Germany and was smuggled into Berlin by one of the escape routes, but we can't prove anything. Since your people went and killed that sleeping-car attendant, we haven't even got one witness.'

'I know that, Herr General, and the officer responsible for Loser's death will stand trial for murder.' Von Zuler sat slumped far back in the seat with his metal leg stretched out in front of him. 'Whatever you say, though, I don't think we should presume that he was taken into West Berlin by one of the escape routes. At this stage we can't really be sure about anything.'

'No, we can't be sure, but in my mind there's very little doubt about it.' There was a sudden break in the cloud and through it Kirk could make out the line of the Berlin—Helmstedt autobahn. 'We know that that woman, Ruth Eulenburg, was a member of the Freiheit Organization which exists for the purpose of smuggling out refugees from the East. We know that she could have been infected by Billy Fenwick and, to me, it appears likely the name she kept repeating, Clever Gretel, was a code name for her contact in the East who brought the boy through. Doesn't that sound feasible to you?'

'Feasible, but not certain, General.' Von Zuler's eyes were half-closed and he looked bored. 'At this stage, we just don't know what happened.'

'But we've damned well got to know.' Kirk's voice was very weary and his torn hand trembled on the arm of the seat. 'Sir Marcus has told you the seriousness of the situation and we have to find the original source before a full-scale epidemic breaks out. If it is in East Germany we must have the co-operation of the M.V.D., which means showing them that we have come in good faith. It could even mean giving them the names of the people who organize the escape routes. I'd hate to do that, but it may be necessary. You could supply me with those names, couldn't you, von Zuler?'

'I might be able to find them out for you, General Kirk, but at this stage I'm not even going to try.' The German stared across at him and his eyes were as hard as pebbles screwed into his face by some revolting surgical operation.

'And would you really expect me to do so, General? To hunt down my own people and betray them to the Russians?'

'Yes, I may expect you to do that, Herr von Zuler. Believe me, I dislike the thought of it as much as you do, but to stop an epidemic it may be necessary.' Though Kirk felt sympathy for the man, it was quite unimportant as he remembered the things he had seen in the laboratory the night before.

'Sir Marcus,' he said, 'once again will you try and explain to Herr von Zuler just how serious this business is.'

'I'll try, General, but as I said before, I can't be very exact. At the moment we haven't got enough facts to be sure about anything.' Marcus turned to the German and heard himself automatically repeating the little that they did know: the production of the spores, the spread of the infection, the periods of incubation. As he spoke, the plane tilted slightly and he could see the city spread out beneath them; the Wannsee lakes like frosted glass, snow on the trees of the Grunewald and the tall mast of the Funkturm sliding away to the west. It was twenty years since he'd last seen it and then he had been locked in a cattle-truck with fifty other human beings. He was more fortunate than most of his companions, though, for he'd been crammed against the side of the truck and through the slats he had looked out and seen a great glow in the sky. He'd felt hope for the first time in years as he watched that enormous light and known it was Berlin burning.

'This is Captain Hanks again, ladies and gentlemen.' The pilot's voice broke into his memories and explanation as the plane sank down to the rectangle of Tempelhof. 'We will be landing in a few moments, so please extinguish all cigarettes. I can't say that I hope you have had a pleasant trip after those bumps just now, but at least we are only twenty minutes behind schedule.'

'Thank you, Sir Marcus. That was a very clear explanation.'

Von Zuler stubbed out his cigarette and nodded. 'I am sure the situation could become as serious as you say, but I haven't changed my mind yet.

'No, gentlemen, though this disease may be all you claim, there have only been three reported cases so far, and that's not enough to make me do what you ask.' His hard eyes were pleading as he looked across at Kirk.

'As an Englishman, General, you can't understand what those escape routes mean to us in Germany. Since the wall went up, only a trickle of people manage to get through, of course, but at least there is a trickle. At least there is some hope that families may be reunited one day. Without them I think we might have a mass hysteria, a group neurosis on our hands which would make your plague epidemic appear almost unimportant. It is likely that their chief organizer is somebody in the East German hierarchy who risks his life every minute just to help others. I don't know his name and I wouldn't tell you if I did. No, Sir Marcus, unless the medical authorities can give me more proof of the dangers involved, I just can't help you.'

'We will, Herr von Zuler. We'll give you the proof all right, or rather that bacillus will. God, can't you realize the speed at which it can spread?' As he spoke a clear picture of the things floating on the slide, dividing and releasing their spores, flashed through Marcus's mind. 'There may be only three reported cases so far, but how many others are there which we don't know about? Can't you try and imagine what will happen once it really breaks out in a big city? We were lucky to get the boy's contacts, but . . .'

'Easy, Doctor. Just take it easy.' Kirk's hand gripped his arm and cut short the outburst. Already the plane had touched down and was running towards the reception building. Marcus nodded wearily and picked up his case, praying for a miracle to change the German's mind.

'Zu Befehl, Herr Kommissar.' One of von Zuler's assistants was waiting on the tarmac. He clicked his heels and bowed stiffly to Kirk and Marcus, obviously impressed by a full general and an internationally known specialist. A porter and two uniformed policemen were standing beside him.

'A car is waiting, gentlemen, and arrangements have been made for you to pass through the Brandenburger check point into East Berlin. But I was asked to give this to Sir Marcus Levin. It is from Professor Mannheim of the Semmelweiss Hospital.'

'Thank you.' Marcus ripped open the envelope. Mannheim's observations were almost exactly the same as his own. Abnormal sporification, abnormal reproductivity, abnormal speed in the life cycle. And so far no antibiotic or bacteriocide to touch it. Everything they knew and dreaded and not one ray of hope. He stuffed the letter into his pocket, preparing to follow Kirk and von Zuler to the reception hall, and then paused. The porter was coming down the steps with their bags now. A heavy, middle-aged man in a faded blue uniform, with a face which was remarkable for nothing except stupidity. But as he looked at his face, Marcus had the strange feeling that he should know him, that he had seen him somewhere before, that it was important that he remembered where.

Yes, the face really was familiar. Thick, stupid features bloated with cold, a curved nose and a double chin which pressed against the folds of his jacket as he lifted the bags on to the trolley. Just where had he seen the man?

'Aren't you coming, old boy?' Kirk frowned back at him. 'Do let's hurry up and get inside. It's freezing out here.'

'Yes, of course. I'm just coming.' Marcus followed him towards the entrance. It was ridiculous, of course. Though he'd never been to Tempelhof before, there could be a dozen explanations. The man obviously resembled someone else or had worked at an airport in West Germany. Hamburg perhaps. He'd been to Hamburg himself three times last year. Yes, that was probably it, and you really must control yourself, he thought. Already his hunch about Rudisheim felt slightly ridiculous, and now this. Anxiety because a porter's face looked familiar.

All the same, it was important. Something told him that it was important. He stopped and turned. The porter was coming up the slope toward him, and though he looked strong enough, he was making heavy weather of it; the barrow zigzagging on the concrete and his breath like a cloud of steam in the cold air. He had to remember where he had seen that face before. A hooked nose between swollen cheeks, bloodshot brown eyes and a heavy double chin straining against the uniform jacket. And then as he watched him Marcus knew that he had been wrong: he had never seen the man before. It was what had happened to him that he recognized. The features couldn't have been merely bloated with cold because the cheeks were so swollen as to appear flat and the jaw was twice its normal size. 'Lion-faced' was the usual way of describing the condition, and the last time he had seen it was shortly before Billy Fenwick died.

'Just a minute, porter. Please put down your barrow for a moment. I am a doctor and I want to ask you something.' Marcus nodded as the man lowered the shafts and stared vacantly at him. His breath was stale and sour and he drew back slightly before it. Was he really safe, he wondered? Could he be sure that the vaccine had taken?

'Anything wrong, Sir Marcus? One of your cases been left behind?' Von Zuler came hurrying back to him, but he waved him aside.

'No, nothing like that, but keep away from us please. And get somebody on to the Isolation Hospital. Have them send over an ambulance right away.

'Now, porter, please sit down on the bench over here and let me look at you. Good.' The man's forehead felt like a hot-water bottle under his fingers and the pulse was racing. 'What is your name?'

'Kubisiac. Franz Kubisiac.'

'Well, don't worry, Franz. Everything is going to be all right.' Even in the bare concrete corridor the smooth, bedside manner came automatically to him. 'How long have you been feeling ill?'

'About two days, Herr Doktor, but it is nothing.' The man shook his head stupidly. 'Only a little chill that will soon pass. Now, please let me get on with my work, Herr Doktor.'

'In a moment, Franz, in just a moment, but first I want to ask you something else. Were you on duty when the little English boy was put on the plane? Did you go near him?'

'Yes, but what if I did? What has that to do with it? As I told you, this is just a chill and I want to get on with my work.' There was anger as well as stupidity in his eyes now.

'I see, just a chill, eh? And you didn't get yourself inoculated, Franz? You knew that you should have done, but you were afraid your arm would swell up and you would lose overtime perhaps? Have you a family to keep?' Marcus's hand reached out towards the tunic as he spoke.

'Yes, a wife and three kids; little girls. They need a lot of money. All the time my wife asks for money. I couldn't afford to go sick. Now, please let me get on, Herr Doktor.'

'No, Franz, not till I've had a proper look at you. But keep those people away, can't you?' Quite a crowd was beginning to gather in the passage and Marcus motioned von Zuler to hold them back.

'And now let me have a look at your chest, Franz. It won't take a moment.' His fingers were undoing the top button when Kubisiac's face altered. A second before it had merely shown stupidity and anger but without any warning it suddenly changed to a mask of almost animal rage. 'No,' he said. 'No, no, leave me alone!' He stood up, his body stiffened, and his arm swung out like a flail. 'Just leave me alone!'

'Stop him! Don't let him get away!' It felt as though the Adam's apple had been torn out of his throat, but even as he fell Marcus tried to make them understand. Typical, he thought, feeling his knees start to buckle and his umbrella snap under his weight. As with rats the will to escape is the only emotion which remains important. Quite typical. The concrete floor rushed up to meet him and the world went dark.

'You all right, Doctor?' They had propped him on the bench and Kirk's face was frowning down at him. 'Feeling better?'

'Yes, I'm all right.' His eyes seemed to blur for a moment and then steady themselves into focus. 'How long have I been out? Only a few seconds? Good. And the porter, Kubisiac? You stopped him?'

'Yes, after he went berserk and hit you, one of the policemen laid him out with his truncheon. They put him in a waiting room over there. But take it easy, old boy. Sit still for a bit. It was a hell of a bang he gave you.' Kirk's eyes were full of concern as Marcus stood up and moved towards the room.

'No, I'm all right. Quite all right, but I must look at him.' He steadied himself against the door frame as the floor seemed to tilt slightly, and walked on. Kubisiac was lying on a sofa by the far wall, and there was a mirror above him. Marcus grinned ruefully back at it. Sir Marcus Levin the natty dresser, he thought. Marcus Levin who takes such a pride in his appearance. Well, you don't look very natty now. Blood was dripping on to his collar from a graze on his cheek, his jacket was covered with white dust and his right eye was starting to blacken. He shrugged his shoulders and then bent down over Kubisiac. The man's eyes were open but he was quite unconscious.

'And I don't want anybody in here till the ambulance arrives,' he said, and then changed his mind, remembering the miracle he had prayed for on the plane. 'That is, nobody except you, Herr von Zuler. I would like you to see this, please.' He watched von Zuler come towards him and ripped open Kubisiac's tunic and shirt. In the V of the sweat-stained vest was the thing he knew he would find: the scarlet rash like tiny roses on the skin.

'Herr von Zuler,' he said. 'A few minutes ago you refused to give General Kirk the information he needs till you have more proof of the dangers involved.

'Well, here is your proof. This man was infected because for a short space of time he breathed the same air as the Fenwick boy. He will probably die and he has a wife and three children who are almost certainly carriers by now.' He gripped the German's arm and pulled him forward.

'Go on, look at him, von Zuler. Smell his breath, examine the rash, better still feel his body.' His free hand undid Kubisiac's trouser buttons as he spoke.

'Yes, that's it. Put your hand into the groin and tell me that you need more proof.' Von Zuler was struggling against him but Levin forced his arm down.

'Yes, you can feel the bubo, can't you? Be very careful because it could burst at any moment. About the size of a small plum, would you say? It's hard and corrugated too though, isn't it? Perhaps rather like a walnut? Go on, make a proper examination, and then tell me that you still refuse the information.'

'Please, please, Sir Marcus.' Von Zuler's body went suddenly slack and then with a single convulsive jerk he pulled himself free and stood staring at Marcus. He didn't seem able to speak for a moment and his eyes didn't look completely sane.

'All right,' he said, when at last he could say anything. 'All right. You win. I'll get you the names you want and may God forgive me for it.' He turned and lurched out into the corridor, fighting to control his urge to vomit.

CHAPTER TWELVE

'AH, there you are at last, gentlemen. Better late than never, and it is a great pleasure to welcome you here.' Gregor Petrov jumped up from behind a desk, bowed, smiled and stretched out his hand, apparently in a single action. He was dressed in what he hoped would impress Kirk as being the best possible taste: corduroy slacks and a thick green Harris tweed jacket purchased in London fifteen years ago. On his little pudgy body they gave him the air of a forest gnome waiting to ensnare the lost traveller in some rather sinister fairy story.

'General Kirk,' he said, beaming up at him and squeezing his hand. 'General Charles Kirk, my old antagonist in person. Walk into my parlour, General. I shall regard this meeting as one of the high-spots of my life.' He chuckled and turned to Marcus, his three chins joggling up and down over his tight collar.

'And you, sir, will be Sir Marcus Levin. A pleasure, too, though I am sorry to hear of your unfortunate experience at the airport. Oh, yes, General, we also have our sources of information.

'But let me introduce you to my colleagues. Colonel Gustav Behr of the People's Police; Dr Glauser from the Potsdam Institute of Histopathology who has kindly offered to help us; my secretary, Miss Tania Valina. Would you do the honours, please, Tania?'

He nodded approvingly as the girl brought over a tray of glasses.

'Good. Now, let's sit down and be comfortable, gentlemen. Take this chair by the fire, General. I have heard of your dislike of badly-heated rooms and only hope that this one is warm enough. I had it specially built up for you.' The stove was almost red-hot and looked big enough to propel a small ship.

'It is most comfortable, Comrade Petrov.' Kirk studied him as he smiled back. He knew that Petrov, for all his benevolent, slightly comic manner, was a very shrewd man who would drive a hard bargain before giving any co-operation.

'Excellent. But please don't call me "Comrade", General Kirk. It is a rather archaic form of address now, only used by our real die-hards; my wife amongst them. I would much prefer "Mister".

'Be careful, though, General. Be very careful which glass you take.' He chuckled again as Tania held out the tray. 'Four glasses contain nothing but good Russian vodka, but perhaps the other two may have been doctored. Sorry, Sir Marcus.' He grinned apologetically, congratulating himself on his colloquial English.

'Perhaps when you drink from them you will both sleep a little. And, while he is sleeping, General Kirk might be persuaded to tell me some very interesting things about his organization. What would you use to make him talk, Sir Marcus? Pentothal perhaps?'

'I'll take a chance on that, Mr Petrov. Thank you.' Kirk picked up the nearest glass. 'I don't think the details of either of our organizations are of much importance at the moment, except in so far as they can help us to locate the source of this plague. And, if they can't locate it quickly, I think we may be both out of business before long.'

'I see. Then your very good health, gentlemen. Your good health and to the destruction of this mysterious disease of which I have heard so much and "do in part believe", if I may quote from Shakespeare.' He raised his glass and knocked back the vodka in a single quick movement.

'Now, let's get down to business, shall we?' He replaced the glass on the tray and stopped smiling. As he did so his face lost all its benevolent flabbiness.

'I have naturally seen your newspapers and listened to your radio, General. I have also read through the very full account you sent us and heard what our own agents in England and West Germany have been able to find out. I'm afraid that I still only do in part believe.' His hand rapped sharply on the table as though swatting a fly he had seen crawling across it and he turned to Marcus Levin.

'Sir Marcus,' he said, 'I understand that you have brought the technical data of this—this scourge with you. As they will probably be incomprehensible to all of us except Dr Glauser, perhaps you would take them over to the desk there and go through them with him. Thank you.'

Petrov watched the two men move away and then looked past them out of the window. The snow was still swirling over the Linden. Clean, cold snow, blanketing the earth and purifying it. He believed every word in Kirk's report, but he wasn't going to admit it; not yet. Though he could die of plague as easily as anyone else, though he dreaded the very thought of an epidemic, it was still his job to exploit the situation.

'Well, General, let's have all the facts. Let's have all your cards on the table. I am prepared to believe that this disease is as deadly and repulsive as your report states, and I agree that we must co-operate with you in finding the source and wiping it out. But . . .' Once more his hand rapped the table. 'Just where is that source, General?

'Oh, yes, I know what you people say. That the child fell from a train which was passing through East Germany and he became infected here. But what evidence can you give us that this is true? Remember that your earlier story stated that we had kidnapped the boy to bring pressure on his father who worked in some signals office. Not a very charitable idea, General, and the present version is scarcely more so. Look for yourself.' He picked up a copy of the *Morning Echo* and handed it to Kirk. The headlines read 'Russian Germs Loose', and a notice at the foot of the column urged the reader to turn to John Forest's report on page 2.

'No, not very friendly, is it? We are accused of running some kind of bacteriological warfare establishment in Germany, letting a culture get loose by accident and then rounding up all infected persons to pretend there has been no outbreak over here.'

'That is not the official view, Mr Petrov, and there will be no more articles of this kind.' Kirk scowled at the page. 'Orders for censorship have already been given.'

'I am sure they have, my friend. Just as we have given orders to stop this.' Petrov tapped a copy of Pravda. 'I don't know if you read Russian, but this is the same sort of thing, except that the parts are reversed. Here it says that the germs came from a Western establishment, the Fenwick child was never in East Germany at all, and the whole business is a trick to discredit the peace-loving Soviet people. "Jackals", "spreaders of filth" are some of the terms used to describe you.' He pushed the paper away from him, as though it were an extremely disgusting object.

'Yes, lies, General. I am personally sure of that. But can you prove they are lies, any more than we can disprove what your Press says about us? Our medical experts seem to be falling foul of each other, though.' The two doctors were arguing violently. Glauser's face was flushed and Marcus appeared to be regarding him with a look of bored contempt: the expression of a man who could make an apology sound far worse than his original insult.

'And let's have the East German view. Colonel Behr, will you please tell the general what your people have discovered so far?'

'There is nothing to tell—nothing at all.' Behr was a tall, thin man with a rather sour and old-maidish expression. He looked more like a schoolteacher than a policeman. 'A most thorough investigation was made and there have been no cases of plague reported anywhere in our territory. Nor is there the slightest evidence that the child was ever in the People's Republic. In my opinion the *Pravda* article is materially correct. If the bacillus exists, it must have come from the West.'

'Thank you, Gustav.' Petrov leaned back in his chair and

nodded. 'There you are, General Kirk. There has been no outbreak here, so why should we co-operate with you?'

'Because you can die of plague as well as we can, Mr Petrov, and I don't think your wall will keep it out.' Kirk turned away from him and looked at Behr. He had never felt more miserable in his life. Von Zuler had kept his word to Marcus. Half an hour after arriving at Tempelhof he had got them the information they needed to bargain with Petrov. Kirk hated the thought of giving it to him, but now he knew that he would have to.

'Yes, we can die of plague, General.' As though reading his mind, the Russian smiled again. 'And you will get the collaboration you ask for. If the source of this germ is in East Germany, it will be found. I will also allow Sir Marcus to go anywhere he wants and provide him with an escort. In return you must collaborate with me. The boy can only have reached West Berlin by one of the escape routes, and to trace his movements we must talk to the people who brought him through. Well, where can we find them, General Kirk? Who is Brother Lustig?'

Brother Lustig? Kirk's head jerked back in his surprise. Von Zuler hadn't mentioned the code name, but it was all fitting together. Another character from Grimm: the soldier who gave away his last crust to a beggar. Iron Hans, Clever Gretel, and now Brother Lustig.

'This is ridiculous, Gregor.' Behr broke in before he could answer. There was an odd expression on his face which Kirk couldn't recognize, though he felt he should know what it was. 'Brother Lustig is dead. He was killed in Heinersdorf six months ago while trying to escape from the police. His real name was Gunter Kirsten and since he died we have closed all the escape routes. You have my word for that, Gregor. No refugees get out today and the whole story is a Western trick to discredit us; a propaganda stunt. Lustig is dead.'

'So you have told me, Gustav; many times.' Petrov stood up and massaged his hands over the stove. 'And once again I repeat that I don't believe you. I think that you are trying to pretend to yourself that your department is rather more efficient than it really is.

'No, Kirsten wasn't Brother Lustig, Gustav. The man, or possibly woman, is still alive. I know it. I can feel it. Somebody we trust probably. Somebody in authority who has fooled us for years. And we are going to get him, Gustav. We are going to get him and we are going to make him talk. When he talks, not only will the escape routes be finished for good and all, but their organizers will be in the hollow of my hand.' He held out his right hand, grinning at it, and nodded to Kirk.

'After that, General, you will not have to worry about me any more. I shall retire, loaded down with honours. Who knows, they might even give me an Order of Lenin? Stranger things have happened.'

'Mr Petrov, it is five o'clock. Time for the British news.' Tania had already got up and crossed to the radio.

'Yes, turn it on, my dear. I expect that our friends will like to hear the recent developments from their country.' Petrov sat down again as the announcer's voice echoed across the room.

'. . . three further cases of bubonic plague have been reported in London this morning and the government is expected to announce a national emergency at any moment. The Queen and the Duke of Edinburgh are returning from Sandringham tonight. At North Kensington this afternoon a number of people were detained when rioting broke out at an immunization centre. The trouble appears to have started when three men attempted to force their way to the front of a queue. In the ensuing struggle a seventeen-year-old youth received severe head injuries. Replying to Mr Dylan Mogg-Rees for the Opposition, the Minister of Health stated that ample stocks of serum were available and there was no undue cause for alarm.'

'You have heard enough, General?' Petrov motioned to Tania to switch off the set.

'Yes, things begin to move, don't they? More cases, civil disturbance, a national emergency, your Royal Family hurrying home to show that all is well. Doesn't that prove that you must collaborate with us now? If we are to help, you must tell us how that boy entered West Berlin.' His eyes were quite unblinking as he stared at Kirk.

'Come on, General, I'm waiting. Who is Brother Lustig?'

'Gregor Ilyavitch, this is ridiculous.' Behr leaned forward, shaking his head. 'There is no such person any more. Lustig is dead. He was killed in Heinersdorf, as I told you.'

'Shut up, Gustav.' Without taking his eyes from Kirk, the Russian turned slightly towards the men at the desk. 'Well, gentlemen, you have had some minutes of discussion. Are you agreed about the seriousness of the situation?'

'We are agreed in part, Comrade Petrov.' Marcus Levin had obviously got the better of the argument and Glauser sounded slightly crushed. 'I still consider that this bacillus is a man-made mutant, probably produced in the West. I do agree, however, that unless we can find the source soon and also an effective bacteriocide, the world is in very great danger.'

'Thank you, Doctor.' Petrov's hand tapped up and down on the desk as he spoke. 'Well, General Kirk, it's up to you, isn't it? Only you can help us to find the source. How did the Fenwick boy enter West Berlin? Who is Brother Lustig?'

'Give me a minute, Mr Petrov. Just one minute.' Kirk looked away from him and stared at the stove. He could see a row of faces melting before it and all of them were his own. Had it been the same with other betrayers, he wondered? Had Judas felt hell fire as he took the silver? In a few seconds he would have to kill the hopes of half a nation and destroy a man for whom he felt deep respect. There was nothing else that he could do. 'National Emergency'—'More Cases'—'Civil Disturbance'. Three short sentences on the radio had destroyed all freedom of choice.

'Yes, I'll tell you,' he said at last, but he was speaking to Behr rather than Petrov. The German looked completely bored and indifferent, the observer of some dull and badly acted play longing for the final curtain.

'The man you want—the man who runs the escape routes and calls himself Brother Lustig is . . . No . . .' His voice became a shout and he jumped to his feet. 'No, don't do it. You mustn't do it.' He hurled himself across the table, but he was too late. Slowly and indifferently, as though the action was completely trivial, Gustav Behr pulled out a revolver, placed the muzzle in his mouth and pressed the trigger.

CHAPTER THIRTEEN

A FOOL'S errand, a wild-goose chase, a labour in vain. The phrases ran through Marcus Levin's head against the clatter of the car chains. What the hell, he thought, just what the hell are you doing and what do you expect to find? Fairy tales, legends, the history of a monastery that has been deserted for six hundred years. While at every minute, in every news bulletin, more cases were being reported and the pandemic was gathering strength.

All the same, though he couldn't explain why, Marcus knew that he was right in going to Rudisheim. He lit a cigarette and stared out through the windscreen. The wipers were having a struggle to keep it clear and the snow swirled and eddied across the flat countryside, though to the left of the road he could make out a railway embankment. The same line, possibly, along which his cattle-truck had rumbled to Belsen so many years ago. In the rich, crowded streets of West Germany he was always conscious of that journey, but today, driving through the untilled fields and broken-down villages of the East, it seemed strangely unimportant, almost as though it had happened to someone else.

'Can I give you a spell, my dear?' He looked across at Tania Valina. 'You have been driving a long time now.'

'It is all right. I enjoy it. Besides I do not suppose your licence will be valid for what they call Iron Curtain countries.' She smiled at him without taking her eyes off the road. 'You speak very good Russian, Sir Marcus.'

'Thank you. It is a long time since I had the opportunity to do so.' He nodded, trying to remember just how many languages he did know. Two classical, four European, Yiddish, Hindi and three Oriental dialects which she wouldn't have heard of.

'But tell me something. Why did Mr Petrov supply you as my escort? Was he merely being courteous, or did he want somebody he trusts to keep an eye on my movements? To see that I don't get up to any mischief?'

'Both, Sir Marcus. You want to go to this place Rudisheim as a private person . . . to question the inhabitants without appearing to have any official position. Mr Petrov thought I would be an unobtrusive escort and also carry a certain authority should you come up against the East German authorities.' She grinned to herself, remembering Petrov's actual words. 'This man is said to be a great medical expert, but in other matters he may be a fool. It is up to you to see that he neither makes, nor gets into, any trouble. To be a little mother to him, in fact.'

'And do you think that Colonel Behr will die, Sir Marcus?'

'He'll die all right. He's probably dead already.' Marcus glanced at the dashboard clock. It was over two and a half hours since Behr had pulled out his revolver. 'If General Kirk hadn't managed to knock his hand to one side he would have died on the spot. The question is, can they make him talk before he dies?' That was ludicrous, of course. The word was communicate, for

Behr would never talk again. The blast and bullet had shattered his vocal cords and torn the tongue to shreds. He had somehow retained consciousness, though. Marcus remembered how the man had struggled against Glauser and himself as they fought to save his life. By some trick of extra-sensory perception he had almost seemed to hear him praying for their fingers to slip from the arteries and let the blood drain away.

Nonsense, too! There was no such thing as telepathy; no scientific proof for it. It was as absurd as . . . Yes, as absurd as his own hunch—the wild-goose chase which was taking them to Rudisheim.

'But he must talk. They must make him tell everything before he dies.' As though to drive home the point, Tania accelerated and the car took the next bend like a sledge. 'They must make him tell everything. Not only about the English boy, but about the escape routes and the people he worked with. To think that during all those years he worked for the Vopo he was betraying us.'

'Yes, I suppose he was a traitor, and I agree that, if it is possible, he must give up his information. But don't you think he was quite a patriot as well? He gambled his life every minute of the day and, when he was finally found out, he tried to kill himself rather than expose his comrades. Can't you appreciate that, Miss Valina?'

'I can appreciate nothing about such creatures.' Another bend loomed ahead and once again her foot came down on the accelerator. 'To me they are just vermin.'

'I see. You are a hard woman, I'm afraid, comrade.' Marcus pulled at his cigarette and then clutched the door handle as the car corkscrewed across the road, narrowly missing a telegraph pole. 'Look out, though. You'll have us over in a minute.'

'It is all right. I am a good driver and this is a very safe car; a lovely car.' She beamed proprietorially at the bonnet of the battered Zis. 'Do you have a car of your own in England, Sir Marcus?'

'Yes, I have a car.' An image of his gleaming Ferrari shone before Marcus's eyes. 'A much nicer car than this, Comrade Valina.'

'I see. Then you are either a braggart or a very rich man. Both bad things, I think. Yes, Sir Marcus Levin, the rich English Jew.'

'Quite right. I'm rich enough. Do you object to my being a Jew?'

'Do I object?' Tania frowned slightly. 'On the question of

the Semitic problem, I naturally follow the Party line. As far as I have any personal views on the subject . . .' Her frown deepened in concentration. 'Mr Petrov has a thing about his staff speaking colloquial English and I took a course last year. Let me see if I can express myself in it.' She took her eyes off the road for a moment and glanced across at him.

'No, Sir Marcus, I don't give a damn about your being a Jew, one way or the other. At the same time, I have been told that all Western Jews are rich.'

'Then, if I may reply in a similar manner, you've been fed a load of crap, my sweet.' Marcus laughed and relaxed as the car finally reached a straight stretch of road. 'Oh, Luba,' he said, humming lightly against the whine of the engine. 'Oh, Luba, my little Bolshevik girl.'

'My name is Tania.' She frowned again and then smiled. 'Oh, I see. You know that song, Sir Marcus? About the woman who hangs about army camps. Where did you hear it?'

'A long, long time ago, my dear. Probably before you were born.' Marcus considered how it had been. The Soviet troops had looked as though they would stay in the town indefinitely, and then one day they had marched out and an S.S. regiment moved in.

'I heard it in Poland during the spring of '40,' he said. 'Let me see if I can remember the words. Yes, "Though your body's like a hay sack and you're barmy, it's your vigour makes us shrug aside the cost. You're the backbone of our mighty Russian army. Without you the Bolsheviki—Without you the Bolsheviki—" ' Marcus waved his cigarette like a baton and Tania joined him in a rich, throbbing contralto. ' "Without you the Bolsheviki would be lost . . ." '

The car clattered over a wooden bridge, lurched up a slope and slid past a sign that read 'Rudisheim 16 Km.'

'In an hour, comrade, maybe two, even in a few minutes. Who knows?' The doctor straightened from the operating table. Above the wad of bandages around his neck, Behr looked as though he were already dead, and tubes ran from jars and cylinders into his body.

'If you ask me, it is a wonder that he is still alive. Without oxygen and the constant transfusions he would have gone out a long time ago.'

'Yes, so you have said before.' Petrov nodded. 'But before he dies, is there any chance that he can be made to talk? He has certain information which it is essential . . .'

'Talk?' The doctor smiled at all lay ignorance. 'There is not the slightest chance of his talking, Comrade Petrov. The vocal cords are shattered and we had to remove most of his tongue before we could stop the bleeding. Even if he wished to talk—even if we pumped him full of EX3, it would be impossible. And this man doesn't want to talk.' He leaned forward over Behr again and shook his head. 'He just wants to die.'

EX3. Kirk pricked up his ears with professional interest. So that was the name of their latest truth drug, was it? Poor devil, though. Behr's eyes were open and they seemed to be pleading for death. Pleading to be able to protect his organization and the names of the people who had worked with him. Kirk felt great compassion as he looked at him.

All the same, they had to make him communicate somehow. They had to trace Billy Fenwick's movements right back to the time he fell from the train. Somewhere along his route he must have picked up the disease and they had to find all his contacts: Iron Hans and Clever Gretel and whoever else had helped him. On the last news flash more cases had been reported; four in London and three in Western Germany. Seven bodies growing black, with the rash like a ring of tiny red flowers on the chest, and the obscene things between the thighs pulsing as though they had a life of their own.

And soon there would be more cases—soon the epidemic would start to spiral. The vaccine appeared to be working all right, but how long would stocks last? Less than an hour ago a Hanover doctor had been almost beaten to death because he had run out of serum. Once infection had taken place there was no drug to help, either, and public confidence would be breaking down before long. They had to find the source, the first carrier, and, though Marcus Levin might have gone off to Rudisheim following his hunch, Kirk was quite sure that Behr was the only person who could help them. Somehow he had to be made to give up his information.

'Excuse me a moment, Doctor,' he said. 'You have made it very clear to us that the man is unable to talk, but you also said that the spinal column is undamaged and there is a motor connection between the brain and the rest of the body. Now, if he wanted to communicate, is it possible that he might be able to write down the answers to a few simple questions?'

'Write!' It was Kirk's turn to receive that pitying smile. 'This man is practically dead already, Herr General. He is under maximum stimulation. You might just as well expect him to get up and walk across the room. Look for yourself.' He took a probe from the tray and held it between Behr's fingers. As soon as he removed his hand they opened and it fell to the floor.

'You see, Herr General?"

'Yes, I see, Doctor. I think that I really do see at last.' Kirk felt a sudden gleam of hope as he looked at Behr. For the last two hours the man's body had lain quite motionless, but now he had moved. For perhaps five seconds after the probe had fallen his right index finger had tapped against the side of the table.

'Gregor Ilyavitch,' he said, turning to Petrov. They had dropped formality from the moment that Behr shot himself. 'Did you notice the way his finger moved just now? As a policeman he will probably know the Morse code, and if he is able to move his fingers, he might . . .'

'Yes, yes, I understand. That could be our way.' Petrov frowned for a second and then his little pudgy hand squeezed Kirk's arm. 'Good, very good indeed. You are a clever fellow, my friend.' He turned to an assistant standing by the door. 'Get over to headquarters and bring back a buzzer and a couple of Morse keys. Be as quick as you can about it.

'Now, Doctor,' he said. 'Just what will happen if you give him this stuff of yours; the EX3? Will it make him want to communicate with us, even though he is unable to do so?'

'It will make him want to do anything you ask, Comrade Petrov, but he is so weak that . . .' He felt Behr's pulse and shrugged his shoulders.

'EX3 is a variant of Psilocybin administered with an accelerator. It has been used in the treatment of certain mental disturbances for years, but only recently has your profession adopted it.

'The general effect is to take the subject right back into the past so that he remembers things which have been shut away for years: childhood terrors of the dark, the feel of his mother's nipple, even what it was like to be a foetus in the womb. All that is relived in a matter of minutes, and afterwards he will feel so free, so contented and cleansed that he will want to answer any question you put to him. All the same, I don't think we should give him an injection. In his condition the initial shock will quite probably kill him.'

'Don't worry about that, Doctor. I will take full responsibility. You said he is dying anyway, so we have nothing to lose.' Petrov stared down at Behr's face. And I trusted you, Gustav, he thought. For years I trusted you. I almost counted you a friend, while all the time, right under our noses, you were betraying us. But now you are going to talk to me, Gustav. It will be the last action of your life, but you are going to tell me everything.

'And how long after the injection shall we know if he has stood up to this initial shock, Doctor?

'I see. Ten to fifteen minutes. Then give it to him. As I said, the responsibility is mine.' He watched him start to fill a syringe and turned to Kirk.

'Well, General,' he said, 'let's hope that your idea works. I don't know if you are a religious man, but if you are, I would advise you to pray. As a good dialectical materialist I am supposed to deny the existence of a personal God, but at this moment I am rather inclined to join you.' The drug had been administered now and they both glanced up at the big electric clock on the wall. One minute—two—three, and no change at all. Four—five; Behr's left eyelid quivered slightly, but nothing else happened. Six—seven; a little spasm of pain flickered across his face and he groaned. Eight—nine; his face became quite rigid for a moment with the eyes opening wider and wider till they seemed to be bursting out from the sockets. Ten—eleven—twelve, his whole body went slack and his eyes closed. The doctor reached out for the pulse again.

'He's made it, comrade,' he said. 'He's all yours, but I've got not the slightest idea how long he will last.'

'Thank you. Yes, give them to me please.' Petrov's assistant had returned and he took the equipment from him.

'Now, just stand to one side, Doctor. You've done all that was required of you.' He pulled up a chair beside the table, laid the buzzer beside Behr's head and very gently placed his finger on the Morse key. 'I imagine that it will be better if I try to contact him in Morse. In that way the reflexes might help.

'Well, are you still praying?' He grinned at Kirk as he lifted the other key. 'I very much doubt if this will work, but it appears to be our only chance.

'Der der dot—dot dot der—dot dot dot—der . . .' The tinny

sound of the buzzer rang across the room. 'Gustav, you must tell me everything. How did the child reach West Berlin? Who are the people who brought him through? Dot dot dot—dot der—der dot—dot dot dot. Who is Hans, Gustav? Who are Iron Hans and Clever Gretel?'

CHAPTER FOURTEEN

'THERE is no truth in it whatsoever.' For the fifth time Sergeant Goltz of the Rudisheim police bellowed the denial. He and his attendant minion, Constable Braun, were two vast men filled with self-esteem and, judging by their breath, several glasses of schnapps. Bearded and suitably dressed they could have brought down the house as pantomime ogres, and Marcus would have been only mildly surprised if Goltz had exclaimed 'Fe fi fo fum,' instead of 'Papiere bitte,' as he demanded their passports.

But, however great their self-importance, Tania's credentials had brought them to heel with much bowing and scraping and 'Gnä'es Fräuleins' and 'Zu Befehl, Herr Doktors'. Once it was established that she and Marcus had not come for any sinister motive, such as inspecting the police station, the giant's hospitality knew no bounds. Chairs had been pulled up before the stove in a small, private office, a bottle of cheap 'Clara' was produced and the fortunes of the Soviet Union, Great Britain, and the People's Republic of East Germany solemnly toasted. After Marcus's first question, however, helpfulness had ended abruptly.

'No, no, no.' Goltz was obviously incapable of normal speech and he shouted at the top of his voice, pacing across the floor with his huge face set in a scowl of disbelief. 'No, no, no.' The boards shuddered beneath his feet and Marcus could almost hear the thud of the big drum as the giant lumbered on to the stage.

'No, it is impossible. How often must I repeat that it is impossible?' His blue tunic was wrinkled and crumpled as if it could scarcely contain the enormous chest, and below it his stomach stood out like the broad end of a pear.

'For three days, Fräulein. For three days and nights people have done nothing but ask questions about that English child and I am getting sick and tired of it. We have had the army searching the district. Berlin has been on the telephone almost every hour.

Even Major Fischer from Magdeburg has been over to see us. And I have told them all that it is just not possible that the boy could have been here.' He came heavily to rest by the table and knocked back another glass of schnapps.

'Comrade Valina, this is my town. Before the war ten thousand people lived here. Now there are less than three thousand and I know them all. I was born here and I know every house and bomb site and rat-hole in Rudisheim. Is it possible that the boy could have been harboured here and I not have known about it?' He swung round to his subordinate for confirmation. 'Comrade Braun, is it possible?'

'It is quite impossible, Comrade Goltz.' The constable nodded in agreement. If anything he was slightly bigger than his superior and a deep scar on his right cheek gave his face a rather sinister and vulpine expression.

'Our investigations have been most thorough, and in my opinion the child never existed at all. The whole story is just a fabrication; propaganda put out by certain parties to discredit the Republic.' He glowered up at the wall above the stove. It was decorated by a photograph of Mr. Mikoyan smiling at a small blond child who had just presented him with a bunch of flowers. Beside Mikoyan was a poster showing a simian creature dressed in American uniform with a rope around its hairy neck. 'We have enough trees in East Berlin to hang every Western war-monger,' read the caption beneath it.

'Do you agree with me, Comrade Goltz?'

'I agree with you entirely, Comrade Braun; all propaganda.' His glass crashed down on the table to emphasize the point. Now that the initial shock of seeing Tania's credentials had worn off, the giants were getting out of hand. They had obviously run the town without check or interference for years, probably making a very good thing out if it, and the recent attention from outside was a sore point with them.

'Yes, propaganda. Dirty Western propaganda.' Again his glass beat on the table and again Marcus seemed to hear the thud of a drum from the orchestra pit. At any moment Goltz would declare that he smelt 'the blood of an Englishmun'. He turned away from the glowering face and studied the pictures on the wall. The photograph looked oddly pitted and pockmarked, as though breaking out in a rash and it only took him seconds to see why. Goltz and Braun might rail against the West for disturbing their peace, but they could scarcely regard themselves as pious Party members. Mr. Mikoyan's face had been used as a dart-board to while away the long winter evenings.

'That is quite enough, Sergeant. You will confine yourselves to answering our questions, please.' Tania's voice broke sharply in, but Marcus scarcely heard her. He was thinking of what Goltz had said, and what he had seen as they drove into Rudisheim. A town of ten thousand inhabitants that had shrunk to less than three thousand since the war. Deserted streets, rows of empty houses and shops with boards nailed across the windows, bombed ruins that nobody had troubled to clear or rebuild, and piles of rubble spilling into the roads and pavements. A place where anything could be hidden. A place where the ground had been disturbed and the rats could multiply unchecked. A sickness of the soil, they had once considered plague: a contagion sent from the stars to trouble the earth and drive the animals up into the world of men. Goltz's claim that he knew all that went on in the town was obviously just an idle boast too. Neither he nor Braun would notice anything a yard away from their noses. Marcus had almost begun to despair of his hunch in coming to Rudisheim, but it had suddenly grown much stronger.

'Plague, Fräulein! Plague in Rudisheim!' A howl of derision from the first pantomime lead brought him back to the present with a jerk.

'No, Fräulein. We keep ourselves informed, you know. We read the newspapers and listen to the radio, but, as I said before, it is just propaganda. If there were any truth in this story of an epidemic there would have been an outbreak in East Germany; cases here in Rudisheim. Apart from a little influenza there is no illness in this town. Ask anybody; the Mayor or Dr Humperdinck. Correct, Comrade Braun?'

'Perfectly correct, Comrade Goltz. We are a healthy people in these parts; perhaps the healthiest in Germany. It may be because of the pine forests around us.' As though to prove the point Braun inflated his chest till it appeared in danger of bursting. A huge grey wolf crouched before the pig's flimsy home. 'I'll huff and I'll puff and I'll blow your house down.'

'Yes, you look healthy enough, gentlemen, but I wonder how long you will remain so. You obviously have no idea of the speed at which this thing can travel, nor just how horrible its symptoms are. No, as a doctor, I wouldn't gamble on your chances of remaining healthy for very much longer.' Marcus had the satisfaction of seeing them wilt slightly before his professional stare.

'Now tell me something. Have either of you heard the story of the Black Virgin?'

'The Black Virgin?' Braun frowned for a second and then burst into a roar of laughter. 'No, that is a new one to me, Herr Doktor. You tell it to us and I will tell you the one about the railway porter who had three testicles.'

'Silence, constable. You should be ashamed of yourself, Comrade Braun.' Goltz scowled at him and nodded to Marcus.

'Yes, I know the story, Herr Doktor, but you have got it wrong. It is not "virgin", but "woman" that she is called. A hag who rides about the woods on the shoulders of a dead man. It is just a legend, of course; a folk-tale like the Rhinegold or the dragons in the valley of the Neckar . . .'

'Or the head of Rudolph.' Braun broke in, quite unabashed by his rebuff.

'You know about that?' Marcus frowned, remembering the account he had read in Vogel's *Great Pandemic*. 'The relic that was kept in the church?'

'But naturally, Herr Doktor. Before it was stolen everybody in Rudisheim knew about it. The head of a monk cast in bronze, I think. It was supposed to be Rudolph von Ginter, the mad abbot who died in the Middle Ages and was taken away by the Devil, but nobody was sure about that, of course. I have seen it, though, and such a face he had: like a damned soul who has been a long time in the fire.'

'There was a story about it, too.' Goltz interrupted him. If there was to be a lecture on local antiquities, his rank obviously entitled him to give it before a mere constable.

'The head was supposed to be hollow and there was something inside it; something very valuable. One day a man would discover the secret of how to open it and then . . .' He broke off, staring sheepishly at the floor. 'It was all nonsense, of course; just a fairy tale for children.'

'And it disappeared at the end of the war?'

'That is right, Herr Doktor. Some D.P.s from Reichburg camp are supposed to have stolen it. That was never proved, of course. All we know is that no local people would have dared to take the relic. At any rate, the church was bombed and it vanished. I was not here myself, but a prisoner of war in England.' He looked at

Marcus as though he were personally responsible. 'In Yorkshire, near a place called Huddersfield. Do you know Huddersfield, Herr Doktor? It is not a very nice town, I think.'

'It is a horrible town. But tell me, Sergeant, is there anybody in Rudisheim who could give me a full account of the relic and the local legends? The priest perhaps? The schoolmaster, or this Dr Humperdinck?'

'No, there is no priest any more and the schoolmaster and the doctor have only been here a few years. There is a local history book in the library, but it won't tell you any more than I can. There's no more to tell really. Just a bronze head and a lot of silly legends about it.'

'What about Karl von Arnim, Comrade?'

'*Von* Arnim, Comrade Braun?' Goltz snorted with annoyance. 'This is a democratic country and we no longer use "von".'

'All the same, if you are interested in our legends, Herr Doktor, Karl Arnim is the man to help you. His father, the old Freiherr, was pastor here till after the war and he lives with his mother in the church house. He works as a sort of park-keeper; looking after the abbey grounds and so on. The family have been here for generations. I think it was his great-great-grandfather who built the church in the first place.'

'Thank you.' Marcus made a note of the name. 'But just now you told us that no local people would have dared to take the relic. Why is that, Sergeant? After all, you mentioned a treasure.'

'Yes, there was a treasure; a wonderful treasure; the most valuable thing in the world, they said. Just a silly story, of course.' Goltz shook his head, but there was a sudden gleam in his eye and all at once he looked more like an eager boy than an ogre. Marcus realized that at least one child had believed in fairy tales; had known that there was a crock of gold at the end of the rainbow; that the noises in the attic were not merely boards creaking; that there really was something walking through the dark woods at night.

'But if there was a treasure, why wasn't the relic removed years ago? Surely somebody would have stolen it before, or at least tried to open it? After all, it wasn't locked up. It just stood there in the church, didn't it? Quite an easy thing to steal, I should have thought.'

'Yes, it would have been easy, Herr Doktor. All the same, nobody would have laid a finger on that relic—nobody from

Rudisheim. There was more to the story than just a treasure—that stupid story to frighten children.' Goltz looked down at the floor and it was clear that as a child he hadn't found the story at all stupid.

'You see, they told us that the head of Rudolph von Ginter had a guardian.'

CHAPTER FIFTEEN

'This is the radio service of the East German People's Republic. We are about to break off transmission for three minutes and will then bring you an announcement of the utmost national importance. Will you please inform your neighbours of this? I repeat that the announcement is of the utmost . . .'

Well, here it is—here it comes at last. Kirk stared through the window of the ante-room beside the operating theatre. The Linden outside was deserted and the snow lay thick and unmarked on the pavements. Not for long, he thought. Soon the crowds would be coming out; pouring down the streets to hospitals and inoculation centres, just as they were doing in England. As he'd said, the wall couldn't hold it back and the thing was starting to spread across the world. He heard Petrov's coffee cup rattle as the radio came to life again.

'Plague . . . bubonic plague.' An announcer with a reassuring voice gave almost the same message as he himself had vetted in London. 'Plague . . . Three cases confirmed in East Berlin . . . Plague . . . No cause for alarm, and immunization centres are being set up at the following points . . . Plague . . . The authorities are confident that the outbreak will soon be under full control, and ample stocks of serum are available . . . Plague . . . Plague . . . bubonic plague . . .' Like a cracked gramophone record the sentences kept repeating themselves and Kirk closed his eyes for a moment. 'The authorities will soon have the outbreak under full control.' Lies that wouldn't fool anybody for long. They might slow the epidemic down while the stocks of serum lasted, but without knowing the source of the bacillus or having a drug which would kill it, the death-roll was bound to multiply every hour.

'Shall we go back?' Petrov switched off the set. Until a few minutes ago he had been working the Morse key for almost an hour and his wrist felt as though it were paralysed. 'I don't suppose there has been any reaction but . . .' He shrugged his shoulders and walked into the operating theatre. His assistant had taken over the key and the buzzer still creaked like a cicada across the room.

Der der dot—dot dot dot dot—dot . . . Where did the boy come from, Gustav? Who brought him into West Berlin? Who is Gretel, Gustav? Who are Iron Hans and Clever Gretel . . .' He shook his head as he saw them return.

'He still doesn't respond then?' Petrov nodded and looked at Kirk. 'Well, our gamble doesn't seem to have paid off, I'm afraid. Any other ideas?'

'No, not at the moment.' Kirk studied the still figure on the table. Behr's eyes were fixed on the ceiling, and he appeared to be smiling at it. His body was quite motionless and his hand on the key looked as dead as that of a wax dummy.

'No, I've no more ideas for the present. Let's just hope that the lab. boys come up with something soon. Let's hope that Marcus Levin's hunch was not as crazy as it sounded.'

'It is no use, gentlemen. No use at all.' Another doctor had joined the first and he ran a lens over Behr's eyes and shook his head. 'The Psilocybin has taken all right. This man wants to communicate, but he just hasn't got the strength to do so. I don't know how long he will live, but I think your best chance is to let him rest for a few minutes. I'll increase the oxygen and perhaps . . .' He shrugged his shoulders and started to adjust a tap on one of the cylinders.

'As you say, Doctor. You can stop sending for a moment.' Petrov motioned to the operator. Though the room was warm he pulled his jacket a little tighter around him.

'Didn't you hear me? I told you to stop.' The buzzer was still working, though the Morse sounded slower and more indistinct. 'Are you blind as well as . . . ?' He broke off as he looked at his assistant. The man was busily writing on a pad and it was the other key that was activating the buzzer. Slow and faltering, but gathering speed at every impulse, Gustav Behr's finger had begun to tap out a message.

The snow had stopped at last and in the thin moonlight the streets of Rudisheim looked as though the war had only recently ended. At least a third of the buildings were bombed ruins; little or no attempt had been made to clear away the rubble. Even the coal-mine that had given the place its pre-war importance was a ruin, with the lift headgear standing out like a blighted tree in the car headlights.

'Just what do you expect to learn from this man, Mark?' Tania frowned as he negotiated a bend. Since reaching Rudisheim they had reached first-name terms and she had finally allowed him to drive.

'I'm not sure. About the local fairy tales perhaps. In which part of the forest the Plague Maiden rides her corpse. What was the thing that was supposed to guard the relic and failed so miserably.'

'You're not serious, Mark? You don't really believe that there can be any connection between those old stories and the epidemic?' She twisted round on the seat, staring at him and laying her hand on his arm. 'You're joking, aren't you?'

'No, I'm not joking at all. Until I've talked to this local antiquary, Arnim, I'm perfectly serious.' Through his coat Marcus seemed to feel the warmth of Tania's fingers.

'I also want to know about the people who live round here. Is there a family, on a farm perhaps or in some remote house, who, for no reason, have been shunned and disliked by their neighbours for generations? A very intermarried family, probably, because few outsiders would marry into it.'

'For no reason? That's ridiculous, Mark! There's always a reason for everything.'

'Quite right. I mean for no apparent reason. If these people exist, nobody knows why they must be shunned except that it is thought unsafe to associate with them.'

'Just a moment: I think I'm beginning to understand what you mean.' Tania's frown deepened. 'These spores you described can exist almost indefinitely, in the soil perhaps. You are suggesting that people living near them might have been infected, but somehow grown . . .?' She struggled for the right word.

'Might have developed immunity.' Marcus nodded. 'Yes, that's partly it. Strange cases of immunity exist, you know. The typhoid carrier is unaffected by the disease, but his faeces pass it on to others. The rat flea, *Xenopsylla cheopsis,* carries the plague bacillus but suffers no ill effects from it.

'What I'm driving at is something called "regenerative mutation": a change in the actual bacillus itself. The organism enters the blood stream of an immune host and at once becomes dormant. For thousands of generations it remains static and the host is quite unaware of its presence and also incapable of passing the disease on. But from time to time and for short periods only, you get a generation which is active. During those periods, the host will be a carrier.'

'And you think that Billy Fenwick might have been in contact with such a carrier? A perfectly innocent person who thought there was nothing wrong with him?'

'I don't think anything, my dear. I'm just clutching at all the straws that come my way.' There you go admitting it, he thought. Sir Marcus Levin, the specialist, the expert, the bringer of hope and confidence, following a blind hunch and clutching at straws because there was nothing else to clutch at. 'All the same, the fact that there was no early outbreak in East Germany makes it a possibility at least . . . This must be it, I think.'

He stopped the car and climbed out, feeling slightly better for the cold air on his face. To their right was a small wood and behind it a ruined church. There had once been a track for vehicles, but a rusty chain was drawn across it and the only entrance was through a wicket gate. He pulled it back for Tania and they walked down the path. Beneath the thick covering of snow there were deep ruts and furrows, and among the trees brambles had been allowed to grow unchecked, almost blocking the way. Karl Arnim didn't appear to take his park-keeping duties very seriously. Probably, like Goltz and Braun, he had suffered no outside inspection for years.

'Brrr! What do you say in English? Yes, it gives me the creeps.' Tania's hand tightened on his arm as the wood ended and a graveyard opened up before them: marble crosses and broken pillars and weeping nymphs bearing urns.

'You can say that again.' Marcus nodded, but these graves didn't interest him. Their tombstones were all modern or late nineteenth century. The dead he feared had been buried for six hundred years. Behind them the church stood out like a great stone ship and, though half the roof had fallen in, it looked enormous in the moonlight with a huge square tower and flying buttresses straining against the walls.

'Listen, though.' In the far distance there was a sharp humming sound coming towards them and growing louder at every second. As it approached the earth shook slightly, the noise increased to the choking roar of a diesel engine and then started to fade away. There must be a deep cutting somewhere behind the church because there was no sight of the train.

A cutting. Billy Fenwick had said that when he came round he was lying in a deep cutting and a woman was bending over him. As far as the route was concerned they could be in the right place. Marcus walked on through the graveyard. Though Karl Arnim might not be a competent park-keeper, he obviously kept his own house in good repair. It stood a little to the left of the church, with its windows brightly lit and smoke eddying from the tall chimneys. Under the snow-covered roof it looked strangely unreal: a gingerbread house tucked away in the forest to lure unwary travellers to their doom.

There had been a lot of fairy stories lately, Marcus thought. A lot of Grimm; Iron Hans, Clever Gretel, Brother Lustig—and now this. As he raised the brass knocker, he half expected to hear a window creak open and a crone's voice intone, 'Nibble, nibble, mousekin. Who's nibbling at my housekin?'

'Come in please, sir, and you too, Fräulein. Come in at once. It is a terrible night.' Frau Arnim smiled at them as she pulled back the door. Though she was certainly old, nobody could have described her as a crone, for she was short and stout and looked as brisk as a terrier, with white hair tied back in a bun and little bulging eyes beaming in welcome.

'Ah, that's better, isn't it?' She slammed the door to as though shutting out an unwanted visitor. 'Now, let's put down your coats over here.' As she fussed around them Marcus had the feeling that they were two delicate children in charge of a nanny.

'My son would have gone down to the road to meet you, but they only telephoned us a minute ago.'

'You knew we were coming then?' Marcus glanced around the little hall-cum-sitting room. The walls were bright with polished brass and flower prints and Dresden china figures. The general effect was of over-cosiness.

'Yes, of course. Fasholt and Fafner telephoned us. Oh, I'm sorry.' She shook her head and laughed. 'We call our policemen, Goltz and Braun, that; after the giants in the Rhinegold, of course.' She radiated cheery goodwill and must have been a model parson's wife; an organizer of sales of work, a visitor of the poor, an encourager of the sick.

'But what is my son up to? Surely he must have heard us.' She bustled to the foot of the stairs and raised her voice. 'Karl, Karl, our guests are here.'

'I am just coming, Mutti. I thought I should put on another suit in their honour.' Karl Arnim must have been at least fifty years old, but his face was quite unlined as though the years had written nothing on it. Apart from a white collar he was dressed in black and, if Goltz had not told him otherwise, Marcus would have taken him for a clergyman.

'Fräulein.' He gave Tania a little awkward bow and held out his hand to Marcus. 'I know of you by reputation, sir,' he said. 'It is a very great privilege to welcome you under our roof. But please come through into my study.' His eyes twinkled as he pulled open a door. 'My mother is very proud of her brass and china; but they make the place rather bright for me. A real palace, isn't it, Sir Marcus? Circe's palace, perhaps.'

'It is very nice indeed.' Marcus felt slightly embarrassed as he smiled back. *A real palace* to describe a bright little hall. *Circe's palace,* the place where men were turned into swine.

'Now do sit down, both of you. Over there would be best, I think.' Arnim motioned them towards a big porcelain stove. 'It is still bitterly cold.'

'Thank you.' Marcus stared around the room as he sat down. 'Den' was the obvious word to describe it; like Arnim's clothes, it savoured of the clerical. Old leather armchairs, leather-bound books in tall oak cases, photographs of student groups and an illuminated testimonial that read 'Presented to Freiherr Walther von Arnim by his devoted parishioners.'

'Did the—the giants tell you what I wanted to see you about, Herr Arnim?'

'Fasholt attempted to.' Arnim sat down very close to his mother and Marcus sensed that if they were alone their hands would be touching. 'Goltz and Braun really are like giants, aren't they? Great, stupid, clumsy giants, but we are fortunate in having them when one considers the majority of the Vopo.

'Yes, Goltz said that you would like to consult me about our local folk-lore. Though I am no trained historian, I will be delighted to tell you all I do know.'

'Thank you.' Marcus studied Arnim, remembering what the police had said about him. The Arnim family had lived in Rudisheim for generations and Karl had been on the point of taking holy orders when the war had come and he had been carried off to the army. He had been wounded in Africa and shipped home like a piece of useless rubbish. By the time he recovered the war was over, the Russians had occupied that part of Germany and there was no church for him to serve. A bitter, frustrated man, one would have thought, but there was nothing except rather foolish good humour in his face.

'Don't thank me, Sir Marcus,' he said. 'I am most flattered by your visit. Just as I was impressed when I read your paper on the "Streptothra Madura Fungus" some time ago.'

'You have studied medicine then?'

'Studied it, but never qualified.' Arnim shook his head. 'I always wanted to be a medical missionary, but fate was against it. Nowadays you could describe me as an amateur in everything, I'm afraid. An amateur botanist, an amateur historian, even an amateur park-keeper. There is no doubt that I hold my job more as a sinecure than anything else.'

'Karl would have been a great doctor, Sir Marcus.' As though she couldn't resist touching him, Frau Arnim's right hand gripped her son's. Her index finger was rather unpleasantly deformed: it had no joint, and the nail grew where the knuckle should have been. 'He was admitted to Heidelberg when he was only seventeen and Professor Mainz described him as one of the most brilliant students he had ever known.'

'Please, Mutti, you are embarrassing me.' Arnim withdrew his hand and reached out towards a pile of papers on the table.

At any rate, let us hope that my small gifts as an amateur local historian may be of some use to you, Sir Marcus.' He picked up a photograph and handed it across to him. 'Sergeant Golz mentioned a few of the things you wanted to hear about. This was one of them, I think.'

'Yes, that is one of them.' The picture was almost life-size, and it showed the face of a man fashioned from some coarse metal. The features were so bloated as to appear scarcely human and the description 'lion-faced' came automatically to Marcus as he looked at it. Though taken after death the expression showed not only pain and terror, but also murderous rage, and he remembered Goltz's description of the relic. 'Such a face he had; like a damned soul who has been a long time in the fire.'

'Yes, that's the death mask of the mad abbot, Sir Marcus. What do you want to know about it?'

'Almost everything that you can tell me.' Marcus considered how to explain. 'Did you hear the news flash on the radio just now?''

'A news flash?' Arnim frowned and shook his head. 'No, we don't listen to the radio very often these days . . . But, Mutti, I am sure that our guests are very cold and would like a cup of coffee.'

He smiled as she got up and hurried to the door, and then stopped smiling. His unlined face suddenly looked much older and there was strain and unhappiness in the eyes.

'Sir Marcus,' he said, as the door closed behind her. 'Please forgive me. I lied to you just now. I did hear the bulletin, but I don't want my mother to know about the outbreak; not for the time being, at least. She has an almost pathological terror of disease, and I'd like to keep it from her till the morning. My father died of cancer, you see. He died very horribly and he took a long time over it. Since then, every room in the house, except this one, has been dusted and polished at least once a day.' Arnim leaned forward and opened the damper of the stove.

'Yes, I heard about the epidemic, Sir Marcus, and I guessed that that might be your reason for coming to Rudisheim.'

'You guessed that, did you? Why, Herr Arnim? Have you some evidence that it might originate from around here?'

'No, no evidence, but surely there must be a connection? An outbreak of *bacillus pestis* in East Germany and a distinguished bacteriologist coming to Rudisheim and asking questions about a man who died of plague in the fourteenth century. Can you tell me why you have come, Sir Marcus?'

'I'll tell you all I can.' As Marcus spoke he realized that there was something in Arnim's make-up that made him an ideal listener: the aura of a priest in the confessional, the manner of a psychiatrist quietly taking notes beside the couch. He told him all he knew and also what he merely suspected; his vague theory about a return to the Black Death bacillus and regenerative mutations.

'Thank you. You have been most kind to confide in me.' Arnim got up and pulled an old, battered volume from the nearest bookcase. 'But tell me something else, Sir Marcus. Do you believe in evil, and the punishment of evil?'

'Evil? I believe in wickedness as part of the human predicament; a necessary piece of the process of evolution.'

'Yes, as a good scientist, I thought you would say that. Human wickedness; as men progress from apes to the Ubermensch perhaps.' Arnim smiled as he flicked through the pages. 'I don't mean that I'm afraid. I mean pure evil which comes from outside; from the devil, for lack of a better word.' He had found his place at last and held the book under the light.

'This is a fairly early account of the head of von Ginter. Please excuse my reading it to you. The print is rather bad and it is in medieval dog Latin.

'"And when Lucifer had taken the soul of Rudolph, our abbot, and all men knew what his life had been, we made a bronze image of his face which will stand in the porch of our church. And in the image we have locked a demon that will watch over this accursed place for ever."

'Yes, we are a superstitious people around here, Sir Marcus. Children still claim to see the Plague Woman riding her corpse. Grown men avoid certain parts of the woods at night because of the wolf-rat on whom it is death to look.' Arnim still smiled, but Marcus could see that, like the policemen, he had once believed the stories implicitly.

'And do you think those legends are all nonsense, Sir Marcus? Don't you think it is possible that there might have been a demon or guardian in that relic?'

'If there were, it wasn't very effective, Herr Arnim. After all, the relic was stolen by D.P.s at the end of the war.'

'It was said to have been stolen. A great many people went to a lot of trouble to blame those D.P.s for it. Does the name Maria Trude mean anything to you?'

'Trude? You mean Frau Trude?' Marcus nodded. Another fairy-tale character to join Iron Hans and Clever Gretel and Brother Lustig. 'The woman who turned a curious girl into a log of wood and threw her on the fire?'

'Oh, no, not the witch out of Grimm. Maria Trude, or Frau Doktor Trude, was a very real person. With your background you must have heard of her, Sir Marcus. After all she was Julius Streicher's cousin. She was also in charge of the S.S. medical research centre at Dachau for a time.'

'Yes, I remember.' Twenty years slipped away for a moment and terror and hatred were like a red screen in front of Marcus's eyes, blinding him. 'She was supposed to have been killed in Berlin, but they never found the body. Why do you mention her now, Herr Arnim? What connection was there between Maria Trude and this?' He looked at the bronze face glowering across at him from the table.

'Because she may have had the relic, Sir Marcus. It was almost the last week of the war and everything was in chaos. We wanted to go to the west before the Russians arrived, but my father was dying and couldn't be moved. One evening that woman came here with a party of S.S. They said they were looking for an escaped prisoner and searched the church. Soon after they left, there was an air raid and the church was bombed. In the morning the relic was missing. It may have been buried under rubble and later found by D.P.s. There may have been an escaped prisoner, but personally I doubt it. You have known those people, Sir Marcus. Doesn't it seem feasible to you that Maria Trude might have wanted that relic?'

'But why, what possible motive could she have had?' Though Marcus muttered the question aloud, he knew the answer. Germany was breaking up and the sane thing would have been to find a disguise and a new personality before the Allied armies took over. Those people hadn't been sane, though. Himmler had sat in Flensburg consulting the Norse runes. Goering had imagined himself to be an honoured guest of the Americans. Hitler had bent over a map and moved armies which no longer existed. It was quite possible that Maria Trude could have based her security on a folk-tale.

'Yes, just a fairy tale, Sir Marcus.' Karl Arnim had exactly read his thoughts, and he nodded across the firelight. 'Just a silly tale for children, but don't you think a woman like Maria Trude might have believed it?'

'She might have. All the same there was pretty clear evidence that she was killed in Berlin . . . Are you all right?'

Marcus broke off abruptly, because Arnim was obviously not listening. He was staring at the door with his lips drawn back and his face didn't look completely sane. 'Are you ill?'

'What's that? No, I'm all right, but listen for a moment. For God's sake keep quiet.' As he spoke the sound of a radio announcement grew in volume and flooded through the door. 'We repeat that there is no cause for alarm and ample stocks of serum are available . . .'

'Mutti. She turned on the wireless.' Arnim lurched across the room like a man in the last stages of Parkinson's disease. 'I meant to take out a valve, but with your coming there was no time; there was no time for anything.'

He pulled open the door and the announcer's voice poured unchecked into the room. 'Immunization centres are being set up at the following points . . .' At the same instant Marcus was on his feet and hurrying after him. Frau Arnim was standing in the centre of the hall swaying from side to side. Her eyes were wide open, as though staring at something which terrified her, and there was a line of foam around her mouth.

CHAPTER SIXTEEN

TRUDE—Maria Trude. As Marcus hurried down the path, the name seemed to beat in time to his footsteps. Was Karl Arnim's story even remotely possible, he wondered, or was the man so obsessed with the lost relic and his ideas of impersonal evil that a vague suspicion had grown into belief? Certainly there was a good deal of mental disturbance in his background. Though he was not a nerve specialist, Marcus had had little difficulty in diagnosing epilepsy as Frau Arnim had pitched forward with the radio blaring around her.

At any rate, true or false, he had to get the information to Kirk and Petrov. The Arnims' phone was out of order, probably the line had been brought down by snow. He only hoped it was a local fault and he could get through from Rudisheim.

'Mark, please listen to me. What I want to tell you is important.' He could feel Tania tugging at his sleeve, but he shrugged her aside and hurried on. He had to concentrate—to remember what he knew about the Trude woman. She had been a bacteriologist, that was certain. Worked on vegetable pathology as well. Oswald Farquhar had mentioned one of her papers in his Presidential Address last year. Yes, something about tobacco blight. 'Uber die Mosaikkrankheit der Tabakspflanze.' Farquhar had used it as an example of how a really brilliant mind could sometimes fasten on to a wrong premise and fly completely off at a tangent.

But was it possible that she could be alive? At the time it had appeared quite certain that she had been killed in Berlin. Though they had never recovered the body, there had been enough witnesses to make it appear definite. There had been a thorough investigation too. Once it was discovered what had been happening at that research establishment—experiments into the causes of malignancy with paraffin and radiation cancers produced on human subjects—she'd been quite high up on the list of wanted war criminals.

But if she wasn't dead? If somehow her death had been faked then he could believe Arnim's story all right. If Trude's mind had run along the same lines as his own and she had suspected what that relic might contain . . .

Marcus shuddered slightly at the thought. A crazy woman hiding under another name for twenty years. Quite an old woman, but still bitter, still carrying on her crusade against the world. He was quite sure now that he knew what the guardian of the relic was, and he could picture her opening the case, studying the thing inside, gloating at the thought of its power, building up her phantasies of destruction. Then, one day, the phantasies had become too strong to be resisted any more and the demon had been released from its bottle to plague the earth.

'In a minute, my dear. Tell me in a minute, but please let me try to concentrate a bit longer.' He climbed into the car as Tania broke in again. Kirk had been sceptical enough about his going to Rudisheim and probably this new development would be received with a good deal of disbelief. All the same it was at least something to go on, and it would be a near miracle if they got anything out of Behr.

'But what on earth! Just what are you doing?' He swung round as Tania reached out and snatched the car keys out of his hand. 'Look, I told you we have to get through to Berlin at once.'

'Yes, so you have told me, Mark.' She laid the keys out of his reach on her side of the seat.

'You have also told me a lot of your theories, but now you are going to hear one of mine.' As though there was not the slightest need to hurry she pulled a packet of cigarettes out of her bag. 'Sir Marcus Levin, K.C.B., whatever that may mean,' she said when at last the cigarette was alight. 'Mark Levin, the great bacteriologist who forgets all his scientific training and rushes blindly off after every shred of evidence that comes his way. No, don't interrupt me.' She held the keys up to the window. 'Just sit still or I'll throw them out into the snow.

'Now, Mark, you were quite right in coming to Rudisheim and in a moment I'll prove it to you. But this story about the Nazi doctor that Arnim told you! You can't believe that. Arnim is trying to hide something and he made it up on the spur of the moment. All that business about the S.S. coming here! Oh, I realize that with your background everything about the Nazis must seem like a personal war, but the Trude woman is dead. She was killed when our troops entered Berlin.'

'Tania, you said that you can prove I was right in coming here. Have you got some evidence? Something I don't know about?'

'Yes, I think I have, Mark, and in a minute I'll tell you what it is, but first I want to ask you a question. When you examined the Fenwick boy, did you notice if he had buck teeth?'

'Buck teeth?' Marcus frowned. He could almost see the rash on Billy's chest again and feel the bubo throbbing under his fingers, but the face . . . ? Apart from the fact that it had been flushed and bloated he could hardly recall what it had looked like.

'I can't really remember,' he said. 'I can't be sure, but I seem to think that he may have had. But why do you want to know? What possible importance can it have?'

'It may have every importance, Mark. It may tell us exactly what happened to him.' Tania fumbled in her handbag and brought out something which glittered under the dashboard light. 'When Arnim's mother had that attack he told me there was a bottle of tablets in the bathroom cupboard and I got them for her.'

'Yes, I remember, but so what? They were only phenobarbitone. A perfectly normal prescription for cases like that. She was much better as soon as she took one.'

'She was better, but that's not the important thing. You see, beside those tablets, I found this.' She handed him the small and rather unpleasant object, smiling at his expression as he looked at it.

'Yes, it's strange, isn't it, Mark? You said that you seem to remember that the boy may have had buck teeth. Doesn't it start to fit together at last? After all, what possible use could an old woman or a middle-aged man have for a child's dental brace?'

'Dot—der der dot—der der der . . .' Behr's fingers still trembled on the Morse key, but the impulses were very slow now and more often than not they were just a jumble of sound without any meaning at all.

'Dot dot dot—der der derrrrr . . .' They finally stopped altogether and his finger came to rest pressing down the connection. The doctor felt briefly for the pulse and shook his head.

'Well, that's it, comrade. He's dead and in my mind it's a wonder that he lasted so long. I hope you've got what you want.'

'Give it to me.' Petrov had been staring over his assistant's shoulder and he snatched the pad from him, studying the disjointed sentences, and the letters which often didn't add up to a word, and here and there blank spaces where the dots and dashes hadn't signified a letter. For a full ten minutes he pored over the pages, his pencil crossing out and adding and joining up as he struggled to make the meaning clear and then his face broke into a grin of delight and he turned to Kirk.

'Well, General, we've done it, I think. This is all we wanted to know and I'd like to congratulate you on a most brilliant idea.' Petrov waved the pad in his hand and he almost capered in triumph.

'Yes, it's all here. The child fell from the train and was befriended by what you would call the "Resistance Movement" and I the "Counter-revolutionary Element". The person who found him was this Clever Gretel of whom we have heard so much. He was later smuggled into West Berlin by what Behr refers to as the "Meister-Route".

'Get my car round to the door, please.' He nodded to his assistant and scowled at the still body on the table. The doctor had already pulled a sheet over its face.

'And I thought that that piece of carrion was my friend, but he knew everything, and rather than betray his precious organization he was prepared to gamble with the health of the world.'

'Yes, I suppose he was.' Though every news flash reported that the epidemic was gathering strength, Kirk still felt sympathy for Gustav Behr. 'But did he tell us who this Gretel is and where we can find him?'

'Yes, he told us everything, but it's a she, not a he, as we thought. Her name really is Gretel, and she's been very clever indeed. Let's go and pay a call on her.' He clapped Kirk on the shoulder and moved towards the door still squinting at the pad.

'And we've done Marcus Levin a grave injustice, I'm afraid. We both thought he had rushed off on a fool's errand and we were quite wrong.

'The woman we want lives at Rudisheim, and her name is Gretel Arnim.'

CHAPTER SEVENTEEN

'ANY luck? Did you get through to Berlin?' Marcus started the engine as Tania hurried back from the telephone booth.

'I got through, but it was no use. Petrov and Kirk left the hospital, but didn't go back to police headquarters. I gave a message for them.'

'Very well.' Marcus glanced at his watch and drove off. Almost nine thirty already; over twenty minutes since Tania had shown him the dental brace. She had been in favour of knocking up Goltz and Braun and taking them round to Arnim's house, but he had quashed that. The men had not been inoculated and, if Billy Fenwick really had been with the Arnims, it would be murder to take them there. He had made her try to contact Kirk and Petrov and now it was up to him.

Not that there was any definite evidence yet. The brace might have belonged to any child; a nephew or niece of the Arnims, perhaps, who had stayed with them and left it behind. He couldn't even be certain that Billy Fenwick had had protruding teeth.

All the same . . . Marcus remembered the hint of mania in Arnim's face as he discussed the relic and how his mother had stood swaying in the hall with foam on her lips and the radio blaring around her. He stopped the car at the end of the drive and slipped the brace into his pocket.

'All right, here goes. Let's find out for ourselves.' He opened the door and climbed out.

It was much darker now. A wind had blown in from the north, bringing thin trails of cloud to obscure the moon. Their feet slipped and stumbled on the frozen path, and among the trees briars clutched at them like small, vicious hands. There was a haze of mist drifting across the tombstones which made them resemble yew hedges, trained and clipped for centuries in an English park, or the strange fungoid vegetation of some distant planet.

But what was he going to say to them? What the hell was he going to say to the Arnims? A dozen scenes from stage and cinema crossed Marcus's mind. The great detective smiling cynically as the malefactor made his glib denials. The flick of a finger, the lost heiress coming in from the wings, and the damning evidence triumphantly produced. 'And how exactly do you explain this?'

'Mark, are you sure that we're doing the right thing? Don't you think we should wait till we can contact Petrov? After all, if these people really are what we think . . . ?' Tania's fingers gripped his hand, making him think of warm things: log fires and double beds and a final drink before turning in.

'No, I'm not sure about anything, my dear,' he said. 'And, if you prefer it, give me that revolver I saw in your handbag and go back to the car. I'm not waiting any longer to contact Kirk and Petrov. I've got to know the truth now.

'Make up your mind, please.' He watched her hesitate and then fall into step beside him, and he knew he was right. There was no time to wait for reinforcements. That child's dental brace was the only real clue they had and he had to check it.

All the same, he half hoped that it meant nothing; that the Arnims were just unbalanced eccentrics with a perfectly normal explanation for the brace. And if the Arnims were innocent, he even hoped that the story about Maria Trude was rubbish too. He hoped that there was no human agency involved and all he had to deal with was a freak of nature.

As before, the little house still looked bright and cheerful, with lights glowing through the curtains and the chimney smoke pluming in the wind. Once again he lifted the little brass knocker, trying to imagine how he could conduct the interview. As he brought it down the door swung back a few inches as though the catch were free but a chain was holding it.

'Herr Arnim,' he called. 'Are you there, Herr Arnim?' He knocked again, feeling the door move another inch and he knew that it wasn't a chain, but something soft and heavy which was behind it.

'Mark, look! Look down at your feet, Mark!' Tania's breath was like smoke in the freezing air and, as he followed her eyes, Marcus stiffened. The cottage floor sloped slightly and in the light from the room he could see a trickle of dark liquid dripping over the door-step and reddening the snow that was piled against it. He hurled his shoulder against the door and forced back the thing which was holding it.

'Let me die.' Frau Arnim lay on her side staring up at him and she looked like a tired child wanting to go to bed. 'Please, please let me die.' She still held the knife in her right hand, but her left couldn't have held anything. She had slashed the muscles as well as the artery and he could see a glint of white bone through the oozing blood.

'Yes, yes, you will sleep soon.' Marcus pulled out his handkerchief and twisted it round her wrist with the door key to form a tourniquet, motioning to Tania as he did so. 'Try and find something for her to drink; schnapps or brandy or anything at all.

'That should do.' He took the bottle of kümmel from her and forced it between the woman's lips. Most of it slopped on to the floor as she fought against him, but at least a little went down.

'Are you feeling better, Frau Arnim?' he said. 'Can you tell me what happened? Where your son is?'

'My son? I have no son, Herr Doktor.' Her lips were like grey worms crawling across her face. 'I killed my son years ago and he became something else. I destroyed him. Didn't you hear what he said, Herr Doktor? Circe's palace; the place where men are turned into swine.'

'Yes, I remember Frau Arnim.' Marcus picked her up and laid her on a sofa by the fire. 'But what happened after we left here? Why did you try to kill yourself?'

'Because I guessed what had happened after I heard the radio and I made Karl tell me everything . . . no, that will be no good to you.' She shook her head as Tania took a revolver from her bag and moved towards the study door.

'Karl has gone. He went away as soon as he told me what had happened . . .' Her voice was so weak that Marcus could hardly make out the words. '. . . to the little English boy.'

'Billy Fenwick?' He leaned forward till his ear was almost touching her mouth. 'He was here, then?'

'Yes, he was here. We found him lying by the railway line and brought him home. Poor little boy, he was so cold and frightened. When he told me who he was and what had happened I made arrangements with my friends to have him taken back to his own people.

'Karl didn't mind my bringing the boy here at first and then something made him angry. I think Billy laughed at him, but I never knew what it was about. I never imagined he would actually harm him though.

'And now please let me die, Herr Doktor. Can't you see that I have to die? I turned Karl into a monster and now . . .' She stared longingly at the knife on the floor. 'I often wondered what he was doing in the crypt, but I never guessed that he would hurt anybody. Please let me die.'

'You will sleep in a moment, Frau Arnim. I will help you to sleep, but you must help us first. Where did Karl go after he left you?'

'I don't know. He didn't tell me, but I think he would go to Berlin. He mentioned something about the new tunnel that our friends have made.'

'To Berlin.' Marcus looked up, but Tania had already hurried to the telephone at the top of the stairs and was rattling the rest up and down in the hope of getting a connection.

'And what did Karl do in the crypt, Frau Arnim?'

'He played, Herr Doktor. He always wanted to be a priest and he played at being one. He wanted power and esteem and the assurance that he wasn't just the pig I made him. Then one day he told me that he found—he found . . .' The eyes closed and her face went quite slack.

'Yes, I know what he found, Frau Arnim. The thing which could give him all the power he craved for.' Marcus suddenly remembered an illustration from a book of Greek legends: the inquisitive woman bent over a casket as she searched for the catch. Pandora's box opening and all the ills of heaven rushing out to plague mankind.

'The line is still down?' He nodded as Tania came back into the room.

'Yes, Frau Arnim should be all right. She's just passed out from loss of blood and nervous exhaustion. Try and tear a strip from the table-cloth, will you? I can't leave her with the tourniquet on. Good.' He bandaged the woman's arm tightly, removed the handkerchief and stood up.

'And now, let's go and see exactly what Karl did find in that crypt.' He shook his head at Tania's revolver. 'Yes, by all means take that if it makes you feel better, but I don't think it will be much use. The person we're going to meet died a long time ago.'

The church itself was just a ruin, of course. Even though the moon was partly hidden by cloud they could see that. The doors had rotted away from their hinges and lay on the floor covered by rubble, and most of the roof had fallen in. Through a gaping hole in the wall the clock hung face down over the nave with its hands set at twenty to three, and bushes and creepers had pushed up through the tiles of the chancel to screen the altar. It didn't look as though anybody had been near the place for years.

But that was wrong. Mingled with the smell of rubble and damp wood they could make out a tang of burning oil and hot metal. Tania's torch flitted across the building and she walked forward. To the right of the chancel a flight of stairs ran down to the crypt, and in the torch-light they could see that it had recently been swept. There was a rusty iron door at the foot of the stairs, but the key was on the outside and it swung open on well-oiled hinges.

'Yes, the blighter really did play at being a priest.' Marcus stared around the room. It was about forty feet long and almost the same width, with a vaulted ceiling and oil lamps burning along the walls. The general effect was a mixture of library and private chapel, for there were two long bookcases by the door and a curtain on the far wall with a rough wooden altar in front of it.

'A priest, and a scientist, too.' He glanced at the books. Hirt's *Conquest of Plague,* Kuhn's *Vegetable Pathology,* Wilhelm Sahm's *History of the Plague in East Prussia,* his own monograph on the Madura fungus. From a hook at the side of the second case a cassock was hanging and he felt a sudden pity for Karl Arnim as he looked at it. A man obsessed with guilt and the sense of failure who had hidden something. A man full of hatred and bitterness which must have come to boiling point in that little cosy house by the graveyard. And, one day, when he was cleaning the thing he had hidden, or merely examining its workmanship, he had discovered the secret and Pandora's box had clicked open.

Yes, Marcus felt that he knew everything now, and he walked very slowly towards the altar and the heap of faded purple cloth that lay on it. His heart was racing as he stretched out his hand and pulled at the cloth. It came away, falling in folds to the floor, something glittered and he looked at the face of Rudolph von Ginter.

The chronicles had been incorrect, though. The thing was brass, not bronze, and time and weather must have given it the rough corroded appearance he had seen in the photograph. Now it had been cleaned and polished and shone like gold in the lamplight. Though cast after death there was no mistaking the agony of the expression, and 'lion-faced' was clear in every swollen feature.

'But how does it open? How did Arnim find what the demon really was?' Marcus took Tania's torch and craned forward over the relic. On the backward sweep of the skull, where the tonsure joined the carved hair, he found what he was looking for: a blur as though an artist's hand had shaken on his chisel; a line of scratches which might mean anything or nothing. He pulled out his lens and bent still lower. The scratches steadied themselves and became words; four lines of verse engraved with a needle on the shining metal.

Very carefully Marcus copied each letter on to his notebook and then looked at the result. At first they didn't appear to mean anything at all; just a jumble of words written in some language he couldn't recognize, though it had a Spanish flavour.

Fincá los Inogos
Que yacé alli l'Arca
Do tusé una Marca
Sobré los tus Ojos.

Yes, of course. He nodded as understanding came. The verse didn't mean anything to him because it was written in a dead language. The words were Cid, twelfth-century medieval Spanish. And that was strange, because the relic itself was fourteenth century. They would have been as incomprehensible to a German of the period as to a present-day Englishman. The message must have been written that way so that it could be read only by a highly educated person.

Well, it was going to be read by a highly educated person. It was going to be read by Sir Marcus Levin, whose knowledge of medieval Spanish might be scanty, but whose linguistic ability was certainly not. He bent over the notebook, concentrating hard and jotting down every word he could recognize from its modern form.

'Marca'—that was obvious. 'Inogos' was knees, and 'Ojos'—eyes; while 'Arca' was a chest—perhaps a treasure chest. His hand ran across the page and soon he had what he imagined to be a rough translation.

Bend your knees
The treasure lies
Where I cut a mark
Above your eyes.

'Bend your knees'? Why so? Couldn't he see every detail of the thing much better by holding it to the light? No, of course he couldn't. The point was that the light had to be above the eyes and he remembered the purpose for which the relic had been designed. It was to stand in the porch of a church and before it the faithful would kneel in terror. Probably its makers had intended anybody who could actually read the message to see what it contained, but the religious community had died, the monastery had fallen into ruin, and oxidation had hidden the words till Karl Arnim's polishing operations revealed them.

Very well, he would bend his knees, if that was what was wanted. Marcus lowered himself before the altar, and he could see at last. In that position the light was reflected from the polished chin to the curve of the swollen, arrogant lip and showed the thing which lay below it; a tiny hairline crack into which a fingernail could be inserted. He reached for the crack and very gently pressed upwards. The front of the relic tilted back like a visor and the demon of Rudisheim stared out at him.

'Yes, there it is. There's your guardian. There's the Gorgon that can turn you to stone.' Sweat was pouring down his forehead, but Marcus felt no horror, nor even disgust. The thing was too sad, too pathetic for that. The dreadful leather thing, wedged in its case, with two huge rubies which were its treasure gleaming in the eye sockets, and blackened teeth grinning between the ridges that had once been lips. The face of a man who had died six hundred years ago and looked like a tortured monkey, buried alive in the shining brass.

'But how did he discover that the stuff was still active?'

Marcus spoke to himself, and then swung round as he heard Tania scream. He had just time to see Karl Arnim rushing towards him, and then something swung out, picked him up, and threw him into oblivion.

CHAPTER EIGHTEEN

He was lying in bright sunlight and it was very painful to his eyes. He was cold, too; lying somewhere high up on the white wall of a mountain, and the summit was only a few hundred feet above him. Soon he would get to his feet and climb up to that summit, but not for a moment. For a few more minutes he had to lie still and wait for the pain to stop.

'Mark, come round. Please come round, my dear.' The snow was pillowed under his head and somebody was speaking to him in Russian, which was ridiculous. What was he doing on a mountain, when he should be addressing the Royal Society on the enterin virus? Why was he so cold, and what was the thing that was beating on his head like a hammer?

'Please open your eyes, Mark.' With an enormous effort he forced himself to obey the voice, seeing a room spin round, as though viewed from a circling aeroplane, seeing a blurred face harden into perspective, feeling consciousness come back.

'That's it. That's right, my dear.' Tania's arm was under his head and her eyes were full of concern. 'And I'm so sorry, Mark, so terribly sorry. There was a door behind that curtain, you see, and . . .'

'Yes, I remember. He came through it when I opened the relic.' Against the hammer blows he recalled Karl Arnim's face rushing towards him and a bar swinging out to beat him down.

'Yes, and it was all my fault, Mark. Petrov told me to look after you and I never saw him till it was too late. He knocked the gun away from me before I could use it and then hit you with that length of pipe.'

'He certainly did.' Marcus felt the lump on his head and pulled himself to his feet. 'And after that he went out, I suppose, locking the door behind him?'

'Let me have a look, though.' He lifted Tania's wrist. It was swollen and discoloured and bent at an odd angle. 'Yes, he gave you quite a knock too. You've got what is called a Colles fracture —a break at the lower end of the radius.' He smiled as he tore a strip from the altar cloth to make a bandage. 'I shall be becoming quite a wrist specialist before long. But did he say anything before he left?'

'Later, but I'm not sure what happened at the beginning because I passed out for a few minutes myself. When I came round, there was no sign of Arnim and I was only concerned about you. I thought you were dead, Mark . . . Then I saw Arnim again. There must be a room through there and he came out of it.' She pointed past the altar. The curtain had been pulled aside to show a board wall and a door fastened by a padlock. 'After he'd locked the door, he stood there for quite a time, leaning against the wall with his hand pressed on his cheek. I don't think he even knew we were there. He kept muttering to himself about his mother: how she had destroyed him years ago and was going to betray him now. I think he was weeping, but in this light I couldn't really be sure. He's crazy though, Mark; quite crazy.'

'Yes, he's crazy enough. Easy though.' He felt her shudder as he pulled the bandage tight and tied it. 'Crazy, or perhaps possessed would be the better word.' He turned and looked at the thing on the altar. In the dim light its withered skin looked like slag, and the ruby eyes might have been smiling at them. There was no question of what had happened now. As an amateur scientist Karl Arnim would have examined the tissue to see what preserving process had been used. And, as he laid a sliver of long-dead flesh on the microscope the moisture of his breath might have touched it. Then, when a stain had been added, he would have known that the spores were still alive.

'And then what happened, Tania?'

'He suddenly seemed to realize we were there. He had my gun in his right hand but he kept his left pressed against his cheek. He pointed the gun at me for a moment and then he shook his head and pushed it into his pocket. He went across to that thing on the altar and sort of bowed in front of it; genuflected I think the word is. He really was weeping as he passed me.'

'And then he went out?'

'Yes, by the door up into the church. He pulled it open and then he turned and looked back at us. As he did so, he uncovered his cheek and I could see that it was bleeding. Then he said . . . He spoke very quickly and I couldn't quite make it out. I think it was . . . "There's gratitude for you. I gave them freedom and one of the little blighters went and bit me." '

'He said that, did he?' Marcus ripped the rest of the curtain from the wall behind the altar. The boards were very flimsy and here and there they were uneven, leaving gaps above the floor.

' "I gave them freedom." The bastard! The crazy, bloody bastard.' He hurled himself at the door to the church tugging at the handle and battering against the iron panels with his shoulder. He might just as well have tried to force his way into the vault of a bank. The lock and hinges were set in mortar and they didn't give a fraction of an inch. He leaned against it, gasping for breath and then turned and walked slowly back to the boarded wall. He pressed his ear against it, fighting to control the sound of his own heartbeats, and as he listened the pain in his forehead faded into complete unimportance. He'd felt fear many times in his life but never as badly as he did now, listening to the noises behind the boards. Tiny pattering, scraping noises that could have been made by sandpaper running over rough timber or light rain falling on grass. Time rolled back and he was standing in his room in the Central Laboratories watching the infected rats and noting his observations on a pad. 'For seven hours after infection, no apparent change in the animal was observed, but this was followed by a three-hour period of intense physical activity, aggression and the urge to escape.'

'He said that, my dear? "I gave them freedom."' He walked across to Tania and suddenly pulled her to him, feeling a great strength and comfort for the touch of her body. He'd always imagined that he'd been through the worst terrors that life could offer, but now he knew he was quite wrong. The things behind that wall were unspeakable and, even as he listened, their noise was increasing. Scaly feet pattering on a stone floor, yellow teeth tearing at woodwork with now and again a scream or a shriek to punctuate them; a miasma, a sickness of the soil, a visitation from the stars to trouble the earth and drive the animals up into the world of men. The lamplight flickered on the thing upon the altar and its brass face seemed to be set in a wide smile of triumph.

'Yes,' he said, pulling Tania still closer to him. '"I gave them freedom and one of the little blighters went and bit me."'

Gregor Petrov smelt strongly of lilies of the valley, but at least his car was warm. Kirk leaned comfortably back against the blast of an enormous rear heater and smiled approvingly as the drab suburbs of East Berlin slid past them.

Yes, things were going to be all right now. He was back on the job he understood, he was earning his keep, and everything was working out; though the last report of the epidemic was the worst yet. Everywhere stocks of vaccine were running low, cases were being reported from as far afield as Paris, and in London police had been brought from the provinces to control the crowds. Through the car window Kirk could see a long line of tense faces queueing in the snow before an inoculation centre. None of it worried him at all. His idea about the Morse code had worked, Gustav Behr had talked, and he and Petrov were both back on the job which they thoroughly understood.

Yes, *à chacun son métier,* every man to his trade. The saying ran pleasantly through Kirk's head against the whine of the engine. He had felt horribly useless until a few minutes ago, but now he was in charge again and everything would work out. Behr had talked, Levin's hunch had been proved correct and they knew all about the Fenwick child's movements. Clever Gretel's name was Gretel Arnim, or von Arnim, and she had been a key figure in the escape organization for years. Her contact in East Berlin was a man called Adolph Wolner, and on the day after Billy Fenwick disappeared Wolner had gone to Rudisheim to fetch him. That was all that Behr had told them before he died, but it was enough. Already the police were looking for Wolner, and he and Petrov were on their way to pay a call on Clever Gretel. It was a nuisance that they should have to go personally, but under the circumstances it had seemed necessary. The important thing was that he was back at his own job and doing something useful. He looked across at Petrov and, as though reading each other's thoughts, they both grinned.

'We have quite a long journey before us, my friend. I wonder if we could pass the time pleasantly.' Petrov pulled a small flat case from his pocket. 'This is one of my hobbies and I think I have heard that it is one of yours too.' He opened the case and the chessmen glinted as the car passed an illuminated sign reading 'Workers' Front Against War'.

'Would you like to give me a game?'

'Very much.' Kirk smiled back at him. 'I just hope that I'm good enough to play with a Russian.'

'Ah, yes, it is our national vice, isn't it? All the same, I'm just an amateur Russian.' He picked up two pawns and shuffled them in his hands.

'And to make things more interesting shall we have a bet on the result? The details of your decoding computer against the name of a certain British physicist who is intending to defect to us at a very early date? . . . no, of course not; that is merely a joke. Chess is too serious a business to mix with such trivialities.'

He held out his clenched fists and shook his head sadly as Kirk touched the left and revealed a red pawn.

'Ah, a pity. That should have been my colour, shouldn't it?' He switched on the roof light and laid the board on the seat between them.

'Now, how shall we start? Yes, you began your military career in the cavalry, so I'll meet you on your own ground.' The Russian smiled as he lifted his queen's knight and then they both stopped smiling. Only the game mattered to them now and neither of their old crafty minds would think of anything else till one of them nodded and acknowledged checkmate.

He was going to die and his death would be horrible, but so what? Karl Arnim laughed as he climbed into Tania's car. He deserved a horrible death, the whole of humanity did, and he would go out like a bomb; like a conqueror with an army of corpses around his funeral pyre.

Yes, here were the leads. The fools had removed the ignition key but it wouldn't take him long to make a connection. 'So what—so what—so what?' He hummed as his fingers tore the wires from the switch and started to twist them together.

A bomb—a great big bomb which he wouldn't waste in the bare fields of Rudisheim. It was going to explode where it could really do damage: amongst the busy streets of West Berlin, where the crowds poured out of the underground stations all day and family parties sat in the cafés on the Kurfürstendamm. That was the place where his bomb would be planted. 'Pardon, gn'e Frau, did I breathe on you?' 'Excuse me, please sir. It is an unfortunate physical weakness. I spit slightly when I talk.'

'Dogs, would you live for ever?' Frederick the Great had asked his soldiers. Well, nobody was going to live long now. Not much longer than Marcus Levin and the Russian girl would live once the rats tore through that barrier.

And how much longer had he himself, if it came to that? Ten hours—twelve, perhaps? The tear in his cheek had stopped bleeding and was really hurting now. Already he could feel the stuff in his bloodstream, poisoning it, killing him. All the same, ten hours gave him plenty of time to do what he had to do.

But it wasn't his fault. Nothing had ever been his fault. At the beginning he'd never wanted to be evil. It was just that all his life he had been let down. Mutti had promised him so much and none of it had ever come true. That he was to be a pastor like his father and grandfather. That he would take a medical degree. That he would live in honour. 'Lies, lies, lies.' He screamed the words as he pressed the starter switch and then smiled as the engine burst into a merry hum.

Mutti would be dead now of course. She'd said that she would kill herself after he'd told her what had happened, and that was one promise she wouldn't break. Silly Mutti. Silly evil Gretel von Arnim. He'd loved her so much, but she deserved to die. 'You and I, Karl. You and I, my darling; always together.' He could still hear her voice and feel her arms around him, while upstairs in the little, stuffy bedroom his father had lain coughing his life away. 'My son can do anything he likes. My son isn't bound by rules or prejudices.' She deserved to die a thousand times for that night alone.

And now she'd let him down again. Everybody always let him down. After Levin had gone she'd screamed and raved at him, told him that she had borne a monster and didn't want to go on living. Well, perhaps she was right, but she had made him what he was and then deserted him. For years her work with the escape organization had taken all her energies and driven them steadily apart. Though that would be useful to him now of course. He took out a roughly drawn map of the route and studied it under the dashboard light. An empty shop in Fruchstrasse with a false wall in the cellar hiding a corridor which came out in the disused railway tunnel that ran through to the British sector. The same route through which they had taken Billy Fenwick.

But damn Billy—damn him to hell! It was Billy who had destroyed everything. He'd offered to help at first; to take the boy to Otto at Helmstedt, but Mutti hadn't wanted that. It was as though she didn't trust him any more, and she'd seemed to go crazy over the child, fondling him, crooning over him. And then he had taken Billy down to the crypt and showed him the relic, and he had laughed as though he were looking at some amusing toy. It was at that moment that he had known what possession was; as though somebody else had reached out for the chloroform and held the child's shoulders against the cage of fleas. Somebody else had opened the visor when Billy came to and somebody else's voice had said, 'You like fairy stories? Then look at one. Come and look at Iron Hans who can destroy the world if we let him loose.'

It all seemed so long ago when it had happened. After the church was bombed he had gone out and hidden the relic; 'an interesting historical curiosity', as the guide books called it, which should be preserved. Then, one day, when he was polishing it, he had made out the lines of verse and realized how to open it.

It took him less than a day to discover that the things which killed Rudolph von Ginter were still alive.

But he hadn't wanted to harm anyone. It was just the feel of ownership that he liked. The knowledge that it was there; that Karl Arnim, the failure, the park-keeper, the man who had committed a sin which would never be forgiven him, held something as powerful as an atomic bomb in his hands. And then that damned child laughed!

And would anybody ever find Marcus Levin and the Russian girl, he wondered? Probably not, because there wouldn't be anybody left alive to find them. The first strain, the original strain could be beaten, of course. It responded to normal Pasteurella immunization, and before long they were bound to find an antibiotic to kill it. But the second form, the strain he had perfected and strengthened and given to the rats, nothing could touch that. 'Excuse me, sir. Is my breath rather offensive?' He chuckled as he considered how it would be. 'My body is rotting, because when I opened the cages one of the little blighters bit me.' He broke off and his eyes blurred with pain.

'Oh, I wish—I wish—I wish . . .' Karl slid the car into gear and took one last look back through the window. Trees obscured his view of the house, but he knew that it was there; cosy and warm and hellish. It always would be there, just like that, till death blotted out his memory.

'Oh, I wish—I wish that only once—just once in all my life—I had slept with a woman who was not my mother.' He released the clutch and drove off: a blight moving across the clean snow into the world of men.

CHAPTER NINETEEN

JUDGING by the noise, there could be scores of them behind that wall, a hundred even and, while the period of activity lasted, the creatures would attack anything that came their way. All fear had been driven out by pain and sickness and they were mad. The smell of man would certainly increase their mania.

But how long was it since they had become infected? How long would the active period last? If only there was something they could climb on to, they might have a chance. Marcus piled the last of the books along the foot of the wall and as he did so the sound of tearing wood seemed to increase. They would be in darkness as well before long. Already one of the lamps had gone out and Tania had checked the others and found that the oil was low in all of them. Her torch battery was almost dead, too.

No, the altar and the bookcases were no good: flimsy structures knocked together out of thin laths which wouldn't support their weight. Besides, rats had no difficulty in climbing up timber.

'There must be a way out. There has to be.' Tania's fingers clutched his arm. 'Let's try the door again, Mark. If we both tried to lift it together . . .'

'No, that's no good.'

He shook his head as he looked at the rotten plank with which they had attempted to lever the door off its hinges. They might as well have used a match stick.

'What we've got to do is to hold them back for just a little longer. Probably only two hours or even less.' He tried to put a little confidence into his voice, but without knowing when Arnim had infected the animals he couldn't be sure of anything. All he was really certain about was what had happened at the end. After the radio broadcast and their visit—after his mother had got the truth out of him, Arnim must have known that the game was up and he would have gone down to destroy the evidence. As he was doing so, he would have heard them come in and one last final blow against life must have occurred automatically to his crazed mind. And, as he opened the cages, 'One of the little blighters bit me.'

'No, it won't be for long. The organism runs down after three hours. Besides, the police are bound to start looking for us when we don't report back.' Once again he struggled to put assurance into the lie. Goltz and Braun would probably have forgotten the whole business by now and be peacefully snoring away beside their Fraus.

But it was impossible. It just couldn't happen; not to him. Sudden anger and disbelief mingled with his fears. It couldn't happen. He was Marcus Levin. When his new thesis on the enterin virus was published he would be well in the running for a Nobel prize. If he were due to die before his time it would have happened earlier; in Poland, or Belsen, or with Rachel in the Vietnam jungle. It was impossible that he should go out now. He looked across at Tania and knew that there was another reason why he couldn't die.

'Mark, Mark, look there—in the corner.' Her voice suddenly rose to a scream and he saw one of the books move jerkily forward. He tore a lath from the altar, knocking over the relic as he did so, and hurled himself at it, beating down at the gap between the wall and the leather spine. Under the stick something screamed, twisted, writhed upwards and then crunched.

'That's one of them we won't have to worry about any more.' Even as he spoke he heard Tania cry out again, and another book started to jerk out. It was right at the far end of the wall, too far for him to reach, and with an almost reflex action he pulled the nearest lamp from its bracket and threw it at the book. The paraffin flared up in an orange line, but there wasn't much of it, and after a minute it dwindled to choking grey smoke.

'You've stopped them, Mark. You've really stopped them.' Tania swung her torch along the wall. 'Listen.' Apart from their breathing there was complete silence in the room.

'I've stopped them for a little while. They'll be back very soon. All the same, there's a chance for you now.' The glare of the paraffin had shown him a niche in the wall which had been hidden by shadow, and he crossed over to it. It was quite small, probably intended to hold a statue, but one person could just get into it and no rat would climb those four feet of brickwork.

'Try and get up in there, my dear.'

'And sit watching you die?' She shook her head. 'No, I'm sorry, Mark, but you can't ask me to do that. It will only hold one of us and I'm staying here with you.'

'Very well, if that's the way you want it.' He turned from the niche and came towards her, shrugging his shoulders. 'Thank you. And, Tania, if we get out of this, there's something I'd like you to remember. Though we've only known each other for a few hours, I think I'm in love with you.' He held out his left hand and, as their fingers touched, his right fist swung at her chin with all his strength behind it.

'Sorry about that, my sweet, but perhaps your husband will be grateful to me one day.' Marcus lifted her unconscious body into the niche. There was a rusty iron hook driven into the brickwork and he took off his tie and fastened her waist to it, grinning sadly as he pulled the tasteful device of crossed alpen-stocks into a knot. He had been very proud when they asked him to join the Il Vagabondo Club. Its current membership included two Nobel Prize winners, a Catholic cardinal, a Cabinet minister, proposed on the strength of his book on Etruscan architecture, and the Archbishop of Canterbury, who had only got in by the skin of his teeth.

'Well, that's one of us taken care of.' He glanced at his right hand. There must have been a nail in the lath he had taken from the altar and blood was pouring from a deep cut in the palm. As he looked at it, a verse from Housman ran through his head. When he first came to England he had thought the people to be without emotion till he had started to read their poetry. '"And here's a bloody hand to shake,"' he said aloud to the almost silent room. '"And, oh, man, here's goodbye. We'll sweat no more on scythe or rake, my bloody hands and I."'

And it would be goodbye soon. The last of the smoke had drifted away and the noise was starting again. It sounded quieter and more subdued at first and then steadily grew in volume as though the animals had been goaded into fresh activity by their setback. Beside him one of the three remaining lamps flickered and went out, and he seemed to hear a parody of the television slogan mocking him: 'Marcus Levin, this is your death.'

But there—over there. Marcus grabbed the lath as another book jerked away from the wall. The creature was already out of its prison, pulling itself up through a gnawed hole in the wood and glaring at him with red, tortured eyes. His stick lashed out, breaking its back, but there was another rat beside it and this one didn't pause. It leapt up at him in a bouncing arc, gripping the lath in its teeth and swinging from it like a bulldog. He dashed it to the floor, seeing it twist away to safety, knowing that there would be another one following it, and another, and another, but concentrating on nothing except killing the first. He never heard the noise behind him: feet running down the stairs, the door bursting open, and the shots. He never saw the beam of light. He just went on slashing at the rat till it turned and sprang at him, it was within inches of his throat when Gregor Petrov's third bullet killed it.

'Yes, we were quite literally here in the nick of time, Sir Marcus. In at the kill, eh?' Kirk beamed at him. 'It reminds me a bit of that H. G. Wells's story, *The Food of the Gods*. You remember, when they hear the newspaper boys shouting "Doctor eaten by stupendous Rats."'

'Yes, I suppose it might remind one of that.' Marcus found

the remark both tasteless and unfunny. It was two hours since he and Tania had been rescued and they had been partially restored by brandy at the local hotel. But now, as he stood at the top of the steps to the crypt again, nausea was coming back. 'If one had a particularly perverse sense of humour, that is.'

'Oh, sorry, old boy. Poor taste, eh?' Kirk sniffed the air and turned to the leader of the decontamination unit which had been sent over from Magdeburg. 'I suppose that it's safe enough to go in there?'

'Perfectly safe, Herr General.' The man clicked his heels and pronounced the title with a flourish. 'We pumped the place full of potassium cyanide, killing everything, but extractor fans have been at work and the air should be quite pure now.'

'Should be?' Petrov raised his eyebrows. 'It had better be, comrade, or I can picture a very miserable future for you and yours. Well, gentlemen, are you ready?'

'I suppose so.' In spite of the hint of a grin on Kirk's face, Marcus took Tania's arm as he went down the steps. High up in the vaulted ceiling of the crypt there was an electric bulb which they hadn't discovered, and in its glare he could see the relic lying on the floor, the lath that had saved his life and the dead bodies of the rats. They looked quite innocent now—just small bundles of brown and grey fur; nothing to do with the things that had slashed and screamed at him.

'Yes, Arnim made himself quite a business-like laboratory.' The door in the partition had been broken open to show the room behind it. More dead rats lay on the floor, there was a huge wire cage in the centre, and benches ran along the walls, piled with scientific equipment.

'He must have worked very hard, too.' There was admiration in Marcus's eyes as he looked at the apparatus. Apart from a modern microscope it was terribly crude and old-fashioned, and some of it appeared to have been home-made. He studied it briefly, and then opened a book at the end of the third bench: Arnim's notes.

'Yes, I see.' He flushed with excitement as he read the spidery writing. 'So, that's it. All the time, right under our noses and we never even bothered to try it. Histocyn 2.'

'What's that, old boy? You've found something important?'

'Yes, I think you can call it important, General.' Marcus nodded without looking up. 'There is a drug to kill the bacillus. According to Arnim it has no resistance to Histocyn." He flicked on through the pages.

'There doesn't appear to be any doubt about it. He used all the standard tests and it was effective in every case. Once we can get production going, there'll be no need to worry about this little beauty any more.

'Have this sent out to all medical authorities at once, will you?' Marcus scribbled a note and handed it to Petrov. 'And don't think too badly that we didn't discover it ourselves. Histocyn 2 was one of the very early antibiotics, developed in Holland soon after the discovery of penicillin. It is thought to be effective only in dealing with certain localized complaints—sinus infections, for example—and rarely used these days. I suppose we would have tried it in time, but very much as a last resort.' He glanced at the dates on the book. 'After all, Arnim has been studying the bacillus for fifteen years.'

'Don't worry, Sir Marcus. Nobody will ever criticize you.' Petrov gave the note to one of the policemen. 'Your hunch about coming here paid off right along the line, and please accept my congratulations.' He mopped his forehead with a very bright silk handkerchief.

'So, everything will be back to normal again, it seems. This—this stuff of yours can stop the bug, and there'll be nothing more to worry about. You can go home, eh, General, and start getting to grips with my successor, and I can look forward to a long and well-earned retirement. Thank you.' Another policeman hurried into the room and Petrov took a message pad from him.

'Ah, good.' He smiled as he read. 'They've located this man, Adolph Wolner, who took the child through to West Berlin. For some reason, perhaps merely luck, he is not infected. He hasn't told us about the escape route yet, but there's no doubt that he will do after my boys have had a little time with him. And when he has talked we'll put an end to this escaping business once and for all.' Now that the crisis had passed Petrov was getting back to his routine problems.

'But Arnim? Any news of him yet?'

'No, not at the moment, but don't worry. We'll find him soon enough. A full description has gone out and road blocks have been set up. It's merely a question of time before Herr *von* Arnim, as he likes to call himself, is shot down like—how do you say—a mad dog.'

'Yes, mad enough, but a clever dog too.' Marcus read on through the notes and a pleasant picture was forming in his mind. A series of lectures, a new mention in the Honours List, his picture in every newspaper, a very rosy future indeed. He looked across at Tania and smiled. He was far too old for her and they would make an ill-assorted couple. Doubtless his housekeeper, Mrs Anderson, who was a staunch Conservative, would be full of disapproval too. To hell with his age! To hell with Mrs. Anderson! She would just have to get used to the idea. He remembered how he had sung on the way to Richmond and almost started to hum the refrain. Then he turned another page and everything became cold again.

'No, no, please God, no. Let him have failed—please let him have failed.' The writing seemed to twist and blur in front of his eyes, but there it was. 'October 15th, 1961 . . . Today I commenced experiments to see if it is possible to produce a strain which will be resistant to the normal Pasteurella serum. Dr Runeberg who is indebted to my mother for his daughter's presence in the West has promised to obtain supplies of the serum for me . . .' Six pages of dates and figures, and at last three lines of cramped writing. 'I have done it. Now to see if immunity to Histocyn 2 can be produced. The key may well be through intense radiation. I will try ultra violet first.'

'Yes, that might be a possibility.' On the shelf over the bench Marcus could see an outlandish piece of equipment which resembled a magic lantern. It had battery carbons fitted as burning elements and the reflector had been taken from an electric fire. Though it looked a horribly botched and amateur job, he had no doubt that the power would be there. He stared at the notes again and he had never prayed harder in his life.

'Failure—failure.' Across every page, covering weeks and months and years, the word had been scribbled in red pencil, obscuring the notes. Marcus felt hope coming back as he looked at it. 'January—August—November—1962—'63—'64. Failure—failure—failure.' Then, almost at the end of the book, dated less than a week ago, the entry that told him hope had died. 'It should now be perfect and I have enough subjects to make a thorough test.'

Yes, he had had enough all right. Marcus stood up and looked at the cage. It was divided into dozens of partitions, but they could all be opened by a single lever if necessary. Beside it was another small cage of very fine wire mesh with what looked like a pile of dust on the floor. Neither of them was of any importance now. Cyanide had killed the rats and the fleas and there was only one carrier left. Just as Arnim had released the rats, 'one of the little blighters bit me.'

'I'm sorry, gentlemen.' Marcus turned to Kirk and Petrov. 'I thought we were home at last, but I was wrong—quite wrong.' The mere effort of speech was almost too much for him. 'Arnim produced a mutant, you see; a species which is unaffected by the Pasteurella serum and also resistant to Histocyn. He is infected with it himself.'

'Only himself? Only Arnim?' Petrov smiled reassuringly. 'Then don't worry, Sir Marcus. The police have his description and . . .'

'And they will shoot him down like a mad dog, as you said before.'

Marcus shook his head and tried to imagine what might happen. If they merely wounded Arnim and he staggered away into a crowd of onlookers. If a bullet grazed him and went on to find another target, carrying a smear of his poisoned blood with it. If a police dog sniffed his breath before he died.

'You'll have to change your instructions to the police, I'm afraid, Mr Petrov. Arnim is a carrier and his one ambition will be to pass on the disease to others. That is normal enough with the sane, and he's a psychopath. Samuel Pepys reported that during the Plague of London, "Ill people would breathe in the faces of well people passing by."

'No, tell your police not to interfere with Arnim till they've got him where they can't miss—where there's not the slightest chance of his escaping. It's not a question of *killing* Arnim any more. He must be completely destroyed.'

CHAPTER TWENTY

It was almost as though they had been avoiding him. As though they knew what he could do to them and were keeping out of his way; avoiding him like the plague. Karl Arnim grinned, partly at the thought and partly to stifle pain; clenching his teeth to try and control the shudders which were running through his body.

Yes, almost as though they knew. It was just after Magdeburg when he had come across the first road block. Two police cars drawn up on the verge and their occupants standing in the road with machine pistols under their arms. He was sure that they would try to stop him and he had prepared to make a dash for it, but one of them had waved him on. And, after all, why should they stop him? Nobody could say that he wasn't a perfectly respectable citizen. Not Mutti, nor Marcus Levin, nor the Russian girl. Nobody could accuse him of anything.

All the same, he'd been careful after that, turning off into minor roads and approaching the city from the south-east. At Friedrichhain he had left the car in a side street, because private vehicles were likely to attract attention in central Berlin and also because he wanted to walk; to feel clean air in his lungs and the snow, which was beginning to fall again, cool against his burning face.

It was soon after that that he'd had his second encounter with the police. Three of them, a sergeant and two very young constables had come slowly towards him down the pavement. He had been almost on the point of running, but the sergeant had said something to his companions and they'd all walked across the road; again as though they knew.

And perhaps they did. Perhaps some sixth sense in their stupid, animal minds told them to beware of him. It was pleasant to think that, and also pleasant to think of them dying, rotting; just as he himself was beginning to rot. In a strange way he almost felt offended that they had not tried to stop him.

After the police had come the drunks. Five horrible, 'for tomorrow we die' drunks lurching along in the centre of the road. One of the men had paused to vomit in the gutter and the two women were howling out a bawdy song. Though it was bitterly cold he could see that one of them had her blouse ripped open, showing a glint of bare flesh.

Yes, 'for tomorrow we die' was right and he loved them, because they were behaving exactly as the human animal was supposed to behave. In the Middle Ages sexual activity had been considered a protection against plague, and these drunks were following the pattern. He would have liked to go up to them, raise his arm to quiet the bawling hags and shout, 'Bless you, my creatures. I made you what you are.'

Then had come the immunization centre near the Ostbahnhof. A long queue standing in the snow and shuffling forward. It was quite an orderly queue, because there was a squad of police watching them, but the strain on every face was clear enough in spite of the reassurances which poured out from a loudspeaker. 'There is no cause for alarm—the only danger is panic—ample stocks of vaccine are being flown in from the Soviet Union—it is just a matter of time before the epidemic is under full control.'

That was true enough. Karl nodded in agreement as he listened. Soon there would be no danger at all. The vaccine would take and before long somebody like Marcus Levin would hit on Histocyn and the strain would be wiped out. Only the original strain, though. It would take a long, long time to get the measure of the second creature—the one which he had strengthened and perfected and which was coursing through his bloodstream now. Once again he had a desire to go up to them, to tell them who he was, but he fought against it and walked on. It wasn't among these small pathetic groups that his blow would fall, but among the jostling, hurrying crowds of the West.

But here he was at last: Fruchstrasse, a narrow, dingy street with half the buildings unoccupied and the scars of bombing still plainly visible. The shop he wanted was on the next corner with a sign reading 'Glass and Novelties' on the fascia.

Before the wall went up, it must have sold ornamental ash-trays, and tiny glass animals, and beer mugs which played a tune when they were lifted from the table. Now it had been shut for years and only people who knew its secret would visit it. On the boards across the window there was a poster advertising some athletic meeting at the Volkspark; two tall, bronzed girls leaping across hurdles. Karl stared at them for a moment and then glanced up and down the street. He was quite alone and there was no need to hurry. Six o'clock of a fine clear morning, the snow blowing away and a hint of dawn coming up in the east. Between eight and nine was the time he wanted. Then the crowds would be flooding the underground stations and he would be with them. He moved to the door and then paused and stared up at the poster as though his eyes were being pulled towards it.

'Oh, I wish,' he said to the empty street, and the cold air, and the faded, torn paper, 'oh, I wish that just once, I could have known somebody like one of you.' He pushed open the door and walked forward to his destiny.

The car radio had been choked with static since they left Rudisheim and now the loudspeaker was almost useless. The operator sat hunched beside the driver with earphones on and he scribbled what he could make out on a pad, handing back each message to Petrov. As he read the last one the Russian frowned and shook his head.

'Well, I just hope we're doing the right thing, General,' he said. 'As you know, Arnim reached the road block outside Lenzfeld shortly after three and, according to instructions, no attempt was made to stop him. We now know that he left the car in Friedrichhain and is going west on foot.' He scowled at Tania. 'Though you were in a hurry, surely you could have remembered to lock the car door?'

'It was I who left the door unlocked, Mr Petrov, and it's a good thing I did. If Arnim had gone by public transport or tried to get a lift, there would be the very devil to pay.'

'Yes, I suppose you're right.' Petrov grinned at Marcus. 'But what an attractive phrase, "the very devil to pay". I must try to remember that.

'At any rate, from what we learned from his mother, it seems certain that Arnim is making for West Berlin. As soon as Wolner tells us about the route, we shall bring up the equipment General Kirk so wisely suggested and there will be nothing to worry about.' He pulled out a case and offered cigarettes all round; the courteous host attending to his guests' comfort.

'And perhaps this will be what we are waiting for.' He pushed away his lighter as the operator handed him another note. 'Yes, Wolner has talked all right. I thought he would after my boys had a little time with him.

'It seems that in the Fruchstrasse there is a shop with a concealed door in its cellar. Behind this, a passage has been dug through to one of the main sewers, and the route finally comes out in the underground railway system. Since we stopped traffic, all inter-city lines are blocked of course, but they have cut an opening in one of the barriers. But . . .' Petrov broke off. He had been smiling as he read, but now he suddenly looked very worried. He handed the paper to Kirk.

'And that's all we do know, General; all that Wolner was able to tell them. For obvious reasons he was only given part of the route.'

'Thank you. Yes, natural enough, I suppose, but it puts us on the spot.' Kirk's maimed hand trembled on the arm rest as he spoke. 'In case he should be caught, Wolner was only given details of the route as far as the railway block. From there on the escapers were escorted by an agent from the west: this woman Ruth Eulenburg, who is dead.' He picked up a map of Berlin and scowled at its mass of railway lines.

'So, I'll have to send the police in after him.' Petrov hated the thought of that, for he could picture a squad of men blundering through the tunnels. The chances were that they wouldn't even find Arnim, but if they did—if he turned on them before a lethal bullet went home . . .

'You may have to do so, if he has already reached the shop, but I don't like the idea at all. As Sir Marcus says, we want him out in the open where he can't be missed.' Kirk bent over the map, trying to put himself in Arnim's place and understand the workings of his crazed mind. Once he was through the barrier separating east from west, he could go where he liked, but he must have some specific destination. He leaned forward to the radio operator.

'You are a Berliner?' he said holding the map out to him. 'Good. Now, this railway is called the "U-bahn" or "Untergrundbahn", but it is really a simple cut-and-cover system which often runs on the surface. Can you indicate which are surface lines in this section here?

'Thank you.' He nodded as the man drew a series of crosses on the map. 'Now, I'd like you to try and contact British Military Headquarters in Charlottenburg. The wavelength is fifteen point five metres and the code words to get them to answer are "Wuthering Heights".' He leaned back on his seat and held the map out in front of him. If he had read Arnim's mind correctly, the man would remain underground till the last possible moment and he would want to make his appearance at a big station. That ruled out the line between the Leipzigerplatz and Yorkstrasse, and also from Friedrichstrasse to the Lehterbahnhof. There was just one obvious choice. He drew a circle around a station and handed the map to Petrov.

'Yes, I think it's going to be up to our people to deal with Arnim now and, unless I'm completely wrong, this is where they should wait for him.' Kirk closed his eyes for a moment as the operator struggled to make the connection he needed. He had made his last move and played his hunch as Marcus Levin had done and, once he had given his orders, there would be nothing more for him to do. He considered the crowds which would soon be filling the underground system and he prayed he was right. 'And, if I'm wrong,' he said, partly to himself and partly to his companions, 'if I'm wrong, God help us.'

Seven forty-five. The little luminous dial of his watch told him that it was time to go, and Karl hoped that it wasn't much farther. His body was hardly capable of obeying him now and his feet stumbled and dragged on the floor of the disused tunnel.

Yes, he'd have to take it very slowly, because he was almost finished. It was like an eternity since he had entered that shop in the Fruchstrasse, crawling on his knees down the narrow corridor and wading through foul water as he crossed the sewer. But at last his torch had found the grating and he had pulled himself up into the railway tunnel.

It was shortly after that that the police had come. Three of them marching officiously up to the brick barrier as he crouched behind a pillar. It had obviously been a routine patrol, because they had merely swung a lamp over it and clumped off as though satisfied. Fools! Incompetent fools! If they had only looked a little closer they must have seen the tiny line of metal in the brickwork. The door which when pushed in a certain manner swung back to show the way to the west.

Clever Gretel. Clever, clever Gretel von Arnim. She'd destroyed him. The sin they had committed together might make his soul rot in hell, just as his body was rotting now, but he had felt enormous admiration for her as he crawled through the door that she and her associates had made. Clever, clever Gretel.

He must be almost there now. The rusty nails between his feet started to throb and hum and, less than a hundred yards away, he could see a string of lights as a train clattered across a junction. He held the torch over his map. The refugee lines had to be kept secret, even in the west, and at this point there should be an air shaft with a loose cover that led up to a piece of waste ground behind the station. To hell with the refugees, to hell with crawling up air shafts, even if he had the strength to do so. It was the station itself and the early morning crowds that he wanted. Very serious crowds probably. Worried people thinking about the epidemic, but still secure in the knowledge that 'it can't happen to me'. It was going to happen though. He grinned at the thought of them standing there, with their newspapers like barriers before them. Then one of them would turn and see him climb up on to the barrier and . . . There was a nursery rhyme that Miss Steele, his English governess, had taught him. 'Atishooo—atishoo —we all fall down.'

Karl threw the map and the torch away and staggered forward. His throat appeared to be furred up and now and again he had to lean against the wall, gasping for breath. That's right, he thought. Not far now, so take it nice and slow and easy. Mind that pillar and look out for trains at the junction. Such a very little way to go, and you must make it because they are waiting for your entrance, for the grand performance. The rusty nails joined others which were shiny with use and he could see the station.

Yes, there it was, though his lungs were bursting with the effort, and at every step he could feel the thing in his groin grate and swell. Such a little way. Fifty metres, thirty, twenty, there. The platform reared up like a cliff, but his arms grasped the top and he pulled himself up till he was kneeling on the edge, seeing nothing but a red glow at first and then slowly opening his eyes and looking at the world he had come to destroy.

But no, it wasn't true. It couldn't be true. It was just his eyes deceiving him—the poison in his body distorting sight. He stared along the platform, seeing confectionery and cigarette machines, advertisements and signs reading 'Kurfürstenplatz' along the walls and a clock showing seven minutes past eight. But nobody was there; nobody at all. Arnim shook his head in bewilderment, and then smiled.

For that was it, of course. Somewhere along the route he had made a mistake and come out at the wrong station. A station which was out of use because it only connected with the east and the lines were blocked. The name signs were just a trick of the eyes; wish fulfilment brought on by disease. Somewhere he had missed the turning, but it wasn't important. He only had to get out into the daylight, into the fresh air, and he would find people to accept his legacy. 'Excuse me, sir, I'm afraid that I spit slightly when I speak. It is a weakness.'

With a gasping, shambling effort Karl moved on. He crawled up the steps to the booking office on his knees; more deserted machines, no porter at the barrier, no woman in the newspaper stand and more signs mocking him; 'Kurfürstenplatz'—an illusion. But, at last, he saw a message with daylight at the end of it.

It was a lovely day too. 'A lovely day to die on,' as the French queen had said on her way to the guillotine. Under an almost cloudless sky the snow-covered buildings looked like Christmas cakes. Their cakes—his and Mutti's cakes—Gretel von Arnim's cakes to be consumed with love while the chestnuts popped on the stove and everything was warm and cosy.

And there were the police waiting to welcome him. Dozens of them standing at the other side of the street with a little group of soldiers in front of them. British soldiers—Tommies. The same khaki soldiers who had given him his wound. They carried no guns, but one of them had two cylinders strapped to his back and held what looked like a length of hose-pipe in his right hand. The sergeant at his side wore a row of campaign ribbons on his tunic and there was a blue cockade on his cap which showed that he belonged to a crack regiment.

Well, a British soldier would be the first victim. Karl stood grinning at them from the station entrance and then broke into a stumbling run. 'Here I come, Sergeant,' he thought. 'Here I come with my present.' He stopped as a car came into the square and drew up beside the soldiers. Four people got out. Two old men in very thick overcoats with faces that looked strangely alike, and after them ghosts—the dead—Marcus Levin and the Russian girl, coming to see his end. Behind him Karl heard the station gates crash together, cutting off his escape, and he suddenly realized what the cylinders meant.

'No,' he screamed. 'No, no, no, don't shoot. Friend, Ami, Kamerad, please don't shoot! I don't mean any harm! I just want to give you something!' He went on screaming like that till one of the old men gave an order, the soldier lifted the nozzle of his flame-thrower and pulled the trigger.

THE CONCRETE KIMONO

John Paddy Carstairs

"The Concrete Kimono" is published by W. H. Allen & Co.

The Author

J.P.C. could be encountered in any of a number of energetic guises: when he's not directing films or holding an exhibition of his own paintings he might be discovered tap dancing, playing squash or doing some rather rapid motoring. As if this is not enough to fill one man's time he has a long string of entertaining books to his credit. They come fast and furious; he has written thrillers (meet his agreeable amateur agent Garway Trenton now in *The Concrete Kimono*), contemporary novels and light novels, some satire, a children's book and some biography and autobiography. When not in orbit Mr. Carstairs lives in Surrey.

CHAPTER ONE

THE bang of my front door had awakened me. It appeared to be about five in the morning, winter-time and pitch-dark and not the sort of day I really wanted to get up at five—if there were any days that came under the category of wanting to get up.

It was true I'd been dancing in Helen Cordet's *Saddle Room* with young Penny Thrale-Thwaite-Popham until four, and it seemed to me that couldn't have been more than ten minutes ago. However, the strident tones of Lily Mertens, my daily, who was never known to be early, convinced me.

I groaned. My head had the little men banging on anvils which Mike Hammer's cretor, Mickey Spillane, writes about; *my* gang were working on double-bubble and I thought if I ever saw a brandy and ginger ale again, I'd vomit instantly. I turned over on my back and sighed heavily. I asked myself *was* it worth it? It wasn't as if I had actually gone to bed with Penny—her 'Mummeh' was home. Usually 'Mummeh' was at Cannes in the summer, Paris in the spring, Kitzbuhl and/or Bahamas in the winter, and New York in the Fall. What was especially embarrassing was the fact that Penny hadn't known 'Mummeh' was home. Nor had I! But 'Mummeh' was not amused and I retired rapidly, leaving among other things, a gold cigarette case Penny had given me. It was a pity about that cigarette case. I liked it and it hocked inordinately well.

Below, stentorian cries could be heard from Lily of *Climb upon my Knee, Sonny Boy*. She had run the gamut from Sinatra to Presley to Darin and happened, by chance, to take her young nephew to a local cinema to see a Disney, and a re-issue of a re-issue of the Jolson story was still going the rounds and Lily had discovered Larry Parks. A pity really.

Intermingled—if one could mix sound and smell—the pungent smell of frying kipper assailed my nostrils. I couldn't be sure which made my stomach turn the worse—Lily's imitation of Jolson or the frizzling kipper. I groaned again.

With some trepidation, in case it was a cold day, I lifted my right hand from under the blanket and gingerly felt the bruise under my right eye. It was bloody painful. That male film-star —one of the few—had no right to throw punches when I was sitting down and looking the other way at his orchidaceous guest (female). It could have been highly dangerous. In the *Saddle Room,* too.

Lily was still singing when she brought in my breakfast tray.

'Oh, put a sock in it, Lilly,' I shouted, trying to drown her vocal efforts. 'And for God's sake, *don't* draw the curtains!'

'Why?' Lily asked archly. 'We got visitors, then?'

'No, Lily, we have not got visitors,' I replied primly.

'Well,' sniffed Lily, 'don't say it as if we never 'ave visitors.'

'I don't want to discuss such matters,' I retorted, 'I just find your "Pop" numbers too loud for the time of the day. Come to think of it, I preferred your Perry Como period to the present favourite' .

Lily sniffed her disapproval of my criticism, but I was on a subject in which she was always interested. As she switched on a very tiny, tender little blue low-voltage bulb bedside lamp, which I had cunningly organized for such mornings, she said, "Ere, Mr. Garway, sir, why don't they ask you to go on Juke Box Jury?'

'I've no idea, Lily,' I replied, thereby terminating the conversation I hoped.

'I mean, though you're not exactly a teen-ager, you do go jiving with them debs and you're still "with it", I mean.'

'Thank you, Lily. Whereas I might not pass the tests to fly a Hunter P1127, I think I could still run the mile in under twenty minutes.'

Lily didn't appreciate the joke.

'You changed your Maserati, then?'

'No, why?'

'This P1127——?'

'Never mind, Lily, I was merely . . .' I began then faltered, for Lily had placed the breakfast tray under my nose and the nauseating kipper's odiferous efforts peppered my postrils. It took me all my time to wave the tray away without fetching up. It reminded me of the time I had had a beating-up by the captain of my house at Eton for a parody of Milton's L'Allégro, *Hence loathèd Melancholy,* in which I complained of an undesirable-brekker kipper, starting it *Hence loathèd Smellin' fishie.* The past repeats itself, if you will pardon the burp.

Suddenly and raucously Lily emitted a delighted yell.

'Cor stone the crows! Look at your eye! That's a real shiner!

What she do,' Lily asked roguishly, 'Give you the brush-off?' I ignored this.

'Is it really bad, Lily?'

'Not 'arf. All in lovely beautiful Technicolour. . . . Oh, wot a surprise,' she started singing. 'Simply for tellin'——'

'Shut up, Lily. Pour out my coffee and go, gal, go!'

'Aren't you going to tell me 'ow it 'appened? I suppose her 'usband was 'ome!'

'Oh, Lily, belt up!' I commanded, using the sort of language she understood.

Lily belted, sniffed, departed.

I played about a little with the kipper, drank two cups of black coffee and felt sufficiently alive to glance at the morning papers. I switched on another light over the bed, groaned as it rained steel shafts into my eyeballs, got used to it, and made my rapid assessment of the news.

There were the usual eclectric, fascinating headlines—*Nun Singer quits as a Pop Star; Wife had Gelignite in her Powder Compact* (That Was The Nose, That Was!); *Husband finds Wife dead under Lodger's Bed; Priest who Lost Girl-Friend becomes Con-Man,* and a quote from a visiting film star personality, 'Your Lord Mayor is a dream-boat.'

Then, on an inner page was a photograph of Roddy Vandaleur. Apparently he had won an Oscar in Hollywood for a screen play of some gi-normous Biblical epic entitled *The Animals Went in two by two*. After the photos of the bustier-star, the art editors of the dailies don't normally find room for shots of the directors or scenarists, but Roddy Vandaleur was such a handsome hunk, I suppose he made the female readers—er—eyes moisten.

He was smiling in that inimitable, slightly-amused, slightly superior way of his. And, of course, in his left ear the 'famous' ear-ring. With his curly black shock of hair Irish blue-black, 'Bible-black', and his flashing white, even, tombstone teeth he looked a splendid swashbuckler. Roddy's ear-ring had caused a lot of trouble at Eton: but Vandaleur was always in trouble at Eton. Some thought he was an exhibitionist, and a few called him Flash——, behind his back of course. We were in the same house (Martineau's) and were both Wet Bobs, members of Pop and in the Cricket Eleven.

He claimed the ear-ring couldn't be removed though I suspected this was sheer nonsense. There was a great to-do with his house master, and his parents, both very handsome and arrogant, backed him up and, finally, it was a sort of *fait accompli*. I think he wore it so that the other fellows would rag him and he could get into fights. He adored fights; and most of the House adored him, but there were dissenters.

I admired him because of his *sang-froid* (he always made a point of striding through a group of Windsor 'Mods' in the hope that they'd engage in battle and usually they did). I used to think of the poem *The Fighting Temeraire*. But, despite his engaging 'blarney', his physical courage, his fantastic, movie-star good looks, he had a strange bad-egg side to his nature.

I remember spending a week-end with him at Buck Brinton's country house. The Brinton's were very proud of their flock of doves. While we were there someone was banging off at them with a pellet-pistol, at least one a day would be discovered with a pellet in his head. The marksmanship was superb. It wasn't till we returned to college that I saw Roddy shooting at our Dame's (Matron's) bottom from his study window with a pellet pistol and when I challenged him he confessed he'd bagged the doves. He did it to see if the Brinton's would catch him out. He was always smoking and wenching in the town. He read a smuggled-in-from-Soho copy of *The Kama Sutra* which he propped behind his algebra book. It was as if he lived life on a dare.

Then one day he was caught in the back row of the cinema in Windsor with a local tootsie of good looks and shocking bad reputation and he was 'asked' to leave. Not expelled, not sent down exactly. He was relieved about this he said, because it meant he could still wear the O.E. tie I wasn't surprised he'd won an Oscar for writing; I remember losing the Richards Prize for English Essay at Eton to Roddy, who freely confessed afterwards that he had swiped most of his 'original' from a more obscure portion of the works of Ruskin, and 'Badger' someone or other had written the rest.

I emerged from my reverie on Roderick Vandaleur by the return of Lily with the morning mail.

She started to snigger.

'*Now* what, Lily?'

'Your shiner,' she said between giggles, 'it's wot they call King-Size, ain't it?'

I ignored her until she said, 'Dunno wot they'll say about that at the studios.'

'The studios!' I sat up quickly and the breakfast tray went for six.

'Oh, my Gawd!' groaned Lily. 'Never a dull moment!'

'*The Studios*! I'd forgotten about the studios.'

'To much noshin' and drinkin' the night before. If you——'

'What's the time, Lily?'

'Well, I was a *bit* late,' she confessed. 'It's—well, a bit after nine.'

'What do you mean, a "bit after nine"?' I inquired, trying to find my watch which was usually under my pillow.

'If you are looking for your watch, you forgot to take it off—it's on your wrist,' she said.

The time was ten to ten.

'Lily!' I shouted. 'I was due at United Studios five minutes ago!'

'Well, don't blame me,' she retorted sulkily.

I leapt out of bed, making for the bathroom, as Lily sniffed again, this time, contemptuously.

Have you noticed in life that people aren't the sort of people you expect them to be? I mean they don't look as one expects them to look. The butcher looks as if he works in the City, the brain surgeon could be a station master. It appears that only painters want to look like artists. The most snobby individuals are the film wallahs who will do anything to avoid looking like villains. It has become the thing for the wealthy writer to wear suits not just sweat shirts and jeans. I know of one film director who wears a bowler hat; the old order passeth. As for top film producers they are, these days at any rate, dolled up like avuncular characters from that *other* school (on the Hill).

To generalize: British film executives look like bank managers though, when I reached the conference room of the London United Studios, there was a sepulchral air about them that reminded me more of a group of undertakers as they sat gravely awaiting my appearance. I apologized and gave some waffling excuse about having difficulty starting the Maserati—this fooled nobody: nor did the black eye and the sticking plaster on my forehead exactly help to convince them.

El Supremo, the executive in charge of production coughed gravely and came quickly to the point.

'Well, Mr. Trenton, the fact is we—we—like your ideas on

how to plan to adapt Miss Sharon Saxbee's novel, and we think the next step is for you to get on with the treatment.'

There was a murmur of agreement from the lesser hierarchy. El Supremo looked significantly at Christopher Lane who was to direct the production. He and I were old buddies, he had made a successful film out of one of my earlier novels, *Bird Singing on a Blitzed Château.*

'Fact is, Garway, we think it might be a good idea if you took a shufty at Mandura—before you embark on the treatment of the Saxbee book.'

'Eh?' I had hoped to write it leisurely in Sardinia among The Quality. 'Eh? When?' I inquired.

'Well, the sooner the better.'

'The studio PRO will fix your air tickets, hotel accommodation and so on."

'Fine.'

'We suggest you have a chat with Miss Saxbee before you leave for Mandura—chances are she'll know all the ropes.'

'Chances are she's never been to Mandura,' I replied.

There was an ominous silence finally broken by El Supremo. 'But,' he reminded me icily, 'her novel *Manduran Sparrow* is about Mandura.'

'Too true, but the best song about New York, in my opinion, is *Transatlantic Lullaby* written by Diana Morgan and Robert McDermott who'd never been there!'

There was incredulity and suspicion on the faces of all except Christopher Lane. Christopher gulped. Only he knew that my *Bird Singing on a Blitzed Château,* which was about the troubles in Cyprus, had been conceived and written on an aircraft carrier off Glasgow.

Chris said quickly: 'I'd come to Mandura with you but I simply must start testing. God knows who we can get to play the star part in Miss Saxbee's story. By the way,' he added, 'you can get her address from the story department.'

I gave him a dead-pan 'thank you'.

'Capital,' said El Supremo as if we had decided on the inlaid gold ebony-embossed casket. The meeting was over.

'You bastard!' I said to Christopher as he walked with me to the Maserati. 'You told me there was no hurry. I'd planned to water-ski at Sardinia.'

'Lots of nice water in Manura—blue lagoons, lovely gals——'

'I can lap up all the atmosphere I need by visiting their Tourist Office,' I averred.

'Nonsense! What did you take this assignment for?'

'Only because I'm a fourteen-carat whore. I wanted the Maserati—badly,' I said, patting the car which we had by then reached—Ming III, by name.

'But why was I tempted? I mean, what the hell has my *Bird Singing on a Blitzed Château* got in common with Sharon's *Manduran Sparrow*?'

'The bird, of course,' Chis mocked, adding in a phoney American accent, 'Not to worry, you're doing a Top Class Job! Will you take Penelope Fitz-Hyphen what's her name?'

'Certainly not and you, Herr Direktor, know too much,' I retorted, adding, 'where the hell *is* Mandura, anyway?'

'Somewhere between Madagascar and Mauritius, I believe,' he said. I stopped in my tracks.

'You wot?' I gasped, in imitation of Coronation Street.

'Well, certainly at the foot of Africa.'

'You're bloody joking.'

'I'm bloody not.'

'What in hell was Sharon Saxbee doing out there, for God's sake?'

'Writing her novel, *Manduran*——'

'I know that!' I cut in, 'but *why* there?'

'You'll have to ask her. In any case, I don't know why you are fretting. I hear it's bloody marvellous there.'

I gave him a look that put a decade on him.

CHAPTER TWO

I HAD a lunch date with Penny at the Pickwick Club. Like all debs. she was mad keen on the world of entertainment and she gazed wide-eyed at the Roscian Gipsies as they gave better performances than when they were being paid for it. She murmured 'Fab' every now and then and was utterly entranced.

When I said I had to go to Mandura to lamp the place for a movie script she was even more thrilled.

'I say! Why can't I come with you?' she asked excitedly.

'I don't think Mummy would like that,' I said, all decent fellow *Floreat Etona,* and all that jazz! I was bloody sure 'Mummeh' wouldn't like it at all, at all.

Penny began what could be a long session of the sulks, so I girded up my Old College sock suspenders and winged it in the Maserati out towards the Chiswick Eyot, where Sharon Saxbee lived on a houseboat. If you know Sharon Saxbee or have read any of her books, of course you'd realize she would live on a houseboat.

I had seen her occasionally at literary cocktail parties. She was 'booksy', very young, very attractive. She wore her blonde hair in what I am told is an Urchin Cut, very boyish, but with her slightly defensive attitude (don't-touch-me-or-I'll-ring-for-the-fire-brigade) gave the appearance that she was far too fey to be interested in men. By that I mean physically interested. Yet no lesbian she. She was enchanting, bird-like and intelligent. However, one felt that one false move towards one's flies would have her reaching hastily for the burnt feathers. This I respected though I found it irksome. I was always uneasy with that sort of woman, probably because I was extrovert despite any whimsey-whamsey in my novels, *Bird Singing on a Blitzed Château* and *Brown Sugar and Jasmins*. I think my generation (the Forties?) were able to be hearty and whimsey-whamsey whereas the Twenties produced the Whimsey-whimsies who were purely aesthetic and never hearty.

Then, too, Sharon Saxbee was always surprising, whereas dear sweet idiot Penny never was; debs. ran true to form—I mean only the Saxbees of this world, pure-looking, virginal-looking, respectable-looking, intelligent-looking would swim the Channel—or so her publicity agent had proclaimed.

Her houseboat was moored off the Chiswick Eyot. Well, actually, it was moored by a catamaran near the bank. Well, actually there were several boats nearer to the catamaran than Sharon's. You had to cross several other houseboats before you reached her boat. To get to the *Sad Geraniums for Dulcie* meant a sort of naval *Permission to Cross your Ship, Sir*? as one made the journeys from one craft to another.

The name of the houseboat was *Sad Geraniums for Dulcie*, and the reason, she explained later, was that this was the title of the first thing that Sharon sold—a short story when she was still at Westfield. Sharon's houseboat was crammed with books, place of honour being given to the better known female novelists—they ranged from Margaret Irwin to Phyllis Bottome, Cecil Woodham-

Smith to Rumer Godden. I found her taste bright, eclectric, modern, romantic, nostalgic. There was also the works of Iris Murdoch; the poems of Rupert Brooke, Flecker's *Hassan,* T. H. Elliot's *East Coker* and an early Bridget Boland.

There were several too-large-for-the-area abstracts on the sides of the boat, too complex for me who couldn't see much after Jackson Pollock. These were by her brother, Hardy, who I imagined to be a bit of an obscure Wet—but this was unfair because I was visualizing a sort of near-male Sharon, and, in all probability, he wasn't like that at all, after all, a number of toughies painted abstract.

She kept a bicycle on the houseboat, a Siamese cat, two tortoises and a budgerigar; they all had names of a twee kind, such as Marmaduke, Lucretia, and so on but, since I had a golliwog called Ginsberg, I guess I was as kookie as she and it gave us something to kick around whilst I sipped the very tolerable Australian sherry she pretended was from Jerez.

When I had seen her around the West End she mostly wore ex-naval bell bottoms (maybe they were ex-Wrens boat crew issue), and a polo-necked white sweater. This outfit was not for the houseboat but, bizarrely, for London interviews; it seemed to get her no end of work in Fleet Street and its environs.

For the houseboat, Sharon sported a cheongsam — brightly coloured and highly impractical I suspected. Maybe it was put on for my visit. I had always visualized dark, alluring brunettes in cheongsams but with her hyacinth-blue eyes and flaxen hair, she looked doll-like, entrancing. She kept picking up the Siamese cat whose eyes seemed to be the same colour as hers and I suggested that in a previous incarnation perhaps she had been a Siamese. This—on the third glass of sherry—took us to J. W. Dunne on Time, Buddhism and Freud.

I said I was a little worried for the Siamese cat who clearly had to make shore trips for his comfort, but Sharon assured me all Siamese cats were intelligent, and none more than Alberto. As for the two tortoises, they knew the limits of the barge exactly and they used a small garden patch on the quarter-deck, disdained by the cat, who required privacy, even if it was a shore trip.

The barge which was large but filled with arty bric-à-brac and far too many *objets d'art* and otherwise, was extremely warm in winter and suicidally hot in summer—in fact, Sharon slept in a hammock on deck, seemingly resisting trips into the interior as often as she could.

She told me she wrote her prose with a quill pen, liked lots of chunky jewellery (effective with the cheongsam), and, just to complete the extrovert picture, she sometimes smoked a clay pipe.

It was all too good to be true and after another sherry, I could not help challenging her with it. To my horror I found that I had instantly made her cry. I felt a right Charlie. I had been nonplussed by her ordinary façade. No one, surely, could be *that* fey, that twee? Yet her work was sincere, warm, very observant, and most significant of all, it was utterly believable.

And the more I became acquainted with Sharon Saxbee, the surer I was that she, too, was sincere, wasn't putting on an act. She believed and did all the twee, all the odd, all the 'front page' stuff because this was Sharon. Just how she had arrived at all this intrigue had puzzled me—was she lonely? Had she no friends? She certainly attended—or claimed to—for I didn't—certain literary parties, booksy folks get-togethers and she had been a guest of honour at one of the Christina Foyle's book luncheons (which was more than I had).

And so I suspected that somewhere in her not-so-distant past Sharon had had some sort of strange experience that had produced this gawpish, garish, this presenting in the most humility-making way Sharon Saxbee, novelist and poetess. It was as if on the one hand she cultivated all the most self-effacingness she could whilst, at the same time she metaphorically rode that bicycle nude all the way to her publishers.

Suddenly, and my arms were still around her, she looked up, her tear-filled eyes made me feel like a Walls ice-cream in a hot sun. She asked:

'Why the hell did they choose you to write the script of my book?'

'I've had this conversation with Chris Lane, the director. It's very simple, the film moguls don't ever read books, just the titles —our novels sounded similar.'

'O.K., then why did you decide to do the script?'

'I answer you in the immortal words of Marcel Achard: "The career of a writer is comparable to that of a woman of easy virtue. You write the first for pleasure, later for the pleasure of others and finally for money".'

'Let's make love,' Sharon said suddenly. I was always to be surprised at Sharon Saxbee.

CHAPTER THREE

SHARON certainly knew how to make love. After, I remember, I tried desperately to keep awake, women get so angry with men if they turn over and go to sleep—their natural inclination *is* to turn over and go to sleep—but an indignant tug's hooter screeched vociferously on the river which awakened me.

'A penny for your thoughts,' Sharon had offered me. If I had collected the pennies women had offered me for my thoughts since I had been a member of Pop, I'd have been a penny millionaire—or do I exaggerate a little? I didn't have to exert myself to think about this one.

'I was thinking about you!' (Same old routine, you horrible old *roué*, you!)

'And?'

'And I came to the conclusion that you are a remarkable woman.'

'Yes?'

'Yes.'

'Like, f'rinstance?'

'Well you are a mass of enigmatic contradictions.'

'Aren't we all?'

'Yes, but not *quite* like you, dear Sharon, you out Mona the Lisa, if you understand me.'

'That's part of my fascination.'

'I'm the one who is supposed to say that,' I said. 'Take your name, for instance, you were obviously born Bessie Beet: no one could possibly have been christened Sharon Saxbee—and what the hell were you doing in Mandura?'

'That's simple—my father——'

'—Major Basil Beet?'

'Lieutenant-Colonel Alfred Crane-Saxbee was Governor-General there for five years.'

'Well, I'm damned!' I exclaimed.

'How else do you think I wrote my book?'

'Well, it certainly read as if you had been there, I do agree.'

'Thanks. And I hope you do it justice.'

'I can't be expected to. I'm the wrong writer for the adaptation.'

Sharon sat up in bed. Her breasts were taut, provocative even after the event.

'Isn't there something about you in the Song of Solomon?' I asked.

'Chapter Two: "I am the rose of Sharon, and the lily of the valleys",' Sharon quoted.

'Clever old you.'

'No, no,' she mimicked a TV ad, ' "clever Vaseline shampoo".'

'Know any more?'

'Song of Solomon?'

'Yes.'

'H'm. "My beloved is unto me as a cluster of henna-flowers in the vineyards of En-Gedi".'

'Nice work.'

'Now you.'

'Think I can't?'

'Think you can't!'

'We are talking about quoting Solomon.'

'If you insist.'

'O.K. "Awake O North wind, and come Thou South". In other words, I gotta go now, lover.' I started to get up.

'Let's make love again!' Sharon suggested.

'Now, Sharon!" I cautioned. 'I've got to get me—to write your lousy screen play—remember?'

'Well, you don't have to go now, do you? The planes only run three times a week!'

'Nevertheless,' I said, quickly getting out of bed and, as always, feeling foolish as I entangled my head in my shirt. I could feel Sharon's eyes examining my torso.

'Did you box or row?' she suddenly asked.

'Both,' I replied.

'Nice,' she commented, adding, 'I sometimes wish I were a man.'

'We've no time for that sort of statement, now, honey-bee,' I said quickly putting on my trousers. 'Tell me about Mandura. Where do I stay? What do I take?'

'I'll fill you in on the details over dinner.'

'Now, Sharon!'

'We'll go to the Hilton—downstairs in their atmosphery Trader Vic's—it'll get you in the mood for Mandura.'

It was at that moment I noticed the cutting from the morning paper. It was of Roddy Vandaleur.

'That's odd!' I said. 'Why did you cut out the photo of Roddy Vandaleur?'

Sharon may not have thought I had noticed the tiny pause before she answered, but I had.

'Do you know him?' she asked.

'Oddly enough, I do. We were at school together.'

'Were you? Was he—interesting?'

'Is any boy interesting?'

'No, I suppose not. Had he embryonic anything?'

'Yes. I suspect so. But you didn't tell me why you cut out his photo.'

'Didn't you know, I'm nympho,' she said, dead-pan.

The trouble with Sharon was one could never be sure when she was kidding.

I decided not to do the flight to Mandura in one long hop, instead I took on B.E.A. to Rome. It had long been a policy of mine to stop off in Rome whenever it were possible. There is something civilized about Rome except, of course, the noise.

B.E.A.'s Harry Berry and Irish Molly of his P.R.O. staff gave me champagne at L.A.P. (and so he should, from my trips to Nice I'd practically paid for the Trident) and B.E.A. turned on the V.I.P. treatment. I liked being a successful novelist going First Class. It avoided the inevitable and idiotic Gadarene rush for aircraft seats.

Being a writer makes one observant I suppose, or was it that I recognized the little man who was reading a newspaper, so obviously watching me at the B.E.A. Regent Street offices? Or should I be honest and say it may have been because he held the newspaper he was studying so intently upside down. At any rate, he certainly was at the departure spot when our flight was called. I didn't think about it till a day or two later.

The trip was pow, pow, pow, and the sun was shining in *Roma*.

I stayed at the *Eden* which was close to the Via Veneto, but quieter than the *Excelsior,* and there was less chance of bumping into film stars. I have never been gregarious and it puzzled me the way film people go off on their holidays exactly to the spot they know they will meet the people to whom they have just said good-bye. When I checked in at the *Eden* the courteous receptionist with the excellent English and the perfect manners, handed me four letters and a cable.

One letter was from Amigo Productions, who had another assignment for me, another was from Tee who always fazed me when I got entangled with her. She had a studio in Rome and painted divinely. There was an air letter from Sharon who said simply: 'It was nice. I miss you.' And one from Penny, which said: 'I miss you like hell. It was wonderful.'

The cable was from Roddy Vandaleur.

I uttered a sharp exclamation.

It caused the receptionist a solicitous 'Anything wrong, sir?'

'No.'

It was the sheer coincidence of it that puzzled me. I hadn't heard from Roddy in years.

'When you get there Steve will contact you. Roderick Vandaleur.'

'When I get there.' How in hell did he know where I was going? 'Steve will contact you.' Why should he? And who the hell was Steve, anyway?

When I arrived at *Mario's* on the Via Veneto a couple at the outside restaurant were just leaving their table and I made a dive for it, causing a young lady with a slightly North Country accent whom I'd jockeyed out of position to squelch me with a 'Don't mind me, I'm sure.'

Since she was alone, I could do no less than ask her to join me, though I suspected, from the waiter's dirty glances at her, she was always hanging around all day for free meals and hoping to be discovered by a famous film producer. Her face was piquant if pinched, and her cough was more T.B. than nicotine. Her outrageously low-cut blouse was dark blue, pretty tatty, but her bosom, pushed up to nigh on impossible heights, was set out for display like two avocado pears. Her bottom, taut as a drum, almost split the seams of her light blue zipper-style man's jeans.

I suppose there are always a few of them, living on in Rome, on the borrowed *lire*, scrounging, praying, living on tick and laid by the minor Italian movie trade who promised an introduction to Ponti, or could fix her a meeting with someone who knew a cousin of Visconti. As we kicked the light *conversazione* around, about the wonder of living in Rome, I heard myself prattling on. . . . 'What was it Oscar Wilde said about London? "London is very dangerous: writers come out at night to writ one, the roaring of creditors towards dawn is frightful, and solicitors are getting rabies biting people".' I waited for her laughter and since it was polite and about as warm as a witch's teat, I realized that she was wondering whether Oscar Wilde was a film name to watch.

All the time I was thinking I'd like to do something for her. She'd probably be holed-up in this lovely city, trapped, unable to get back to Batley or Ashby-de-la-Zouche. It's all right being in love with a city and starving, but to be in love with ambition because of its location, that was—but nothing.

I hoped Tee would be late. Tee was sufficiently unfemale to understand my scribe's interest in the girl. Hell! Had I been Scott Fitzgerald I'd have written a piece about her with her appealing little northern face, her too-anxious-to-please conversation (the periodic darting away of the eyes, eyes surrounded by gigantic false lashes, in case she missed the appearance of a film producer over one's shoulder). She and the others were still living on *Cleopatra*. What would happen when there was no epic turning at Cine Citta?

I was still talking as I mulled over in my mind how I could discreetly offer her her fare back to London, when a big-set oaf in an American type straw hat with a Sinatra hat band, lurched for a table, knocking the contents of a waiter's tray—two very nasty little espresso coffees—over my cream-coloured suit.

'Now you're truly launched!' said Miss Bolton, laughing stridently.

I accepted the joke. Amid the profuse apologies I made for the cloakroom. The obese gook followed me. As I strode to the gents, my trousers sticking unromantically to my hams, I suddenly thought, Methinks he does protest too much. Then, when I went inside the loo his mate was waiting. I quickly side-stepped his blow with a small black-jack which hit his pal straight across the forehead. He slumped without so much as an 'Oops, pardon!' and as his chum, now off-balance, swung in an attempt to catch me on the return swing, I ducked and sunk a very quick left hook into his large guts. He grunted and slipped into the classical position for me to give him the traditional upper cut, the knock out, the *coup de grâce,* the matador's despatch. I took it too quickly and missed the point of the jaw, instead I clipped his nose so that an almighty flush of blood, like a loo flush, exuded from his nose. He yelled like a stuck pig. The combination of blood and sound frightened the life out of me. I fled.

Regaining the outside my Lancashire companion had departed

and, instead, Tee was sitting in icy composure, where the local slut had been. I slapped enough money on the table and grabbed her arm, forcing her to her feet.

'If there is one place in the world a lady does not like to sit alone it's——' Tee began.

'It's Sevilla!' I said, grabbing her arm.

'Look at your trousers!' she said.

'No time to look now. We are off.'

'Where are we going?'

'To my hotel.'

'Same old Gar'.'

'To change my trousers.'

'Same old Gar'.'

'Oh shut up, Tee! Villains are pursuing me,' I explained as I moved her across the street, despite the protests of cars and the whistles of the police, and the wolf-whistles of the Italian males.

'Why do you have to do everything so *loudly*?' Tee inquired angrily. 'And why in hell must you get involved with Mods and Rockers when I am wearing my latest Nina Ricci?'

'Tee, forget the past. I am a reformed character. I am minding my own business——'

'Picking up some local tart——'

'Oh! Did you meet her?'

'I did.'

'Where's she gone? I wanted to give her some money.'

'No doubt.'

'I mean, if I were Scott Fitzgerald, I'd—what I mean is—did she leave a message?'

'She'll call you,' Tee imparted icily.

'Oh, good. I mean, that's fine.' We were almost at my hotel. 'I wonder how I missed that upper cut? I must be getting old.'

'Now Gar',' Tee retorted in her most cutting tone, 'don't let's say that. Let's just say second childhood, shall we?'

I ignored this.

I bought her a copy of *Playboy* from the messenger's stand in the lobby and I crossed to Reception. The young man who was on duty earlier looked solicitously anxious as he handed me my key.

I returned to Tee, saying:

'Wait here a second, while I go up and change.'

Tee looked surprised, or pretended to.

'Aren't you going to ask me up to see your etchings?'

'You,' I reminded her, 'are the artist. I plan to see yours, after dinner.'

In the ride up in the elevator I was still wondering why I had been jumped and was in a suspicious frame of mind therefore when I reached my room door.

In my time and mostly, let me add, minding my own business, I had been jumped in my hotel bedroom before. I approached the door with extreme caution. Not to my surprise there was a pass key in the lock. I grinned smugly. O.K. I'd goofed (for by U.S. readers) or cocked-up (for the British) my last attempt at the Saint stuff; this time I'd show just how I'd gained my College Boxing Colours.

With surprising speed (and I write this modestly, for I am a big fellow, and *en-passant,* handsome in an obvious sort of way, I suppose), I flung open the door and came face to face with a figure coming towards me. I had no room to use a jab or upper cut and so I did the next thing possible, I grabbed quickly catching two arms and in a quick twist I had the miscreant in a Boston Crab. Help was at the door.

'Ring for the cops!' I commanded, wondering about the interloper's perfume.

'Do you think that's a good idea?' Tee inquired.

'Get help!' I yelled. 'I thought I told you to stay below!'

'I'm not surprised,' Tee retorted, making no effort to telephone. By now my enslaved thug began to emit distressed signals—in a shrill, female voice. I began to get the message. I looked up at Tee who sat on the bed, grinning cheerfully. I must have looked a right clot. I had grabbed the night staff chambermaid. It appeared that she had just turned down the sheet—in the course of her duties if you understand me—and was admiring my golliwog, Ginsberg (who had the honour to wear my R.N. ribbons) when I made my stealthy pounce. Apologies, plus a large tip to be used for medicinal purposes, appeared to pacify her—indeed, when I was able to detach myself, I had certain regrets that Tee had appeared.

'What the hell did you come up for?' I repeated this time irritatedly.

'Reception forgot to give you this note,' Tee said.

I glared at her and grabbed it. Maria bobbed an old-fashioned curtsy and with disarranged hair made her departure.

I grunted, took a pair of trousers from the closet, and crossed to the bathroom, leaving the note.

'What did your note say?' Tee shouted after me.

'You didn't give me time to read it,' I called back. 'It's on the bed. Open it and read it.'

I thought it can do no harm, if it's from the studios, Tee will be impressed, if it's from another woman, ditto.

I heard Tee whistle incredulously.

'So?' I shouted questioningly.

'I think it's a gag.'

'If it's from Mastroniani it's no gag. It's about a film.'

'No such luck. Well! Well!'

I was intrigued by Tee's tone of voice and the exclamation. I wandered out, trousers in hand, and took the note. The paper it was written on was cheap and the message to avoid detection was made up from words cut from newspapers or magazines. I was rather pleased about this. I'd never had one of these before although, in the past, Ginsberg had been stabbed as a warning and, once, some gang of non-cultured types had even had a little coffin made for him.*

The note read:

> ALTER YOUR PLANS. DO NOT GO TO MANDURA.
> YOU HAVE BEEN WARNED.

'I say, is it a joke?' Tee inquired.

'Well, if you think two chaps setting on you in the loo's a joke,' I replied.

I could see her considering a reply but I beat her to it.

'—and never mind the funny cracks!' I snapped.

'You mean you think those men at *Mario's* had something to do with this?'

'Indeed I do, Tee,' I replied. 'They weren't just ordinary thugs after my wallet.' I stood, trousers in hand, also reflecting about the note from Roderick Vandaleur. 'And that's not all. . . ."

I got no further, my voice was drowned by a vociferous banging on the door.

'Come in!' I yelled.

A man burst in, surprised I think at the invitation, but pleased when he saw the trousers in my hand. He looked positively gleeful.

* *No Wooden Overcoat*

'Aha!' he said and burbled something in Italian. Tee rocked with laughter.

'What's *his* particular beef?' I asked her.

In between ripples of mirth she replied: 'He is the hotel detective.'

CHAPTER FOUR

WE managed to placate the hotel detective and I asked Tee what our plans should be for the evening.

'You're the guest,' she said.

'When in Rome, we do as the tourists,' I paraphrased.

'Like what?' Tee asked.

'Like—er—dining at Fontonello's for the spaghetti, and taking one of those horse carriages round the city.'

'Garway Trenton, there are times when I think you are——'

'Bonkers?'

'No—perfect!'

'Really. What did I do?'

'When anyone takes me out it's always to the *Excelsior*, they *must* visit Oddy's, and they never, ever want to eat spaghetti or drive in a horse drawn carriage.'

'It's nice to be popular. Nevertheless, as a precaution, I'll use the toilet here and *not* at the restaurant—I like a lot of room when I'm swinging lefts.'

'I thought you were a Judo black belt?'

'Red, but this wasn't Judo or boxing, just a crude punch-up.'

Tee was silent for a moment, then inquired:

'Do you think Rock Hudson does all his own fights in movies?'

'Shut up!' I snapped succinctly. Tee sighed.

'Go to the toilet while I powder my nose.'

'That's a whatever the opposite to a *non sequitur* is,' I replied.

Rather to my surprise it all worked according to plan. Nothing went amiss, possibly because I had taken Horace along with me. Readers of my thriller fiction will have met Horace, my trusted Betsy, my equalizer, my gat. I don't think I was entitled to have it—I mean I don't think my driving licence exactly covered it—and yet there had been occasions when I was jolly glad I had it, and so was the Law. I suspect the Law (Interpol and M.I.6) knew I still had it, certainly after the affair of *Gardenias Bruise Easily* they didn't request I hand Horace over. Today, though I knew they weren't really as effective as other places, I was wearing Horace in a shoulder holster, under my *right* armpit for two reasons. The first: wise guys looked to the *left* of you to note any significant bumps, and this fixed them. And two: I was ambidextrous.

We ate our Spaghetti Bolognese at Fontonello's (Tee had to take out a portion of the Bolognese for the inevitable hungry Roman cats by the door), and we took our espressos at Doney's —*de rigueur*. Though I wanted the cloakroom (isn't it always the way?) I was determined not to use it. When we hailed our carriage I gave the ancient Jehu who was driving a very critical look. *Were* those whiskers phoney? He misunderstood my penetrating stare and cut the price of the Grand Tour!

The night was crow-black with a peppering of stars, silver-sweet, and the melodious clip-clop of the horse and the beauty of the Borghese Gardens, the warmth of Tee and the perfume from her hair made it very exciting. I hope I remembered correctly but it used to be Sciaparelli's *Shocking* on the body and Lanuin's *Arpège* behind the ears and around the bosom.

'Can't we stop for a moment?' Tee suggested.

'Why do you always read my thoughts?'

'But can't we get rid of Speedy Gonzales?' With a flick of her lashes, she indicated our driver.

'I'll try,' I murmured. 'We'd like to stop,' I called out to the driver.

'*Si, si, bellissima!*' he agreed, indicating the gardens with his whip, and paying no regard.

Tee chuckled and translated my request. He replied and Tee nodded.

'What's he say?'

'It seems it's a good idea. There's a restaurant in the neighbourhood and he wants to spend a penny.'

'Well I hope he doesn't bring out a couple of pals, that's all,' I said, my dander up.

'Oh, Gar'—time was when you believed your own publicity, now you've got worse, you are believing your own stories.'

'Very funny,' I retorted tartly, slightly toffee-nosed.

'Kiss me!' Tee ordered.

'Let's wait till Ben Hur's got into the convenience,' I replied. 'Women!'

We clinched and it would have been divine except I couldn't help keeping one eye open on the Men's—I didn't want to be jumped with Tee's arms round me. Tee got quite narked.

'Gar'—your eyes are open?' she said accusingly.

'Well, who cares?' I replied.

'I do. You know I do. I don't think it's quite the same if your eyes are open.'

This made it very difficult, you understand, but we embraced, and she undid my shirt buttons to fumble with the hair on my chest. It was one of the things she like to do when she necked with me. Suddenly her closed eyes opened wide. Her hand had come across and closed with Horace. I was still a little apprehensive, the shadows in the park were enormous.

'Christmas, Gar'!' she suddenly exclaimed. 'What the hell's that?'

'Well, we know what it's not!' I interjected.

'What are you toting a revolver round for?' Tee asked part-aghast, part-exhilarated.

'Tee, you don't seem to have taken in what happened today at all.'

'You're not still on about the pick-pockets?'

'They weren't pick-pockets!' I shouted in contradiction.

'There's no need to shout!'

'Oh, yes there is when my life's at stake.'

'You don't have to be so melodramatic.'

The cabby came running out with his whip at the ready. I dam' nearly raised my hand for Horace but stopped myself in time. He was still alone.

Tee said something to him in Italian and he gave me what I took to be a contemptuous look. He shrugged his shoulders and climbed back in front. Tee gave him her address. We clipperty-clopped to her studio in silence. Suddenly I loathed Rome.

'Why do we always quarrel?' Tee asked me, softening a little.

'I dunno. Perhaps if we got married we'd stop,' I replied.

'You've proposed five times to me but you never do it in a way I'd say yes to.'

'Six times lucky, I'll try on the way back from Mandura,' I said sadly.

I kissed her on the top of her nose and watched her go into her studio.

'Good scripting!' she wished.

'Happy painting!' I replied.

I felt like hell.

'I'd like a drink.'

The cabby seemed to understand. He must have been a very patient fellow. Waiting, shadowing in the hope I'd want a cab. Then there was that taxi which kept cruising past Doney's refusing other fares. I know I looked a right Nana in the typical British way, but that was *some* of the time surely not *all* of the time?

They jumped me as he slowed down at some small bar. It was an excellent place for a beat-up. I kicked the first one right where it hurt most as he clambered up to pull me down, and the second I caught with my left hand as I whipped back an old throat trick. Number Three had a knife and he appeared alongside the comatose cabby who was pretending the whole thing wasn't happening. I wasn't sure if Number Three planned to throw the knife or plunge it, but I didn't wait to find out. I reached for Horace, fumbled and cursed all shoulder holsters but whipped him out just in time.

Horace acted as a splendid deterrent. Number Three yelled a warning and scarpered. He was followed at a less rapid rate by the cabby. Number Two was gasping for breath and Number One lay screaming on the pavement. I was about to find out more about the attack when a cop hove into view. The best thing to do was drive off. I did so, erratically and, as I found out after avoiding a Ferrari, two Alfas and another horse-drawn cab, on the wrong side of the road.

Pulling the nag to a halt, I tethered it to a tree, patted it and apologized for startling it and stayed not upon my stooging but shot off very smartly. I was sorry Tee hadn't seen me in action, I reflected as I dropped to a walk. I lit a Blue Gauloise and made for the Via Veneto. I was feeling ten foot tall. I was great. I began to recite Kipling's *If*—corn my mother taught me—hell! I liked corn. . . .

I saw two lovers in the shadows and I stopped abruptly but they had heard and decided I was bonkers.

I approached another cop, and I passed him whistling, 'I'm Not Afraid' from *The King and I*.

Yes, I thought. I know the feeling. I glared all the way to *Mario's,* frightened a man out of my table, sat heavily and ordered a double-scotch on the rocks in an emotional voice.

''Ullo, luv!' said a voice.

It wasn't how I'd played it. I had expected Tee or Penny or Sharon, certainly not the bright but grubby presence of Miss Bolton.

It was a tremendous temptation not to gallery-play to the lassie from Lancashire but I managed to control myself and not tell her of my strange ordeal. Instead, I said to her, I hoped not too sternly:

'Miss Bolton, I'd be very obliged if you'd keep very quiet while I think, I——'

'My name's Entwhistle,' she interrupted.

'Yes, it would be, of course.'

'You what?'

'Look, Miss Entwhistle——'

'Martha Entwhistle.'

'Is it? Well——'

'But for films I thought I'd call myself April Shower.'

'Good idea. Miss Shower, look——'

'I'd recognized you, of course.'

'Yes, well—er—I don't think that's possible. Apart from an occasional photo in the *Queen* or the *Tatler*——'

'Oh, yes. But I asked just to be sure. I'm very glad to make your acquaintance, Mr. Brassano.'

'Eh?'

'I hoped you would help me with my career. Give me some advice, I mean.'

'Look Miss Bolton——'

'Entwhistle.'

'Entwhistle—I am not Brassano. I am only vaguely connected with the film industry—in fact, my connection is infinitesimal, but I feel very sorry for you—stranded all this way from home. Now be a good girl. I want to sit here and think, so I'd be very obliged if you'd let me pay your fare home. Look, don't thank me, thank Scott Fitzgerald. In any case I'll probably use the idea for a short story. I don't know what it is one-way tourist to London, or would you rather go direct to Manchester?' Whilst I was trying to work out the amount of lire to a pound (I reckoned about 1,000 was equal to a ten bob note) a policeman appeared, he seized my wrists triumphantly shouting:

'Ecco!'

Rome seemed to be lousy with cops.

'Look, Mr. Sir Echo, if it's about a horse and carriage,' I began but he shouted me down.

'Madame,' he said with little accent, 'is this man importuning you?'

'You what?' Miss Entwhistle repeated again. I got the impression that she was finding the whole thing too much.

By now one of the waiters, who had earlier on glared at Miss Bolton, stepped forward to add his few centimos worth.

'No, no, no!' he exclaimed. 'This-a young-a girl soliciting this man.'

Another waiter stepped forward to add his *Si* to the first, and a few people from nearby tables decided to record their impressions of the scene. This caused Miss Bolton to deny the implications in no shy manner. That I had a bundle of lire in my hand was unfortunate, but matters were brought to a head by the appearance of a large woman of about forty, over-dressed, domineering and determined.

'What's this then?' Her bassa profunda, plus her impressive appearance, soon brought order to the brawl.

'Madame, would you kindly mind your own business,' I requested with some bravado, seeing that she had an unopened parasol which she seemed to be waving somewhat belligerently.

'Eh?' At least I had taken the wind out of her voluminous sails.

'That's my mum,' Miss Bolton introduced her in the subsequent silence.

'What?' I gasped more stunned than I had been by any gangsters.

'Yes. I wanted you to meet her, you being so nice to me when I was waiting for her earlier.'

'What—what's your mum doing here?' I spluttered.

'That's a pretty daft question, isn't it?' Mum retorted. 'We're on holiday, of course, *And* her da' *and* her Uncle Fred and our Walter, 'er brother.'

I quickly turned to the policeman.

'I think there has been some mistake.'

By now he was looking pretty mystified himself. Mum panzered on.

'Martha told me about you. Says you are going to get her into films.' She looked pointedly at the bank notes in my hand. 'What's the idea, then?'

'Look Mrs. Entwhistle,' I replied. 'Tomorrow, tomorrow, come round to my hotel at lunch time.'

'Well, that's very nice of you. Where are you stopping?'

'The *Excelsior,*' I replied quickly. ''Bye, 'bye, *A rivederci* et cetera! Cheers!' I made a very rapid exit. The copper did not stop me.

I was very glad Tee hadn't been a party to the scene. My trouble was of couse that I was too romantic.

I hurried back to my hotel. The receptionist I knew was not on duty. I was not sure about that receptionist. Maybe he had wised-up the boyos who had tried to sort me out. I don't know. There was no more mail, no more threats and there was no maid to grapple with in my bedroom. Ginsberg, my golliwog, had not been disembowelled and no one tapped on my window during the night.

Yet, there was still the note, the slightly sinister note, telling me to lay off. And I had been attacked in the cloakroom and I had been 'jumped' after I left Tee. Two lots of robbers, two lots of simple footpads? Could be. But the note. . . . Yes it was funny about the note. I locked my door, placed Horace under my pillow and dreamt I was pulling the carriage; the horse *and* Mrs. Bolton were sitting in the carriage. Tee and Miss Bolton were on a bicycle built for two, shouting encouragement, and chasing us and catching up fast were bandits and bandits. Freud might have been able to explain it.

Next morning I sent Sharon a cable saying, 'Wish I'd never agreed to write your lousy script. Garway.'

I caught the early plane to Madagascar. The one that leaves well before lunch time.

CHAPTER FIVE

THE flight was uneventful: there was a charming mother of four, wife of a British chap named Butterworth-Urn in the Colonial Service, who breast-fed her youngest. Davina, her five-year-old, imitating Mummy pretended to breast-feed her teddy. The other two, about nine and thirteen, decided to tell me about life in Uganda, that is when they were not singing off key. These antics were interspersed with attempted cartwheels down the aircraft aisle to the fury of a silent, saturnine sharp-faced gent whom I had eyed with grave suspicion, but who turned out to be an innocuous air line ground official in civvies *en route* to Mauritius where he was based.

Two African chieftains, urbane, sophisticated in their English-type lounge suits and London University ties, retired to the lavatories just before we arrived at Nairobi, then emerged dressed in African finery, including lion skins, to the starry-eyed enjoyment of the enchanted children. The Africans had two groups of loyal, vociferously cheering supporters awaiting them at Nairobi. They made their Press statements in the airport lounge and departed, one by car and one by helicopter, to their local destinations.

I was sorry to see the delightful British depart here. On the flip to Madagascar we were joined by two saffron-robed Buddhist priests—even these worthies I watched suspiciously for the first hour or two, then decided I ought to re-read Sharon's novel.

Once more I was puzzled that she had especially requested I do the screen adaptation, the novel wasn't my cup of tea at all. The story bore no relationship to the kind of thing I wrote: and it wasn't that Sharon was being kind in getting me the screen play. I wasn't at all in need of the job; in fact I had refused the assignment twice. But, I mused, I certainly wasn't the right scenarist for Sharon Saxbee's twee, fey, sensitive novel.

The journey was now tedious but uneventful. The airline official who had been told by the aircraft crew I was a minor celeb, chatted me up about a story he wanted to get made into a film or onto TV but he departed at Madagascar where my next contact with my strange adversaries took place, this time a contact less violent but, nevertheless, intriguing.

We had put down for an hour's refuelling at Tennairive Airport Madagascar, green, lush enchanting island to which I planned to return. The female air staff of Lufthansa and Air France take some beating, but the delightful, bijou, small size, beautifully proportioned, slant-eyed Madagascar girls chosen to represent airlines were the *crême de la crême*. It was while I talked to one of these delectable creatures over Instant coffee in the small airport lounge, that a courteous young man approached. He was a local or appeared to be, in a westernized suit with a panama hat which he doffed with a super courteous flourish.

'Mr. Trenton? Mr. Garway Trenton? I represent the *Courrier de Madagascar,* I wonder if I might have a few words with you, for my paper? My name is Hico Sen.'

'It's very kind of you but I have nothing to say to the Madagascan *Courrier* except that I think your airline hostesses are wonderful,' I replied.

He flashed two rows of perfect teeth at this, as did the lovely stewardess who, taking his unsaid hint, departed leaving me with the young man.

'May I join you?' he inquired not waiting for my reply but sitting himself at the table. We were alone and the other passengers were drinking at the bar.

'Help yourself—have some coffee and tell me why it's Instant, I thought this was the home of the coffee bean."

The journalist shrugged his shoulders.

'Perhaps it has gone for export—everybody in West drinking coffee, everybody in East on the Instant kick.'

I looked at him with new interest.

'Kick? That's a hep word for this part of the world,' I replied with a grin.

'Everybody hep all over the world now, thanks to jet aircraft, Tel-Star and H-Bombs,' the young man stated with simplicity. 'Everywhere everything Instant—Instant everything.'

'Nearly everything.'

'Mr. Trenton I am told you rich man,' he said soberly, having the usual Asiatic trouble with our Rs. The word came out 'lich' no matter how much trouble he took with its pronunciation but I wasn't smiling, not even inwardly. I couldn't speak my own language well, let alone several others.

'Well, I'm no Paul Getty but I get the odd crust,' I replied.

He smiled politely.

'But everyone has his price,' he continued.

I suddenly realized that this nice coffee-skinned young man was the Opposition. I mentally tautened.

'H'm,' I grunted, offering him a Gauloise. 'I'm not so sure about that oldie.'

If he was disappointed he didn't show it.

'Excuse me, Mr. Trenton, I couldn't help overhearing——'

My grin stopped him but he went on urbanely, 'I couldn't help hearing you talking to the stewardess, you said you would like to come back to Madagascar.'

'That's right. I have only seen the airfield but already I like the place. On my return from Mandura.'

'Why go to Mandura, why not stay here now?' he said, suddenly becoming more matter-of-fact.

'Because as you are perfectly aware, I have to *recce* for a film script I am to write.'

'But you know Mandura very well already, Mr. Trenton.' He was looking at me challengingly.

'Yes?'

'But of course. At the age of nineteen you were a torpedo-bomber pilot on the aircraft carrier *Revenge*.'

I looked at him in utter astonishment.

'Well, I'll be damned! The Madagascan *Courrier* certainly knows its facts!' I gasped.

He pretended to smile then he said: 'Does one hundred thousand pounds interest you?'

My eyes must have boggled.

'Merry Christmas!' I replied facetiously after I had regained my composure.

'Unfortunately——' he began, but I cut in, 'I know, it just so happens you haven't got it on you at the moment.'

'That is true,' sighed the journalist. He had made for his inside wallet pocket. I was trigger-happy and in no time my hand had darted up towards the shoulder holster carrying Horace. The journalist's eyes reacted with a quick flicker. I changed direction and went for my breast pocket.

'Cigar?' I offered him.

Mr. Sen smiled properly again.

'You have just given me a Gauloise,' he reminded me. I felt a real oick.

'I see, too, that you are holding your own cigarette with the left hand,' Mr. Sen observed.

'In other words, you've noticed I'm toting a Betsy.'

'Betsy?'

'Equalizer, rod, gat, iron.'

'Oh, yes. Gun. Sorry I hadn't heard the word. Would you repeat it for me,' requested the inquiring Mr. Sen.

'You were about to say when I sort of flew off the handle?'

'I was about to say that, as a preliminary payment, would ten thousand pounds be all right?' Mr. Hico Sen proceeded to pull out a wallet which was stacked.

'Excuse my rudeness, but I can't help noticing all those lovely £1,000 notes—have they the correct metal strip running through them?'

'Oh, they are genuine enough, Mr. Trenton.'

'I think I'll have a drink,' I said, pushing the Instant coffee away from me.

'Good idea. May I recommend a Gin Sling?'

'By all means,' I murmured.

Mr. Hico Sen ordered the drinks.

There was a little but profound silence. Then—and I couldn't resist it—I questioned, 'You did say one hundred thousand pounds?' My voice seemed tiny, ridiculous.

Hico Sen nodded. 'You see, we want you to work for us.'

'You certainly must do,' I gagged. 'You don't represent M.G.M. who plan a Todd AO version of the Sharon Saxbee story?'

The little journalist was non-plussed. 'I am sorry I——'

'No. Silly of me. But when you say "us" who do you mean?'

'I mean "other interests".'

'Other than who, or is it whom?'

'Now you are joking with me, Mr. Trenton.'

'Indeed I am not.'

'We think the "cover" is excellent. We think your organization went to excellent, even admirable trouble to give the whole thing a good front, but we'd rather you didn't go.'

'It would appear not! Let me get this straight. For some reason you are prepared to pay me one hundred thousand pounds not to go to Mandura!'

'Yes. That's right. And we will pay it in any currency you like into any bank in the world—or you may have bank notes if you like. They tell me the Swiss banking security box arrangements are well liked in Europe.'

I laughed at his preposterous suggestion, but he continued placidly, 'Of course we can only give you the ten thousand now —in dollars American or Mexican. Yen, if you like.'

'I certainly have a yen for American dollars!' I quipped. Hico Sen looked non-plussed again.

'So sorry. Your Gin Sling or the idiotic offer has made me light-headed.'

For the first time Hico Sen looked cross. '"Idiotic"?' he snapped; almost viciously.

'Apologies, I didn't mean quite that. I meant fantastic.'

'You find it generous?'

'To the point of absurdity.'

Now the cordial Mr. Hico Sen turned quite angry and in anger he became quite ugly. 'You want more? I am not able to offer you more—obviously we can't offer you more until we have it.'

'It?'

'You know perfectly well what I mean,' he retorted icily.

At that moment my flight number was called. I finished my Gin Sling saying jokingly, 'I take it this is drugged?'

Mr. Hico Sen reacted as if to a deadly insult. 'You think you play funny games with me, Mr. Trenton.'

'No. I don't. I mean I like you, I like the place, the people, the customs.'

'I am not Madagascan, Mr. Trenton. As you well know, I am part-Japanese.'

' "As I well know"?' I repeated parrot-like. Out of the corner of my eye I could see the passengers giving up their transit cards and making for the aircraft.

'Why should I know you are part-Japanese?'

'My name isn't Madagascan and those ridiculous jokes about yen,' Mr. Sen hissed. 'So, one hundred thousand pounds isn't enough for you, eh?'

'Well, I'd like to know a little more about it,' I stalled. 'Look, when I've taken a wee gander at Mandura, I'll come back. I've a date with that enchanting airline hostess anyway, and——'

By now I was being tannoyed.

'Do excuse me—my flight.'

Hico Sen made one last attempt to tempt me. His mask of civility had dropped.

'Mr. Trenton you stay for twenty thousand pounds."

'Sorry, chum, it's very tempting but——' I picked up my transit card from the table. 'If you can't tell me a little more about the proposition, I'm afraid we'll have to leave it till I get back—say in a couple of weeks.'

'If you get back, Mr. Garway Trenton.'

'Eh?'

'If you get back.' The pseudo-journalist said; his oriental-shaped eyes narrowed. 'Maybe you want measuring when you get there.'

'Measuring?'

'Yes,' Hico Sen positively hissed. 'What you asking for—a concrete kimono?'

CHAPTER SIX

FIFTY minutes flying time and we sighted Mandura—'a rich jewel in an Ethiope's ear'. It lay lush, glistening with dense wet foliage smiling serenely in a silver sea. As in Hawaii, there were daily short quick rains which kept the vegetation almost as green as Ireland.

H'm! with Mr. Hico Sen's one hundred thousand pounds, I mused, I could probably buy the lot.

Idly, I speculated on what I could do with that amount, apart from buying islands in the Indian Ocean. A yacht or two, two more Maseratis, an E-type and a fast motor boat? The odd thing about money is that when you think about it in gargantuan terms you rarely know what to do with it. A more interesting consideration was why I should be offered so much money not to fly in. Well, only time now, would tell.

The pilot—D.S.O., D.F.C. and bar—tooled in to chat. He had noticed my tie earlier on the flight. He grinned at me, indicating my tie. 'You must have been even wetter than I was behind the ears!'

I smiled back. 'A tender lad of nineteen.'

He nodded. 'Fighters?'

'Yes, finally, but firstly on T.B.R.s—so slow Jerry couldn't ever believe it.'

We both laughed.

'Here to write a script, I'm told.'

'Good old B.O.A.C. publicity department!'

'Yes. You'll love it. Fabulous beaches, peace, tranquillity—and those Creole girls!' He winked at me, pretending to be madly 'with it'. Whereas I was sure he had a wife and three kids tucked safely away in Carshalton where he watered the roses on his weekends off, and his only vice was to study the still photos outside the Soho strip clubs on the few occasions he had to go up to Terminal House. A nice guy. Salt of the earth. And I bet he hadn't earned his D.F.C. biting his fingernails.

As I said, the air hop from Mauritius was a mere fifty minutes and we landed at a small but good modern airport. Like Mauritius, Mandura was getting on to the tourist bandwagon—it was very convenient for rich South Africans and, as I had read in

Sharon's novel and could verify as we circled the island to land, the beautiful beaches were abundant and beautiful.

The Customs formalities were informal. I was asked to open my one case. (I had travelled light, determined to shop locally if necessary.) On top of the case was Ginsberg, the golliwog. The Manduran Customs official froze for a moment as if Ginsberg's colouring was an affront to his own skin then he saw the war medals and grinned. He closed the case making the usual custom hieroglyphics in chalk. The French Passport Officer was white, less lax, but maybe he had been warned. I never really knew how much my help to M.I.6 had been, and whether they were tolerant of Horace because of services rendered, or services about to be rendered to Interpol. He merely indicated the bulge beneath my coat with a cryptic:

'Got a licence for that?'

It saved a lot of time to nod affirmatively. He nodded and stamped my passport—the usual farce. I wondered how many thousand times I had had my passport either stamped or not, depending on the state of the official's liver, how many custom forms I had deliberately gagged up, falsified: domicile, the Scrubbs. Reason for visit: I plan to blow up Government House, and so on. All religiously stacked with thousands of other pieces of bumpf in thousands of government storing houses all over the world!

But the business of Horace always perplexed and pleased me. It could have been tied up with that curt little message I had once received from D.D.N.I. asking me if I was willing at any time to help H.M. Government in matters of security. It was vague, innocuous but covered a multitude of emergencies. I was wondering if, indeed, this was one of them. What had started out as an innocuous trip to write a screen play was assuming astonishing suppositions.

My reverie was interrupted by the arrival of a short stubbly little man, perspiring in the rather wet heat of the day, in a crumpled white suit and carrying a panama.

'Trenton?'

I nodded.

'I'm Uncle Steve.' He introduced himself. This was a bit swift. I had expected Roderick Vandaleur's uncle to ring my hotel but not appear at once.

'Roddy sent me a cable,' he explained. His moustache needed a clip. He had protruding eye-balls that gave him a permanently surprised look, and wet lips. I wasn't mad about him.

'This way,' he said. He led me to an ancient Rolls Royce, first indicating to a young porter to pick up my grip. The first thing I saw outside the airport was a large Coca-Cola sign, fringed by palm trees, the next a Lux ad. The world was getting smaller every day. By way of conversation I mentioned this to Uncle Steve. He didn't 'get it', so I didn't press it.

'Good flight?'

'Yes, except from the Via Veneto onwards where people seemed very anxious I shouldn't get here.'

He looked at me with his soft-boiled eyes mildly surprised, '*Shouldn't* get here?' he reiterated, emphasizing the *shouldn't* questioningly.

'Yes. In fact I was sorely tempted in Madagascar not to turn up, but natural curiosity, you know. . . .' I left the sentence unfinished.

'Oh, you'll like it here,' he said, he winked one of his protruders. 'Wait till you meet a couple of the Creole women!' he added with a leer and much innuendo. He was the sort of chap who thought sitting drinking beer in some stygian night club with two girls was positively satanic.

The Rolls was driven by an Indian in a turban and Uncle Steve noticed my glance at the chauffeur.

'Polyglot population. French possession and French still the main language. Lots of French in administration, lots of Chinese in commerce. British shipping and beer interest. The Japs are trying to get in but this you know.' I didn't. He sniffed contemptuously and added, 'The local lads do f.a. Lazy lot of bastards! Indians are industrious, though. Then, as I said, there are Creoles—rich, too, and many mixed "jobs". Lazy, though.'

'But they are very friendly people I believe?' Uncle Steve shrugged his shoulders. 'What do you do here?'

'I have a tea plantation.'

'Oh, yes?'

'Come and look it over if you like. Put you off tea for a bit once you've seen it.'

'Really—why?'

'Dirty lot of buggers,' Uncle Steve said, 'pee on the tea bushes.'

I made a grimace and changed the conversation.

'What's the Royal like?' I asked of my hotel.

'Bloody horrible,' Uncle Steve replied succinctly. He wasn't exactly gay with enthusiasm. He uttered something harsh to the Indian, who promptly increased the speed.

'Patois,' Uncle Steve explained.

I nodded.

'I was puzzled how Roderick knew about my trip.'

'Roderick knows everything about everything,' Uncle Steve said platitudinously.

'It's very nice of him to have me met, I rather expected someone from the local legislative.'

'Oh, the P.R.O.? Englefred? Lazy bugger, he'll turn up at the airport this afternoon. Time means nothing to these people.' He cast his marble-shaped eyes gloomily around the maroon coloured earth.

'I thought this was a tropical paradise,' I said, by way of conversation; I didn't give a dam' whether Uncle Steve liked it or not.

Uncle Steve sighed tolerantly. 'That,' he said, 'depends on what you want in life.'

I nodded. 'True,' I said fatuously, 'very true. Anyway, the country's picturesque.'

We were approaching a group of basalt-like mountains, teeth-like in shape, sienna coloured, sharply etched against the almost cerulean sky. The rain clouds were fluffy, fleecy, gay as in a Dufy painting. Occasionally we passed through a small village, small huts with gaily coloured tin roofs. There was a profusion of palm trees, red and yellow iris-like flowers, plum-coloured leafy bushes, red ochre earth. Occasionally a palm or banyan tree uprooted. Noticing my interest, Uncle Steve volunteered the information cryptically: 'Clara!' he said.

'Clara?'

'Last cyclone.'

'Oh, that's the snag.'

'One of 'em. But it's typical of this part of the world, get 'em in Mauritius, too, of course. Effing awful. One bugger's tin roof blew off into my tea plantation.'

'Hardly his fault,' I ventured. Uncle Steve glared at me. His eyes reminded me of the old-style lemonade bottles that had glass balls for stoppers.

I said: 'I remember Roderick talking about you at Eton. He had a great admiration for you.' Come to think of it, Roderick's description of Uncle Steve hadn't been madly good.

'You were Navy, weren't you?' I said.

'Hell of a long time ago. Just a kid.'

I thought of my conversation with the B.O.A.C. pilot. Funny; two generations taking time out from the valuable, so short years to do what? What had been achieved?

'Yes, I made Commander,' Uncle Steve said, 'youngest they had.' It was an odd expression 'made Commander' and it puzzled.

'You were at Eton, too, weren't you?' I said.

'That's right. Same house as Roddy.'

'Oh, yes? Which was that?'

He hesitated for a fraction of a second. 'Rowlands,' he replied glibly. I let it pass.

'Roddy said you were on H.M.S. *Heron*.'

'That's right.'

'Torpedoed, wasn't it?'

'Yes—but I was O.K.'

I nodded.

'I suppose they mentioned it on your Flimsy.'

He was really stuck now. He paused, praying for the answer to that one. 'Oh, yes. Yes, they mentioned it on my Flimsy.'

'Do forgive me, Uncle Steve, but you are really talking the most arrant balls. Rowlands isn't a house at Eton, it's a café and if you'd been in the Navy you'd know what a Flimsy was. And *Heron* is a naval air station difficult to torpedo, a stone frigate or shore station!'

Uncle Steve wasted no more time. He stuck a revolver into my belly and said curtly, 'Shut your gob. We're here.'

CHAPTER SEVEN

'SILLY-BILLY me!' I exclaimed, 'I goofed, didn't I? You're not Uncle Steve at all!'

'That's right.'

'I suppose your name is Smith.'

'That's right.'

'How surprising.'

'If you don't shut up I'll get Umesh to take some action.'

'Umesh being the driver.'

'Exactly.'

The Indian, bearded, turbanned, turned and with one hand on the steering wheel produced a long sinister-looking knife with the other.

'Look sharp!' I gagged, feeling anything but pleased with myself. 'Fancy my not checking Uncle Steve's credentials. What's his speciality—disembowelling?'

'Umesh is very partial to ears.'

'He eats them?'

Smith ignored this. Great rivulets of sweat trickled down his face, down his neck to reach his damp khaki bush shirt.

'Possibly they are a great delicacy, like rattlesnake,' I suggested.

Smith turned his protruding eyes in my direction.

'Stop the car, Umesh!' he ordered. I realized I'd goaded him a bit too far, but I couldn't resist one last jibe.

'Be very careful, I'm ticklish,' I said.

The ancient Rolls stopped. Umesh got out of the front seat and came round to the near-side of the back seat where I was sitting, his gun in his hand.

'Get out!' Smith ordered, there was seemingly pleasure in his voice. I did so, thinking how I was going to escape, plotting speedily on the way I was going to seize the Rolls and make a bid for freedom. I took my time getting out and for it I got a sharp kick in the small of the back which sent me sprawling into the road. I gasped for breath, regained my feet before Smith had another kick. Umesh laughed softly, sadistically.

'Temper! Temper!'

'You're one of those funny lads, are you?' Smith said, reaching back into a side pocket of the Rolls.

'Fancy thinking the Jerries had torpedoed a shore station! I ask you, I blame myself for not checking on you. You could never be Uncle Steve. I mean, Uncle Steve was a gent, so I'm told.'

By now Smith had produced from the door pocket a machete, a short, powerful, broad knife.

'No, Trenton, I'm no gent, but in no time I'll have you—who I take to be a gent in view of your old school tie chat and your effing condescending manners—I'll have you, my fancy gent, not only screaming for mercy but also admitting you're no gent at all. In fact,' Smith said softly, with relish, 'I think you'll be grovelling!'

Umesh laughed delightedly. He held his knife in one hand and Smith now transferred the revolver. It was a Victory Model

Smith and Wesson which could do a nasty lot of damage provided it was aimed reasonably in the right direction.

Smith advanced with the machete raised slightly above his head. 'This is called a machete. It not only chops very nicely, it leaves a very nasty bruise round the cut.'

'Charming!'

'Run out of funny chat?' Smith inquired.

I edged away not really having to feign fear; I really was due for a nappy change.

'No more high class jokes?' Smith inquired. He spoke quietly but he was very excited, and I realized he had been hopped-up, probably on P.H.s, before we met.

'Aw, c'mon, Smith, gimme a fix!' I jibed, still easing away.

'Umesh!' Smith snapped and Umesh quickly approached me, the revolver in my back, the Indian's long knife just behind my ear. That was a pity. I was relying on a Judo throw that would take Umesh over my shoulder and hit the perspiring Smith just as he swung the machete.

'Don't cut him too much, Mr. Smith,' the beared Indian said. 'You know what Minoru Oko say! Just let me take an ear. I love taking ears.'

'Now Umesh, you heard what Minoru Oko say!' I taunted.

Angrily Smith swung and, since I couldn't go backwards, I made a swift dive forward grabbing his arm as it descended with the fearsome machete. I dived forward and with the full weight of his throw held the arm and the machete skywards for a second, then with a quick flip I had him screaming with pain and the machete out of his grasp lying on the road.

I swung Smith's body round as Umesh made his stab at me with the knife. It tore a clean flesh wound in Smith's dangling arm, and before Umesh could fire I kicked him where it hurt most. He doubled up like a jack knife too hurt or surprised to yell.

Since I had last been jumped (on the outskirts of Tetuan) I had learned a lot. I learned that the Marquis of Queensbury rules were jolly nice if both parties were observing them but if they weren't the quicker man to unobserve them was the better able to get out of a *fracas*.

Umesh lay writhing on the ground and Smith stood staring disbelievingly at his dangling arm, which I had broken, and which, for good measure, Umesh had practically severed. It was still too early for him to yell.

'What a caper!' I shouted exultantly, grabbing the machete.

'Don't!' Smith finally screamed, 'don't!'

I couldn't resist waving it above his head menacingly as if I were about to swing it down on his cranium. Smith yelled. I laughed and made for the Rolls. I had just stepped into it, and was about to flip on the engine, when an armoured car came at quite a rate round the bend in the road in the direction I was facing. The sight threw me for a moment. Furthermore, the tank was an old Jap model from the '39-'45 war. I stared at it in astonishment then, since it was bearing down on me fast, I turned the ignition key and slung the Rolls into reverse, but too late.

To my utter astonishment the tank did not pull up but rammed the bonnet of the Rolls good and hard. I landed up on the floor in the back. I rolled over quickly, having had the sense to keep a tight hold of the machete, and threw open the off-side door. The business-end of an old British Sten glared balefully in my direction. Behind it was an ugly looking geezer who certainly didn't use Palmolive for his complexion; his uncleaned teeth, too, could have done with some scaling. He had been chewing betel nut juice and a blood-like trickle flowed around his gums.

It was clear he didn't like me. Another colleague, whom I had no time to turn and see, jabbed a piece of cutlery in my back and before I could say N.A.T.O., I received one hell of a bash on the back of the head. I went out, not like the proverbial light, but slowly and before it really hurt. And I could still hear Smith screaming.

Mickey Spillane's little men with hammers were bashing around in my head when I came to.

I was in what appeared to be a nineteenth-century Colonial French-style building. I was seated on a chair and a native was gently slapping my face.

'He's coming round now, I fancy!' said a cultured voice with an Oriental accent.

'Aha! Honourable Mr. Minoru Oko!' I hazarded a guess.

'Correct, Mr. Trenton!' Oko had the usual Japanese difficulty with our r's. He was short, mean-looking, about fifty and he wore a silk shirt, pale blue, elegant, expensive and monogrammed. He wore darker blue trousers and sandals. I had the feeling of quiet strength and great evil. For a moment I thought he was wearing perfume then I realized there was someone else present. Seated on the edge of an ornately carved desk was a girl.

She had blue-black shoulder length hair, a sunburned complexion, she had what the pop novelists called a 'generous' mouth and what I call a highly kissable one. She was possibly part Spanish. She was tall, delectable and slightly cold. She wore a man's type white shirt with pockets she filled amply. She wore men's type riding breeches and short, soft leather boots. Around her waist was a belt and an elegant little 25 Beretta, a nicely-tooled leather holster. She held a jewelled-top horse whip in one hand, the other was stuck nonchalantly into the top of her riding breeches. She had one very, very brown eye—her right one. The left was covered by an eye patch.

'Take me to your leader,' I quipped. She smiled. 'I *am* the leader,' she said.

'What's your name, doll?' I inquired.

'Reba.'

'Just Reba?'

'Just Reba.'

She motioned to Minoru Oko, who offered me a cigarette. It couldn't have been more welcome. Reba came towards me and flicked on a lighter. It was in the top of the riding whip. 'Neat,' I observed, 'but slightly gaudy. *Coursi,* in fact!'

'So your curiosity tempted you more than the money?'

I inhaled then slowly blew out smoke, saying:

'Are you so efficient you knew I smoked Gauloises *bleu*?'

She laughed. Her teeth were marvellous and her own. She shook her head negatively. 'Now what am I going to do with you?' she mused.

'I'm told I'm very good in bed.'

She chuckled. 'Such talk! You sound like the back streets of Rio.'

'I don't get the accent—American-Argentinian?'

'Not a bad guess.'

'Will you tell me if you had anything to do with trying to deter me from coming here, as far back as Rome?'

'You know I did.'

'Now why does everyone think I know what's going on. I don't—I really don't.'

'Oh, come now, Mr. Trenton——'

'You can call me Garway!'

'*Trenton,*' she re-affirmed. 'You're smooth, don't let's play childish games.'

'No. Not childish. By the way, what are you doing for dinner?'

Mr. Minoru Oko made hissing noises and then spoke in what was not Japanese, but Reba seemed to understand it. He had clearly had enough of my chit-chat.

She said, a little wistfully I thought, 'You really won't go back—not even if we raised the ante?'

'What, *more* mazuma?'

'Say two hundred thousand pounds or the equivalent in any currency you like?'

I pulled at my cigarette and studied it intently.

'May I have about a hundred aspirins for my head?'

'Of course!' She gave the necessary order to one of the boyos I had met on the road.

'Thanks,' I said, 'you know, I find it difficult to believe I can possibly be worth all that money. What is it I've got?'

'Knowledge, Trenton.'

'How did you lose the eye?' I asked.

Reba flushed angrily, she was very sensitive about it. 'Suppose you mind your own business!' she retorted.

'O.K. Horatio!'

This really angered her. She stepped forward and slashed me across the face with the whip.

'Ouch!' I exclaimed. 'That really hurt.'

Reba bit her lip as if she regretted that she had lost her temper. 'I thought you were a tough guy,' she sneered. 'You mussed up Smith & Co. quite a bit.'

'"Mussed up"? Then you *are* of American extraction?'

She didn't answer. Once again Minoru Oko broke into the conversation in a language I didn't savvy.

'What's his lingo?' I inquired. 'It's not Japanese.'

Reba and Minoru Oko exchanged what appeared to be significant looks, then he spat the words at me 'You talk Japanese!'

I looked at him in perplexity then I thought I got the message.

'I've got it! The whole thing plops into place! You think I am someone else!' I said excitedly. The back of my head began to give me jip again and I gave an exclamation of pain.

'Your poor head!' Reba said pseudo-solicitously, then, changing her tune, 'What about Smith's arm?'

This time it was my turn to laugh. 'Poor old Smith,' I kidded.

'And who is Smith? Oto von Smidt? Who are you? What kind of set-up is it? You want to keep me out of something pretty big, but the fact remains you've got the wrong Trenton.'

Reba reached for an ornate cigar box on the desk, took out a cheroot and lit it from the whip top.

'Oh no!' I pleaded, phoney-serious, 'moonlight becomes you, it goes with your hair, stay feminine, girly! Not ceegars!'

Minoru Oko cut in angrily. All I could understand was the name Kunhke-Schultz. In spite of my splitting headache the name vaguely tinkled a little bell.

'I still can't see how you reckon I'm your man,' I said. 'All I do is take out my little Parker and scribble words on virgin pieces of paper, and nice gentlemen buy them and equally nice gentlemen print them and even nicer gentlemen buy them. I'm a writer, get it, not—not'—now I was guessing—'not a uranium expert.'

'Yes, yes,' Reba concurred testily, 'you're a writer—even I've heard of you, though I personally don't read your kind of novel——'

One of the local henchmen moved a step forward. It was clear he would have liked to have clipped me across the face with the nose of his Stirling. Reba waved him back. Minoru Oko made further chat about Kunhke-Schultz. I got the impression that Oko wanted to crease me and that Reba was reluctant to go ahead with the idea.

'Look, Gorgeous! Let's reason this thing out——' I began.

'You're wasting your time, Trenton.'

'I don't see that. I'm here on business—writing a screen play, I think your Manduran police are marvellous.'

The joke misfired.

'Police?' Oko positively hissed out the word. 'Police?'

Reba laughed.

'Nice laugh,' I said, ' "Soft and low, an excellent thing in woman",' I paraphrased, 'perhaps Shakespeare is more your cup of tea?'

'More than your kind of cod's wallop!' Reba returned. She said to Oko: 'No. I don't think Trenton called in the Police. Not Trenton'—she paused then added—'not Sharon Saxbee—and not Roderick Vandaleur.'

There was a potent pause, then Reba said: 'You do know these people, don't you?'

'Yes, of course,' I replied. 'Why should I deny it?'

Reba paused in front of me, puffing the cheroot. She was an impressive sight and I told her so but I was getting nowhere pretty fast.

'Look. I'll give you thirty seconds to decide whether you'll agree to be shipped out—if you don't go voluntarily we'll have to send you.'

'And it won't be first-class, Mr. Trenton,' Minoru Oko added darkly. I could tell he was 'for real'.

Would it be worth a dive through the open french window and a zig-zag dash for the thick undergrowth beyond the—what, about fifty yards of garden? But I'd never make it. Reba and Minoru Oko approached me and at the same time signalled to the local stooges who, on a command from Oko, began to tie me to a chair.

Reba read my thoughts. 'Well, gallant Commander Trenton,' she began, 'feeling a trifle uneasy?'

'I feel like I felt the first time I went out to an airfield——'

'A naval airfield,' Reba corrected me.

One of the stooges appeared with a bucket containing something that was very black and smelling of something like tar.

'Pitch?'

Reba nodded. 'Pitch,' she agreed. I was puzzled. Reba answered my unasked question. 'Minoru Oko, a man of some sensitivity, thinks the simplest thing to do is *muss* you up a bit.'

'Like I did to dear old Smith?'

'Oh, much better than that. He's quite an artist.'

'A disembowelment, perhaps? The ancient Japanese art of Hari Kari?'

Reba shook her long black hair, 'Oh, no. Something far less dignified.'

The hired help brought the pail of pitch nearer. I felt a nasty little trickle of fear-sweat run down my spine to my belt. Minoru Oko went to the wall and took down what I imagined to be a local knife. It was long and curved.

'Minoru will give you a chance to tell us all you know before he. . . .'

'This suspense is killing me,' I said. The cord round my wrists bit into my flesh, my head throbbed, my face was raw and tender from the whip lash. All I wanted was my mum, I said, 'I'll gladly tell you all I know. . . .'

'Good!' They relaxed.

'But I honestly don't know what you want to know.'

They looked exasperated. Minoru Oko nodded to the stooges. One came forward and undid my belt.

'Hey!' I said. 'What is this?'

'A little trick the Ethiopians played on the Italians in the Abyssinian War. That is, when they occasionally managed to get a prisoner,' Reba said, adding, 'I met an old waiter once in Positano—it had happened to him. They did it, then dabbed a bit of pitch on and that was that!'

'Did what?'

'Oh, don't be too embarrassed. I shan't be present.'

'Just what is your Japanese associate planning?'

'Oh,' said Reba, all innocence, 'didn't I make it clear? He plans to castrate you!'

CHAPTER EIGHT

I SEEMED to be running oceans of cold perspiration. Just how much was Reba bluffing? The leather thongs round my wrists, the sinister long thin Manduran knife, the presence of the evilly-smiling Minoru Oko and his side-kicks. All this could be bluff but I was with dangerous men who had a lot to lose. Come to think of it so had I! I wet my lips and tried one last sally.

'Then this is "for real", Reba? You mean that you and I could never be lovers?'

'Well,' she agreed, 'certainly not after today.'

'But Reba, beautiful. . . .'

'You still have time to talk.'

'You mean—tell all?'

'I mean tell all.'

'I don't quite know how to begin.'

'Minoru Oko does.'

'Yeah, I can see that. I suppose he owns all the butchers' shops on the island!'

Reba lit another cheroot and inhaled, blew out the smoke, enjoying it.

'You could be a great delicacy,' the beautiful, raven-haired bitch had the temerity to suggest.

Oko gestured that we were wasting time. I'd never seen a man so anxious to cut another.

'Is this *your* particular kick? Are there lots of young men going around less a vital part thanks to your special vice?' He approached me and spat in my face and then deliberately rubbed the spittle on to the weal made by the lash of Reba's whip. I winced and he saw it and was glad.

'You sadistic little bastard!' I shouted.

Reba laughed. I thought she must be kidding, she's a double agent. She *must* be. She must be working for Roderick Vandaleur: any moment the big switcheroo will happen.

Benevolently, like a genial dentist, a sympathetic surgeon, Oko approached. He motioned to his escort. After the belt they unzipped my trousers.

'Bye-bye, Trenton,' Reba said, 'I wouldn't want to embarrass you.'

Then, as Oko took hold of me, I broke.

'Look, honey lamb, I'll talk. Mam, I'll certainly talk.'

'How nice,' Reba remarked jubilantly, returning from the door. 'Cover the gentleman up, Minoru, we don't want to embarrass him in front of a lady.'

'You could wear two eye patches,' I mocked.

She stepped towards me with her whip raised. 'O.K., let's have it.'

'Lady, not right now. Some wise man said that when a man was frightened his hair and another portion of his anatomy could not rise together.'

'I meant the information,' she cut in impatiently.

'Ah yes, the information. Now where shall we start.'

'At the beginning.'

'Good. I was born a baby. . . .'

Oko had had enough of my stalling, he grabbed me by the hair and pulled back my head. He held the Manduran knife close, very close to my face.

'No cut-throat type, thanks, I always use an electric razor,' I said. Oko spluttered with rage.

'Start when you switched from fighters to torpedo-bombers,' Reba commanded.

'Torpedo-bombers?' I repeated, taken by surprise.

'Yes. You changed from fighters to T.B.R.s because. . . ?'

I was so astonished I flicked my eyes from the knife across my throat to Reba's face. 'Your Intelligence Section *is* something. You've got a positive army here. Is it an army?'

'Not quite, but you could call it a military operation.'

'Who are you fighting?'

'We aren't fighting anyone but there's a lot of work entailed in salvage.'

'Salvage?'

'You'll be so much salvage if you don't stop playing the innocent, Sub-lieutenant Trenton!' Oko assured me.

'It's a long time since I was a sub,' I reflected, wondering when did the rescue party arrive, or wasn't I going to get one?

'Yes. You were nineteen.'

'Mam, you sure do flatter me!'

'But it happened when you were nineteen.'

'Oh, it happened when I was sixteen, man, and I reckoned I was backward.'

'For a man about to be severely—er—damaged, your insistence on sex talk means you're going to be a very unhappy fellow two minutes from now,' Reba said.

'Reba, I'm talking. Just ask the questions.'

'You must have had quite a party in the Ward Room after you bagged it.'

'Bagged what?'

'Oh, come now, we've been very tolerant. I'm deadly serious, *talk*!'

'Can I have a drink of water?' I tried one final throw, but no dice. Quite suddenly Oko kicked me. He kicked me where I kicked Umesh but luckily, in his hurry, he misplaced the kick, but he hit me all right and I groaned.

'Your first direct hit,' Reba said harshly. 'Your first submarine. You got the D.S.C. for it, didn't you?'

'Oh, that, you mean when I torpedoed the Nip? Yes. Yes I got the D.S.C. but shucks, it was nothing! They gave one out with every other packet of cornflakes, why, we used to say——'

'When you torpedoed the Japanese submarine you——'

Reba got no further. The door was suddenly kicked open and there was the short, sudden surprised cough of a sub-machine gun and the acrid smell of shots being fired. All hell was let loose. The noise seemed vociferous.

There were shouts and screams intermingled with the crash of glass as someone fell into the frame of the french windows. Reba was on the desk but I couldn't be sure if this was self-preservation. Oko had leapt behind the desk, but whether he had been hit, I couldn't tell. One of the guards was lying very still and, from

the pool of blood spurting from his chest, looked very dead.
Suddenly I received what must have been a cosh with a rifle butt. I flopped out for a second and it was as if I had been suddenly rushed skywards. Actually, I had fallen off the chair.
By now, someone had released me, my bonds had been severed and my hands were free. I was helped to my feet and two men rushed me very speedily from the room through the open door. As we reached the exterior of the fine Colonial house, I saw another man, a local, I presumed, slashing with a machete the tyres of the car in which Smith had transported me.
An old Cadillac, with engine gunned and driver at the wheel, was waiting at the ready as the two men hurried me to the car. I was flung ignominiously into the back, falling at the feet of an elderly man who stooped to help me on to the seat beside him. He was thin, with an aquiline nose, wore a thin cream-coloured cotton suit, old but well laundered. He wore an old Carthusian tie and a monocle in his left eye. He was as lined as Clapham Junction or Grand Central, clean shaven, and he had the imperious dignity of an Indian chief. His voice was cultured, his accent clipped. He was an obvious product of the 'Twenties.
'How do you do?' he murmured. 'My name's Uncle Steve.'

CHAPTER NINE

It seemed an eternity while we waited there for the two men who had created the fracas and were covering our escape. Suddenly they came pelting towards us, unhurt but breathless. Uncle Steve had the door open for them and we were on the move as they fell into the car. We moved away like a jet-propelled rocket.
A bullet crashed the back window glass behind my head, I hastily slipped to the floor of the car. One of my rescuers poked his Sten through the window and fired a quick burst. There seemed more bloody flak about than on the Taranto raid. Uncle Steve asked urbanely:
'How is the Old Country. Gone to the dogs a bit, hasn't it?'
I couldn't believe my ears. He had me laughing, laughing till I cried.
'What?' he asked primly, 'What's so funny about that?'
'Apologies, I was amused at your coolness in the face of the "enemy"—who are they, anyway?'

'Oh, Reba and Minoru Oko—don't you know, they're part of the Kunhke-Schultz mob.'

'Apologies for my ignorance and just who are the Kunhke-Schultz mob?'

Uncle Steve looked at me suspiciously.

'Didn't Roderick tell you *anything*?'

'What in hell has Roderick got to do with it?'

Uncle Steve looked at me in astonishment.

'Roderick has everything to do with it. It was Roderick who brought you here!'

'Now don't be daft—what do I call you?'

'Uncle Steve is all right since you are a friend of Roderick's.'

'Very well, Uncle Steve, I came here for the British United Studios to write the script of Sharon Saxbee's novel.'

'We know all about *that,*' Uncle Steve said quite stuffily, sniffing down at his co-respondent shoes, 'but that's a front.'

'By the way, there's an old Jap tank about here——' I began, but I'd left the warning too late, we sped round the corner in the Cadillac and braked quickly as we ran slap facing the tank. It was astride the road fifty yards away and it instantly opened up with a Bofors. Only a clot could have missed us and I can only conclude he was doing his Manduran football pools when we hove into sight.

'Hard a starboard,' yelled Uncle Steve, obviously enjoying it. The driver instantly left the road, crashed through a crude but luckily ancient fencing and on to rough terrain full of bushes and undulations. The driver went like Jehu. By the time the tank gunner swung round we were zig-zagging madly but the first shot whined uncomfortably close.

'Nasty things,' Uncle Steve remarked, 'make quite a mess, what?'

Uncle Steve's accent was splendid. His era was clearly the Charleston. He clipped his final g's and words like nasty came out as 'Nasteh'.

'Yes,' he reaffirmed, 'naughteh, very naughteh.'

'Exactly what is Roderick Vandaleur's stake out here, what is he doing here?'

'Well, actually he's in California. Like you he's writin' a kinematograph scenario.'

'And that, I suppose, is a front, too.'

'In a manner of speakin', yes,' Uncle Steve agreed.

I groaned.

'Head hurtin'?' he inquired solicitously.

'Yes, but I'm not groaning about that. Look, Uncle Steve, for gawdsake, please tell me the score. Fill me in on the details. I don't like to be whanged-off by a Bofors, and offered two hundred thousand pounds, and have my privates almost shaved off without knowing the reason behind it all. I just like to be in the picture.'

My language caused Uncle Steve some loss of prestige. He took out his eyeglass and polished it, giving his colleagues a furtive look. Clearly this was something one didn't talk about in front of mere gun-toters.

'Toppin' lookin' girl that Reba, eh, what?' he observed.

We had swerved back on to a second class road and were going too fast, but the driver was making sure we had a clear get-away. Occasionally we would go through a small village, scattering the inevitable scrawny chicken. Pretty coffee-skinned, big-eyed children turned from making mud castles too near the road, and a few anxious mothers in tatty cotton dresses screamed incoherent abuse at us.

Every now and then there were temples, bright, attractive, made of thick white stone or the local basalt with the inevitable domed cupola and tiny flags flying gaily against the background of a cerulean sky.

'The little flags, I remember when I was out here in wartime, it has some significance, a burial or a wedding, hasn't it?'

Uncle Steve shrugged his shoulders.

'Always thought it was their national colours,' he replied, then murmured, because he was obviously impressed, 'A cool two hundred thou' eh, well! well!'

'Are we near your H.Q.?' I inquired. 'I feel a bit sick.'

'Yes, won't be long now. Very naughteh of them to beat you up. Didn't get any change out of you, I suppose?'

'For the very simple reason that I didn't know what they wanted me to tell 'em. A somewhat awkward situation.'

'Stop pullin' my leg,' Uncle Steve requested. 'It's got bells on.'

I sighed. Uncle Steve patted my arm. 'You'll be tickety-boo in next to no time.'

We were approaching a small town at the fringe of the ocean. The sky was fantastically bright. There was the same vivid brightness of Greece about Mandura.

'The island's circled by a ring of coral, isn't it?' I said. 'Keeps out the sharks.'

Uncle Steve chuckled. 'Oh, yes, my boy, keeps out the sharks.' His chuckle became a tickling cough. 'I like that. Very funneh. Comic. Rather rich. "Keeps out the sharks". I like that,' he said approvingly.

Now it was my turn to say, 'Have I said something funny?'

'You'll like the hotel,' Uncle Steve said. 'Not bad, not bad at all. Hassamal runs it. Indian—decent fella. Very good business chappie Hassamal.' He gave me a sharp scrutiny. 'Soon put you right at the hotel. A stingah or two and you'll be right as rain, eh?'

'Do you think it wise to go to a hotel?' I inquired.

'You're booked into the Royal, aren't you? They've given you a very decent room and bath.'

'But haven't you some H.Q., some hide-out—I don't really want to find part of me in the market as a *specialité* of the day.'

'Kunhke-Schultz mob, you mean? Don't think they'll try anythin' in Babalu. No, shouldn't think so. Anyway, I can give you some of what Roderick calls cutlery.'

'I don't think a knife will be much good and I do have this——' I tapped Horace, which was snuggled under my coat. 'I was lucky they didn't realize I had a Betsy.'

Uncle Steve was fairly impressed.

'Oh, that. No. I mean something really damagin', like a Sten, maybe.'

'Uncle Steve, just tell me one thing, is this a political thing, 'cos frankly I'm not interested in politics, I think they are all charlatans——'

Uncle Steve looked thunderstruck. 'I say, you wouldn't include the Tories, would you, not the Tories?'

I was becoming tazzy now, the reaction to my experience with Minoru Oko and Reba, and I was a bit battle-sore. 'The *lot*!' I repeated with finality, asking again, 'Is it political?'

Uncle Steve's eyeglass glinted.

'You know dam' well it's not,' he tartly replied. It was clear he couldn't quite fathom what I was playing at, and I was bloody sure I hadn't perceived his drift one whit.

We drove through what was the main drag of Babalu, the capital of Mandura. The houses and shops were of concrete, wide but not tall, built by the French for the locals to withstand typhoons. There were multi-coloured markets festooned with fruits, vegetables and flowers—it looked like something out of Glorious Technicolor. The road transport was mostly bicycles and old cars, though there were jolly red buses, old stock sold off by London Transport to the French, and very welcome in a distant clime. I remarked on this to Uncle Steve who sighed.

'Miss the Old Country, you know,' he said, 'but it's pretty bad now, isn't it? I mean, not what it was? Understand they question the umpire's decision at Wimbledon.'

'Afraid so.'

'And as for soccer—by jove! What about soccer? The players are liable to clock the ref., I'm told. Throw bottles, argue with the linesmen, eh?'

'Afraid so.'

'And even cricket's got nasteh, very nasteh. Play to win, don't they? It's got a lot to do with the Americans.'

'What *is* Roderick's racket, Uncle Steve?'

'You mean the one he wants you for?'

'You mean there is more than one?'

'Yes, of course,' Uncle Steve panzered on, 'now you take the time when I played soccer for Charterhouse—I liked the Repton match, you know, decent lot of fellows. Of course Roderick went to Eton——'

'Yes, I was there with him.'

'Of course. Top-whole school. Gentlemen at Eton. What were you saying about Roderick's racket?'

CHAPTER TEN

OUR arrival at the hotel put paid to further quizzing. A laughing local lad, ridiculous in a pale pink uniform and pill box hat, came out to greet me; he was the only concession the local hotel made to the West. With him was an ancient but wiry Manduran, with no more than a loin cloth and turban, who took charge of my baggage.

'You'll be quite comfortable here and just to keep you happy, I'll leave Mango with you.'

Mango was one of the two armament boyos.

Uncle Steve gave some cryptic word of command and a very cheap brown fibre suitcase, which was in the back of the car, was opened, and one of the Stens was placed inside with loving care. The suitcase was closed and Mango carried it, following me to the hotel reception, nor would he let the aged retainer touch it.

The Royal Palace and Continental with its reception hall-cum-lounge-cum-writing-room-cum-cocktail bar was hardly Hilton in its conception.

There were beaded curtains to keep out sunlight, and ancient bamboo chairs. The *décor* had become lost over the years, though from the odd tapestry on its walls it appeared that ritual killings of wild boars seemed to predominate any scene that would be determined. Bric-à-brac there was a-plenty, from imitation Ming vases to, bizarrely, an old Army stock table (for letters home) still with its W.D. arrow on one leg left behind on the leap-frog recapture of Madagascar. Ash trays were everywhere on tables, on arms of elephantine sofas and on long trunks as if the manager was afraid of the whole building suddenly igniting. The only thing I missed in this mausoleum of an ancient hotel was a picture of shaggy Highland cattle or an aspidistra, nothing else had been omitted.

The pert bell-hop plunked a brown pudgy hand on the bell at the reception desk and a yawning Indian, scratching his head, appeared from a back room. He wore a crumpled cream suit, no tie, open shirt and on his left sleeve he wore a piece of cloth covered criss-cross with ink marks. I soon realized why. He picked up a pen, cleaned the nib on the cloth and handed it to me diffidently.

'Your name, please?'

I told him and his manner changed instantly. He was positively reverent.

'*The* Meestaire Trenton?'

I shrugged my shoulders. As I signed the registration form, he added spectacularly, 'Welcome to the Royal Palace and Continental!'

Behind the reception desk were two posters, one announced a football match at Agar's Plough. It gave me a nostalgic giggle. It was between the Muslim Scouts and the Fire Brigade. The other poster advertised a local dance. Al Metaxa and his Jazz Group. I pointed it out to Uncle Steve.

'I bet that Al is a swinging cat,' I observed. This was wasted on Uncle Steve who no doubt still thought the Beatles were somethin' you trod on, or that the Rolling Stones carried no moss.

The hotel receptionist indicated that I should follow him to a lift which was operated by tugging on a steel wire covered by a thick pad of cloth to avoid severing one's hand. Uncle Steve said he'd drop by in half an hour but Mango followed me into the lift until the receptionist ordered him out. Mango had to climb the stairs. I reckoned the receptionist would have changed his tune pretty promptly had he known the contents of the fibre suitcase Mango carried.

We ascended, snail-like, to the first floor. 'My name,' announced the receptionist, leading me along a spacious corridor to my room, 'is Hassamal, *Mister* Hassamal,' he emphasized. 'If you want the manager, I am also he. I am at your service. The entire staff,' he added, making a magnificent gesture, 'is at your service. We are here to do you justice.' I nodded gratefully.

The bedroom was large. The windows, in addition to Victorian-style faded flower pattern curtains, had mosquito netting, and overhead there was an ancient fan which had one broken blade. It was not working. The bed was double, and the bathroom as big as any at the George Cinq in Paris.

'Ring for anything you need, anything at all.'

He gave the weal on my face a long, interested look, then he bowed low and, with a flourish, handed me the key. Need I tell you it didn't lock the door?

He paid no regard to Mango, who now squatted outside the door, embracing his fibre suitcase. I couldn't be sure if this was acceptable practice in Mandura, or if Mr. Hassamal was determined not to see him.

I had noticed the vase of flowers when I gave the room the once-over and I now crossed to put the hotel key onto the dressing-table. The flowers were poinsettias. Vivid, blood-red. It was then that I noticed the envelope attached to one of the flowers. The envelope was typewritten, the message in a large feminine hand, the i's circled ostentatiously. The message read:

> 'You will be interested to know there is a plane departing for Madagascar tonight.'

It was signed 'Reba'.

I laughed. There was no doubt the girl was still in there pitching. Though she had had the crudest of ideas for me, and one that wouldn't have helped us to get to know one another, I couldn't entirely dislike her. In fact, I had to confess I wanted to see her again.

I shrugged my shoulders and began to unpack. I thought I would like a drink. I crossed to the bell pull and gave the ornate sash a tug. There was a hell of a report and I leapt back like a startled faun. Now, in addition to a weal on my face and a clout at the back of my head, I had a .38 bullet furrow down my forehead. The door burst open and I promptly dropped unheroically behind the bed.

The would-be assailant rushed round, and I just had time to boot him into the upholstered arm-chair. It was Mango who had come to see if I had been assassinated. Sheepishly I helped him up. He was holding the Sten in one hand and the fibre case in the other. He looked startled and probably nearly as ridiculous as I did. I crossed to the bathroom, blood dropping on the carpet.

'What happened, master?' he inquired. This was the first time he had spoken since we had met. I pointed to the unobtrusive .38 craftily set at the top of the bell pull.

Mango nodded sagaciously.

'You want to know, master, I think these people mean business,' he predicted.

'Mango, that is the under-statement of the year,' I replied.

Mr. Hassamal—receptionist, manager, cook, bottlewasher, exterminator (?) knew nothing about such treachery. The miscreant couldn't have come through the anti-mosquito netted window, so the lock would have to be changed immediately. Who would do this thing in the hub of the city—the very nerve centre—the Royal Palace and Continental, Mr. Hassamal inquired of Mango, who picked his nose disinterestedly. I suggested that if the right key be found, it might be a deterrent.

It was a foolish idea because soon after, bringing me a large whisky as a gesture, Mr. Hassamal carried also a wooden box. As I drank, Mr. Hassamal tried assorted keys from the box. None of them fitted.

I took a couple of sleeping tablets with the whisky and despite the throbbing weal, the soreness of my forehead, the kerplunk at the back of the head, the kick in the back and the desire to shake like a leaf, I did finally drop off.

A stentorian banging on the door awakened me. Since my trusty Betsy was in my hand, I merely lined it up with the door and said, 'O.K., come in and I guarantee I'll take the first one of you!'

Uncle Steve appeared. Very smart, very clean, immaculate in a new suit. This time a straw hat with the O.C. colours replaced the panama.

'Well, Trenton, havin' forty winks, me boy?'

'I was,' I replied tartly.

'Nothin' like it. Now Winnie once said to me——'

'Winnie?'

'You know the fella. "Never have so few" and all that——'

"Oh, Sir Winston Churchill."

'That's the chappie—told me, it was on a tour of the city after a Jerry raid, he could take a cat nap anywhere, at any time. Very useful. Go ahead and bath, I'll sit on the edge and talk.'

'Uncle Steve, give me five minutes and then we're on the town.'

'On the town?' He looked mystified. 'What town?' he inquired. 'No, dear boy, I'm takin' you to the Sportin' Club.'

'A night club?'

'No, well certainly not yet—too early for that sort of thing—no, the social club. Very cosmopolitan, decent sort of people, you'll like it.'

CHAPTER ELEVEN

THE ancient Cadillac was parked outside the hotel, the grinning page boy holding the door open. The turbanned driver grinned conspiratorially, betel-nut juice made it appear as if he had acute pyorrhoea. I was followed out by Uncle Steve and the faithful Mango carrying the cutlery in the fibre case. The night was full of promise, of sweet scents, the tintinnabulation of Cambodian bells. I felt fabulous, but Uncle Steve viewed me with alarm.

'Where's your necktie?' he inquired.

I had put on a nice clean white shirt, a single-breasted navy blue blazer with F.A.A. buttons, light grey Daks, hand tailored, and a pair of elastic-sided tan shoes which were not made by Lobb but, in fact, came from Texas, and it's too long and too dull a story to impart at this time. I didn't think I had erred sartorially in the Tropic of Capricorn, and that a few hundred miles east of Madagascar I would need a necktie.

'Where are we going,' I quipped, 'Tiffany's?'

'The Sportin' Club, dear boy. You can't possibly go to the club——'

'Tieless in Gaza?'

'Well, I mean to say. As a matter of fact, we've got a case on now——'

'We?'

'The committee. Fella—new chap, didn't know the rules, arrived in a stock, if you please.'

'What's wrong with that?'

'The by-law clearly states a necktie must be worn after seven in the evening.'

'But surely a stock is even more impressive than a necktie, Uncle Steve?'

'A necktie's a necktie. And by-law seventeen clearly states——'

'That gentlemen must wear neckties. And women, I suppose, tops to their dresses.'

Uncle Steve looked askance. I turned to go back into the hotel.

'I say, Trenton, I'd esteem it a great favour if you made it an O.E. tie.'

At last, properly dressed, with a nod of approval from Roderick Vandaleur's uncle, we cruised down the main drag. In addition to French billboards, there were advertisements for Heinz, Daz and so on and, it appeared, Mandurans were very partial to *Guinness*. The buildings were only two or three storeys high, solid, French Colonial, *circa* 1870. The tawdry shops with goods ranging from contraceptives to pineapples, were lit poorly by electricity or naphtha flares. The names over the shops were occasionally Indian, nearly always Chinese—Lin Hing, Sam Fat, U Sin Tan and, inevitably, Ah Fook.

The Indians, with their love of colour, the women's vivid saris, the boys' gay shirts, splashed it around like a kaleidoscope; pale pinks, pale greens, scarlets, puce, vivid blues. They were garish and gay in contrast to the sombrely dressed French. The Mandurans, Negroes and Hindus stood or sat tranquilly around a pacific existence. Occasionally, a very beautiful Madagascan girl walked slowly along the pavement, walking like a princess with giant bundles poised, seemingly perilously, on her jet black, well coiled hair. On one occasion I grunted admiringly.

'Wait till you see the Creole gals!' Uncle Steve said and flicked his fingers incongruously as if he were about to do a fandango.

'If the nights are so beautiful, I'll need to,' I predicted.

There was an air of happy poverty about the place and I remarked upon this to Uncle Steve. 'Is there any colour bar?' I inquired. 'They all seem to get on—the different races——'

'Yes. Yes. They get on. It's a very tolerant community. It's going places. Or it will, when we get it goin'. A few Jap factories, eh what?'

'Jap factories?'

'Cars, cameras, you know the Japs.'

'There don't seem to be many.'

Uncle Steve roared with laughter. 'Roddy didn't tell me you were a bit of a wag,' he complimented me. 'There will be, when they, *if* they, amend the legislation but until then . . . until then, eh?' He leaned towards me cabalistically. 'Maybe tonight, eh? A short baptism of fire, and all that?'

I didn't know what the hell he was talking about. I asked:

'Legislation? Why, is there a quota?'

Uncle Steve looked at me as if I had said a 'naughty' word in front of a Mother Superior.

'I should say so. Disgustin'! After all, it should be a free country, can't get the little blighters in. Very bad for business, eh? But you know all about that.'

'But Uncle Steve, I don't.'

Uncle Steve took out his monocle to give me an over-the-top wink.

'What about the colour bar?' I inquired.

'What about the colour bar?'

'Is there one?'

'What, here?' Uncle Steve looked at me as if to say 'you've got to be joking!' 'Aha! Here's the Sportin' Club,' he said proudly. 'Very exclusive. No wogs, no Indians, nothin' like that.'

I looked at him in blank astonishment, but he was quite serious. 'You mean the Governor can't come in.'

'Great heavens no, the fella's a Manduran,' Uncle Steve replied frostily.

The Club grounds were generously large. In the moonlight I could see hockey grounds, rugby football grounds, tennis courts, a golf course. The Club house was a replica of a course I had played on near Chantilly. A Manduran indicated obsequiously where we might park among the French Dauphins, the Renaults, the old British Bentleys, Lancias, Rolls, Daimlers, open E-types and Triumph Heralds. Jazz—of a sort—came wafting out from within, intermingling with the babel of chat.

'Al Metaxa?' I hazarded a guess. It stopped Uncle Steve in his tracks.

'Good gracious, how did you know?' He eyed me as if I were M.I.5—or 6. 'Extraordinary,' he murmured, adding, 'toppin' band.' Then, confidingly, 'Some Sundays they let me take over the drums.'

'Oh, you're a percussionist?'

'No, my dear fella, a drummer. Love it. But of course only on a gala night, bit tricky, you know, it puts the real drummer's nose a bit out of joint. You see, tho' I say it myself, I'm rather good.'

I couldn't wait for gala night.

Meanwhile we had wandered through the hall into a spacious lounge. Parties of well-dressed British and French women were drinking with their menfolk, some of whom were even wearing white tuxedos. There was ungainly dancing in the middle of the room. The British are good on horses but not on the dance floor. The French, one presumed, were good in bed.

Uncle Steve left me to dance with a very tall girl in a strange dress cut into diagonal pieces of pink, green and apricot. Uncle Steve was having himself a gay time, not only was he spinnin' the gal round for dear life but, to get into the party mood, was wearing a false nose (retroussé and red) and a clip-on moustache.

The atmosphere and period was set between Lonsdale and Coward, the wit, I fancied, of about the same period. Certainly there was nothing Lonsdale or Coward about Reba, who broke off from a group of the younger set to cross to us.

She wore an exclusive French, almost austere, white grosgrain dress, exquisitely cut, one string of real pearls round her neck, and a small white velvet bandeau which would have looked idiotic and adolescent on someone else. Her eye patch was, bizarrely, also white grosgrain, probably the same material as the dress. In the exciting valley between her beautifully moulded breasts there nestled provocatively one scarlet poinsettia. Her hair, the fascinating blue-black sometimes seen on beautiful young Israelis, flowed about her cheeks, wave-like, as she moved. She walked with the dignity of the Manduran women but I am sure she would not have found that a compliment. She dazzled me with a smile.

'Well, surprise, surprise!' she said cordially.

'What a delightful dress—Lanvin?' I inquired.

'Nina Ricci, but thanks for trying. What's the perfume?'

'Yours or mine?' I gagged. 'Yours is Balenciaga's *Le Dix*.'

She nodded, impressed.

'I spend hours in the Rue de la Paix, genning-up,' I imparted.

'"Genning-up"—that dates you,' she replied.

'Yep. Ancient old roué. "There was I upside down over the *Tirpitz,* etcetera, etcetera",' I parodied.

'Yes, but it wasn't the *Tirpitz,* was it? It was a submarine, wasn't it?'

My mouth opened in astonishment.

'Your first.'

I corrected her. 'My *only* sub. As I said earlier, your intelligence system——'

But Uncle Steve cut in brusquely. A new Uncle Steve, angry, tough. 'Listen, woman, what the hell's the idea? What were you and that arch-bastard, Minoru Oko, doing to my nephew's friend, eh?'

'Oh, Nunky, be your age! We're after the same thing! All's fair in love and war——' She turned to me, giving me the full treatment. 'Dance me, tall man.'

'Your wish, my command.' I turned to Uncle Steve. 'May we, sir?'

'Of course not,' he protested. 'Dam' it, boy, she's the enemy. No fraternization! Anyway I want you to meet the Assistant Governor.'

I turned in surprise. 'The Assistant Governor? But I thought you said——'

'Oh yes, but the Assistant's French. Er, white French,' Uncle Steve explained.

Reba pulled me away towards the dance floor.

'Tell her nothing, boy, nothing!' Uncle Steve positively shouted it after us.

I held her close and she didn't mind. Her nose flared slightly and I knew that the bitch found me attractive, too.

'You know,' I murmured in her right ear, 'what I can't understand is that since you are mad for me, you wanted to castrate me.'

It was unfortunate that this remark was heard by a splendid dowager festooned with rubies. She shook so much her ear-rings fell off.

'But, darling, how do you know I felt that way *then,* how do you know it hasn't *just happened*?'

'Well, I can't be sure. I think a woman knows at once if a man is attracted to her but I think a woman's more cunning, she can deceive a man about the whole thing.'

'Oh, Trenton, you've been reading your own books again!'

'Was Minoru Oko really going to—er—give me surgery?'

She pulled her cheek away from mine and looked at me. She was ice cold and furnace hot at the same time—a sort of Robert Carrier Baked Alaska. She looked at me calculatingly then changed the subject. 'What are your first impressions of Mandura?' she inquired. She couldn't care less.

'Good natured people, polyglot races, all seem very tolerant and therefore liable to be exploited.'

This amused Reba.

I added, 'I see it's the Chinese who own the stores. I see the rich houses of the French, the tin shacks of the poor locals——'

'Oh, a crusader.'

'Not at all,' I continued, 'no colour bar, but of course the governor of the island isn't allowed in here.'

Now Reba looked angry. She was as attractive angry as she was when she was serene. 'That's typical of the tourist. He's here two hours and he knows all the answers.'

'You're annoyed and it becomes you, and you are behaving as if you lived here. I didn't think you cared.'

Reba shrugged her shoulders. 'Let's have a drink.'

Clearly any magic in being held in my arms had lost its charm. As we proceeded to the bar, I said: 'Is it a crime to hold views that differ with yours?'

'There's no point in talking to you. You haven't studied the subject.'

'And you have?'

'I only talk about things about which I have some information or knowledge. But anyway, one can rarely hold an intelligent conversation with a man, they all want one thing.'

By now we had reached the bar. We made the usual beaming faces at our fellow imbibers as we stood and sipped our drinks. The men, white cotton suits or white dinner jackets, hot, shiny, looked crafty-lustily at Reba.

'What do they do?' I inquired of Reba, 'when they are not trying to roll you in the hay.'

'Sugar, tea plantations, shipping, rubber and coffee. Tuna

fishing.' At this she flashed a knowing look. 'But then of course, you know about fishing.'

'Not much,' I replied.

She laughed sarcastically. I asked: 'Is this, the Club, a sort of no-man's-land?'

'In what way?'

'Well, I was a little surprised after the fracas today—how are you able to, as it were, bury the machete and appear here, clothes by Nina Ricci, perfume by Balenciaga and no questions asked.'

'I am a respectable member of the community,' Reba replied. There was mockery in her voice.

'Albeit there is a *pax*, is there? Both sides engaged on whatever it is they are engaged upon—respect the Sporting Club territory as neutral?'

'Not at all. There is no let up.' She finished her drink, adding, 'as you will see!'

As she said this the lights suddenly fused. It was my guess that this wasn't any accident. I did what I had always done in that kind of crisis. I flopped to the deck but with pronto speed. My old college manners prompted me to grab Reba and take her with me.

There were a few exclamations of irritation at the sudden black-out which became screams as a scuffle ensued somewhere by the door. There was a revolver shot and renewed screams and the crash of glass.

Rather surprisingly Reba didn't resist as I held her tightly in my arms on the floor. Above the din she murmured in my ear.

'You are crushing my poinsettia, Mr. Trenton.'

I refrained from the obvious.

'Not wearing your Betsy tonight?' she added.

I really was surprised at that.

'Oh, we *had* noticed it when we had you—er—closeted with us. You looked so heroic we didn't want to spoil the manly impression you were trying to make.'

'You were going to spoil the manly impression, at least Minoru Oko was!' I reminded her. She giggled as she lay in my arms.

There was a sharp noisy cough of something more sinister than a .38. More screams and now panic. Some people began running and tripped over Reba and me on the floor. They fell, shouting out in surprised fear.

'I suppose this is Oko's high spirits—this horse play?' I said.

'If he's trying to grab me again I swear I'll wring your elegant little neck.'

It was then that Reba relaxed. Suddenly she grabbed my hand and I realized it was about to be a Judo lock. I tensed myself to make a counter-move against the same balance when, astonishingly, she kissed me and she kissed as I hoped she'd kiss.

I felt a right Berk when all the lights went on and we were found locked in a passionate embrace on the Sporting Club floor. Perhaps it was fortunate that the brouhaha took precedent over good conduct.

People were still at panic stations, several tables were upturned, and some of the members were crouched behind them. No one else had the sense or bad manners to be on the floor, but a surprising number had managed to get behind the bar and now peered over the top anxiously. The light switch had clearly been pulled, this was no fuse.

I broke from our embrace and looked round warily. I was determined to use Reba as a shield if it meant I could get to Mango and the car. People were talking noisily, discussing the raid but oblivious of the real motive of it—a snatch.

'Don't you think we ought to get up, handsome Trenton?' Reba suggested. I was so tensed I think there were sparks coming off my eyebrows.

'Well,' I said and by now people were becoming 'curiouser and curiouser' about us. 'They didn't make it that time.'

'Oh, yes they did,' Reba replied with assurance, asking femininely, 'Is my hair a mess?'

'What do you mean—they did.'

'We thought you'd be a bit too much on your guard so we snatched Uncle Steve. Bye-bye, Trenton!'

'Uncle Steve? Now wait a minute!' I grabbed her arm but she saw it coming and I knew, since I was right off balance. I suddently went flying. So she *did* have Judo! By the time I had picked my ignominious self up, Reba had made a buffalo to the door. 'Stop that girl!' I shouted.

Since she had just thrown me for six, and me in my O.E. necktie, not a man stirred. I heard the rev. on an E-type. Reba was clearly on her way. People were still excited, chattering like the little monkeys in the island zoo when Mango ran in, the fibre suitcase in one hand. He looked for me and rushed over.

'They got Mr. Steve, suh!' he exclaimed. I nodded.

'The bastards!' I growled. An elderly gentleman in a white suit and a Shop tie came up to me and glared, 'Kindly ask your guest to leave, sir!'

'I beg your pardon?' I'd forgotten where I was.

'Damn it, sir, you know the rules!'

'Oh, how stupid of me,' I said with super apologies, sending him up, 'Mango, my dear friend, you're not wearing a necktie and you know it's after seven o'clock.'

I took Mango by the arm and we made a leisurely exit. I expect they set up a sub-committee meeting right away.

CHAPTER TWELVE

WE went like hell back to the hotel, *en route* there was a Manduran policeman on duty at the only real intersection of the main drag. We went past lickety-split and he started blowing his whistle as if it were Judgment Day.

I sat in front with Mango. 'What happens now, Mango? Will someone call me?'

Mango nodded. 'Top Blass.'

'Who?'

'Top Blass.'

'Oh—top brass?'

'Yes. Top Blass.'

I was half toying with the idea of getting Mango to drive me to the airport. They had told me Mauritius was very peaceful. Mandura was losing its charm rather rapidly. Then I thought Hell, why should I be pushed around! And, anyway, I was some sort of highly valued property—like plutonium.

'I'm worried about Mr. Steve,' I said

Mango nodded glumly. 'Bad business.'

'So you reckon the Board of Directors of Uranium Ltd. or whoever you—and it appears *I* work for—will contact me?'

'I go.'

'Oh, you'll get a message to them?'

'Yes.'

'Wouldn't it be simpler if I come with you?'

'No. Better you not know hide-out.'

'Don't you trust me, Mango?'

Mango grinned. He was as bright and as active as a lizard.

'Tlust you,' he said, 'but better you not know hide-out. Minoru Oko catch you again, he squeeze you somewhere, you tell where place is. You not know where place is, how can you tell?'

'I reckon that's pretty good Manduran logic.'

'Logic?' Mango was out of his depth.

'Skip it.'

We were at the hotel.

'I come back, *avec grande vitesse*,' Mango said.

'You do that, chum.'

There was no one in the hotel lobby and, worrying like mad about Uncle Steve, I skipped the slow lift and took the stairs rapidly. It wasn't until I got to some yards from my bedroom door that I stopped in my tracks. I remembered just in time how often I had been surprised by bouncing into my bedroom because I hadn't taken precautions. I grinned. This time I wasn't going to be a mug.

I reached into my coat for Horace and then groaned quietly. Of course, I had left Horace in my hotel bedroom!

I turned downstairs to borrow Mango's Sten, only to see the tail light of the Cadillac winking provocatively as he sped up the main street. I cursed aloud and went back slowly, more thoughtfully, into the lounge and stood there and started to count up to twenty very slowly. It wasn't a bad idea when one was in a flap. If I had been thinking carefully, I wouldn't have let Mango skip off like that. I had reached eleven when I was conscious that Mr. Hassamal, the manager, had appeared from the door behind reception. His eyes stood out like organ stops.

'Can I be of any assistance?' Mr. Hassamal inquired.

'Well if you happen to have a Smith and Wesson, yes.'

'What is it, a dictionary?'

'Not to worry.'

'You mean I can't be of assistance? We at the Royal Palace are——'

'Well, if you haven't a derringer——'

'A what?'

'An equalizer, a gun——'

'*Gun*?' Mr. Hassamal practically shot himself at the very idea. I thought he was going to have the vapours. I was about to ring for the burnt feathers.

'A gun?' he repeated.

'Not to worry, *chalky,*' I said, 'the blood'll drain back in a moment. Got a meat axe?'

'A m-meat axe?'

Mr. Hassamel went into the hippy-hippy shake. How I could ever have imagined he was Opposition I'll never know. As a judge of character, writer-wise, I had always thought I was the top Banana.

'How do you defend yourself?' I inquired. 'Suppose the hotel was robbed?'

Mr. Hassamal screeched like a parrot. 'Meestaire Trenton, you fool with me.'

'I fool with you not. Never mind, if you hear a blood-curdling yell, send for the cops—there *are* cops on Mandura?'

'Meestaire Trenton, you jest with me.'

'Who dare jest with you who never felt a wound, or words to that effect?'

I slipped off my elastic sided Texans. Mr. Hassamal looked amazed. I think he thought I was about to face Mecca and pray. Instead I hopped up the stairs at a rate of knots. I tip-toed rapidly to my bedroom door and listened. There was silence, and so my nostrils went in to bat. My sense of smell was titillated. I smiled. Reba's perfume hung faintly around the door. They did think I was a Charlie!

I considered the situation for a moment.

If I went below and got a cop or two what could I say? Of what was I afraid? So someone—a burglar—ten burglars, had broken into my room. So ten burglars had jumped me. What was the charge assuming—idiotic thought—that there were going to be enough Manduran cops to surround the hotel. No, the thing to do was to give whoever the intruder was a scare and to get them scattering instead of me. It was the surprise attack technique.

I looked around for some sort of armament and then noticed the ancient fire hose by the lift. I darted back and unscrewed the heavy brass nozzle. I crept along to my bedroom door with it, paused again and then, yelling as if Old Nick was after me, and banging the brass nozzle on to the floor, I kicked open the door, carefully darting back and falling quickly to the corridor floor. The staccato message from the Stirling which I had expected did not occur. Instead, bedroom doors were opening and voices raised, some in fear and some in anger.

Clearly the intruders had flown. I waited a few more seconds, beating the fire hose fiercely and loudly on the deck, but I desisted as the pyjama and nightdress brigade began to gather round. Giving one final, phoney rallying call, heroically brandishing the fire hose nozzle, I leapt, Crane-like into my room. Sitting puzzled, but by no means afraid, was Sharon Saxbee. She was cuddling my golliwog Ginsberg, and she had Horace levelled at my heart.

'Well! Well!' I exclaimed, 'you've changed your perfume.'

'Oh, for heaven's sake, stop trying to be a gay boulevardier, and come and kiss me.'

'What, with that nasty thing in your hand?'

'I didn't know you were one of these tough guys, fancy you toting a gun.' She pointed the gat at Ginsberg. 'Who's he and what's his history? You got a thing for or against racial discrimination?'

'I've had Ginsberg since the age of two——'

'He could use a new suit, I must make him one. And I suppose like all bird men you have to take him flying?'

'Well, that's his history.'

Sharon jangled the miniature medallions sewn on Ginsberg's coat. 'What's that one?' she asked.

'Now, for gawdsake, Sharon, don't be impressed by that—we all got them.'

'I don't recognize the blue and white one in the front.'

'I got that for beating Harrow at cricket.'

'Ha! Ha! Is it true you were Captain of the School, a Member of Pop, in the College Eight, in the Cricket Eleven, in——'

'Oh, dry up, Sharon! Don't be so bloody impressed by the heartiness of youth. Later comes delusion. Even the tie doesn't help any more. It don't mean a thing if you ain't got that swing.'

'You *were* Captain of Cricket. Roderick told me.'

'Yes, yes,' I said, pretending to be weary, pretending not to enjoy it. 'I *was* Captain of the School which entitled me to some very pleasant privileges—I was allowed to wear a beard, I was entitled to a house and, what is more, also a wife!'

'A *wife*?'

'Yes.'

'You don't mean to tell me——'

'No, I don't. I didn't claim the privilege, and I expect it would have embarrassed the jolly old Provost if I had.'

'I knew you were having me on.'

'Look, Sharon, as for having people on, you've got a bit of explaining to do.'

There was a loud bang at the door. I deftly took Horace from Sharon and slipped him into his 'scabbard'. 'Yes?'

Mr. Hassamal entered, speaking as he came in. 'Meestaire Garwise-Trenton, it come to my notice you 'ave a woman——' he stopped short and goggled at Sharon. I don't know if he thought I'd trundle her into the bathroom or bundled her under the bed, but he spluttered and nodded and then bowed and inquired: 'Is there anything the Royal and Continental can bring you?'

'Yes. Two large Suffering Bastards,' Sharon said.

I thought poor old Hassamal was going to have a haemorrhage. I quickly put him out of his misery. 'My guest is merely showing off. Even if you've got the formula from Shepherd's, Cairo, send up two Wahines.'

'Wahines? Wahines, Hawaian girls,' Mr. Hassamal spluttered.

'I meant cocktails. Never mind, do you make a Bahia?'

Mr. Hassamal looked pleased and proud. 'Of course.'

'Two please.'

'With the greatest of pleasure.'

'When my man Mango returns get him to sample them before you send them up. If he drops dead, I'll sue the hotel.'

'Meestaire Trenton-Garfield!' Hassamal looked offended.

'It's Garway Trenton and this is my Mother, Lady Burton-on-Trenton,' I said solemnly. Mr. Hassamal apologized, bowed again and retired. Sharon giggled.

'Now we can go to bed,' she said, putting Ginsberg down and started to take off her clothes, adding 'Will I like the Bahia?'

'For heaven's sake, Sharon!' I rushed across to prevent her and she grabbed me and pulled my face down to her and kissed me passionately. I tried to disentangle and as I came up for air I said, 'Darling, what are you doing here?'

She kissed me again very fiercely before replying.

'I fell instantly in love with you, tall honey, as soon as you stepped across the bow onto the good ship *Sad Geraniums for Dulcie*.'

'Liar!'

'You don't think I hop into bed with every good-looking male novelist I meet?'

'Will you tell me why I saw a newspaper photo of Roderick

Vandaleur on your barge and why you told me you had a thing about him?'

'Because it happened to be true.'

'*Happened*?'

'Oh yes, past tense. I met him in Hollywood.'

CHAPTER THIRTEEN

'LET'S tell the manager we're married—because we're going to be,' Sharon said, 'and so we can go to bed and practise.'

'Good grief, Sharon!'

There was a tap on the door and I yelled a fierce 'Come in.' The beaming young page boy arrived with the drinks. I tipped him and he looked at Sharon, and then flipped his right wrist about as if he had broken it, saying with an admiring if lewd look, '*Guapa*!' I bundled him out. Sharon was enchanted.

'What's *guapa*—some local compliment?'

'Spanish for you're the most, I think.' I gave Sharon her Bahia. I said, 'Come on, Saxbee. What's going on? Ever since you conned me into writing the script for your lousy book, I've had trouble—oh, and I've become a very expensive property since I last saw you. I was offered a fortune—no, two fortunes, not to turn up here.'

'Oh?' Sharon couldn't have been more innocent.

'So let's make with the truth, eh?'

'Darling, you're so handsome and tall and you must have been brave 'cos of that piece of ribbon on Ginsberg—you do find me a little bit attractive. I mean, I do appeal to you just the teeniest?'

'Sharon. I loathe girls who ride bicycles, live on barges, wear sweat shirts, know hunks of the Bible and Shakespeare. I detest girls who. . . .'

'Oh good,' Sharon said, 'I knew you loved me.' She drank thirstily and then said, 'Now what bothers you?'

'First things first—why did you want me to do your script? You know bloody well that Bryan Forbes is a much more sensitive and better scriptwriter for your sort of caper. So why me?'

'Because you knew the terrain.'

'What you mean is I was on the China Station for a short period during the war as a wet young sub.'

'Exactly, but it wasn't just *that*, and you know it.'

'Sharon, if you don't tell me. . . .'

Again there was a bang at the door but this time it was opened almost as it was knocked. Mango appeared, the trusty fibre case in one hand.

'Mr. Trenton, Sahib, Uncle Steve——'

'Yes?'

'Maybe on Minoru Oko boat—we go!' He paused, looking at Sharon. 'Oh, good evening, Missy Vandaleur,' he said, recognizing her instantly.

'Missy Vandaleur!'

'Well I'll be a——' I altered what was going to be a lewdness to—'a hot cup of tea!'

'Wonders never cease!' I said fatuously.

But Sharon was serious. 'There *is* a chance we could head them off if we drove to Bains Doux——' She turned to Mango, 'Is the M.T.B. there?'

Mango nodded.

'We must rescue Uncle Steve—it's not that *he* can tell them anything——" She pointed at me. 'You are the only one who knows.'

It was no good asking her what.

She said: 'But he's an old man, and——' she left the sentence unfinished then turned to me. 'Do you want to come, Gar'?'

I had been clumped, kicked, clocked, punched, gouged, hit in the guts, socked on the back of the head all within the last two days but I lived on; besides adventure always tasted good. I answered: 'Yes, I'll come because in a way it was my fault. I should have stayed with Uncle Steve. I should have realized that these people mean business.'

'Yes, and so do we!' Sharon snapped, an alive, with-it-on-the-ball Sharon—to me, a new Sharon with a fanatical gleam of excitement in her eye.

'Let's go,' she said, 'and bring that deringer. You'll probably need the dam' thing.'

We ran down the wide, creaking stairs and across the olde-worlde lounge. We brushed aside poor Mr. Hassamal who stood requesting words with us.

'Mr. Trenton—Lady Garway, would you——?'

'Not now, Mr. Hassamal,' I yelled, 'we're off——'

'Off? Eloping? Er—leaving?'

'No. We are off to see the Wizard.'

'Wizard?' Mr. Hassamal repeated in a high-pitched voice.

'Yes. The Wonderful Wizard of Oz,' I yelled back.

The pale pink-suited page boy held the ancient Cadillac's door open. Sharon and I tumbled into the back as Mango started up. He revved too much and we lurched back as he spurt-started. I couldn't resist glancing back at Mr. Hassamal, he was talking excitedly to the page boy. Clearly he was asking '*What* wonderful Wizard of Oz?'

As we approached the town's only big road junction the grey uniformed policeman (white shorts and a sun helmet), on traffic duty spotted us. He began to blow his whistle stridently and put up a commanding hand for us to halt.

'Pity!' murmured Sharon Saxbee, 'if he hits the tyres, I mean.'

'You think he'll shoot?' I asked, beginning to slide down to the floor of the car.

'Yes,' she replied almost cheerfully, 'but they're frightfully bad shots.'

'Great!' I said. 'And I said they were a tranquil people.'

The first shot whined past us well to port. I reckoned the next would be to starboard and the third would hit us. It was unfortunate that Mango had to turn slap right, for the second shot acted as I predicted. It whammed through the car side window which was now amidships to the cop's aim and the broken glass just missed my leg.

'Lucky break, Gar',' said Sharon in a shrill excited voice.

We were soon at the outskirts of the small town and heading fast for the basalt mountain range. A big, unbelievably yellow moon helped our route, though the Cadillac headlights had been enhanced by a grossly unfair spotlight—more like a searchlight which had been screwed to the car's roof top. I felt sorry for the occasional cyclist, the soft blinking-eyed oxen pulling small carts, and the inevitable woman with head bundle, protesting at our caddish behaviour.

I noticed Mango's fibre case on the car deck, I opened the case and made sure the Sten was in working order.

When we reached the foothills of the mountains, the car going like a bat out of hell, I suggested I ought to whang off a few rounds just to ensure the toy could cough nicely. Sharon agreed. I pointed the gun out of the broken window and loosed off a short, staccato burst. Certainly there was something satisfying about it when you were at the blunt end, but I hated the acrid smell of cordite. Sharon, however, was breathing it in as if it were something by Patou.

'I say! Isn't it exhilarating!' she exclaimed. 'I do hope we manage to board them!'

I blanched. I asked sarcastically, 'Cutlasses, yet?'

She didn't think I was joking.

'I wish I were standing in my morning coat in the Royal Box Enclosure at Ascot.'

'Snob!'

'Or Strawberry Mess at Rowland's.'

'Snob again.'

'Or Brand's Hatch or down the Thames on a P.L.A. launch.'

'What's a P.L.A. launch?'

I ignored it.

'Or watching the beefy Russian crew from the Zjalghiris Vilnnjus or those gallant Harvard oldsters of seventy paddling the course again, at Henley, or——'

'Or cricket at Lord's—you in your top hat and cornflower—how perfectly ghastly!' Sharon said.

'*A chacun, son goût.*'

'*Chacun à son goût,*' Sharon corrected me.

'You pays yer money and yer takes yer choice.'

By now we had started to climb steeply.

'Golly, Miss Molly!' I exclaimed, 'we don't have to climb that great whopper.'

Sharon said 'Not entirely.'

'Well, thank God for that! I can't stand heights.'

'I suppose you made a pact with the Captain of your carrier that you never had to fly above a hundred feet.'

'It would have been a very smart idea, come to think of it. I'll suggest it to the strategic reserve.'

Quite suddenly the road narrowed and we were now going down again. I was mightily relieved because there was no room for any more traffic than the Cadillac. We swung a corner at too high a rate of knots when Mango banged on the anchor with such intensity that Sharon and I fell on the floor after hitting the back of the driving seat. Mango ducked and so avoided going through the windscreen.

Ahead of us was a large boulder. Whether by accident or design we were *ümstuck,* stymied or up that well-known creek.

'Well,' I said, 'that's that!'

While Sharon made sure Mango was all right I ran to the boulder to see how far imbedded it was. It was well and truly astride the road. We had certainly had it.

Sharon and a head-shaking Mango joined me, I patted him on the shoulder. 'Nice driving, Mango. You O.K.?'

'Me O.K.' He gave a simian-like grin.

'But the rescue. . . ? Poor old Uncle Steve. . . .' Sharon broke off her sentence.

Then Mango clicked his thumb and second finger together and uttered a Manduran exclamation. In his excitement he broke into the native language so that I couldn't get it but, whatever he said, made Sharon enthusiastic. As Mango ran back to the car she turned to me, eyes agleam again.

'Gar'! Mango's had a perfectly wizard idea! Come on!'

She started to scramble round the boulder and ran down the road beyond. We hurried to catch up. To Sharon, running down a moonlit road in Mandura with a Sten gun on a hi-jacking operation exclaiming, 'A perfectly wizard idea' seemed normal procedure.

'What are we going to do?' I shouted after her. 'No one tells me *anything*!' I complained. Mango caught me up. I took one of the Stens from him.

'You see!' he said. 'I fix!'

We ran a considerable distance, the weight of the guns making us pant. We caught up with Sharon as we approached another bend in the curvaceous road.

'Another road block?' Sharon inquired.

'One, I fancy, was enough,' I replied.

'A blast of gunfire?' She hazarded a guess.

We all stopped. We hadn't considered that.

'I mean they may just conceivably have placed it there and they might just conceivably be waiting for us,' I added. 'On the other hand they could have ambushed us when we were stopped by the boulder.'

Sharon looked at me with pleasure. I was obviously a keen type at heart.

'Nevertheless,' I cautioned, 'I think if Mango discreetly left the road and made a recce. . . .'

My soaring stock with Sharon took a nose dive. 'Why don't you go?' she asked.

'A good point, but I reckon he knows the terrain better than

I do. Besides, I told you,' I added, 'I can't stand heights.' Sharon sniffed contemptuously.

'Look!' I panted. 'Roderick was *Victor Ludorum* at Eton, not me.'

'Very funny,' Sharon said. 'Save your breath, Gar', you're going to need it.'

'I must say you're doing nicely. I suppose you ran for Roedean.'

'Westfield, actually.'

'May I inquire where we are going?'

'Round the next bend——'

'What another?'

'Mango says there's a small village.'

'With a tank, I suppose.'

'Not exactly, but he thinks transport.'

'I wish we had Ming, my Maserati right now,' I grumbled.

The transport proved to be three antediluvian bicycles. The owners sleepy, disgruntled, changed their tune when they saw how much Sharon was prepared to pay for them.

'Thank goodness it's a one-way deal. I didn't really want to ride the bloody thing back,' I said, adding, 'If Lily Mertens——'

Sharon stiffened.

'I know about Penny something Hyphen someone and your painter friend Tee in Rome, but Lily is new to me.'

'Lily happens to be my "daily". My char. House-keeper——' I explained.

'Girl Friday?'

I nodded.

Sharon looked at me longingly.

'Oh Gar'——' she said. 'I'd love to be your——'

'Now, now, Sharon!' I backed away from her. 'There's a time and place for everything.' She certainly looked bewitching in the moonlight. 'Remember Uncle Steve!'

Amidst the garrulous, gesticulating villagers (we had managed to waken most of them in our hunt for bicycles), with Sten strapped to our backs and led by Sharon, we freewheeled down the mountain road.

'If only me Da' could see me now,' I said trying hard to avoid potholes and keep my balance. 'To think he wanted me to join the Bengal Lancers.'

'Lucky there's a moon. It would be impossible without,' Sharon observed.

'It's well nigh impossible *with*,' I corrected her.

I prayed that the bike brakes would hold. We sped, fell, tripped, sprawled, jogged, jolted, crashed and skidded our way down and round until suddenly a small fishing port with a beautiful sandy beach alongside appeared.

'That's it,' Sharon said.

'And it so happens you have a Cruiser or two here!' I said sarcastically.

'We do have an M.T.B.—old, but serviceable.'

'This is quite an organization. Doesn't the Manduran government mind?'

'Why should they mind? We bring a lot of trade to the island, well money, anyway. As far as the law is concerned that's a converted M.T.B. There are plenty that have been converted, just as there are around Chelsea at home.'

I nodded.

'I can imagine just how you've converted it!' I said.

The village was utterly quiet and the only lights were from boats in the harbour. As we dismounted and wheeled the bikes along the tiny quay, a figure appeared on the M.T.B. and waved. Sharon waved back and gave a musical sort of whistle to which the character on board replied.

'We're not taking the bicycles with us?' I asked.

'No, leave them here,' Sharon said, stacking her bicycle by a convenient bollard. I glanced round at the other craft in the harbour. They were mostly fishing boats, with the occasional pleasure boat and a powerful yacht or two.

The beach looked fantastic, unreal in the moonlight, fringed in silhouette by palm trees. Seawards, the coral reef which surrounded the island could just be discerned.

Sharon noticed me gandering the spot. 'It'll be tricky, negotiating the reef——'

'But you'll do it.'

'That's right.'

I sighed. 'What a horror you are! Remind me to marry you sometime.'

Mango stepped aside to let us across the short gangway onto the M.T.B. The figure on board was now whistling. Sharon stopped and tautened. I bumped into her and said, 'What's up?'

'That tune. It's a German folk song!'

I was about to say 'so what' when I felt the barrel of Mango's Sten in my back. The figure on the boat raised his arm in the moonlight, there was a glint on the barrel.

'That's right, Fraulein Saxbee, a German folk song. Won't you come into my parlour, said the spider to the fly?'

'Gar'!' Sharon cried out.

'Honey,' I said trying to keep the shake out of my voice, 'I don't quite know what you think I can do but Mango has the Sten slap in the middle of my back!'

'Mango?' Sharon repeated incredulously.

'Yup!'

'Please to walk forward,' Mango said softly.

'Yes, *kommen sie, bitte*!' added Kunhke-Schultz.

CHAPTER FOURTEEN

'WHAT happened to——?' Sharon started anxiously when Kunhke-Schultz cut in with:

'Your crew? Safely tucked away. *Bitte!*' He waved the business end of his Betsy indicating that we should proceed below. He said something to a member of his mob who emerged from the shadows and who joined Mango on deck. We went below.

'Yes, an admirable crew. They had a most excellent man on watch. Unfortunately he kept watch on the quay, looking at the port.'

'And you came up the sea side of the boat?'

'Correct, Commander Trenton.'

We were now in the M.T.B.'s wardroom where another stooge was ready, also with ample deterrents.

'Drink?' Kunhke-Schultz cordially offered us.

'Strychnine or cyanide?' I inquired. Schultz laughed—a laugh that was mirthless.

'Got any ice?' Sharon inquired.

I certainly admired her gall. I felt as if I had suddenly been let into a bull-ring with one pass, a *veronica*. This man, tall, with not an inch of fat on a powerful frame, who moved as lithely as a puma, was cold, calculating, humourless. The fascinating thing about him was that he was an albino. His white hair crew-cut and shock-thick. His eyes were as blue as Sharon's.

'I don't think Hardy will erase us, Gar', at least not yet.'

Schultz had put his deringer into his hip holster but his cohort, an Asiatic whose finger seemed very itchy on the Sten, watched us through his Oriental-shaped eyes.

Schultz crossed to the adjoining galley, took out a tray of ice cubes from the small 'fridge and returned to a sideboard screwed to the bulk head. He poured out a Scotch-on-the-Rocks for Sharon without asking her preference. He looked up at me awaiting my verdict.

'The same, thanks,' I said, adding: 'You two have met before.'

Again he laughed his humourless laugh.

'Well,' snapped Sharon, 'What have you done with them—the Concrete Kimono, I suppose?'

Schultz handed her the Scotch. He moved so cat-like I felt quite scarey. The man was walking nuclear fission. I was glad I hadn't been jumped on the mountain side. The deep-throated M.T.B. engines jumped into life—a powerful, impressive sound.

'Nice day for a sail out, Kunhke old Schultz,' I said superciliously, but this wasn't Minoru Oko whom I could rile easily. He smiled urbanely, the sixth carbon-copy smile, that is.

He replied courteously. 'During the short time we will be associated, you may call me Hardy.'

'"Kiss me Hardy",' I said facetiously.

Schultz looked at me with sad dignity, he was as warm as a polar bear's behind. He said, still urbanely:

'It was Kismet, wasn't it?'

'Very funny, Ha Ha!' I snorted.

'He'll never make the coral barrier,' Sharon said suddenly and surprisingly. He turned to her acknowledgingly:

'*Ja!* That is so but I'll do that myself—little sister.'

I looked astonished. 'Little sister?' I reiterated.

'Yes, Garway. I am his "little sister".'

'And she loathes my guts, don't you, *schöne* Hildegarde?'

'Yes, dear Hardy, I do.'

'I always said Sharon Saxbee was a *nom-de-guerre,*' I retorted, 'you could knock me down with that ole proverbial feather. So you are on opposite sides of what ever it is we are fighting about.'

Schultz imitated me, 'Very funny, Ha Ha!'

He spoke softly to the stooge.

'Manduran?' I asked Sharon but her brother answered:

'No, not Manduran. Hildegarde—er—*so sorry* Sharon understands Manduran. We lived here as children. We were anxious to come back but by then we had—er—lost confidence in one another, and so I teamed up with Minoru Oko because, of course, he was there as you no doubt know.'

I didn't.

The M.T.B.'s engines were suddenly pulled down to almost zero. Schultz cocked his leonine head and listened, then nodded.

'The barrier. Do please excuse me. It's a delicate operation. I won't be a moment, I must pilot us through.'

'What's the itinerary. Round the lighthouses or Southend Pier?'

He paused as he reached the companionway—paused dramatically then said: 'You know something, Trenton? I don't think you'll ever see Southend Pier again.'

'Charming!' I exclaimed.

'If Mango wasn't Robespierre——' I began, trying to wrap it up so that if he understood English he couldn't translate. 'Maybe he isn't either.'

'I don't dig you.'

'Robespierre, you know. Didn't Roedean teach you anything?'

'Westfield.'

'Oh yes, sorry. Robespierre—the "sea-green incorruptible", get it?'

'Nearly.'

'Well if our chirpy double-crossing chumsie wumsie did the dirty. . . . I mean, maybe every man has his price.'

Sharon 'got the message', contemplated the idea for a moment, sipped her drink. This movement put the guard on his mettle.

'No throw dlink!' he cautioned.

'I don't think our goon will take any mazuma,' Sharon said, also wrapping it up. I thought how strange to hear Sharon, formerly Hildegarde Kraut, using the word 'goon'.

I said, 'I've got one gag I can pull. It won't work, but it just might throw the jolly old geezer off centre, if you perceive my drift.'

Our armed thug had had enough. He wasn't getting what we were saying, and so he played safe.

'Shut up!' he commanded. He was still expecting us to hurl the glasses so he raised the Sten ominously.

The M.T.B. engines were now back at half throttle. I chanced one more sentence. 'Confucius he say best time noisy-noisy M.T.B.'s go, man, go.'

'Shut up!' The guard moved forward to clout me with the

Sten, thought better of it, for if he got within range I just might pull a fast one, eased back. Then I pulled my stunt. I drank another gulp of my whisky and as the engines zoomed to full throttle, I uttered a garbled half choked throaty rattle, gripped my throat, assumed the most terrible agony, made a splendid topple to the deck—a performance that would have had Alfred Hitchcock giving me a standing ovation from his aisle stall.

I moaned and writhed. Sharon screamed and the guard did *absolutely nothing.*

Clearly Hitchcock wouldn't have been very pleased with my performance after all. Amid her cries of terror and splendid efforts to revive me, Sharon slipped in a couple of pig Latin comments. 'Onay Ixnay!' She shouted in stentorian tones, 'ipskay itnay!'

By now the guard was laughing and I reckoned I'd had it. I was just about to get up and admit I was *crême de la crême* of the Berks when there was a sudden lurch and Sharon and the guard fell on the deck. The Sten fell out of the guard's grasp and I had that gun and was on my feet before you could say Danger Man.

There was one hell of a bloody noise on deck and, intermingled with his cries of terror, I made it pretty clear to our erstwhile guard that to make a sound would be a very foolish thing to do, not that he could have been heard due to the rumpus on deck.

'How marvellous Hardy has cocked-up getting through the barrier reef!' Sharon exclaimed excitedly.

'Is that tricky?'

'Oh, my word, yes!'

There were shouts above and a rasping sound as one of the ship's sides scuffed against the scaly crustaceous side of the reef. Without my cueing her, Sharon was looking around to find something to tie up the goon. She located some rope in a lower cupboard and I motioned the guard to sit on a chair. Sharon seemed to relish tying him up and ramming a gag in his mouth. All the time I was wetting my lips and swallowing and watching the companionway, expecting trouble, but, from the noise above us, Kunhke-Schultz had plenty of trouble on his hands above deck.

It would appear that he had, after several nasty smacks broadside onto the barrier reef, which because of the tide was difficult to avoid, at last managed to get clear and had returned to the quiet of the bay and turned to try once again.

'Hold onto your hat, Gar'. He'll make another stab at it any time now,' Sharon predicted, and added with a snigger, 'I'll laugh like hell if he cocks it again.'

I forgot my fear for a moment or two while I looked at her, I suspect admiringly and with astonishment. It was a mad, mad, mad world. It was the womenfolk who were the pioneers, the doers, the ones who girded up their suspender belts and went out pioneering. It was the women who wanted adventure—Sharon, like One-Eyed Reba, obviously thrived on adventure. The sudden throttle-up of our twin Rolls engines brought me back to the present.

'About now!' Sharon warned me.

We gripped the wardroom table as the M.T.B. zoomed towards the gap in the reef. There was another nasty rasping, scraping sound and I thought the bottom was about to be torn from the boat. It shuddered as if it were hurt.

There was a little hysteria in Sharon's laugh. She yelled: 'He's not dead centre! He'll break her back, the idiot!'

There was another terrifying rasp and then, as we held onto the goon's chair to ensure that he didn't fall, we shot upwards as a wave carried us through the cut and we were over.

'He's made it!' Sharon said. 'Now, this is probably the best time to jump them—while they are still talking about the reef.'

'Good-o,' I said. 'Good luck! What's the plan?'

'Over to you, my Captain.'

'Lissen, Sweet Doll, this Captain hates the sea.'

'Nevertheless. . . ?'

'Nevertheless we'd better go straight for your charming brother——"

'The bastard!'

'Was he? I didn't. . . .'

'Let's get weaving. You jam that Sten right——'

'In the small of his back. Check, dear Sharon, or should I call you Hildy?'

'If you ever do, I'll take that self same Sten. . . .'

'Not now, dear heart, later, if and when we escape.'

'Oh, there's just one thing,' Sharon cautioned, making for the companionway, 'try not to fall overboard, at any rate till we're back inside the barrier reef—there are sharks at the bottom of our island.'

'Sharks?' I said in a small voice.

'Man eaters. Whoppers, and they love Old Etonians.'

'Very funny,' I whispered, 'let's go.'

I held the Sten away from the ladder and started to climb when there was a shattering crash, the lights promptly went out and an unholy cacophony of sound smashed against our ears, a combination of reversing engines, the scream of burst pistons, of escaping steam, the signature tune which meant a machine gun.

I had fallen back on Sharon and the guard, tied to the chair, had fallen on his side. I knocked him as I got up.

'What in hell's happened?' Sharon asked. Even she sounded frightened.

'I don't know except we've been holed!' I shouted. I could feel the sea surging ankle-deep into the wardroom. 'Get up that companionway, fast!' I ordered. I pulled Sharon to her feet.

'Yes, but which way is it?'

'Close your eyes for two or three seconds, then try,' I suggested. Already the water had risen and was around my calves. I followed my own advice and when I opened my eyes Sharon was already several rungs up the ladder.

I remembered the goon. I waded quickly across and got to him just in time. His mouth was underwater and partly open because of the gag, he was gulping in part sea-water, part air. With a bit of an effort I was able to pull the chair to an upright position and yanked the gag out of his mouth. He gurgled and gasped for air and I tried to untie him. Sharon had done an excellent job and, coupled with the fact that the sea water had tautened the knots round his ankles, it was tricky.

In desperation I rushed to the table drawer, which I could just discern silhouetted in the darkness and found a large carving knife. I think the Manduran thought I was going to take the easy way out. His face was terrified. I cut the ropes and quickly freed him and, taking no chances, preceded him to the companionway with the Sten pointing at him. I was often a mug, I agree, but some of the time, not all the time.

It was lighter near the hatchway and I could see Sharon's trim ankles on a rung above. I butted them with my head and she moved up and out of the way. The ship was listing to starboard and was fast going down by the stern. The noise was nearly deafening. We had come up by the bridge end and a member of the crew was loosing-off a sub-machine gun at another M.T.B. which was fast backing away. I clobbered the boyo with my Sten and as he fell sideways I gave him a neat trip so that he fell for six. I was just about to kick him overboard when I remembered the sharks.

I looked round for more assailants, and one in particular, but Kunhke-Schultz wasn't to be seen. If he was hiding on deck, he was doing a good job.

'Duck down by the helm!' I ordered Sharon.

Tracer from the other M.T.B. was ripping the side of our craft, fortunately below the waterline. Suddenly there was a nasty deafening kerwhoosh! as something below blew up. We were knocked back several paces by blast. There was a sort of sub-human cry from one man as he was swept into the sea. I picked up Sharon, who was winded and lying beside a deserted Pom-Pom gun, and as I helped her to her feet the boat shook violently as if in the middle of a typhoon. It was as if some mighty super-natural force had taken us and was shaking us to pieces.

'Let's go! Let's go!' I called out. 'She's sinking.'

In the distance I was conscious of a dinghy with an outboard motor skimming fast across the lagoon back to the port. Kunhke had scarpered and I certainly didn't blame him.

'Come on, woman! You can swim, can't you? Well, jump, girl, jump!' I started to lug Sharon to the ship's rail, the lower rung was well under water. She screamed piteously, 'No, Garway! No. Sharks I tell you, man eating sharks!'

In her fear she fought me with the strength of ten. And then as if to confirm what she had shouted, there was a terrifying, almost sub-human scream from the sea. The Manduran who had been swept overboard disappeared from view. The other man, the one who had been guarding us, lay gripping the rail praying to whatever God he believed in.

I knew we'd be sucked under with the ship but there was just a chance we could swim back to the reef before those snapping jaws got us. I began to tug Sharon to the stern shouting my plan. I cursed the day she had persuaded me to write the script of her wretched book. I wasn't winning and I wasn't winning fast when the M.T.B., which had apparently caught Schultz unawares as she moved away and presented a three quarter stern view, flicked on a searchlight. We were caught in its beam and were a splendid target.

As suddenly as it had been switched on, the searchlight went out. But the M.T.B. swung hard round and made towards us again. By good luck someone had, I presumed, seen Sharon.

Soon they were alongside. They swerved broadside on, and with a very slick piece of seamanship whipped us off—the three of us, for we still had the fear-crazed, praying guard. They pulled clear as Schultz's boat started to crack up.

As we were helped aboard and sheered off, a voice I would for ever love spoke up, carefully clipping the final g's in most of his words.

'Astonishin' near thing, eh? A bit naughteh on a nice evenin'.'

'Good God! Uncle Steve!'

'Uncle Steve!' echoed Sharon exultantly. 'We—we thought you'd had it.'

'To use a phrase I deplore,' Uncle Steve replied, 'not on your Nelly!'

CHAPTER FIFTEEN

'Come on, Uncle Steve, out with it—what happened?'

'Oh, you mean at the Sportin' Club?'

'Of course we mean at the Sportin' Club?'

'Very naughteh, very naughteh indeed, cuttin' those wires, puttin' us in the dark like that. Where was Moses when the light went out—what?'

'So?'

'Well, I realized something might be up. Hope you didn't mind, I thought they were after you, Trenton, after all, you were dancin' with Reba.'

'What?' Sharon positively exploded.

'Yes. Bit smug of her turnin' up there. After capturin' our Prize Specimen here.'

'You mean to tell me you actually danced with Reba?'

'Is that so crazy? She was at the Sporting Club. Come to think of it, I think it was an *Excuse Me*, anyway.'

'Tommy rot,' growled Uncle Steve. 'Never have the things—think it's some bally palais-de-dance, Trenton?'

'Well, anyway, Reba came up and asked me to dance,' I continued, rather lamely.

'You—you Rat Fink!' Sharon spat vituperatively.

'Go on, Uncle Steve,' I said, trying to change the subject. 'What happened to you?'

'Well, because that minx was dancin' with you I reckoned they'd cut the wires in order to abduct you again,' Uncle Steve said.

'I ruddy well wish they had!' Sharon added petulantly.

'Frankly, I nipped out the back way.'

'And where were you when all this was happening?' Sharon demanded.

I decided it wouldn't be diplomacy to tell her about Reba and I lying on the Sporting Club floor. Instead I said, 'I thought they were after me, but nothing happened. When the lights went on again Mango rushed in.'

'That was the double-bluff, everyone at the Club would now be able to alibi Mango——'

'Mango! Now there *was* a Rat Fink!'

'We fell right into the trap—we followed Mango thinking you'd been snatched, Uncle Steve.'

'I wouldn't be any use to 'em.'

'Well, that's as maybe. They could have been very, very unpleasant, you were a perfect hostage——'

'Instead they were after bigger game—they wanted Garway *and* me,' Sharon said. There was a pause whilst she thought about it, then: 'That dam' brother of mine! You've got to hand it to him,' she added admiringly. 'It was nicely executed.'

'What's the next move—report your brother to the police?' I asked.

Sharon turned to me and looked at me in utter astonishment.

'Moonlight becomes you,' I sang softly, 'it goes with your hair, et cetera, et cetera.'

'Garway Trenton, are you completely bonkers?'

'Sharon Saxbee, *née* Hildegarde Kunhke-Schultz, you must be the only girl I know who uses the expression bonkers.'

'Don't try to evade issues. If you really think I'd go to the cops, well I—I don't think I want to marry you.'

'Boo hoo! I was going to ask you if we could change *our* name from Trenton to Kunhke-Schultz, it would look good on the front of my novels next to my colophon.'

The dawn was coming up, Kipling-fashion, in thunderous great squall-like clouds, billowing wrathfully on the horizon, the greys, indigos and deep purples, and the windsor blues were giving way to cobalts and ultramarines and. in the distance, there was a slash of scarlet like a great knife wound—this was the dawn of another day in the tropical island of Mandura. But Uncle Steve did not eye it with a painter's relish, he was biting his underlip. For a man who pretended not to worry, Uncle Steve was, nevertheless, worried.

'"O, what can ail thee, Knight-at-arms alone and palely loitering?"' I inquired. Sharon was thrilled. I stopped her waxing enthusiasm.

'I know! I know. It's your favourite poem—or one of them.'

'Yes, how did you know?'

'I also know you like *Morte d'Arthur* and ballet and the balcony scene from *Romeo and Juliet*, you like thick wool stockings in winter up to your knees. You light candles to St. Francis, on account of your animals—and by the way you can get them to stop hunting deer here, the bastards, they keep 'em as pets all the year round, then let them loose and shoot them—charming! And you also go on holiday to Florence, subscribe to the Home of Rest for Horses at Elstree and think bullfighting has something. You crazy, mixed-up, enchanting Kunhke, you!' I said.

'Quite finished?' Sharon inquired icily.

I nodded, 'Except,' I continued, 'to ask Uncle Steve again, what ails *him*.'

'Bloomin' dawn. I shouldn't have rescued you, we'll be late for the rendezvous.'

'Thanks!' I said sarcastically. 'What rendezvous?'

As always I was ignored. It was clear that as a youth I should have subscribed to some of those magazine adverts, sent for the pamphlets, you know the ones, 'They laughed when I sat down to play' and 'Are you shy? Do your hands perspire because people ignore you?' Clearly I hadn't the right presence. I remember once at an Admiralty Selection Board I was asked, 'What happens when you go into a bar and order a beer?'

'I wouldn't, sir!' I had said with super *savoire-faire*. 'Up spirits, eh, sir?' I nodded knowingly. I all but winked.

'I don't give a dam' what you'd order, man.' The gent in the gold uniform with the bit of blue on it snorted, 'What I want to know is would you get service?'

'Eh?'

'Do you command respect?'

'I beg pardon, sir?'

'Have you a *presence*? Do people take notice when you enter a room, do you command respect when you order at a pub?'

I recall I had contemplated that for some time before deciding that honesty was the best policy.

'No, sir,' I had admitted. 'I don't think they pay much regard.'

I remembered Uncle Steve. 'What rendezvous?' I asked again.

'Oh, dry up!' Uncle Steve retorted.

'Now look here!' I began belligerently.

'Shut your trap!' Uncle Steve commanded. 'In fact,' he added, 'fry your face!'

He muttered something to Sharon and then took the wheel. To starboard lay the island and to port a group of small islands, probably no more than half a mile across. They stood up, razor sharp, jutting imperiously in the crimson flush of dawn behind them. Uncle Steve was now making for these at a terrific rate of knots.

'Dear kind, patient Sharon whose novel I am so keen to adapt for the screen, please to tell me just what are we up to now? Please, take thirty weeny seconds from your crowded day *and tell me what we are a-doing of*!' I shouted.

Sharon sighed. 'We are about to earn our bread and butter,' she explained as if to a child, 'and with it we will be able to pay for all the things—the equipment——'

'The tanks, M.T.B.s, sub-machine guns, Oerlikons and Stens——'

'The equipment,' she repeated, 'to finance the real scheme.'

'The real scheme?'

'Oh Trenton, *please*. . . .'

I was about to persist when I noticed a light flash about seventy-five degrees to port. The look-outs hadn't seen it so I mentioned it to Uncle Steve. He berated his crew and thanked me. 'It should come on again in another thirty seconds,' he imparted.

We were all looking in the right direction when the light flashed on again. It gave a call sign—just 'Hi'.

'Good!' Uncle Steve murmured.

'Would I be *de trop* in asking if Hi is as in Hi ya or Hi as in High Noon?' I inquired.

'Hi is O.K.,' Sharon replied.

'Once again, thanks for absolutely nothing. All I want to know this time is do we want to keep our equalizers at the ready?'

'It's always a good idea but I can't believe Sharon's charmin' brother knows our call sign!'

'I wouldn't put it past him,' Sharon replied acidly.

As we approached the port of rendezvous everyone was very quiet. Even I decided that this was not the time to ask questions. One of the crew, a squat, thick-set Manduran with a sweat band round his head, dark skinned, proud flashing eyes and wearing only old Chinese-type trousers, went to an ancient Bofors and made it ready. It was quite clear he wasn't wearing L plates. Uncle Steve took out his eyeglass and with slow deliberation polished it on a silk handkerchief. I goggled at his cad shoes, out-of-this-world, so utterly ridic'. I couldn't resist saying to Sharon, 'Uncle Steve's shoes——'

'He is rather *outré*.'

'I suppose to the people of his generation he was a toff,' I said to Sharon.

She nodded. 'Heart of gold.'

'Tough as tungsten,' I added.

She looked at me, you know how it is, sometime when a woman does this and you know—there's an inner glow. It wasn't now a sort of nympho-possessiveness. It was a genuine—for want of a better word—togetherness. We were man and woman drawn to one another, not so much by admiration as by the fact that we had shared emotional experiences, albeit sex, adventure, excitement, danger and our adrenalin had tingled danger high. We had come out of these experiences knowing how we had behaved, knowing our strength and frailties and upon totting these up a fusion, warm, appreciative, pleasing had formed: Sharon and I now co-existed happily where before there had been tension, attraction by contrast, calculation, animal desire probably, and friction, attraction-friction. I slipped my hand over hers.

'Big hands, Gar'!' She would have liked it to have been a murmur, but that was impossible because of the powerful noisy throb of the engines. But no one else heard.

'Big hands, cold heart,' I said gaily.

'You've got it wrong, it's warm hands cold heart,' Sharon contradicted me.

'I know. Only joking. So I've got warm hands and big ones and please don't be coy and tell me they are artistic.'

She took one and, peering round to make sure we were unobserved, cradled it against her face. A wind-swept, sun-tanned face albeit soft, peach-like, utterly feminine. 'Artistic, though,' she decided.

I emitted a mock groan. 'Oh don't!' I pleaded. 'I'm about as artistic as a hippo!'

We were now leeward of the nearest island, behind which glowed the first rays of the sun, apricot, saffron and a rift of gold; shortly there would be a swift change as dawn took over from night.

I gently mocked my Juliet but already I had lost her, already her eyes were intent upon the scene above, anxious for action, breath abated for possible danger. I realized I could never hold this one; she was like some quivering race horse crossed with some Machiavellian spirit sired by a Borgia!

I sighed. No, this one really wasn't for me. I mean for keeps. And what of Clytemnestra, the ice cold, torrid Reba? She was all Sharon was not.

'Stand by!' Uncle Steve said. We stiffened the sinews and summoned up the blood as we went to half throttle. We approached a medium-sized fishing vessel, etched in burnt umber against the rapidly changing sky. Sharon handed a megaphone to Uncle Steve. I moved nearer the bridge and saw that his free hand held a .38 and that he had itchy fingers. I knew that he was going to signal with the other a pull out, 'full astern both', as fast as he could say it if we had become snarled-up in another trap.

'How many, Louis?' he asked. A voice with an accent, probably French, answered:

'Two.'

'Two. O.K. Louis.'

'No trouble?' the man called Louis inquired.

'Slight altercation with Schultz,' Uncle Steve said, 'a bit naughteh.'

I enjoyed that 'slight altercation'.

'O.K. See you.'

Uncle Steve called down to the engine room and altered course. To my surprise we swung away from the fishing boat.

'Is that it? Is that all?'

'Hold your horses,' Sharon said.

We throttled back and sped away from the fishing ship screened by the little island and we churned our way seawards where ahead of us lay another island. We sped past this, Uncle Steve cursing the rapidly approaching daylight.

'Blinkin' brother of yours. We'll be too late, it'll be too light,' he moaned.

Past the island, a mass of palm trees, lush vegetation and dangerous tips of rock and reef. We gave it a wide berth and made for yet another island farther to seawards. Once again there was a quick wink of a recognition signal. Several of the crew saw it at the same time and indicated it to Uncle Steve. He nodded.

We approached at great speed and this time there was not quite the same anxiety. Presumably Louis had had some contact already, perhaps by radio. The new ship was a small steamer, the sort of craft that traded between Mauritius and Mandura, short, stocky, plenty of room for cargo. Funny to think it was possibly built at Jarrow or on the Clyde and was now plying its trade in the Indian Ocean.

We went back to half-throttle and then made a seventy-degree turn to starboard, not yet approaching and not stopping our engines, this time we were greeted by a loud hailer.

'Hallo Steve, how many?' a voice with a clearly north-country accent inquired.

'Two, skipper!'

'Two! Oh 'eck!'

I laughed softly.

'That's a fat lot of use!' the voice continued.

'Don't blame me, Barney, blame Neptune or God or Buddha, or whoever it is you do blame!' Uncle Steve retorted.

'Well, they say God made little fishes——'

Sharon and Uncle Steve appreciated this. I didn't comprehend.

'And it'll 'ave to be two. By gum, let's 'ope 'E's more charitable next time!' Barney added, 'O.K. port side!'

We moved round to the port side of the small vessel where a companionway had been lowered. And then, as the crew steadied it, two small figures were hurried from the ship down to our M.T.B. They came down rapidly and we cast off in no time. No more words were said. The two men were hurried down to the wardroom. They were Japanese.

We turned and made for the original contact boat, the fishing craft, and were alongside in a matter of minutes. The two Japanese were brought on deck and hastily transferred to the fishing smack.

'Two it is!' Uncle Steve said. There were some *ad lib.* good-byes and we moved off, returning to the port where the battle with Kunhke-Schultz had taken place.

'H'm!' Uncle Steve snorted, 'Barney's right, you know, you can't get rich on two. Never mind,' Uncle Steve added, 'perhaps tomorrow, four. . . .'

Tomorrow four? What were they up to and how did this fit into the chicanery?

CHAPTER SIXTEEN

As we approached the port the sky suddenly went mad in a frenzy of swiftly changing colours, salmon pink, apricot, orange, carmine and rose tyrien, and then an all-over citron yellow that held for a few moments. Finally the sun was up in full splendour, the sky cerulean and it was daytime in Mandura.

I gasped audibly. 'Old Sun God Phoebus is certainly doing his nut,' I said.

'I thought you'd be impressed,' Sharon who had been studying me said, adding, 'if you had read my novel properly you'd have remembered a very vivid description of dawn breaking over the lagoon.'

'I do remember. I did read it, but somehow—the real thing. . . .'

'Thanks very much,' Sharon snapped tartly.

'Toppin',' Uncle Steve observed, rather shyly. One felt that such things as poetry, discussing sunsets and sex (other than physical joke sex at a stag dinner or Soho Strip Club) were strictly taboo.

'Look!'

On the reef, in their caiques Mandurans were attempting to salvage what was left of Schultz's M.T.B.

'I suppose your brother is now on shore behind a battery of naval guns?'

'If I know my brother he's fast asleep—and not giving a dam' about us until he's had his kip.' Sharon looked sideways at me. 'Probably with Reba.'

I though for a moment and pretended to be jolted. 'You mean he and Reba are lovers?'

Sharon shrugged her shoulders in pretended indifference. 'I should be very surprised if they weren't.'

I was suitably silenced for some seconds, then inquired: 'How did she lose her eye?'

'I don't know—there are plenty of rumours—the most idiotic of which is the one about an indignant Creole wife who had an attractive Creole husband. . . .'

'What is alleged to have happened?'

'The wife appeared at a most undesirable moment with an umbrella!'

'Surely no one believed that version?'

'It's the most charitable version there is.'

'People! Take Roderick Vandaleur, for example, the stories about Roddy's slash on his cheek.'

'What about it? It happened when Roderick was a student at Heidelberg,' Sharon stated categorically.

I laughed out loud.

'You're joking, of course.'

'What do you mean?'

'Uncle Steve, was your favourite nephew ever at Heidelberg?'

Uncle Steve chuckled. 'Don't involve me, young fella.'

'You know jolly well, sir, if Roderick was at Heidelberg, he was flogging fencing swords to the students,' I retorted.

'But he got it, he received the cut in a duel, you know that,' Sharon averred.

I laughed again. 'There are other versions, a knife fight in Cuba, rescuing a tart in Limehouse and in a beat-up over a poor old horse that was being thrashed in Mexico City. Good old Roddy!' I added sarcastically.

'What the devil are you trying to say?' Sharon furiously spun me round.

'I'm not trying to say anything. I'm telling you the various stories I have heard about Roddy's knife cut.'

'You are insinuating that they were all composed by Roddy.'

'I'm not insinuating anything of the sort but I will tell you what Roddy told me.'

'About what?'

'How he really received the knife cut.'

Sharon was silent as if she anticipated that she would not like the answer. It was Uncle Steve who broke the silence.

'Well, go on, then, Trenton,' he requested.

'We really don't want to hear about it,' Sharon said sharply.

'Indeed we do. It might be different from the one I heard,' Uncle Steve said with a chuckle. Sharon sniffed angrily.

'It was after we'd won the Inter Collegiate Boxing Cup for

Balliol. Roderick was a bit stoned and confessed he had paid a Harley Street surgeon to do the necessary for him—to make him appear more attractive to women.'

Uncle Steve slapped his thigh in appreciation of this.

'That's the best version of them all because it's more than likely the truth,' he said.

As we came alongside the quay a grey uniformed Manduran policeman, unshaven and untidy, revolver in his belt, approached the M.T.B. When the bow was out he stepped aboard, politely saluted and spoke in Manduran to Uncle Steve who replied. A few of the native crew exchanged quick looks. He proceeded below and, on finding nothing, returned on deck. I inquired 'Does he do this after every trip?'

'Oh, they're around. Trouble is the Roberts are also the Customs chappies—you never quite know who you're dealin' with.'

By the wheel were two tatty old fibre cases. They were similar to the ones the treacherous Mango had used. I didn't have to be told what was in them.

Uncle Steve looked intently at them for a moment and then to my surprise, brought them forward to his ankles.

'No use tryin' to hide 'em, he whispered to me. 'That fella Churchill had the right idea: "Be Bold!" Good motto, eh?'

The copper returned from an abortive trip below and, while we waited permission to disembark, ignored the two prominent cases and crossed to the ship's armament and examined it intently. He sniffed the breach of the Bofors, appreciated that it had been fired, asked Uncle Steve about this. Uncle Steve played it very cool and apparently the cop was satisfied. He nodded, saluted and left the boat.

'What did he want?'

'Wanted to know if we were involved with last night's fracas.'

'I should think he bloody well must have known about that!' I averred.

'They're a very tolerant people.'

'What about all this bloody cutlery?' I inquired, indicating the ship's main armaments. 'I suppose you told him this was for rabbit shooting.'

'Not at all necessary to be facetious, my boy. Protection!' Uncle Steve patted the Bofors with affection.

'Protection against what?'

'Hostile tribes——' Uncle Steve began smoothly.

'Hostile *what*?'

'Natives — er — maraudin' tribes, bandits from — eh — Mauritius. . . .'

'Mauritius? They're known to be as friendly as they are here —besides, it would take them days and nights to paddle here,' I said accusingly.

'Then, too,' Uncle Steve urbanely pattered on, 'there are whales, of course.'

'Whales?' I simply didn't believe him. 'They certainly are a tolerant lot, the Manduran cops!' I said.

Uncle Steve took out his eyeglass, polished it and refixed it before reprimanding me. 'Bless my soul, Trenton-Garway, whose side are you on?'

'His name's Garway Trenton, Uncle,' Sharon corrected him.

'I don't care if he's Freeman, Hardy and Willis. He's no right to question my authority, especially when the police have upheld it,' Uncle Steve said. It didn't really make any sense but I let it pass. 'Come on, *avanti*!' Uncle Steve added. 'Don't forget the suitcases.'

The crew crossed to pick them up. One of the cases opened and out fell a Sten. There was a quick attempt to close the case before the cop, now on the quayside, noticed. Fortunately, he was discussing the wrecked M.T.B. with one of the local inhabitants. The fibre case was closed and we trundled past him to the end of the quay where stood the ancient Cadillac.

As we approached it I said:

'That's funny.'

'What?'

'The car. I mean, we left it half way up that mountain,' I reminded Sharon.

'Of course we did!' She turned to Uncle Steve. 'Hardy?'

'I dare say.'

'But surely my charming brother would have destroyed it, shoved it over the mountain rather than deliver it. . . .'

'You don't think?' I began, approaching it with a certain amount of newly acquired respect.

'He could have. . . .'

'He wouldn't dare.'

'Well, there's one way to find out.'

'Gar' be careful. What are you going to do?'

'See if the car key's in the switch.'

'Well, if it is, don't for God's sake turn it on.'

'What do you take me for?' I approached the car as if I were a Colonel in the Bomb Disposal Unit. I stopped pretty quickly when I got to the car door for, as I peered in, I could clearly see the ignition key in the starter. I gulped and turned to Uncle Steve. 'The key's there.'

Uncle Steve frowned trying to work it out.

'It's a trick, of course.'

'The swine!'

'First thing you know, the chappie who turns on the switch gets sent to Kingdom come,' Uncle Steve pronounced dramatically. 'Now I wonder who'd volunteer?' he murmured looking round for a hero.

'Uncle Steve, for God's sake!'

'Now that policeman. . . .' Uncle Steve moved off to talk to him.

'Uncle Steve, you wouldn't dare!' I shouted in my anxiety. I turned to Sharon. 'He mustn't do it, he simply mustn't. Is he mad?'

Sharon did nothing but stare in horror as Uncle Steve, having talked to the policeman, approached the car himself. Then, galvanizing herself into action, Sharon started to run towards him, trying to pull him back. He had almost reached the car when I, too, joined in and was able to hold him back.

'Oh, didn't I tell you?' he explained.'It's O.K. It was the police. The locals up at the village moved the boulder and the police brought the car down here. This chap——' Uncle Steve indicated the local cop who was now taking a statement from a fisherman about the Schultz boat debris. 'Sorry if I frightened you. Pindo!' He called one of our crew and spoke to him. Pindo took the fibre cases and put them into the back of the Cadillac.

'Suppose I better tip the Peeler for bringin' the car down for us,' Uncle Steve said.

'Tip the policeman?' I reiterated, parrot-like.

'Yes. It's not Scotland Yard, you know. Bribes are accepted.'

I looked at Sharon and raised my eyebrows in despair.

'Come on, I'm dying to get some shut-eye,' I said taking her by the waist and moving towards the car.

By now Pindo was in the driver's seat. He switched on the ignition and was blown to hell.

To me the most extraordinary thing about it was that nobody screamed, for in the distance the noise had set the dogs barking and I recall a flight of birds which rose from the nearest trees screeching, but on the quayside there was silence. People were stunned by the incredibility of it. One moment there was Pindo stepping to the car and the next, after the Godawful bang, there was no car and no Pindo. We were shattered. It was the police sergeant who, giving several strident blasts on his whistle, brought us back to the ghastly reality that it *had* happened, that this was no dream.

All hell broke loose. Sharon started to have hysterics but I shook her so fiercely that I was able to pull her out of it. The police were running round in small circles screaming themselves hoarse. Islanders from their tin huts near the quayside appeared jabbering vociferously. Most terrifying of all, and it took us all some time to comprehend, of poor Pindo there was absolutely no tiny trace. Whilst another car was laid on we retired to the small wooden shack where the local 'harbour master or customs wallah' was housed. The ever-persuasive Uncle Steve assured him that, medically, he ought to open the bottle of brandy housed there in case of emergencies. As Uncle Steve said: 'Damn it, man, if this isn't an emergency I dunno what is!'

We sipped the brandy and pulled ourselves together. I stopped Sharon from crying when I told her her brother was a real charmer—suppose *she* had decided to drive the car? Suppose we had all been in the car. . . ?

Sharon shook her head disbelievingly.

'Hardy couldn't. . . . Hardy wouldn't have. . . .' She was utterly confounded. It stemmed the tears.

When another car arrived, the first thing I said: 'Will somebody identify the driver I don't want to be driven straight to Hardy, Reba and Minoru Oko.'

Uncle Steve took it seriously, looking piercingly at the man. 'You're Maolo,' he said. 'I've been studyin' you.'

The Manduran seemed pleased at being recognized. He cheerfully assured us that he was.

'Believe he has Hawaiian blood.'

'Eh?' I gasped incredulously. 'Hawaiian—aren't we a bit off course?'

'No. Captain Kidd and that other fella, Morgan—they both brought slaves, prisoners, here. Some stayed, either by accident or design. Mandura is teemin' with mixed nationalities, teemin',' Uncle Steve stated.

We took the coast road back for fear of ambush, and the lads with us removed the Stens from their cases and had them handy in the event of trouble. The lush verdure of the countryside made all this velocity and violence seem the more incredible.

'I look forward to the Comet out of here,' I said. 'I feel like Sisyphus.'

'Very funny,' Sharon said, adding, 'who was Sisyphus?'

'He was the bloke who eternally shoved a large boulder, probably the one Oko pushed in the roadway last night, to the top of a mountain only to find it rolled back to the bottom, and he had to start all over again.'

CHAPTER SEVENTEEN

It was a fabulous day when we reached my hotel and Sharon said, 'Tell you what, why don't we go to Purple Baie and swim. You have a late breakfast and a sleep and I'll stop by for you.'

'Good idea,' Uncle Steve said. 'We'll leave Maolo. He'll look after you.'

They handed him out one of the fibre cases which he took comprehendingly. One of the others took over the chauffeuring. I thought, as Maolo followed us into the hotel, this is the third bloke assigned to me. The shark's got the first, the other was blown across to Manila, what were the chances for this chap? I hoped he wouldn't push his luck.

Mr. Hassamal, our splendid manager, orchid in buttonhole was being very unctuous to some new people who were getting into the elevator. The cherub in the pale pink uniform was taking them up to their rooms.

'Ah, Mr. Garway Trenton, an enjoyable evening? Out all night no doubt at the Club Rouge et Noir.'

'Don't tell me people actually become abandoned enough to stay at clubs all night here?' I exclaimed.

'Very droll. Very droll. Can I offer you a cocktail?'

'No. Just some breakfast—and then no calls. I must get me some shut-eye,' I replied. 'By the way, who were those people—dynamite experts?'

Mr. Hassamal laughed at my sally, too much and far too long.

'Steady, it wasn't that good.'

This only increased Mr. Hassamal's desire to give his best. He laughed again, wiping a tear that hadn't materialized from his eye. He should have been at the Old Vic. When he was able, he said:

'No. No. Mere tourists. We are at last stealing a little of Mauritius' thunder—getting some rich South Africans here at last! We're going places in Mandura.'

'I'm going places out of Mandura—if that means there's a 'plane in. It'll be going out soon, won't it?'

'Yes. Midnight.'

'Good. Book me on it. London Airport direct!'

Mr. Hassamal was (it appeared) heartbroken.

'Alas! I have to go. I must pop home and change my library book,' I said.

Baffled, defeated, Mr. Hassamal turned away. 'I'll cook your breakfast immediately,' he said sadly. 'I did so hope you'd write about our island.'

'Don't worry,' I assured him, 'I will!'

The faithful Hawaiian-descendant, Maolo, sat cross-legged outside my room, to the fascination of the newcomers, and my breakfast arrived soon after I had showered. I only half completed an excellent local breakfast of pineapple, coffee, frizzled up eggs and bacon, topped up by a delicious local bread with honey and clotted cream when I simply had to hit the sack. I slept undisturbed but not peacefully. Violent dreams shattered my serenity but I felt better for the rest and I was ready when Sharon called.

She had changed into a Thai silk dress, deep purple with emerald green overlaid in a leaf motif. Green straw sandals that clearly came from St. Tropez. I admired her and she made a mock curtsy. I added, 'as for the shoes, anyone who is anyone knows that St. Trop' has been dead for years.'

'Phooey to you, Garway Trenton—you're just not with it.'

'On a day like this I wish I had Ming here.'

'Ming?'

'Not my Chinese concubine—my Maserati.'

'Oh.' Sharon brightened. 'Well, I have a little something without, which you won't object to.'

It was a white E-type Jag. 'May I drive?' I asked Sharon. 'I love making the cylinders spin.'

'O.K. but no burn-up. I'm fragile.'

'Where are you taking me?'

'Purple Baie.'

'Is it really purple?'

'Yes, about seven in the evening. This is a beautiful island.'

'Yes. That's the irony,' I retorted. 'The scenery's fantastic but raise this idyllic back-drop and you see the poverty, the Sten guns and the volcanic lava! It's a funny thing, but I can't get people to see the wood for the banana trees. Uncle Steve, you, Reba——' I could see that this shaft went neatly home.

'You turn left at the intersection,' Sharon said icily. We passed a crowded open air market. Indians, Chinese, Africans, bartering, lolling, chatting, often laughing.

I asked 'Is the Purple Baie anywhere near the Sporting Club?'

'We pass it.'

'You know, I'd dearly like to look in for a wee moment.'

'Thirsty?'

'Thirsty to see it all again. I just didn't believe it the first time.'

This made Sharon frosty once more. 'You forget I spent my childhood here.'

'Not at all, but I don't see why that should mean that it's a golden island.'

Sharon turned to me. 'It's going to be, Mister, it's going to be!'

'Stop talking like a "B" picture and gimme the facts, Mam. All I want is the facts!'

'I estimate that you'll get the facts in exactly twenty-four hours,' Sharon solemnly stated.

'You mean it?'

Sharon nodded. 'Turn right here.' Having whetted my appetite she then pretended to dismiss it.

' "I'm on a see-saw, you throw me up and you throw me down".' I sang her an oldie, but she grimaced.

'Save it for Reba. In any case, you are out of tune.'

'Are we liable to be hi-jacked by Reba and her cohorts?'

Sharon shook her head. 'I don't think they've got anything that can catch the "E"-type—correction, with you driving, I mean.'

Whether she meant it or not, I acknowledged the tribute gracefully.

'What are the mountains called?' I inquired.

'The Dents de Midi.'

I laughed. 'Who named them, some Swiss miss?'

'Don't forget this is French owned. Whenever they can they name things in French—the main boulevard where your splendid hotel is, that's Boulevard de la Liberté and the intersection. . . .'

'Avenue General de Gaulle?'

'How did you guess?'

We laughed together and Sharon was herself again.

'Great heavens, there's been a Communist uprising!' I indicated the blue bus ahead, the driver had put out a red flag which he was flourishing excitedly.

'*Vive la Revolution!* Up the rebels!' I said.

'Clot. Be careful! That's to indicate he's about to make a right turn!'

In the lush, vivid emerald green fields enchanting doll-like Chinese children were flying kites. Sleepy old men, purporting to be watching bullocks, indolently scratched themselves. The countryside was ablaze with red and yellow irises, plum coloured leafed bushes, light amber palm trees with umber trunks, and banana trees with bunches of vivid green bananas beautiful in their clusters. 'It always seems odd, the way the bananas grow the wrong way round—I mean sort of upside down,' I commented.

'Keep your eyes on the road. We don't want to be gaoled for knocking someone down. You only say they are upside down because you expect them to be the other way up.'

'So?'

'So if you were born here you would have accepted them hanging with the stems down and the bananas in the air and it wouldn't be odd.'

'O.K., you win. You're obviously in a tazzy mood.'

'Never felt less tazzy in my life. Right at the little bridge then left,' Sharon said. Suddenly, surprisingly if one wasn't used to it, a full voluminous white cloud with a swollen grey belly wept and rain pelted down for a few seconds.

'I wish it wouldn't do that,' I complained.

'What? Once a day and then beautiful sunshine.'

'It's like that in Hawaii. It used to annoy me.'

'Some people are never satisfied. It makes everything so lush you should be grateful.'

'What's that stuff?'

'Sugar cane.'

'Really? Mind if I try it? I've plucked oranges in California, tapped rubber in Malaya and I've eaten a coconut straight from the tree in Ceylon but never had sugar cane.'

'O.K. It's quite delicious and it really is sweet.'

'You don't think we'll be jumped?' I looked cautiously into the mirror. We certainly weren't being tailed, or if we were, the pursuer was doing a crafty job. I stopped the E-type.

'Mark you,' Sharon warned, 'the sound of those Cambodian bells and the scent of wild roses and the conveniently tall sugar canes—I mean I couldn't guarantee that I wouldn't feel amorous!'

'Sharon!' I reprimanded, starting up the chariot. 'After that shower the ground is very damp. I'm surprised at your outrageous suggestions. You really are the *derrière*.'

She shrugged her shoulders looking petulant. 'Next right and we are at *Le Club Sporting*.'

We were back in the Club precincts. In the car park were the ancient dependable Citrones (the French Civil Service?), an aggressive '36 Lagonda (the British Consul?), a Renault Caravelle (the new French shipping magnate's daughter?) and a gaggle of Austins, Dauphines, Armstrong Siddeleys and Hillmans.

The Tricolour waved in the sunlight. Under parasols watching the lawn tennis, sat chubby well-corseted French ladies and their men in too-long shorts. At other tables tall bony, equine British women with short hair, long cigarette holders, their men in cream coloured suits, well worn but clean suits and a good sprinkling of Lord Hawke ties. It was all very splendid. Sharon bid good-morning to an elderly foursome playing bridge. Indian servants watched lynx-eyed in case of a sudden signal that some memsahib wanted her chota peg repegged. Occasionally, if they missed a cue, a stentorian 'Boy!' thundered from an oldster whose complexion indicated too many pink gins. It was all very halcyon and dream-like. Sharon and I sipped a Lime Rickey on the terrace.

'I refuse to believe it all happened here only last night.'

'Yes, and the fact that if you pop across to Mauritius you can get a Comet and be back in England in a day.'

'And that's exactly what I'm going to do,' I said finishing my drink. Sharon looked worried.

'Gar', promise me one thing—please stay at least twenty-four more hours.'

'Why?'

'Well for one thing, you haven't seen the island. You came out here to steep yourself in atmosphere, so you could script my novel—you can't leave yet.'

'I've got enough atmosphere to write ten scripts. What's the real reason, Sharon? Come on, you've given me the double-talk —the script jazz that's strictly San Marco stuff.'

'San Marco stuff?'

'Yes. Don't give me those big innocent eyes. Strictly for the birds—the old spinacho! In other words, Alfalfa! Come on, Sharon, give!'

She finished her drink and then turned and said, 'I promise to tell you everything by this time tomorrow.'

'Why not now?'

'Because—oh for God's sake, Gar' why must you be such an annoying bastard? Will you promise not to leave for Mauritius for twenty-four hours?'

I looked down at those innocent, beautiful brown eyes, enormous eyes with fantastic lashes.

'Are your lashes false, Sharon?'

'No more false than anything else—try me?'

'Sharon we are in the grounds of the residential Club. There is as much privacy here as a roller towel in a public convenience. Before you embarrass me, I promise not to leave the island for twenty-four hours but that is my dead-line.'

I said this making it appear final but, in truth, I had no intention of leaving until I found out why Sharon wanted me to stay and Reba wanted me to go.

'Well, if we're going to look at *la maison*, and swim, we'd better go,' Sharon said.

I finished my drink and followed her to the car park. As I opened the door of the E-type, three little Manduran ragamuffins appeared, practically in rags, begging. I fished in my pocket when the Indian car park attendant ran on to the scene, laying about him with a stick. I just managed to get between him and the kids before he could strike them. I thought Sharon was berating him then realized that she was shouting at the children. I called the kids back and gave them more money than I would normally have done. This seemed to infuriate Sharon the more. I tipped the Indian who was now trying to placate me; it appeared that the sahibs and memsahibs didn't like the urchins hanging about.

'Wrong colour, I suppose,' I said giving him his *pourboire*. He didn't really dig me.

Sharon was pretty huffy as we departed for the Legislative Assembly, known locally as the Maison. She couldn't resist a final sally: 'You're typical of all tourists, Garway. You've been here forty-eight hours and you think you understand the island.'

I let it go, what the hell, but my silence only seemed to goad her.

'I knew you were the wrong writer for the script,' she blurted out then bit her lips.

'Well,' I said, 'we agree about one thing!'

'What I meant was——'

'What you meant was that you got this script writing assignment for me as a complete cover for some nefarious scheme I'll be lucky if I hear about before I'm given the deep six and probably not even full Naval honours.'

She was silent, writhing mentally under my sarcasm, then, in a small voice, said, 'If you'd rather not go to La Maison.'

I was about to say I'd go back to the hotel when I thought what the hell. . . . I said, stubbornly: 'I may as well see as much as I can of the lousy place before my parole is up. Remember, I gave you twenty-four hours then I'm off!' Sharon did not reply. Apart from directions, she was silent and seemingly abject and humble. There is always something highly suspicious when a haughty beauty is humble. I suspected arson, treason and great chicanery.

The Maison, or local parliament, was at the other end of the town. One of the Napoleons (not the one who told Josephine he was tired) had once visited the island, and there was a statue to commemorate the visit.

As we parked the E-type, Sharon said: 'Gar'—your coat!'

'What about it?'

'Where is it?'

'At the magnificent Hotel Royal *et* Grand *et* Continental, or wherever it is I'm holed up.'

Sharon grimaced.

'*Now* what?'

'Well, you simply can't appear in the Strangers Gallery at the Maison without a coat.'

'Now don't be silly, Sharon. We are in the tropics not at the Quai d'Orsay, Paris.'

'I give you my word, we won't get in.'

I paid no regard but strode towards the entrance to the building. A splendid Sepoy in a sort of Spahi costume, a bit like the chaps outside Rainer's in Monte, leapt out of a sentry box with a speed that was commendable. Since he thrust a '14 type Lee Enfield with a '14 type bayonet, long and rusty, at my belly, I felt compelled to stop.

Sharon cruised up alongside. 'See what I mean?' she said serenely.

'So where can I buy a jacket?' I inquired, completely tamed.

The shopping centre was a mixture of TV sets (they had no TV!), refrigerators, coconuts, American-style drug stores, a barber's shop—and a gent's outfitters. The salesman—Chinese, of course—could fit me with a nice Harris tweed, off the peg job for ten quid. I refused to pay ten pounds for the benefit of visiting the Manduran Parliament.

'O.K. O.K. Buy *anything* so long as it's a jacket,' Sharon said.

There was a row of terrible blazers purporting to be flannel, of a royal blue that positively revolted the eye. They all had what appeared to be R.E.M.E. badges on them. They were going begging, the Chinese owner said, at two pounds each. The snag was they were all small sizes.

'It's your own fault for being so bloody tall,' Sharon expostulated.

I caught a reflection of myself in a tatty old cracked mirror and I reckoned I could have got a job in a Norman Wisdom film. I said: 'Don't you think the Hon. Members would find me less comic in my own shirt?'

'Rules are rules.'

I kept a watchful eye on Cerebus when we reapproached the Maison. Instead of rocking with laughter at my ridiculously taut blazer, he presented arms. I guess it was the badge on the pocket. Sharon produced an impressive pass and seemed to know the way.

'Do you think Uncle Steve's employed the sentry to look after us or is he always here?' I asked her.

'Very funny,' she said, 'my sides are splitting.'

When we entered the Assembly I realized that the interior had been made to look as near the genuine article in Metropolitan France, the original Paris Assembly. We were ushered to the Strangers Gallery.

I felt a proper twit in my schoolboy blazer, and even more indignant to find half the Parliament in their shirt sleeves. I glared at Sharon and began to divest myself of the coat when an usher hurried up to remonstrate. Reluctantly I put the coat on again. The debate was in French, but I got enough of it to realize that a coloured gent was making an impassioned speech for the poor children of the island. What, he said, was needed more than anything were football boots. With football boots the Manduran children could in time meet Real Madrid in the final of the World Football Cup tie. There were loud exclamations of agreement with this until an aged French diplomat, choleric pink in skin texture, got up and with the Speaker's permission said he was of the opinion that—and it had been proven time and again—the Mandurans, like many other nations, played better football *without* football boots.

At this there was an uproar. The Speaker banged on his desk with his gavel to no avail. Fighting broke out and the ushers tried to intervene.

A rather triumphant Sharon indicated we should go.

We made our way out to the E-type. 'Feel like a swim?' Sharon asked sweetly.

CHAPTER EIGHTEEN

WHEN I reached the hotel the new man, Maolo, had plopped himself outside my door with the inevitable fibre case. Winking knowingly, he playfully tapped the side of it.

'Not to worry, sir. Maolo take good care of you.'

I was almost too tired to worry about this. I nodded and bade him good night.

I don't know if you have tried to sleep in a shoulder holster. It's bloody uncomfortable and so I took it off. I took Horace into the bathroom while I had a shower. I popped him under the pillow when I lay down, clad only in my trousers, and fell asleep.

It was dark when I awoke and someone was shaking me, commanding me to wake up. It was night-time and for a brief moment I couldn't think where I was. I reached for Horace but Horace had gone. A curt voice bade me get up.

The lights flicked on and I found three Manduran policemen in my bedroom. There was no sign of Maolo.

'What's the trouble?' I inquired sleepily.

One of the three cops had what appeared to be sergeant's stripes on his half sleeve. He held my Betsy in his hand, the other was still shaking me. Another policeman was by the light switch, the third was going through the chest of drawers. All three had revolvers, but they were in button-up waist holsters.

'What you do with this? You got permit for this?' He waggled Horace under my nose.

'Of course I have a permit for Horace.'

'Horace—who's Horace? Where's Horace?'

'If you stop shaking me I'll tell you where Horace is,' I replied, narked by his belligerent attitude.

'We find Horace, don't you make no mistake about that. You put on shirt and come with us. What man this Horace? What him do?'

By now I realized what had happened. Reba and Oko had gone one step better this time, they'd sent three phoney policemen. Obviously Maolo had been easily duped. I decided I wasn't going to fall for this. I stalled for time. I said: 'Horace is the name of him.' I pointed at the gun in the sergeant's hand.

'Eh?' He blinked and decided he hadn't heard me correctly. 'What you say?'

'The gun.' I tapped the barrel but he jerked it clear.

'Don't you try to take gun. You try take gun from police—very bad for you. Anyway, you no right to have gun.'

'Chum,' I said wearily, 'all I am saying——'

But I got no further, for the cop going through the drawers had found Ginsberg, my golliwog mascot. By now, the third cop, vastly intrigued, came forward from the light switch. Number Three was clearly a member of the Party. Said he sternly in French: *'Pourquoi est-il noire?'*

'I beg your pardon, I'm afraid I don't *sprechen* the old *deutsch*,' I said with assumed nonchalance.

'French is the official language of the island,' the sergeant said imperiously. 'Now, this doll, why for——'

But the Party Member was back in native Manduran and going it ninety to the dozen. What he lacked in persuasion he was clearly making up for in garrulity, and the sergeant and the other policeman were now nodding in agreement. Finally the sergeant turned to me and said: 'So you mock the citizens of Mandura?'

'Him, full of precious stones,' I said.

There was a puzzled silence.

'In him, jewels, diamonds! Stolen. Stolen diamonds!' I said in bad French. The sergeant got very excited. He put Horace on the dressing-table while the other two policemen crowded round him and began to try to open-up poor old Ginsberg. It only gave me three clear seconds but it was enough. I was across to the bathroom, through the open window and down the fire escape before the sergeant could shout stop in French, English or Manduran.

At the bottom of the fire escape there was another policeman, this one held a .38 in his hand and he was holding it straight at my bonce, and he wasn't shaking me one tiny little bit. I reckoned that the chance of his hitting me from that distance was about ninety-eight per cent. I decided I didn't want to take that sort of chance. I put my hands up.

By now the sergeant and the two coppers came lumping down the fire escape making a fine old hullaballo. This was backed up by the sudden appearance of a cop jeep from the front of the hotel. Two more police jumped out.

'It's a fair cop!' I said. 'And if you were real police you'd appreciate the joke. O.K. take me back to dear old Minoru Oko or, preferably, Reba.'

They were all behaving in such a vociferous and excited manner I was surprised a posse of real police didn't show up to see what all the commotion was about. The sergeant looked pretty silly holding Ginsberg but it takes all sorts to make a world and, anyway, it was my dolly.

I was bumped very unceremoniously into the jeep, protesting my innocence and demanding to see the British Consul, and I shouted to several intrigued onlookers to send for the police. On reflection, I realized why they did nothing since I appeared to be surrounded by the bluebottles.

The jeep moved off smartly with as many of the police as could be accommodated, including the sergeant who seemed reluctant to part with Ginsberg. We drove quickly through the main street and along a route I began to recognize. We were going back to the little fishing port.

I tried a few questions but the sergeant was angry at my attempted escape and he refused to talk. It wasn't until we were back on the quayside, and I recognized the fishing boat the Japanese had been transferred to the previous evening, that he said anything.

'You recognize this boat?'

'I think so—tho' they all look much alike.'

He snorted derisively. He and his colleagues rushed me aboard. Standing in the scuppers, guarded by more 'police' was one very small, very frightened Japanese, beside him the carcase of a large shark. Nearby was another shark.

The sergeant crossed to me and putting his face close to mine he shouted: 'Now I show you, how you do it, eh?'

He issued an order and one of the 'police' went to the shark and with a long sharp knife slit the side of the shark. From its carcase out rolled a very small, very frightened, very alive Jap.

My eyes boggled. I smiled affably. 'Ingenious idea,' I volunteered.

The sergeant crossed back to me, his face contorted with rage. He shook Ginsberg in my face and screamed in fury: 'You think it funny, eh? You enjoy making fun of the island of Mandura, eh? How much you get for smuggling in Japanese?'

I looked at him in blank astonishment then I realized. Of course! This was Uncle Steve, this was Sharon's pocket money, this was their second-string racket!

'Actually,' I began, 'this has absolutely nothing to do with me.' I began to suspect that the suspect police weren't suspect at all.

'Oh, yes?'

'No. No. My name is Garway Trenton. I'm a visitor to the island——'

'Visitor to the island?' repeated the sergeant in his fury. He rapped out another order to one of the policemen who produced sort of notebook, local credentials of some kind.

'So your name is Trenton, is it? Spelt like this?' He flourished the notebook under my nose.

There in front of me was a passport photo of myself and my own name in good clear letters. 'What is it?' I inquired wearily.

'This is the log book, this is the owner's book of this fishing boat. It says here in French, in English, in Manduran that you are the owner of this boat.' His voice though elated now assumed a more dignified manner. He was clearly no stooge of Reba or Oko, this was the gen-u-ine article.

'Garway Trenton,' he intoned. 'I arrest you for smuggling Japanese into the island of Mandura.'

I glugged and was removed once more to the jeep, this time *en route* for the local Bastille.

The gaol was real all right; the gaol was no more phoney than the police.

I was in one of three cells, two were pack-jammed with locals who, I learned, had been on a binge the previous evening. The third cell, mine, was fairly full, but we were special offenders.

There was a man who hadn't paid a local tax, another who had had an *affaire* with his best friend's daughter; the best friend didn't object though the daughter was a minor, he just felt he needed financial compensation. There was another man who had put a brick through his neighbour's window because he didn't like the colour of the curtains. I was prepared to admire this one, clearly an artistic nonconformist but one of the police assured me that the man was colour blind. There was one other 'guest' with us in cell 3, the man who had 'thrown' the party.

All the cells had bars between them but communication was easy. There seemed to have been a lot of people at the party. The binge was called, in local parlance, as far as I could ascertain, a *dinge-ho*. I couldn't find out if they were held for religious, patriotic or just bibulous reasons. They would be started by a Manduran who had a few pence and would announce to his chums that he was going to hold a *dinge-ho* that evening. He then went to his local grocer, usually an avuncular-looking Chinese, from whom he bought a local wine. This was very cultured; it came in a bottle and not a can. It had a French label on it which clearly stated it was *Vin Ordinaire* and it could have been a combination of red biddy, paraffin, shellac, cochineal and meth. spirits. I speak only from short experience with the potion. I was offered some from a generous soul in one of the other two cells. It not only scorched my mouth and took my breath away but I am pretty certain it made my hair stand up straight for two seconds.

One did not only drink at a *dinge-ho,* one danced. One danced as long as one could stand up. The *dinge-ho* usually took place on one of the enchanting pale-cream coloured beaches that were fringed with palm trees beside the super tropical sea. A few of the oldsters appeared with bottles and the local drums, a couple of sad, reedy flutes, a tambourine or two and maraccas. Whilst the musicians warmed-up the drum skins they also warmed themselves with the *dinge-ho* wine.

By the time the chap who was throwing the *dinge-ho* had arrived with his pals, the musicians were really swinging, but it was a sound that would have pained Liverpool.

The police sergeant who had taken Horace and Ginsberg from me had not divested me of my money. I asked in bad French how we could get some wine into the prison. This apparently was no trouble, all we had to do was to be sure that the police had their fair share of it! Accordingly, a sum was donated to police 'charities'.

The police had no objection to a *dinge-ho* being reconstructed in the town gaol because the belligerents were already under lock and key.

For a time I quite enjoyed the *dinge-ho,* but the heat of the gaol and the fact that no enterprising firm had yet introduced any, coyly termed, anti-perspirants, meant that the atmosphere became rank and foetid. I obtained—with the aid of a British five pound note—permission to walk in the small prison yard. This would have been pleasant except that I had a large ball and chain attached to my leg. In order to walk a step I had to hold the iron ball in my arms, like some giant metal suet pudding, which was not only exhausting, but made one appear something of a *cretin.* My guard smoked my Gauloise, while I sucked in great gulps of fresh Manduran air.

I was standing like this when a police corporal appeared and gesticulated that I was to return to the interior of the gaol again. Since I didn't feel I had had my five quid's worth of fresh air, I protested but was informed that I had a guest.

I realized that my visitor would be Sharon. I had no real desire to see her, and since it was clearly Sharon and Uncle Steve who had framed me, I sent a message back that I wasn't seeing visitors. This was agreed by the guards, who benefited financially. Unfortunately the Corporal returned with a glum face—the Sergeant had pulled rank on him (I suspected it was a larger *pourboire* than mine) and my visitor followed the Corporal into the yard. It was not Sharon, it was Reba.

CHAPTER NINETEEN

In the gaol the *dinge-ho* was at its height. The noise—a cacophonous caterwaul, which had grown on me, perhaps due to the *Vin Ordinaire*—was deafening.

'Having a party?' Reba shouted cordially.

'Got any money?' I asked.

'How much do you want?'

'Enough to stop the party.'

Reba nodded and produced some Manduran notes with instructions to the police. She noted the metal plum pudding I was holding. She eyed it thoughtfully for a moment and then said: 'I've enough to get you out of that, too.'

I smiled.

'Surprise!' I said. 'And I imagine for an even larger sum you could bail me out.'

Reba nodded. She looked just as marvellous to me as she did the first time I saw her, though today she wore a simple, exquisitely cut ice-blue shantung dress with matching handbag and no jewellery. Blue dyed buckskin shoes and her eye patch, ice-blue to match the dress. It was a pity about the eye patch and yet there was something rather fascinating about it.

Reba said, 'What are you thinking about?'

'I was admiring your Nina Ricci.'

She laughed, showing off those fabulous teeth. 'No. Not today. Perrugi, but thanks for trying.'

'You get around, clothes-wise.'

'I get around.'

'Would you like me to gaze into the future? Shall I tell you what is in store for you?' I asked and made a few idiotic passes across the metal ball as if it were a crystal.

'I think,' Reba retorted, 'the situation should be reversed. I should predict *your* future!'

'I got the impression that you didn't think I had one.'

'Oh, yes. Yes, I think you have a future.'

'Do *you* share in it?'

She looked steadfastly at me, the most beautiful Cyclops in the world.

'Are you really cruel, Reba?'

'About as cruel as Sharon Saxbee!'

'H'm! *Touché*.'

'I suppose Sharon finds you attractive—in a sort of animal way,' Reba said calculatingly.

'Yes—like you,' I taunted.

'You don't think I'd have left you to the tender devices of Minoru Oko if I had found you attractive,' Reba replied scornfully.

'Maybe I grew on you.'

'Let's get back to basic things——'

'We couldn't be more basic, surely?'

She gave me a wry smile.

'Lift your mind, dear Trenton, above the navel for a few moments. We were discussing your future—and put that dam' thing down, it bothers me.'

I obligingly did so.

'Probably,' I said, 'the biggest clanger I've ever dropped.'

'Do you,' she asked, 'want me to bail you out?'

'It's jolly nice of you, but I think I am safer here.'

'Incidentally,' she asked, 'what did you do to be picked up by the police?'

'Well, that's the puzzle. You see, I could understand *you* wanting me framed——'

'Don't tell me the enchanting Sharon framed you?'

'Possibly, but I have a strange feeling it might be termed protective custody.'

'Look, Trenton, the other day I offered you a lot of money to get you to leave Mandura. Today I'll make you an alternative offer. I can get you out on bail or——' at this she put the cheroot case back in her handbag and produced the Baretta.

'Hey Ho!' I said. 'Haven't I seen that somewhere before?'

'Cut the comedy!'

'You wouldn't dare!' I taunted her.

'No?'

She took careful aim. I gazed at her in blank astonishment, she really looked as if she meant it.

'Bluff!' I said.

It was very silly of me. The gun spat out her answer. There was a searing pain at the top of my left ear. For a moment I couldn't believe it, then, as a warm trickle of blood flowed down into my ear, I emitted a Bashan-like roar. 'What the bloody hell! You cow! You've wounded me!'

I reached down to pick up my incarceration bauble to hop it while I had the chance.

'I nicked your ear,' she said, 'and you still look quite pretty. What are you belly aching about?'

I had expected the gunshot would have brought the prison guard but no one appeared. There was a sudden spurt of sound to the right and just ahead of me, followed by shot number two.

'Hold it or I'll put one where it'll really embarrass you!' Reba said. I obeyed instantly.

At that moment Sharon appeared with the police sergeant.
'Talk of the devil!' Reba said.

The blood was cascading down my neck when the sergeant rushed forward with Sharon. 'What you make, what you make?' he shouted excitedly. He tried to get out his revolver but had the usual trouble with the holster catch. Reba was not one whit worried, the Baretta was back in her handbag and as far as she was concerned all was right with the world.

'I make blood, that's what I make,' I shouted. I felt it a bit unsporting to tell him to search Reba's bag for the weapon; I agree I clearly went to the wrong school.

'How this happen?' the sergeant asked.

'I cut myself shaving, idiot!' I yelled at him.

'Idiot, eh? Cretin, you!' He still struggled with the gun.

I turned to Sharon.

'Lend me a handkerchief, will you, Saxbee?'

She produced the usual stamp-size job that purports to be a hankie if one is a woman. It wasn't much use. I put down my metal plum pudding and dabbed my nicked ear and, realizing that Sharon's hankie wasn't going to be adequate, took off my shirt and began using that.

The sergeant gave up the attempt to draw his gun (I hadn't decided if he planned to use it on me or Reba) and, selecting a key from a bunch attached to his belt, tried to undo my leg guard. It was the wrong key.

As he fidgeted, trying first one key, then another, I stood between two of the most attractive girls I knew, one brunette, one blonde, and I could positively feel the claws. It was as if I had been plunked into some zoo and left between a tiger and a puma, yet the scorn, the vituperation, the enmity they felt for one another did something rather extraordinary as it was as if they realized that I, poor bleeding male, was the real cause of the trouble. Quite suddenly these two seductresses, these divine temptresses, united. They ganged up on me! Their animosity suddenly melted, they were in tune. They were affable, but puzzled. They were pals under the old Lysistrata act. I was Pubic Enemy Number One.

'You didn't come to bail him out?' Reba, one-eyed goddess, inquired, puzzled.

'No. Of course not.'

I resented that hotly. I was worm, I was dirt, I was a lousy maggot of low degree.

'Look here, you two. . . .' I began. My shirt was now covered with blood and the police sergeant still fumbled around trying to unlock my leg guard.

Both women paid no regard to me. Sharon said: 'But you did, of course.'

Reba nodded. 'We don't want him here if he won't join us.'

Sharon nodded. She was beginning to get the same excited expression she had had when we were on the M.T.B. 'I came to apologize for putting him in,' she said.

'Oh, it was you who incarcerated him.' Reba was intrigued.

'Great!' I added my two cents to the fund. 'All I want to do is write a movie script.'

Reba was frowning. 'Now I wonder why you wanted to frame him?'

Sharon didn't want to tell her, instead she said: 'You know my brother dam' nearly killed me when he fixed that car.'

'Oh, that was Oko,' Reba said. 'He's a Jap with a complex—he always resents the fact that the Chinese discovered gunpowder. Actually, your brother was hopping mad.'

There was a pause then Sharon said almost coyly, 'I say, are you going to marry my bro'?'

'Hardy?'

'Don't mind me, ladies, I'm only bleeding to death.'

The women of Troy, Junoesque, impervious, utterly captivating, turned to me, as if in surprise, but only momentarily. Then Reba turned back to Sharon to say, 'I might.'

She looked back at me and then at the guard. I believe she had half a mind to take another shot at me, for she slipped her hand into her bag. I was on the deck, crouching behind that sergeant, before you could say Clytemnestra. I peered round the cop's shoulder as the two girls looked at me contemptuously. Reba brought out her cheroot case and offered it to Sharon, and Sharon actually took a cheroot.

'Going my way?' she inquired. It was as if they were on the Rue de la Paix. They strolled out of the compound as I got to my feet. I really had been made to look a right Charlie. I decided to protest.

'After them!' I yelled to the sergeant. 'That dark one's armed.' I ran forward, forgetting the leg guard, and I fell flat on my face.

By the time the sergeant had found the right key, the ladies had disappeared.

I was taken to the second floor of the two-storey gaol building where there was a section devoted to medical cases. A local doctor was found who bound up my ear asking no questions. My leg guard had been removed and I had been granted permission to buy it. I thought it would make a splendid 'Oscar' for the Screen Writers, which I would donate for the best film script with an oriental background. I was permitted to take a shower and then locked into the small cell.

Suddenly it was nightfall. There was no long twilight. Night suddenly, rapidly enveloped one; from a splendid day there was a rapid switch of colours from crimson to purple to indigo in a matter of moments.

The *dinge-ho* had re-started in the cells below but since I complained I not only had ear-ache but back-ache as well, the prison doctor had given me a pain deadener and I drowsed through most of the noise and finally slept.

I was awakened by an insistent tapping. The *dinge-ho* was still in session. The noise came from the cell window which, of course, was barred. I crossed to it. At the window on a ladder was Roderick Vandaleur.

'Well, I'll be b——!'

'Hallo Gar'. Welcome to our island. Sorry I wasn't here to greet you.'

'What the devil are you doing here,' I said.

'That's a question I could well ask you,' he retorted affably.

CHAPTER TWENTY

'RODDY VANDALEUR—what in hell are you doing?' I repeated.

'Taking a Sabbatical!' he grinned.

'Now come on, Roderick, out with it—what's the game?' I asked accusingly. 'I knew instinctively when I saw a newspaper cutting of you in Sharon's houseboat that you'd have something to do with this.'

'Then why did you come?'

'I came because I thought this was a straightforward writing ticket for the British United Studios.'

Roderick grinned. 'Well, no one's stopping you from scripting—why don't you ask the cops to supply you with pen and paper? I'd have thought a prison was the ideal place to write——'

'You haven't heard a *dinge-ho*!'

'You're joking, chum, I invented them!'

Roderick had not been idle as he talked to me from his ladder. He had a haversack slung around his shoulder and as we chatted he brought out various items which he placed on the outside of my cell window.

'Anyway, I haven't had time or inclination to write since I have been here. I have been gouged, kicked, dam' nearly castrated——'

'Minoru Oko?'

'Yes. I have been bonked on the head, dam' near blown to glory in a wired car——'

'The Cadillac—pity about the Cadillac!'

'Thanks for the sympathy.'

'Hardy Kunhke-Schultz?'

'Who else?'

'He's mad, of course——'

'*He's* mad. Pardon my girlish laughter! I have had my ear blown off, well, nearly. . . .'

'Reba?'

'Reba.'

'Good shot. Reba wouldn't do any real damage unless she wanted to.'

'So considerate for a young woman!'

'What's your beef—you're in the money now.'

'Mate,' I said earnestly, my voice getting louder, 'I've been in the money—for some time.'

'I don't mean a Maserati and a yacht at Monte—I mean aircraft, golf links, winter quarters in the West Indies, I mean——'

'Look Roddy, just what *is* the racket?'

'Hold your impatient horses, Garway Trenton. Let's get you out of here first.' Roderick surveyed the gadgets he had laid out on the sill, biting his lips as he considered the problem.

He hadn't changed much, a little older and no doubt more attractive, thick curly hair, long, black, shiny. The angry glare of the knife cut was very romantic on that almost too handsome face.

He lived for women, and I suppose it wasn't exactly his fault that he was over-sexed, there must be many men who envied him this and his good looks. It was certain that many men, although they derided it, wished they could get away with the ear-ring he wore.

He looked up sharply knowing I was scrutinizing him. He said, half smiling, half quizzical, 'So?'

'So I wondered how it felt to be a bastard?'

'*Et tu, Brute?*' he retorted.

'That phoney scar, the curled hair, the pirate's ear-ring!' I derided.

'Mate, do I grudge you your snares, your wiles—your props?'

'Mine?'

'The Maserati, the inevitable O.E. tie—*have* you got any other ties?'

'Yes, a Fleet Air Arm one!'

'The Gay Boulevardier act, the dinners at the right places, the *premières*—arriving at just the right number of minutes late—the 400—is it still going strong? And Cordets? No! Gar', don't give me the stuffed shirt routine.'

He looked thoughtful. 'I've got to decide the best way to get you out—geli' might be too noisy—on the other hand, to file through their bloody bars is going to take time.' He considered the problem for a moment. 'I wonder if it would be best to rush the gaol?'

I chuckled. 'They haven't used a Sten around here for at least an hour, I should try that.'

'Don't be so sarcastic,' Roddy replied beginning to wire up the window cell bars.

'Why is it Sharon framed me to get me into this place and now you are trying to get me out?'

'Very simply, you told Sharon you "wanted out". Sharon had orders to keep you here until I arrived.'

'Orders?'

'Yes—orders, things you used to get in the Queen's Navee.'

'So she framed me?'

'Well, if you want the explanation about the sharks and the Japs it'll have to wait.'

'But my name was down as the owner of some bloody fishing smack——'

'Yes, I hope you don't mind. I've signed your name to a number of things.'

'Charming. Now see here, Vandaleur——'

But Roderick put his index finger to his mouth indicating quiet.

'Back in a sec',' he whispered, winked and bobbed down out of sight.

I turned away from the window as a cop appeared with a tray. On it was a bowl of fruit, bananas, oranges, sliced coconut and a bottle of *Vin Ordinaire*—this, the guard explained, was with the compliments of the man running the *dinge-ho,* he was sorry I had been 'drafted'. There was a small door in the grille-work through which the tray could be passed without the cell door having to be opened and, gingerly, because I had once attempted to grab the guard's gun as he had opened it earlier, the policeman handed me the tray.

'What, no eggs, beans and crumpets?' I joked.

The cop was not amused. 'You are lucky to get the *vin,*' he assured me, 'after you try to steal my gun.' He shook his head sadly. 'And all the time I have been told the English are gentlemen.'

I gave the guard time to get out of sight and returned to the window just as Roderick did the same.

'Peep-o!' he whispered cheerfully, adding gustily, 'Now, let's just complete this little wiring job and we'll have you out of here before you can say Honor Blackman!'

'What have you decided?'

'A teeny weeny bit of geli', I think. It's neat, effective——'

'Don't blow the whole bloody gaol down.'

A pseudo-crucified look appeared on Roderick's handsome face.

'Look, give me the griff—what's my drill?'

'*Très* simple old buckyorum—you lie on the floor over there!' Roddy indicated just where. 'As soon as the charge is blown you nip out and hop down the ladder. I'll be waiting below in the E-type.'

I nodded. 'I'll have to come back for my brass ball.'

'Eh?'

'A leg guard, I got sort of attached to it. Joke,' I explained. 'I want to give it to the Screen Writers—ah well, I'll apply for it later—it'll be pretty expensive as excess air baggage.'

'I don't know what you are burbling about but go and lie down and double yourself up to protect your head.'

'I am not exactly a half-wit.'

'I know, you've done this bit before.'

'Exactly.'

'O.K. I'm going to pay off the wire now. When you hear all hell let loose in the front of the building, you'll know it's kick-off time.' He must have noticed my expression for he paused on a lower rung of the ladder to say, 'No, no violence. This way, only you will be blamed for the escape.'

Before I had time to answer, he ducked away. There was a pause of what seemed many minutes but probably was only a few, when there was a devil of a rumpus in the front of the gaol and a swift, sudden quick bang as Roderick detonated the fuse, a mighty rush of wind and I felt as if my chest was going to cave in. A shower of rubble cascaded on me. Choking because of the dust and the smell of the cordite, I made my way swiftly to the place where the window bars had been, only their stumps remained. It was a typical Vandaleur job, neat, orderly, Machiavellian, to mix metaphors.

I was out to freedom.

We were away in the E-type as the revolver shots whined past us.

CHAPTER TWENTY-ONE

WE made for the basalt mountain range, and we made for it lickety-split. Roderick Vandaleur drove the E-type exactly as one would expect him to—like Jehu, but his dexterity at the wheel was probably better than Jehu's horsemanship.

'Now that you've raised the alarm and I'm a wanted criminal, perhaps, you'll tell me what dirty deeds you have involved me in, chum,' I suggested.

'You've waited—not very patiently till now they tell me. Another few minutes won't hurt.'

'I always said you were a scug at Eton and scug you still are, Vandaleur.'

Roderick was no whit put out, he looked at me urbanely. 'You didn't. You secretly admired me. Light me a cigarette.'

I sighed. Same old Vandaleur. I took out my case and as I took out two cigarettes he said:

'They're not Gauloises are they?'

'Bleu.'

He made a mock shudder. 'You were always full of ostentation—member of Pop weren't you? I seem to recall your "over the top" waistcoats.'

'"Over the top" sounds more like Hollywood than Eton,' I retorted, lighting him a Gauloise which, despite his protestations, he accepted.

'What's this about your winning an Oscar?' I inquired.

He took the cigarette without thanks and dragged deeply. The small warm glow from the lighted cigarette lit up the scar on his cheek making it sinister.

He replied: 'Piece of cake, it was like your gong in the jolly old Armageddon, they dole 'em out in batches—this year was my turn to win.'

'In your hat!' I retorted succinctly. It was typical of the man that in replying he tried to de-bunk and rile me but I'd had a lot of experience in adolescent days dealing with Roderick Vandaleur. Waterloo wasn't the only thing won on our verdant playing fields. I played it his way. 'What you really mean is you had a ghost-writer?'

He swung round in surprise, for a moment losing control but he quickly looked back at the road ahead.

'Seemed to flick you on the raw, *amigo*?' I taunted.

'How the bloody hell did you know, you crafty bugger you?' Roderick inquired incredulously.

I had said it as a joke but that Roderick had someone else doing the writing was no surprise to me. The thing to do with Vandaleur was to jab while you were in a position to jab. I said: 'Takes you back, doesn't it?'

He pretended not to understand.

'The jolly old English essay prize.'

'Eh?'

'Come off it. The year you won the Richards. You openly boasted you had paid young—what was his name, we called him The Badger. A hyphen name. . . .'

Roddy turned to me in mock horror. 'You realize, Trenton, that you are being highly libellous!'

'Come off it, Vandy old Roderigo! Once a Borgia always a Borgia. I bet you paid this stooge a dam' sight more than the fiver you gave "Badger".'

'It didn't cost me a cent.'

'Not much!'

'I repeat it didn't cost me a cent.'

'But you do admit you had a ghost writer do it for you?'
'But natch,' he replied airily. 'How you go on so! Let's talk of less mundane matters——'
'I bet we'll be mundane all right when we talk about your reasons for registering fishing boats in my name, and shipping in illicitly Japanese tucked into the sharks' tum-tums contrary to the Manduran regulations—what do you get per head for that little dodge?'
'Chicken feed, Gar', chicken feed. Don't be angry with your old Col' mate. All to pay the Manduran rent——'
'The rent including such things as M.T.B.s——'
'Very ancient M.T.B.s.'
'Cadillacs.'
'Very ancient Cadillacs.'
'Stens.'
'Yes, yes, ancient Stens.'
'Not to mention the fishing smack!'
'But you have mentioned fishing smacks and you go on so. Wouldn't you like to talk about my success in Hollywood? Now there is a fascinating city, Trenton.'
'You mean women-wise?'
He made a mock grimace. 'These awful expressions, "women-wise", where do you pick them up?'
I glanced back to see if we were being tailed but there was not a vehicle in sight. We were now climbing the foothills to the mountain range but it was not the same road Sharon, Uncle Steve and I had taken before we had had the fracas with Schultz.
'Don't worry, *amigo,* they won't get you back in the calaboose, it's important to me that they don't. We were talking about women.'
'*You* were talking about women. No wonder someone else won your Oscar for you, you were too busy satisfying the gals to do any writing.'
'I must admire you, Trenton, at least you find time for the occasional piece of tripe.'
He didn't faze me, I had had my anti-Vandaleur vaccine years ago when we sang treble.
'By the way,' I said, 'will you ask your Uncle Steve to remember my name's Trenton?'
'What's he call you, Simon Templar?'
'Everything but Trenton.'

'What do you think of my gay uncle?'

'Out of this world!'

'He is rather splendid, isn't he? Have you seen him do the Charleston?'

By now we had turned off the main road and were approaching a very large white wooden French-Colonial style house, very elegant. The driveway was long and straight between two rows of tall palm trees.

We were silent as we approached and then I couldn't resist, 'Another little item *I* help to pay for with my fishing fleet?' I said dryly.

Roderick turned and flashed me the smile that launched a thousand *slips*.

'You know Gar' I always liked you, you're, you're so—so——' the words tapered away as he searched for the right one.

'Droll?'

'Droll. Exactly.'

As we swept up to the veranda I noticed that we hadn't made the driveway unobserved. One of the ship's crew was standing behind a balustrade, the inevitable Stirling at the ready. Roderick Vandaleur struggled out of the E-type, he was even taller than I and I don't know how he had tucked his legs into the chariot in the first place. The air had a pungent, aphrodisiacial quality.

'Welcome to my Old Kentucky Home, par'dner!' he parodied.

'No par'dner of yours, I trust.'

Roderick stopped and looked intently at me.

'Oh yes, mate' he replied very definitely. 'Oh yes, indeed. Maybe not a willing par'dner. Not yet. But a par'dner, a par'dner all right.'

As we moved up the veranda steps the front door was opened by another of the crew and just for safety, if one could so term it, he had a ·45 in his other hand.

Roderick Vandaleur ignored him. Roddy rarely bothered to turn on the charm for minions. I followed him into the large living room. My eye swiftly took in the fact that steel shutters were fixed to the windows and that they were closed, a coal and log fire burned merrily at one end of the room where Uncle Steve stood, sipping brandy and smoking a cigar, and Sharon ludicrously, in view of the banditry, in an ankle length crimson

Paris or Italian evening dress. She looked startlingly provocative and just to underline this she had a matching hibiscus in her hair.

'Hallo Gar'.' As opposed to our last meeting, she now greeted me with cordiality. 'Hi Van Gogh! How's your ear?'

'Painful,' I replied, 'like the bump on the back of my head, the kick in the middle of my back, the——'

'Garway's become a masochist since you last saw him, Roddy,' Sharon chipped in.

'How's your friendship with Reba?' I countered.

'Now, now! No sly innuendos. It was like——' she searched for a smile—'like two wrestlers who find they have one another in the same hold, they mutually agree to desist, temporarily.'

'What do you know about wrestling—and don't give me a sexy answer.'

'I often went with Roddy to down-town L.A. Great fun. Ridiculous, of course, but amusing. Good showmanship.'

'I didn't know you had been to L.A.'

'There you are. You hardly know a thing about me.'

I thought back to our first meeting when she had invited me into bed practically before I had set foot across the gang-plank of the houseboat *Sad Geraniums for Dulcie*. I tried to keep my eyebrows from travelling skywards.

'I was at Desilu for a time when Roderick was at Culver City.'

I nodded.

'Hungry?'

'No thanks.'

'Brandy?' Roderick invited.

'Thanks. No splash.'

'Here, Trinton,' Uncle Steve said, 'have one of these.' He proferred a silver box in which lay a row of Corona-Coronas. I took one.

'Excuse the fact that I've left the band on,' he said pompously, 'done it on purpose, ole man. A habit one gets into in tropical countries.'

'Oh yes?'

'It's done, you see, in case a fella's perspirin'. Keeps the sweat from trickling down the cigar.'

I nodded, then, sending him up, in case he was doing it to me. 'It's not because one doesn't know any better?'

'Good Lordie, no!'

'Well, how did you like our local Scrubbs?' Uncle Steve inquired.

'Apart from the fact that you've given me a criminal record, I rather enjoyed it. We had—let's see, what's it called, a Bung Ho or something——'

'Dinge-ho.' Roderick corrected me.

'Yes, *dinge-ho*. Highly entertaining.'

'There you are, you see, another bit of Manduran histriona!' Sharon said. 'You'll know more about the island than any of us soon.'

'What with a sentence in the calaboose and smuggling in Japs in the interior of sharks, a gun battle at sea, I think you could say I'm learning the subtleties of the island fairly rapidly.'

'Trenton! Trenton! This sarcasm doesn't become you!' Roderick chided.

Sharon laughed reflectively.

'Now what?'

'I must say you looked super holding that bowling chuck and blood pouring out of your ear.'

'Glad you thought it comic.' I turned to Roderick. 'I suppose I will get an explanation before I catch the midnight 'plane for Alabama?'

'Now, now!' Uncle Steve soothed. 'Steady the Buffs! Hold your horses!'

'Of course my dear fellow,' Roderick replied, 'but I can't help thinking you know it already.'

'I am not bluffing. I haven't a clue.'

Roderick nodded. For a change, it seemed one of them believed me. He demolished a brandy very quickly, then crossed to a beautiful hand-carved Chinese cabinet, selected a key from a thin gold chain attached to his trouser pocket and opened it. He brought out a rolled up map. He took the map to a large table where there was a jade vase with parchment shade on which exotic birds had been hand-painted; there was also a Chinese vase full of wild orchids. I thought, they have everything on Mandura except, of course, civilization—they had had that once Roderick Vandaleur and Kunhke-Schultz moved in.

Sharon moved the vase, Uncle Steve switched on the lamp. Roderick Vandaleur unrolled the map. It was a nautical map of the island. He looked at me triumphantly.

'Recognize anything?'

'The island.'

'Of course the island.'

'It's a Navy map.'

'You bet it's a Navy map. Anything else?'

I studied it more carefully.

'It's a flying map—R.A.F. or F.A.A.'

'Good lord, take a pound out of the till,' joked Uncle Steve taking out the monocle and polishing it with one of those greeny-brown mottled silk handkerchiefs beloved of haberdashers serving the military.

'So it's an R.A.F. map of Mandura?' I said.

Roderick looked at me, waiting for my reaction. Then, since he waited in vain, said, 'Oh come on, Garway, give man, give!'

'What *is* the sixty-four dollar question?' I inquired. '*You* tell *me*!'

They looked at each other, not quite sure if I was pulling their legs.

'Come on you cabalistic plotters——'

'You can't have a Cabal if it's a trio—there must be five!' Sharon said.

'Oh come now, don't be pedantic!'

'Bet you don't remember their names?'

'You're joking. You forget I was educated.'

'Clifford, Arlington, Buckingham——' Sharon began shamelessly showing off.

'Well?' I challenged, 'still want to bet?'

'You're bluffing——'

'Oh yes?' I suddenly caught sight of something I hadn't observed before. On a desk, in the corner of the room, stood a gold statuette. I had only seen photos of it before. I recognized it instantly. It was a Hollywood Oscar.

I grinned. 'I see Mi'lord Vandaleur has brought his Hollywood prize with him!'

They looked at the Motion Picture Screenplay Award and laughed concertedly.

'Oh shucks, it was nothing!' Roderick gagged.

'I'll wager you the Oscar against my Maserati I can complete the quintuplet,' I said.

'You're bluffing?'

'Want to be bet?'

'Yep.'

'You're on!' Uncle Steve said for Sharon.

'O.K.—you lose—the others were Ashley and Lauderdale!' I said.

There were shouts of approval from the others.

'Hand him the Oscar!' Uncle Steve said jokingly.

Entering into the spirit of the mood, Sharon got the Oscar and crossed to me and presented it to me with a curtsy.

I held it for a moment and put it on the table by the map. 'How can you give me something that belongs to Roderick?' I asked.

'Correction, please!' Sharon said.

'Eh?' I blinked.

'I thought you knew. You said you did, Trenton,' Roderick added. I was beginning to perceive their drift.

'The ghost writer!'

'Exactly! Sharon won it for me.'

'It was Sharon's screen play!' Sharon! Of course, Sharon wrote his Oscar-winning script.

'Exactly. Got to keep these things in the family! Well now, the sixty-four dollar question—the map. Look again, Trenton and stop clowning.'

I studied the map intently.

'Is it—is it one I might have had when we liberated Madagascar?'

'Good man!'

'You're getting warmer.'

'It's a F.A.A. map of Mandura and it was of the type issued to the Striking Force on the *Revenge*.'

'Warmer! Warmer!' The others were treating the whole thing as a game but I was getting irritated.

'Oh, for heaven's sake tell me the mystery.'

There was a moment's pause. Roderick looked at me very intently and then put a finger on the map, to the north-east of the island.

'Somewhere here,' he said. 'You torpedoed that Japanese submarine.'

CHAPTER TWENTY-TWO

I LOOKED at Roderick Vandaleur then I looked at the map. His finger pointed to a place that certainly was in the area.

'Yes. Somewhere about there.'

'Come now, young fella,' Uncle Steve said. 'Have another look.'

I still didn't get the message. 'I don't dig you,' I replied, 'what do you mean?'

'Chum, they handed you out a D.S.C. for copping him, you must know where he went down.'

At last it dawned on me.

'Man, I'm beginning to see the light,' I replied. 'What you're asking me is where did I torpedo the Jap sub.'

'Bright boy!' Uncle Steve said patronizingly.

'Trenton rides again!' Sharon said.

'Exactly! But you knew all along, you're just playing foxsy-locksy!' Roderick averred.

' "Sweet Prince",' I mocked. 'Why the hell should I? who cares? So I torpedoed a Jap submarine off this coast about where you're pointing. It was nineteen years ago.' I went into the usual F.A.A. and R.A.F. send-up of ourselves. 'There was I upside down over the *Tirpitz,* ailerons shot to hell, observer riddled with flack, inter-com not working. . .'

'Trenton, exactly *where* did you cop that Jap sub?'

I blinked at him owlishly, trying to read what was going on in that highly dazzling but highly dicey mind.

'Have you brought me all the way here to ask me that?'

'Yes,' Roderick replied blandly.

I looked round at Uncle Steve. In his excitement he had let his cigar go out. I panned round to Sharon, she had that excited look in her eyes, the over-the-top danger look. I said suddenly, 'Do you take Purple Hearts?'

If I had expected her to look embarrassed it didn't work. Roderick laughed softly.

'She doesn't need them. Pure excitement gives Sharon all the kicks she needs—a mere shot-gun has to go off and her adrenalin starts swinging!'

'I'll have another brandy, if I may,' I said, all the time trying to get it in the right perspective. While Uncle Steve poured me a beauty, what Peter Cheyney's characters used to call a three-finger deep one, I said, 'Let me get the continuity. I am in the immortal words of the late Damon Runyon, standing on the side walk, minding my own business, enjoying the amenities of the London scene, you recall what dear old Doctor Johnson said "When a man is tired of London, he's——" '

'Oh fiddle to Doctor Johnson!' Sharon retorted sharply.

'Carry on with your one-line continuity,' Roderick urged dryly.

'I am doing the Gay Boulevardier act, having just sold the Italian rights for a very nice dollop of lire.'

'Never mind the personal publicity, stick to your subject!'

'When Sharon Saxbee, whose novels I knew well,' I said, not being truthful for I hadn't read any of them—'when out of the blue I am asked to write the screen play of her best-seller.'

'Check!'

'If you mean cheque with a "que", they certainly dazzled a nice fat one in front of my money-loving eyes.'

'So you accepted the job, we know all this,' Roderick impatiently tried to cut me short.

'Just a tick, Roderick old chap, let the fella sort it out for himself,' Uncle Steve said.

'"He knows, you know".'

'I don't. Leastways, I am beginning to see the light,' I continued. 'I call up Don Donati at Hatchards and ask him to get Audrey Morrison to send me a copy of the book round——'

'All this name dropping! O.K. so you read my novel,' Sharon said sharply, 'speed the action—you take the job.'

'Not so fast, Sharon, you Song of Solomon you!'

'Have you finished getting your mind acclimated?'

'It's acclimatized, Vandaleur, you've spent too long in Hollywood, and I'm still trying to work out how you get into the act.'

'Proceed, *amigo,* proceed!' Roderick helped himself to a further drink.

'I read Sharon's novel and quite frankly I am surprised.'

'That it was so good?'

'That it really wasn't my cup of tea at all.'

'What do you mean?'

'Well, frankly, I didn't think I was the right script man for it.'

'Why not?'

'Well, if you're not a half-wit you get the bloke who is in cahoots to write the screen play in tune with the original. For instance, you'd probably get Pinter to script Mortimer—certainly not Trenton to script Saxbee. It doesn't make sense. And so, having some slight integrity, I refuse and so they raise the ante; it appears the authoress is mad-keen for me to do the screen play. I am puzzled but I suppose at least I am a very expensive call-girl. I refuse, knowing that they will come back again—isn't it the way of life?—and they do, and I can't resist all those kopeks, so I say O.K.'

'Right, so you fly into Mandura to recce the front.'

'Now, now! Take it easy! You forget Sequence B. Oh, yes, for the record, as they say, I noticed a clipping of you my dear Roderick in Sharon's barge.'

'He came over to chat about the book,' Sharon explained just in case Roderick didn't get any wrong ideas.

'Let's have Sequence B, as you call it,' Uncle Steve said impatiently.

'Sequence B takes place in Rome.'

'Oh that! I heard about that!' Roderick stated with assured indifference.

'Once again I am standing on the side walking minding my own business when I am jumped by a series of chaps who clearly aren't just ordinary "chummies", and it is made abundantly clear that there are a number of people who do not want me to go to Mandura.'

'My brother's mob,' Sharon said.

'Exactly, Barbie-doll, but I'd never heard of Hardy Kunhke-Schultz at that time, remember?'

'Sequence C fade in on the tropical island of Mandura. . . .' Roderick said.

'It doesn't, you know!' I corrected him. 'Sequence C fades in on B.O.A.C. Comet touching down at Tennarive Airport, Madagascar, *dissolve* to airport lounge, cut to medium shot a chappie purporting to present the *Madagascan Courrier*, approaches famous author and this time a nice bribe is offered to Mr. Garway Trenton, a big, big sum of money for Garway Trenton to Harry Scarpa—to take it on the lam! It's a vast organization or rather, there are two vast organizations!'

'They tried that on in Madagascar, did they? I never knew that!' Sharon claimed.

'Stap me!' the intrigued Uncle Steve said incredulously.

'Yup. But by now I'm pretty intrigued. I say to myself H'm, my dander is up.'

'Your pecker is high.'

'Yes, but *not* for the American market.'

'And so at last, Gar', Sequence D gets you here.'

'And now the fun and games really start!' I said.

The trio exchanged anxious looks and finally Sharon spoke. 'Look, Gar', we can explain everything.'

'Good! I hate mystery stories when clues are sprinkled all over the shop, but none of them explained,' I retorted icily.

There was an uneasy silence then Uncle Steve tried to mollify me. 'Trinton, my dear chap——'

'The name is Trenton—with an e,' I cut in frostily; I was on a very high horse.

'Yes, of course, dear fella, with an e——'

'You were saying?'

'I was just sayin'—if you're worried about makin' you the owner of the fishin' smack, is that such an awful curse? I mean the boat's yours, it's a present——'

I couldn't help laughing at the preposterousness of the statement. 'Uncle Steve you're marvellous! You make me the owner of a fishing smack, probably a fleet of 'em for all I know and that makes the whole thing O.K. In a court of law it was a Deed of Gift, I take it?'

'Well, you see——'

'You are illicitly smuggling in Japanese to Mandura in a boat owned by me—that's great!'

'The fact is, me dear fella——'

'Let me handle this, Uncle Steve,' Roderick cut in.

'Yes—give the noble lord the floor!' I taunted.

'It was convenient for us to make you the owner. O.K. we lost out and you were gaoled. We'll make it up to you.'

'What, serve my sentence for me? I don't know the law in Mandura, but I don't think they'll wear that.'

'Look, we've got bigger things at stake——' Sharon began when I shouted.

'Big things at stake when you frame me and get me imprisoned for——'

'Look—it would be true to say that we can get you out of this——'

'How?'

'Well, it is possible to corrupt——'

'Shockin' to have to confess it but it's true.'

'And in a short while we'll have the money to do so—with your help.'

'With my help! *Ca commence*—now we get to it!'

'It's very simple. It is so simple, you'll laugh when you hear it.'

'My laughter will, I fear, have a hollow ring.'

'Not, my dear Garway, when you hear the fantastic news.'

'What do I have to do, apart from not write Sharon's script?'

'The script—of course you can write the script if you want to —it'll depend if you can be bothered. You'll be so rich you won't want to move from the Bahamas for the rest of your natural!'

'I repeat, and this is my final word on the subject—what do I have to do?'

Roderick took a deep pull of his cigarette, inhaled and slowly blew out the smoke with dramatic slowness.

'Locate the Jap submarine you torpedoed.'

'Locate it?'

'Exactly.'

'But how?'

'We know approximately where it is, you know exactly.'

'You mean you think the latitude and longitude are engraved on my heart twenty years later?'

Roderick looked at me critically.

'Listen, Gar', I've known you a long time—when you put in your report you gave all the details, and I am willing to take very long odds that you know *exactly where that sub is*!'

CHAPTER TWENTY-THREE

I DID know. You don't forget those sort of details—not when you're nineteen and they give you a D.S.C. for it. I remembered every exciting moment of it, even though it was twenty years later. I was in *Revenge*, the Commander, Flying, was 'Drunkie' Lewin.* Drunkie and I had been messmates earlier on in the *Glorious*, he was a marvellous bloke, one of the youngest and later to be one of the most decorated fighter-pilots in the F.A.A.

We had had a briefing for a dawn strike. Intelligence said there was a Jap sub working as a 'lone wolf' off Mauritius. A hell of a lot of shipping had fallen to this energetic Nip sub-mariner, including a Hunt Class destroyer, and we were out for vengeance. I recall my Squadron Commander, Tommy Harrington, jokingly saying, 'if you nab him, Gar', I'll give you the biggest party you've

*Later, Captain (A) Duncan Lewin, C.B., C.B.E., D.S.O., D.S.C. and Bar.

ever had when we get shore leave!' Maybe Tommy had second sight.

My Flying A—H—, the photographic observer, was 'Ginger' Bier (who has appeared in several of these narratives). The dawn take-offs had always excited me. The large mugs of tea sweetened with condensed milk, the first rays of dawn's early light, the dry, good-humoured 'cracks' of my Scots air mechanics, and all the time the terrible fluttering of butterflies in the tummy. The Bunting Tosser still using his Night Aldis, just the tiny cross of light, the rest blacked-out.

'Drunkie' Lewin's few words, no bull, no big-time 'Rah-Rah' pep talk; the way we 'drivers' had our own superstitions just before talk-off—Boteler liked the mechanics to take away his left choc first, never the right; O'Casey always made the Sign of the Cross; Jamie Drummond patted his tail plane; I made sure Ginsberg was secured to my parachute. The final move into the wind, the final engines rev, the final O.K. from the Flight Bridge and the zoom off into space. . . .

Somehow we hadn't expected the Jap to be just off the coast of Mandura. We had searched abortively around the Port Louis of Mauritius. It was nine-tenths cloud and a pretty futile mission, and certainly we hadn't expected him to be on the surface. Ginger's voice on the inter-com was almost strangled in his incredulity.

'Gar', forchrissake, starboard forty!'

The cloud had cleared for a brief moment and there in the lee, in the shadow of the coral reef, presumably taking in fresh air, just discernible in faint silhouette, was a submarine. My first thought was that it was one of ours and I said:

'You nit! It's——'

But then the cloud closed in and as I swung round for a closer inspection, I did what must have been the only sensible thing I had ever done in my years with the Royal Navy I anticipated that he had spotted me and would crash-dive. And I anticipated and gauged just about where he would go, and just where I had a chance of hitting him—most of the glory, if you can call any of it glory, belonged to 'Ginger' Bier for spotting him and for plotting me on course when I yelled my plan.

We came down through the skies to zero, sea level, to locate him and I knew that once I had found him I'd have to get up sufficiently clear so that the explosion of my torpedo didn't cop me, too. My anticipation was spot on. We found him crash-diving almost within a mile of my turn.

I made the shortest circle I dared, went up to five hundred feet, came down to three, yelled to 'Ginger' to give me the angle of drop and we got a series of perfect pictures with the P.39 to prove exactly how we copped him. There will never be, I reckon, another moment in my life as exciting, the sudden whoosh as the torpedo caught him, the underwater explosion.

Then, after the enormous exhilaration and exultation followed the nausea, the feeling of disgust and despair as I thought of the Japanese matelots trying to surface. We circled round and 'Ginger', using an R.A.F.F.46 camera (the F.A.A. had R.A.F. photographic issue in those days) photographed the oil splurge on the water, the *débris* and the clamouring oil-gorged Japanese submariners. I think I got my gong for dropping all the life saving equipment I could and radioing for help for the survivors. At least, that's what 'Ginger' and I decided at our investiture. Of course in those days I never thought of sharks . . . yes, I remember exactly the spot, longitude, latitude. I don't know how long I had been dreaming. It was Roderick who brought me back to reality with a gentle 'Well?'

'Sorry chum, day dreaming,' I said apologetically.

'I said,' reiterated Roderick, 'I am willing to take very long odds that you know exactly where that sub is.'

I grinned. 'Could be,' I replied non-committally.

'Of course you do!'

'That's my Gar'!' Sharon said, I thought a shade too possessively.

'But what's the interest? All the gear's a mess after all these years, there can't be a thing to salvage.'

At this they grinned. 'Oh, no?'

'Shall I tell you something interesting,' Sharon said. I adored her when she was serious, everything became so very profound. I said so, and this irritated Roderick. It appeared I was spoiling the drama.

'O.K., beautiful Sharon. *Dis-moi*—give!'

'Do you know what my brother's profession is?'

'I dunno, tax collector?' I quipped.

'Hardy is a salvage expert.'

This surprised me and I must have looked surprised because Uncle Steve couldn't resist a, 'That shook you, my boy!'

'So there *is* something of interest down there!'

'Exactly.'

'Another biographical fragment that will interest you, my old *amigo,*' Roderick said, 'you knew, of couse, there were survivors?'

'Yes, thank God!' I said vehemently. 'The whole mad bloody business. . . .'

'Never mind the too-late sermons,' Roderick panzered through my speech, 'just listen to this—one of the survivors was——' he waited triumphantly for me to guess. Then I got it. 'Of course, Minoru Oko!'

'Right, as they say on TV guessing games, *absolutely* right, Garway, and you got a major prize.'

'They never have any *minor* prizes, do they?' I reflected then asked, 'What was Oko—the Sub-Commander or Johnny-the-One?'

'In those days, a punk kid like you—just a Jap matelot—no specialist. That's why he doesn't know where she went down, but he did know something else and he's got on in the world, has Minoru Oko. Took his little Jap war pension or whatever they gave him when he went home to Kobe and worked and sweated and saved and now owns a fantastically successful Japanese photographic business. You may even have one of his cameras—the Oko?'

'Velly lich man, Minoru Oko,' Uncle Steve had to say and enjoyed it far more than anyone else.

'Reba?'

The three exchanged their superior, know-it-all looks again.

'Reba,' said Roderick, 'was my first wife.'

'Well I'm damned!' I exclaimed. 'Reba—Reba—she was a movie star, wasn't she?'

'For a time, until I took her out of it. Reba Revere they called her, though she preferred the surname, like Garbo or Bergman or Swanson. You can't blame her.'

'It was my nephew Roderick who interested her in the story,' Uncle Steve said proudly.

'Yes. I'd always remembered the rumour we had heard about the sub torpedoed off Mandura in war-time.'

'And I, spending my childhood here, was able to confirm it to Roderick when I met him in Hollywood,' Sharon added.

'When Reba left me, whether out of spite, or because she wanted big dough I don't know, she took up the trail herself.'

'But where did she start?'

'It wasn't difficult,' Sharon explained. 'My brother Hardy was working on a salvage job for a company based at San Pedro. He spent the week-end with me at my house at Westwood. They became——'

'Good friends!' Uncle Steve interrupted and followed it with his inevitable guffaw.

'We don't know how they made contact or found out that Minoru Oko was a survivor or interested in the sunken submarine——'

'It could be he was flogging his cameras on the West Coast at the time.'

'But Minoru Oko was interested because he knew it was true.'

'What was true?'

'The story about the sunken Jap submarine and what was in it.'

'What *was* in it?'

'What is still in it,' Roderick said, enjoying his moment, '*gold bars*!'

'Gold bars?'

'Yup—gold lovely gold bars.'

'Well, why haven't the Japs done something about it before?'

'The situation is somewhat delicate—the submarine is off the coast of a French possession——'

'Torpedoed by a British pilot,' Sharon added.

'I don't see that that matters a dam'——'

'You are right except for one thing——'

'Yes.'

'The Japs weren't supposed to have the gold bars in the first place!'

'What do you mean?'

'It's *loot,* that's what. It's stolen property and they know bloody well if they go after it they've got to return it——'

'Whereas we are able to claim it as salvage.'

'As, indeed, is brother Hardy, Oko and Reba.'

'Or any other smart cookie who wants to go out and get it.'

'What about the Admiralty?'

'The Admiralty do not know that there's treasure aboard so why should they want to raise her?'

'Of course, there was the difficulty of finding her.'

'Only the pilot of the aircraft who sunk the sub would know

the exact position he torpedoed her, and of course the Jap captain and maybe his Navigator——'

'Both of whom were drowned.'

'Frankly, we hadn't reckoned on any of the Jap crew—of which there weren't so many survivors——'

I made a grimace.

—'Getting in on the act. Who was to know that a go-ahead young Jap naval rating was going to become a photographic gear baron with oodles of cash to spare, who remembered only too well what that Jap sub carried that fatal dawn Garway nabbed her!'

'But, surely, anyone who was able to locate the wreck and get out the loot would have to return it.'

'That *is* the difficulty,' Roderick answered grimly, 'you see, the gold bars didn't start out as gold bars.'

'Eh?'

'No—they were gold certainly, but gold from teeth——'

'Charming!'

'Gold from temples——'

'Gold from anklets and ear-rings——'

'Hindo and Buddhist gold——'

'And even Chinese gold.'

'Lots and lots of it, Gar', and the victorious Japs had looted it from Burma and Malaya and Singapore—it had been melted down into nice, solid, velly velly valuable blocks of pure solid gold, my lad. Fascinatin', eh what?'

'And it lies there on the sea-bed waiting to be collected. Now you see why the business of importin' Japs into Mandura is a sideline—mere chicken feed—that's to help the real object of your visit, Trintin!'

'*Trenton!*' chorused Sharon and Roderick.

'Sorry, *Trenton*!'

'Jolly convenient if you'd imported a Jap who was the son of the sub's captain who knew about the gold and wanted to get it!' I ad-libbed.

Sharon shook her head. 'There he goes, it's a funny thing about writers, but you can be sure they simply have to over-elaborate.'

'*Et tu,* Brute?' I countered.

'And so, my beamish boy, you now realize why we simply had to have you along.'

I nodded. There was certainly a simple logic about it. I contemplated for a moment, drawing on my cigar. 'You're forgetting one thing,' I said finally.

The three looked worried.

'I doubt it, but fire away.'

'The submarine won't be where I copped her.'

'And who has spirited her away?'

'Monsoons, typhoons, storms.'

It was clear that they hadn't considered this. There was a silence while they contemplated it then, very anxiously, 'Yes, but how much difference?'

'Not necessarily a lot but she certainly won't be lying at the same longitude or latitude.'

'You can still locate her?'

'I might. I can't go further than that—yet, at any rate.'

'Capital! Capital! Have another brandy, my boy?' Uncle Steve invited.

I nodded my acceptance. 'Thank you, sir.'

As Uncle Steve poured out the drinks I looked up sharply to find Roderick's eyes gazing steadfastly at me. 'I know what you are thinking,' he said. He did, too, for he added, 'never mind it comes second nature to you, doesn't it, having been to England's premier Col'!'

I shook my head. 'Roderigo, you are incorrigible, you really are!'

Uncle Steve handed me my brandy.

'Why,' I jabbed at Roddy, 'don't you take that bloody silly ear-ring out and try and behave less like Pheeno and the Barbitones?'

'It looks jolly marvellous!' Sharon said, rising instantly to his defence.

I shook my head. 'It's a funny world, women seem to be glad men don't look like men any more.' I didn't mean this, I was only taking the Michael, since no one could look more manly than Roderick.

'Quite agree! I hear some of these Mods or is it Rockers, actually wear make-up—I mean, make-up!' Uncle Steve exploded.

Roderick was giving me the fish eye again. 'What else, Gar'? You're still working it out, aren't you? What else, my bonny bucko?'

'Sharon's brother, Kunhke the MacSchultz,' I began.

'What about him?'

'What was his plan? I mean, they had several alternatives as far as I was concerned—to offer me more to join them, to capture me to give them the information as to just where the sub was, or to deter me from coming along with my information.'

'Yup!'

'But suppose they succeeded, say, in Rome in deterring me, there must be some other evidence, some other person or information on its way.'

'I don't get it—what are you drivin' at?' Uncle Steve inquired.

'What Gar' is saying is that if Schultz and Oko were able to stop him they were postponing their job, as they were eventually able to do with someone else's knowledge!'

There was a long silence while the realization of what I meant sunk in. Then, I said, enjoying a dramatic moment like Roderick. 'This is their unknown factor.'

Roderick nodded approvingly. 'Point taken. There is one more unknown factor and Sharon's bro' has it but, since you are here and not deterred and since we are still a jump ahead—the sooner we act the better.'

The others became jubilant again.

'What is your plan of campaign?' I inquired. 'You won't attempt to raise the sub?'

'No. Not now. We suspect, since he didn't know where he was torpedoed except that it was somewhere off the north-west coast of Mandura, Oko engaged Hardy because he was a salvage expert. We had made tentative reservations in Mauritius for a salvage boat, claiming we were looking for oil, but we thought we'd wait till we'd seen you.'

'It could be due to the typhoons that she may have rolled and dropped into very deep water.'

'In which case we'll have to use the vessel—but if you are able to pin-point her and she isn't too deep, we thought divers.'

I nodded.

It all depends if I can locate her,' I said, but knowing Roderick, doubt still gnawed at me. 'You're quite sure the gold is flotsam or jetsam or——'

'Finders keepers?' Sharon finished it for me. 'Of course, Gar', Roderick's been into all that.'

I sniffed derisively.

'Isn't he a positive scug!' Roderick shouted boisterously. 'I make him a millionaire overnight and all he does is query every bloody thing.'

'How do we recce? When do we recce?'

'Good man! Well, we've got the M.T.B. even if poor old Hardy's lost his. We also have the fishing smack and Alf's boat that brings the would-be immigrants——'

'Hasn't the fishing boat been impounded?'

Uncle Steve looked at me as if I had hurt his pride. 'We do have another one or two, Trenton,' he assured me.

'We should do the first recce by air,' I said, thinking aloud.

'I had a feeling you'd say that, my intrepid bird man,' Roderick said gaily, 'it just so happens——'

'Oh, no!' I said. 'You're not going to tell me——'

'Only a small one—a Rave six-seater but very comfortable.'

'Ye gods, and where have you secreted *that*?'

'It's only a few miles away, a war-time airstrip. The French built it to keep out the Japs, just the right size runway.'

I looked suspicious. 'I don't happen to own that, too, do I?'

'What do you mean?'

'I mean, I suppose I've another gaol sentence coming up for flying in Japs as well as bringing them in by sea!'

Roderick shook his head in mock sadness.

'Tch! Tch! How could one man be so mistrustful,' he said.

'Dinner is served,' a plump and grinning Manduran cook announced.

'Want to wash, Gar'?'

I did. I suppose the idea of being a millionaire had raised my temperature.

We ate in a splendid dining-room at the back. The view, however, was marred by the specially improvised steel shutters and a spice of drama was added when one of the locals sat at the door to the hall with the inevitable Sten.

For my part, I was far more disturbed by the serving hatch, any moment I expected the business end of a Sten to protrude from it followed by a short sharp burst—of which I'd only hear the first cough, if that!

I said, by way of conversation to Sharon, 'I suppose this simple scene is being enacted at your brother's H.Q.?' I offered her a cigarette.

She nodded. 'Yes. I've been there a couple of times.'

'What?' I dropped my cigarette case in surprise.

'Well, we met at a rendezvous and I was blindfolded. That's how I met Reba.'

'I must say you two struck up a strange friendship.'

'It's probably *not* a lasting one, however.'

'But your brother might have killed you when the Cadillac was wired up—did you trust him, wasn't the fish poisoned?'

'No. You see we both knew that neither of us had any information valuable to the other, that is, until your arrival. He simply bided his time.'

The first course came in. It was *Bouillabaisse,* and was delicious. It was served in ornate white porcelain goblets. I said, 'Well, I know one thing, brother Hardy *can't* be eating as well as we are!'

Roderick was pouring a Pouilly-Fuissé. 'That's true, though I think his wines are pretty good, aren't they?'

'Yes, except that he reverts to type and we had Alsatian with the fish. And, of course, as a sop to Oko, there was saké on both occasions,' Sharon said.

Our meal was positively Lucullan, and when we had completed it there was Cointreau, another cigar and the local coffee.

We had agreed we'd make the first recce in the Rave just after dawn. It meant we had to be up at four to make the airstrip on schedule and so we turned in early.

The bedrooms were large and would have been airy but for the improvised barricade at the windows—corrugated tin, my old school chum wasn't going to be caught napping, if you will pardon an awful pun. After the gaol escape and the splendid meal I was asleep almost as soon as I had crashed my swede.

A light insistent tapping at my door awakened me. I reached hurriedly under the pillow for Horace only to realize in dismay that the local police sergeant had it. I was disinclined to open the door. I switched on the light over the bed and, since I was nude, slipped on the bottom half of a pair of pyjamas Roderick Vandaleur had thoughtfully provided. The tapping persisted. I looked round for something with which to guard myself, found an ancient iron poker by the unused fireplace and thought the best thing to do was to open up fast and stand-by to clonk.

I opened the door as if I had been Sykes (Bill, not Eric) in a previous incarnation. Then I flung the door open wide and stepped swiftly back swinging the poker over my head like an Indian club.

In a pale pink frilly nightdress, utterly feminine, irresistibly adorable, stood Sharon Saxbee. I gasped, swung back the door to close it but too late; a beautifully proportioned leg was thrust quickly in the jamb and I narrowly missed banging the door against it. In my split second of indecision, Sharon had slipped into my room.

'Sharon!' I whispered. 'Are you crazy?'

'For you, honey bee, you know that.'

'But this is madness! Aren't you and Roderick——?'

'Courting is the word,' she whispered, clinging to me and standing on tiptoe trying to reach my mouth. 'Or, as the Americans have it, going steady. It sounds so suggestive, doesn't it?' She couldn't reach my mouth so she pulled my head down by my hair and forced my lips on course to hers. Not, I must confess, that there was too much evasive action taken on my part. 'Sharon, please, you can't stay here!'

'Yes, going steady is very suggestive.' She found my lips and her tongue forced open my teeth. I luxuriated for a moment and then broke away from her protesting, backing from her.

'Sharon. Be reasonable. I thought you were "that way" about Roderick.'

'Of course I am, darling,' Sharon turned and swiftly locked the door, ran to the bed and switched off the bed light. A diffused moonlight crept in provocatively over the top of the corrugated tin where it didn't quite fit.

'Sharon, I simply can't let you——' I began but by now she was on the bed and pulling me towards her.

'"Methinks you do protest too much".' She misquoted.

'Sharon, you sweet idiot——'

'Oh, Gar' darling. It's been so long—too long! Remember your visit to my barge?'

'How could I forget it?'

'Exactly, darling, exactly.'

She pulled me to her ravenously. . . . *Had* she been on French Blues?

CHAPTER TWENTY-FOUR

We lay palpitating in each other's arms. I said suddenly, sleepy, 'What about Roderick?'

'What about him, darling, I adore him.'

'You're a strange girl!'

'Why? Why is it men are allowed to love more than one girl but women have to be—what's the word——'

I was nearly asleep, lulled into a false security by her proximity. 'Polysomatic,' I murmured somnolently.

'Gar'! Gar'! Hell! Don't you dare sleep. I think men are the end, they always want to go to sleep.'

'If not poly something, then mono something,' I burbled, then thought about it and said, 'Roddy? Suppose he's outside with his old Manduran shotgun?'

'Not Roddy—not *se soir*!' Sharon reassured. 'Remember the Chambertin?'

'Could I forget it?'

'I filled the glasses——'

'I though Roddy did.'

'Roddy filled the Pouilly.'

'And so?'

'I slipped him a Mickey!'

I was wide awake now. I sat up in bed as if it had been wired electrically 'You gave Roderick a Finn?'

It was Sharon's time to be drowsy. 'Darling, you don't think you. . . ?'

'No I don't!' I said pugnaciously. 'Cor suffering cats, he'll know as soon as he wakes.'

'No, he won't. It was a very mild one and he usually drinks too much anyway and has a hangover. Don't worry my love, all you have to do, Gar'. . . .'

'Honey, I'm so tired—are you sure Roderick didn't——' I could hardly get the words out—'are you sure that suave boy-friend of yours didn't——?'

I couldn't have been more drowsy. Now Sharon was shaking me. 'Gar',' she whispered fiercely. 'Gar', wake up. What are you saying?'

'The Chambertin, are you sure you poured the Chambertin?' I said, sleep-sodden. My head dropped onto my chest.

Now Sharon was smacking my face. 'Gar', you can't go to sleep!'

'But Sharon darling I've got to. I simply must sleep.'

Sharon was shaking me as if I were a rag doll, all I could do was giggle hysterically.

'He fooled you! That Roddy of yours! Didn't trust you—or—correction—didn't trust me. Thought *I'd* sneak along the corridor to find *you*!'

'Gar', wake up, Gar'!'

I chuckled. '. . . "Jocund night" and all that sort of jazz . . .

tip toe to the stars . . . Sharon my Song of Solomon . . . beautiful, crazy, mixed-up, sexy Sharon. Not, dear Sharon, tonight Josephine, he switched the glasses. . . .' I burbled on.

'My God! I think he *has* switched the glasses!' I heard Sharon say as if from many miles away.

'Outer space. I'm in outer space. Sharon, light of my love, I hope . . . I hope Morpheus is . . . is female,' I made a great effort to complete my sentence whilst I was still able, 'because, dear heart, those are the arms I'm going to be in . . . good night, sweet princess!'

I heard from miles and miles and miles away, Sharon saying: 'That rat fink! He switched the glasses!'

A thunderous banging on my door startled me out of my wits. I cursed the fact that I hadn't got Horace around. I leapt out of bed pulling the top sheet off the bed and looking for Sharon, eyes half closed.

'My God! Roderick and the blunderbuss! Quick. Under the bed or something.'

As I stood dazed and bleary eyed, the door opened and the beaming chubby Manduran cook appeared. It was broad daylight and she carried in my breakfast tray. The door was unlocked and Sharon had long since flown.

'Bleakfast—flied lice.'

'Not for this boyo,' I said firmly. 'Good morning, Lotus Fragrance——'

'Babette,' the porcine chef corrected me. Shades of some all conquering French marine of—perhaps the Napoleonic Wars? 'Babette, sorry! What I do need is the world's longest drink! My mouth is like the proverbial——'

But Babette cut in and finished it for me, 'Like pallot's cage!'

She poured me out a Jumbo size glass of pure fruit juice. I drank greedily. 'Marvellous!' I exclaimed when I'd drained the glass.

She passed me a basin of ice cubes and a small towel. 'Hold at back of neck. Excellent for hang-over,' she laughed silently and her Asian eyes disappeared in folds of flesh.

'What's the time, Babette?'

'Four o'clock,' she announced imperturbably.

'Four o'clock?' No wonder I was sleepy.

'Long dlive to air-plane,' she explained.

I drank the piping hot coffee, coffee from the Manduran hills and began to wake up.

'We have splendid meal for you when you come back,' Babette said.

I dressed and went downstairs. The triumvirate were there.

'Sleep well?' Roderick inquired, also playing it cool.

'You scummy bastard!' I retorted.

'Eh?'

'Oh, don't give me that,' I said pugnaciously. 'You know bloody well what I mean.'

'Well, there aren't two meanings about scummy bastard, but——'

'Now you two, it's far too early to quarrel!' Uncle Steve interjected. I wondered if he had an inkling as to what had transpired. Of course he was a wily old bird, perhaps he slipped us both Mickey Finns to avoid any bloodshed on the mandate of Saxbee terrain.

Sharon in jodhpurs and a Mexican embroidered blouse, a souvenir no doubt of a trip to Tijuana when she was ghost-writing Roddy's Oscar-winning script in Hollywood, didn't look as if privation had made her petulant. I felt a sudden gnawing jealousy.

Perhaps I'd been cuckolded and in frustration she had spent the night with Roddy—as he had possibly planned. I took it out on the time of day. 'Fine bloody time to be groping around, I must say!'

'Groping,' Roddy said superciliously smiling, 'being the operative word.'

I gave him a sharp look, but he gazed blandly back at me.

'Something bothering you, Gar'? You're binding like an old hen!' he said.

'Get,' I said succinctly, 'stuffed!'

'Charming!'

'Let's go, all of you!' Uncle Steve said in peremptory fashion picking up his panama with the Old Carthusian hatband. 'This is a moment I have been waiting for for a very long time.'

'Don't be disappointed if I can't locate that sub,' I said.

He swung round and suddenly, surprisingly he was made of steel. 'You'd better find that submarine, Trenton,' he snapped.

CHAPTER TWENTY-FIVE

As we drove to the airstrip, Roderick occasionally looked back to see if we were being tailed.

'You seem to suspect treachery,' I said.

'Yes. It's a nasty side to my nature,' Roderick retorted sarcastically. 'We seem to be in the clear but they have a means of communication, be it bush telegraph or smoke signal.'

'Or even a simple 'phone call!'

'Look! sun up!' said Sharon, and, indeed, the fantastic business of sunrise began. On the horizon the sky began its incredible, swiftly changing colour hues as if some demented painter had gone mad and in a frenzy kept changing his mind—apricots, pinks, saffrons, and the landscape a patina of gold, with day clouds of Kipling-like indigo being changed in a trice into plump fleecy, cotton wool ephemeral things that could only house cherubs. Then suddenly the sun was fully up and for a few more moments, everywhere was gold. The sea beaten gold, the sky a gold cupola, the clouds gold as if from some giant Hollywood production in Technicolor.

'Impressed?' Sharon inquired.

'Naturally.'

'When you've cashed your first million why don't you settle here? It's less spoiled than Tahiti, less commercialized than Hawaii.'

'Too far! And, anyway, I like the contrast of other places. Even these clouds—magnificent though they are—can't compare with the rain clouds over Ireland, say, and what is more pleasant than rain over the Malvern Hills?'

By now we had turned off the coast road and travelled inland by a rough road. Suddenly we came to a clearing. It was a typical war-time improvised, semi-camouflaged air-strip. There was a sad old windsock (I idly wondered if it was Japanese or French) and the remains of a few anti-aircraft gun emplacements. At the side of the concrete strip—wide and fairly long—was a small bamboo building which, I imagine, was continually repaired or replaced after any hurricane. Two medium sized hangars at the far end of the strip had lost any camouflage but were solidly built.

By the 'official' building was the Rave aircraft, neat and compact. Two Manduran mechanics were fuelling from a small petrol bowser. A Peugeot and a Land-Rover were parked nearby, and two lanky young airmen in khaki peaked caps, bush-type shirts and khaki officer-type material trousers walked, rather like subalterns at Buck House, up and down. They both wore revolvers. I thought, the place has more guns than the average American city.

We cluttered out of our chariot, Roderick greeting the crew of two cordially with his usual, easy charm. I was introduced and, looking at these youngsters, felt ninety. I think Roderick must have given them 'the chat' for they saluted me as if I really had made the Big Time. Both spoke with South African accents, and I was quite sure no one would volunteer how they had come to join the party.

They wore no insignia such as pilots' or observers' wings, and I couldn't identify the badges in their peaked caps. One—Alan—who was the senior technician said something to the other who nodded, entered the aircraft and produced a thermos of coffee and plastic cups. As the Mandurans completed their task of refuelling we drank the coffee and, because of the magical moment of dawn and the mood of anticipation, I felt it was the best coffee I had ever tasted.

It was then that I noticed the silver charm round Roddy's neck. 'What's that, Roddy—name, rank and number in case you are captured?' It was one of the few occasions I had ever seen him embarrassed. Sharon nudged me in the ribs, causing me to spill my coffee.

'Watch it!' I growled jokingly, but from her expression realized that Roddy was put out. I suppose this made me press the point. 'What's at the end of the chain—down by your belly button nestles a police whistle?'

Roderick sipped coffee pretending not to hear me.

'Or maybe a waterproof torch?' I continued to probe. 'We had a fellow in our squadron who always wore one. Had a horror we'd be torpedoed and he'd never find the companionway. Always wore a tiny waterproof torch, even under the shower.'

'Sensible bloke,' one of the South Africans said.

'That's nothing. There was a chap in my Company used to wear a St. Christopher *and* the Star of David—took no chances!' Uncle Steve led his own laughter, but still Roderick wouldn't bite.

And then, impulsively and rather to my own surprise, I playfully grabbed the chain and pulled it out of Roderick's shirt. At the end of it was a strange device I'd never seen before. 'What is it, Roddy?' I inquired examining the silver trinket. 'It looks like Somerset Maugham's colophon.'

Roderick pulled the chain away from me. 'It's that sort of thing—it's—well it's a joke really,' he said, but too glibly. 'It's to ward off the Evil Eye.'

'Oh!'

'A—a girl gave it to me. It's Moslem or Arabic, I don't know.'

'You mean you're superstitious?'

'No, of course not.'

But I couldn't accept this. 'Well, well!' I said unkindly, 'fancy the bold bad buccaneer with the eighteen carat ear-ring being superstitious!'

'Oh dry up!' Roderick snapped, just as he did at Eton, years ago.

'My!' I added, just to rub his nose in the red dust of Mandura. 'I never realized you had an Achilles' Heel, you heel!'

'Very funny, Garway!' Sharon snapped in his defence. 'Drink your coffee and save your quips for your corny novels!'

It was then that I realized *she* was the 'some girl or other' who had given him the magic charm.

CHAPTER TWENTY-SIX

I WAS still childishly glowing at the discovery that the gargantuan Roderick Vandaleur was the same size as the rest of us poor mortals when Alan, the captain of the aircraft, announced they were ready for take-off. The Rave was a neat aircraft with four comfortable pullman seats, so that passengers could face one another; there were two other seats facing the nose and a communicating door to the crew of two.

Sharon, Roderick and Uncle Steve sat in the pullmans and the co-pilot sat in one of the two seats that faced the engines so that I could sit alongside Alan in the cockpit and—to use an old service expression 'gen-up' or 'get with' the controls. Roderick had provided the excellent map of the area and, if the sub hadn't shifted too much in the years that ensued, I was pretty confident I could locate her. We cruised at one hundred and fifty and were soon over the north-west tip of the island.

The young pilot said, 'By the way if you want any iced fruit juice to cool you down, sir, there is another thermos in the cabin.'

I thanked him and then, glanced down at Mandura and noting on the map where we were, requested that I be allowed to take over the controls. I got used to the aircraft very quickly and made a couple of swift turns to gauge exactly what I could pull away in the event of trouble.

We had left the communicating door open so that we could talk to the others and when I called out that we were approaching the area, they unfastened their safety belts and crowded the open door. I cautioned them back explaining that they had better comply with regulations. Reluctantly they returned to the cabin.

I studied the map once more, lowered the stick to take her up a bit then going into a sideways slip, brought her down to two thousand and levelled out. There, by the Grace of God, the love of Allah, the word of Buddah or pure bloody luck, we should see a torpedoed Japanese submarine. Alan scanned the sea from his side, I kept my eyes peeled on mine . . . not a trace. We cruised, then turned and started to search, allowing for the sub's drift. I could sense the atmosphere in the cabin, the keyed-up Sharon, the phlegmatic Uncle Steve, and Roderick with his calm façade inwardly consumed by tension.

And then, suddenly, Alan shouted, 'There she is!'

And sure enough, deep, deep down, with her nose in the mud and a great, ugly, leering gap in her side was the submarine I had torpedoed twenty years ago.

In the cabin they had been studying the wreck with binoculars and were now vociferous. I suppose this caused me to react in the opposite direction.

'We haven't got to her yet!' I yelled. 'And, when we do, the stuff may have been where that bloody gap is!'

'What do you mean, Garway?' Roderick asked indignantly.

'It's pretty obvious if the gold was where the sea could get it, it's probably gone.'

'Oh God, no!' Uncle Steve's call to the Deity was tragicomic: no longer the stiff upper lip.

'Or, for that matter, if the wreck is reachable it could be that someone's got in ahead of us.'

'Don't worry, Garway!' Roderick said, 'we're the first and I mean us to stay the first. Garway, are you absolutely pin-pointed?'

I nodded assent.

'Then the sooner we get the salvage caper going, the better!'

'Hear! Hear!' Uncle Steve echoed, 'and to celebrate our discovery I took the precaution of bringin' a bottle of bubbly with me!' He unbuckled his seat belt and went to a small 'fridge at the rear of the aircraft and took out a bottle of champagne.

'You certainly live rough in these here parts,' I said.

'After all, Garway, Mandura's a French possession, you can't blame us for following their lead. When in Rome and all that jazz,' Sharon retorted, adding, 'thar's gold in that thar sub!'

'I hope you're right!' I shouted back.

Roderick opened the champagne, and though there were no fancy Swedish glassware from which to drink it the plastic mugs were acceptable.

Roderick had just proposed a toast as I turned the aircraft into the sun. It was then that I had—as indeed I believe often happens to people about to experience a terrifying experience—a sudden shiver of anticipation; a tiny tremor of fear, a premonition of some imponderable kind caused me suddenly to break out in a cold sweat of fear.

'I have a nasty feeling,' I began, but I got no further. The first burst of tracer ripped through the top of the pilot's cabin as, in a reflex, automatic action, I slewed round the tail plane, gunned the stick back and instantly lost height.

There was a concerted cry of fear from those in the cabin and Uncle Steve, who had left his seat, crashed heavily against the rear of the compartment. I had only time to glance round and call to the co-pilot to strap him back in his seat and get the hell back to his own, lickety-split.

'What the hell's happening?' Alan shouted.

'Bloody aircraft, perfect attack, straight out of the sun. I'm going to try and take evasive action but he's got the drop on me.'

The aircraft had come out of the sun, fired and made the loop and was now on my tail. I prayed that his second burst would be as bad as his first. The Rave responded to my sudden plan, and though the wings shuddered in protest they stood up to my spiral dive. I could see the tracer zoom past where we had been only two seconds earlier.

'Who the effing hell are they, the mad bastards?' Alan shouted.

'Didn't you know: Oko had a Zero fighter?'

'No, I bloody well didn't,' he shouted, 'and if I had I'd have effing well resigned!'

'It's probably held to pieces by the odd replacement and bits of string, but it's working.'

'Too bloody well, if you ask me!'

The Jap 'plane was still on my tail and the next burst of tracer ripped through the starboard wing but mercifully missed the engine.

'We've got one chance,' I yelled. 'I just might be able to pull it off. Stand by with the rubber dinghy. Warn the others to keep their safety belts fastened until you order them to release. It could be your chum'll have to open the cabin door very fast.'

A further burst from the fighter plane ripped through the cabin. The co-pilot had just strapped-in Uncle Steve and was making for his seat when we heard a terrible scream then silence.

'What?' I shouted.

I was now down to zero, just clear of the sea, zig-zagging in a vain effort to get out of the way of the enemy's pilot who kept pressing the gun-tit whenever I accidentally came back into his sights. The bastard must have been enjoying himself.

'What?' I repeated. 'Sharon?'

'No. My mate, Tim. He won't be opening that door. He's dead, very dead!' Alan yelled. I could hear Sharon's agonized cries. I guessed Tim wasn't exactly a pretty sight.

Ahead was a long wide stretch of sandy beach.

'Now!' I yelled, forgetting that only I knew what I had schemed. I suddenly made straight for the beach. Beyond it the inevitable clump of palm trees fringed it.

The enemy pilot, now anxious for the kill, merely followed on my tail. It was just about curtain time as I suddenly feigned that I was going up then, as soon as I rose, I rammed the stick back, levelled and cut both engines. We crash-landed with a terrific bump on to the beach, ploughed our way along it, scuffing the sand back in great banks, and the Jap fighter shot straight into the palm trees and burst into flames. As he did so we hit a sand dune and tilted so that the aircraft was standing on end, the engines and nose in the sand. After what seemed centuries of time, and must have been merely seconds, we flopped back with a crunching finality onto the beach, upside down.

CHAPTER TWENTY-SEVEN

ALTHOUGH slightly concussed and shaken to hell by the crash, I suppose the desire to survive was sufficiently powerful to galvanize us into activity. The difficult thing was to free the others who, upside down and suspended by their safety belts, on reflection probably looked comic but for the presence of the dead South African, Tim.

As I shouted to them, exhorting them to pull themselves together, the pilot had made his way to the small safety box where he had an axe and was busy clearing a hole in the fuselage to get us to safety.

Uncle Steve, still moaning from his fall in the cabin, was difficult to help. And there came a moment when we had to heave him through the gap in the fuselage to Roderick, who had already leapt out. Due to the distance Uncle Steve had to drop, all Roderick could do was attempt to catch him, but the distance was too great and Uncle Steve slipped from Roderick's grasp and fell heavily on the sand.

Sharon was concussed and did not seem to take in the full implication of the flaming aircraft a short distance from us; the blaze had ignited several palm trees. She kept staring at the funeral pyre saying over and over, 'Oh my God!' but it was clear that she had not thought at that time of the possibility that her brother was on the aircraft. When I mentioned this to Roderick he pulled a small pouch from his back pocket and took out some white phials.

'Sedatives. Strong ones. I'll get a coconut and we'll make her take them. They'll knock her out for a few hours.'

I watched the last few burning pieces of the Japanese aircraft blaze. The heat was tremendous. Roderick said: 'Poor bastards! I bet you've said that before, Garway.'

'Unfortunately, yes.'

Alan, the South African, came over from Uncle Steve and reported that his ankle seemed broken and probably his shoulder from the earlier fall. He was badly concussed.

'You'd better give him a couple of knock-out drops, too,' I suggested to Roderick. He nodded.

As he walked unsteadily to the trees to locate a coconut, I

noticed he had lost his shoe, I looked down and realized that I had, too. I remembered on the other occasions when I had crashed, I had lost my flying boots—normally, difficult to get off. I supposed that about the time of impact one felt fear, one's feet contracted and the boots slipped off.

I had often mentioned this odd phenomena in reports and to Medicos but never got a satisfactory reply. All I knew at this particular moment was that we had no shoes and no transport and, it had appeared from the aircraft and from the map, we were a long way from a village. I didn't like the idea of spending the day and maybe night without medical attention for Uncle Steve; and I was afraid of Sharon's reaction when she realized that her brother had probably been burned to death in the other aircraft.

We got Uncle Steve under cover of the trees and cleaned ourselves up with the cool, salty water of the ocean and Alan, who was a tower of strength, went back to our wrecked aircraft and was able to find and bring out several useful things, including a brandy flask.

Fortunately the noise of the crash and the fire brought help sooner than we dared hope. The first arrivals on the scene were two Mandurans in a bullock cart. They lived nearby and we were able to travel in the cart to their home. Uncle Steve was feverish by now, moaning and talking most of the time, while Sharon just stared stupidly into space, occasionally murmuring 'My God. Oh, my God!'

The house owned by the Mandurans was no more than a large barn-like shack with the inevitable corrugated tin roof, but it was shelter, and in no time more people appeared with many excited children.

We rested at the barn while the farmers resumed work in a paddy field nearby—the tragedy, excitement, drama, divertissement over, the daily toil had to proceed; they weren't rich enough to take the day off on our account. We managed to buy some native shoes and Alan borrowed an old bicycle and rode down the track road to the nearest village to organize a car to come to our rescue.

Whilst we waited and Roderick held Sharon's hand, patting it reassuringly every now and then, I wondered if Uncle Steve could make the journey back to Roderick's hide-out. He was an old man and he'd taken quite a pounding. There was another anxiety gnawing away at me, and I think Roderick sensed it, for he left Sharon for a moment and crossed over to me.

' "O what can ail thee, Knight-at-arms"?' he quoted.

'You brash bastard!' I flung at him. 'You are all façade! Aren't you a bit perturbed?'

'Great race the Chinese, Gar', you could learn a lot from them.'

'Confucius he say 'you big nit", why?'

'What's rotting you?'

'Just that Minoru Oko's boyos might be coming out in a posse, just to see what's happened, and all the protection we have is a scout's jack knife.' I exhibited it.

'I have,' said Roderick gravely, 'a golden toothpick. It's quite a revolting idea, isn't it? But a producer at Paramount who thought he had European culture, gave it to me last Christmas. It even has my name on it. And, of course, this old equalizer.' He tapped his revolver.

'Great but since you boyos are all in the Big Time, I don't think Oko will stoop to mere pistols.'

'Point taken. Let's just keep our fingers crossed.'

'Or,' I jibed, 'rub our Aladdin's lamp or touch the magic eye on our manly chest and hope for the best!'

He looked at me a long time then said:

'You don't like me a great deal, do you, Gar'? You never did.'

He laughed softly. He was a handsome bastard and I could readily understand the girls falling for him. Sharon among them, but it was on my door Sharon had tapped the previous night.

Again he looked at me a long time, a cool, slow appraisal. 'You do O.K., Garway Trenton. You do O.K.'

We had an apprehensive moment when the sound of the car was first heard. I was badly frightened at the possibility that it would be an Oko recee car armed with Stens. We crouched down in the barn scarcely daring to breathe and poor Uncle Steve's groans were stifled for a few seconds while I muffled them with one hand and held his protesting arms with the other. We had as much chance as the occupants of the Jap aircraft—but it turned out to be Roderick's driver in Roderick's jeep.

We paid the two farmers handsomely and packed into the jeep and drove as fast as we dared. I quarrelled with Roderick about this, suggesting that we should take it slowly and snail our way back but he retorted that this was the best plan. To save time an ambulance would meet us halfway and Uncle Steve would be rushed into the town for proper treatment.

'*Now* what ails thee?' Roderick asked, a trifle anxiously.

'I was wondering whether they shot us up because they had also spotted the sub and could find it again, or whether they thought they'd just rub us out and then have plently of time to reconnoitre.'

'Point taken again. Which do you think?'

'Since they were ten thousand feet up and at an oblique angle and coming out of the sun, with all that coral camouflage provided, I don't think they saw it.'

Roderick nodded. 'Suppose Schultz got to the wreck, would they be able to find the sub?'

'His task would be considerably easier, obviously, but we were a long long way from the wreck when we belly-flopped onto the sand.'

Roderick nodded again. 'In other words, they just lost out.'

'I think so,' I said He was highly elated, his moods evanescent, one minute ebullient, the next murderously low, and it made me wonder if he took snow or maybe purples. More to rile him than to be ethical, I said: 'This treasure, doesn't it belong to the French government?'

Roderick looked at me as if I was demented.

'You've got to be joking.' He said it with such incredulity I simply had to laugh.

As we approached the driveway to Roderick's palatial hideaway, I noticed that the driver placed a large red disc of cardboard by the windscreen, clearly this was the colour of the day. Roderick noticed my smile of approval, saying, 'I see you, too, aren't particularly keen for a burst of ack-ack to greet you as we turn the bend in the drive.'

'You think of everything!' I kidded.

Roderick nodded far from modestly. 'Unless you've got a desire for the Deep Six, it seems a good idea.' He then talked in Manduran to the driver. What he said was self-evident when we stopped near the character in the driveway with the Sterling, and Roderick gave him some details about the ambulance, 'I 'got' this from the mention of 'Red Cross' for which I presume there was no translation into Manduran.

Several men ran out to help take Uncle Steve into the house.

Roderick chanced giving him a mouthful of brandy and Sharon, too, had a short snorter. She was still under the influence of the sedative and remained that way until the ambulance arrived. Uncle Steve was lifted gently into the ambulance and was soon on his way to the hospital at Babala.

While Sharon rested on the sofa, and I sipped Cognac and smoked a calming cigar, Roderick was busy on the long distance line to Mauritius. I had persuaded him that we ought to be able to get to the sub without a salvage craft, but that we did need full underwater equipment from flippers to oxygen cylinders and certainly experts.

Roderick looked at me through half-closed eyes, contemplatively summing up whether he should spend out more money. Now that the prize was within possible reach, he was already getting greedy.

'Stop looking like Minoru Oko and be sensible. Who's going down to get it out? You'll need deep water oxyacetylene gear—all sorts of bloody things.'

Roderick re-considered it with reluctance. 'Well, I'll be bloody well down there,' he said.

'What for, to make sure they don't nick a couple of gold bars? Where the hell will they shove it, they'll be in skin-tight rubber suits.'

Roderick glowered at me but proceeded to order up the men as well as the equipment. The excitement was making him quite uneasy and this amused me.

'You look,' I derided, 'like you did the first day of the summer half when we were allowed our first swim—as if you were afraid the water was going to be bloody cold.'

'Well, it usually was.'

'Yes, but it was the *anticipation* wasn't it, that gave one the goose pimples?'

'Eff you, Garway Trenton, I wish I hadn't been at school with you.'

'You poor old bleeder!' I condoled.

It was then we had a nasty scare. Sharon who had been pacified by the pills, suddenly emitted the most shattering cry of terror and getting up ran towards the door.

'Hardy!' she screamed. 'Oh my God, Hardy!'

We had a difficult time restraining her and then, as if a minor miracle had happened, the 'phone rang. As Roderick held her, shaking her into normality, I answered the 'phone, thinking it was a call from the salvage people in Mauritius. It was Reba at the other end.

'Hallo, Tall Type!' she drawled.

'You'll have to talk louder,' I shouted. 'What's on your beautiful if tiny mind?'

'What's the noise? Sharon having hysterics?'

I didn't answer.

'Tell her to relax, Hardy wants to talk to her.'

'Thank God!' I murmured.

Reba heard me.

'Then it *is* Sharon I can hear!' Again I didn't answer. 'When are we having dinner, Tall Type?' she inquired.

'What—first course cyanide soup? Fish with prussic acid, and with the turkey baked potatoes loaded with arsenic? Not this poor sap!'

'Come back when Sharon's been reassured.'

Sharon's joy was touching. It seemed strange that as brother and sister they were so different. I had read about love-hate relationships. I was touched. When Sharon moved away from the 'phone, brushing her tears from her face with the back of her hands, she told Roderick he wanted to talk business. Roderick sniffed contemptuously.

'Whatever it is, no!' He took up the receiver. He listened impatiently and cut in on Hardy as the latter tried to make a deal. 'No dice!' he snapped.

Now it was my turn. I went to the telephone.

'Did you say you were taking me out to dinner?' Reba asked. The audaciousness of it appealed to me.

'Don't be fatuous,' I said.

'No. I mean it. We could call a truce.'

'I'd trust your truce about half as far as I could see your white flag.'

'We could meet in a neutral corner—say the Sporting Club?'

I laughed scornfully. 'Last time we were at the Club you tried to kidnap me.'

'But that was when we needed you.'

'You don't need me any more?'

'No. We don't need *another* hostage.'

My heart sank. '*Another* hostage?' I repeated hollowly. Roderick hurried swiftly to my side followed by Sharon.

'That's what I said.'

'Another hostage?' I repeated it yet again idiotically. I was beginning to realize how we had been tricked. 'The ambulance!' I said.

'That's right,' Reba was almost cheerful.

'You mean you've got Uncle Steve!'

'That's right.'

'You're bluffing?'

'That's right.'

'You're bluffing?'

'Oh, come now Garway! You know me better than that by now.'

And as if to confirm what she was saying a second ambulance drew up at the front door—the genuine one.

CHAPTER TWENTY-EIGHT

I HAD never seen Roderick so humiliated.

'The telephone must have been tapped!' I suggested.

'More likely someone double crossed us.' He dismissed the second ambulance, and called in his men and spoke harshly to them in Manduran. It was pretty clear what he was saying. I was still holding on to the telephone.

'Having fun?' Reba said. I cursed softly, cupping the receiver.

'Reba—what'll I tell her?' I shouted at Roderick. He gave his men some orders and they hurried out.

'Tell her to—— Hell!'

He was really up the proverbial gum tree.

'Tell her—— I don't know. In the immortal words of W. C. Fields, give her an evasive answer.'

'What's that?'

'Tell her to —— herself!'

'Charming!' I said, indicating that Sharon was present. Roderick apologized.

'Look, Reba, can you call me back?'

'I'll give you five minutes,' she replied.

'Big of you!' I hung up.

'So Hardy doesn't know where the sub is!' Roderick said, 'so we're still ahead.'

'We are level pegging,' I reminded him, 'they've got Uncle Steve.'

'Yes. Poor old bastard!' Roderick replied.

'I don't like the way you said that, Roddy boy!' I said.

'No?'

'No. They've got Uncle Steve. We've got to make a deal.'

'In your brandy!'

'What are you trying to say, Roddy?' Sharon asked, the truth dawning on her.

'He's trying to tell us that Uncle Steve is expendable!' I accused.

'Roderick! You can't! You simply can't!' Sharon said.

Roderick didn't reply, instead he crossed to the decanter.

'Roderick!' Sharon went to him but he shook her away and poured himself a four-fingered dram.

'Who can say if he'll last out after the crash, anyway?'

'You haven't time to stall and you know it!' I accused. 'They're offering you a deal, or I'll go and dine Reba—they'd prefer me. Besides, I know more than Uncle Steve anyway!'

Roderick was aghast. He put his brandy glass down and crossed slowly to me. 'What are you saying?'

'I'm saying that I'll make a deal with them—to free Uncle Steve.'

'You won't!' Roderick said.

I noticed that his right hand had slipped down to his waist, very near to his gun holster.

'Are you bloody well threatening me, Vandaleur?'

'Yes, by God I am!'

We were interrupted by a commotion outside. Roderick spun round and this time went for his gun. His men came in clamorously, dragging one of the guards with them. It was Maolo. Again there was a fierce conversation in Manduran and now and again the word Red Cross was interspersed in the conversation. From the fierce protestations from the captive Maolo, it was clear who was suspected of giving the information to the other side. The man, screaming his protestations of innocence, was dragged from the room. I looked at Sharon who was chalky white.

'Get the message, Gar'?' Roderick said boisterously, his gun hand idling with the butt of his revolver.

'They've found the one who double crossed us—the chappie who told Oko that we needed an ambulance.'

'Roderick, are you sure it was Maolo? He's always been so loyal.'

'Save it, Sharon! Like Mango he double-crossed us. He admitted it.'

'He didn't!' Sharon said. 'My Manduran's better than yours. He didn't, he denied it.'

Roderick paid no regard. He was still having at me. 'I take it you've heard about the Concrete Kimono?'

I nodded.

'Know how it operates?'

'No. Not madly keen to hear, either.'

'Oh, it's quite interesting. I'd listen if I were you,' he continued smoothly. 'They wrap it round him . . . the prisoner.'

'Wrap what around him?'

'The concrete. When it hardens, they dump him into the sea. It's a favourite trick of Oko's. Sometimes the kimono washes on to the coral reef but maybe months later, after a typhoon.'

'And you'll give that poor fellow the same treatment?' I gasped. 'You inhuman bastard.'

'Oh, not Maolo. No, we'll shoot Maolo. I was talking about you, Trenton, I was talking about you!'

It wasn't my happiest moment. I lit a cigarette and I'll never know how I controlled my hand. I said, 'My! but your trigger finger's itchy! You ought to take a couple of those sedatives you gave Sharon.'

The telephone rang and caused all of us to jump.

'I'll get it. It's for me anyway,' I said. I was outwardly icy calm. I was James Bond, the Saint and Chandler's Marlowe all rolled into one. Inwardly I was Jelly Roll Trenton.

'Trenton,' I announced casually. 'Reba? What's new?'

'Where did you suggest we met?'

'The Yachting Centre.'

'Another Club?'

'Yes.'

'No colour bar, but only pink people admitted?' I hazarded a guess.

'Very funny.'

'In half an hour?'

'I look forward to it.'

'Flattery will get you nowhere!'

I hung up. Whether because of my safety or her own vanity, I don't know, but Sharon ran across and held me by the shoulder.

'This is madness, Gar'! What proof have you they'll let Uncle Steve go?'

'They'll let him go. They won't need him if they have me! I won't make a deal until I am sure.'

'You won't make a deal; period!' Roderick said.

I turned to find the revolver was now in his hand. He was shaking a little. I thought if he could see the butterflies looping the loop in my belly! I lit a cigarette. I hope I looked cool, casual, in command of the situation. I said pseudo-contemptuously: 'You're trembling, Roddy!'

'Gar'. Please! My God, Gar', don't!'

I kissed Sharon on the forehead. 'Be seein' you!'

I turned and walked slowly to the door, my back to Roderick all the way. Somehow I got to the door and I was thinking, when it comes I hope I don't feel a thing. Icy calm, Trenton, icy calm. I had one pace to go to the door handle. I couldn't swallow but sorely wanted to. It's now, when I put my hand out to open the door, I told myself. I'll never know if it was to have been then. Before I put my hand out I said casually, 'By the way, can I borrow the car?' I reached for the door, made it and opened it.

'Sure! Help yourself—rat fink!' Roderick said, bitter humiliation pierced the careless way he said it, embarrassment tinged the deadly sarcasm. I turned and then coolly, and now that the tension was over I was cool, walked back to him. 'O.K. Roderick,' I said, 'merely proving a point.'

He gasped. Sharon couldn't help let out a delighted 'Gar'!'

'"The Duplicity of the world",' I said. 'Who was it—Pecksniff?'

'No, Mrs. Totters!' Sharon corrected.

'Look,' I continued, 'I've got an idea!'

One of Roderick's henchmen drove me to the Yachting Centre. This, too, was a club and, again, it was strictly for the white population. It was very attractive, with a club house and open-air restaurant overlooking the harbour where yachts, rowing boats and cabin cruisers were moored. Some of the craft had gaily coloured sails of vermilion or petrol-blue stripes on a white background. Yawing slowly on a turquoise sea with the voluminous fleecy clouds in a hyacinth sky gave the place a halcyon atmosphere of never-never-land. Only the presence of the very real Reba sitting on a high stool at the bar made me realize that this was no dream world.

She was wearing a very simple, beautifully cut turquoise blue Thai silk pyjama-type top with matching three-quarter length trousers. It had a square neck and very short sleeves, high heeled white shoes, no stockings and no make-up except for a slash of scarlet on her lips. She was devoid of jewellery except for a small diamond crucifix round her neck. The idea of Reba and religion was bizarre. Her hair, which was usually festooned in a *soignée* beehive, had been allowed to drop to her shoulders, its blue-blackness contrasting with the lotus blossom in her hair, the long silky tresses washed her high cheek bones. She wore no false eye-lashes—unnecessary; and no bra, unnecessary. Again her eye patch matched her dress. Her 'good' eye, deep, pupil very brown flecked with sepia, positively pierced me.

She looked like a sophisticated magazine cover with one exception, instead of the usual characterless or pleasantly vacant expression, Reba's face was full of character, of determination. She was a personality plus a beauty. I wouldn't tell her but she was Cleopatra, Clytemnestra and Marie Antoinette.

'When you dress to—er—kill, you dress to kill,' I said.

'Subtle joke.'

'No topless dress?'

'I leave that to the natives.'

'Sensible girl! In any case I understand in Bali the locals are buying bras, like mad—gotta be different.'

'Another joke—you've been drinking?'

'Charming!'

'Have another?'

'Whatever yours is.'

Reba indicated to the barman to bring another.

She surveyed me quizzically over her glass. 'Ever considered parting your hair on the other side?'

My drink arrived. 'Good grief, what's that?'

'It's a Barbados.'

'It's strayed a bit!'

'Yes. Daiquiri and Barbados Rum.'

'Is it, by golly! The drinks out here are as varied as the way they give you the Deep Six. No, I haven't considered parting my hair on the other side, the left's for little girls, isn't it? Leastways, that's what they told us as children.' I looked around. 'Nice place you've got here.'

She nodded. ' "Paradise enow", why don't you stay—now that we're in partnership.'

'We're in partnership when I see Uncle Steve in the local hospital with an armed guard.'

'I can do better than that.'

We finished our drinks. I said to the barman, 'Keep two more on ice, we'll be back. Lead on, you would-be Croesus!'

If she had a 'cruiser' escort, they were skilfully concealed among the rich Anglo-French *clientèle*.

We made for the car park and my eyes boggled. 'Well I'll be damned!' I exclaimed.

In the car park was my Maserati Type 3500, convertible, Ming III.

'How the devil. . . ?' I stared at her number plate. 'Where the devil did you. . . ?'

Reba laughed, two rows of beautiful white teeth good enough for any toothpaste 'ad.', I wanted to flick my tongue across them.

'Don't look at me like that.'

'Where did you get my car? How did you get it here?'

She laughed again. 'Hardy said you'd—what was the expression—"take it big"!'

'You bet I take it big.' I was beginning to get angry.

We got into the car. I opened the door and let her get in first.

'Now don't get alarmed!' she said sarcastically.

'Thanks, but I do remember poor old Pindo and the Cadillac.' I went round the back of Ming III and got in and then I realized, just from the 'feel' of the driver's seat, it wasn't mine.

'Very simple,' Reba said. 'Hardy's idea of a joke. He'd ordered one some while ago—same colour as yours, same make. Had a special delivery.'

'But the number plate?'

'Alas, dear Garway, fake—like so many things on the island—there! I said it just ahead of you—didn't I?'

I grunted. I turned on the ignition and revved. It was a wonderful feeling to be behind the wheel of a Maserati again.

'Straight up the hill ahead,' she said. It was a one in ten and the view was marvellous. When we reached the top she said, 'Turn right.'

We were in the drive of a small R.C. church.

'Don't tell me that the church falls away and there behind it is the hide-out of Hardy Kunhke-Schultz and Oko!'

'No. This isn't camouflage—it's genuine.'

'If you're trying a shot-gun wedding, we haven't any witnesses——' I glanced in the rear mirror, 'unless we're being tailed.'

'No. I'm sorry I don't know the right denomination—but anyway it's the only church in the vicinity and they've been very kind, very co-operative.'

I took my eyes off the driveway and gave Reba a quick look. 'Reba. I suspect treachery.'

She flicked me a look, deep, intent, as honest as a sheriff in a Western.

I said, as we reached the church and got out, 'What's happened?'

'We've got you here on slightly false pretences,' she confessed.

'You mean Uncle Steve?'

'Your—or rather Roderick Vandaleur's Uncle Steve is dead.'

'*What?* You mean, when you——?'

'I mean, when we made the deal we were bluffing—Uncle Steve was already dead.'

'You lousy bitch!' I shouted, but she remained maddeningly cool and unruffled.

'Perhaps you'd like to see him,' she suggested. She indicated the church door and we went in.

CHAPTER TWENTY-NINE

It seemed preposterous to see Uncle Steve lying there with a tall candle at head and feet, his hands clasped together, his cad shoes never to move again. It seemed wildly improbable that someone devotedly, or derisively, had carefully placed his monocle in his sightless eye. It seemed incredible that there would be no more missing g's, no more funny false noses to wear on festive occasions, no more excitin' adventure, and certainly no gold bars.

I was bitterly angry and I turned to Reba only to find that she had taken a silk handkerchief from her handbag and covered her head and that she was weeping. Somehow I had never thought of Reba crying. I was taken aback.

'He was a gay old man.'

'You bastards!' I said absurdly, causing her to look up in surprise. The tears wrought havoc with her eye make-up.

'He was dead when he arrived, really, Garway!' she added imploringly. 'Please believe me. All we've done is double-cross you.'

'He was dead when you made the deal, in fact.'

Reba nodded.

'Leave me with him. I won't nip off through the vestry door, I promise,' I said sarcastically.

She flashed me an indignant look as if to say that Death was an all-pervading Truth. She gave Uncle Steve a last pitying look and genuflected as she left the church.

I looked round to be sure I was alone. He was not my Uncle Steve, but I felt someone should be related to him just for that moment, and said softly, a fragment of Brooke, '"Think only this of me, that in some corner of a foreign field. . ." So long, Uncle Steve. . .!'

I walked out from the heady, musty smell of that cool church on the hillside into the garish bright hot sun on a beautiful Manduran day.

Reba sat in the car and I looked round quickly and smiled cynically. By the lychgate standing far too casually reading a newspaper stood a lolling local, far too casually. I presumed that the gents with the Belgian machine-guns, the Stens, the Machetes and the revolvers were stashed away among the gravestones.

I walked slowly to the car and got in.

'You continue up the hill,' Reba said.

I was surprised. I suppose I had thought that Hardy Kuhnke-Schultz and Minoru Oko would have the same sort of hide-out as Roderick Vandaleur—long winding drive with plenty of cover for the guards, and a big mansion with a wide amount of free surround so that no one could get too close without being observed.

We drove to the very summit of the hill and stopped outside a walled garden. Wrought iron gates barred our way, nor were they opened. We left the car and proceeded on foot. When we reached the gates they swung open automatically.

'Tut! Tut!' I chided. 'The money you people put into crime! I suppose big brother Schultz and velly honourable Minoru Oko are watching us on a TV screen.'

'I'm afraid so,' Reba replied, almost guiltily.

There was no drive, just a long steep row of stone steps leading up to a veranda which faced the harbour below. We walked up the steps, Reba, who clearly knew the routine, taking it nice and slowly.

'Composure at all times. No deep breathing, eh Reba? What happens when you have sex?'

'There's absolutely no reason to be crude, Trenton,' she said.

She didn't say 'you'll find out'. Perhaps she knew I was still angry at Uncle Steve's death. I didn't mind walking into the lion's den. My silence must have intrigued her.

'What are you thinking about—Uncle Steve?'

'No, I was thinking in my next incarnation I might be a vet.'

That shook her.

'How odd! Not a Buddhist priest?'

'Why the sarcasm?'

'You are so proud of your curly fair hair, I thought you'd want to humble your pride at once by having your pate shaved.'

I nodded, appreciatively. 'The way you keep cutting me down to size pleases me.'

'So?' She was a little out of breath, despite the slow pace and the composure, but she tried not to show it. 'Why?'

'Because it clearly proves I have got under your skin!' I replied.

'The vanity of men! How can one respect a man one has laughed at?'

'Laughed at?'

'At the local gaol. Holding your metal ball in your hands and blood trickling from the nick I made when I took a piece out of your ear—which I see has healed nicely.'

'I'm rocking with laughter!'

'Never mind, handsome Garway Trenton, no doubt the fair Sharon Saxbee has been consoling you.'

'"Take me to your leader",' I wisecracked, but again she slapped me down.

'You said that once before.'

'Is that a crime?'

'No, but continual originality might help your cause.'

We stopped outside the front door.

'You think I have a future?'

'Why not?'

'I think once you three have split the money, you'll do your best to erase us. One hundred per cent is better than fifty.'

'I don't think we'll be that greedy.'

'Only time will tell.'

The door, massive and obviously reinforced, creaked open.

'May I lead the way?'

'Do. I'm strictly an Aristotle lover, female only, and I'd adore to follow you, especially since you qualify for the major prize.'

Hardy was too subtle to have men loaded with hardware in the hall, but I wasn't fooled by the placidity of the place. I followed the elegant Reba into a large lounge facing the sea and noticed the TV set which was for ever facing the front gates.

'Lovely little shack you have here,' I said, I hoped nonchalantly.

Hardy stood looking down at the harbour. Minoru Oko sat in an arm-chair with a tall back to it. To my surprise he was smoking a hookah.

'Don't,' I said, 'offer me a suck, I'm highly fastidious.'

Hardy swung round, his handsome face cruel, strong, angry. 'You can skip the facetious remarks, Trenton. You're no longer at Eton!'

'True, Sweet Prince.'

I glanced at Minoru Oko puffing at his hookah.

'And Oko,' I panzered on, 'looking like some malevolent Oriental, which of course he is.' I wasn't going to be put in my place by Hardy.

'Whose civilization goes so much further than yours,' Oko reminded me.

I made a mock grimace. 'Now I'm cut down to his size,' I said to Reba. Schultz strode angrily across the room to confront me.

'Now! Now! No fisticuffs—I must warn you I was in the Eton and Balliol Boxing Eights, and your methods of gelignite and Sten are no match for the more orthodox and ancient methods like boxing.'

I so enraged Hardy he telegraphed a left hook which, if I say so myself, I neatly side-stepped.

'Hardy!' Reba warned him. 'Can't you see Trenton's deliberately trying to provoke you. He's angry about Vandaleur's Uncle Steve—thinks it was our fault.'

'I don't give a dam' what he thinks, he can——'

'Don't—what is the expression?—push us too far, Trenton,' Oko said suavely. 'We might *extract* the information from you.'

'Like you tried to do before? I knew you'd never be happy until you *unmade* a man of me!'

Oko drew on his hookah at an increased rate of knots. I contemplated this for a moment saying, 'May I have sippers? And is it neaters?'

'Stop being adolescent, Garway,' Reba requested.

I was very mindful of Hardy's proximity. He swung a right wildly and I ducked and slammed in a right to the body. He grunted, doubling up and I gave him a classic left across the jaw which sent him reeling on to the Aubusson. It was positively classical. He seemed rather surprised. He looked at me and shook his head. Having spent some time with Sharon I was able to see a family resemblance.

He said, now more even tempered, 'I thought you were bluffing!'

'Shucks! It was nothing,' I replied. He scrambled to his feet and I stood ready for the counter-attack but he merely rubbed his jaw, shook his blond head and grinned.

'Now perhaps you two kiddie-winks will kiss and make up,' Reba suggested.

'I still prefer his sister!' I said.

'Leave Sharon out of this,' he warned, getting narked again.

'Exactly. Covet not thy chum's wife, there's a dear boy,' Reba added, winking her uncovered eye.

I blinked. 'Eh?'

'Don't look so innocent!'

'What was that about wife?'

It was Reba's turn to blink. 'I suppose you didn't know Sharon is your friend Roderick Vandaleur's wife?'

Now I gasped incredulously. 'Sharon Saxbee is Roddy's wife——?'

'Oh come off it.'

Oko stopped bubbling at his hookah.

'As you so charmingly put it, "pull the other one, this one has bells on it"!'

'Cambodian bells!' I said, but the news was making me think furiously. 'Mrs. Vandaleur, oh it's rich!'

'I thought you'd enjoy the joke,' Reba said.

'O.K.,' Hardy snapped, 'the pleasantries are over.' He indicated a large-scale map of the island which was on a refectory table by the window. 'Perhaps you will be good enough to show us where the submarine is lying.'

I crossed to the map. 'I take it we then fix a rendezvous with Roderick to arrange the salvage operations?'

Hardy laughed harshly. 'You have got to be joking,' he said.

'I beg your pardon?'

'You don't think we'll go fifty-fifty with Vandaleur now we have the pleasure of your company?' he replied.

I nodded. 'You mean it's a real double-cross?'

'Exactly!'

'Then I expect once you've located the gold, I'll get one of Oko's concrete kimonos.'

Oko smiled not so inscrutably. 'You *are* suspecting,' he replied.

'I've every reason to be.'

'Don't worry, Reba's interceded for you.'

I flashed her a quick look.

'I think she rather fancies you,' Hardy sneered.

'It makes me sound like a pigeon.'

'No, rather a turtle dove!' Reba purred. 'I'd like to find out what it is that Sharon finds so attractive about you.'

Hardy looked up sharply and glared at her. Reba was just using me as bait to make him angry.

'The position of the submarine!' he commanded.

'Of course if you plan to double-cross Roddy I could refuse to tell you and accept the Deep Six with as much grace as I can muster. Drape me in the Balliol colours and slip me quietly over the side.'

'You are stalling, Garway Trenton,' Oko said quietly.

'Don't worry,' Schultz assured me, 'if you're washed ashore, we'll see that the concrete gives you correct billing.'

'Charming!'

'The position of the submarine if you please,' Oko said, for the first time he was quite sinister.

I said, 'I made one error when I torpedoed the sub—I should have deflected a little to the left and copped you!'

'Wrong again, Mr. Trenton, I was in the forward hatch.'

'With the gold?'

'I didn't know about the gold then.'

'The position of the——'

'Yes, yes! I heard you.' I crossed to the map. 'The position of the sub is there!'

I plunked my index finger to the west of the island, several nautical miles seawards from the coral reef. It was, of course, nowhere near where the submarine really lay.

CHAPTER THIRTY

HARDY KUNHKE-SCHULTZ had his salvage vessel cross from Mauritius before you could say 'nineteen carat'. The next day, the first frogman went down at dawn. The wreck wasn't difficult to find despite its layer of seaweed and coracles. Hardy was jubilant. While a careful watch was kept for any intruders, he invited me to join Reba, Oko and himself in a celebration bottle of champagne.

I inquired: 'About that 'plane of yours——'

Hardy, about to drink a toast, frowned.

'I was intrigued about it, where did it come from?'

'From here. It was one of the 'planes shot down when the French re-took the island. It was repairable. We got hold of a couple of good men and they got the spares from here and there and made it flyable.'

'But the lads who——'

'Kicked the bucket? Two young friends of Oko's, sons of former Kamakaze.'

I nodded. 'I'm sorry,' I said.

Oko shrugged his shoulders. He was of the Oriental old school in that life wasn't that important; perhaps that was why he was so free with other people's. I looked at Reba, fawn eye patch, to match the British-cut cavalry twill trousers, the same fawn coloured man's bush-shirt, the breast pockets swollen in delightful cupolas not seen on men—well, not *this* season, perhaps next. She returned my salute as news came that the first frogman reported he had reached the wreck.

As if cued, the first frogman clambered down into the salvage vessel's wardroom. This, I thought to myself, is the time to have another glass of champagne.

'The wreck,' he reported. 'It's an ancient frigate—or something——'

'What?'

'About the time of the Napoleonic Wars, I don't know. Certainly it's not a Japanese submarine.'

There was an ominous silence.

'Any treasure on board?' I inquired casually.

Oko, who was never really amused at my facetiousness, gave me the old fish eye.

The others turned, silently awaiting an explanation. If it had not been that Hardy might think I was reaching for my Betsy, I would have reached for a cigarette. Instead I said, 'It's very simple, Hardy——'

By now he had his hand on his revolver butt.

'You won't believe that Roderick Vandaleur put me in the same predicament forty-eight hours ago.'

'Talk very fast, Garway. Very fast and very clear.'

'It's a double-cross,' I began and his gun was aimed square between my eyes before I had said 'cross', so I continued very quickly, 'but it's a double-cross with a difference.'

'Hurry, Trenton,' he commanded. His fury was ice-cold, frightening. Even Oko and Reba were in awe of it.

'I did bring you out here to survey this wreck because I had paid a visit to the Maritime Museum and I had "genned-up" on it. It was one of Captain Kidd's and, in case you are interested, there *is* supposed to be a treasure of doubloons aboard, but many expeditions have failed to find it, tides, monsoons, you under——'

'Listen, you bastard, you've tricked us!' Hardy shouted. 'Why—this is the only thing I don't understand—why did you sacrifice yourself? You must have known we'd kill you when we realized what you had done!'

I wasn't too sure of myself or rather of Hardy, but I made a great pretence of enjoying the champagne.

'It was really a question of saving lives,' I said.

'But not yours, my friend.'

'I think so. I think when you hear me out the twisteroo will appeal to you.'

He still had his gun pointing clearly at my temple. He would have made a bloody mess if he gave that trigger the necessary pressure. 'I hope so. I really hope so, Garway,' he said.

'Well,' I began, trying to infuse some jollity into my tale. 'I cabled an ex-naval chum of mine, "Ginger" Bier——'

'Ginger Beer,' Minoru Oko said, in a condescendingly nasty tone, 'is a non-alcoholic beverage. Trenton, you are stalling.'

'No, my dear Oko, not at all. This fellow's real name is Tarquin, but well I *ask* you—and you know, service slang, after all I expect they have service slang in the Nip Navy——'

'Thirty seconds gone, Trenton,' Hardy said.

'O.K. O.K. I cabled former Lieutenant-Commander Tarquin Bier and asked him the following: "Inquire Naval Intelligence re gold in Jap Sub I torpedoed", the reply was interesting; here it is.'

I handed the cable to Hardy.

Some days later I was staying at the Hotel Malgache near the airport at Madagascar as planned when I received the 'phone call from Roderick Vandaleur. His voice was vociferous. He was in a state of tremendous excitement. 'We've got it, Gar', we've got it! We'll meet up in Honolulu in six months time as arranged. 'Gar', you're a genius and, man, have you ever seen a real live gold bar?'

'No. What do they look like?'

'Real live gold bars,' he said, roaring with laughter.

'Are you in Nairobi?'

'Yes.'

'You didn't waste any time!'

'You've got to be joking. See you in Hawaii six months from now,' he added. 'Here's Sharon.'

Sharon came on the 'phone. She sounded breathless, excited. I cut her down to size a little. I said: 'You didn't tell me you were married to Roderick.'

She tried to cover up by changing the subject. 'Do a good job on my novel for the studios, won't you, Gar',' she said quickly.

'What's the matter, is Roddy too near the 'phone?'

'It's marvellous about the bullion. We'll see you, as arranged.'

'What about all those animals on the houseboat?' I chided. 'I'll talk to the R.S.P.C.A. about you when I get home.'

'Don't be silly, Gar', my aunt is looking after them.'

'Then I hope you'll send her a gold brick or two for their keep.'

'Of course,' she said, slightly angry, slightly ill-at-ease. Her natural female curiosity got the better of her. 'I suppose Reba told you!' she accused. I could hear Roddy asking 'told him what?' I couldn't help laughing.

'*Ciao!*' I said.

'Gar'!' Sharon's voice was positively plaintive.

'We *will* see you in Hawaii, won't we?'

'Of course—or maybe we'll go to the London *première* of the film together,' I said. 'Bye-bye, you booful blonde beauty, you!'

I cradled the 'phone and turned to Reba. She lay completely

naked on the double-bed. Naked, that is, except for the eye patch. It was a deep blue-black and it matched the only possible thing it could match.

'I suppose you're still keen on her?' Reba said pseudo-petulantly.

'She's mad about me!' I gagged, 'like you!'

'I suppose you do have a certain rustic charm.'

'Rustic?'

'O.K. O.K. Suave, then suave. They'll be awfully mad when they find out the gold bars are phoney,' she said.

'It was lucky I checked with "Ginger" Bier. Naval Intelligence knew all the time that the gold bars were phoney—that's why no one in authority bothered about the stuff.'

'The Japs had actually gone to the trouble to make them for use in their occupied countries?'

'Yes. There are still a few floating around Malaya.'

'But won't Roderick Vandaleur be simply livid when he finds out?'

'Of course, but I didn't know any more than he did,' I said innocently. 'In any case I expect, like Hardy and Oko, I think they'll *finally* laugh.'

'Hardy certainly took it well. He would,' Reba said.

'I don't like Hardy,' I said. 'His teeth are too pleasant.'

Reba ignored it.

'And Oko,' I added.

'His teeth are false.'

'I mean, Oko laughing.'

'Yes, that was quite a moment. It took him longer but at least he did see the comic side of it.'

We were silent for a moment.

'Your teeth are nice too, Gar'. Very nice.'

'Then let's clash them!' I suggested.

We kissed for a very long time. When we broke away, Reba had closed her eyes. She laughed silently. Her lashes fluttered jet black, like the eye patch.

I had to know. I said hesitantly:

'Reba, your poor old bad eye—how did it happen? Was it a stick or something?'

She looked surprised. 'A stick?'

'Did someone accidentally knock the poor thing out while you were a kid?'

Now Reba looked bemused but shy. 'Good heavens, no!' she replied. 'The eye's there all right.'

'Oh.' I didn't pursue the subject. I realized it was wonky, or crossed or something fearfully embarrassing for a girl. I held her more tightly as if to compensate.

'No,' she volunteered, 'the eye's perfectly O.K. but it is embarrassing. You see, it's a different colour from the other one. Like an Odd Eyed white.'

'What?'

'Odd Eyed—that's a rare cat—they have different coloured eyes, like me. You see I have one brown one and one green.'

I looked at her perplexedly and I said: 'Is that so awful?'

'It's odd and so people are inclined to laugh.'

'May I see it?'

She seemed reluctant. 'If you laugh I'll die,' she said.

'I promise not to laugh.'

'Well,' she said, taking off the eye shade, 'you've seen everything else.'

The green eye was the same size as the brown one. They were odd only in that they were different. They both smiled at me wondering. 'You, my darling, are a crazy mixed-up kid. I suppose you read the story about the gal in the steel corset in *Memoirs of Hecate County*.'

'I've never heard of Hecate County.'

'Never mind, honey. I adore your eyes. I shall love them separately on alternate nights.'

'Pull that blind down, Gar',' Reba said, 'the sun's getting into them.'

'You know something—I never did meet a Creole gal on your island.'

'And so?'

'It doesn't matter now.'